Arlene T hayer

By the Same Author:

THE WORLD IS NOT ENOUGH

Zoé Oldenbourg

THE

CORNERSTONE

Translated by

EDWARD HYAMS

Pantheon

THIS IS A TRANSLATION OF

LA PIERRE ANGULAIRE

LIBRARY OF CONGRESS CATALOG CARD NUMBER: 55-5062

MANUFACTURED IN THE UNITED STATES BY

KINGSPORT PRESS, INC., KINGSPORT, TENNESSEE

A.B.

CONTENTS

PAGE

PART ONE

PART FOUR

PART FIVE

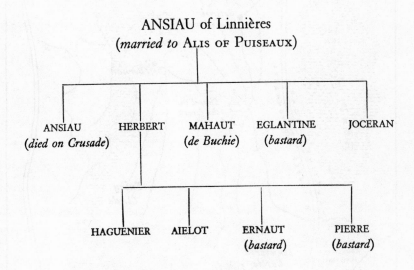

ANSIAU of Linnières
(*married to* ALIS OF PUISEAUX)

ANSIAU
(*died on Crusade*)

HERBERT

MAHAUT
(*de Buchie*)

EGLANTINE
(*bastard*)

JOCERAN

HAGUENIER

AIELOT

ERNAUT
(*bastard*)

PIERRE
(*bastard*)

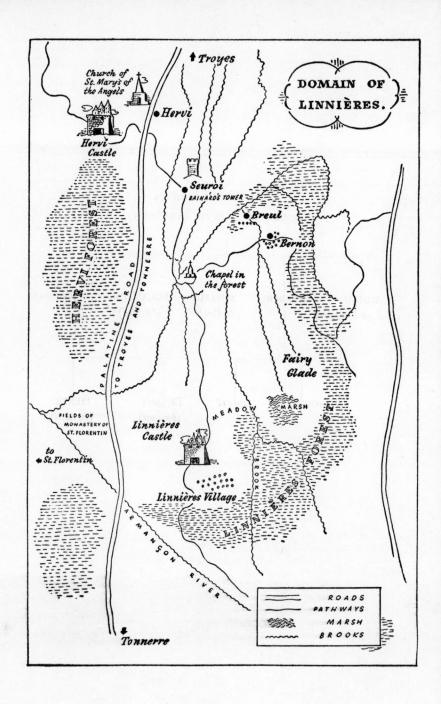

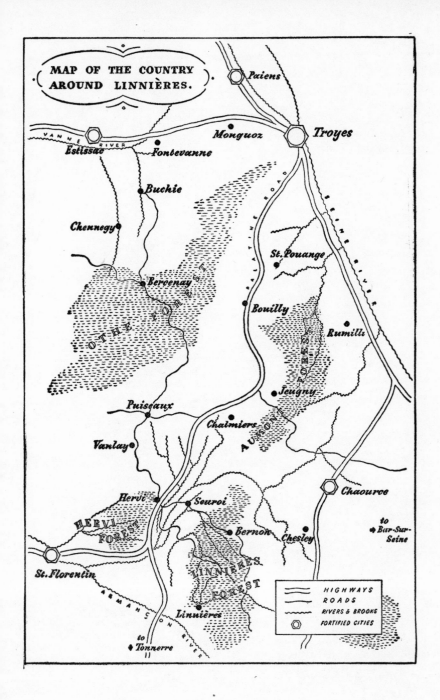

MAP OF THE COUNTRY AROUND LINNIÈRES.

Paiens

VANNE RIVER
Estissac
Fontevanne
Monguoz
Troyes

Buchie

Chennegy

St. Pouange

Bercenay

OTHE FOREST

Bouilly

SEINE RIVER

PALATINE ROAD

Rumilli

AUMONT FOREST

Jeugny

Puiseaux

Chalmiers

Vanlay

Hervi

Seuroi

Chaource

HERVI FOREST

Bernon

Chesley

to Bar-Sur-Seine

St. Florentin

LINNIÈRES FOREST

ARMANSON RIVER

Linnières

to Tonnerre

HIGHWAYS
ROADS
RIVERS & BROOKS
FORTIFIED CITIES

Part One

FAREWELL

S O NOW le Gros was to be master.
Yet he was not accepted as the real lord; people still believed
that the old man would come back. He had always come back;
impossible to believe that this time he was gone for good.

He had left three Sundays before Christmas.

He was well known in all that countryside. He was a very big man,
burly as a wild boar, his face more swarthy than a farmhand's who
works in the fields. He wore no hat to protect him from sun and wind,
and to spare his horse he would walk a league through the marshes,
leading it by the bridle. Singlehanded he would attack boar or bear.
He could track his game by scent, with a nose as sensitive as a hound's.

He was a simple man, not too proud to sit on the floor of a woodman's
hovel and be satisfied with a chunk of bread and cheese for his supper.
Whenever, caught by bad weather, he spent the night in some peasant's
cabin, he always slept on the outside so as not to occupy the whole
pallet himself. And he could not see a little child without caressing its
hair.

He, the old master, had suffered a great misfortune in his life: he had
lost his son, a youth of twenty years, dead of a sickness in the Holy
Land. True, he had other sons, but it was this one, the eldest, whom he
loved best. And it was said that since his death he had had no joy in the
love of his other children. But when he heard that any man of the countryside had lost a son of twenty years of age, he would have the sum of
the man's poll-tax for that year returned to him, and if the man be-

longed to the monks, or to the commune of Chaource, he paid the tax for him. And since his child's death he had had nothing but misfortunes and bad luck, fifteen years and more, so that there was no man of all that countryside who did not mourn for the fair young man who lay in the earth of the Holy Land. For everyone loved the old lord, although he was thought too simple and too easy in his character. Too gentle a master, they said, makes bad servants.

But now he was gone, and in this manner: he was not old, still of an age to bear arms, but two years ago his eyesight had failed because of wounds received in the Holy Land. He hardly left the castle, a hardship, surely, for so great a hunter. Then he fell ill. Le Gros, his son, had come to see him. And one fine day he was seated in his hall with his son and his people and his men, and at his feet was a little page, son of a cousin, Bernard by name. Le Gros had ordered Bernard to bring him beer, and the old man had said: "Bernard shall not go," and nevertheless the boy had gone. Then the old lord had covered his face with his hands and sat thus, a long time, without moving.

Two days later he left with his son for Troyes, to yield up his fief and invest his son with it. Then he confessed and communicated at Troyes cathedral, took leave of his friends and donned the garments of a pilgrim. The country folk saw him pass by Linnières, wearing the short brown coat and the cloak, his head shorn and his beard slashed. But for his blind eye and his great bulk, they would not have known him.

Nobody was surprised that a man should wish to put so unchancy a life into the hands of God: sick and half blind, he could do no better than go and pray for his sins, and surely God would be kinder than le Gros; it is never good when a man is weaker than his son.

The old man had remained three days at the castle, for love of the old lady his wife; for she was a most worthy lady, and he had never wished to be apart from her although she had neither lands nor rich connections and was his first wife.

During three days he stayed at the castle, sleeping in the straw with the servants, and eating below the salt with the grooms. And his lady, seeing him thus, wept for pity and shame, and God knows that not even for any of her children had she suffered so.

He lay stretched out upon the floor of the chapel, his face pressed to the naked stones. And his lady came and knelt beside him and placed her hands on the massive head with the hair still more brown than grey. And he made no movement. And she took one of his hands which lay upon the other in front of his head, and carried it to her lips. Then the man raised himself upon his elbow and looked at her out of a troubled eye.

"Friend," she said, "friend, it may be that you find in me faults of which you have not spoken."

"Lady," he said, "do not torment me. Why do you say this to me?"

"Friend, what fault have you found in me?"

"Sister, why do you torment me?"

"Friend, you must bear hate against me in your heart. What will they say of me in the countryside when they know that I let you take the roads alone, blind and sick as you are, in the depth of winter, your hair shorn, and dressed like a poor man? Friend, a man of your age quickly falls ill when he has no woman who knows him to care for him. And who will take care of you? You are old, yet you have no more sense than a child. I tell you, friend, once for all, if you go now you will never see me again, neither living nor dead. When you want to come back to me it will be too late. And if I curse you as I die it will be a sin for me and for you."

"Sister, if you will use such words to me, I would rather leave as quickly as I can. And if you forgive me not you will do a great injustice, for it is God who has made me see that I must go. And it is for God that I leave you, sister, and you will see if He is good and just, and knows what He is about. Look on me, lady, as I am: had I my eyes I should have another five years at least in which I might bear arms, and my body is younger than my years. I have yet ten or fifteen years of horsemanship left in my body, and when a sound man sits in the chimney corner his strength turns to fat and to folly. God has given me to know this. And I shall tell you, lady, the three great mercies He has granted me, so that I must thank Him: first, He has so chastised me in the child of my sin that now I can no longer love her and she is dead for me. Thus has He shown me that we should not cleave to our own flesh and blood, and that it is but rottenness. And then, He has seen that although I lost an eye in His service it did not make me a better man; and so He is taking the other from me that I may no longer look upon the things of this earth, but only upon those of Heaven. And finally, He has given me a son who has neither pity nor respect for me, that I may learn to live without pride, like the poor wretch that I am. And I should be thankful to my son Herbert for making me understand what I have to do: yet that will not bring him happiness, lady."

And on the morning of the fourth day the old baron had knelt before his lady in the great hall and bowed his head to the ground to ask her forgiveness for all the wrong he had done her in his life. And she had placed her long hands, now knotted and discolored, on the old man's head, and had gone on her knees to kiss his mutilated eyes. At her side were her two youngest children and of them too he asked forgiveness; and he blessed them.

Then he rose and turned towards all his people, cousins and vassals, who stood together near the great hearth. They were so sorrowful that they dared not speak, and all were within a little of weeping. The old lord bent the knee before each one of them, his head bowed, and he kissed them all on both cheeks. And when he came to le Gros he did not kiss him and he said:

"Thank you, fair son, for your great goodness to me. May your son honor you as you have honored me. Be a better master than I have been. Take nothing from your mother's dower nor from your sisters' portion. You have two sisters still to marry: give them to men of whom your mother is not ashamed."

"I have done you no harm," said Herbert.

"Which is why I am going, and leaving you free of your place." Thereupon he slowly bowed the knee, "Forgive me, fair son, for all the wrongs I have done you. You have promised me upon oath to be good to all the people who are here. Let them be witnesses to your promise."

Then he rose and called for his cloak.

On his great grey horse with the clipped mane he crossed the green and the village, followed by his old squire Guiot-Thierri whom he loved in memory of his friend, the squire of his youth, fallen in the Holy Land. And a crowd of servants, women and vassals followed him, matching his horse's paces, holding to the harness, clinging to the skirts of his cloak and to his shoes. A cold wind was blowing, carrying off the last brown leaves, and the flight of the crows was broken by gusts. The old man huddled in his brown cloak and the wind found out his head, shorn like a poor man's, and filled his eye with dust. Before the iron cross he bowed his head and crossed himself: then he took leave of those who were with him and bade them return to the house.

The two horsemen skirted the forest and were lost among branches tossed by the wind. In the sky long, black clouds drove down upon more clouds of yellowish grey.

The old man bore with him a thorn in his flesh, for he had a daughter, born of the damsel who had loved him, this daughter a girl with a kind of madness in her body, and a kind of innocence; and of her he had not had the courage to take his leave. He had sent her for a time into a convent, where he had another daughter, a religious. Throughout all that countryside the girl was known, the dark girl who haunted the hazel-nut hedges and grassy rides in the company of handsome youths; yet there was none so harsh as to despise her, for it was known that her father loved her.

A BITTER LOVE

IN THE month of March, in mid-Lent, the cool waters flowed about Puiseaux; and in the still earth-dark fields village lads and girls danced, with budding branches of elm and birch in their hands. The breeze was already soft, and young women, seated upon the parapet of the well, shook out their tresses. The castle of Puiseaux possessed the finest well of the region, its water so cold and pure that it was said to be enchanted, and it was not for nothing that the ladies of Puiseaux had, for generations, been reputed knowing in witchcraft: such was the lady Hermengarda, mother of the baron Joceran now dead, and the lady Hodierne of sainted memory, and the lady Irma killed with blows of an axe in the inner court of the castle, and the lady Brune, wife of the reigning lord. The women of Chaource, and even those of Saint-Florentin, came to ask help and counsel of the lady of Puiseaux. It was said that the fairy of Puiseaux endowed the lady of the place with her powers. And the castle folk preferred their own well even to the spring of Saint-Anne, in the forest.

It was a large, square well shaded by an elm; two iron hoops crossed above it, joined and protected by a cross. In spring the young girls decorated these hoops with apple blossom and sweet briar. This evening, in a sky of tenderer blue than a pigeon's wing, white clouds drifted over grey forest and the road was like a white lace between meadows of acid green and the dark fields.

The lookout on the roof was watching two horsemen approach by the road, with falcons on their wrists, and seeing them take the turning towards Puiseaux he sounded his trumpet. The young servants, who were practicing archery, climbed on to the wall to see. The sentry at the door cried, "A horseman on the green!" The two damsels of the castle, Ida and Mainsant, exchanged swift glances.

"You will see," Mainsant said.

"You are stupid," said Ida. Their gowns of light blue linen were all creased, and their faces flushed with laughter beneath light, soft hair, hanging in tresses.

At that moment a horseman with a falcon rode into the courtyard; he was a young man, fair and well built, dressed in a russet habit which reached to his knees. He jumped from his horse and bent the knee to the lady of the castle, the falcon upright on his right fist.

"God save you, Ernaut," the lady said, "my lord is in the hall. You may go in." The young man sighed and made towards the great house: passing near the two girls he greeted them with a motion of the head, without daring to stop, but he let his eyes rest upon Ida with a look so warm that she turned away. Mainsant nudged her. "There, you see!" she said. Ida shrugged.

Joceran, master of Puiseaux, second of his name, was taking his siesta, reclining in his wide easy chair. His little niece Marguerite stood by him holding a bowl of white wood in which was a large pear preserved in honey, a sweetmeat which the lord of Puiseaux enjoyed after his sleep. A boy entered to announce the arrival of his cousin Ernaut of Linnières, and the little maid took advantage of the diversion to steal a sip of the syrup from the cup; Joceran saw her, administered a good slap for her greediness, and began to sip the syrup himself. At that moment the young man entered the hall and halted to greet the master of Puiseaux, his wide, grave countenance expressive of an overstrong wish to please. He held himself before Joceran in the attitude of a beaten dog, while the other had a smile at once hard and amused at the corners of his lips.

"God be with you, fair cousin," the youth said. "I am come to announce my father's arrival; he will pass the night in your house."

"Thanks be for the honor," said Joceran. "I shall be glad to see him. That's a fine creature you have there." The young man smiled quickly and held out the falcon.

"Take him, fair cousin, he has been well manned, he will obey a touch of your thumb." He set the bird gently down on the arm of the chair. Joceran took up the falcon and began absently stroking the beak and neck-feathers.

"Will my fair cousin of Hervi be long in these parts?" he asked.

"Two or three weeks, perhaps, he wishes to prepare the house for the knighting of his son."

"It will be a great joy for you to see your brother," Joceran said, with a smile at the corner of his mouth. "They say that he is a handsome young man, with fine manners."

"All is handsome which comes from afar," Ernaut said.

"He is to be dubbed at Troyes?"

"At Troyes, after Easter. But he will hold a feast for Hervi afterwards. He has promised me my spurs also, on that day," the youth added, with a sidelong glance at Joceran.

"And to your brother Pierre likewise, as I hear," said the lord of Puiseaux. "You must indeed love your father. Is it his intention that you should hold land from him, a fief to maintain your arms?"

Ernaut blushed and hung his head. "If I wed I am to have the revenues of the Bernon vineyard and apiary."

Joceran said:

"Then marry, fair cousin."

"It is well said," replied Ernaut, "that it takes two to make a marriage; and, as it happens, there must be four in agreement; and it may happen that three agree and one does not. My own father will never put any obstacle in the way of my marriage."

"Fair cousin Ernaut," said Joceran, "I love your father well; but every man is master in his own house."

In the courtyard the servants were already preparing for the reception of the stout lord of Hervi; when he passed through the country with his women, his bastards, his rout of servants, his falcons and dogs, the whole life of the castle was disturbed for several days. Twice the usual amounts of hay, straw and flour were used, and the village ransacked for eggs and poultry. In the stables the horses which had to be shifted snorted and knocked against each other and the grooms had difficulty in calming them.

"Hey, Jacquet, don't put so much hay in le Gros's mangers; our horses are as good as his—mix a bit of straw with it, and they'll not notice. We've taken no oaths to le Gros, it's all the same."

"I say, Girard, what about an extra layer of planks across the moat? What for? So that the bridge won't break when le Gros crosses it!" Laughter and taunts filled the stable, mingled with the neighing of horses.

On the road the cortège of the stout lord of Hervi advanced, horsemen in the lead, then two burly horses drawing a litter covered with red cloth, next mules laden with boxes and bags. The lady Aelis, wife to le Gros, cantered circling in the rear with her maid of honor, and flew her falcon at crows and magpies.

When le Gros's litter entered the courtyard Joceran was waiting for him, standing with his nephews and squires. First out of the litter was a girl, fair and bedizened and carrying a little white dog in her arms; next two tall, russet greyhounds, slender and quick, tails and muzzles brisk and busy. Finally, le Gros himself appeared, and when he put his feet to the ground the whole litter shuddered and creaked on its axles and the red cloth curtains shook as in a gust of wind.

The man was so big that all the others seemed suddenly like children or youths; he topped them by a head. From his shoulders and chest a long green tunic fell in heavy folds, and his handsome, square head, as big as a bushel, was held up by folds of fat under the strong, shaven chin divided in the middle by a vertical cleft. The eyes, heavy and pale, were slowly lowered to Joceran who, swarthy, lean and agile, seemed like a greyhound beside a bull.

Joceran, in the presence of his mighty cousin, became obsequious from pleasure, turning his house upside down to entertain him; yet it brought him nothing, nor did he owe Hervi money. But he had the vanity of a poor relation and nowhere was Hervi better served than at Puiseaux. After the customary courtesies he led his guest to the bath, where the lady Brune herself served him, helped by her daughters, while Joceran, lounging in a cushioned seat, amused him with gossip.

From their small, high room, to which their lady had sent them, the two damsels of the castle looked out upon court, fields and forest.

Ida, leaning her large, fair head against the edge of the small window, looked down with curiosity at cousin Herbert's women. Standing by the well, they were laughing very loudly and arranging their hair and girdles.

"They have beautiful dresses," Mainsant said, leaning over her cousin's shoulder. "Look at the fair one, oh look!"

"What a number of necklaces she has!" Ida said. "Like a Blessed Virgin in procession." The blonde, tall and slender, with a great mane of very curly hair, flung up her slim, white arms behind her head, stretching and yawning; her very full skirt of red muslin was edged with a heavy braid of gold embroidery.

"You would like to be dressed like her?" Mainsant asked.

Ida made a face, "You can see her breasts through her shift. It is not decent."

"But of course! She's one of the damned. And they say she is only seventeen."

"The German girl? She's been with Herbert at least five years!"

"What beautiful braid," Mainsant said. "What a task, embroidering that!"

Ida sighed and gently shook her heavy, tawny hair.

"Why," Mainsant said, "there's Ernaut looking at you!"

Ernaut, standing with his back to the well, had his eyes fixed on the little square window from which the two young heads, the blonde and the brunette, emerged. Ida frowned and withdrew from the window, and Ernaut still stared, fascinated, imagining God knows what paradise of cool purity beyond that dark square, in the little room where his golden-eyed girl with hair like ripe corn hid herself away—the well of joy, cool waters—and he had been so thirsty, for so long!

After Lauds, Joceran served his guests a light evening meal; Herbert always made a high ceremony of eating and his two bastard sons, Ernaut and Pierre, served him, holding back his sleeves, cutting up his meat before him and filling his cup. His wife contented herself by sharing a dish of cheese and onions, beer, and some dried fruits, with the lady Brune. The evening was so mild that the young men had gone out into the courtyard to chat together seated on the parapet of the well.

Joceran, facing his cousin, his elbows on the cloth, the left cheek wrinkled by his eternal crooked smile, listened to the two bastard sons of his guest disputing as to who should first cut their father's meat.

The two lads had always been jealous of each other; their father had reared them like two cocks trained to fight.

"You have two fine sons, cousin," Joceran said, "and soon to be knighted."

Herbert smiled. His smile was heavy, without gaiety, and only the fleshy lips moved.

"I shall be very glad when it's all over," he said. "This feast is giving me more trouble than a departure for the Holy Land. What I can raise from my lands will not cover half my expenses, and I shall be in debt for three years."

"You have good news of your son?"

"Good enough. But I am in much haste to see him."

"That's life," Joceran said. "You lose your father and recover your son. He must be at least eighteen now."

"Nineteen, I think. I am not sure what they have been teaching him in Normandy. But a lad who has travelled a little is worth two, as they say. As soon as he's knighted I shall marry him off and send him to do his forty days' crusading in the south, since I can no longer go myself. Let him learn the weight of a hauberk; it will teach him something about life."

"Why, yes," Joceran said, "it's not a good age for a young man to stay at home. They think too much of matrons and maids. As for me, with my girls, I take my precautions, ha, ha!" Ernaut cast him an evil look from beneath his straight fringe.

After the meal the two cousins rested, and the young men took advantage of this to go down to the courtyard. Ida and Mainsant, duly chaperoned by their old serving-woman, were amusing themselves by looking at their dark reflections against the rectangle of white sky cut into four by the iron hoops in the deep mirror of the well. Herbert's noisy escort had withdrawn into the castle. Ernaut seated himself beside Ida and took her hands in his.

"Are you pleased to see me?" She gently shrugged her shoulders. Mainsant laughed.

"It's getting cold," Ida said. Ernaut kissed her cheeks, her lips, her neck and, lazily, she put him aside, fidgeting a little, as if to drive away a too persistent fly.

"You have spoken to your father?" he asked.

"Why, yes," she said, indifferent.

"And he will not have it?" She shook her head.

"Because I am a bastard?"

"Yes."

"He is mighty proud! At least I know *my* father!"

"You are not to speak ill of my father," the girl said.

"If you desired it, he would wish it too," Ernaut said, "but you are too false." And he kissed her again, and again she put him aside. Since some time ago he had taken to kissing her too often and too hard, and she did not like it.

"Is it true, Ernaut," Mainsant asked, "that your brother will soon arrive from Normandy?"

"Who asks what he knows wears out his tongue in vain."

"They say he is very fine," Ida said.

"Old Girard says that he can read, and sing poems," Mainsant added.

"And write songs," Ida said.

"You will see," Ernaut said, "he will talk to you through his nose, with his Norman accent."

"Is it true," Ida asked, "that you will serve him as his squire on the day of his knighting?"

"I shall do as my father bids me," Ernaut, very flushed, replied; he had had enough of serving as target for the girls' wit. "It certainly will not be you who lace his hauberk; there are more beautiful ladies than you in Troyes."

"You have only to love *them*, then," Ida said, laughing. "Come, Mainsant; and here are snowdrops for Ernaut, to make himself a crown on the day of his knighthood."

She picked up from the ground a handful of faded flowers and threw them over Ernaut. Bursts of cool laughter sounded there, under the elm. When the girls were gone, Ernaut sat and watched the sky whiten at the bottom of the well.

HAGUENIER:
I. FIRST ENCOUNTER

HAGUENIER OF LINNIÈRES, or of Hervi, as he called himself, from the name of his maternal heritage, was returning from Normandy with the old squire whom his father had sent to accompany him. Before Troyes he dismissed the old man, who was charged to convey letters from the baron of Coucy, the young man's old master, to Haguenier's father. It was Haguenier's intention to spend a few days with his sister who would be in the town, with her husband, for mid-Lent.

He passed along the streets of Troyes, unable to get over his surprise at finding them so small and narrow. He had difficulty in finding his way by his ten-year-old memories: there were the turreted jetties of the Seine; and the square before the castle. The black and grey waters of the river were cluttered with boats under a fine March rain, and, against the pale grey sky, above pointed roofs of wet tile, the church towers reared, dominant, Saint-Pancrace and Saint-Nizier and Saint-Pierre, and also—square, and protected by wooden shuttering—the towers of the new cathedral; for years the building had made no progress. Count Henri's castle, with its round turrets and blue banners, was reflected in the puddles of rain-water.

The mid-Lenten court had been held and was over, so that the streets were crowded with petty, rustic knights who, wrapped in travelling cloaks, their coffers loaded on the backs of mules, were returning home with their wives and squires, hailing each other as they went forward to make up parties going towards Bar, Reims, or Provins. Haguenier knew nobody and felt himself an alien. He wondered whether he would find his brother-in-law still in Troyes. He passed the great portcullis of the castle and entered the courtyard, clamorous with festival uproar, there in permanent session; people coming and going, a-horse and a-foot, forced their way through a crowd of idlers waiting for the countess to show herself. There was no great entertainment at the castle that evening and Haguenier hardly hoped to find his brother-in-law there. But he got as far as the guardroom and humbly asked the old sergeant who was standing in front of the door whether he happened to know the baron of Pouilli.

"Why, yes," the man said, "his wife sleeps in the countess's suite. It is she who tends the candles during this week. You're sure to find them at the castle." Haguenier was very glad of the honor which had fallen to his sister, and set out to look for her. But he made his way by the back courtyard, not daring to appear in travelling garb before the countess.

He set himself to wait in the servants' hall, where the servants of gentry who had come in for the feast guarded their masters' boxes, played at dice, or dozed while waiting the time to serve as tiring-men when their masters went to bed. Haguenier stretched himself on the straw, wrapped in his great cloak: the chamber was cold and damp. He felt very melancholy.

He had left friends behind him in Normandy. In Troyes he had no one but his sister from whom he had parted ten years before, when she, a tall child, fair and pale, had sobbed as she bade him farewell. Now she must be twenty. Haguenier had had a sorrowful childhood. Not always had his mother, his sister and he had bread for every day of the week, and in winter he went in clogs, like a peasant, and had chilblains on his hands and feet. His father—he could still see him in memory—was a handsome man, young, fair and plump, always well groomed and perfumed, whom their nurse took them to visit on feast days, Aielot and himself, after having washed them and clothed them in red garments; their father took them on his knees and pinched their chins. Everyone feared him, their mother more than anyone. Aielot had told her brother, in great secrecy, that this man beat their mother, and that it was for this reason that she had lost her teeth. And when their mother died, he learned, again through Aielot, that it was because their father had beaten her too much. At that time they were living at Hervi and in summer they went to their grandparents at Linnières, where the old lady, in her white coif, stuffed them with cakes and apples, washed them and combed them and called them her pretty white doves, and her ermines, and her little falcons; and Haguenier loved this lady, because his mother had never much caressed him. He played with his grandfather's youngest children and built mud castles in the courtyard puddles. After their father's new marriage, they had to leave his house. Aielot was sent to a convent, to learn to read and to bear

herself correctly, while he, Haguenier, was sent into service with the
baron of Coucy, in Normandy.

Haguenier saw himself at the mercy of a father who, he believed, did
not love him and was suspicious of him. He had no brothers; he did not
count his father's bastards as such. He believed that his father had sent
him far away on purpose to make him a stranger to his family and his
house. He knew it well—his father was rich, he held three domains, a
good five leagues about, and he, Haguenier, was heir to the best two of
these lands: a man often distrusts those whose interest it is to see him
die.

And yet Haguenier's own nature was not distrustful. He had been
taught courtesy and good manners and that benevolence which a good
knight should show towards those about him, he was ready to love the
lord to whom he was going to swear fealty. He was not of those who
think one thing and say another, because he knew himself well born and
well bred.

He was young, and gay by nature, and desired to live his life well and
bravely.

On the following day Haguenier asked one of the castle servants to
point out the baron of Pouilli as he went to morning mass. This baron
was a well-looking man of about thirty, his beard black and pointed.
Haguenier introduced himself and apologized for his appearance. He
said that he wanted to see his sister before going on to Hervi.

"This falls out well," Jacques of Pouilli said. "We are returning home
tomorrow, you will spend a few days with us. Come with me, and after
mass I will take you to the ladies' chamber; my wife will be happy to
see you. . . ."

The countess took her meals in the suite of rooms on the second floor
which were light and hung with tapestries into which were woven the
arms of all the fiefs of Champagne on a red ground decorated with light
blue foliage. The fire in the great hearth, lit as soon as it was morning,
cast a pale and yellow light into the room and upon the high table
covered with a white cloth. The countess, with her ladies and her
chaplain, was already finishing the meal, the pages were carrying finger
bowls to the guests, and the minstrels were coming to table to eat what
remained of the meal. The household knights were waiting for the meal
to finish, to salute the countess and the ladies. And when grace had been
sung and the tables put aside, the countess led her ladies to the windows,

beneath the carved shields, to admire the Seine and the roofs of the town which gleamed like gold in the sun after the rains of the previous evening.

When the ladies had installed themselves on the benches or with cushions on the ground, setting about embroidery or playing at knuckle-bones, the men could join in conversations, as was proper, after having bent the knee before the countess. Then Jacques of Pouilli took his wife aside and told her that her brother was come from Normandy and wanted to see her. Haguenier held himself humbly, near to the door, admiring the ladies' beauty; from afar, in their light but brightly colored gowns and with their hair skillfully braided and rolled, each seemed lovelier than the others, and he could not guess which was his sister.

Then she had run to him and he suddenly found himself hugged, squeezed, kissed more than twenty times on his cheeks, his mouth, his eyes—by something, someone, tall and warm, drowning him in a strong scent of nard and of flesh. "Niot!" she was saying. "Niot!" She was sniffing and he, too, wanted to weep. He took her by the shoulders.

"Let me at least look at you a little!" She wiped her eyes. "O my Niot!" She pressed his head into her shoulder, raised it again, again wiped her eyes. She was a big woman, almost as big as himself, her face not very pretty but with a skin so white that her white dress seemed yellow beside it; her flaxen hair fell in heavy tresses beside her neck and breasts, and her eyes, large and very blue, all wet with tears, shone with joy. Aielot had her father's full lips and cleft chin, a slightly flattened nose and light eyebrows. But in the light of her hair and her eyes and her soft skin her face was better than beautiful. Now she was laughing, pressing the young man's face between her large hands, milky and warm, and so soft that Haguenier, for all he was her brother, was troubled. They stood so, looking at each other, unable to say a word.

"Come," Aielot said at length, "come near to the window so that I may see you better. My Niot! Say something, so that I may hear you speak." She wiped her eyes with the tips of her fingers. He said:

"So I find you, tall and beautiful." She made him sit in the window seat, saying:

"You're not tired by your journey? You're not hungry?"

She could not remain long with him that day, but on the morrow they left Troyes together, very early in the morning, to arrive before mass at the manor of Pouilli, which was two leagues from the town. Excited by the freshness of the day, the young woman laughed and sang at the top of her voice. On the hills before Troyes the sky was very pale blue, and a mist, dazzling white, lay upon the town with its turrets and ramparts and its great churches all clamorous with the sound of bells; the last lights were being extinguished on the walls.

At Pouilli the hall was small but light enough, the walls hung with painted canvas and the floors covered with hay. Aielot had a bath prepared for her brother and the tub was carried into the hall, near to the hearth; she served him herself, supervising her women, who massaged and rubbed the young man with sweet-smelling herbs.

"Scratch his back well!" she cried, and, "What a handsome white body it is! You've a pair of archer's shoulders on you. Jacques, come and look! There are not many men with such arms, under twenty years of age. Sybille, you'll be getting soap in his eyes." She had taken a white shirt and a woollen gown from her husband's chests and laid them out on the bench.

"You shall see how handsome he will be," she said, full of pride, to her husband. "Ah, how glad his father will be to see him!"

"And how is our father?" Haguenier asked. Aielot stretched wide her arms. "Like this. As stout as three canons. He no longer rides a horse, excepting on feast days."

"At his age! Already!" the young man said.

Aielot laughed her fat, rather hoarse laugh. "It cannot be very comfortable for his women," she said. "At the moment I think he must have all the braid-makers of Troyes at work for your knighting. And he has found a hauberk of Toledo steel for you, the scales so fine that you cannot get a needle between them. Jacques has seen it, haven't you, Jacques? And the cloak is to be of raspberry-red silk trimmed with marten fur. And I am to hold your shield, my Niot. And as for your spurs, there's my friend, the most beautiful lady of Troyes, who has promised to buckle them on for you, for love of me."

Haguenier listened, his eyes sparkling at the thought of the feast and of the fine clothes he was going to wear.

His sister took him over her house—her pigeon loft, her stables, her children—she already had two. "And a third here," she said, putting her hand to her body. "It will be born after Assumption: it is going to spoil my hunting season." She pinched and tickled the two pale, plump babies, wrapped like larvae: her handling ended by making them cry, and she put them back into the cradle.

"They are tiring," she said. "At an awkward age."

A hedge separated the orchard from the copse of willows, beech saplings and mulberries which fell away gently down to the Seine. A six-foot wall of stone pierced by a postern was built along the river bank. Here, among the willows and the burgeoning oaks, in springtime they gathered strawberries by the basketful. Aielot, in little clogs, walked the place, herself, to see if she could find snowdrops to give her brother. It had rained in the night and each branch that she put aside sprinkled them with raindrops cool as dew.

"Look there," Aielot said. "On the far bank, behind that wood of elms, the round tower, where the road bends. That is Foulque of Mongenost's castle, and there lives the lady of whom I spoke to you. If you can make her love you, I will do all I can to help you. But it will be very difficult, for she is proud and, I think, she has never loved."

"You are certainly not like her, little sister!" Haguenier said, laughing.

Aielot stood upright and whistled softly.

"No, indeed! I am not one of those women who think a man no good as a lover until he has broken his bones and torn out his eyes to prove his love." At that Haguenier was shaken by laughter.

"As far as I can see, you are good—and, it seems, would have me break my bones and tear out my eyes!"

"Oh, I hope there will be no need for that. But, seriously, if you could win this lady it would bring you much glory, for she has scorned all our best knights."

THE FEAST OF WOLVES

IN THE white forest, under a sky yellow and heavy with snow, the crows flapped their wings and clamored with hunger.

In the fringe of the forest, among dead bushes on the slope down to the ravine, the snow was red with blood and the tracks of paw marks ran hither and yon, crossed, and streaked the snow all around, for a hundred feet: for there was a notable feast served here, a living horse. The pack had flung themselves upon it, hanging on to the throat and legs; and now, pulled on to its back, the heart still beating, the entrails smoking, it moved no longer. At first entirely covered with a hairy, snarling, struggling mass, it was soon nothing but a bloody mess of bones and hanging tendons, and the animals danced about it, tugging at the blue and black tubes, licking the excrement, nosing between the legs, beneath the flanks, between the jaws, drinking the eyes from their sockets, gnawing at the hoofs, choking on the hair of the tail—the cubs rolling on the ground in the blood, fighting over a bone, and the older beasts, strong in the leg, slashing with a stroke of their claws any that came nosing into their own meal. But hunger was stronger than fear, and the bodies of two wolves were also eaten clean to the bones, and then the pack flung itself upon the saddle and harness and the blood-stained snow all fouled with excrement; and the starving crows, attracted by the scent of blood, were snapped in full flight and devoured, feathers and all. And when nothing remained on the bones but well-licked blood-stains, when the snow all about had been melted into mud and eaten, the pack set off again in search of game, licking their blood-stained chops and still howling aloud the great hunger of the forest.

And then the snow began to fall, confusing scents and spoors.

A man was walking, alone, through the great deadness of the forest and above his head the crows flapped their wings, waiting to see him fall. He was tall, and took long, slow strides, going forward without direction; and the frozen branches knocked against his face. There was snow upon his head and shoulders and his beard was white with rime. He had lost his horses and his companion and his fire had long since gone out. He was walking in order not to die of cold. Wolves howled in the distance. But never had this man been less afraid, for he was enclosed within his thoughts as in a tower. He was calm. Says the proverb —he sleeps well who has nothing to lose. He was praying. It had become his habit, and when he was so weary that no memory could reach his mind, then the rhythms of prayers mixed with the refrains of war songs served him for thoughts. He was a man of great hardiness under suffering.

Not a month had passed since he had left his house, but so well did he know that he had left it forever that for him time had stood still. It seemed to him that he had been walking so, alone, in the snow, for centuries, and that he had never had any other life. *You will not see me again, neither living nor dead.* And the crows cried aloud the great hunger of the forest.

The trees opened a way before him and the brambles flattened themselves beneath his feet. He well knew what it was to fight, and that only he who does not guard himself is strong. Hard is life for a man who is full of fears: all those things which he had feared had happened to him. Hard is life to the man who has love for creatures, harder yet to one who loves the creatures of his own flesh.

O just King, who never lied!

By that Lady to whom no man has ever prayed in vain, open Your joy in paradise to all the poor who go upon the roads in cold and in hunger and who are alone in the world. The great packs of wolves hunt yonder in the valley and howl from their hunger-torn entrails. Today I have no longer a comrade because You saw fit to send the wolves upon him and to nourish them upon his entrails and his brave heart and his flesh, exposed in Your service in the Holy Land and pierced by heathen arrows. Friend, friend, you will not see me again. Neither living nor dead.

O Friend without falseness, only friend of all men, have pity upon them who go hungry in winter, upon crows and wolves, upon the hare in her form and the stag in the wood, and upon all the beasts in the air and upon the earth; and upon the sheep and the goats bleating in their folds, and upon the poor folk of the villages who have naught but bread of straw and chaff to fill their bellies. And upon them who take the road with neither bread nor bacon in their wallet, nor wine in their gourd. O Father most good, if my child goes thus upon the roads, let her not live for long.

Giraud the Hare, sergeant of the guards of the castle of Moustallet, in the Auvergne, returned from his rounds with five of his company; the wind had fallen and it was no longer snowing. The forest lay, black and grey, upon the hills; and the village and the white slopes of its fields seemed lost in the immensity of the forest, as an island is lost in the sea. The castle, on a hillock of open woodland, dominated the valley at the bend of the river. A cheerful plume of grey smoke rose from the chimney of the keep and spread across the white sky. The six men blew on their fingers and walked fast. The wolf pack had been seen from the other side of the hill.

"A man in the woods," one of the soldiers said, suddenly. In the skirt of the forest, near the trees which had been felled the previous evening, a tall figure, still and withdrawn, seemed to be watching for wayfarers at a hundred paces from the road.

"Take a shot at him, Robert." Robert raised his bow but found it stiffened by the frost. "For a poacher, he's taking things very easy," Giraud said. "He'll be dead of cold, in this weather.—Hie, fellow, hie! no good hiding yourself, we can see you.—Go and see, Garin.—Go yourself. A great pagan like that!—Listen, Giraud: his back and head are covered with snow. As sure as my beard, the man's lost."

"D'you see them, Robert?" Far down the valley, on the cleared slope, a long, black mark was moving slowly. The men crossed themselves.

"Accursed devils!—hie, fellow!" Giraud shouted. And since the man made no movement two soldiers went to him, to shake him.

Seated on the stump of a felled tree, his elbows on his knees, his temples between his fists, the man seemed to be sleeping. Robert took him by the shoulders. The man raised his head; his face, reddish mauve, the short beard and mustache covered with frost, gave him the look of a church porch Saint Peter. He was blind of an eye; his good eye blinked and his mouth was tranquil. He seemed to smile.

"What are you doing here, jail-bird?" Robert demanded. "This is all Moustallet land, hunting reserved. Let's have a look at your wallet."

"You can see for yourself it's empty," said the other soldier. "He's a pilgrim. Look at his clothes."

"Funny weather to go on a pilgrimage. For all we know, this man's murdered his mother and father. Where are you from, fellow?"

The man said:

"I am a knight."

"Knight of the dagger, maybe. Come with us, old'un. There are wolves abroad."

The man rose slowly, making his joints crack. At once the two soldiers were afraid, for he topped them by a head.

"Fair lads," he said politely, "I can walk well enough, but I do not see well. Lead me. It is this snow which hurts my eye." He put his big hand on Robert's shoulder, and began to walk, hobbling. "Much thanks, brother," he said. "Without you I was finished. When I can, I shall repay you that debt."

Thereafter, came a good soup of peas in a great, warm kitchen. The men, seated on benches or on the ground before the hearth, dried their shoes and gaiters, sodden with snow; the smell of wet leather and burning mingled with that of the broth. The lord himself ate nothing else that day, for it was a fast, the Eve of the Kings. The vagabond, seated on a bench beneath the hood of the hearth, his basin on his knees, rubbed his naked and blackened feet in the warm ashes. Since he had no spoon, the soup had trickled into his beard and dried there and he was too weary to wipe it. And when the lord of Moustallet came to ask him who he was and whence he came, he answered that he was a knight but that he had left his fief to his son, to go on a pilgrimage to the Holy Land. He was of the country of Othe and had held his land from the count of Champagne, but now he owed fealty to none but God and it was because of this that he wished to journey to His country. There he had buried his son and his best friends.

The lord of Moustallet, whose name was Gerbert of Moirans, was a courteous, open-hearted man. He knew the world and, hearing this man speak, he recognized that he was well born, and might be believed without oath taken. He said to him:

"Since you are a knight, I will ask you to share my bed for this night, and thereafter you can consider what you have to do. You will be welcome here for as long as you like."

"I lost my squire and two horses in the forest," the man said. "If you can help me to find them, I will make you a present of the horses. The man is an old comrade of mine and a servant of great price; I should not want to lose him."

Gerbert sent six mounted men towards the river, with orders to sound their horns as loudly as possible, but they did not dare venture too far because of the wolves. And on the morrow Giraud brought his lord a belt of iron plates, the leather of which had been chewed, and a hunting knife, the sheath torn by teeth. They were taken to the tall, swarthy man where he sat within the hearth. He rose and felt the blade and the sheath with his hands and said:

"This was made in Troyes; I know the craftsman."

Gerbert said:

"Yesterday, in the forest, a man fell among the wolves. My lads found these things."

Then One-eye sat himself down again, without speaking a word, and hid his face in his hands.

It was the Day of Kings. In the townships, their streets full of snow trodden into mud, cortèges marched in procession, celebrating the Kings of the Golden Star in songs; and the people of the villages went into the neighboring towns to see the procession of the Kings march towards the church, all clad in gold, and bearing their gifts. At Moustallet, isolated by the snow, the castle chapel was decked with em-broidered banners, and lit by ten white candles. In the courtyard, at the chapel door, the young girls, hoods covering their unbraided hair, sang canticles in honor of the royal Magi; and the kitchen, hot as a furnace, smelled from afar of the fat and spices of roasting poultry and the honey and saffron paste of the cake of Kings.

During the meal the old one-eyed man, seated between the lord and his wife, drank with them, recalling all the Feasts of Kings of his life-time, and thinking of the Kings, Melchior, Balthasar and Gaspar: of their long beards and their crowns set with pearls, and their long cloaks woven of gold and borne by pages.

Ten days after Kings, Ansiau of Linnières left Moustallet. For his journey Gerbert gave him a strong roan horse, a mule, and a little boy from among his servants, Auberi by name; and Auberi was very glad to go with the tall, dark knight who had seen so many beautiful lands and who promised to lead him to Jerusalem. But on the eve of parting he wept in the arms of his elder brother, for his mother lived ten leagues away, up country, and he had not had time to take leave of her.

AUBERI

DESPITE the thaw it was cold and Auberi whimpered and huddled into his cloak and stooped to protect himself from the wind. His new master was none of the gentlest: his sight was bad, yet still he saw too much, pressing forward his horse and stooping to strike the child lightly on the back, with his fist.

"Sit straight, son of a bitch! Fine I shall look, going to Jerusalem with a boy who sits a horse like a peasant."

"I am cold," the child said. The other swore.

"Don't whine! Not even a girl complains, when she is of good blood. What, are you all naught but bastards in Auvergne?"

And the child, too tired to be moved by this outrage on his country, said only:

"I have never been so far. I want to go home."

The rain drenched them and the horses' hoofs sank into the mud.

"Hey, there! Stop, we will dismount," the man said. "We shan't get through like this, the beasts are already tired enough."

"A lot of use having horses, if we're to go on foot," Auberi said. One-eye slapped him with the tip of his glove and made him dismount with a tap on the bottom.

"And what if your mule dies, eh? Would that help you on? You'll see, he'll be in mud up to his belly. It's all streams about here."

So they went forward on foot, seeking in vain for traces of a firm path on which to put their feet. No one had passed that way for three days. They were making for Puy-en-Velay, thinking to join up with a band of pilgrims who were going to Marseilles for the spring. It was well to ask protection of the Virgin of Puy for so hazardous a journey.

They found no other shelter for the night but a shepherd's hut. The dead wood was too damp to make a fire. They ate some of the bread and salt pork which they carried in their bag. Auberi had to wait until the old man had finished before he might eat; and he was so hungry that tears ran down from his eyes and he was shaking. But he could not eat much; the pork made him thirsty and the bread was dry and lay heavy in his stomach. Night fell early; outside, gusts of wind were breaking branches from the trees and the rain drove in through the door, which would not close. The child remembered tales of brigands and of the souls of the dead crying in the wind upon deserted roads.

"Come," said One-eye, "lie here against me and warm yourself." And the child huddled against him, his face to the ground, and began to cry.

"Now he's crying, the son of a dog! Auberi, how old are you?"

"Twelve, my lord."

"At twelve I was stronger than you, boy. Listen, Auberi, you must understand that a child is worse than a beast, for he is wilier and lazier.

You can do nothing, ever, with a child who is not handled harshly. I, myself, had an old and wise father who flogged me so much, for so little, that I had no more skin on my buttocks than this meat we're eating. And when you've borne that, without complaint, there's not much you're afraid of later on."

Auberi said: "Yes, my lord." But he was by no means wishful of being so hardened. He wanted a bowl of good, hot soup, and a good bed. And he cried so much that his head hurt him.

He reached Puy so ill that he could no longer sit his mule. The cold wind was freezing the puddles and once again they had to dismount and go on foot because of the icy roads, the horses' hoofs sliding and slipping on the rising slope, and in the streets of the town the trapped wind formed freezing drafts. Too poor to lodge at the inn, the two travellers stopped before a shoemaker's shop, and the old man bargained lengthily with the shoemaker, offering his belt in exchange for several days' hospitality—the belt, he said, was a good two thumbs wide, of new leather, worked in Reims, and so strong that it could be used to sole ladies' shoes; the shoemaker hesitated, but the man had an honest look about him and the child seemed really ill. He took the belt and gave them a corner of the apprentices' room. Auberi was laid upon a pallet and the old man dried their travelling cloaks by the fire to cover the child. Auberi was coughing so grievously that it seemed as if his frail chest were being torn inside, and One-eye, seated beside the pallet, his hands clasped about his knees, listened, puzzled and a little ashamed, to that rattle of the dying.

This Auberi was a child of great charm, tall for his age, thin, strong in the joints and straight of leg; his chestnut hair fell in tufts, unconfined, even over his eyes. He had a tip-tilted nose and grey eyes which laughed or cried for a trifle. It was most piteous to see him, all red, and shaken as if by an evil spirit. So piteous that the old man rose and went to the horse market with the mule.

There the people fell foul of him and nearly beat him, because he had a northerner's accent and thrust himself full before the customers, barring their way. He explained that his sight was bad and that he was no merchant—if anyone wanted a mule he would let it go cheaply. The price he asked was indeed low, for prices were lower in Troyes than in Puy. But the look of him was so strange that he was taken for a thief and had to talk hard and swear on the cross that the beast was really his own. And as he was not familiar with the coinage of the region, he received only half what he asked.

With this money he returned to the shoemaker's and begged him to find him a man learned in curing maladies of the chest.

Throughout the whole winter and until the end of Lent he remained in the cobbler's shop, seated in a corner of the workshop, hammering hard leather to soften it, plaiting laces, sharpening the knives and razors. The apprentices about him sang as they beat with their mallets or tugged at their needles. Sometimes he would sing with them, because he liked to learn new songs. His sight grew worse and worse; they had put him in a dark corner, behind the rolls of leather, because there was no room anywhere else. The room was small, the two square windows covered with stretched bladder to let in a dim and yellow light. Candles were lit early, but then only for the master and the senior workman.

Auberi, not well recovered from his sickness, sometimes came to the workshop; but he preferred to stay in the kitchen, where he helped the housewife to peel vegetables. The saucepan hanging over the fire made a noise suggesting that a hundred imps were shut up in it. The good wife went to raise the lid, and Auberi would seize his chance to slip half a carrot or a bit of bacon into his mouth.

The old man who, God knows why, had been nicknamed Master Pierre, was well liked by the apprentices. He told them stories of the Holy Land and advised them to abandon their trade and take to soldiering: at their age it was still possible to make something of them, although it was better to begin at the age of six or seven. They should take service with some lord about to set out for Palestine: since the kings and the high nobility were too evil to deliver God's tomb, it was up to the lesser people to do it. The land which God had chosen to inhabit was every man's only true fatherland and it was shameful not to go to its defense.

The master also listened joyfully to the old man, for it seemed to him that these were the words of a pious pilgrim. But at last he realized that his lads were so busy listening that they worked less quickly. After Easter, seeing that Auberi was better of his sickness, he told One-eye that he could keep him no longer. The other took it well, packed the few things which remained to him in his wallet, and said:

"Much thanks for your goodness, Master. We have caused you anxieties. When we reach Jerusalem, we will pray for you." It was the only recompense he could offer, for the horse had long been sold.

At the gate of the town, at the sight of hills turning to green, and the lambs leaping in the meadows, and of the sky above the blue mountains, he sighed like a man released from prison. And he began to walk, with the measured pace of a pilgrim, singing the apprentices' songs. And Auberi marched beside him, limping, for he was still weak and tired.

At their first halt One-eye said to him:

"My lad, if you do not wish to come with me, I shall not hold you to me. You are nearer to your home than to Jerusalem. I can manage as well by myself."

The child looked long at him out of great grey eyes brimming with tears.

"I will go with you," he said. "Beat me if you want to."

THE LADY OF BEAUTY

MARIE OF BAUDEMANT, lady of Mongenost, had neither child nor lover. She was twenty-four years old. And she was bored.

Two men loved her, the count of Bar and Pierre of Joigny, seneschal of Provins. As for suitors of lesser rank, they were beyond counting. But she did not dare show preference to any, for fear of making them objects of hatred to the two barons; and to give her love to one of the two she could not, without making a mortal enemy of the other, for both were very much in love. In any case, neither of them pleased her. She had no children by her husband and was content that it should be so, for as long as she had no heir he was obliged to treat her with consideration. He had married her for her inheritance and it was she who paid his debts.

When the lady of Pouilli spoke to her on behalf of her brother from Normandy, the lady of Mongenost turned a deaf ear: it was not the first time that a friend had spoken to her for a brother or an uncle or a cousin. But she told herself that the young man was not known in Troyes, that the castle of Pouilli was near neighbor to Mongenost, and that if the youth really had the manners and distinction which his sister claimed for him, it would perhaps be worth while to try him.

Haguenier had good hunter's blood in his veins and loved game which was rare and of great price. Not that he was difficult in the matter of women; but he had certain ideas concerning love; he believed that once knighted he should love none but a very noble lady and be faithful to her. Had he foreseen all the trials to which the lady of Mongenost would submit him, he might perhaps never have engaged himself to her. But she was to seem so gentle at the beginning; afterwards, it was too late to draw back.

Love, it is said, goes in through the eyes to reach the heart. Those who set eyes on Marie had good reason to say so, for never was lady lovelier to see. Her skin was so soft and clear that her face was like a lamp of alabaster lit from within; and her eyes, of color changeable, like the sea, were so eloquent that even had she been mute, she would none the less have been loved—better perhaps, indeed, for she had a false and subtle tongue, more cruel than the serpent's who misled the matriarch Eve. Her hair, light in color as ripe oats, ranged in fine tresses beside her cheeks and, interwoven with threads of silk and with pearls, suggested rich embroidery. There was, indeed, a quality excessive, precious, in her elegance which sometimes made her resemble a statue of a saint in a church porch. To young men drilled from childhood for the military life, taught to exalt every kind of fidelity, this mixture of delicacy and stiffness seemed the ultimate in feminine perfection. More than one petty squire of Troyes had vowed his life to Marie without even the hope of ever winning a smile from her.

Marie was learned, for having nothing to do all day she read much. Often, indeed, her eyes were red and her eyelids drooping from much reading. Her suitors undertook to lend her books; and she liked to copy those songs which pleased her, for herself, with the music, and to decorate them with little drawings in red ink. She was also very clever with her needle and herself designed the patterns for her embroidery, the greater part of which she had done by her women; as she was pious, she embroidered chiefly decorations for the Church. Reading, music, works of art and prayer had occupied her, to the point of passion, for years. They comprised her only life—she had no affection for her husband. But now she was beginning to think of love, like any ordinary woman.

Haguenier had seen her for the first time in the countryside about Troyes, with Aielot; she had stopped, with her women, near a clump of

birch trees and was playing at blind-man's buff, her eyes blindfold, her
head and neck uncovered. Seeing the lady of Pouilli approaching, with
a man, her damsels began to laugh and call and to gather up their cloaks,
which had been thrown on the ground. Maliciously, they left their
lady in the meadow as she was. Marie laughed and tried to untie the
knot of the blindfold. When the riders had dismounted, she tore off
the bandage, and was all astonishment to see a young man on his knees
before her.

And he saw her so, rosy and luminous, her hair a little disarranged,
her glance lost in surprise, her eyelids blinking. Then she blushed and
raised her eyes to the lady of Pouilli and said to her gently:

"Friend, it was not well-mannered in you not to warn me that you
were with a man. Brigitte, bring my cloak and my veil. Sir Bachelor, I
do not know you but I think that you are this lady's brother; you will
excuse me for my appearance, you can see that it is no fault of mine."

And Haguenier found her even more beautiful for her politeness—
how could she fail to be gentle to a lover, who was so considerate of a
stranger?

She led the brother and sister near to a spring, where sheep sometimes
came to drink, in the shade of willows and beech trees. The water filled
a small, flat tank edged with stone and ran over into the meadow as a
stream. Aielot scooped water into the hollow of her hand and drank,
and then wiped her hand over her hair and her cheeks.

"Brother," she said, "you should ask the lady to let you drink, in
this manner, out of her hand, for courtesy. Lord! how much sweeter the
water would be, drunk from her hands."

"I should never dare to do it," Haguenier said.

"My friend the lady Aielot loves jesting," said Marie, gently. "Only
my animals drink out of my hand. The noble bachelor will find much
better drinking-cups."

"Better there cannot be," said Haguenier, "unless it be the chalice
which contains God's blood. I should never be bold enough to dare touch
it."

Whereupon Marie took water in the hollow of her hand and carried
it to the young man's lips.

"You shall see," she said, laughing, "that I yield nothing to you in
courtesy. And now we are quits."

He drank, taking care not to press his lips too firmly against the
small wet hand.

"I should not ever wish to be quits, lady," he said. "And you did very wrong to remove the blindfold from your eyes."

"And why so, Sir Bachelor?"

"That I cannot tell you, it would vex you too much, and you would not want to see me again."

The lady pretended to be displeased, and turned away and began to look for snowdrops. She found two, which she gave to the lady of Pouilli, saying:

"You will give the second to messire Jacques, from me, with my remembrance."

"Messire Jacques is not the man to care for such gifts," Aielot said, laughing. Marie also laughed.

"Do as you like with it, they are not such rarities."

And after that day Haguenier had no other thought than to see the lady of Mongenost again.

"You must know," Aielot had told him, "it is not wise to go often on to her land, for the husband is jealous, and not only the husband. She is much watched over. If you are seen with her too often, you will throw away your chances, for you well know that a woman does not like to be reproached because of a man. Return, rather, to Hervi, since our father awaits you. I will talk to her of you, in the right way."

"But she will forget me," Haguenier said. "Since I am so fortunate as to be within half a league of her house, the devil would be in it if I do not contrive to see her. She will think me very backward."

"Not at all," said Aielot. "I will prove to you that I am right: she is a lady much sought after; if you are forever under her eyes, you will be acting like any bumpkin who thinks himself already loved because of the two or three words of politeness she has spoken to you. You are not even a knight yet. It is your business to make her see that you know how to keep a proper distance, that you are sensible and prudent. No woman ever wants a madcap or a vain man for a lover."

"True," Haguenier said, "but I do not want her to think I am afraid of my rivals."

"In love," Aielot said, "patience is everything. You must see that a woman like her, who has only to choose, will not choose a man whom she cannot be sure of."

HAGUENIER:
II. A FATHER AND A BROTHER

HAGUENIER found the castle of Hervi in all the bustle of a general house-cleaning; the women were down at the river for the great wash and were spreading the sheets in the meadows to bleach them, for the sun was already strong. The door of the castle was wide open and masons were working on the wall, the courtyard full of their mortar. Servants were washing the floors and walls of the hall with great quantities of water, so that a black stream carrying bits of straw was pouring out of the door.

Puzzled, Haguenier stopped in the middle of the courtyard. He knew nobody here and nobody paid any attention to him.

"Hey, friend," he called to an old servant passing with a bucket of water, "the lord is not here, I suppose?"

"Le Gros? You'd see him all right if he were here. He's at Linnières, a league below by way of the forest."

"Worthy man," Haguenier said, "you should know me: I know that you were already here in my grandfather's time. I remember your face well."

And the old man's countenance lightened into such a beaming that the young man was surprised. The old servant seized the horseman's foot and kissed it several times.

"Little Niot!" he cried. "Ah, God knows, we were waiting and hoping for you, my lord, God knows it."

Haguenier understood exactly what this meant, and was offended for his father's sake; he frowned.

"I shall be very glad to see my father," he said. Then he took leave of the old man and followed the road to Linnières, thoughtfully.

Herbert was taking his ease in the meadow in front of the castle, propped up by woollen cushions. He was so great a lover of fresh air that he often even had the tables set in the meadow, to take his meals there. Near him was the beautiful Ortrud, his leman, who, seated by his side, was untangling his hair with a little horn comb. She was a very beautiful girl but most exceptionally stupid—despite which, or perhaps because of which, Herbert was very fond of her. It was said, indeed, that he did not sleep with her, preferring for that purpose girls not so beautiful and not so well dressed, but the little German girl was the only one he would bear near him when he was in a bad mood and he was hardly ever seen without her.

From time to time the young woman amused herself by pulling her master's hair a little, and he responded by a little grunt of pleasure; whereupon Ortrud would laugh aloud her clear, shrill laugh. Two squires, seated somewhat apart, held ready the spiced hydromel which the master liked to drink before the mid-day meal.

Haguenier dismounted and went forward twenty paces on foot, holding his horse by the bridle. He was a little vexed to find his father in the company of a girl, but let nothing of his feeling appear and respectfully bent the knee.

"So," Herbert said, "here he is, the fine gentleman. We're lucky he did not postpone his arrival until after Christmas. Come here." And he raised himself on his elbow. Haguenier was forced to bend double to kiss the hand which his father did not even take the trouble to raise. They looked at each other and the young man dropped his eyes, despite his strong wish to examine his father closely.

"He is handsome," Herbert said, "but as for taking after me—no. Yet your mother was no beauty, eh, son of a bitch? Could it be that you are the son of some handsome country fellow, fair youth? You may sit beside me."

This kind of pleasantry on Herbert's part surprised nobody, but Haguenier was not used to it.

"You receive me ill," he said. "If I have displeased you, tell me so, but, in God's name, speak no ill of my mother. It is not fitting to make a jest of such matters."

"Who knows?" Herbert said. "It is very clear that that strumpet Aielot has been talking to you against me. She knows how to do it. But God knows I bear you no grudge for that. As for me," he added, "I am loyal to those who love me; I am not like others whom I shall not name." He raised the young man's chin with his hand.

"No beard yet," he said. "Pleasant to touch. A pretty mouth, too. And you run after women like the devil, I can see that from your eyes.

In that he takes after his sister—and this I tell you between ourselves, my lad—Jacques of Pouilli's sons are little Swiss soldiers of fortune or wandering minstrels, as true as God lives."

This time the young man became angry.

"Listen," he said, "for a man of your age you talk very wildly. It does you no honor to defame your own daughter, especially before this lady or damsel. Tell me to go up to the castle, to see the lady my grandmother. When you are in a better humor, you will send for me again."

Herbert, in point of fact, was in an excellent humor, and even a little moved to tenderness by his son. Seeing him angry, he frowned.

"As you please, my fine cockerel. I do not know what that trollop told you against me, but understand that I love those who serve me well and that I have eyes in my head. God knows a loyal son will have no cause to complain of me."

Haguenier took leave of his father and again mounted his horse. Herbert followed him with a look long, thoughtful and hard. He was wondering whether the brother and sister were not conspiring together against him. Haguenier could claim full control of his fief of Hervi. He was past his majority and the sole legal holder; his father merely administered it in his name. But to claim it would have been to go against custom, and to succeed in his claim he would have need of powerful friends in Troyes. Get him married as quickly as possible, Herbert was thinking, let him get an heir, and then away to sow his wild oats in a foreign country.

Haguenier was disappointed to learn that his grandmother no longer lived at the castle but at Bernon, beyond the forest. Nevertheless, he stayed for the meal. Herbert placed him on his right, next to his wife, the lady Aelis, and the better to do him honor caused him to be served by Ernaut, the elder of his bastards; the other, Pierre, who was very jealous of Ernaut, was delighted to see him humiliated and said:

"It is a great joy for my brother Ernaut to serve the young lord, son of a noblewoman." (It must be explained that Pierre was himself the son of a bastard daughter of Herbert the Red and boasted of having good blood on both sides. Ernaut's mother was a village girl, a peasant.) Then Ernaut said that no man could force him to serve one who was not a knight and that there were younger lads for that office.

"Be silent, you cur!" Herbert thundered. "It would be a fine thing, indeed, if the spawn of a whore, like you, refused to serve my son!"

Ernaut did not dare to disobey. But when he had to go down and saddle Haguenier's horse, he wept with mortification in the stables.

Haguenier, who was good-hearted, was distressed at having been the cause of wretchedness to his half-brother. He sought him in the stables and said:

"Ernaut, fair brother, I remember you well; we used to play together. You are even, as far as I know, older than me. If it pains you to serve me, we will find means to arrange otherwise."

"Your words are fair," said Ernaut. "Meanwhile, I am to attend you to Bernon."

"Fair brother," said Haguenier, "do not think I am trying to flatter you; I speak in all frankness. Do not be distrustful of me. We are of the same blood, we should not quarrel."

"The honor is too much!" Ernaut said, surly. "And I have never quarrelled with you."

On the way to Bernon they rode side by side and Haguenier succeeded in cheering his companion by talking to him of the customs governing the tourney and the hunt which he had learned in Normandy. Ernaut had a passion for tournaments and had journeyed to them throughout all Champagne in his father's train. He soon forgot that he was dealing with the brother he had resolved, in advance, to hate and began, in his turn, to tell of the handsome jousts he had seen. But when they arrived at Bernon he resumed his sulky face and coldly obsequious manners. He was thinking of Pierre and his taunts.

The grandmother now lived at Bernon, which her husband had left her as a dower; thither she had summoned Milon of Cagne, her bailiff, her youngest son, her granddaughter, and the damsel Eglantine, her husband's bastard. Bernon was no more than a large farmhouse, long and flat, built of cob, the only windows two small square openings, one in the north wall, one in the south. In fine weather the women worked out of doors, a little apart from the house, in the meadow; all about the house was a vast field of dung, clay and rotten straw, planks being laid across it to make a path to the door. During winter the cows and sheep were taken into the house and from behind the wooden division of the interior their great heads would peep, curious or hungry, lowing for the straw stuffing of the pallets.

The lady was not yet accustomed to this farmhouse and was always knocking her forehead against the low door, and complaining of the darkness. But she held her head high. She always attended the church at Hervi, as she had formerly done, dressed in her old red gown, now worn and repaired; she sent Milon to buy candles and spices at Chaource, and on Sundays spread her table with a white cloth. She wished everyone to see that she had no need of her son's charity to live. Herbert had long begged her to remain at Linnières. She had refused, preferring to be the lady of Bernon rather than housekeeper at the castle. And she knew that she had thereby done Herbert a very ill service, for he had no one to keep his house; Aelis, his wife, did not understand the business at all and the servants served the new master against their will. Herbert had not yet forgiven his mother this "woman's whimsy" as he called it, this "mad pride." During Lent he had seen her again, in church, and had again begged her to return to his house.

"You shall have hangings of silk and a table service of oak, and as many candles as you wish, to pray to God."

She had answered:

"Fair son, your expenses are already too heavy, without that."

And she had returned to Bernon with the two maidens and the young Joceran, her youngest living son. This Joceran was seventeen years of age and Herbert was asking for him, for his service; but the mother feared that he might put the youth to tasks beneath his rank, and said:

"I need him at Bernon."

Herbert loved his mother well but he could not prevent himself blaming her for her woman's pride.

"Fair child," the old lady said, "lovely youth, sweet offering of spotless white." With her lips she touched the young man's hands and shoulders. He was astonished to find her so little changed: there was the same tenderness in her eyes, and the same smile.

She talked to him a great deal about her new house. It was now her chief preoccupation. It was, she said, hard to make such a change in one's life at her age; on the other hand she had fewer worries with this house than with the other—she could live on her ewes, her cows and her field, and she even had enough left to buy candles and embroidery thread for her women: she made beautiful things which could be sold in Chaource and even in Bar. Her baron, who was wise, had made good provision for her. She was very glad that she had not remained at the castle, for Herbert was engaged in turning the place into a brothel and she could not abide immorality. God be thanked that she had the means to teach her maidens to make a dower for themselves.

She offered Haguenier ewe's-milk cheese which she had made herself. The two young girls, standing before the table, stared admiringly at Haguenier: their lady had so often told them that "the child" was as beautiful as Saint Michael, and learned, and strong, and that he would be lord of the two domains. Marie, who was seven years old, was small, thin and as if transparent, as children are when born to elderly parents. But the other, Eglantine, who was already more than sixteen, was a beautiful girl, tall, rather thin, robust as a peasant, brown-skinned; her large cow's-eyes, dark and full of dreams, were very like Ernaut's.

"My lovely Eglantine has grown into a big girl," Haguenier said, "will she be married soon?" The lady looked long, with pitying severity, at the girl.

"Eglantine is a wild girl," she said. "There is something wrong with her mind. I tell this to my fair grandson Haguenier because he is already a man, and first of our family after Herbert. He should be informed of all that is happening in the household. At the moment we have no husband for her," she added, with a sigh. Eglantine gave her a harsh look, then turned her back and left the room, her head high.

"It is true, then, that poor Eglantine is mad?" Haguenier asked Ernaut, on their way back.

"It seems so," Ernaut said. "They say she was bewitched when she was little and that the lady grandmother had something to do with it at one time. She has a devil in her."

"So young a girl? It is not possible."

"They say she brings bad luck. There was a lad called Pierre whom the old baron had killed, because of her—that was a good three years ago. Then there was Jacques of Vanlay, you know, our father's cousin on the Puiseaux side—and yet he's not young—they say he had his way with her and that afterwards he fell into a sickness, like a man who has seen a fairy. There's a lad of Puiseaux, Girard by name, who is languishing after her, so much so that he no longer eats but weeps all day long. And I can tell you something very strange—and I tell you to warn you, for it's a thing the lady our grandmother must never know —our father himself has lain with her and for him to have done such a thing it's certain that the Devil must be in it."

"But it's appalling!" Haguenier said. "I'd not have believed it from anyone but you. He'll get himself damned. She is his sister."

Ernaut shrugged his shoulders.

"After all," he said, "they are not from the same belly. Anyone can have sisters like that, without even knowing that they are sisters."

He had been so long accustomed to his father that nothing he did could shock him. He loved him, and that passionately.

But Haguenier thought differently. He was much tempted to say to Ernaut:

"And you, yourself, what sort of brother are you to me?" but he bit back the words and held his tongue. Nevertheless he was distressed, both for his father and for the young girl and for Ernaut, so honest a lad, who yet could speak with indifference of such a sin.

"And suppose I tell the lady?" he said.

"God! Don't think of it, our father fears her more than twenty bishops. She would make a scandal. And this is a thing to keep to ourselves, in the family."

Haguenier sighed—to how many such secrets would he have to be a party, in this household?

EGLANTINE

Nobody knew how that unnatural relationship had started; certainly both of them must have willed it, for it was not easy for them to meet. It is well said that the Devil snares men where and when he pleases. Eglantine sometimes came to Linnières with her little sister, to gossip with friends at the castle. Herbert had hated her while her mere existence threatened the interests of his own children: his father might find her a powerful husband and eat into their property for her sake by making over land to his future son-in-law. Once Herbert had clearly understood that the girl was not marriageable, he had laughed with joy; and, well pleased with the old man's humiliation, he had forgotten his hatred of the bastard girl. When she had returned from the convent, in despair at the loss of her father, he had put himself forward to console her—after his own fashion.

No child whose mother had given it a stone instead of bread would have been more broken-hearted, more confounded, than Eglantine the day she learned that her old father had left the country. When he had fallen sick she had cut off her hair, offering it to God that he might get better. Ah, that she had rather let him die! Ah, God do thee hurt, old liar, false traitor who has abandoned me to my enemies! And may God send toads beneath thy shirt and ants into thy beard and flies into thine eye, old wickedness, old black devil! Never more will I love thee nor pray to God for thee, neither night nor morning. Through thy fault I shall die and damn myself forever and I shall become the wildfire above the marshes, misleading wayfarers on autumn evenings. And I shall become the black fawn of the forest, leading huntsmen into the bottomless mud, and I shall change into a swallow and seek thee in the hot countries and forever fly about thy head and make thee afraid: and when thou shalt have killed me thou shalt see thine Eglantine dead at thy feet, her head crushed by a stone. And never again shalt thou know joy. And thou shalt weep for me so bitterly and long that it will burn out thine eye and never shalt thou see again. On every road I shall be with thee, crying in thy heart, thou who hast wronged me because thou feared to see me weep.

At first she had tried to hang herself from a branch in the forest, but her girdle was too frail and had broken. Afterwards, she had gone back to the lady, at Bernon, and promised to be good and obedient, for she loved the lady. But it seemed that the heart of her heart was a black hole filled with little grey flames which gave neither light nor heat but burned like quicklime. Ah, what loveliness was hers, what noble blood! Daughter of a golden-haired damsel—and Herbert would give her in marriage to some servant of his squire, a man who must work to get his bread—Herbert the jealous, wolf-heart, vulture-eye, cursed be whoever loves and serves thee. And I shall laugh loud on the day that devils drag out thy brains through thy great nostrils and fill thine eyes with spiders.

On a Sunday in Lent she had come to Hervi on the way back from church and had sat down in the courtyard, near to the drinking trough, to talk with her friends. Herbert had taken her on his knees and had said to her, as if in jest:

"And you, my pretty, what would you ask of a man, to lie in your arms?" And she had said:

"A golden ring," as a young girl should. Then Herbert took a ring of chiselled gold from his little finger and put it in Eglantine's hand. She flushed red with anger and flung the ring into the mud, saying:

"From you, fair brother, I ask nothing."

"Well done! That, I like," Herbert said. "Since my ring does not please you, tell me what else you must have."

"Me?" she said, lifting her chin, "I must have the two eyes—blue as water—of a horse, upon the two wings of a snow-white falcon."

Now, as all knew, Herbert had an Arab thoroughbred with blue eyes and a white falcon of Hungary of which he was very proud. And he broke into a laugh and said:

"That is how I love a girl to be! You have spoken well. If you come tomorrow at noon to the chapel in the forest, you shall have what you want."

And Eglantine came to the chapel to see whether Herbert wanted her badly enough to sacrifice his horse.

He had brought her the bloody gift, wrapped in a silken cloth. Eglantine had with her her spaniel dog; she threw it the blue eyes and scattered the feathers of the white wings with her knife.

"Well," Herbert said, "and my prize?"

"For you, fair brother," she said, "no prize. You are too old."

"And was Jacques of Vanlay young, then?"

"And though you brought me your own eyes out of your head, I should do as I have done with these."

"Good," he said. "And what if I take you by force?"

"That will not make you handsomer. And I shall be very glad of it, for it will surely cause you to be damned, since I am your father's daughter."

"Little ugliness," he said, taking her head in his hands, "I can do as I will with you, but listen a little: I am miserly or generous at will; but I prize money no more than a nut. You can see that I do not regret the horse killed for your sake. But that is because I wished it so. I knew well that you would come. I carry such charms upon me that every woman I desire comes and offers herself to me."

Eglantine replied that that was most fortunate for him, for that otherwise he would have gone short of women. For a good hour she rallied and insulted him as much as she could, all the time wondering when and how he would punish her. And the bolder her words, the greater grew her terror and drunkenness at insulting the man who had all power over her.

She took pleasure in making him wait and sometimes hid from him on purpose, behind a tree, to watch him pace in a circle or up and down in front of the chapel, his arms crossed on his chest. And when he took her in his arms she beat his face and bit him and thrust him away with her elbows, and he accepted it all; it was in the rules of the game. At first she had been frightened at committing such a sin, in a chapel and beneath a crucifix, but afterwards she took pleasure in it.

"Since we are damning ourselves," Herbert said, "we may as well damn ourselves for good." It amused him to hang his gloves and his belt on the crucifix.

Herbert boasted of knowing love secrets such as would subdue the haughtiest of women. He greatly exaggerated; but Eglantine was not a haughty woman. Lost, terrified, full of rancor against their father and amorous hate of Herbert, she had let herself be drawn body and soul into this bitter relationship. She knew that this was by far the worst thing she could do to her father and perhaps the only thing he would be incapable of forgiving her. At night, with her face hidden in her hands, she devised and uttered long litanies against the old man and against Herbert, mixing them together to make one object for her hatred. She believed herself able to do Herbert harm. She thought that he loved her. He must surely love her, to have done what he had done. And she recalled with joy everything which was ugly about him—laughed because she knew him so profoundly and burned with desire to shout their relationship to the whole world.

Before the lady of Bernon she had to lie and be gentle and act the role of repentant sinner, for before that lady she cast out her mad spirit and became like a nut without a kernel. At noon, during the siesta, she escaped, stole the keys, oiled the latches, followed the wild boar's paths and neither the marsh nor fear of wild beasts could stop her. Her head was full of the hard words she would say to Herbert. And her head sang with never-ending refrains—Herbert le Gros, Herbert the Fat, iron-head, bull-face, Herbert the Jealous, wolf-face—she knew that the village children sang these things on the road when they saw any of the castle people. The snotty little urchins of the village hated him like the plague while she, daughter of a noble mother, what did she do? Yielded her body to the Jealous as to a lover, a beloved friend.

Ah! the sky is clear and brooks sing in the meadow, every girl has her lad, and I have mine. The largest, the strongest, master of the countryside. The one whom nobody loves, unless it be for his money. Me, I've no use for money. I would fling his money into the water, to the fishes, his necklaces would I scatter in forest clearings for the magpies and starlings and spread his fine cloth in the mud for the ewes to trample. Friend, lover—to no one, not even to God at the Last Judgment shall I dare tell what you are to me, of what blood you are; and if it be found out I shall be excommunicated and burned at the stake, and you—the lady will curse you and you will be driven from the country barefooted, in your shirt, to go and pray to God for your sin.

At all these things Herbert laughed. Nothing could ever be proved against him. At heart he was less at ease than he pretended. Throughout the countryside the girl was known to be his sister and passed for a simpleton, an idiot. If the lady learned the truth, she would be capable of withholding forgiveness: women are by nature obstinate and proud, unable to understand to what lengths desire in love can drive a man— and that the longer love is denied, the more it torments a man. Such is the law of nature and Herbert did not claim to be a saint. When he thought of Eglantine he sometimes experienced unavowable pleasures of pride revenged—this blow dealt to his old father repaid God knows how many scoldings, petty injustices, insults swallowed in silence. The one-eyed old man had not really been a bad father to him—rather, indifferent, rough in his manner, and that was all. But Herbert had too good a memory; the beatings suffered at fifteen and even at seven years of age still smarted.

ERNAUT, OR THE HEAVY HEART

ERNAUT was the son of a peasant girl of Bernon, Gauchère by name. At the time when Herbert had known her she was a handsome girl with thick hair and flat lips. She had loved the excessively fair, gently born youth who had seduced her, with the strong and simple love of a decent and virtuous girl. She suffered both blows and shame and ended by seeking help from the lady of Linnières; she was about to be brought to bed and swore that the child was Herbert's indeed; she did not want to abandon it but knew that her parents would not let her keep it. The lady had had almost enough of girls who complained of having been seduced by Herbert, but Gauchère had pleased her; she had made her welcome at the castle and had consented to be the child's godmother. Herbert's wife had as yet borne him only a daughter, and he was not a little proud of having a son: of what is one not proud, at sixteen? The lady, who was not fond of her daughter-in-law, hoped that Gauchère's influence might help her son to settle down. After the men had departed for the crusade Gauchère remained at the castle, counting the hours and making her *novenas* like any crusader's wife. Then Bertrade, Herbert's wife, bore a son—Haguenier—and the lady changed her attitude to Gauchère: she even sent her away to the farmhouse at Bernon, to please Bertrade: but she did not forget little Ernaut who was still, after all, the eldest of her grandsons.

After an absence of three years Herbert returned, tall and strong, arrogant as a captain of free-lances. The death of his elder brother had made him the heir of Linnières; the death of his wife's brothers made him the future master of Hervi. And now everyone feared him, for he was known to bear malice. He began by relegating Bertrade to the servants' quarters: she had been disfigured by the smallpox and he claimed that the mere sight of her froze his blood; but his aversion to her was older than that—he had been married against his inclination and could not forget it. For Ernaut's sake he brought Gauchère back to the castle. But his current companion was Isabeau, one of the castle girls, whom he had also got with child—Pierre—before the crusade;

until he married again Isabeau was to be his official mistress. Gauchère, weary of Isabeau's taunts, had finally gone back to her family at Bernon, but Ernaut had stayed with his father.

Pierre was the oldest of Isabeau's sons and Herbert was very fond of him: he was a pretty child, intelligent and lively, some months younger than Ernaut. Ernaut and Pierre had hated each other from the first, because of their mothers, and when Herbert took them both into his service it was not long before they were jealous of each other. Their father cunningly fostered this jealousy, finding their quarrels amusing, like the fury of pretty little animals. He also realized that this was a good way of stimulating their zeal to serve him well and also a guarantee —one can be sure of a servant constantly overseen by a colleague who hates him.

He had given Ernaut to his son as a servant and companion; thereby he intended to underline the difference between his legitimate son and his bastards, for he was anxious to show respect for custom. Haguenier's knighting was to be the grandest feast ever beheld at Linnières, and on the following day the two bastards were to receive their spurs, with other young men of smaller consequence—Herbert could not act otherwise, for there were already complaints that the two lads were treated with too much favor. In this also his fat lordship demonstrated a certain singularity of behavior: he loved Ernaut far more than his other children and yet insisted upon humiliating him before Haguenier whom he regarded, rather, as an enemy; doubtless his object was to make his bastard sons hate his heir from the beginning.

Now, from the first days of their association, Haguenier and Ernaut appeared to get on wonderfully with each other. They were seen riding together in the forest and on the banks of the Armançon; they competed in shooting, leaped ravines together, and fought endless fencing duels with some old swords which they had found in the cellar. Then they would dash towards the well, hustling the servants to draw them water, drinking from the very bucket, and laughing so much that they could hardly stand upright.

It was well known at Linnières that Ernaut was not of a laughing disposition. He had his reasons for not being gay and never let anyone forget the fact. He was distrustful. But whoever won his confidence kept it forever. Haguenier had begun by dazzling him with his knowledge of fine manners. He had just spent ten years at the court of a count and had not wasted his time; and he was a youth so frankly and clearly good-hearted that not even Ernaut could suspect him of hypocrisy. He spoke neither good nor ill of anyone and had a wide, boyish smile, creasing up his nose and his eyelids and making the flecks of gold gleam in his grey eyes. He laughed easily and for small cause, having a deep laugh, a little like neighing, so droll that it was as contagious as the itch; it was impossible to hear it without the mouth and throat opening of themselves in their desire to laugh.

Ernaut learned to laugh almost as much as his brother. He was a little surprised at it himself; never had he had a comrade so gay and carefree. At first Ernaut had not been sparing of rebuffs and bitter-sweet answers and took the smallest jest in bad part. He soon saw that it was wasted effort. Haguenier shrugged his shoulders and then came to make it up a quarter of an hour later, ready to ask forgiveness.

They went to Puiseaux together, and all the way there Ernaut begged his friend not to speak to Ida and to do nothing to please her: he was wildly jealous in advance, yet could not resist showing off Ida's beauty to his brother.

"There is no other like her," he said. "She has eyes like the sun, hair like the sun, too. So sweet, also, when she looks at you, it makes your heart turn over. As true as I live I have never cared for any woman, excepting for her."

Haguenier found Joceran of Puiseaux and his wife very pleasant hosts, but Ida was not at all to his taste—for him she was no more than a rather plump girl with rustic manners and poorly dressed, but what most displeased him in her was her manifest indifference to Ernaut, who must surely, to keep his illusions, be making truly heroic efforts. Any other girl in her place, Haguenier thought, would think herself only too happy to be so loved. She must be made of wood: a man like Ernaut is not to be despised, even by the daughter of a count. He was careful not to communicate these impressions to his brother, but from that day Ernaut admired him more than ever: he saw a grand proof of brotherly loyalty in the fact that Haguenier had not fallen in love with Ida.

Herbert seemed to feel a pinching pain in his heart at the sound of Ernaut's laughter.

"Ingrate," he thought. "At his age they've naught but folly in their heads. You rear the sons of bitches, spend your money on them, your bread and your woollen cloth. No more heart than a buzzard, and your training all wasted."

"Fair son Ernaut," he said, "I know you are sober and well-behaved. To look at you now one would never have thought it. I am very glad to find you so prudent."

Ernaut was silent, turning his glove over and over between his fingers; he knew his father's bitter taste in praises only too well. Herbert put his hand on his shoulder.

"My fair son knows very well who will be master here after my death. He is well aware that there is more to be had by serving a young master than an old one."

Ernaut looked at him somberly from beneath his thick fringe.

"An ill thing to say," he said.

"Pierre is simpler than you," Herbert continued. "When a man grows old there is neither joy nor profit in serving him. But I am not so old, fair son, fat though I be."

"You do not speak justly," Ernaut said, quietly.

"I am thirty-seven years old, fair son. But fathers with grown children are wrong to live to old age. Pierre is a simple lad, he does not understand that. And I shall remember that. Never mind, I am well pleased to see that you will not lose much by my death."

This was too much for Ernaut. He drew himself up and bristled like a wild-cat.

"What I shall lose by your death—if I live to see it—neither you, nor any other knows—unless it be He who knows all. And you shall not mock me, bull-face! Go and seek one who loves you better than I do! You will search until Christmas and the Last Judgment!" He burst into sobs and rushed from the room. And during three days he was very cool towards Haguenier and said no word to his father but yes or no. Herbert was never offended by Ernaut's ill humors. He said:

"The lad's in love and it sours his blood." And his secret thought was:

"I did well to speak to him; he will see that he must distrust his brother."

The two young men slept in the same bed and always talked together before going to sleep. Ernaut's feelings were too strong to permit him to conceal his thoughts for long. He said to Haguenier:

"For your sake I have drunk from a bitter cup. I shall not be caught like that again. Because of you I have been blamed and treated as a traitor."

Haguenier said:

"I know nothing whatever about it."

"Swear to me," said Ernaut, "swear by your dead mother and by your lady and by the cross and by the Holy Virgin—say, may my mother be flayed and quartered by devils in the other world—"

"God!" Haguenier said. "I shall never say that. What would you have me swear?"

"Swear first," said Ernaut.

"Tell me what it is. I was taught never to swear without knowing why."

"Very well, I will tell you; but promise me not to speak of it. Swear to me that you wish no ill to our father."

"But of course I will swear it," Haguenier said, surprised. "By anything you like. By my mother if you wish it. Such ideas have been put into your head by people who wish me ill. I have never wished our father ill—and yet God knows . . . fair brother, it is he who is not very fond of me."

"Don't say that. I got myself blamed because of you, for the sake of your friendship. Our father is not a fool, he has more brains than a bishop. He can guess a man's thoughts: I cannot do that."

"That hurts me," Haguenier said. "If you must listen to what they say about me, then never speak to me again. I shall never love people who think me false. God knows I am not false."

There was a long silence. At length Ernaut said:

"Are you asleep?"

"I only wish I could sleep," the other said. "I am too sad to sleep. I see that I am not loved here. I shall arrange matters so as to live always at Troyes or with my sister or to go to some other country. Our father shall not blame you for my sake, neither you nor anyone else."

"I can see," Ernaut said, "that you are trying to turn me against him."

"Say what you like. All I know is that when I lived at Hervi I went barefoot, like a peasant, while you ate white bread every day; my mother was put with the servants while yours was with our father's women. God knows I never bore you a grudge for that—God knows it. I have no evil thoughts. But for you loyalty and courtesy are not worth two nuts. I am not blaming you, but it is so much the worse for you."

After another silence, longer than the first, Ernaut again said:
"Are you asleep, fair brother?"

"No."

"Brother, my heart is very heavy. I know that I have not long to live."

"Who told you so?"

"Myself. For if ever Ida lies in another man's bed I shall kill myself. I know it. I am very fond of you, brother. If you reproach me, you will regret it when I am dead."

Then Haguenier set himself to prove that Ida would never marry another man. The next day the two brothers found that they were more united than ever.

NOBLE YOUTHS AND MAIDENS

HERBERT's great red litter slowly descended the slope of Linnières meadow.

The young men had gone on before with the whole troop of squires, young and old, and the Lady Aelis, with her damsels and servants, followed them closely. She was to call at Puiseaux and Bercen to bring away the ladies and damsels of both castles, for Herbert was inviting them to the feast and offering to lodge them at his expense.

At Puiseaux the lady Brune was folding the young girls' festival gowns in coffers, while Ida and Mainsant were constantly going up on to the walls to see whether the lady Aelis was coming: they had never yet been to Troyes.

"Will you bear Ernaut's shield?" Mainsant asked. Ida shrugged her shoulders: her cousin teased her so much about Ernaut that she had long since grown weary of his name. She said:

"Do you think he—the bachelor—looked at me, the other day?"

"Of course not! He's Ernaut's friend."

"He certainly took no notice of *you*."

"Foh! You know they say he lies with shepherd girls."

"Perhaps it's only Ernaut who says that."

The watch sang out:

"The lady of Linnières on the road!"

The young girls flew from the walls like startled sparrows. Joceran was waiting for them near the well. He said:

"Go at once, my doves, and braid your hair and tell Jacquet to put a new saddle-cloth on your horse. And he is to check the stirrups of my own."

The lady Brune, wearing her travelling cloak, was strapping the coffer while Jeanne, her sister-in-law, knelt on it to force the lid shut. The young girls were hastily doing up their hair while looking out of the window: the lady Aelis entered the courtyard with her sister-in-law, the lady of Buchie.

"They say the lady of Buchie was the most beautiful woman in the region," Ida said. "Oh, look, look—what a beautiful black horse she's riding. Like silk."

"Or oil," Mainsant said. "By my mother! What a waist!"

"Pooh! She's too thin."

"Not like you then!" Mainsant taunted.

"Look at Lady Aelis's horse, with the blue fringe on his bridle."

"She uses blue everywhere because it's Our Lady's color. It's a vow."

"It's the color that suits me best," Ida said. "When I am married . . ."

The young men, down on the road, were arguing about the relative strengths of the various castle households which were going to take part in the tournament. Pierre said that the Reims contingent was by far the strongest. Ernaut held that the count of Bar had the best knights: the count himself had proved very skillful at the last feast at Eastertide, so successful that his lady had been queen of the tournament for three days. And Haguenier bit his lip, knowing that this lady had been Marie of Mongenost. "Surely she loves him," he thought, "and only pretends not to, to avoid betraying her secret." He was almost tempted to give up all thought of her, to avoid competing with so noble a knight.

"Me," Pierre was saying, "I still back the Reims people. Our own are too poor and have bad weapons. We have no real fighters since Jacques of Coinci died and our father gave up jousting."

"There are the younger ones," Ernaut said.

"Yourself perhaps?"

"Listen, my children, I am going to tell you what old Barthélémi, our father's squire, told me: a lad who can manage to say seven thousand *Aves* during his vigil of arms, neither one more or less, and without thinking of anything else—he'll overthrow seven men in his first joust."

"Superstition," Ernaut said. "Your man would be so stupefied, counting his seven thousand *Aves*, that he'd be completely woolly-minded the next day."

"Oh—so by your reckoning the help of Our Lady means nothing? I know that my cousin Gillebert of Jeugni tried the thing at his dubbing, and, as you see, it worked well."

"Your cousin by father Adam," Ernaut said.

"You're picking a good day to quarrel," said Pierre. "At least my uncles didn't harness themselves to the plow with their oxen."

"And my grandmother," Ernaut said, "was not . . ."

"Peace!" Haguenier said, "the best way is still this one: we shall all three offer candles, one to Saint Paul, one to Saint George and one to Saint Michael."

His two brothers looked down their noses a little: they were both remembering that Haguenier would have a hauberk of Toledo steel and the countess's ladies to put on his armor.

THE BITTER CUP

HERBERT had stopped his litter at Bernon, wishing to see his mother. He had to get out and walk the plank path, which sank into the mud at every step he took. The lady welcomed him at her door, placing both hands flat on his chest. He stooped to kiss her. He was come, he said, to ask her to go with him to bless his son on the eve of his knighthood: she would be doing him a great honor if she would go with him.

"I had already blessed him when he left here," the lady said, "nor should I do you honor, for I have neither fine clothes nor a pretty face nor rich kinsfolk. You have enough other things to do you honor."

He repeated his request three times and thrice she refused, politely, as she knew how to do. Then she offered him beer and ewe's-milk cheese, for it was a fast day.

He sat down on a bench and Eglantine served him, upright and stiff in her simple dress of dyed linen. And when she drew near him the blood beat and boiled in her veins and she wanted to throw the cheese in his face.

And he, possessed again by his evil desire, forgot the lady, and Haguenier, and the feast. "Great is the misery of the flesh," he thought. "This girl is the devil." Oh, to be in their chapel with her, hearing her laugh and cry and call him wolf-face! She was hot and savage and wild, tormented by the devil in her blood. They were stupid oafs who had known no better than to take her and leave her. He, Herbert, had a better understanding of her quality, being skilled and experienced in women. He must contrive something which would keep her near him. Incest? What then? His father himself loved the girl not as a man loves his daughters but he had never dared face the fact. He, Herbert, dared, because he was candid.

"Wicked one," he thought, "I am going to take you in hand and you shall see what a fine life we can have together." To the girl he said:

"Listen, little ugliness, one thing I know: I shall give you a good husband of my choosing, a squire living on my bread."

She stared at him open-mouthed, too surprised to be angry.

"Cocks will lay eggs the day I marry one of your servants," she said at last.

"Wait: he's quite a well-bred man, his mother a freewoman. He's been in the castle service for forty years and he loves me like his son. To be sure, he is not young but that is all to the good, is it not?" And in a low voice he added:

"Who saddles a horse for his master does not mount it."

"Who mounted the horse shall mount it no more," Eglantine said loudly, tossing back her short curls. Now she was letting herself go in the drunkenness of anger. "Lady!" she cried, "he says that he will marry me to a servant!" The lady, at the other end of the room, had turned round and was looking at her son with surprise. Affronted by the girl's impudence, Herbert became coarse:

"You are, after all, of the family," he said to her, "and it is my business to find a father for your bastards."

She said:

"Old swine!" And spat in his face. Then she bolted, knocking over the stool and the jug of beer.

At that Herbert had one of his rages which frightened even the lady herself. He rose, put aside the table as if it had been a little stool, and the veins in his temples were like thick cords. There was silence in the room and everyone was still, pressed against the walls, as if confronted by a wild bull about to charge.

The lady's hands were full of the dough which she was engaged in kneading, and she lifted one of her hands to her brow as it was, without wiping it; Eglantine, too, raised a hand, but slowly, with an effort; her eyes were dull, as if sleepy, and her mouth open. Then little Marie began to cry and hid herself behind the lady's skirts. All felt guilty, as if they had committed a crime.

Herbert slowly wiped his face and took one step forward.

At that the lady placed herself between him and the girl, her arms raised and crossed before her face.

"Herbert! By this womb! Herbert! I will punish her so that there will not be one part of her body unbeaten! Do not touch her, you will make me perjured before her father. Herbert! I will break every tooth in her mouth! She shall never do that again."

And before her poor, worn hands covered with dough, Herbert lowered his eyes. His anger was of that order which grows in intensity as it becomes calm. He had forgotten what the girl was to him. There are things which, in the midst of caresses, and unseen, are permissible and do not count as an offense. But this time the affront was public. He was the master. She, a mad little slut. She needed a lesson, one which she would not forget.

"You have never loved me, as I know well, lady," he said to his mother—he spoke slowly, his bottom lip trembling with anger—"I see that you are defending a girl who brings shame on you, shame on my father, shame on our house. As I know, you do it to displease me. Out of consideration for your woman's folly, I am forced to tolerate her about my lands. It is very fortunate for her that you are here."

"I shall punish her," the lady said, a little calmer, wiping her hands on her apron.

"I shall punish her myself," Herbert said. "Hey, you, there, fetch me my chaplain. Before I quit this house she shall be married to Macaire, the Bernon swineherd."

The lady dared not protest: Eglantine's fault was too great. The Bernon swineherd was a fat lout, with flaring nostrils big enough to put nuts into and lips like raw meat. The lady hoped that by the time the priest had come Herbert would have changed his mind.

Herbert seemed no longer to be concerned with Eglantine. He had gone out into the meadow and was playing with his dogs. The lovely Ortrud, having got out of the litter, was running among the bushes already budding with green, clapping her hands to frighten the sparrows: she laughed aloud as she watched them flapping their little wings and fluttering about her in the grass. Her fair hair floated loosely about her pink and white face and her red muslin dress made the grass look greener. She was so pretty to see that all the Bernon servants stopped their work and followed her movements, quick and abrupt, like those of a tame antelope.

The Linnières chaplain came up in haste upon his mule, a little anxious, for he always feared his fat lord's whims. Herbert raised his head to take him in, slowly, as if he had already forgotten his reason for sending for him. But the remains of his gust of anger still twitched at the corners of his mouth.

"Ah," he said, "here you are then, old shaven-pate. Not in a hurry, today; brewing your beer, perhaps?"

The chaplain got off his horse and humbly excused himself; his wish to obey his lordship, said he, was as swift as lightning but his mule was as obstinate as Balaam's.

"Never mind the chatter," Herbert said. "I have need of you. It's for a wedding. And get it done quickly; I must be at Bercen this evening."

"Will his lordship be present himself?"

"The devil! May I be a cuckold like your father if I shift from here! Off with you, get on with it. Fetch them here, and quickly, and if the lady starts talking nonsense to you, shut her up."

Presently Father Martin came out of the house on to the planks, followed by the lady and Eglantine; the girl was hanging on to the lady's sleeve, pressing herself against her as if trying to hide herself in the folds of her dress. Macaire arrived from the pig-pens, trembling all over, his hands red, for he had just washed them. He kept his back bent and his head hung down, and he hardly knew where to put his big feet, which were wrapped in skins full of holes.

"Come, my fair lad," the lord said, "here is the pretty bride we're giving you! You shall have her dower, there's my word on it—the income from the Linnières vineyards, plus her trousseau. And I shall make you master of the Bercen swine. You'll be better off there than here. Breed handsome children together and I'll be their godfather."

"Son," said the lady, "it is a sin to make a jest of God's sacrament. The girl is a wicked slut; lock her up, kill her, but do not put her to this shame."

"As for shame," Herbert said, "this lad is from Adam's rib, like you and me. It is better to marry than burn. You don't imagine a man of noble birth would take her?"

"Son, if your father returns I shall not dare to face him. If you do this thing I shall not forgive you."

"Lady," he said, "I have yielded to you enough. I know what I am about. Father Martin, you may begin your *paternosters*."

"There are no rings," said the priest, hesitating.

"What! Refinements and affectations! Rings—here's one—"

He took a ring from his finger. "Here, Ortrud, my pretty, come here." The lovely girl came to him, smiling her eternal, roguish smile. "Give me your hand. Give me a ring from your finger for this girl. Her hands are bigger than yours but for this purpose it will pass."

Eglantine stood still, mute, her hands behind her back, her eyes so hard that it was frightening to look at her.

"You are very bold, Herbert, my big brother," was all she said, in a hoarse voice.

Then she allowed herself to be married without protest. Not once had she looked at Macaire. And he, awkward and sheepish, sniffed with emotion, wondering how long the joke would last. He was well aware that this marriage humiliated him, that he had been chosen because no man of lower estate could be found. As for the dower, he did not consider it. There was nothing he could do with it. He could already hear the taunting laughter of his cronies and feel its smart; a man has only one name and when shame is joined to it, it sticks. No man likes to be shamed. He could only hope that they would soon unmarry him.

After the benediction, Herbert told the bridal pair to pack up their things. He would take them to Bercenay; they could take the road with the servants who were carrying the baggage. Then there was a delay—Eglantine had tried to cut her throat with a kitchen knife; she had lost a little blood and was trembling so much that her teeth chattered. The lady herself helped her into the cart, promising to come and fetch her in a few days—once at Troyes Herbert would forget the whole business and forgive; he was not really bad, at bottom, only he must not be crossed.

"And it's your own fault, poor foolish creature. Why did you provoke him? You know what he is." Eglantine was not listening. She was seized by such a trembling that her knees and arms shivered and twitched as if shaken by the jolting of a wagon.

"You are sick," the lady said. "You shall stay here, whatever Herbert may say."

The girl shook her head and pushed her away.

"Leave me alone," she faltered. "I hate you. I curse you. Curse you! I curse the Holy Virgin." When the lady took her hand she shouted:

"Leave me alone! Old witch!" and fell back into the cart, huddled, her head hidden in her arms. The cart moved forward, the wheels creaking on their axles.

At Bercenay the newly-weds were shut up in the watch's lodge, where they passed the night, each in a corner, avoiding even looking at each other, such mutual hatred and disgust did they feel. Herbert no longer gave them much thought. He had other worries. Several times a vision of the couple crossed his mind, never for long; sometimes he thought of the business as a good joke, sometimes as an act of justice, sometimes, again, his senses were disturbed—but not much; his desire had changed to disgust after a last flare-up—the spittle on his face, Macaire's muddy feet, the shame of having been enslaved during a whole long month, his revulsion from flesh all too closely akin to his own —all this was confounded in a single sensation of dirtiness, from which he was glad to be delivered. He was not likely to be short of a woman! He had a day of travelling before him. Afterwards, he must visit the armorers to see that everything was ready. He would be lodging with a wool-merchant who was giving up half his house to him—it would be necessary to have the rooms decorated, to buy wine—he had so many friends to receive, to introduce his son to them; the boy was handsome and good-mannered, he would not put him to shame. As for the marriage, it was all arranged, the lady was a widow with a rich dowry;

he had gained the viscount's consent—not without difficulty—and the woman's relations were willing; even so it would be polite to send a gift to the future father-in-law—say a live peacock and a pebble from the garden of the Holy Sepulchre. True, the lady was no longer very young, but she was still capable of bearing children; she already had sons, handsome, vigorous and pugnacious.

Listening to the sleeping Ortrud's even breathing, he began to think of the little red gash in Eglantine's throat—supposing she tried it again? But no, girls like her never really killed themselves. The suicides are the calm and gentle ones—Permelle, the woodman's daughter . . . No, it was as well that this particular adventure had finished as it did. There are bitter pleasures which are sometimes as keen as the other kind. To put a red-hot iron to a poisoned wound hurts but it cures at the same time. To kill by disgust a love which has gripped you so hard —that too was a pleasure, one which turns your very entrails. He was not a brute, by any means; he knew pity; and pity, again, was not a disagreeable sentiment. In any case it would have been necessary to have done with the girl, since he had to go to confession and take Communion for the Easter celebrations.

ARABESQUE

O N Easter Day, after high mass, the countess was entertaining all the barons to a meal in the great hall. The windows were open and the sun made the arms on the wall shine, and the painted escutcheons were brilliant with bright colors. There were a hundred people at the high tables and more than three hundred at the lower ones, not counting the knights and squires on duty. The countess, under a canopy of red brocade, presided over the central table, the archbishop of Troyes over the right-hand one, and the very young count Thibaut over the table on the left.

The ladies of Pouilli and of Mongenost were at the foot of the count-ess's table, being of the petty nobility, but they were very glad to be there all the same—for the sake of their beauty and their good manners, the countess liked to see them near her. The marshal of Troyes, to whom a stuffed pigeon decorated with white feathers and surrounded by little red and green peppers had just been served, had it carried to the lady of Pouilli, with the request that she taste of it, thereby doing him great honor, the red standing for his love, the green for hope, and the white for the lady's beauty. Aielot accepted the gift, flashing a lovely smile across the table to the marshal, her cheeks showing not two but four dimples. She shared the pigeon with her husband, who ate three parts of it. She herself nibbled the peppers, liking no foods so much as those which burn the mouth. To the lady of Mongenost she said:

"You see the young man who is standing behind my father, there, at the archbishop's table? Do you recognize him?"

"I should need very good eyesight," Marie said, with a little grimace.

"I have a heart to see him with," Aielot said. "It's my brother. The day I fasten on his spurs I think I shall cry with joy. You have a hard heart, friend."

"He is not my brother," said the lady of Mongenost, smiling.

"But he can be something more; you have only to wish it. And I know of beautiful ladies who would be happy to love him. But he will be satisfied only with the most beautiful of all."

"Please, friend, you do not well to flatter me. If he wants me, he is very wrong, for he will never have me."

"I shall talk to you so much of him that you will end by loving him."

The meal was long, the dishes being brought to table in order of importance—first the poultry, then various game, then stags and antelopes, seated as if alive on dishes an ell in length, their graceful heads raised, decorated with foliage and ribbons and their horns gilded, with spices about them on large vine leaves, arranged in red and black arabesques in the shape of plants or beasts. Each of the castle cooks had insisted on having a hand in the work, and the master cooks of neigh-boring castles, lent by their masters, had wished to show their skill. Each had been allowed to compose at least one dish: they crowded about the doors of the hall to hear the Ohs! and Ahs! of admiration provoked by the appearance of each dish as the squires carried them the length of the tables, raising them on high so that they could be admired, then passing them to the knights charged with serving the meats, who carried them still further, to the countess or the archbishop. But nobody, neither the countess nor the archbishop, was more delighted with the beauty of the dishes than the master cooks themselves.

There were swans for dessert, and peacocks with their tails spread, and little quails set in flocks on spiced greenstuffs. Then there were candied fruits, and honey served in small, brightly colored pots, and marzipan.

Since the feast must please not only the palate and the eye but likewise the ear, there was soft music, and by each table rebec and lute players played new airs, accompanying them with song. But the best music was by custom reserved for the dancing and concerts in the ladies' withdrawing-rooms, after the siesta. There were at the time several good musicians at court. They were seated at the foot of the archbishop's table, taking their pickings from the remains of the dishes served above them; and from time to time some noble admirer sent them something from his own portion.

The dancing had started in the hall decorated with massive garlands of yellow and blue flowers, and benches covered with rugs had been ranged against the walls. To these the countess had led the older ladies and barons of high lineage; the young knights of the noblest families took part in the dancing, while the others, standing at the end of the room, were forced to be satisfied with the role of spectators—but the spectacle was well worth the trouble of watching. The ladies were very elaborately dressed in gowns with long sleeves falling almost to the ground and deeply pleated bodices clasped at the base of the neck or in close-fitting dresses decorated with richly wrought girdles entwining their bodies like glittering serpents. The figures of the dance formed and dissolved with the lightness of swarms of dead leaves rocked and rolled over by a billow.

Haguenier watched the lady of Mongenost from afar, in despair to see her so beautiful. "Simply for the joy of looking at her," he thought, "I would exchange the love of all these other ladies, though they were emperor's daughters. And how could I succeed where the count of Bar has failed? For sure, should she love a man of these parts, he must be her choice. And if even he is not worthy of her, I must serve her without hope. Perhaps she loves the emperor of Germany's son, or the king of Spain's, and hides it for fear of jealousy. It is not cowardice but wisdom to flee her, for she must despise insolent men."

She was seated, all luminous in her gown of periwinkle blue, on a bench covered with a rich rug of dark-red patterns on a violet ground; the count of Bar and the seneschal of Provins both stood before her and she raised her fair head and pearly throat towards them.

She was not proud, had no pretensions to a consequence beyond her rank—such, at least, was the impression she wished to give the two men—and so answered them always gently and modestly; both were asking for a favor—a sleeve or a scarf—to bring them luck in the Easter jousting.

"You press me in vain," she said, "and are both wanting in courtesy. But I owe you too much respect to be angry and, for the sake of this day of the Resurrection of Our Lord, I forgive you. I cannot give my veil to one of you without being impolite to the other. For this tournament I shall lend my scarf to some young man soon to be knighted, who has as yet no lady of his own; and I shall be glad if it brings him luck in his first bouts."

"He will be mighty bold," said the seneschal of Provins.

The lady gave him a severe look.

"So much the better. Ladies like a bold man." She turned to Aielot, who was standing by the window talking to her escort. "Lady, fair friend, do me a service; will you summon your brother of whom you have talked to me?"

Aielot fetched her brother, holding him by the hand and laughing loudly at his diffidence.

"The lady won't eat you," she was saying. "Hold up your head and stop looking like a fried carp."

Haguenier saluted the two barons, then bent the knee before the lady.

"Lady," he said, "command me." He had raised his head and all three were looking at him, and Aielot, very proud, was trying to read in their faces what they thought of the lad. Certainly the two men found him too handsome for their taste: wide, deep eyes, a short, straight nose, a large and gentle mouth, chestnut hair in plump curls, a neck rather long, held stiffly, and the head well poised on wide shoulders. Aielot could see that Marie was at the moment engaged in judging him, and that a frown from the count of Bar could do more in Haguenier's favor than all the words she might utter.

"Fair bachelor," Marie said, "you are only just come from Normandy and your sister has told me that you have no lady for your first tournament. Out of love for your sister I willingly lend you this scarf for the three days and I shall pray that it may bring you luck." She took the scarf of mauve and purple silk from about her waist and held it out to the young man.

"Lady," he said, "it is more than I should dare ask: my mettle has not yet been tried. The honor is too great for me."

"You will put me to shame if you refuse," she said, frowning a little —but in jest, for her eyes were gentle. "Come, take it, and try to acquit yourself well, so that I am not reproached on account of my knight. You will return it to me after the festival."

Haguenier thanked her, kissed her hand, and rose, after having bound the scarf about his left arm.

"You see, my lords," Marie said, raising her eyes to her two suitors, "how frankly and loyally I deal with you. You see that I have neither vanity nor partiality. And I hope you will be the first to wish this young man good luck."

"Since my lady wishes it," said Count Henri. As he was very jealous of the seneschal, he was more glad than not at what she had done. Nevertheless both rivals were thinking the lad too handsome, and the lady of Pouilli as cunning as a demon—she must certainly be intriguing in her brother's favor.

Haguenier, after his passage with the lady, remained very thoughtful: he told himself, indeed, that no doubt she had been making fun of him a little, but everything is permitted to so perfect a lady. He was glad to have seen her so close, but how the devil, he thought, was he to live up to it? He was no stronger than the next man and, with that scarf, he would look ridiculous if he did not succeed in unhorsing at least five opponents. However, he counted a good deal on his weapons and armor; his father understood such things, and had not spared his money.

As he came out of the hall Haguenier felt a tug at his sleeve and turned: the count of Bar confronted him, looking him straight in the eyes. This man had a somewhat disturbing way of looking at people: his gaze was keen and anxious, almost, indeed, painful; his mouth was

marred by his habit of chewing at his lips. Haguenier lowered his eyes—
the count was the same height as himself and he wanted to show, if only
by his bearing, his deference towards so brave a knight; he was telling
himself that in the matter of feats of arms he did not even reach to the
count's ankle.

"Listen," Henri said, "don't take my demand in bad part. I know
that you are the son of Herbert of Linnières, who was famous for his
strength and your grandfather Ansiau of Linnières was one of the
best knights of Troyes in his day and I held it an honor to serve him at
tournaments when I was a squire. Do not think me presumptuous or
discourteous, nor that I value myself higher than you, age and experience apart. If you are willing to serve me, I will give you the revenue
from the tolls of Sézanne bridge as a fief, plus clothes, and oats for your
horses. Moreover, you can ask what you will of me, I will grant it, in
exchange for a service which means a great deal to me."

"I should like to do you a service," Haguenier said, "and without
asking anything in return. But I do not know whether I can."

"Listen," Count Henri said again, "that scarf which the lady gave
you—lend it to me for the tournament, the lady will never know; I
will find you another of the same color in exchange. I will hide this one
under my armor and I will give it back to you afterwards and you can
return it to her; I shall not damage it. You cannot know how much it
means to me."

Haguenier turned as red as a carrot and his eyes filled with tears. He
did not even deign to answer, turned his back on the count, and joined
his comrades. He did not know what to do nor what means to take to
avenge himself; he thought that the count of Bar had meant to show
his contempt for the Linnières family and for the nobility of all the
Othe low country—for the count could hardly have supposed him
capable of selling a lady's favor.

He did not know that Henri had made his request in perfect good
faith; he had supposed that the young man would not refuse him a
service of courtesy, knowing how much the scarf meant to him. But
such a haughty refusal only exacerbated his desire to obtain the purple
scarf. And he ended by being as jealous of the young man as if he had
been the lady's lover: he constantly imagined him with the scarf
knotted across his chest like a streak of red and violet light. For years
his love had had nothing but such occasional favors to nourish it, until
these trifles seemed to him as precious as the lady's very body.

THE ARROWS OF THE SUN

O H! the dusty roads under the sun, the water of rivers shining like a steel knife; oh! golden rays of lovely Easter month straight as pointed swords, like arrows, beautiful, beautiful light, cruel light; all, heaven and earth, is naught but a pattern of golden, pointed arrows.

As they walked, the man preferred to close his eyes and keep a hand on the child's shoulder, for the light made his head ache too much. He did not complain—he had known much worse—but the pain in his forehead prevented thought. Beneath his eyelid a mass of white-hot arrows burned, crossing at the root of his nose, and it was like a fierce fire devouring his sense of sight.

They went down the valley of the Rhône from village to village, from castle to castle, getting their bread on the way; the old man understood the care of horses and the repairing of harness; by touch alone he could find the thorn beneath the hoof, the swelling on the haunch; his hands were deft with bandages, dressings, and at lancing wounds. He loved animals. When he spoke to them it was in short, guttural sounds, *hor* and *haii*, like neighing, and there was such a caress in his voice that the most restive horses came and rubbed their noses against his shoulder. The lord of Mirac had, indeed, wanted to keep him as mastergroom and when he refused had turned him out without a penny or a bit of bread for his trouble.

In the village he repaired the ox-teams' harness, he knew how to sew and drill leather and braid thongs to resist any strain. Thus he would remain two or three days at a house and afterwards they would give him bread and wine for the road. Only, his sight grew dimmer and dimmer and he worked slowly, by touch, his eye closed. Auberi did not know how to do anything at all; he might just serve to carry in firewood or water; but he was a nice child and people gave to him willingly; in a small town an old woman one day gave him a whole chicken ready roasted, begging the pilgrims to accept it for the love of God.

"Auberi," the old man said, "understand that a free lad must neither steal nor beg. Yet I would rather see you steal than beg, for begging is shameful. When a gift is freely offered with a good heart, accept, but never look as if your stomach were in your eyes. To show that you are hungry is the same as begging."

"Ha!" the child said, half laughing, half sullen. "But I've no rouge to color my cheeks nor yeast to swell me up. I'd have to put a notice on my back saying 'I am not hungry.' But then, I can't write and the good folk can't read."

The old man laughed open-heartedly.

And because this month of April was fine and there was much sunshine, the old man suffered what seemed like a burning wound within his forehead; and the light completed the destruction of his eyesight.

HAGUENIER:
III. FIRST RIFT

H AGUENIER was not fortunate in his first tournament.

It was to some extent his own fault. He had fasted too much during the preceding days and prayed too much during the vigil of arms, not that he was thinking of Pierre's seven thousand *Ave Marias* but he was by nature inclined to exaltation, so that for him this first trial of manhood was rather like initiation into an order. Indeed it was no small matter to become a knight, not simply a matter of money and apprenticeship. It was necessary to be worthy of knighthood. But God was not to give ear to him in the way he expected.

To begin with it had been a question of pure bad luck: his horse, a fine Persian, had suddenly taken fright at the clamor of armor and trumpets and had started bucking and backing, refusing to obey his rider. Nevertheless, he was a good horse, well trained and tried, but God knows what had come over him. He danced about, reared up on his haunches, wild, his eyes all whites, twisting his long, nervous neck which was dressed with fringes and festoons. Haguenier almost tore his mouth with the bit, but nothing would do, he was held back behind everyone in the lists and at the high barrier hung with garlands above which were the ladies' seats. As he was one of the best equipped of the new knights, all the more attention was drawn to him by this backwardness and the crowd, behind the enclosure, began laughing.

"Look at the big roan! Look at the great plumed pheasant!"

Herbert, in the front rank of knights and notables on the left of the tribune, had a reserve horse sent to him, which two grooms brought into the lists; but in dismounting, mounting the fresh horse, and getting back into position, Haguenier lost a good quarter of an hour. When the heralds at last announced him, the best knights were already engaged in combat and there was hardly anyone against him but insignificant, ill-equipped young men against whom he would have considered it ridiculous to turn his lance. He had such an ache in his heart from this first accident that all seemed lost; he would have had to be very strong-minded not to be put out by such a bad augury.

In the course of the day he crossed lances with several young men among the strongest in the lists, without, however, succeeding in unhorsing a single one. Yet he was keen and well trained but on that day he first discovered his major fault; he had a weak heart, and, after so many days of fasting and the excessive joy of his morning of knighthood, it subjected him to spasms which almost caused him to lose consciousness. He gave no sign of this but held on until near the end of the day, when an ill-directed blow from his adversary flung him against the grandstand and dislocated his right shoulder. Pain blinded him and made him drop his lance; thereupon the umpires separated him and his opponent, declaring that the blow had been foul. He had just time to see, above the garlands of apple blossom, the heads and heavy headdresses of two young ladies, and two hands gripping a fold of a blue cloak. The trumpets were still clamoring and heralds were proclaiming the victors' names: "Hear ye! Hear ye! Jacques, sire of Chassericourt, Ernaut of Vanlay, André of Tassigni, Thierri of Baudemant, Archambaud of Monguoz, Ernaut of Linnières, Robert of La Châtre!" And then Haguenier recalled the lady's scarf which he had defended so badly, and told himself that he was forever dishonored.

He came to himself in the mansion Herbert was occupying, on a comfortable bed of cushions. A physician was massaging his shoulder and it was pain which had restored him to consciousness. Herbert was standing beside the bed, his arms crossed on his chest. Haguenier was prepared to hear well-merited insults, but his father only said:

"Well, bitch's son, they've made a pretty mess of you in your first joust, eh?" Then he touched the young man's cheek with his hand, loaded with rings. "Well, well," he said, "there's no horse so good but it may stumble. I have a good eye. You have all that's needed to do well, everyone has been telling me so. Some envious persons must have ill-wished you, to bring you bad luck."

For Haguenier that idea was like sunshine breaking through clouds, and in fact his nature was such that he could not long be sorrowful. He smiled at his father and asked whether his shoulder would soon be better: perhaps he could ride again on the third day of the tournament?

"The Devil! You're in a hurry! You're out for five or six days at least. Just in time to return to Linnières for the feast I am giving. Above all, keep still and sleep. I've other things to do than looking after you."

On the evening of the third day of the tournament Pierre and Ernaut were seated on their brother's bed, joyfully recounting incidents of the jousting. Ernaut had been lucky: on the second day he had even been proclaimed champion among the younger men. He had unhorsed six adversaries and had borne his arms in triumph to the feet of Ida of Puiseaux, who thus became one of the queens of the tournament. That day even Pierre was proud of his half-brother and his wide, handsome brown face was beaming with joy.

"Eh!" he said. "You should have seen how he showed all of them, the dog! And then when they all shouted 'Ernaut of Linnières'! At first I thought it was the other Ernaut, of Vanlay, and then, you know, they said *of Linnières*. Oh yes, our house made a good showing this time!" And he slapped his brother's thigh with all his strength.

Haguenier, too, laughed with delight for Ernaut. He did not want to spoil his brothers' pleasure, and joked about his accident.

"You, at least," he said to Ernaut, "fought well for our house. And now, when's the wedding to be?"

Ernaut flushed.

"When Christmas falls in summer time, apparently. Do you know what Joceran said to me, the cur?"

"Yes, do you know what he said?" Pierre put in. "Word for word then: 'Fair cousin, what is good for a lady is not good for a damsel; I want to marry her well, not have her the talk of a tournament.'"

"He's an oaf," Haguenier said. "But never mind that, now that you are such a good knight the girl will love you in spite of her father."

Then the two bastard brothers began discussing their brother's accident: both maintained that the blow had been foul, against all the rules. Possibly the man had even done it on purpose, he might have been paid to do it; both of them knew all about the purple scarf and firmly believed that the two barons had contrived something to spoil the tourney for the young man. At bottom they were very proud of the honor which the lady of Mongenost had done their brother and they were, on the whole, flattered at the idea that Haguenier's failure was due to the powerful count of Bar's malice.

"Everyone is saying it, your horse was bewitched," Pierre said, "for there's no better horse between here and Reims. Joubert, our father's head groom, broke and trained it himself and he has never seen the horse take fright."

"And as for the man who gave you that foul lance blow," Ernaut said, "they ought to send him back to the kitchens, for there was not a fouler stroke dealt in the whole tournament. They ought to take his spurs away for a stroke like that."

At that moment, heralded by a throaty laugh and the sound of rustling skirts, breathless, Aielot appeared, raising the heavy tapestry across the door; and at once the little room seemed even smaller, half the size; a large woman always seems to take up more room than a man. Aielot, in her long gown, her cloak in heavy folds, her massive tresses, the almost sickening smell of her scents, seemed at once to absorb all the air in the room.

"How like our father she is," Haguenier thought.

The two bastards had risen to greet her but she seemed not to see them, sat down on her brother's bed and kissed him on both cheeks.

"Niot!" she said. "Oh, I was so hurt for you! I cried with rage." She stroked her hand across her eyes. Then, with a sudden start, she turned towards the other two—their eyes were hard for this woman who could forget nothing; and indeed it was strange to see how her own magnificent, brooding eyes could blaze with hate and contempt.

"Still here, little boys?" she asked, in a voice which seemed to hiss with anger. "You are not sending them out, brotherkin?"

"Oh, we're going, lady," Pierre said. "There's no salary for listening to you, never fear."

"Gone, the puppies," Aielot said, stretching. "Poh! Just seeing their snouts makes me ill. They must be very pleased with themselves, eh? Ernaut must have pissed in his peasant breeches for joy! They can hardly contain their delight at seeing you in that state, with your shoulder out. I can see it in their filthy dog's eyes." She spat on the floor and wiped her mouth. "But they'll get no profit of it. They won't be laughing long, the little louts."

"Don't let's speak of them, they're my friends, sisterkin," Haguenier said.

The young woman burst out laughing.

"Niot, what a simpleton you are, really! Friends, with that? Does that sort so much as know what friendship is? Villeins! Every word out of place you may utter they will sell to our father. They know how to flatter, of course. That's how they got round our father. Me, I never flattered him. Don't trust the nasty little snakes. While the death rattle was in our mother's throat Isabeau was in our father's bed and I could hear them laughing together. Do you think Pierre didn't hear them and laugh with them? *'Your mother is ugly,'* he said to me, and then *'Mine is beautiful,'* that's what he said to me." She put her hand to her eyes, and spat again.

"Ah! well, never mind. Only don't trust them and don't make a friend of Ernaut. I'm telling you, he is not going to be fortunate. He'll come to a bad end. I have a gift for seeing such things."

Haguenier knew his sister too well to try and argue with her.

"About the lady, Niot?" she said, suddenly. "Have you thought about her, about her scarf?"

"God, don't speak of it! When I think of it I want to die. Here's the scarf! Take it back to her, I don't even dare to see her myself. I can't write, with this shoulder, but I'll dictate a letter to her. Is she very angry?"

"Why no, Niot, she knows very well it was not your fault. You're a very good fighter. I know good fighting when I see it and so does she: she is distressed, she says that she brought you bad luck."

"She is very good," the young man said, "but she says it out of courtesy. She must really despise me."

Aielot sent for ink and a roll of paper and prepared to write. Haguenier dictated the letter as well as he could; he was, he said, sick and dead with pain and shame and suffered in his body, but a thousand times worse in his soul, because he had failed to be worthy of the lady; despite all he could do, fate and his enemies had been too much for him. He no longer felt himself worthy to serve the lady and did not know if she would still want to keep him in her service. To close the letter he said that he would surely die if the lady did not pardon him.

"I shall give her this today," Aielot said, "and tomorrow she is leaving for Mongenost. But I shall bring you a favorable reply, you may be sure."

Herbert, furious at his son's failure, had had his head groom flogged with rods to punish him for having neglected to keep a watch on the horse. In the household there was already talk of a little grey man who was supposed to have been seen sidling about the courtyard on the eve of the tournament. In point of fact nobody had really seen him but after the event everyone thought they remembered him. It was supposed that the count of Bar had sent him, or the knight Jean of Chassenay, who had a grudge against Herbert. And Herbert was forever to bear malice against these two men. At heart he was much angrier with his son than he wished to show him. To save face it was very necessary to pretend that it had been a matter of fate, luck, that the young man had nothing to do with it. But his pride had been harshly tried; he felt that he was having to make himself ridiculous, obliged as he was to celebrate, with so much pomp, the knighting of a lad who had cost him such a humiliation.

Aielot brought the purple scarf back to her brother with Marie's reply: the lady did not wish him ill because of the tournament but she was very angry that he had made his sister the bearer of the scarf instead of bringing it to her himself: he must return the scarf into her own hands, not hide from her like a coward.

"Ernaut, fair brother, I have been bedridden four days and my shoulder is nearly better. And we leave for Hervi in two days. I shall die unless I find means to go out before then. It is to render a service to my lady. If you could take my place in bed and pretend to be asleep for an hour or two, in that time I could be well away. If our father scolds you, you can tell him that otherwise I should have killed myself."

Ernaut consented, for he knew the beauty and fame of the lady of Mongenost: Haguenier would have been mad not to obey her.

Haguenier mounted Ernaut's horse as best he could and left the town as quickly as possible. There were three leagues to ride to Mongenost but the roads were crowded and it took him two hours. When he knocked at the castle gate the porter asked him from the watch-tower what he wanted: his lord was not returned from Troyes.

"Friend," Haguenier said, "I am come on behalf of the lady of Pouilli, to see your lady."

"Come in," the man said. "The lady is in the garden. But if you happen to be one of the count of Bar's people, I'm warning you she'll have you put out: she's already done it once, yesterday."

Behind the keep Marie had a tiny garden six feet square, about the well; sweet briar grew there, roses of Arabia and jasmine; ivy and the wild vine clambered over the parapet of the well and the ground was blue with lavender. There the lady had a stone seat, above which she had had fixed a small canopy of yellow canvas to protect her from the sun. She came there with her damsels during the siesta; sometimes she made them sing and play the rebec and taught them new songs, for the count of Bar frequently sent her very pretty ones. Sometimes she sent for her small lectern of carved wood, placed a book on it and read, her elbows on the margins of the book, her temples clasped in her hands. At such times a thunderbolt might have fallen into the well and she would not have noticed it.

Haguenier entered the little garden, and the damsels, who were playing at lowering the buckles of their belts into the well, rose, laughing and nudging each other. The lady did not notice her visitor and they did not dare recall her too brusquely from her reading. Haguenier looked at her, sitting in the golden light of the canopy, her fair head bent; the breeze was playing with the light muslin veil which covered her head; her dress of deep violet silk was shot, by the sun, with amethyst and russet-gold lights.

Haguenier thought that she was refusing to notice him on purpose, out of contempt: the damsels had fallen silent, looking at each other and laughing soundlessly, and nothing could be heard but the sound of the birds twittering in the trees.

Surprised and distracted from her reading by this sudden silence, the lady raised her head and her veil fell on to her shoulders. She had the swollen eyelids and rather wild look of someone waking from a dream, she fluttered her eyelashes and touched her eyes. Haguenier drew near to her and went down on his knees, asking forgiveness for disturbing her.

Whereupon, without knowing why she did so, she took his head

between her hands and tilted it backwards, the better to look into his
face. They looked at each other thus, both a little astonished; he felt
pity for her swollen eyelids which, as it seemed to him, made her lovely
face even sweeter; and she was deeply moved by his look, in which she
read so much gentleness and something like pity.

At last she said:

"Thank you for coming, Sir Knight. You are still suffering from your
wound. I was mad to ask you to bring me back the scarf."

He drew the scarf from about his neck with his left hand and offered
it to the lady. She lowered her head and he stared at the play of light
on her gown, purple in the yellow light of the canopy and casting rosy
reflections on to the lady's cheeks and throat. "How can one believe
that women are of the same flesh as ourselves?" he was thinking.
"These hands are not like real hands but like long iris flowers, pink and
animated. How comes that about, how is it possible? What is there in
common between her and me?" And his heart seemed to contract.

Marie, her mouth tender and her glance sad, looked him straight in
the eyes.

"I have not brought you good fortune," she said. "You are right to
return this scarf to me, for you have had no joy of it. Leave me. Find
some beautiful young girl to give you her veil or her sleeve, and may
she bring you victory everywhere and make you happy."

"You know well that I shall not do so," Haguenier said. "I put myself, once again, in your power. And when I shall have won the right to
serve you, then I can ask you to take me for your servitor."

She smiled.

"It is from courtesy that you say so. It is a thing, I know, which is
always said to ladies."

He spoke, then, as eloquently as he could to persuade her of his
constancy, and this was hardly necessary, for Marie had too good an
opinion of herself to doubt his words. She was aware of a sudden whim
in herself for this young man with the wounded shoulder, chiefly and
above all because she believed his accident to have been engineered by
the count of Bar. She pitied him. He was young. And, she was sure,
madly in love. And she had brought him bad luck, without wishing to.
And then there had been that look of grave pity which had so moved
her. In short, she was gentle with him, as she could be, gave him back
the purple scarf and promised to put him to the proof. If she found him
worthy she might consider granting him her friendship—chaste and
pure, of course.

DEVIL IN THE HEART

THE whole nobility of the countryside was to come to Hervi castle to celebrate the dubbing of the son of Herbert le Gros. After his ceremonial assumption of arms, and the tournament, all his kinsfolk had taken the road again, in parties, in separate groups, on horseback, in litters, riding mules, with baggage, dogs and falcons, keeping company on the road with others of the neighborhood also returning from the jousting. Herbert was inviting everyone he encountered. It was enough if he had met a man twice or knew his parents; the castle of Hervi was large, moreover there was room at Linnières where the lady Aelis did the honors helped by Cousin Joceran. Joceran was a man very useful at all weddings, festivals and funerals. He oversaw the meals and never forgot either the rank or age of the guests and he could be relied on to settle quarrels by a word in place or a cup of good wine.

Herbert had had all the carved escutcheons at Hervi freshly painted —and God knows there were enough of them, as well as arms and armor; he had brought some of them back from his second crusade and he had also had the whole armory of his late father-in-law, the old Haguenier, hung upon the walls. Striped woollen tapestries were stretched on the walls and half the tables dressed with white napery. Polished wooden table utensils had been borrowed from all the neighbors for three leagues round. And there was not a peasant in the whole countryside from whom a chicken, a lamb, a veal calf or a dozen eggs had not been taken.

The villagers came out on to the roads to see the handsome youth pass dressed as for a wedding, surrounded by his half-brothers and cousins, mounted on his handsome Persian horse which cavorted and snorted, proud of its fine harness and its rider.

Herbert's litter had stopped at Bercenay, before the castle, where the horses had to be changed. Herbert brought away with him his brother-in-law of Buchie and Barthélémi of Chapes, Haguenier's future father-in-law, both too old to make so long a journey on horseback. The litter was parked in the meadow before the wagon gateway, and the three men and the ever-present Ortrud had got out to stretch

their legs. Their servants had made for the castle, taking advantage of
the halt to have a drink in the courtyard which was decorated and full
of a joyful crowd; the whole rabble of servants had gathered there to
see the master pass. Lads and girls had also come up from the village,
bringing gifts to the intendant on this occasion of the young master's
knighting, and the intendant had ordered a small barrel of wine up
from the cellars and parcels of dried fruit, as it was customary to do
during the week after Easter.

In the courtyard, with freshly cut twigs of willow and elm, the castle
maids were weaving enormous crowns, trellises and little tents, for that
evening there was to be dancing and games in honor of spring's coming.
Eglantine was there, too, her hair loose, like a damsel's, her head dressed
with jonquils; and she was singing at the top of her voice while she
decorated a dummy made of branches to represent Saint Odile,
patroness of the castle, with wild roses and flowers of hawthorn. She
was pretending to regard her "wedding" as a pleasantry and held her
head high.

When she knew that the master was at the castle gate she hid behind
the dummy so that the Linnières servants would not see her; she wondered whether Herbert would think of her and whether he would at
last allow her to return to Bernon; if only it would occur to him to
enter the courtyard and to see her.

Before the wagon gateway a burly, stocky lad was struggling with
Herbert's servants. He was shouting: "I want to talk to the master!
Let me go! I've got to talk to the master."

"Are you mad, Macaire? You can see he is with two rich lords, his
kinsmen."

But the man succeeded in shaking them off and ran straight to
Herbert, who was just handing a cup of wine to the aged Garnier of
Buchie. The man had flung himself towards the master with such
precipitancy that he nearly caused him to upset the cup.

"What's this, fellow! Have you been seeing Morgan the fairy? Or are
you looking for a flogging?"

"Mercy, my lord, pity! I am Macaire, the Bernon swineherd."

"Ah—so—Macaire—why yes, of course, Macaire. Yes, yes, I recognize you. What do you want?"

"My lord, for pity's sake; don't let them mock me, my lord—the
people here mock me! Unmarry me, my lord."

Herbert was in too good a humor to grow angry.

"What's this?" he said. "What! is it so shameful for you to be my brother-in-law? You're hard to please. Why, here is my lord of Buchie who has long been my brother-in-law, and he doesn't complain much." He turned to the old baron to explain the jest.

"I have a sister—on the wrong side of the blanket—whom I was obliged to marry to this creature. What of it? I am not proud. He's a decent lad." He clapped Macaire hard on the shoulder.

"Drink with us, son of a bitch. Wait now: your late father was groom at Seuroi. As a child you used to help him; I remember you. How would you like me to make a groom of you? With your wife's dower, it would not be a bad situation; you would certainly be better treated than if you remain a swineherd. You shall have old Joubert's place."

"Very much thanks, my lord"—Macaire fell to his knees and kissed the hem of Herbert's dress—"but, for God's sake, unmarry me."

Exasperated, Herbert thrust him away with a kick on the chin.

"Do you take me for a bishop? I married you, it's said and done, I can do nothing more about it. Get out, before I grow angry."

"My lord, order me to return to Bernon; my mother is there."

Herbert hitched his shoulder and shifted his hand to his dagger. Macaire did not wait for any more but fled as fast as his legs would carry him.

Thoughtfully, Herbert followed him with his eyes for a moment. That thing's wife? Certainly he could never have found a better method of curing himself of his madness.

"And I'm as well pleased," he told himself, "that he did not take my offer. It would have made me sick to see that bestial thing touch my horses."

Back in the courtyard Macaire swore and spat and tore at his hair with rage. His cronies tried to console him.

"You're very stupid, Macaire, it takes a bishop to unmarry a man and even the pope. D'you think the pope's going to put himself out for you?"

"Never you mind, son, disgrace can be borne when it's profitable, and it's le Gros who's robbed, since he's got to pay you the dower."

"The dower, the dower!" Macaire said. "What do I want with his money? Am I a free man? What use can I make of money? Make wash for my pigs with it? I've my intended, at Bernon."

The others roared with laughter.

"Look at the handsome fellow! Him, with his pig-face, thinking of intendeds! What you need is a sow, not a girl. Come on, lad, let's drink, it's still the best thing there is."

Macaire swallowed four cups, one after the other, wiped his beard and spat.

"Right. I'll show you my intended. There'll be one, at least, this evening, who doesn't do any laughing, not likely." His voice was thick and his breathing hoarse with fury.

Macaire went and snatched the jonquil crown from Eglantine's head and slashed her face with willow twigs. The other maids, seeing him drunk, placed themselves in front of the damsel, to protect her, and he struck them as well.

"Bunch of whores, she's my wife, I tell you; le Gros gave her to me, we were married by the priest. I'm le Gros's brother-in-law, just like the lord of Buchie."

He dragged his wife to the pig-pens and beat her for a long time with his leather belt and when he saw that she was too broken by pain to resist, took her by force. She wept and supplicated.

"Beat me, Macaire, beat me if you want to, but don't touch me! Macaire, if my father returns it will be the worse for you; I'll have you hanged, I'll have your nose and lips cut off, Macaire."

"Le Gros is master here. I don't care a damn for your father."

"Macaire, I am not like just any girl; I tell you I know such words that if I will it magpies will come and peck out your eyes and rats eat you alive."

"You should've done it before, then. Now you're going to learn who's master. Me, I'm le Gros's brother-in-law."

Eglantine hardly had the strength to drag herself to the back court-yard, to wash her bleeding face in the tub of rain-water beneath the gutter. Her ears were humming, she could hardly hear the sounds of laughter and singing coming from the castle. There they were laughing and dancing while she was here, abandoned by everyone, alone forever. Never again would she dare to look anyone in the eye. Macaire—she did not even blame Macaire—do you blame the horse that crushes you beneath his hoofs? They had made him furious and he had forgotten himself. She would have killed him had she been able to; but without hate, simply to defend herself. But the man who had exposed her, in cold blood, to the ultimate shame, *he* knew what he was about: to complete his own pleasure he had to be sure that she would lie in that villein's arms.

To think that she had hoped it was all a game, a cruel game, such as he liked, and that he would say to her: "Go back to Bernon," and would contrive to annul the so-called marriage. She had undertaken that hellish game they had played together without reserves or haggling; she had not damned herself for fun. Because of it she had been unable to sleep, had become as if mad. During the fifteen days she had been at Bercenay she had thought of nothing else; she was ready to forgive, ready to like even this marriage with Macaire, because she thought that afterwards she would weep over it in Herbert's arms. She had thought that he was humiliating her out of spite because he loved her overmuch and that he would be the first to avenge her if ever Macaire dared lay a finger on her.

In her madness she had thought that during the fortnight at Troyes he had had no other desire than to see his little wicked one again, in the chapel, under the black crucifix.

"Fool that I was," she thought, "did I not know that his heart was not big enough even for that? He will have confessed everything to some priest in Troyes, paid out some money and got his pardon, while I was thinking that he was willing to be eternally damned for my sake. I, who have lied in the confessional and will lie again, and always and unto death. Oh yes, he has a son, he has made a knight of him, he has to get him married—important matters these, he has no time to think of trifles. What has such a man to do with a swineherd's wife?

"Oh thou," she thought, "who hast allowed me to be dishonored by a villein, though I be thine own father's daughter, let the shame fall upon thy head and upon all thy family, since thou hast allowed thine own blood to suffer such disgrace. In all the country there is not one free man whom thou hast not outraged by that act, bull-face; and worse than a beast hast thou been, in giving up thy sister to a beast. Ah, bull-face, thou art feasting thy son in the great house and I am not bidden to the feast. But I shall learn such words and spells that I shall make him die, thy fair son, and his children, and all thy cursed race; I shall make images of their hearts with the wax of their own candles and I shall pierce them with red-hot needles until even a small flame will melt them."

THE BODY'S DARKNESS

THAT day the old man was awakened by the singing of birds and he thought himself in Linnières forest, fording the river very early in the morning on the track of a big boar, and he was astonished to see the spoor so clear in the riverside mud. "I still see clearly, after all," he thought. And the birds outdid each other in singing—*pia–pia–pia–pia, quic–quivic–quic, fiu–fiu–fiu—quic–quivic*—it was unending, and then he stretched and opened his good eye.

And it was still dark.

At first he thought that all the birds had gone mad and that this might be a bad sign, something dreadful was going to happen in the country. But the darkness was so black, not a streak of light anywhere on the horizon, not even a star; and the grass was drenched with dew. Suddenly he was terribly afraid, like a little child, and cried out: "Lady, lady, sister," and his own voice, weak and foolish, seemed strange to him and he was ashamed of it.

Then he remembered; the previous evening he had lain down in the grass on the slope of a hill with Auberi; they had been on the move, he was weary, he had a headache—now, at least, his headache was gone. But he could see nothing—not even red blurs or golden arrows. He rubbed his eye. He might as well have rubbed his nose. Nothing. He called: "Auberi."

He could hear the child yawning gently and stretching, his voice was drowned in sleep.

"My lord?"

"Do you think it is late, Auberi?"

"We've certainly slept well," the child said. "The sun is already fully up behind the hill opposite: the trees on the ridge are all golden, the light comes through all combed."

"Auberi, turn me towards the sun."

"But you're facing it," the child said, surprised. And the old man raised his hand before him as if he were trying to touch the sun.

"Auberi, my son, I can see nothing, I don't know what it is, it has never happened to me before. Perhaps it will go off; it's being so tired."

The child took him by the shoulders and looked hard into the wide-open eyes.

"Look—look hard," he said; the old man's fear was infecting him. "But you must be able to see! Your eye is the same as before! No!" he cried, "no! no! You are frightening me. You can see, say you can see!" His voice became whimpering, and still the old man said nothing. He took Auberi's head in his hands and passed his fingers over his face. The child burst into sobs and pushed him away.

"I don't want you to! Don't touch me like that! Don't be like that!"

The old man lay face downwards on the ground, his head on his arms. He, too, was sobbing, great, dry, barking sobs, and his shoulders shook, and it was so painful to hear him that Auberi began to tug at him and put his arms about the old man's neck.

"Don't cry like that. Come, look, it will go away. Come now, we'll go and pray to Our Lady and it's sure to go away."

"Auberi," the old man said, "leave me alone, go away, go back to your home. I want to die."

Auberi clung to him, wailing like a baby. "No, don't die! You must not! I don't want to be left alone!"

An hour later the man raised himself on his elbow, sat up, felt for his bag and his cudgel. Auberi watched him with his mouth open, unable to get used to the uncertain movements of a blind man.

"Auberi, where are you? We will leave here."

"Yes, my lord."

The old man rose with difficulty, took a step forward, leaning on his stick, and stretched out his arm—he thought he could feel holes beneath his feet and he dared not go forward—the earth seemed to crumble and shift in all directions.

"Auberi, give me your arm. Auberi, tell me, what are your eyes like?"

"Grey, I think, my lord. Or yellow."

As they were passing beneath a tree a branch wet with dew touched the old man's face and he started violently, then slowly wiped the dew from his forehead.

They went down towards the valley and every step was a plunge into the abyss.

"Auberi," the old man said, "is the sun up?"

"Yes, my lord, it is just above the mountain. It already hurts the eyes."

"Hurts the eyes," said the old man. "Look well, Auberi, look well. It is so beautiful! . . ."

He had to learn to walk straight and to cut his bread and to drink from a bowl without spilling it over the side—it was not as he had sometimes done it before, at night time—now the certainty of not seeing made all his motions so clumsy that he did everything wrong; seated at some peasant's table, he felt endlessly about to find a bit of bread which was right under his nose and his hand went all round it but could not seize it; if Auberi gave it to him he became angry, because he wanted to learn to find everything for himself.

Yet he had thought that since his sight was so bad he would not lose much if he went blind! Ah! what would he not have given for one bit of grey sky, seen through a half-open door, at evening; to see the moon shiver in a drinking-trough, even to see the sun as a red blur through closed eyelids; but no, nothing, he was like a beast which has never had eyes, just a head of wood with a hole in it to swallow bread.

No matter which way I turn there will be no more sun for me. No matter the hour of my awakening, there will be no more day. All roads will be the same, I shall see none new; all men will be faceless, I shall see none new.

Friend, friend, you will not see me again. Neither living nor dead.

There was once an old man so blind that he mistook the skin of a kid for the hand of the son he loved and blessed in his stead the son he did not love, and the son became strong, and fathered the twelve patriarchs, for it was not given to the beloved son to be blessed. But my beloved son has long been dust and earth and no longer has eyes, ears nor voice; and it is the one I do not love who will possess all—children and name and land. And it is for that reason I must go out blind on to the roads, to find the child again who has lost eyes of flesh and heart of flesh. Such is God's will.

Ah! may he who has stolen blessing and heritage live in peace and increase and multiply, since it is God who has willed it. I know well that the will of God is not the will of men.

And on the Wednesday following Quasimodo they came to a large township where there was a church dedicated to Saint Peter; since

Saint Peter was the patron of Troyes and Ansiau had often prayed to
him, he went and knelt before the church porch and asked Auberi to
guide his hands to touch the image of Saint Peter carved in the door.
He raised his hands and clasped them on Saint Peter's foot and leaned
his forehead against the column on which the saint stood. There he
stayed, talking to Saint Peter as he would have talked to an uncle or a
godfather.

"I have always loved and honored you. In my prayers I have never
forgotten your name. In the time of my youth, after each tournament,
I made offering to you of a candle. Now I can no longer give you anything. I cannot even see your face, for I am blind. I have nothing to ask
of you unless it be the health of my lady and my children. I shall love
you faithfully even though I have nothing to ask for myself, better
even than before, now that I have need of nothing. With my sad heart I
am very happy to find you again, father and friend. There, in your
Paradise, before the Mighty King, think of me, a poor pilgrim. In your
great church in Troyes remember me sometimes, during the mass.
O best of all men, no one loved God as much as you did at the time
when He was on earth, and how dearly must we love you, for none has
ever been able or will be able to love as you loved. If only I had a small
part of your great love for Him, I should surely have the strength to
bear all without complaint, father and lord."

The sun beat directly down upon the old man's uncovered head. He
was so still that the pigeons which fluttered about the porch began to
settle upon his legs and shoulders. And the longer he stayed there,
pressed against the column, his hands grasping Saint Peter's foot, the
more he desired to remain there forever; he did not feel the blood withdraw from his numbed arms and since he could see nothing he felt his
body grow vast and rise and grow out in all ways. The column was like
an enormous cathedral pillar and Saint Peter's statue a great tower
reaching towards the clouds and the door of the church raised itself
higher than mountains and dominated the whole country; if he took
but a single pace he would bestride the Rhône; he had but to reach out
his hand to touch the sea. And, what was strange, this did not frighten
him. He experienced neither vertigo nor drunkenness but only a great
tranquillity. It was as if he had just understood that this was natural,
that he had always been bigger than the mountains without knowing it.
He saw immense vistas of mountains bathed in sunshine, their blue
darker with distance, their outline strangely jagged, green-banked

rivers bearing fleets of sailing boats, fields of ripe wheat to the horizon and beyond, vast forests of ancient oaks and great hoary pines and beeches with deep hollows beneath their roots, and beneath the coppice wood there were earths where foxes hid with their cubs, stags bounded across the clearings and vultures glided above the summits. He had only to extend his hand to cover all that with its shadow.

As of a dream he wondered what could be the meaning of his vision. Why did God show him, at this particular moment, what he could never see with his eyes? "Are you telling me, Friend, that I still have my heart's eyes and the memory of what I have seen? I know it well but it does not console me; when a man is hungry, is he satisfied with the memory of yesterday's meal? O Friend, why have you taken that from me which you left even to the holy man Job, whom you tried so hard? Why torture me by showing me all the beauty of the world which you created for the delight of our eyes? There it is—I see each leaf on the trees and the small birds in the branches and the dew drops in the grass, and yet, Lord, I see them not. I see them not, I see nothing! If I could only see my hand, my staff. O good Saint Peter, ask God to give me back my eyes. I know well that for Him it is less than a little speck of dust, but for me it is still very much."

Someone touched his shoulder and asked:

"What are you doing here, poor man?" He raised his head. The statue of Saint Peter, and the column, shrank so quickly beneath his hands and arms that he seemed hardly to have time to realize the change. He was aware of his body as a bit of flesh, formless, colorless and so small that he would have to walk and walk forever even to reach Marseilles. The porch of the church, too, felt small; and small the man who spoke to him.

But he could not forget his dizzy ascent; and he stayed there, his face stupidly turned towards the man who had spoken, yet not knowing whether he was still there. Yet for eight days now he had believed himself able to detect people's presence by their breathing.

"What am I doing here? You can see for yourself: I am praying to Saint Peter."

"Are you mad, old man, to speak in that manner to a priest of God? Are you a heathen?"

"I am blind. I could not see that you were a priest."

"Forgive me, poor old man," the other said, gently. "Come with me, we will eat together. I have, as it happens, fresh eggs and lettuces."

"There's my boy, somewhere," the old man said. "He should be playing here, near the drinking-trough. He will certainly be hungry, hungrier than I."

"Come, I will beckon him. Take my hand. There are three steps."

In the priest's little house there was a window cut into the stone, rounded at the top; the floor, paved with irregular flags, was strewn with herbs.

The two men, seated at a small, square table, were finishing their meal. The priest offered his guest a cup of water reddened with wine; he was poor and could not afford wine every day. The table was of well-polished wood and smelled of wax. The priest's gown was carefully darned, his face red-brown, lean, and marked with deep lines, like a peasant's, and his eyes were grave. He talked at length with the man, urging him to confess so that he could receive Communion on the morrow. It would be of much help to him, he said.

"Confession is too bitter a thing, Father," the old man said, "and if I were to confess now I should speak rather of others' sins than my own, for my heart is heavy with them. As for my own sins, God has already chastised me more than I deserved. I well know that I should not say such a thing and that He knows better than I what is good for me. But there it is—I gave up everything of my own free will, my house and my children and my country; and yet I was attached to them. And He has deprived me of the only thing I should not have had the strength to sacrifice myself."

"He will take even more from you, if He judges you worthy, my son," the priest said. "Is it for us to haggle with God?"

"Father, I do not haggle, but if you knew how hard it is no longer to see anything! You are perhaps thinking that since I am old the thing has hardly any importance. Father, even toads, even flies can see the sun. I should never have told any man what I am telling you now; I don't like to complain. But you are more learned than I—tell me why God has done this to me."

The priest made no answer and Ansiau's head fell lower than ever; since he had been sightless it seemed to him that all his hidden thoughts were written on his face and he was ashamed to be so exposed to a man he could not see.

"Son," the priest said, at last, "we are here in the hands of Saint

Peter and I see that you honor him and pray to him, which is well. You show good sense, for Saint Peter is so great a saint that the heavy and terrible keys of Paradise are confided to his care, and entry into Paradise to his judgment. Know that, after our most sweet and most pure Lady, Mary, the Crowned Queen, it is he who is our great intercessor with God, for he holds a place in Heaven that no other saint could ever fill, how great soever the marvels which he wrought. For before God there are twelve thrones all made of gold and light, for the twelve holy apostles, and of these apostles Saint Peter is the highest in dignity. And never could you conceive the beauty of these twelve thrones, for you must not think that they are twelve chairs decorated with gems like the thrones of kings and bishops, but surely high, spiritual glories beside whose beauty that worldly beauty which you regret is naught but a dung-heap.

"Do you suppose, my son, that Saint Peter was a sinner like us? Know that he was a man clean of all stain and he came very near to being a perfect man, for he was guilty of only one sin in his whole life. Even so, when he was tempted by the Devil, who came to him in the shape of the high priest's handmaiden, it was not from cowardice that he denied God, nor any other evil feeling, but only because he had trusted overmuch in his own strength and God wished to teach him a lesson. And even so, my son, learn that no sinner, though a parricide, no truly repentant sinner, not even Saint Mary Magdalene, ever wept for his sins as Saint Peter wept for that one backsliding; they were surely tears of fire and blood that he wept for his sin and even until his death he did not forgive himself. As you can see, my son, there is a vast difference between him and you, and yet 'when he was become old one took him by the hand and led him where he did not wish to go.' And do you think that *he* said: 'I have not deserved it?' "

His elbows on the table, Ansiau listened, and his dead eye blinked; he was fighting back his tears.

"And that is the great lesson, my son, which Saint Peter and all the Saints give us. It means that we do not attain to joy by a pleasant life and making good cheer, but by such agonies and martyrdoms that the mere thought of them makes your hair stand on end. If you have ever seen a criminal flayed or quartered, think of it, and do not forget that not otherwise were the holy martyrs treated. And know this, when Saint Peter yielded up his body to the great agony of death, he asked his executioners to crucify him not as Our Lord was crucified—though that is suffering unspeakable—but with his head below his feet, which is harder still and more shameful. That was how he considered that he deserved to be treated, after the most holy life he had led. And after that, friend, what suffering and what shame have you to fear on this earth? Come, do not call yourself unfortunate. And if worse happens to you, do not hold it an evil, but a good thing."

The worthy priest had succeeded in his aim: the old man was now thinking of Saint Peter and his heart contracted with pity. "Simon called Peter, dost thou love me more than these others love me?— When thou art old they shall bind thee and lead thee where thou wouldst not go—Lord, you know well that I love you." Beside such a love what did his own wretchedness for a little ball of flesh and water and a dead nerve amount to? He was not the first nor the last to whom that had happened. And after all he was free and was going where he wished. *Domine, tu scis quia amo te.*

On the morrow the man and the child took the road early in the morning. It was cool, the birds were singing and the sky above the valley was white. A thick white mist hung above the river, slowly rising. In the east the face of the hills began to glow.

The blind man, with his hand on Auberi's shoulder, kept to his rhythmic pace, rather slow, forced to match his long strides to the child's shorter, irregular steps. His head was empty and he was thinking of nothing.

THE SONGBIRD

At a couple of hundred paces from the town a man in a red bonnet was lying in the grass of the verge, and another, a muscular ruffian in rags, with a bandaged eye, was engaged in slitting his pockets.

Auberi, very amused and excited by this spectacle, at once began clapping his hands and shouting, "Hi, there! Hi, there! Thief! Thief!

Murder!" The man with the bandaged eye, seeing the two pilgrims and no doubt impressed by the old man's imposing stature, dropped his knife and made off. The man in the red bonnet, woken by the shouting, jumped to his feet asking:

"Who cries thief?"

As his whole posture was that of a man offering help, Auberi stopped and, bent double, his head thrown back, burst into such a wild peal of laughter that the old man began laughing too, without knowing why. Then Red-bonnet, thinking himself the object of a practical joke, advanced on the child with raised fist.

"I'll teach you to wake folks up for nothing, you urchin!"

Auberi could not stop laughing.

"Look at your pocket, you big goose," he said, between two hiccups, "y-y-your pocket!"

The other, seeing his pocket slit open, grasped what had happened and began to laugh himself.

"So," he said, "I'd have certainly been done for but for you, good people. Thank you. I'll repay that one of these days." He began pulling up his worn hose which hung down his legs like sacks and the two pilgrims resumed their way.

They had hardly taken twenty steps when the man in the red cap overtook them. He put his quick, strong hand on the old man's shoulder.

"Who are you, good people?" he asked. "I can see you are not from these parts. If there is anything I can do for you?—as for money, I've certainly no more than I need but, if you've need of it, we'll share."

"Why, blockhead," Auberi said. "Have you ever seen folks who've no need of money? Come, share it out, and then we'll see."

"I'm speaking to your father, you little Auvergnat piglet," the man said, and pulled the boy's curly hair but without appearing in the least angry.

"My friend," Ansiau said, "we are pilgrims and do not live on alms. If you have money more than your need, I accept willingly. You must have a good heart. But do not be concerned for us."

"At least you're no Auvergnat, old 'un," the other said. "You look to me like a Burgundian. And, by Saint Trophime, you've been a soldier. Now that," he added, "is something I should never want to be. You get old, the captain recruits younger men and out you go to beg your bread on the roads; and then people complain that there are brigands about! By Saint Macaire, a soldier has a stomach to fill, same as any other man, hasn't he, old 'un?"

"It's a trade, like another," the blind man said. "And understand, my lad, that I never served for pay[1] but to fulfill my oath as a liegeman. I am the son of a noblewoman and my servant is also free born, and you must take a different tone with us."

The man in the red bonnet whistled a little, disconcerted and surprised, and for some time walked at the old man's side in silence. Auberi watched him, rather slily, triumphing in his embarrassment. The man in the red cap and grey jerkin was quite young—he could hardly be twenty-five—handsome of face, with a small, aquiline nose, a strong, rounded chin, a good color in his cheeks and lively blue eyes. A few locks of straw-colored hair strayed from under his bonnet. His lips seemed to smile even when he was serious. He walked with his hands tucked into his belt, whistling the tune of a sad song, and Auberi noticed that he whistled very well. The old man also listened, trying to pick up the tune.

"But," the young man suddenly exclaimed, "by the tripes of Saint Fiacre! you've a queer way of looking straight ahead of you. By Saint Eloi, you're blind!"

"Have you never seen a blind man?" Ansiau asked. "God's grace, they're not scarce like freaks at a fair!"

"And are you going far like that?"

"To Jerusalem."

At that the young man raised his eyebrows and his face expressed pity for the old man's simplicity.

"But Jerusalem is a long way, comrade," he said, smiling. "You don't know the road. You have to cross the whole country as far as the sea, embark in a ship, cross the wide sea; and it's dangerous. And such journeys are costly."

"I know a little about it," the old man said. "I've made the journey twice. This will make the third time."

"God!"—the young man crossed himself—"have you travelled so far? As a pilgrim or a crusader?"

"Crusader, my lad. Both times. As you see, I've seen the world."

For some time they walked in silence.

[1] *la solde,* hence *soldier,* one who fights for pay.

"And you," Ansiau asked, "what's your trade? You've a burgher's manner of speech."

The man seemed somewhat embarrassed.

"Oh, me, I'm not from these parts. I was on my way to Avignon, not that I have any kin there, but they say it's a fine town. I also like seeing the world a bit. I'd willingly go so far as Marseilles. Look," he added brusquely, "I'm going to suggest something: suppose we travel together? It's always safer; and it's pleasanter. What with the war and all these men-at-arms crossing the country, it's always better to be in company—and with a good knife in your belt. There's more than one kind of crusader, as you know. And, after all, you have a child with you."

"Bah!" Ansiau said. "In this season, between Avignon and Marseilles, there's always plenty of people on the road. But as for coming with us, faith, I'll not refuse. The way is not so hard when there's someone to talk to."

Their new companion, who said that his name was Riquet, was a merry-spirited fellow. He sang and jested the whole time. Auberi was glad to have someone young to talk to and moreover happy to make their new fellow traveller realize that he was nobly born, treating him with a certain condescension, and this slightly disdainful and protective manner greatly amused Riquet.

"Now where, exactly, do I find the nobility?" he would say, laughing. "Here he walks on the holes in his sandals and is still at wetting his knickers and yet he puts on all the airs of a bishop! It's like what they say—that a pedigree dog will never drink from the same bowl as a cur." And he would tap Auberi on the cheeks and the child would shrug his shoulders, half-offended, half-won by this affectionate gesture.

They stopped to eat, that evening, near a stone cross, and all three first fell on their knees to say a short prayer.

"Hi!" Auberi said, suddenly, to Riquet. "Heathen! What, is your bonnet stuck to your head or have you a leprosy under it?" And he snatched off the bonnet and threw it on the ground.

Riquet picked it up quickly but Auberi had raised his eyes to the other's head in surprise: in the middle of a crown of tangled golden curls was a circular area covered with short, thick hair like the bristles of a brush.

"What a queer haircut!" Auberi cried, laughing. "Is that the fashion in your parts?"

"Little puppy!" Riquet said, confused, and replacing his bonnet.

"What is it, Auberi?" the old man asked. The child was still laughing.

"Why, that he's a monk," he said, at last. "A fine monk, in his red bonnet! Have you taken a penitential vow to dress like that?"

Hangdog, Riquet sat down beside the old man and began to eat his bread.

"Well, what of it?" he said. "What is it to you that I'm a monk?" The old man received the news with indifference.

"At least," he said, "there's no risk of your getting yourself hanged."[1] The three ate in silence. Finally, Riquet asked the old man:

"Say, Master Peter, good lord, do you still want me for a companion on the road?"

"I don't concern myself with other people's business," the old man said. The young man continued:

"I don't want you to think I've done anything bad. I will tell you the whole story. It's very simple. I was journeying to Valence with another brother, with some crown pieces which the provost owed the father abbot. I had the coins in a belt round my waist. When we came to Saint Matthew's Church the other brother went in to pray while I held our mule. While I'm there a pretty girl speaks to me . . . well, what with one thing and another, come evening, I climbed out of the window of the monastery where we were sleeping and visited the girl. And when I woke up—no girl, no belt and no money. Then I didn't dare return to my companion, and, faith, I threw my frock into a bed of nettles. As you see. That was three months ago."

"That sort of thing happens, when you're young," the old man said. "But you would do better to return to your monastery and confess everything. They won't punish you more than is necessary."

"Oh, I know," the other said, with a deep sigh. "I know it well. The father abbot was so fond of me that I should get off with a few strokes of the lash and three months' duty in the farmyard. The father abbot would never have believed I stole the money, not he! But it's the disgrace! There it is—shame. Ah! misery of me! If ever I were to meet the father abbot, my heart would break. And now, whenever I see a Black Friar on the road, I run till there's ten leagues between us, that's what I've come to! Misery!"

[1] i.e., he could always plead "benefit of clergy." *Trans.*

He shook his head with an air of such sadness that Auberi was sorry for him and clapped him lightly on the back.

"Never mind," he said, "poor little brother! We shan't like you the worse for it."

In Riquet's company their way was merrier and the days seemed shorter. Riquet chattered like a magpie, and he had a fine voice and a taste for music. During their halts he and the old man sang in harmony, for Riquet had a quick ear for a tune and a good memory for the words and the old man had an inexhaustible repertoire of songs merry and sad, war songs and love songs, songs of Champagne, Burgundy and France. For in camp and garrison, on the eve of tournaments or during rests in the course of hunting, there could be nothing pleasanter than to listen to a good song and to sing the refrain in chorus.

Riquet was the son of a rich peasant from the neighborhood of Montélimar and had become a monk to satisfy a taste for study. He had learned to read and write and to copy music and could compose tunes himself. He sang the songs which the girls of his village sang in their dances, and minstrels' songs heard during feasts at the castle. Since he had been on the road he had often tried to join up with troupes of minstrels, but they were, he said, a rough lot, treated people not of their brotherhood like dirt, were thieves and cheated at games of chance or skill.

He was forever making plans. He could play a little on the rebec—if he could get hold of one he would go from castle to castle on his own account; all that was needed was to learn many love songs to please the ladies. Perhaps he might manage to compose some himself and then he really would do well, and be able to wear cloth and silk—perhaps he might even win some lady's love. There had been troubadours who had been so fortunate, and no more born in a palace than himself.

"For they say," he reasoned, "that a handsome face counts for much —and my own is by no means ugly—but that that's nothing compared with a beautiful voice for arousing a woman's love. They say there's neither charm nor witchcraft equal to sweet words of love well sung."

And then—why, then a famous singer may well be received by a duke or a count, be given rewards and honors equal to a knight's—in short, Riquet had made up his mind to try his luck as a minstrel.

As he had little singleness of purpose, however, there were other days when he dreamed of turning sailor, voyaging to Palestine or

Venice—or even joining a ship in the spice trade. He had read books about the Indies and Japan and had such marvels to tell concerning them that Auberi, incredulous, shook his head; Indians there were, half-man, half-dog, others with the heads of birds; flowers grew in those parts so big that they could eat a man; there were winged gryphons with feathers of gold and elephants with a tail growing from their noses so strong that they could root out a tree with it.

"A lot of silly tales," Auberi said.

"No, no, my boy," the old man said, "it is all perfectly true. And there are even greater marvels, only no one has ever seen or told them. For there are things so strange and frightful that a man cannot see them without instantly falling dead. All that Riquet tells us I have already heard, told by older and wiser men than he."

Riquet nodded, half-thoughtful, half-smiling. He said:

"The father abbot was so kind that he let me read all his books. Lord, what fine books he had! And bound in such leather! They were as smooth as oil. And parchment like silk, full of pictures painted in all colors and smothered with gold. We had a brother who did them himself; he did one of the whole history of Alexander."

"I had a son," the old man said, "a monk, who worked at illuminating. He was buried on All Saints' Day. The prior showed me some of his work." He stopped, feeling his voice unsteady.

"Last year," Riquet went on, still among his memories, "the archbishop of Grenoble himself sent our father abbot, out of courtesy, a brand new bestiary, the binding gilt. To read it makes your heart beat with delight, it is so full of instruction. The father abbot liked my voice and made me read it aloud—ah, God! what a good abbot he was! When he was in a good humor he would stop me—" at that Riquet sighed profoundly "—to ask me, 'And what do you think of that, Brother Frotaire?'—they called me Brother Frotaire at the monastery. Yes, it's quite true, it was just like that; he'd say to me 'And what do you think of that, Brother Frotaire?' And I'd tell him what I thought as best I could, and then the father abbot would be quite content. Sometimes he'd say: 'If ever I am ill, don't call a doctor, call Brother Frotaire, he'd revive a dead man.' Oh yes, and there were even some who were jealous of me because the father abbot was so fond of me." And Riquet changed suddenly from smiles to tears, since for him the monastery was now become a place of joy and a haven of peace, the promised land where milk and honey flowed. And, in fact, he had lived well there. Three months of wandering had not been able to efface his air of joyful health, sign of a youth free from hunger.

"Well, there it is, you see what comes of running after pretty girls," the old man said, calmly.

"Ah, well," Riquet said, quickly consoled, "what could I do? I'm young and the Devil is strong. Now, at least, there's no more risk of my losing the monastery's cash. You've been young yourself, you must have loved beautiful girls."

"Oh, I had other things to do. It only happened to me once, and that when I was no longer so young, and God knows it did not bring me happiness. It's not so much a sin, my lad, as foolishness; you always lose a thousand times more than you gain. And I'm saying this chiefly for Auberi's benefit, for I'm not the one to teach *you* anything about it."

"Her name was Talasia," Riquet said suddenly, after a silence. "She had eyes as black as jet."

A troop of crusaders from the north came down the road and the pilgrims had to climb on to the roadside bank and flatten themselves against the rock to let them pass. It took a long time—the horses passed in pairs along the stony road at a light trot, swinging their cruppers and tossing their heads, hooded in canvas: their hoofs clattered, the harness creaked and the iron medallions on the reins clinked together. The horsemen came in single file in their white or grey tunics with a red cross in the center of the breast. They were already wearing their armor and their helmets were protected from the sun by canvas hoods or a scarf of light-colored stuff knotted about the head. They bore themselves upright and stiff, their eyes fixed on the horizon; each squire carried, slung against the side of his horse, his master's long, pointed or oval shield, in bright, crude colors intended to be recognized from a distance—squares, bars or bends, birds, trees and crosses. They were French and many of them also had the royal *fleur de lis* among their arms. Some few were from Champagne or Lorraine and marched behind their own colors. Here and there groups of men were singing. From time to time a lance struck against a shield.

Their whole movement was absorbed into the monotonous clatter of hundreds of hoofs striking the stony road in cadence.

The pilgrims, flat against the rock, were several times brushed by horses' tails and long crupper-cloths or the horsemen's tunics. Ansiau, head high, mouth open, stood there shivering and panting like an old war horse who hears the trumpet sound—and the sounds were so close—the clatter of arms, creaking of saddles and the breathing of horses. They made him wild and since he could see nothing he was lost in it, letting himself go, his heart torn by the sound of them, the old cavalier, blind and naked of arms, without horse or armor and unable to go with them. So strong was the call of familiar sounds and scents, that he wanted to throw himself under the horses' hoofs rather than survive the moment when he would cease to hear them.

"Auberi, Auberi, mark their banners well. Can you see Champagne?"

"There's one that looks like it, blue and silver. But the sun strikes right in my eyes, I can't see very well."

Ansiau was astonished that anyone who still had his eyes could not see very well.

"Blue and silver, how many bars? With crowns or not? Can you see Blois? Bar? Imperial eagles in simple quarterings, cope in sable and azure?"

"They pass so quickly," Auberi whimpered. "I haven't time to see."

"Ah, ah!" The old man was gasping aloud in his suffering. "That I should have such a fool with me—at his age, and nothing learned! Ah, if only I had my sight, misery—brothers, oh brothers—my little ones—my sweet lads—oh, comrades, oh, my blood!—to die, to die!—to go forward with you!"

Now they could see nothing on the road but a distant cloud of white dust and the last banners swinging to the monotonous amble of the horses. The blue sky rested gently upon the green and grey mountains. The road was marked here and there by still-warm yellow dung in which rooks and crows were pecking calmly. Two belated horsemen went by at the gallop, raising a dust, then silence fell upon the road. The three pilgrims walked slowly, without talking, deafened. And the earth seemed still to shake beneath their feet.

And because, after that troop had passed through, there remained nothing to eat in the townships near the road, they had to go up into the hinterland and take to the mountain roads.

THE FESTIVAL

AT Castle Hervi meals lasted from morning till night and the guests did not leave the table until None, when the light in the hall began to fail.

The grass in the paddock was all trodden down, and canvas and mats had been spread for such ladies as wished to take their rest there. The servants carried out sweet wine, candied fruits, honey, and clean water for the hands; Herbert had caused swings and hammocks to be slung from the stoutest apple trees.

He was in the hall almost the whole time, shifting his voluminous person from table to table followed by two servants; he was making a round of all the guests of most consequence, begging them not to disdain his food and wine and to accept this or that titbit of boar or partridge or a cup of claret or a stuffed chicken—others he asked what music they would prefer to hear, for he had brought several minstrels from Troyes and himself chose the tunes they were to play. Whenever the guests relaxed between two good courses, the master of the house set the musicians in the middle of the hall and gave the signal for them to strike up.

Seated on a wide, high-backed chair, a little apart from the tables, cushions under his feet and with his blue falcon on his left arm, he surveyed the hall with his heavy-eyed, piercing glance, occasionally beckoning one of the minstrels to him. He was well-instructed in music —he was said, indeed, to have the finest voice in the parish—and would indicate how a tune was to be rendered or ask for some of the words of a song to be changed in honor of one of the ladies present at the feast.

Haguenier occupied the place of honor at the high end of the table, beneath the great Hervi shield, facing the windows. He was dressed in a long gown of bright red silk, and the white shirt, emerging from the wide collar embroidered in gold, was pleated and clasped at his throat. The sleeves of the gown were so long that they dragged on the ground when he cut his meat, and for each major dish, as at the beginning of each meal, two ladies held up the ends of his sleeves; the first day they were Mahaut, the lady of Buchie, his aunt, and the lady Aelis, his step-mother; but thereafter they were Ida of Puiseaux and Beatrice of Jeugni, his cousins, whom he greatly preferred, for he felt less uneasy, could joke with them and pass them the best bits from his plate.

Ernaut and Pierre, seated one on his left, the other on his right, stiff and correct, shared the honors of the feast with him. Ernaut, grave and gloomy, was chiefly engaged in not soiling his gown and ate little. Pierre, confident in his beauty, proud of his handsome clothes, doing his best not to let his delight be too apparent, kept his handsome brown eyelashes demurely lowered.

In point of fact the three days of feasting were something of an ordeal for all three but especially for Haguenier, for their business was to re-main in their places to be admired and congratulated. Haguenier spent his time thanking the minstrels for songs in his honor, saluting ladies and replying to compliments. All too often Herbert sent his page to tell him: "Send some of that game to such-and-such a lady—she's my aunt" or "Such-and-such a knight—he's my cousin" and Haguenier knew perfectly well that these orders meant: "You are an unmannerly ignoramus who does not even know how to do honor to my guests." Yet God knows that, coming from Normandy, he had not had time to get to know his kinsfolk in Champagne.

It was at this feast that he made the acquaintance of his future father-in-law and brothers-in-law, the barons of Chapes; the father, Barthélémi, was so old that his nose curved down to his mouth and his head was entirely bald and shone like a ball of wax; his sons were mature men, the youngest being forty. Their sister could hardly be much younger than themselves. She had not come to the feast herself, it would hardly have seemed decent, the wedding being so near. Hague-nier was resigned in advance to a marriage of interest, knowing that the heir to lands can never be quite his own master; he would never have been so foolish as to choose a young girl as the lady of his thoughts. He only hoped that the lady Isabeau of Chapes, widow of the sire of Villemor, would not have too unpleasant a disposition.

At nightfall, having heard Vespers at Saint-Mary-of-Hervi, the lady Aelis conducted the ladies and damsels to the castle of Linnières where she was lodging them for the night. The men remained at Hervi where, for want of beds and pallets—there were only four beds in the castle—they lay down pell-mell in the clean hay. Herbert himself had to make do with a pallet, the beds being occupied by the older uncles and cousins. Haguenier took advantage of the clear, warm evenings to wander in the meadows or to amuse himself a little with the castle maids. He could put off his silken gown and his fine manners; the guests were otherwise occupied and nobody troubled about him. These were the best moments of the day. There were young men of his own age among his cousins and he was happy to be making new friends.

They went off into the meadows like a team of stallions freed from harness, running and rolling in the grass, wrestling together, then lying down near the stream, in the damp shade beneath the willows, singing songs or listening to the sounds of the nearby forest; the cool of the evening sobered them and the tunes of songs rang in their heads, carrying them far across God knows what dark forests, what moonlit clearings, down what unknown rivers, towards the country of faery, where every lady loves her suitor.

A wounded stag was bellowing for water and the cry of a heron echoed remotely in the forest; the sound of wings among the branches seemed to send a long shivering through the silent forest, and the young men strained their ears. "Woodcock"—"No, pheasant." The owls began hooting and they crossed themselves, their hearts suddenly filled with melancholy—God knows whose soul was crying in that voice. Night came down, damp and sweet, and the young men went back to the castle. There, once near to the barns and stables, their laughter grew free and light again; all the castle and courtyard lights were extinguished and somewhere throughout the castle there were always a few girls to be found, easy of virtue and loving laughter and pleasantness on feast days when wine and song had turned all heads.

Herbert had long talks with his cousin Joceran whom he had to sleep beside him. God knows why he valued Joceran higher than anyone else in that countryside. He was not accustomed to ask for advice; yet he took Joceran's advice into account. Herbert was very proud of his Puiseaux blood, his mother's blood, and Joceran was the head of the house of Puiseaux.

"The maternal connection," Herbert would say, "is necessarily closer than the paternal connection," and he was a little inclined to consider Joceran as the real head of the family.

"Fair cousin," he said, "you know that I consider you my friend, and I say it without flattery. I wish that this feast were already over; it disgusts me, and I am ill with so much eating and drinking. Then there is still the wedding to come in a fortnight and my stomach will be so upset that I shall be taking purges for three weeks. That, until now, is the sum of pleasure I have had from my son—apart from the question of the heritage. Now, tell me frankly, what do you think of him?"

"A fine lad," Joceran said. "And he knows how to bear himself. He does you honor."

"A pity, however, he made a fool of himself during the tournament and that everyone's talking of it as a bad augury. But I am not going to break my heart over that—it's like what happens to some lads who are too much in love and are totally impotent on their wedding night; it's soon over. The child has stout hams and a taste for jousting. I'm not worried about that, no. But—his nature, his character, tell me how it strikes you."

"I don't know him," Joceran said.

"You are too cautious, cousin. I know that you have eyes in your head. Do you think he has bad notions in his mind?"

"I believe," Joceran said, "that he has none but very good ones."

"Fair cousin, I have already told you: speak candidly and without flattery."

Joceran smiled his crooked smile which creased his right cheek.

"I know what I'm saying. The lad's without malice. But as to his not causing you troubles—I do not say that."

"Eh?" Herbert said, anxious immediately. "You've heard something then? Oh, I knew there was something."

"Why, fair cousin, what is there to know? All it amounts to is—I'm older than you. And I have intuition. The boy has his head in the clouds and he needs watching. You know what young people are like nowadays. One of these fine days it wouldn't surprise me if he threw himself off a belfry, just to please some beautiful lady."

"It couldn't be much worse," Herbert said. "He's silly enough to do it. But he hasn't got his head in the clouds. He takes after his mother. It's just my luck that my only legitimate son should also be the son of that slut. May the devils in Hell flay her! Soft as tripes and stubborn as a mule. Ah, God! if only my strumpet of a daughter were a boy!"

He turned over on the pallet, seeking a more comfortable position for his wine-heavy limbs. Wine never went to his head but it made him rather sad and set him thinking of his soul and all kinds of disagreeable things.

"Cousin," he said, "I am going to ask you to do me a favor. I was involved, this past Lent, in a very ugly business. My priest has ordered me a pilgrimage to Rome, afoot and in a hair shirt. I want you to find me a reliable man who'll do it for me. I'll pay whatever is necessary. If there are children or his parents dependent on him, they shall eat at my own table. Someone you know well, whom I can count on."

"I'll think it over," Joceran said. He guessed what the business must be, for there was a lot of talk about the damsel Eglantine's singular marriage and evil tongues were saying it was the vengeance of a lover betrayed. Joceran passed no judgments. Instead he racked his brains to think of the right man for Herbert—afoot and in a hair shirt—the Devil! It would need someone robust and badly in need of money. But he'd find someone; he knew, after all, that he would get a share of the promised reward.

MISUNDERSTOOD

HERBERT frequently wondered why he was considered to be a man who had been lucky, who had, indeed, had more luck than he deserved. He, on the other hand, considered himself exceptionally unlucky.

In the first place, it is always bad luck for a man to have a father who, having married at sixteen, is barely eighteen years older than himself; still worse, to be the second son, the cadet, with, at the most, right to a suit of armor, a horse and a squire but no inheritance to count on. The younger son he was born and so remained all his life. Nearly twenty years had passed since his elder brother had been buried in Acre cemetery; during nearly twenty years it had seemed to Herbert that everyone looked at him reproachfully for usurping another's place. They all seemed to be saying: "He profited by that death." Profit! What his brother had meant to him none knew, not even his father, his father least of all. Bow and bow-string, axe and haft, a pair of oxen under a single yoke, so had they been to each other, Ansiau and himself. It seemed to him that he had lost more than his father had by that death. True, he had not spent his life in lamenting, that was not in his nature, but after all the dead brother's heritage fell to him, his best friend, by right; no one could dispute that.

Nor was it his fault that both Jacques and Renaud of Hervi had died at Acre. At the time of his marriage no one could have foreseen that Bertrade would one day be sole heiress to the whole domain. It could not even be said that he had survived by a discretion exceeding theirs in battle, since the Hervi brothers had died of disease. True, he had wed Aelis of Bercen because her brother had died on crusade, leaving her sole heiress; but what man does not try to win a rich legacy if he can? Now, to be treated as a cuckoo because, in the place of four lads lying in Acre's graveyard, he was master of three domains.

Oh yes, it was indeed bad luck to have too young a father, especially such a father as One-eye had been, an indolent and incompetent man, squatting on his lands like a dog in a manger, not knowing what to do with them and not allowing others to profit by them. He would have let castle and enclosures fall into ruin and mortgaged the land for twenty years or let it lie fallow. "At that rate," Herbert thought, "in ten years we'd have been forced to restore the land to the count, to see his provosts and bailiffs take it over, and engage our sons as mercenary soldiers. I could see it coming. And yet did I even once forget myself in his presence? Did I ever speak one word out of place to him? Because he had enough sense to realize that he ought to go away, was that my fault? Yet even at Linnières they don't accept me as the real master and I am accused of driving my father out of his own house."

Since the death of the elder Haguenier, his father-in-law, he had felt himself at home at Hervi; he had managed the land and maintained the castle better than any paid intendant could have done. Then at the very moment when he seemed to have won a little breathing-space, with both properties running easily, here came this lad, falling, as it were, about his ears; and the men of Hervi were beginning to make him feel that Haguenier was the real master of the castle.

"They can think again," he thought, "for they won't be taking their oath to him tomorrow. I've certainly earned the right to hold the land as long as I like—if the ninny has to wait until he's thirty-seven, as I did, then wait he must. I'm not the man to go off on a pilgrimage because of a hard word from him.

"But why is it my fate never and nowhere to find my proper place?" He should have been born the son of a count—elder, not younger son, oh, no! What father would not have been proud of such a son, a boy who, at fourteen, could bend bows too stiff for a grown man and break wild stallions. The fact was that his father could not forgive him for being stronger and defter than his first-born. As a child everything he could do to please his father turned against him because his father was jealous for his eldest son. And although he, for his part, had never been jealous of his brother, yet not even for that was he given credit.

It seemed to him that nobody ever found anything but faults in him, whereas he felt himself full of good qualities; consequently he was obliged to manage without the good opinion of others and to live as seemed good to himself. He was thought avaricious and lewd, but he was sure that others were equally so, only too hypocritical to admit it. There his thought took a pleasanter turn: avarice—well, but was it a fault? He was simply a rational man who knew that the stronger a man is the freer he is; if he contrived to carve himself out a great fief by uniting a number of properties in his own hands, the better was he able to stand up to the count's bailiffs in their constant encroachment on the ancient liberties of the landed nobility. By so doing he was helping all the nobility of the region and the lesser among them gave him no more than his due when they put their sons into his service. If he could add Buchie, Baudemant and Ermele to his holdings, he would have the largest fief in the county, could dominate the local roads, and even parts of the county roads. In that event he could fortify and improve Linnières and make it a major garrison.

But what shall it profit a man to gain the world and lose his soul? The *world*, indeed! Herbert thought—a handful of land seven leagues long and four across! Had he not seen fabric and woodwork, fine enough to buy the whole estate, burn like straw at Constantinople? A pretty mess that was! Ah, he had seen some fine things in his time. He was no wool merchant nor banker, he knew how to enjoy life. Money—he had emptied his coffers for his son's knighthood and did not give it another thought. There were men enough to serve him gratis, merchants enough to give him credit, and sufficient legal and illegal revenues to make up the sum in two years.

He had only to look a man straight in the face for the other to lower his eyes. He was not liked—he knew it, but nobody was anxious to make an enemy of Herbert le Gros. With a hard smile he stared at his white hands, so disproportionately small. "And yet," he was thinking, "I'm not ill-natured." He became calm and self-satisfied again—and he knew why—an idea which had crossed his mind had just crystallized and taken form: Garnier, lord of Buchie, was old and in bad health; his wife was Herbert's sister; if she became a widow he might find means to take her under his guardianship and so get control of the fief. He would have to discuss it as soon as possible with the viscount of Paiens.

"The old fellow's liver is rotten, he can't drink. He was taken ill at the feast, yesterday. If I can make him drunk enough at my son's wedding he'll be a dead man within three weeks. He can't get much out of life at his age! He does nothing but torment my sister and his family."

And already Herbert was planning the reorganization of the Buchie domain.

PITY

THE noon air lay ponderous on the blackened stones of the houses. The hamlet had recently been burned and the acrid smells of charred skins and smoldering wool were still apparent; here and there, on the piles of rubbish in front of the houses, rotten straw still smoked. Perched on a slope among rocks, the little black township breathed out the heat of death into the blue air, already heated by the sun.

"No luck," Riquet said, "not one house inhabited. The parishioners have quit! It remains to be seen whether they haven't left us a nice, plump little calf, *vitulum saginatum*, roasted alive."

"The only calf in these parts is you," Auberi said. "We'll be lucky to find a goat dead of starvation."

"Pah! A pretty spectacle, isn't it?" Riquet said. "By Saint Eloi, it'll be crows' droppings for our supper tonight! We shall not find a living soul between here and Avignon. If the knackers came up as far as this they must have been hungry."

"All right," Ansiau said, "but we can at least see if there's water in the well, to fill our gourds."

The young pair leaned over the abandoned well. A fetid stench ascended. There was no water to be seen.

"It's full of dung," Auberi said.

"And other things," Riquet added. "Let's go down, we're sure to find a stream at the bottom of the defile, after last Sunday's rain."

The stony way climbed and turned about grey rock with moss growing in its crevices. Vultures hovered in the blue sky. The pilgrims went down towards the Uzès road with the idea of following the bank of the Gard to strike the Rhône again at Beaucaire. From time to time they could see armed bands in the valley below, famished rovers moving swiftly towards Nîmes and Montpellier in the hope of pillage or employment as soldiers. When he knew they were so near, even the old man crossed himself and held his breath and said:

"I wish we were already beyond the hill."

Hunger became so painful to bear that they had to bind their stomachs with their woollen cloaks, wound three times about them and knotted. Auberi had a colic, lay face downwards upon the ground and cried. Riquet had a humming in his ears and claimed to hear the bells of Paradise. After two days' walking they came to a fortified castle whose master refused to lower the drawbridge, for fear of a trap; but he had black bread and dried figs lowered to them from the watchtower window.

The old man, with much experience of hunger from his two crusades, knew how to treat famished stomachs; he stowed all the provisions in his wallet and would not at first give his young companions more than a couple of figs to chew as they walked. He told them:

"When we reach the fountain you shall have a slice of bread." Auberi's tears ran into his mouth and down his chin but Riquet was of better mettle; he still joked as he had, no doubt, during his happy days as a monk.

"It's a pity," Ansiau said, "that you never engaged yourself to some knight in your parts, as a servant. You might have made a good squire. But at your age—pah!—with your woman's arms, you wouldn't even get taken on as a groom."

Auberi said:

"Riquet, look, there's a man by the spring."

The drinking-trough for sheep lay a little aside from the road; beside the meager trickle of water which overflowed the stone trough the grass grew more thickly. Flocks must have passed that way quite recently, for the stream was muddy and the grass trampled and there were mule and goat droppings and the marks of wheels. No doubt the peasants of the burned village had taken this road.

A man with his head bent towards his knees was seated on a large stone which had been rolled up to the trough. His feet were soaking in the mud of the stream. At the sound of voices he sat upright with difficulty and began, in a cracked voice and a whistling accent, to chant:

"*Beati misericordes quoniam ipsi misericordia consequentur—Beati misericordes.*"

His eyes were covered with a dirty bandage of yellow linen and his grey beard hung in locks down beside his neck. His long garment of good black wool was covered with mud and torn on one shoulder.

"What bird have we here?" Riquet said. He stooped to fill his gourd, when the man, extending two long, swollen hands, seized him by the lapel of his coat and clung to it, still chanting his "*Beati misericordes.*"

"Hey, old Lazarus, let go! We've nothing to give you. You've chosen a fine place for your begging!"

"Have pity on the blind," the other mumbled, "noble lords, noble ladies, good people, brothers in Christ, for the love of the Holy Virgin, Queen of Paradise, a bit of bread for pity's sake."

"Blind?" Ansiau said, and his hand went to his wallet.

"Wait," Riquet said, "he's no more blind than I am. Let go, I say, old Cut-purse! I know this kind of blindness. He's not even good at it; there's others do it better. I'd be quite as blind with a bandage over my eyes. It's a lucrative trade and costs nothing to learn."

"Riquet," Ansiau said, "a man would surely not do that where there is no one about. The poor old man is blind. Lead me to him, I am going to cut him a slice of bread."

But Riquet was confident in his judgment. At the word bread the man had stretched out his arms before him and was groping about in the air with open hands.

"He'll be worth a good laugh," Riquet said. "All right, old man, never mind the play-acting or it will be the worse for you; those tricks will cost you a beating!" With a swift movement he ripped the bandage from about the man's eyes.

The other did not even cry out, but uttered a kind of gulp followed by a sigh, then raised his hands towards his head but without even daring to cover his face. Where his eyes had been were two dark red cavities, clots of dried pus were stuck to his eyelids, a thread of blood trickled from a scab which had been torn away with the bandage. Auberi crossed himself and huddled against Ansiau.

"Poor man!" he said, "his eyes have been put out."

Crestfallen, Riquet said:

"We weren't to know—how does he come to be like this? And then, to be left here alone, by Saint Eloi! And those aren't a beggar's clothes."

Somewhat recovered from the shock, the man again stretched out his hands and took up his *Beati misericordes*: he did not seem to understand what he was saying. Emaciation had made his nose as sharp as a bird's beak, his lips enormous, his cheeks as yellow and smooth as bone.

Before such ugliness Riquet was moved to hatred rather than pity.

"Let's move on," he said, turning away in disgust. "Give him a bit of bread if you like but I don't advise it. He looks very like a heretic to me."

Auberi's eyes opened wide with fear, for he had never yet seen a heretic. Ansiau had sat down on the ground and was cutting up the bread by touch. It was actually easier to divide it in four than in three parts.

"You're a heretic, eh?" Riquet said, taking the old man's beard in his hand. "Otherwise you wouldn't be walking about with your eyes put out. It's what I was saying—he looks like a townsman. Aye—to think a man can win his way into Paradise simply by killing one of these wretches! I don't know what stops me. Come on, old cur," he added. "Cross yourself, to show."

The eyeless mask, the gaping mouth and swollen tongue hardly looked like a human face: a stone gargoyle, rather. And Riquet found it so grotesque that he burst out laughing.

"Hey, what a face! It's a fright. Come on, cross yourself, we'll give you bread if you cross yourself."

The man raised his hand and let it fall, to the great horror of Auberi and Riquet: they thought that the Devil was holding back his hand.

Riquet was serious again.

"Let's go on," he said, "we must not stay here. He really is a heretic. Give him some bread quickly and let's go. I've already filled my gourd; we can eat further on."

Ansiau rose slowly.

"Perhaps he is no heretic," he said, thoughtfully. "We might take him with us."

"Never!" Riquet said. "Never! I'll leave you if you do. I've no wish to travel with a devil, thank you."

"Riquet, fair son," Ansiau said, "I shall manage very well without you. You are free and so am I. If this man can walk, he comes with us. We have no right to leave him here."

Riquet bowed his head, half-ashamed, half-sulky.

HAGUENIER'S MARRIAGE

ISABEAU of Chapes, the lord of Villemor's widow, was thirty-eight years old. Her husband had been dead for six years and she lived alone in her manor, her children being reared by her husband's sisters. For want of a master the domain's revenues were falling and the handful of vassals attached to the holding talked of transferring their service to neighboring lords. Isabeau's brothers had been long in making up their minds to arrange a second marriage for their sister. They had been bargaining over her for five years, unable to find a suitor to their taste. Herbert had, at last, overcome them, backed by the viscount's support and the approval of the woman's father, who liked him. Haguenier was Herbert's only legitimate son: Gilles and Gillebert of Chapes told themselves that if their sister gave him an heir they might, when Herbert died, get a share in the administration of his domains. Weary of holding her lands alone, Isabeau had agreed to the bargain, but she was none the less somewhat anxious at the idea of marrying a lad of twenty.

Isabeau was a large woman, dark, formerly handsome, but thickened by eight pregnancies; her complexion was muddy, her eyes darkly circled, and the wide, thin mouth was puckered or drawn out, as if on purse strings. Since being widowed she had neglected herself and spent

her days seated by the fire, her hair greasy and ill-kempt, long locks
loose from her plaits and her chemise black with dirt. Her only pleasure
was in eating well and, as she moved as little as possible, she had fat-
tened. But, despite her laziness, she was an able woman and as capable
of caring for her interest as any man.

The young husband they were giving her pleased her more than she
was willing to show. After the wedding day they left together for
Villemor, to spend their first weeks together; it was agreed that thereafter Haguenier was to resume his freedom and seek service with some
baron setting off for the crusade in the Toulousain.

Haguenier, pleased at being master of a great house at last, spent his
time in feasting and gaming. He had brought with him several friends
of his own age and he invited there all the damsels of Villemor, the
neighborhood, and even the daughters of blacksmiths and bailiffs, installed them on the ramparts round the lady Isabeau and organized
displays of archery, leaping and wrestling. The lady Isabeau enjoyed
watching her husband polevault the great palisade of the castle or,
mounted on a horse at full gallop, pick up a coronet of flowers from the
ground—which he would then present, on the end of the long wooden
lance, to his spouse. Dame Isabeau would not have believed that she
would ever again be the object of such attentions and could not but be
a little touched by them. Laughter continually filled the meadow and
the courtyard. Haguenier always rose before dawn and went riding,
fasting. Then he practiced with lance and spear with his comrades in
the courtyard; he had become so accustomed to this that on the days
when he had to forgo these morning exercises he felt ill at ease. Lady
Isabeau would see him return, flushed, his hair disordered, ravenous,
and would feel tenderly towards him, as if she really were a young
bride. She noticed that sometimes his nostrils were pinched and his
hands looked bluish, and then she showed anxiety. He laughed at it:
"Another care you've acquired, sweet friend! My blood flows too
heavily, that's all it is." At heart he was not so much anxious about
these crises of weakness, which he had experienced since the tournament, as ashamed; he reproached himself with having neglected his
training.

Isabeau rarely saw him alone but in the evening. He showed himself
courteous, almost tender, towards her: but he was so with all women,
instinctively seeing them as weakly beings in need of consideration and
protection—an attitude which, in the case of a matron inclined to be

masculine and managing, was not without a touch of the comical, yet
Isabeau could not prevent herself being moved by it.

She advised him to take an active interest in the business of the estate
and brought him the box in which she kept the list of vassals and an-
nual rents and the securities for loans—for she lent out much money;
he shrugged and said: "Eh, my dear friend, leave all that to your clerk."
But his indifference was only affected, for in fact he understood figures,
which he had been learning since he was a child, better than she did,
and he was very well informed concerning the business of the Villemor
estate. On the eve of his departure for Hervi he took the lady's hand
and led her to the corner of the room where she kept her desk and
papers, to speak to her alone. Then he firmly laid down his conditions.
She was free to accept or refuse them, but if she refused, he said, she
must not count much on his help.

He had, he said, given the matter careful thought. The estate
brought in so much. He undertook to be responsible for the provision
of forced labor for public works and the payment of debts and all accounts would be submitted to him by the lady's clerk. For his expenses
he wanted half the revenues of the estate, plus the expenses of running
the house, paying soldiers, forage, candles and spices. The remainder
would be the lady's to dispose of as she pleased. He undertook to spend
an average of one week in every month with her, excepting for those
months when he was away campaigning. He undertook that at Christmas and Easter he would give a feast at his expense to all the vassals
and subtenants of the estate; to give a suit of woollen clothes to every
squire of noble blood in the household and a horse to every nobly born
son on his eighteenth birthday; to entertain, at his own expense, his
lady's sons and brothers provided they paid no more than six visits a
year, visits in excess of that number to be charged to her in the matter
of extra spices, candles and wine. In addition he undertook to espouse
the cause of any estate vassal, to stand guarantor for any man of their
domain who had a lawsuit, and to support the lady's kinsfolk in any
business not contrary to the interests of his own family. He agreed not
to keep a concubine in the house, not to strike any member of his
lady's personal staff, and to make her a gift on major feast days.

"If you keep your word to me," he said, "I shall stand by my word
to you and you will not have anything to complain of in me."

"My friend," the lady said, "it is very clear how young you are: you
think that everything can be accounted for and arranged in advance.

You will find your money quicker spent than got. And should you run into debt, must I undertake to pay it off?"

"Do not concern yourself about me, friend. Simply tell me whether or no my proposal suits you. Considering my undertakings, I certainly deserve half the revenues. As to debts, if I contract any, I undertake to repay you, never fear. I am not the kind of man who makes his wife keep him."

Isabeau gently shook her head.

"Men say that, my friend. But I know very well that as long as your father lives I shall not get a penny of the dower he has promised me, and, as he is almost exactly my age, you will be forced to live at my expense. That, I suppose, was the reason for marrying you off."

"My opinion was not asked. Your relations were at liberty to look to that more closely. If you have so little confidence in me, perhaps you would prefer it in writing, sworn to by my friends?"

"Don't take it like that, friend. I am not reproaching you. I am simply taking into account that your expenses will be heavier than you think. I've been told that you carry the colors of a lady in Troyes."

Haguenier flushed very red at the memory of the unfortunate tournament and the lady was put out, but then told herself that at her age it was absurd to be jealous of so young a man.

"Come," she said, "I wish you good luck. And don't worry overmuch about your debts—for you will make debts. I have sons of your age, which is why I am talking to you like this."

That same evening she told him that she believed herself pregnant. In fact, she was not at all sure, but he was leaving; she had only that one trump to play and she did not want to miss her chance to make use of it. Haguenier was delighted but a little incredulous.

"At your age?" he said. Then he told her to take great care of herself, to say nothing to anyone before the fifth month, to cheat ill-luck, and to cause candles to be offered to Saint Roch in order that the child should be a boy. In short, he said everything that was proper in such a case; but the lady Isabeau was enough of a woman to sense all his indifference beneath that natural kindness.

DEPARTURE

THE gear was all ready, Herbert had seen to that. He had had the hauberks packed in boxes, checked the wheels of the cart, tried the war horses.

"If you put me to shame this time, son of a bitch," he said, "you would do better never to return."

For once, Haguenier lost patience.

"Which is, I think, what you would have preferred," he said. "However, have no fear, I'm leaving my wife pregnant. As for me, you need have no concern. God will protect me all right, without your prayers."

"What's this?" Herbert said. "Villein's spawn! My friends, did you ever hear a man speak so to his father? And who was it gave you knighthood, arms and armor, Devil's pup?"

"He who holds my land," Haguenier said, lifting his chin. Then he bent the knee to take leave of his father. Herbert gave him his hand to kiss, then, very coldly, they embraced. But when the young man was on his way, the father, leaning against the main gate of the castle, followed him with his eyes, shaking his head; in three months he had grown accustomed to the lad's singing and laughter.

Haguenier took with him Pierre, two squires and ten men-at-arms. They were all to take the Cross at Troyes, with the baron of Chantemerle, and leave for the south during the first week of June. There would be time to do their forty days and return to Champagne before the autumn. The troop numbered about one hundred and fifty men— the majority of crusaders had left in the spring.

In Troyes the new crusaders were solemnly blessed by the archbishop and had a large red cross sewed on to the front of their tunics. Among those who were going only Haguenier and Pierre were newly knighted and they were more moved than the others. The troops included some who had been to Constantinople and two knights who had already fought in the Albigensian war and were hot with impatience to fight again in so sacred a cause.

The priests were proclaiming, in every sermon, that this Albigensian crusade was holier than the others and more profitable to Christianity. They were not going to fight against heathens, who sinned only from ignorance and could be converted, but against men inspired by the Devil himself, baptized men who trampled on the cross, Christians already saved by the blood of God who had yet turned against Him— sacrilegious wretches who used the consecrated Host in their orgies and kissed the bottom of a cat, believing that animal to be the incarnation of their master the Devil. They massacred priests and profaned churches, transformed convents into houses of debauchery and preached incest and suicide on all sides, claiming them as acts tending to the salvation of the soul.

That such things should be possible was enough to make your blood boil with indignation, and the crusaders who were going to the south were determined to give no quarter to people capable of harboring such doctrines. But the war had now lasted three years and enthusiasm was no longer what it had been in the beginning, those who had been on crusades already returning disappointed at having had to fight against men like any others, mostly Christians for that matter. The whole eloquence of the preaching brothers sent from Rome was required to explain that the leprosy of heresy is not necessarily visible in the face.

Haguenier had difficulty in imagining what this leprosy could be like but he had no doubt that it must be something frightful—he was too pious not to tremble at the idea that there existed men who could soil the image of God in themselves and hate Him who is all Love.

"Christ's executioners," he reflected, "knew not what they did and we hate them even as our worst enemies. Whereas these others know what they are doing and rejoice in injuring God. It is as if they were already in Hell and turned into demons." It was the duty of every man of good feeling to defend his God and protect Him from outrage. Would he have stood by and seen his father injured? And yet Herbert of Linnières was a very imperfect image of God. What, then, was not due to that Father who was all goodness and love?

In Normandy, however, this crusade was not as popular as in Champagne and he had often heard discussions on the subject; the Norman nobility was too closely allied with that of Guyenne where many Normans had relations and friends. Haguenier could speak the *langue d'oc* almost as well as his own language and he loved the songs of the troubadours. He became quite sad at the thought that many southern knights, good Christians, were obliged to defend an evil cause; being a layman and a soldier he could readily understand that a vassal's oath might sometimes be set above God's interests; perhaps he might have done the same himself. In Normandy it was often said that heresy was the Church's business and that different means of finding and burning the real heretics could have been found; that the pope was certainly a very holy man but misled; that Raymond of Toulouse had never worshipped the Devil; that he might be a traitor and a knave but it did not mean that a war waged against him was a holy war.

Haguenier knew all that. He thought that these were probably somewhat quibbling considerations—you go to God's defense, or you do not. But he did sometimes wonder whether the right way of defending Him had been found.

The troop had hardly cleared Troyes and was stopping to rest the horses; the crowd of women, peasants, beggars, gathered on the verge, was watching them pass. Children threw plucked grass beneath their horses' hoofs, women smiled, raising their hands in greeting, old men blessed them—great was the power of that red cross on their breasts, great also the thirst of poor folk for love and pity. These men who were going so far, for God, were men of Champagne like themselves, fellow countrymen, local lads—soldiers and eaters of the poor though they were. And they were going into great danger to do noble things— for God.

A LADY'S GAME

THE crusaders were about to set forth again when a slight young girl in a blue dress emerged from the crowd and caught hold of Haguenier's leg.

"Lord Knight," she said quietly, "you bear about you a purple scarf which you neither found nor bought."

"Fair friend," he said, "I see that it was my lady who sent you. Does she require some service of me?"

"Yes," the girl said. "You are to go at once to see her, at Mongenost, in her garden."

It was Marie's means of putting the young man's love to the proof, to see whether he would not be afraid of making himself ridiculous or of passing for a coward. Haguenier was not the man to care about that; he saw the trap at once. He said to Pierre: "Don't wait for me, I'll rejoin you in two hours," left the ranks at the risk of trampling the crowd, turned his horse and set off at a gallop on the road to Troyes under the surprised eyes of his companions.

The road ran beside the Seine. The heat was great and the horse became dark with sweat. Out of pity for the animal Haguenier was forced to go more slowly.

"Never mind, you shall rest and eat well at Mongenost," he thought. "O lovely lady who is costing me this—how she makes her own fool of me! Well, it's her right, God knows." With how many caresses would he make her pay, with how many kisses buy each minute now lost! "Most sweet, most gracious and most false, my patience shall be more enduring than your hardness and you will be mine; and then you will see that I shall never be hard to you."

He had himself conducted directly to the lady who was astonished and even confused to see him arrive so quickly. She readily justified herself: it was not her intention to distract him from his duty to God; on the contrary, she had sent for him to give him a precious relic which would help him in battle. They had, it is true, seen each other several times since Easter but always in the presence of the sire of Mongenost; now her husband was in Troyes and she felt more at liberty.

"For, friend," she said, "there is no wrong between us and never will be, and that is why I do not want to rouse suspicion in evil minds. Out of regard for your sister I have a friendship for you and I want to confide this little iron cross to you—it was my father's, dead in the Holy Land; to whom could I better trust it than to a man setting off to fight for the first time, and to fight for God?"

She lifted the little cross on its silken cord from about her neck but it caught upon other necklets and ribbons which she was wearing, while the cord became tangled in her hair so that one of the rolled braids came loose and fell down upon her shoulder. Haguenier, tense and still, was forcing himself to quench the fire in his glance, not to see—oh, perdition!—the sun-blaze of her hair, the rosy cheek, the eyes as full of movement as the sea.

"Well," Marie said, "you are hardly very agreeable, fair friend. Another would have offered to help me with this cross. I am getting mixed up in all these knots."

He sat beside her, with the resplendent, candid smile which lit his face despite himself when he believed that he was pleasing a woman, and began to unhook the cross, to disentangle necklets and medallions, taking care not to touch the lady's face or neck; he wanted desperately to do so, but such was the game, and the least suggestion of too bold a movement might lose it. He knew by experience the cost of taking proud ladies' coquetries too seriously.

When he had restored order among the necklets and medallions, Marie hung the little cross about his neck and kissed him on the cheek.

"God keep you," she said. "I should blame myself if I delayed you any longer."

The damsels seated at the lady's feet and on the parapet of the well were chattering and laughing together, and the lady clapped her hands and said to them,

"Come, my friends, sing a pretty song for our knight's pleasure. I should not forgive myself for entertaining him so badly. Gillette, go and order that he be served with wine and fruit, and something to take with him on his way."

The girls began a song in chorus.

"Fair friend," Marie said, softly, "there are things I should like to say to you without being overheard by my damsels. You know the way here by the orchard, and from the orchard you can get in through the meadow by climbing the oak against the east wall at the bottom of the hill. If I can, I will be here, tonight, after Matins."

Haguenier left the castle after taking leave of the lady and set out to follow the east wall in search of the oak. The day was waning. He had to conceal himself in the bushes to keep out of the watchman's sight; and it began to rain.

The bells of Saint-Nicholas convent sounded Matins. The air was cool after the rain, and in the sky a thin sliver of moon swam swiftly among small clouds which were breaking and spreading in wisps throughout the dark heavens, pursuing each other between the meshes of lace sketched against the sky by the wet foliage of the cherry trees. The orchard grass and the ivy about the well were drenched with water, and little streams were still trickling over the fine gravel of the tiny garden. Lavender and wallflowers breathed out a poignant, sad perfume after the rain. In the wood a screech owl cried.

Haguenier sat down on the stone seat and began rubbing and shaking his soaking clothes and wrung out his drenched hair; the downpour had been so sharp that neither trees nor wall had afforded protection. The castle reared, a looming darkness, above the garden; not a light anywhere. And nothing to be heard but the pacing of the watch on his tower. Haguenier was wondering what the lady could possibly have to say to him. But he was certain, God knows why, that she would not come, that she had simply been making fun of him. He thought of his comrades who must by now be far on their road.

"False friend," he thought, "I shall not love you any less for this, but, as God knows, I shall remind you of it one day and you will not be proud of having made me look foolish. Sweet and fine—through what would a man not pass to enjoy your body?" And he seemed to see her beside him again on the seat, warm and roseate and smelling of milk of almonds and jasmine.

He waited all night and at last fell asleep on the seat. When the sky began to lighten, a little maid came to the seat and woke the sleeper. "My lady was not able to come," she said, "but asks that you be here tonight."

Haguenier went out by the orchard, climbed the wall and mounted his horse, shivering with cold and, for once, furious with the lady. He had not been able to deny her but she was already costing him two days' delay; God knows what his comrades were thinking. Pierre would not be sorry to see him labelled coward and to put himself at the head of his men—a good lad, Pierre, but with his eye overmuch to the main chance. He did not care about Pierre, though, it was the baron of Chantemerle he was thinking of.

There was nothing he could do but swim the Seine with his horse and beg his sister's hospitality.

"In God's name, sisterkin, neither your husband nor anyone else must know that I am here, it might injure my lady. Tell your women to keep quiet about it."

Aielot brought him a shirt and breeches and had his clothes dried on the grass in the sun. There he spent the most exasperating day of his life, watching birds hop from branch to branch, the sun climb the heavens and presently decline against the great blue vault with irritating slowness, as the shadows of bushes grew slowly longer and turned from north to east and the grass changed from green to yellowish. The crickets chirped in the meadow, the sounds of voices, laughter, shouts, the neighing of horses and the clatter of pans came to him from Pouilli castle and Haguenier thought:

"They seem bustling enough, over there—whereas I—! And I'm certain of another sleepless night for nothing." Well, it did not matter; he was caught in the game. That evening he crossed the Seine, in a boat this time, and found the oak again, furious, yet determined to return to the rendezvous ten nights running, if the lady required it.

The night was fine and mild. After Matins he was again at the well, listening to the crickets singing in the meadow. The silence of the garden was so profound that he did not dare move his feet for fear of rattling the gravel. The shadow of the castle covered the garden, then the moon swam out from behind the tower. "She will not dare come," the young man thought. "There is too much light."

But this time she came, shining white in her light dress under blue moonlight, her long hair knotted in a dark veil. Haguenier was so surprised that he felt his heart fail him. Marie sat down beside him on the parapet of the well and spoke for a long time, her hands clasped on her knees. She spoke of the respect due to noble-hearted ladies and of the purity of true love. She said that never would she take as a friend a man who would not love her in all purity and without sin and that she had already rejected all the men who had loved her, seeing that their love was nothing but sensual desire. As for him, she did not yet know him but he was young and had as yet no lady; she was willing to help him in his education in love, provided she judged him worthy.

"If you acquire good fame in this campaign, perhaps I will accept you as my servitor."

"Lady," Haguenier said, "I am not of those who boast before the event. But if I fight well, you shall hear of it."

She looked him in the eyes and her eyes were like two dark holes in her delicate white face. Haguenier felt the earth roll under his feet: he took the small fair head between his hands and began to smother her chin, her cheeks and her lips with kisses. Out of pity, and also to see whether he was sufficiently master of himself to cease at her bidding, she did not resist. When, with both hands, she pushed him gently away, he did not protest but for full five minutes remained with head bowed, his elbows on his knees, his hands clasped. Marie felt that this silence bound her to him more than words and kisses, and she was afraid of wanting to love him. At last he said:

"Lady, you are both too hard and too gentle, in the manner of women. God keep me from blaming you: you have accorded me much more than my deserts, and for this I thank you with all my heart."

"Friend," she said, putting her hand on his shoulder, "think no evil because of the kisses I allowed you out of pure friendship. Know that on the day I take you for my friend I shall accord you much less as to the body, for you must indeed understand that not thus is true love."

"False joy, false sweetness," he said, his voice harsh in his throat, "how well you speak of it! Yet you know that your heart is as cold as an icicle and he who wins it will die of sorrow. But for your sake I would go into the flames of Hell without remission; and I should not complain."

Marie judged that the conversation was becoming too tender, and rose. He knelt before her and she placed her hand on his head.

"Go," she said, "and be worthy of me. What I have promised you, many men have desired, and never until now have I promised it to anyone."

In the town of Troyes the bells of the churches and monasteries clamored their music, grave, clear and sweet, the changes following each other in harmonious order; the morning air quivered with their music for a league around and the streets of the town so rang with sound that it found echo in all hearts and set them singing the joy of morning mass in unison.

Kneeling on the cold flagstones of Saint-Pancrace Church, Haguenier watched the hands of the celebrant priest rise towards God, bearing the resplendent chalice against the background of the altar with its tall white candles. And his heart beat with renewed joy in the Divine Presence and a thousand candles burned in his heart. Always and everywhere and to all eternity, grant me I pray thee O Fount of Goodness and Pity without end, most pure Lady, Queen of Glory, grant me the body of my lady that I may be saved the torments of Hell. Farewell, land of Champagne, land of my birth. Guide me, Star of Pilgrims, Consolation of the humble. . . .

The roofs of the houses gleamed in the red light of the rising sun and the bells were still ringing; at the main gate of the town the sentries hailed each other from rampart to rampart, their pikes sharply black against the lightening sky. The rays of sunshine penetrating in clusters from beyond the wall drove pointed like arrows between steeples and gables, the wings of swallows were sharp-edged as keen knives and, beyond the wall, on the slopes, the trees stood like a portcullis about the town. The faces of men on the road were all beautiful and austere, like the faces of angels on the Day of Judgment, and in every eye Haguenier read his own pain at parting from Marie.

And then the sun absorbed and drowned town and fields and woods in its light. The meadows sang and the fields were all of gold and in the distance the wooded hills were lost behind a veil of sunlight.

Part Two

Part Two

MISFORTUNES OF WAR

O GOLDEN sun, green meadows, lovely spring! O flowering may, green branches in the lanes, blue heaven!

The bird in the forest, the lizard on the rock, has eyes. The vilest of beasts can see where they are going. Accursed be ye, dogs, who made me less than the beasts!

Accursed be ye, beasts yourselves, crows that stabbed out and drank my eyes, my light of day. May you have neither peace nor rest, may wolves devour your entrails, worms your tongues, may your eyes rot from within and run out upon your cheeks, accursed dogs!

O my eyes, bright daylight, let my tongue wear out in cursing them who took you from me! May their wives be shamed, their sons quartered and flung to the dogs! O my eyes, my light, may I sing forever the shame and death of the carrion crows who foul our earth! O my eyes, my eyes; let me strike at the wounds to make the blood run, since I have no more tears!

The man seated at the roadside rocked himself from side to side as if he were drunk, and tore at his cheeks with his nails. His ill-appeased hunger, after making him as importunate and whining as a child, was now making him light-headed and excited. From a monotonous chant, his lamentations became a shout like the howling of an animal. The old man seated beside him seized him by the shoulder and shook him.

"Enough!" he said. "Isn't it time you were done with bawling like a woman? You're making yourself ill. You've already got hiccups."

"And who are you," the man said, "to speak to me in that fashion? Give me back my eyes and I will be silent. Give me back my eyes or I shall never be silent. Accursed, wolves, let my voice be so loud that you hear it always! May the Devil your father flay off your skin inch by inch! Let me but drink your blood, accursed, and eat your flesh, then never again shall I be hungry!" He let his head drop forward and fell to rocking and shaking himself more than ever, almost to the point of vertigo.

"You shall have a blow on the head if you continue," Ansiau said. "Stop that ear-splitting noise!"

"Dog!" the other shouted. "Kill me, I prefer to die. You would not be so high and mighty if you, like me, had no eyes."

"I also am without eyes," the old man said. "I am blind."

The man started and raised his head, feeling about for his companion's face. He said in a hard voice:

"You are not deceiving me?"

"Why should I deceive you? Would to God I could tell you the contrary."

The man sought Ansiau's hands and pressed them in his own.

"Then you, too, they put out your eyes? Brother! Forgive me. A man no longer knows who he is talking to."

"No," the old man said, "it came following a wound; I have only one eye destroyed and the other sightless."

The man whose eyes had been put out dropped Ansiau's hands.

"Ah," he said, "I should have thought of that: you're from the north, of course." And once more he covered his face with his hands, but he no longer lamented.

Auberi and Riquet had gone to seek a hamlet or a castle. They had climbed to the crest of the hill, and there the wind whistled and the big stones slipped and rolled beneath their feet. On the far side the slope was so steep that it made them giddy—below, trees grew thickly, there was nothing resembling a path—in the distance, in the sun-shot mist, extended crest upon crest, rocky or wooded; towards the east, perched among rocks, a small grey fortress reared two square towers, with a banner and a wisp of smoke lifting towards the sky.

"They, at least, have something to roast," Riquet said, clutching at his hair which the wind snatched and tangled. "If we made our way round the crest we could climb up again along the valley, but with that wretch and his swollen feet we're not likely to get there."

"Do you think he's really a heretic?" Auberi asked. He was astonished at the idea that a heretic could be hungry, could groan, bemoan himself like any poor unfortunate—it was surely not worth while selling your soul to the Devil to achieve that; but perhaps the man was only doing it to hide his maleficent power.

"Of course he is," Riquet said, "you don't know this country. It's full of the dogs. Master Pierre is too simple, he won't see evil. For my part, I'd have hanged him from the first convenient oak. He can cause us trouble."

The child was amusing himself by rolling stones towards the ravine and watching them leap and bound down the slope. The wind howled and tore into the bushes, breaking their branches, beating at the ears and cheeks of the man and the boy; vultures, carried away by gusts, flapped their great wings from which feathers flew and sailed upon the wind, twisting and turning. Riquet and Auberi had to shout to hear each other.

"Riquet!"

"What?"

"Riquet, Riquet—can you hear the mountain fairies calling? Hear them cry, Ohé!" The wind sang and whistled. A large bird fell injured to the ground at Auberi's feet, beating his legs with its thrashing wings. The child cried out and jumped back.

Riquet stooped, cut the vulture's throat with his knife and began drinking its blood, sucking from the wound and spitting out feathers and down. Then he held out the warm prey to Auberi, wiping his blood-filled mouth on his hands.

"Here," he cried, "take it and drink. It's good. Drink quickly, while it's still flowing!" And he crossed himself several times, shaking all over with excitement.

They went down the slope, leaving the wind behind. Auberi carried the vulture whose long wings trailed on the ground; he was smiling dazedly. Riquet was quivering with joy and gratitude.

"Ah, Auberi, lad, you can see that God hasn't forgotten us. We shall have something to eat this evening." And from that day he no longer complained against the man whose eyes had been put out.

On the morrow they succeeded in reaching the castle which they had seen from the top of the crest. Thence, with a big loaf of bread in their wallet, they went down into the valley again and took to the road, the two blind men walking together. The man whose eyes had been put out—he said that his name was Bertrand—had sores on his feet, limped, and dragged one leg, hanging on to his companion's arm. Ansiau leaned on his staff and his belt was tied by a cord to that of Auberi, who walked ahead as guide.

They came up with a troop of peasants on the road, going from Cajarc, with their sheep and two-wheeled carts drawn by mules, towards Uzès. It was this party which had been before them at the drinking-trough. From there they had taken a shorter road, over the pass.

"Worthy people," Riquet begged, "give some bread for the two blind men."

But nobody would give them anything and they were regarded with mistrust. In the end Riquet succeeded in begging a few handfuls of corn and some olives. An old woman told him that, though the man with his eyes put out was doubtless to be pitied, they had to be careful. They had taken him in at Cajarc village and then a roving band had come and burned down the houses; the man must be bad luck; that was why they had had to leave him by the drinking-trough.

"But who is he?" Riquet asked.

"Ah, God knows! But we certainly shall not travel in your company."

"Good man," Ansiau asked his companion, "where would you have me lead you? Have you friends in Uzès?"

"Where should you lead me? To the top of a cliff and near to the edge, and then push me over. That's where I want to be taken," Bertrand said.

"Do not talk foolishness. Do you know anyone at Uzès?"

"I know nobody anywhere."

"You are mocking me," Ansiau said, somewhat vexed. "Well, I will wait until you get over it."

This Bertrand was not so old as he had appeared to be at first. He could not be more than forty-five. His delicate face, bony and regular, was not yet lined but his hair was nearly white. Formerly, his hands must have been beautiful and shapely and from his manner of speech he seemed to be of the comfortable merchant class or perhaps a cadet of the petty urban nobility. Such, in fact, was his status, but he would not say so; he was so suspicious, thrown at once into a panic by the least question, so obviously afraid of not being believed, that he might be taken for God knows what kind of evildoer. He claimed to have been robbed and blinded by brigands, and as for his country of origin, he avoided speaking of it.

Ansiau told him:

"Listen: I should warn you that I am going to Marseilles and thence to Jerusalem if God wills it. I believe you will not wish to go so far yourself, so that I am bound to take you somewhere first."

"Then leave me on the road. I am neither your brother nor your friend."

"My friend, understand that I am a knight and that never would I do anything so base. I cannot leave you to die of hunger on the road. But I could take you to a monastery where the brothers would give you shelter for the love of God."

The other started.

"No—above all, not a monastery. In these parts they are not safe."

"Have you so bad a conscience, then? Perhaps you really are a heretic?"

"God forbid! No, but in time of war, you never know."

That night, after Riquet and Auberi had gone to sleep, Bertrand told the old man his story.

"I can tell it to you, for I know you will not betray me. I am of Carcassonne, my brothers hold a fortified manor. Never have I been a heretic, at least, willingly. I consider myself a good son of the Church and I curse the evil doctrines of those who have brought such misery on the country. But my wife was my ruin and it is well said that, since Adam and Eve, woman has been the cause of all our ills. May God forgive her all the harm she has done me, for without her I should still have my eyes. I shall tell you how, through my wife's fault, I was betrayed—and that because I tried to save her, understand—Ah! may God judge her, now, before His heavenly judgment seat and may He credit her with my sufferings: it is for her that I underwent this martyrdom. Listen, then: I, as I told you, was no heretic, but my wife was; all her family, but herself especially, so much so that she was known and honored throughout the land as if she were a holy woman. And she talked to me so much and so well, begging me to embrace the true faith, like herself, that I did as she asked and I let her go, with her daughters, and live in a retreat for women of the faith. And when she had received the Consolation I saw her no more, excepting at reunions of the faithful.

"Then, when this accursed war began, I took her back, her and the little girls, into my house, since it was becoming dangerous for them, and that is the whole extent of my fault, Lord Knight, for I know of no other. Had I not done so I should still be at Castres, with my brothers.

"I was telling you that my wife was well known throughout the country. We had taken refuge in Carcassonne and, after the viscount had been betrayed and the town yielded, we fled in nothing but the clothes we wore, leaving all our goods behind us in the town; I went to my brothers; they were not willing to harbor my wife, and so she and I and the three little girls went to Uzès, where she had friends. She took with her another heretic, whose name was Alonsa, and her friends received us into their castle and there we were shut in and in safety.

"But my wife was possessed; she could not be still, and every day went about the country to hamlets and castles to preach the true faith and bring the Consolation to the dying, for all the Good Men were taken or were in hiding and you can have no idea of the number of people who died without Consolation because of the war. Of course, I understood; had she been alone, without family, I should have said nothing. Well, Alonsa went everywhere with her; they were afraid of nothing. People brought the dying to her from ten leagues round to receive Consolation.

"You will understand that this could not last. At Easter a troop of soldiers, led by a monk, came up to the castle. They succeeded in setting it on fire and we were forced out, all just as we were. Then they took my wife and Alonsa and the three little girls—and before we went out Constanza had had time to adminster the Consolation to all of us, for we knew it was all up with us—so, then, they took Constanza first and bade her abjure and worship the cross. She took the cross and flung it on the ground and spat on it.

"And then—and then—they smashed in her face with blows of an axe and flung her into the river from the top of the rocks. And Alonsa said: 'I also desire to be martyred like that holy woman,' and she too spat upon the cross.

"That was what they did. And if you have children, you are lucky to be blind, for you will never see what I saw then: my three little girls with their throats cut like lambs in a shambles and their bodies bouncing on the rocks headlong towards the torrent, and Laura, my eldest, caught on some bushes by her dress—and the dogs stoned her, to make her fall more quickly. Oh, I knew perfectly well that she was already dead, still. . . . They led me to the edge so that I could see it. The lord of the castle and his sons had their throats cut too, because they were ashamed to abjure after witnessing the women's faith so strong, and they were all flung over, so that the stones and bushes were red with blood and the water of the river ran red.

"And to me they promised my life if I would abjure. But afterwards, the dogs! they put out my eyes."

Bertrand was trembling so much that he could no longer speak. His teeth were chattering and he was shaken by dry sobs which excited his feelings instead of calming them.

"Dogs, dogs! They left me there, alone. A beggar led me to Cajarc and taught me how to chant to beg for alms. Ah! The dogs, carrion crows, eating our flesh! May their entrails rot! Oh, my pretty children! My eyes, my light of day, my eyes which ran down my cheeks, my eyes!"

Ansiau listened, thoughtful and calm; he was not at all inclined to be sorry for people mad enough to spit on the cross; naturally the soldiers had killed them, anyone would have done likewise in their place. But, even so, poor Bertrand aroused his pity. What man would want to see his children's throats cut, though they were heretics?

"Listen, brother," he said. "You well know that I shall not leave the son of a free man to beg for his bread on the roads. Tell me where you want to go and I will go with you. No one shall harm you."

"Where are your vassals and men-at-arms, Lord Knight?" Bertrand asked, somberly. "Your horses and lances and swords? You hide them so well that I cannot hear them. It is boastfulness to offer protection when there is nothing you can do. With all you northerners pride is everything."

"Do not say that, brother. Without me, you would already have died of hunger."

"Comrade," Bertrand said, softened, "there really is no one at Uzès to whom I could go. My son is at Castres, with my brothers. That is, he was when I left there; I don't even know what has become of him. Perhaps he has already taken arms."

"I also had a son," Ansiau said. "I will willingly go to Castres with you."

THE BURNING ROADS

I. THE MOTHER

THE narrow, stony roads, and the June sun, so torrid from early morning that the dust of the road burned their feet through the worn sandals—the old man's feet had long been harder than horn and no longer felt the stones; but the heat softened and penetrated the callus little by little, causing sores which, towards evening, became as painful as burns. Progress was made all the more painful, and the stones of the way hotter, by Bertrand leaning with all his weight on the old man's arm. The sun struck at his head through the woollen bonnet and his shirt stuck to his back and shoulders.

The great, fiery spider crushed him; he lived in a dark furnace. Before and behind, above and below and always—the same burning darkness, for now the sun was forever black, without a gleam of light, illuminating neither heaven, no longer there, nor earth, reduced to as much road as he could feel beneath his feet. Always the same four spans of road. That and breaths and sounds about him, the heat of human bodies and the smells of animal ones, oaths, lowing, the screechings of wheels. From Nîmes they had been obliged to keep company with a crowd of pilgrims and country folk flying from their burning villages, hoping to find asylum in the hills about Toulouse and Albi.

Little children, seated on the straw, bundles and baskets piled in small carts, watched the crowd with big, dark, candid eyes. Pots of grain and strings of onions swung between the creeking wheels; asses and mules with their bones protruding, hides peeling and bloody beneath the cords of the harness, went forward slowly, their eyes and sores covered with flies which children, running about the carts, vainly tried to drive off with withered branches. Sheep wandered away to crop the grass of the roadside slopes, already burned and yellowed. The poorer women carried their children on their backs or at the breast, slung in a swaddling band, some of them, as they walked, giving suck to still the infants' cries. The men, armed with scythes and forks, guarded the carts, for there were always thieves in mountain country; and young boys were constantly climbing the nearest hill or tree to make sure that the road was open, for it was said there were licensed bands roaming the countryside.

After Quissac, at the crossroads, a party of peasants took the northerly road, having been told by beggars on the way that there were soldiers moving up the valley of the Hérault. Beyond Saint-Hippolyte the sky was red; the bush was on fire; from sacked castles women and children, with bundles and water-pots on their backs, were making their way down to the road. Wounded lay at the roadside displaying their festering sores and holding out a hand for a bit of bread or a drop of water. It was necessary to hurry, before the fire, driven by the rising mistral which was flinging gusts of hot air and smoke at the pilgrims, reached the road.

Standing in a small group of refugees lying by the roadside, a young girl, with dark golden hair loose, was chanting a plaint in a shrill voice as monotonous as bird song. Her short brown frock was so torn that she could barely cover one breast without uncovering the other, and her bare feet were purplish and swollen. A big woman in a grey coif was seated by her, head drooped, arms flaccid.

"Don't stay here, my pretty," Riquet said, "unless you want to be caught by the knackers."

"Wine, good my lord, a drop of wine for my mother."

The two blind men had stopped and Auberi was devouring the girl with admiring and pitiful eyes.

"Oh, tell her to come with us, Riquet, do tell her!"

"I am waiting for the soldiers," the young girl said, "to get some wine."

"I have wine in my gourd. Come, nightingale, you must not stop here."

Docile, the child helped the woman to rise and followed Riquet. The woman walked slowly, with a regular pace, leaning on a staff with one hand and pressing the other to her chest. The girl went lightly, springing, at her side, her white body gleaming through the rags of her torn frock. Her sunken eyes, shaped like peach stones, had the inexpressive candor of the eyes of a young animal, but her small mouth, covered with scabs, was grave and sad. From that day mother and daughter shared the four pilgrims' meager meals.

They were from Cadière, which had just been burned by marauders. The mother was very ill, for they had cut out her tongue and cut off both breasts; the daughter had only been raped. They did not know where to go and might just as well keep company with the others until they reached a town where they might be in safety.

There were some rich pilgrims in the crowd, two merchants and a Benedictine abbot mounted on a handsome mule; he was accompanied by three monks and two soldiers. He was going to Carcassonne and at Nîmes had made provision of wine and biscuits; the soldiers with blows of their lances drove away the beggars who flocked round the mules. But Riquet, pity overcoming shame, had succeeded in rousing the sympathy of one of the monks by confessing that he was a cleric, though unfrocked, and the monk sometimes gave him a little wine from his gourd or put a few biscuits into his wallet.

Then, proud of his booty, he would rejoin his companions; the wine was shared between the woman and Bertrand, the two invalids; the others were glad enough to get water.

"In any case," Riquet would say, "drinking on the march makes the legs heavy." But the woman—nobody knew or asked her name, they simply called her Mother—reached out a hand for Riquet's gourd twenty times a day; she only drank a mouthful at a time, however, keeping it for a long while in her mouth; she was very calm, maintained her monotonous walking-pace and did not seem to suffer from either heat or weariness.

She was a tall, lean woman, her face still very handsome, though brown, severe and, as it were, dried up; long locks of blue-black hair fell from beneath her coif and her large black eyes were fixed and clouded, as if for ever immobilized by too great an agony. Mute she paced, indifferent as a sleepwalker, staring in front of her but seeing nothing out of eyes like those of a mortally wounded beast. Her cheeks and lips already had the inhuman greyish color of dead flesh, and the trickles of blood which sometimes ran from her mouth seemed the only living attribute of her face.

The daughter—her name was Afrania—could hardly be more than fifteen years old, perhaps less. Despite her thinness, her cheeks and shoulders were rounded like a child's. She was neither merry nor sad, and spoke little; sometimes, to stretch her legs, she would run along the roadside bank, stroke the goats, dart curious glances beneath the canvas coverings on the carts, then return to her mother's side and rub her cheek against the woman's shoulder.

The mother kept going for three days. On the evening of the third day she fell to her knees, dropping her staff. Afrania tried to raise her, but she fell back again, her head lolling to one side; the girl knelt beside her and cradled the woman's head against her little, naked shoulder. The mother's mouth was wide open and her large eyes clouded and sightless. The fierce sun shone into them without causing even a quiver of the eyelids.

Riquet had run to the women, Afrania was gaping at him, her eyes wide with astonishment.

"She's dead," she said. Riquet helped her drag the body to the roadside, leaning over it to make the sign of the cross. *In nominem* . . . But Afrania, swift as a bird to defend its nest, flung herself in front of him, closing his mouth with her hands. She seemed to be terrified. "Not that! Not that!" she gasped. Trembling all over, she began dragging the body on to the slope and rolling it into the bushes. There she stayed, kneeling, looking down, her eyes void with horror, her hands clapped to her cheeks.

Riquet took her by the shoulder.

"Come, wicked one, our party has gone ahead."

Refugees from Lodève were passing; the men, harnessed to a cart, were drawing the sick; the children peered curiously from the bank at the woman's corpse upon which a vulture was already standing. Riquet and the girl set off, running, to catch up with their companions. Ansiau asked him,

"What's happening?"

"It's the mother. She's dead," Riquet said.

And they spoke no more of the mother. Afrania did not appear any sadder than before; only she seemed suspicious of Riquet, watching him covertly out of big, frightened eyes. She still sang as she walked, and played with the goats; little by little she had made friends with Auberi; they spoke very few words but walked side by side exchanging timid, questioning smiles. They did not quite know what to think of each other.

II. THE STRICKEN BIRD

Ansiau would not beg nor let Auberi beg, but meanwhile made no objection to Riquet and Afrania begging for the whole party and did not question the provenance of the bread they brought him. Sometimes, indeed, Afrania brought whole loaves, figs, onions, and once a small ham hidden under her skirt. Auberi looked on her with admiration and found it quite natural that the good folk could refuse her nothing: he himself was so sorry for her that he willingly gave up his share of the figs to her; and she took them without thanking him, only looking him full in the face with her round, bright eyes.

But on the evening when she brought in the ham Riquet said:

"She will get us all cut in pieces one of these days, the wicked one." The two blind men paid no attention but Auberi said: "Why?"

"Have you any idea what a ham costs, eh?"

Seated on the ground, Afrania, her legs tucked under her, calmly chewed her bread and stared at the reddening sky with empty eyes.

"In a town," Riquet said, "she'd have been put in the stocks for that, with a hundred lashes for good measure."

Auberi told himself that Riquet was joking, no one would ever have the heart to do such a thing to Afrania. But it was only too true that she was a thief of the first order. She was afraid of nothing, took what she wanted under the owner's nose and was never caught. She seemed to do it for fun, to amuse herself, for she was not greedy, eating very little and without noticing what she ate.

The band of refugees had to turn off into the mountains, and then down towards the next valley, following a dry watercourse; a large troop of crusaders was approaching and, despite the hope of alms or gain, the refugees were afraid—God knew what sort of crusaders they might be. Although Ansiau was very wishful to wait for the soldiers and mix with them, the others, especially Bertrand, were too much afraid. They had, consequently, to clamber over rocks, make their way through woods, and lose three whole days travelling.

Therefore Ansiau was in a very bad temper. The soles of his feet, torn by thorns and pebbles, became septic, heat and fatigue were stupefying him completely, and the man who hung to his arm with all his weight became such a burden that he was sometimes conscious of nothing but his weight, his close, humid body-heat, and his limping, irregular walk which slowed their pace. Withal, he was an ex-heretic—a man who, perhaps, brought bad luck—and a bad companion into the bargain. But, after all, he was a free-born man, son of a noblewoman; it was out of the question to abandon him.

Bertrand grew little by little to hate the old man, companion of his misery—perhaps it was the stench of his festering feet or his shockingly vulgar northern speech, for he spoke the *langue d'oc* as mercenary soldiers spoke it, clipping his words, pronouncing *e* for *a* and *ou* for *o* and all the time believing that he spoke it well. He was always correcting Auberi's faults of language. But above all Bertrand could not bear the man's frivolity, as it seemed to him, his attachment to all that reminded him of arms, hunting and good cheer. When they halted he would ask Auberi what birds were flying in the sky and how many there were; if there was word of a troop of soldiers, he wanted to know the colors of their banners, the armorial bearings on their shields, and then he would ask: "Is the sun low, what color is it, what are the clouds like?" Or whether there were stars, if they could be seen clearly, whether the sky was clear. Why the Devil must he know these things, be constantly recalling things which he, Bertrand, would never see again—never, never—while the old man, fallen into second childhood, dotingly thought he could see the starry heavens or a red sun because the child described them! Bertrand seemed to hear nothing but the insolent little Auvergnat's thin, hard voice which hurt his ears, and saw nothing, nothing, and wished that nobody else could see anything either; never again would he see his son's handsome face, his great dark eyes under the pure line of eyebrows clean-drawn as a swallow's wings—and what mattered to him dead sky and dead sun—and voices, strangers' voices, voices to which he would never fit faces? And he wondered whether his brothers had had time to shut themselves up in their castle, whether his son was already wearing a hauberk—children take arms so young in war time; whether he had not been caught in an ambush and was a prisoner, tortured perhaps; he was not of those who deny their faith, not he. . . . Meanwhile he must drag himself over the mountain and among the thorns on the arm of this dull old idiot who was blind into the bargain, which was like a further insult to add to his wretchedness.

At evenings, after they had halted, when the heat was declining and the chirping of the crickets became more strident than ever, Riquet sang old Provençal songs which Bertrand, too, had known in his youth, before the accursed conversion which Constanza had imposed on him. O God! Why had he listened to his brothers and made that unhappy marriage, and what, O God, had they done to him, to his life, what had had they done to him, all of them, Constanza and her family and his own brothers? But for his brothers, but for their harshness, their cowardice, he would be at Castres still with his son, and his little girls would still be alive. "O God, that which they did to me, do unto them also, to them, my brothers, my wicked brothers who put the safety of their skins before the claims of their blood."

Riquet's deep and lovely voice, meanwhile, was singing of true love, nightingales and springtime, as if such things still existed. Who was this Riquet? Bertrand had never wondered, nor whence he came. He detested him, as he detested the other two, but a little less than the other two because he spoke without accent. The rest was of little importance. Sometimes it was Afrania who began to sing in her shrill, pure voice, a little drawled and so shrill that it must surely pierce not only the air, but earth itself, and stones.

For Bertrand her voice was like a trickle of pure water in a great swamp of mud—a trickle of cool water, such was Afrania for him, and when he heard her speak he felt less lonely.

She never spoke to him. But he knew that it was for him that she stole bread and figs, for him that she sang; for the other three were not even human creatures in her eyes, whereas he was her brother in the true faith.

In her little head, the head of a peasant girl, these men had no place— they were too remote from what her life had been before her hamlet had been burned. Since she had been on the road the world had appeared to her like a sort of painted canvas with moving figures provided with small, bright beads which looked at you like eyes, but then sometimes she came across familiar objects—goats, sheep, strings of onions, or, again, little children (her own small sisters and brothers had had their throats cut but that, too, had no place in her mind). But the man with his eyes put out, perhaps because his eyes had been put out or because of his manner of speech, recalled something known, familiar; he was like a hole showing real light through the painted canvas; as is possible with children, she had sensed, without having to think about it, that he, too, had listened to the preaching, that he, too, rejected the cross, and she thought that he might even be a holy man. When she looked at him she felt not pity, she could not feel pity, but the vague sense that if she had formerly encountered such a man as this, her parents would have ordered her to serve him; and she considered herself obliged to keep him provided with food. This bond of a brotherhood mute and invisible to the others had been formed from the first day— the brotherhood of accomplices or of human beings among brute beasts.

Certainly Afrania was not one of those girls who prophesy, or fling themselves into the flames; she was a very ordinary girl who had simply listened, with her mother and her aunt, to the Good Men's preaching without understanding very much. At the sack of Cadière she had been violated by soldiers. She hardly remembered it; but if any of the men from whom she asked alms tried to pinch her or take her by the waist she began to shake so much that her teeth chattered and she almost fell into convulsions—and then they let her alone. Otherwise she was tranquil and, on the whole, merry.

It was evening; the band of pilgrims was resting on the slope, scattered in small groups; the peasants were sleeping under their carts, the sheep patiently grazing off the thin and withered grass. Where the sun had just set the sky was white and stars were beginning to shine at the zenith. The heat was declining. The men lying on the ground were beginning to relax and breathe easily. Great vultures glided about the encampment, perhaps in hopes of a meal—that summer, like the two preceding it, had been good ones for them; there was no want of carrion.

Ansiau, lying on his back, was trying to believe that the darkness was that of deep night, that he was campaigning, in the Holy Land, and that on the morrow he would rise and put on his hauberk and see the sun rise red over the *tels*—he frequently indulged such day-dreaming before he fell asleep completely. It was then, then, that he saw many things, saw his old comrade Thierri, dead in Palestine, who said to him: "You see, I am not dead, they have disinterred me," and showed his hands, almost cut from his arms at the wrists with blows of an axe; and Ansiau embraced him and said: "And I, as you see, am not blind." And they were both very glad.

Auberi was seated beside Afrania watching the long black clouds against the white sky. The clouds were like elongated islands in a river of milk. Small stars, lamps lit by angels, flickered, as if the angels' hands were shaking as they held them, and Afrania, at his side, looked all pale and white, her hair in locks which hung beside her face and her eyes very black. So often had he wanted to take her arm and stroke it, as you stroke the feathers of a bird, especially when they looked so white, as they did this evening. But Afrania would not allow even her hand or the ends of her hair to be touched.

"Afrania." She turned her head towards him. "Why don't you want me to touch you?"

She answered calmly: "Because you are a devil."

Auberi started under the insult. He wanted to strike her but controlled himself because she seemed so gentle and sweet.

"Oh, oh," he said, "that's really too much! It is you who are a devil, since you do not wear a cross."

He had thought to wound her but she paid no attention to his words.

"And the tall black one, he too is a devil," she continued, thoughtful, "and Riquet too." She stretched a hand towards a group of sleeping peasants. "And all of those are devils. All men are devils."

"Really! And you?"

"Me too," she said, as if she were repeating a lesson. "I am a devil. All who have not received the Spirit."

Auberi told himself that she was mad and shook the old man, who was dozing near him, by the shoulder.

"My lord, my lord, she says we are all devils, she is mad."

The old man raised himself on his elbow.

"Well, let her say it."

"But," Auberi said, indignant and anxious, "it's not true, say that it's not true!"

The old man made no answer but the child's words had disturbed him. At last he asked the girl:

"You see devils, do you?"

"When a man dies without Consolation," Afrania said, placidly, "a devil, black and with horns, comes out of his mouth."

"And you've seen that?"

"At Cadière, when they killed the good folk, there were black devils no bigger than crows coming out of every mouth. And I saw them. Everyone saw them. And men who wear the cross have the Devil's mark on their bodies."

Bertrand, who was also listening, told himself that the girl must be wrong in the head to say such things aloud but he did not dare advise her to be silent.

Ansiau lay down again, his head on his arms, and said no more.

In the morning Riquet asked him in a low voice whether they ought to allow a girl so manifestly "wicked" to go with them. The old man suddenly turned very pale.

"Let be, Riquet," he said. "You are too young. You don't know what the Devil can do with a little child who understands nothing. We must not blame her."

His voice was so broken that Riquet told himself he must be thinking of someone other than Afrania. And he dared say no more.

Some days later, when they were only ten leagues from Castres, the Devil himself undertook to rid them of Afrania. She was caught by some peasants with a loaf of bread under her skirts, and, since fugitives are not always tender with the "wicked" and she seemed a suspicious character, they tried to make her cross herself. She was so frightened that she would have done it; it was not unwillingness but ignorance which prevented her. She did not know how to do it.

She was tied to an olive tree and beaten with forks by the men, while the children stoned her. Riquet was in the crowd, watching.

The peasants were saying: "Carrion-crows, who've brought war on our heads; accursed!—we ought to nail them through the heart as we do owls."

When evening had fallen Riquet and Auberi took the girl down and carried her away; she was still alive, moaning softly and asking for water.

Auberi was shaking so that he could not put two words together and clung to his master.

"My lord, she's not going to die, is she, my lord?"

It was a hot night: on the far side of the valley, all along the high-road, the grass was on fire, the bushes were like torches, crackling as they burned, and the sky full of red smoke. The incendiaries attached to a troop of crusaders had just passed that way. The peasants were hastily getting their goods together, lambs were bleating, earthenware pots knocking together; the mules, barely awake, snorted and whinnied, while the men, stupefied by fatigue, set off in silence, calmly, too accustomed to such nocturnal flittings to complain; even the children only whined because they had been half-asleep.

The four pilgrims stayed where they were until morning, for Afrania began to scream when they tried to move her. Bertrand was very gloomy and again started to vociferate against the carrion-crows from the north who came to devour his countrymen. And Auberi cried, and the old man said to him:

"Come, she had given herself to the Devil, and he is responsible for this. You must not cry for her."

In the morning, as they had no water left, they were obliged to set off again. There was no knowing who the approaching crusaders might be. Ansiau picked the little girl up in his arms and she passed her own arms about his neck: she was not strong enough for him to carry her on his back. And they began the descent into the valley.

The sun, even just after dawn, was burning. Pebbles slipped and rolled under their feet. The little girl's body grew heavier and heavier, the clasp of her arms relaxed, she was slipping down and at each attempt the old man made to raise her, she screamed. And she felt burning hot to him, as if the devils which possessed her were heating her body with hot coals.

"O God, most great King, may it never be my own sin, the child of my flesh, that I bear thus, to know her dying and see her die, and close her eyes. O Lord God, if you have permitted that she, this one, a child, a little child, and mad, should damn herself, may she who is my heart's wound not die a worse death. Do not moan so, white lamb, we will stop. Must devils so torture an innocent child?"

They had to stop by the shrunken river, almost dried up, where a few thin trickles of water ran between banks of sand. The sun was already declining in a sky red with the smoke of fires. Afrania was delirious and screaming. Her hands were clutched to her temples and her eyes wide with terror. And her voice was piercing, yelping:

"Aie! But what are they doing! What are they doing! What are they going to do? Oh, no! Oh, no! No, no, no." And she clapped her hands over her eyes with an inhuman screech—it was as if a stake were being driven into her belly. Then again, "Aie! What are they doing! What are they doing!" And then she stretched out her hand and began to repeat in a rasping voice and with hard eyes:

"Accursed! Accursed! Accursed! Accursed!" And then began screaming again.

Her face, covered with bruises and scratches, had turned a blackish grey, her nose and lips had become thin and sharp. Towards evening she no longer moved, the rattle of death was in her throat and froth on her mouth and in her nostrils.

Riquet, seated beside her, watched her somberly: he did not know what to do. She might not have been baptized, as is often the case with children of the wicked, in which case he ought to baptize her to save her from going to Hell. On the other hand he did not know, she might have been baptized after all, in which case he would commit sacrilege if he baptized her a second time. Another might not have thought twice about baptizing her but, as for him, he knew that you do not safely play fast and loose with the sacraments. But since he was full of pity he made up his mind and took water in his hand to pour it on the dying child's forehead.

While he pronounced the prayers Auberi watched him, his hands clasped, his eyes big with admiration and happiness: he hardly dared to breathe, for fear of disturbing the ceremony. Once the baptism was complete he clung to Riquet's arm, saying: "Now she'll go to Paradise, won't she, Riquet? And see how it has made her more beautiful; the devils have come out of her now, Riquet."

The girl's head slowly fell back and her eyes clouded. Her face, strangely fine-drawn, became rigid. Auberi still watched for the light of life in her round, black eyes and suddenly he was seized by fear and began shaking the girl by the shoulders.

"Afrania, little flower, little bird, little sister, don't go away!" Her eyes remained wide open and became more and more clouded.

All that night was spent by Riquet and the two blind men digging a grave in the sand with their knives for Afrania, the newly made Christian, born, at the same moment, into the Church and the after-life. It occurred to the old man that the grave would not be very deep and that the vultures would soon smell the body and roving dogs uncover it. He thought how he would have wished to dig such a grave with his hands in Linnières clay for the other child, the wicked one, she who had rent his heart, the misnamed Eglantine, for Thorn should have been her name. And Bertrand's thought was this: "Accursed, accursed, accursed, accursed, accursed."

At break of day the body was laid in the grave and Riquet said the prayers for the dead, happy to have a chance to use his knowledge. The chance was not wasted; Auberi, kneeling beside the grave, his palms devoutly pressed together, gave the responses and drank in the Latin words with admiring tenderness in his eyes. His eyelids were red and swollen but his thin face, all soiled with earth and tears half-wiped away, was already resuming its fresh color.

III. OLD COMPANIONS

Throughout the day they had to wander about the mountain. It was not easy to find the road again. They were afraid to go up towards the forests; the peasants had talked of old, cast-off soldiers who lurked there, catching and eating pilgrims. At the going down of the sun they came out into the wide valley where a belated troop of crusaders was encamped, so that Castres seemed further away than ever.

Hastily erected tents, heavy baggage-carts, and cooking-fires extended along thirty yards of the river bank. Soldiers were leading horses and mules down to water them. This must be a mere rearguard, there could not be more than three hundred men, including the servants. A banner displaying the cross surmounted by the *fleur de lis* flew above the principal tent.

Riquet thought that the French being less dangerous than Germans they might try asking for alms. Bertrand was strongly against this, saying that all northern men were as bad as each other. But Ansiau, seduced by the idea of hearing northern speech and conversing with military men, had himself led to the camp by Auberi.

It happened that there were a few knights from Champagne in the troop; two, indeed, had even served in Troyes. An hour later Ansiau was installed on cushions in the chief tent with a dozen knights, while the cup passed from hand to hand, and Auberi could hardly distinguish his master, blackened and unkempt though he was, from the other men in the tent, so similar were their language and their smiles; the old man smoothed his short beard, still nearer black than grey, with his fingers, put questions concerning the chivalry of the country and laughed with the rest at the good stories which were told.

He learned that his grandson had been knighted in the spring and must be somewhere in the country with the baron of Chantemerle's crusaders.

"A pity that I should not have seen him," he said. "He took after the Hervi side of the family more than mine but he was a fine child, and Herbert would certainly have equipped him properly; he understands that thoroughly."

The men from Troyes knew Herbert. It was, indeed, quite difficult not to know him. "It must be the first time," they said, "that anyone has seen a man knight and arm three sons, all about the same age, on the same day. Saving your presence, it's a thing you're more likely to see among the Moslems."

"Ah," the old man said, "there's never been any lack of men who live like Moslems in the matter of women, and it's no fault in a young man to father a bastard: I don't blame Herbert for that. What I do blame him for is to stay amassing goods for himself, like a banker or a

Jew, when the Holy Sepulchre is in such great danger. It's cheaper for him to send his son here than to send him to Jerusalem."

"Comrade, how can we talk of a crusade against the infidels when the Church is in such great danger in a Christian country? It's like running to put out a fire next door while your own house is burning."

"You say so because you're young. For my part, I tell you this wicked heresy comes from our own lack of faith, because Christians are betraying God out of cupidity and kings think only of enlarging their territories instead of serving God. If we had reconquered Palestine instead of making peace with Saladin, God would not have sent us this heresy to shame us."

The other Champagne men were not of that opinion and recounted all the miracles which God had performed in aid of the crusaders in the south, proving that He was with them.

"It is a mistake," they affirmed, "to think that God is shut up in the Holy Sepulchre, holy though it be, and that it is territory we have to conquer for Him. Now, it is souls we have to conquer for Him, and souls tainted with heresy are in far greater danger than those of Christians persecuted in the Holy Land or even than those of heathens."

But it is by no means easy to make an old Holy Land crusader see reason. Ansiau held out for his Holy Sepulchre. That was the most beautiful as it was the holiest place in the world, and neither the pope nor the bishops could alter that; what good was it to try and repair the walls of a church, when you left the altar soiled and profaned?

And so they argued back and forth until half the night was past.

Riquet and Bertrand, fetched by Auberi, were resting, stretched out on straw near the tent. It was a long time since they had eaten meat or drunk wine. Riquet was joyful and Bertrand very somber; he was no longer afraid and was all the more disgusted at finding himself in such ill company and at being soiled by contact with monks and crusaders; for he believed his safety was only due to their stupidity.

"And could there be anything stupider," he thought, "than that old, blind soldier, neighing like a horse because he gets news of his country? And who knows nothing on earth more beautiful than an empty tomb, a place of shame and the Devil's triumph."

FEAR

CASTRES was decked with flags to welcome the reinforcement of crusaders, and the banners flying from the towers bore either the *fleur de lis* or the imperial eagles. The town was full of soldiers. It was morning and the bells of the churches were clamoring. The four pilgrims made their way up the steep streets in the crowd of townsmen who were going to mass and were forced to keep close to the walls for fear of being kicked out of the way by some citizen's robust and zealous servant—"Out of the way you stinking beggars, this isn't the church close here—getting in a lady's way with your snotty noses!"

The space before the church was full of people. It was market day—a wartime market; bold men were those few horse copers who had brought in foals with their legs chained, the rare cattle dealers whose goats and sheep were grey with dust. To the right of the church, in front of the houses, pastry cooks and cheese mongers had their goods laid out on the ground and sat looking upwards at the citizens' wives and their servants who paraded before them, almost sweeping the cheeses with their long skirts.

Riquet and Auberi, installed near the court before the church, were watching the count of Blois and all his escort of knights cross the square and climb the steps of the church, dividing the crowd which fell back before them. Bertrand, with his head in his hands, was still thinking: "Accursed, accursed, accursed," remembering that these churches were not so crowded three years ago and that many of those now entering did so with death in their souls. . . . And what of his son? Might he be among them too? No, surely not he. His brothers, perhaps. . . . And he was afraid of being recognized.

Riquet spent a good hour asking people in the streets where he could find the lords of Castans; nobody had heard of them. But Bertrand recalled that he had a friend in Castres, one Roger of Gaillac, and finally a child led them to the fairly opulent house of a citizen where, he said, the lord of Gaillac was staying. In the mansion courtyard the four pilgrims sat down on the ground in the shade of a wall, glad enough

that the porter had not driven them away. The lord of Gaillac was
expected back from mass soon, with his brother-in-law, the master of
the house.

Their lordships came back from mass in their long gowns of fine
cloth, surrounded by their servants. Riquet ran to them to ask which of
these lords was messire Roger of Gaillac. One of the men in long gowns,
very pale and hard-faced, turned to him.

"What is it? Roger of Gaillac is not here. What is he wanted for?"

Riquet looked him straight in the eyes.

"A friend, who wants to see him."

"What friend, wretch? He'll have a long way to go, for Roger of
Gaillac is no longer in Castres."

"A friend who has had great misfortunes, my lord; come and see him.
He is here, in the courtyard."

The man started, looked about him, then signed to the other gentlemen and the servants to move farther away.

"Who are you?" he asked Riquet, gripping him by the wrist.

"My lord, come, and you will see for yourself," the young man said.
He drew him towards the two blind men. Bertrand rose and held out
his hands in front of him.

The man stared at him for a long time and at last threw himself into
his arms.

"Gaucelm!"

He recovered himself quickly, turned and again looked about him.

"Gaucelm, are these people reliable?" he asked.

Bertrand was shaking, he did not appear to have heard. At last he
said:

"Very reliable, Roger." He was laughing nervously, in little gasps.
"Roger, it's really you? You recognized me? I've not changed so very
much, have I?"

The other was not listening, he was wringing his hands like a man
stricken with grief.

"Oh, Gaucelm of Castans! Gaucelm of Castans! In what a state do I
find you! Oh, cursed be the carrion-crows who come to devour our
flesh! Oh, Gaucelm, your eyes, your light of day! Ah, miserable land—
may it all be upon their heads, Gaucelm!"

He was weeping. Bertrand had taken him by the shoulders and was
shaken by dry sobbing.

"And your wife, Gaucelm?" Roger asked, suddenly.

"Where no harm can ever reach her, God be thanked."

"Your daughters too?"

"Yes, Roger."

"God be thanked, Gaucelm. And you—what will you do?"

"Find my brothers. I thought they were in Castres."

"They left a month ago, for Pamiers."

Bertrand had become very pale. In a low voice he asked:

"And do you know if they have taken . . ."

"Alfonse was with them," Roger said. "That's all I know."

"Roger," Bertrand said, "listen, I shall stay with you for a few days, resting, and then you can give me a horse and a servant to get me to Pamiers. I must find Alfonse. You have sons yourself. I need just a few days' rest, for I have sores on my feet. After, with a horse and a guide, I shall manage."

Roger's face hardened a little.

"Gaucelm, I am not in my own house here, but that of my brother-in-law. I shall have to ask him whether he will harbor you. I'm sure he will be willing. Wait for me, I shall be back in a moment."

"And supposing he won't?" Bertrand cried. But the other was already gone.

He came back half an hour later with a small purse of chestnut-colored leather in his hand. He appeared embarrassed.

"Gaucelm," he said, "Gaucelm, don't be angry with me. It's nothing to do with me. I argued for a long time with my brother-in-law."

Bertrand raised his head, and a very hard smile shook and twisted his mouth.

"He refuses, Roger?"

"He says only a madman would harbor the husband of Buona Constanza, at a time when they're looking for our people in the town. I'm under suspicion myself, Gaucelm. You must not hold it against me. Everything of my own is at Gaillac. I've nothing here. My brother-in-law lets me stay here, but I'm at his mercy."

"And I at yours, Roger."

"Don't say that, Gaucelm. As you are now, no one will harm you. The people who brought you here can take you to Pamiers; at the moment it's no longer so very dangerous, with autumn coming on. I am not rich, but I will engage myself to pay them when I am back at Gaillac—they can come and seek me there, I shall know how to reward them. Your brothers will surely do that, in any case. Gaucelm, Gaucelm, do not believe that I. . . . Here, in this purse, is half of all I possess—five marks, it will do to buy your food on the road—it will be enough, Gaucelm. Gaucelm! I tell you I'm helpless, don't look at me like that!"

"I am not looking at you, Roger," the blind man said, slowly. "I no longer have my eyes, as you can see for yourself. Thank God—I have no eyes and cannot see you. Your face cannot be very beautiful at this moment."

"Gaucelm!"

"Thank you, Roger," Bertrand continued, in a voice which was almost caressing, softened by hate. "Thank you, Roger of Gaillac, for the service you have done me. Thank you for having welcomed me, for having helped me so much. May God grant that you be always as well served by your friends, Roger; God grant that your friends be always as brave and as faithful as you. You can keep your thirty pieces of silver, Roger; I am well used to being on the road without money. And neither in this world nor the next, Roger, shall I forget the good you have done me."

Roger, nevertheless, put the purse into his hand and said:

"God forgive you, Gaucelm."

"Oh," the blind man said, "He will forgive me, but not you. When I reach Pamiers my brothers and all my friends shall learn how you received me and it will not be a tale to your glory, Roger; you will not boast of it. Come, Riquet, brother, lead me away."

Roger of Gaillac tried to detain him but Bertrand was too angry to listen. Two minutes later the two blind men and the two young people were out in the street again, walking towards the church square.

"Well then," said Ansiau, who had not listened to the two friends' conversation, "so you are still with us, companion Bertrand."

Then Bertrand, thinking of his old friend, began to laugh, harshly.

"Yes, my lord of the castle, my lord crusader," he said. "If you're looking for a good reward after the end of this war, you will take me still further, to Pamiers, which is in the mountains, fifty leagues from here, and thereafter you'll have nothing to do but make your way to Gaillac, near Toulouse, where Roger, perhaps, will give you a cast-off suit of his clothes."

"Ah," the old man said—he had not understood very well, for

Bertrand was speaking too quickly and with froth on his lips—"we've to take you to Pamiers? Well, in any case we shall get to Marseilles before the spring."

"What's this?" Bertrand said. "Why, leave me by the church, man, can beg as well as another."

"Come, I also had a son. If we have to go to Pamiers to find yours again, I am ready. What is the good of complaining?"

Bertrand was not listening. Anger was making him talkative.

"Tell me, you who come from the north, does it also happen in your country, between men of noble birth, that a friend abandons his friend, like this, out of fear? You must think we are all the bastard sons of servants, eh?"

"I don't know," the old man said, "we've never had a war like this one in our country."

MÉLUSINE

SAID Riquet: "Messire Bertrand, since you are now our treasurer, what would you say to buying some good cream cheeses to put on our bread?"

Bertrand flung the purse on the ground.

"Take it, but I cannot eat any of his money. He was my friend. We were pages together."

Riquet shrugged his shoulders; a stall of goat's-milk cheeses had been attracting him for some time, and not only for the sake of their creaminess.

"Hi, cheese-wife, anyone can see you're a haughty miss! You'd only to raise your eyes and the last cheese would have been sold two hours ago!"

"On your way, silver-tongue. Fine words won't buy my cheeses."

"You take me for a beggar, pretty one, but I've the means to buy all your cheeses, your goats and your house into the bargain."

"You must have stolen it then. On your way, I say."

"Come, give me a dozen cheeses, and here's a silver mark."

"And where do you suppose I'm to change it, buffoon that you are? You're a wandering mountebank, your face gives that away."

"Not a bit, little miss, they're an ugly crew. Don't take me for one of that lot. I'm a respectable citizen. Tell me where I can get change without too much discount."

"A fine citizen I must say, with holes in your hose. Minstrel and thief, that's what you are. Go to the Jew at the far side of the square, he'll only take two deniers to change your coin—and look for your cheeses elsewhere, afterwards."

"Oh, what lovely eyes!" Riquet said, "they're the color of honey and ripe corn. It must be nice to look into them when they're merry and kind."

"You're not the one who'll ever see them so, clown. Away with you for your change, now!"

"D'you take me for a fool, pretty miss? Between now and then, you'll have left the square."

"What, take down my stall just because of you? Get along with you!"

The girl was all golden tan beneath her coif of coarse linen. Her brows were frowning but her eyes laughed from under them. To Riquet the whole square seemed a festival and he had forgotten everything but the cheeses and going to the Jew for change.

"Riquet must be mad," Auberi said, laughing. "He's been an hour in the market and comes back with nothing but a pile of cheeses. What is it—a custom of your monastery? Not allowed eggs or hard bread on Tuesdays?"

The two blind men devoured the cheese in silence. Bertrand had begun by refusing, but he was hungry. Ansiau listened to the laughter and chatter of the two young ones; it recalled his soldiering past; the young camp servants had had the same ringing laughter, the heat of the sun was the same, and the cheese had the same taste, the same smell of goat. He forgot that he was a beggar in the shadow of a church in an alien land. Before God, are we not all beggars—all, even to kings and the pope? The years he had passed by his lady's side, at Linnières, were a dream from which he must awaken.

So many of his companions had died in the east that he could no longer think of the Othe country as his fatherland. He thought: "Monks serve God withdrawn into the peace of their cloisters. But the soldier's obedience is stricter, for it is his trade to lose all without complaining and to find asylum nowhere and yet not to be sure of his salvation. God has deprived me of my eyes and I can no longer serve as a soldier. But even such as I am I will go where God wills."

He thought that as soon as they got to Palestine he would put Auberi into the service of a knight of that country, to make a good man-at-arms of him, while himself—God knows, he might perhaps weave reed baskets on the steps of Saint-Anne's Church, at Acre. First, however, they had to reach the Holy Sepulchre and there cause masses to be said for the souls of his friends who had died in the Holy Land.

These were so many that he passed the time repeating their names and each time remembered names he had forgotten. It was a matter of remembering the list correctly in order to recite it without hesitating when the moment came. Garin, and another Garin, Geoffroy, Thierri, Ansiau, Garnier, André, Simon, Jacques, Garin, Ansiau, Bernard . . . Jacques, Haguenier, Pierre, Aïoul—ah yes, Aïoul, dead of sunstroke the day they arrived—Thierri of Puiseaux, Eudes of Vanlay, Jacques again and another Pierre, Adam, Guy . . . Dysentery, fevers and scurvy: those were the great scourges of camp life, far more so than the weapons of the heathen. And rotten water. May God keep Auberi from such miseries.

"My lord," Auberi said, "there's Riquet sitting over there, in the porch of Saint-Jacques, with a woman."

"Then I hope he's keeping his eye on the purse. He already knows what women cost."

"I'll take charge of the purse. But she looks a very nice woman."

They heard Riquet's deep laugh, and the grave and beautiful voice of the girl.

"What tales he tells," the girl said, "in his Provençal speech! We know the Provençals, here! Sailors who've stolen spices from the cargo, to sell it under the rose!"

"Could you love a sailor, eh, Mélusine?" The girl laughed her clear laugh, tranquil and candid.

"Mélusine he calls me! Another mountebank's trick, I'll wager! He can't talk sensibly like other folk."

"Mélusine is a fairy. In my country we say that whoever sets eyes on Mélusine will languish for love of her the rest of his life."

"Oh, the wily one! Here, we say different."

"And what do you say, O Queen of Sheba?"

"That the fool seeks his like, the king the queen, and the villein a villein's daughter. You've only to find a madwoman to make a couple."

"Why no! I am the king and you the queen."

They both laughed so that it was pleasant to hear them. Ansiau was listening and the woman's voice warmed his heart, so sane it was, so calm and clear—if good new bread or the good wine of the south could speak their voice would be like that.

"Well, Riquet," Auberi said, approaching the pair, "you're being very proud. You won't even look at us any more."

Riquet flushed and the girl burst out laughing.

"Is this boy your brother? You're with your people here?"

"Oh, travelling companions. I don't know them very well."

"Come and let me see them. Fine companions, I'll be bound. More minstrels, like yourself."

The girl rose and followed Auberi; Riquet, red with shame, remained apart.

The girl was tall and gracefully slender, her face tanned, with golden eyes and long dimples in her thin cheeks. Auberi thought her very beautiful. She stopped in front of the blind men who, seated on the steps, their elbows on their knees, had raised their heads as they heard her approach.

"Why, Holy Mary!" she cried. "Good my fathers! God's poor! It will be for you that this poor lad stole the piece of silver."

"Good maid, he did not steal it, it was given to him," Ansiau said.

"Never mind, you must have needed it. Come—you shall lodge at my father's, for the love of God. Our stable is empty and there you will at least be warm for the night."

The blind men rose and took up their staffs. Auberi took the old man's hand. Riquet came running to join them, his face radiant.

"Is she not good?" he said. "Was there ever a better?"

The girl smiled at him with good-humored indulgence, while supporting Bertrand by the arm.

Riquet was well and truly caught. He followed the lovely Maguelonne out into the fields to watch her milk her goats, he stood by her side while she span, seated in the doorway, and ran to fetch dry wood for her from the hill near the town. The girl's parents lived without the walls in a small village which had been preserved from pillage by the neighborhood of the town. At evening the shadow of Castres castle walls entirely covered the village. Most of the inhabitants were wine-growers, but some raised goats and made cheeses which they sold in Castres. Now the vineyards were badly damaged and the war had prevented the making of the vintage in time. Moreover, the summer having been dry, the goats had barely enough to eat.

Maguelonne's father and mother had not been too cold in their welcome to the strangers—the blind are not dangerous and in wartime people are forced to give shelter to all manner of men. Ansiau was not very pleased at having to listen to his hosts cursing northern men all day long, but he said nothing.

"After all," he told himself, "it's only too true that war brings misery to poor folk, and here are their vineyards, which were their livelihood, ruined."

The house was very small, the room and the stable being one, divided by quite a low partition, so that they lived in a dense odor of goat, fermented milk and dirt; Ansiau would have preferred to sleep out of doors but did not dare offend his hosts.

At night Riquet hardly even lay down to sleep; he wandered in the meadow and sometimes Maguelonne joined him there and he told her the names of the stars and their stories, and described the fantastic beasts which live in foreign parts. Maguelonne laughed and called him a liar, for she thought he was inventing it all to make fun of her. When he tried to kiss her, she repulsed him calmly, as if he were a child. Riquet was too much in love to try being rough with her.

"Beauty, won't you take me for your sweetheart?"

Thoughtfully, Maguelonne shook her head.

"No, you talk too much."

"Stop a man doing and he'll always talk. If we made love together, you'd find me silent enough."

"Bah, I don't believe you!"

"Try me and you'll see."

"They say round here that there was a man killed his hen to see if she was a good layer. Talk or be silent, it's all one to me."

The moon swam up the sky, lighting up the great wall of the town and the clay and thatch roofs of the hovels. The vines became visible as dark lines on the slopes. The watch's lamp shone from the corner tower of the ramparts and the bells of the churches rang for Matins. Maguelonne crossed herself and, shivering, pulled her brown woollen shawl about her shoulders. Now nothing was to be heard but the strident noise of the crickets in the meadow.

Riquet, seated on the parapet of the well, stared at the sky and fiddled with the rope of the bucket.

"Mélusine, come closer. And consider a little—why should you not love me? My heart is full of songs and merriment and foolishness. Isn't that better than marrying some dirty peasant who'll beat you with his great clogs?"

"Oh no, I shall not sell my maidenhood for your songs, fair minstrel. Go and seek a singing-girl."

Maguelonne sighed and slipped into the barn where her mother slept. Riquet thought he had seen tears in her eyes by the light of the moon.

Riquet stayed there, still fiddling with the rope; he felt his breast swell as if something bigger than himself had entered into him. "To the Devil," he said, "to the Devil, to the Devil . . ." but without knowing precisely what it was he was consigning to the Devil. He rose, stretched, and spread wide his arms as if to embrace the whole sky.

A long limber shape emerged from the shadows and glided towards him; he started and came back to earth. Auberi put his long arms round Riquet's neck.

"It's fine, Riquet, isn't it? She is so beautiful. She loves you, doesn't she?"

"Little spy. What are you doing here?"

"I wanted to see. Oh, she will love you, Riquet, and then you can bring her along with us. I should like that so much."

"To the Devil with taking her roving about the roads! Oh, to the Devil with living like this!"

The next day Ansiau said to Riquet:

"Lad, we've been here eight days. If we want to reach Pamiers before the cold weather we must set out. I have promised our good friend to help him find his son."

"Did you also promise him my eyes and my feet for his service?" Riquet asked, angrily. "You want us to be at the beck of a man who ought rightly to be burned."

"I, too, had a son. I cannot leave the man as he is. He is terribly anxious."

"What can it matter to you if we stay another week?" the young man asked, sulkily. "You're both in need of rest."

"I gave him my word. We must not stay, lad. Besides, I have had enough of that stable and I want to reach Marseilles before Christmas."

"Marseilles! In any case you'll never find a ship. And the roads are going to be dangerous, now, with the military being discharged after their term of service. It seems the whole country's full of free bands."

"Riquet, fair friend, I know all that and it's not your place to teach me about life. Whether you like it or not, we leave tomorrow."

"When people are travelling as companions they ask each other's opinion. My opinion is we should do better to stay."

"Very well," the old man said, "then we shall leave without you."

Riquet was not expecting that. For a long time he stared at the old man and he flushed.

"Why the Devil not wait another week? After all, a week is not much."

"But with you, fair friend, one week may turn into three weeks. One can go with one's comrades or court a girl. Not both together."

Riquet remained silent for two whole minutes, biting his lips; then he drew himself up sharply, and shook his head as if to drive away importunate thoughts.

"After all," he said, with an effort, "every man for himself. So much the worse—but I stay!"

Bertrand, indifferent to everything, supine by the threshold of the stable, was humming troubadour songs in a low voice.

It was Ansiau who was in a hurry to leave. He said that they must not be caught in the mountains by wind and frost and that from Pamiers to Marseilles the way would be hard. He did not want to admit to himself that he was weary of hearing Riquet laughing and joking with the girl.

He would not have believed that at his age he would be troubled by thoughts of a woman. It was not that he desired her—was he capable of that? But her voice was so good to hear and Auberi and Riquet said that she was so beautiful—Auberi was almost as mad about her as Riquet—and he imagined her vaguely as fair, white and pink, a little like the lady Alis, when young. It was hard to be still a man, as capable of feeling and thinking as that little chatterbox, and yet be treated like a poor human remnant and relegated to the chimney corner. He,

Ansiau thought, was supposed to be satisfied with his bit of bread and garlic and his stoup of sour wine. Yet he knew more stories and songs than Riquet; and the girl's voice became so gentle and gay when she spoke to that little vagabond monk—and the lad had no thought but to seduce her, that was how he would repay these good people for their hospitality. That Ansiau would not have at any price. Riquet must be handsome; the girl had eyes, so had Riquet. It's through the eyes that people get to know each other, through the eyes that love passes, and an eyeless man is worse than a eunuch, he rouses as much interest as a lump of wood. No, he thought, at fifty-five a man cannot want a young girl, but when you've no eyes you're also defenseless against bad thoughts, and it's better to be plodding the highroads in wind and rain than to stay like a dog in its kennel, envying the happiness of others.

And it seemed to him that he hated Riquet.

Auberi was very sad when he learned that Riquet would not be going with them.

"But, after all," he thought, "since he's lucky enough to be loved by a girl who is so beautiful and so good, how could he leave her? He will surely marry her. Nobody here knows he's a monk."

Riquet accompanied his friends as far as Castres and there took leave of them. Auberi cried and so did Riquet. He saw that the old man was displeased with him and he felt some remorse. But he tried not to show it and to maintain his air of assurance. It was only when he came to embrace Auberi that he could not hold back his tears.

"There, little Auvergnat piglet, there! The fact is I'm fond of you," he said, forcing a smile. "Who knows? We may meet again."

CROW'S FIELD

THE road along which the three companions were making their silent way was deserted. The weather was still fine but the evenings were cool and they could no longer sleep in the open. Auberi was melancholy; it was hard to be alone in charge of two blind men, yet he was accustomed to serving them. Moreover they had already become skillful in the management of their staffs and could walk almost like anybody else. But it was sad to be always with people who could see nothing. He felt shut out from the world, so much so that sometimes he closed his eyes and tried to feel his way forward. He asked himself: "How can they go on living and still be interested in anything? How is it that one wants to find his son again, the other to go to Jerusalem? What good does it do them? In their place I should have been dead long ago. And then, they're so old already, as it is."

He was not yet thirteen years old and he tired more quickly than the two men, but they would take no account of that, thinking that, since he still had his eyes, he ought not to complain of anything; and they were hard on him. When Riquet had been there he had not noticed it.

Of Riquet he thought with admiration; had he not succeeded in conquering the heart of the beautiful Maguelonne? "If only I were his age!" he thought. In that case he, too, might have stayed behind. Yet he knew that there were boys of his age who had known a woman; and he thought of it with envy. No doubt it was what made a man of you and made the beard sprout on your chin. But for the time being it was useless to think of it.

Two days out of Castres, at Saint-Papoul, while buying bread he imprudently allowed the purse to be seen. A fat rogue with plump cheeks and the eyes of a mouse, who was standing at the street corner, began to follow them about. When they were clear of the town Auberi saw him behind them on the road which was otherwise deserted, running between vineyards and meadows without so much as a small wood to hide in. He said to the blind men:

"There's a man I don't like the look of following us; let's walk more quickly." But then the man began to run and in a few minutes he came up with them. He had a knife in his hand. Auberi said to him:

"What good will it do you to kill us? Take the purse."

And he held the purse out to the thief, who put his knife back in his pocket and made off.

There was nothing the three companions could do but sit down at the roadside and discuss the adventure. They decided that they were lucky; the man had not made use of his knife. But now they must start begging again.

On the following day they came to the foot of a steep and rocky hill dominated by a castle. The castle walls were blackened and the roof of the keep had collapsed. It had evidently been burned out recently, for rain had not yet washed away the soot. But wisps of grey smoke were still coming from the few houses of a half-burned village at the base of the castle walls. A man and a woman, harnessed to a plow, were working on a slope beyond the rocks.

"I smell smoke," Ansiau said, "but my impression is we should have to climb high up towards it."

"I shall not go up," Bertrand said. "We're well out of the wind down here. If you find bread up there you can bring me some when you come down."

"My lord, the country looks very poor to me, the soldiers must have been this way," Auberi said.

"If they can give us bran bread, that's better than nothing."

They set out to work their way round the rock face. The path was narrow and so cluttered with large stones that, despite his staff, the blind man kept stumbling. They came out on to the plowed field and from there Auberi could see the village with its well and its little church which was also blackened by smoke. The wood which covered the top of the great cliff of rock was charred and the undergrowth of bramble and mulberry trailed, blackened, beneath the dead trees. Auberi saw the corpse of a man hanging from a great oak, twisted by the wind; a vulture, perched on the branch above the hanged man's head, was flapping its wings to drive away the crows flying round the carcass.

Frightened, Auberi turned away his eyes and ran across the field towards the man and woman who were plowing, dragging the blind man behind him.

The two peasants stopped working and the man left the plow and advanced a few steps towards them. The woman made a trumpet of her hands and began yelling stridently for help towards the village. A flight of startled crows rose and began to fly in circles above the wood. A few children, two youths, and a woman with her skirt trussed up came out of the houses and began running towards the field.

Far from reassured, Auberi took a step towards the peasant, saying:

"I'm seeking alms, good people, for two poor blind men—one is here, the other has stayed behind. We've eaten nothing since yesterday."

"Nor have we," the peasant said, "we eat grass. Go and beg somewhere else."

"Good people, God will repay you," Auberi persisted. "An onion and a little bran—anything you can."

Ansiau stood waiting, trying to interpret the meaning of the sounds and voices he could hear in the distance. The peasant was examining him suspiciously; the woman had drawn near. She was thin and swart, with a swollen stomach and her eyes darkly circled.

"The man's a soldier," she said.

"He looks like it, by God," the peasant said, "a thorough soldier."

"I am blind," the old man said.

"No, it's only one eye he's lost," the woman said, huddling against the man. "And his speech is northern." The peasant stared at the stranger with a mixture of hatred and disgust and slowly wiped his hands on his hose.

"Get out, carrion-eater!" he said, snarling. "Get out I tell you!" The woman stooped, scooped up a great handful of earth and flung it in the old man's face; he staggered and wiped his face. Frightened, Auberi tugged at his hand to lead him away. By that time the two youths and the woman in the short skirt were near. The first woman had stooped again, to pick up a large stone which she swung above her head. And she shouted:

"Help, it's a soldier, kill him!"

Then there arose a yell of hate, all shouting together. The stone struck the old man in the small of the back and he fell. Another stone grazed his cheek, another struck his forehead, and another hit Auberi on the chest.

The child managed to get the blind man to his feet and was dragging him away with all his strength; they both ran, stumbling over the stony, plowed earth. The two women screamed:

"Catch them! Catch them alive!"

Auberi could see men running down from the village, carrying forks. He was panting and pulling at the old man's arm.

"Quicker, run quicker!"

Ansiau had dropped his staff and lost all idea of direction and it seemed to him that Auberi was dragging him now this way, now that; he stopped, skidding . . . At last they found themselves among the brambles and, after tearing their clothes and the skin of their legs, they reached the wood, Auberi still dragging his master by the hand without looking behind him, so that the blind man crashed his head into tree trunks and caught his feet in their roots. Then they slid into a ravine full of young oaks and dead branches. There, prone on the slope, they were still at last, their hearts beating fit to burst and both breathing like animals at bay. There was such a murmuring in their ears that they could not even hear whether the hue and cry was still after them. Auberi's ears still rang with the yell of "Catch them alive!" and he was no longer sure whether or not he could really hear it still.

Time passed, and Auberi still thought he could hear shouts; the beating of his heart was shaking his body, yet at last he realized that all was still about them. Only the crows moved, above the ravine. The old man had collapsed beside him, his head fallen back, his face and beard all covered with clotted blood. He made no movement, so that Auberi was frightened and said:

"My lord, can you hear me?"

"Yes, lad. Is there any water about here?"

"I don't know. I'm afraid to go and look. Are you very thirsty?"

"It doesn't matter." The old man spoke with an effort. "I'm drinking my blood."

Auberi tried to wipe the blind man's face with the tail of his shirt. He managed to wipe away the clots with fresh blood and to clean the wounds. The old man moaned a little when the child rubbed too hard. Then, making a great effort, he clenched his teeth—there was a sound of bone grating on bone—and he came near fainting from pain, recovered, and with his head on one side, spat out broken molars. The bleeding grew worse, his mouth was constantly full of blood and he could not stop spitting.

Auberi rose, rubbed his flayed legs, and began clambering up the slope in search of blackberries. His hunger had become stronger than fear. His heart was beating less wildly; he could hear nothing but the croaking of the crows. The blackberry bushes had already been stripped but by searching he managed to get a handful of berries. At the least crackle of undergrowth he stopped, remained motionless for several seconds, holding his breath, and then again advanced a few steps, crushing the thick, thorny brambles beneath his feet.

He ate a berry, then another, and then suddenly he had almost none left. At that he grew bolder, crossing a small clearing on his knees to clamber up a rock face above which was a large thicket of brambles.

Now he could see the plowed field and the smoke of the village; twenty paces beyond him were the first charred trees and burned earth. He found another twenty blackberries, withered and eaten by flies, and then the heavy stench of carrion which hung about the place forced him to stop; he lay down, suddenly sick, and vomited up the berries which he had just eaten. When he raised his eyes he saw that he was almost beneath the oak, with its hanging corpse.

The man was wearing a linen tunic with a red cross on the breast; his hands and feet had been cut off; the face was gone. Auberi uttered a cry of terror, leaped from the rock, and ran, dropping the blackberries which he had in his hand. He stopped to listen for a few moments; perhaps his shout had been heard, perhaps the villagers were on the watch beyond the burned coppice, and would come after him, led by his shout—they would catch him and cut off his hands and feet. He glued his ear to the ground. No, he could hear nothing. He waited, faint with fear, then, remembering the old man, he pulled himself together, and returned in his tracks to pick up the berries. For fear of seeing the hanging corpse he dared not raise his eyes. Disturbed, the crows were circling about the tree.

Auberi began running towards the ravine, clasping the berries in his hand, his heart bursting with horror and with pity for himself, he who, having wronged no man, was yet hunted and in danger of being tortured; he almost felt that he must be guilty of some frightful crime unwittingly committed. He must hide, otherwise they would cut off his hands and his feet. He thought he saw the man with the red cross hanging from every tree in the forest.

He rejoined the old man and huddled against him as if this were his surest refuge. Ansiau could feel the child's heart beating so unevenly that he was afraid.

"God," he thought, "to what have I brought this child? What will his mother say to me on Judgment Day? Auberi, my lamb, my squirrel, child of my heart, how shall I shield you?" Aloud, he said:

"Come, eat up your blackberries, I'm not hungry. Try to sleep. We shall not try and reach the road again until nightfall."

Auberi said that he was too frightened, there was the body of a man with his hands and feet cut off, a man bearing a red cross on his breast. Ansiau crossed himself.

"He must have been French. God keep his soul."

"My lord, he will make us die of fear. He must be haunting the wood."

"No, no, child, it is a sin to say so. When a man dies like that, it's the sin of those who took his life that haunts the place and it only harms those who have themselves done evil. You are an innocent child. And you must know that the priests teach us that when a man dies in such agony as that, though he has been the worst of criminals, yet God Himself takes his soul in His hands to console him, in memory of what He suffered on the cross. It is very likely that this man is already among the beatified, looking upon the face of God and able to pray for us. May God give us all such a death."

"Oh, *no*," the child said, and Ansiau thought:

"True, he's still very young."

After sunset the child and the blind man went down to the road through the wood and managed to find Bertrand, who was huddled into a niche in the rock by the roadside.

"You've taken your time," he said. "Is it morning yet? The cold woke me."

"Ah, master Bertrand," Auberi said, "as for bread, you could say that we've had plenty! Big, heavy loaves, and hard too, flung at our heads! And lucky to get off so lightly at that!"

"Then we must die," Bertrand said, "I can already feel my body swollen with hunger."

Ansiau did not speak. The pain of the bones broken in his mouth was almost depriving him of consciousness and he was afraid of the wound becoming infected. Moreover his back was painful. Auberi was weeping, but silently, swallowing the tears which ran from his eyes and nose.

On the morrow, towards noon, Auberi saw two monks of the Order of Saint Benedict mounted on a large, grey mule. He ran to meet them; one of the monks, startled, raised his staff. Auberi called out:

"Pity, Father, have pity, we are dying of hunger."

At the sight of the two men lying on the ground, one with his eyes put out, the other with his head covered with blood, the monks stopped and dismounted.

They gave the blind men a little wine from their gourd and placed them, as best they could, on the mule.

"They must not eat at once," said the older brother. "It will do them harm. They must be taken to the abbey of Saint Peter and put into the hospital."

They followed the mule on foot; Auberi shambled beside them; he hardly had strength to drag his heavy feet along the road.

REFLECTIONS
UPON THE END OF THE WORLD

THE monks spoke together of the new miracles which God had worked for the true faith. A knight in golden armor had appeared among a troop of crusaders just as they were about to attack the heretics. Nobody knew whence he came. He had transfixed several heretic knights with his lance but afterwards no wound of any kind had been found on their bodies. He had spoken with no one, and at the end of the battle he had suddenly vanished into thin air; but the crusaders had clearly seen him and noticed the dragon on his shield. Later, they had learned that the church of the neighboring village was consecrated to Saint George.

"We shall witness many another marvel, Brother Enguerrand," said the older of the monks. "You have only to read Saint John's *Revelations* to see that time has run its course and that everything is happening as it was foretold."

"Not at all, Brother Humbert, not at all. The same thing has often been said but the signs and portents are not in accordance. In the first place, a great earthquake was foretold, and we should certainly have noticed it if it had happened."

"You talk like the vulgar people, who take everything literally. I shall prove to you, Brother Enguerrand, that these things are to be understood in a spiritual sense, and that everything happens in the hearts of men. For an earthquake is nothing in itself, nothing but a work of nature. There are mad people who also deny the signs of the times on the ground that they have seen no angels nor heard their trumpets. There are also those who interpret the Scriptures to suit themselves and maintain that Antichrist is none other than the count of Foix and that the horsemen with flame and hyacinth-colored cuirasses are the northern knights, because some of them put a kind of lion's head between their horses' ears! And that leads to much confusion and shocks the faithful. One must have the sense of things spiritual."

"Still, Brother Humbert, the signs described are very precise, and it must be a bold man who would deny them."

"And have you not seen water changed into blood by massacres, Brother Enguerrand, and a third of the trees burned and the waters grown bitter by reason of the number of corpses flung into the rivers and wells? Have you not seen the light of sun and moon veiled by the smoke of burning villages and the locusts devastating our fields and men tormented and wishing for death and men killed by horses and by fire and by smoke—all this have you seen with your own eyes, Brother Enguerrand? But spiritual signs are to be sought in the agony of one's own heart. The Antichrist foretold by our Saviour is here, and that Antichrist is heresy itself, with its deceitful air of holiness which seduces the people; and it is also heresy which is the Beast. For there are so very many seduced by it that neither the Church nor the crusade can prevail against it. It is written: all the peoples of the earth will adore the Beast! And observe that already it is spreading to the north and even as far as the Empire. It has the horns of a lamb but the voice of a dragon. Have you not seen our brothers and the village priests persecuted and put to shame throughout all the country?"

"It is not the heretics who wage war on us," the younger monk said, bitterly. "My parents' house has been burned down and my sisters raped."

"You fail to grasp the spiritual significance, Brother Enguerrand. Evil begets evil, and out of evil only evil comes, until there shall be no more time. You are uttering a shocking blasphemy when you say that the heretics wage no war on us. What are all the miseries of war—miseries all too common in all ages—beside this rotting of the soul which has infected the whole country? If a wound is septic, you have to apply a red-hot iron, and our holy father the pope saw clearly that that was the only remedy. Would you, like the vulgar people, curse the crusaders because they are northern men and do not speak our language?"

"God forbid, Brother Humbert, but think you that God will give the victory to sinful men and the secular arm? He has clearly shown the contrary, since all their chivalry could not save the Holy Sepulchre from being retaken by the heathens. Consider—these people make use of thieves and highway robbers against our chivalry, and make a holy war serve their ambitions."

"Frivolous words, Brother Enguerrand. Nothing that man can do is perfect. Yours is the very diabolical pride which leads to heresy. If scandal surrounds even the name of the holy war, even in the hearts of monks, how can we fail to believe that time has run its course? For Antichrist will win over even the most faithful and turn them from their obedience. He is trying, even now, Brother Enguerrand, to seduce you by means of false pity and false charity. Do you suppose that the souls of innocent victims of this war have not already received twenty times the celestial beatitude due to them? And that they are not full of gratitude towards those whom you believe their executioners? *They* are the blessed ones, and not we who remain exposed to the terrible temptations of the end of time."

Bertrand listened to the monks' words with malicious joy.

"See how they console themselves," he thought. "They are native here, their houses are burning, their kinsfolk also; they can reckon the price of the war which they've brought down on the country. And their pope promises them heavenly beatitudes for murder and rape! Why not? That's cheap enough! How can some of our people be so foolish as to see Antichrist in him? Innocent! What a name he chose! Oh no, we are nowhere near seeing time run out. Not thirty-three centuries would suffice to come to the end of the foulness in the hearts of men."

"Celestial beatitudes," he thought, repeating the monk's words to himself. "O facile promise which absolves and consoles for everything! O supreme lie of the Beast! How easy it is for them to suffer life, with that lying hope. No—never shall I adopt their faith. A man may be weak, with the assassin's knife at his throat, but you don't cheat your own conscience." No, God knows he felt no remorse. The fault was all Constanza's. How right the old Church was not to entrust the sacred ministry to women! By her impulsiveness, her woman's want of sense, she had brought about the deaths of the little girls and of her friends, and caused his own misery. In bringing them all the Consolation, she had brought them to their deaths. And, after all, would it have been so great a sin to abjure, to save their lives? She had flung him into an even worse wretchedness; through her he had received the Holy Spirit only to profane it thereafter by abjuring; so that now, although he lived another thirty years, never again in this life would he have a chance of salvation. That was why he was sometimes tempted, coward that he was, to yield himself to that faith in which, after all, he had been reared. Unhappy are they who, though their eyes be open, have not strength to bear the light!

Then there was Alfonse. To be sure, Alfonse would never know that his father had abjured, nor that he had already received the Spirit. Alfonse would have let himself be burned alive rather than renounce his faith. Was it worth sacrificing your life to avoid making the sign of the cross? No, he thought, no, now that I am going to be with him I will manage things so that he is always by my side and cannot do anything foolish; in my state, I shall certainly have the right to do it. And the thought almost consoled him for his blindness.

The three pilgrims stayed at the hospital of Saint Peter for ten days. The old man was in a bad way; he had lost a lot of blood. But his physical endurance was almost miraculous. Pain and fatigue seemed, as it were, to affect only the rind of his being, and since he had been blind he had become increasingly insensible to physical suffering. Such suffering fell from him like a worn-out garment. It seemed as if he was blind to suffering too.

When he was able to walk again, he set out with his two companions. Pamiers was now only ten leagues away and Bertrand was growing more and more impatient. He had been visited by dreams, and felt, he said, that his son was gravely ill. He bore the old man ill will for staying so long in the hospital and begged Auberi to take him on alone. The child would not hear of it. Never would he abandon his lord, not even for a single day.

"And what an idea," Bertrand thought, "to go begging from wretched peasants in that northern accent. It's not surprising that they were badly received. We've seen enough of northern men in this country."

Bitterly did he regret the loss of Riquet. As a rule the three companions hardly spoke of him. They bore him a grudge for having abandoned them. It was now Auberi who was the least inclined to be indulgent and never mentioned his old friend excepting as "the unfrocked" or "the ribald." For he was more than ever devoted to his old master and could not understand how Riquet could, even for

Maguelonne, have abandoned so noble a knight. Little by little he had built up a magnificent image of his master's past: he would have sworn by all the saints that the old man had been a count in Champagne and had had a hundred knights to serve him.

Ansiau's head was full of Brother Humbert's words concerning the end of the world. He told himself that since, after all, nobody knew the day nor the hour, it could just as well happen immediately. An immense cross would appear, spanning the heavens like a flash of lightning from Orient to Occident. But would he be able to see it? He could not but believe that he would, since even the dead were to see it and quit their graves. He thought that he would have wished, when the time came, to be in Acre graveyard, near to the tombs of his son and of Thierri.

"What a crowding and bustling," he thought, "if all the dead really come out of the earth and put on their flesh again, as foretold by the prophet. They will come out everywhere and the cemeteries will be more crowded than the public square on a fair-day. Lord! The little dead children alone, if they all came out together in their little white shrouds, would cover the earth like the fallen flowers of a cherry tree." And it seemed to him that it would be happiness far surpassing all earthly joys to see God Himself appear with His Cross in the heavens. He, whom even angels hardly dare to look upon! "God knows, it may be farther away than they think. Maybe I shall die first. But the dead, too, will see it."

THE HEART OF DIAMOND

IT WAS not easy to find the lords of Castans at Pamiers. Auberi had left the two blind men at the great gate of the town, and was running from house to house, and nobody knew of the lords of Castans—they were foreigners, people from the Carcassonne country; and the town was a Noah's Ark. At last, while he was making an inquiry, a man dressed in black, who was passing, said to the child:

"I am Bernard of Castans. What do you want?"

Auberi seized the skirt of his coat and began pulling him away, saying:

"Come. Come with me."

"Let go of me, wretch. You are not of these parts. What do you want of me?"

"Have you not a brother whose name is Gaucelm?"

The man turned very pale.

"You have news of Gaucelm? We thought him dead."

"Come, my lord, he is here, waiting for you at the town gates."

Both the man's hands went to his heart and Auberi thought that he was going to faint; but he recovered himself, and set off, almost running, towards the main gate, Auberi could hardly keep up with him.

"My lord, I ought to tell you, you will find him greatly changed."

"What's that you say? They've disfigured, mutilated him? You may tell me, I fear nothing."

Yet, as he spoke thus, he was almost sobbing.

They found the blind men, seated on the ground; Ansiau was talking with the soldiers on guard duty. Horses were passing, splashing them with mud, for it had been raining. Bertrand had his back to the wall, his head resting against the stone, and he started at each new sound. Bernard of Castans saw him and ran to him.

"Gaucelm!"

The blind man was on his feet in an instant, his hands groping before him.

The lords of Castans were living in a small house built against the outer wall. Bernard, weeping hot tears, led his brother and his two companions to the house. Bertrand was shaking so that he could hardly speak.

Then the two brothers were seated near the hearth in the small, smoky kitchen, while Bernard washed and dressed his brother's feet; Bernard's eldest son had brought his uncle one of his shirts and almond oil for his hair and beard.

"Bernard, tell your son to care for the people who brought me here. They are not of our people but they have been as brothers to me. Roger of Gaillac threw me out like a dog; you will not forget that."

"Gaucelm, we live in an age accursed, and Antichrist has come to try us. We must be surprised at nothing. They are many whom the Beast will yet win over. Roger is not a renegade and therefore he is obliged to be careful."

Gaucelm said nothing; his lips shook. At last he made up his mind.

"And Alfonse, Bernard. He is not with you? Tell me everything."

Bernard did not answer at once.

"Bernard! Speak, man."

"He is with us."

"And well?"

"He has been very ill, Gaucelm. We believed him dying. He wept and begged. . . . We let him receive the Consolation."

Gaucelm, his face hardening, sat up.

"Childishness! He was pretending to be dying. I know him. Had I been there I should not have allowed it. Foolishness! A fine state the faith has brought us to! But he will soon learn who is his master. Well, tell me about him. He's better, isn't he?"

"He was cured by a miracle on the day he received the Spirit. We did nothing to cure him. Yet he was cured."

"And then?"

"He is much changed. He sees visions."

"You are not telling me everything, Bernard."

"I dare not tell you, Gaucelm. It will be very hard for you."

Gaucelm gripped his brother's shoulders and shook him.

"You and Anselme shall pay for this. You and your holy men, you've tried to take him from me, but he shall know his master. Tell me all."

"For fifteen days he has refused food; he takes nothing but a little water. He even says that he no longer feels thirst."

Gaucelm uttered a cry and rose, knocking against his brother.

"I knew it. Take me to him. At once."

"He is very weak, Gaucelm. We had better warn him."

"Not a word, dog! Let him see me first. If, after that, he still wants to die, then—then let him die and rot, I want no more to do with him!" He was seized by a convulsive sobbing and fell into his brother's arms.

"Come," Bernard said.

In the loft, near the skylight, a young man lay upon the floor, his arms behind his head, still as a corpse. He was dressed in black; his hair, too, was very black, curly and carefully combed. His face, the color and texture of the finest wax, was extremely beautiful, feminine in its sweetness and gentleness, with a very small mouth and eyebrows which seemed drawn with a pen. His enormous brown eyes were wide open, almost staring.

Bernard half-opened the door but the youth did not even start.

"Alfonse, a man wishes to see you."

"Who is he, uncle?" The voice was thin and musical, like that of a ten-year-old child. At the sound of it, the father lost consciousness and fell forward on the threshold of the door.

Bernard managed to drag his brother towards the skylight and Alfonse sprinkled water from his jug on to his father's face. He looked at the unconscious man with calm and saddened astonishment.

"Ah," he said, "it is my bodily father. Uncle, with what temptation would you confront me?"

"You see what those dogs have reduced him to," Bernard said.

"Uncle, let me go, before he comes to himself."

"No, Alfonse, you must speak to him. Come, help me to loosen his collar."

But the boy had retreated towards the window, his face hidden in his hands. Gaucelm, coming to himself, said:

"Alfonse, are you there, Alfonse?"

"He is here," Bernard said, and joined their hands.

"Leave us, Bernard."

The father ran his hands over the child's face and hair, felt his shoulders and wrists. And the boy was crying. "Father, oh father, what have they done to you? Father, how I pity you!"

"Alfonse, you will come with me now. You will come downstairs and eat and you shall be my prop. I have come from Uzès to Castres and from Castres to here to find you, my only thought has been of you, my dear, beloved son. You know well that your mother and sisters were not half as dear to me as you. They are beyond reach of harm now and for their sake I am glad. But I could not bear it if you were to leave me."

"Father, my father, receive the Spirit and die with me and you will be delivered from this misery."

Gaucelm thrust the youth away so violently that he knocked his head against the wall.

"It was not for that that I travelled the roads. Your Consolation is folly. You shall live and you shall wed. I'll have no more of this faith of

yours which has brought war upon us. Do you suppose that having my
eyes put out has taught me nothing?"

The youth looked at him with horror and lay down upon the floor
again, without speaking.

"Alfonse! Do you hear me?"

"I don't want to see or hear you. This is a last temptation sent me by
the Devil. Why do you let yourself be the Devil's tool, father?" he
added, in a plaintive and suddenly very childish voice.

"Me? Alfonse, take hold upon yourself; it is you who are possessed
by the Devil. Yes, I know, I was carried away, I was wrong. Well, then,
you shall not marry, eat no meat, wear black—but live! Can you abandon me in the state I am in?"

"The good God does not abandon His own. Return to Him."

"Alfonse, I am your father. It is written: honor thy father and thy
mother."

"That is the old law. You are my father according to the flesh and
the Devil. But that is the very reason why the new law says: 'Whosoever
shall not hate his father and his mother and his brothers and his children
is not worthy of Me.' "

"I know the law as well as you, Alfonse. It is also written: 'You saw
me starving and nourished me not; naked, and clothed me not; sick
and in prison, and relieved me not.' Your own father begs his way to
your side, what other sign do you need of the will of God?"

"I have no more need of signs, I know God. I am on my way to Him.
You are my father according to evil and sin, you begot my flesh from
which God wishes to deliver me. You love only my body. Leave me,
you are a temptation and an instrument of Satan."

"Beware lest I curse you!"

The boy, his eyes wide open, stared at the ceiling rafters with a look
of ecstasy as if he were looking upon the angels of Heaven. A smile, at
once triumphant and painful to see, hovered on his lips.

"You will but curse yourself. You can do nothing to me. I am in
sanctuary. My body only can still be hurt, but my spirit is delivered."

"Alfonse, just now you wept over me."

"They were tears of the flesh and pity of the flesh. Now it is over."

With his hands Gaucelm found the boy's feet and seized them.

"I no longer have my eyes. You are only a child and do not know
what misery that is. Some poor people, beggars, an old, blind man,
found me on the road and cared for me and brought me all this way to
you because the old man pitied a father trying to find his lost son. And

you—will you show less charity than a stranger, a heathen, a man who serves the Devil's church?"

"The man is the companion whom God placed in your way, as he sent the Samaritan to the man who was wounded. But my way is elsewhere."

"Alfonse, and what if I despair, what if I blaspheme?"

"You alone are master of your heart. I am bound to do God's will. He has bidden me go to Him. I go. Leave me, father, leave me"—his voice had become supplicating, full of pain, almost tender. "By the love and respect I once had for you, father, leave me now. I must collect myself and take counsel of God. This evening I will talk to you."

After that he returned no answer to his father's words. With his eyes closed, he was hardly breathing, and Gaucelm thought that he had fallen asleep through weakness. He summoned Bernard, went downstairs, and called upon his brother to mix a little wine and honey, secretly, with the water which the boy drank.

"If he gets his strength back," he said, "his taste for life may come with it. All this is nothing but foolishness. As I am now I have suffered so much that I can face no more trials. It is hard enough to know him already dead to this world. Let him preach, let him console the dying; the country has need of men like him. As things are now, a man needs more courage to go on living than to die."

"You are right," Bernard said, "but I am afraid that Alfonse will not give in."

When, that evening, Bernard went up to the attic with his brother, he uttered a cry of surprise: Alfonse was no longer there. The skylight was open, he must have fled across the roof, which joined the outer wall of the town.

Gaucelm's anger was appalling. He accused his brothers of spiriting the child away on purpose. He would not believe that he had got away through the skylight, weak as he was.

"I am blind," he said. "You were able to get him away without my perceiving it."

Bernard succeeded in convincing him of his good faith, caused a search to be made for the child throughout the whole town, and visited the Good Man who had administered Consolation to the boy. Nobody knew where Alfonse was. Everybody was sure he must have drowned himself in the Ariège.

Three days passed thus. Gaucelm, sick and shaking with fever, sent for Auberi and the old man, who were still resting from the journey in Bernard's house.

"I no longer wish to remain with my brothers," he said. "They have cost me the loss of my son. The whole fault is theirs. This very day I shall leave with you, going where you will, to Jerusalem or elsewhere. But I shall certainly die during the journey and I do not care, provided I am not with them."

Auberi's face dropped, for he thought it hard to have to care for two blind men. Nor did Ansiau seem very pleased.

"You will regret it," he said. "Your brothers love you, and you will be well cared for here, you are among your own people. And then perhaps your son is not dead, he may yet return."

"You do not know him. And what does it matter to me whether he returns? For me, he is dead."

He suffered another bout of his shattering dry sobbing.

"I do not want to wait until they find his body. Let us leave."

That same day they left, in spite of Bernard's tears and prayers. The lords of Castans gave them money for the journey and a plow horse, the two men mounting it as best they could, while Auberi went on foot, leading the horse by the bridle.

The mountains on the horizon were deep blue beneath iron-grey clouds. The forest was all purple, copper and bronze with here and there the black streaks of pines; above the summits, kites, like crosses, hovered. A somber splendor which Auberi devoured with his starved eyes as if, forced to see for three, he saw three times as much. The two blind men were silent and the child, serious, kept his eyes in front of him. These two men who had loved beauty and light so much and were now shut up in darkness forever made him conscious of his own riches. Things which he had never thought to look at before—the shape of clouds, the colors of dead leaves, the flash of sunlight in a puddle, became objects of contemplation and surprise: "That, too, is beautiful, and this. God created it for my enjoyment." And the painful weariness of his body stupefied but no longer crushed him. It brought him to the state when he no longer thought of anything, so that only the blues and russets and browns, the sharp and delicate lines of the countryside, sang in his heart.

They had to call a halt in a wood and the horse moved off to crop the dry grass and mosses. The bread had become as hard as a shoe-sole. And it was very cold; the north wind, the tramontane, was blowing and bringing big branches down from the trees. Huddled against each other, the travellers waited for nightfall and Auberi watched, above the blue-black line of the horizon and against a sky of lucent coral, long violet clouds racing and scattering. Higher towards the zenith of the sky the color changed abruptly to sapphire and the stars lit up one after the other so quickly that it was difficult to keep track of them.

"The night will be cold," the child thought, "cold and beautiful."

There was no darkness for him, but only stars and more stars, without end, and dark branches like lace against the deep blue of the sky; and with the passage of time the sky became more and more radiant because of the stars shining ever more numerous to infinity. Because the two men beside him were forever in darkness, he felt himself forever in the light, and when he closed his eyes to sleep he pressed his fists into them and saw cascades of colored sparks.

"O Alfonse, Alfonse my son, lily without blemish that they have broken and marred. I have no eyes now and no tears in their sockets to weep over you who have wounded me so cruelly. Cursed be the day I begot you on the woman who was all our misfortune. Yet had you been born of another woman you would not have been the Alfonse I loved.

"And if I was only his father according to the flesh, why must my soul cleave to him so painfully?

"And if that cleaving is such a sin, how does it happen that we bind ourselves to what is most beautiful and most pure in our sight?

"Companion, had you but been able to see and to know what a sweet child he was! Not the child Jesus himself can have had more beauty and wisdom and goodness of heart; you cannot conceive the divine loveliness there was in that child."

"Why should I not? I, too, had a son whom I loved."

"No, you will never understand. He was like no other that ever was. With their preaching of the end of the world and the reign of evil, they broke and seduced him. They drove him to deny me. But his heart was pure and good and he loved me, I know it, for otherwise he would not have fled as he did. He sinned only through too strong a faith, I know that. But, for a father, it is a hard thing to accept.

"Comrade, you serve the God of the old law, and life for you is simple as it is for heathens and animals; but as for us, we are so torn this way and that that we are no longer sure if we should love good and hate evil. The good God's Son spoke truth indeed when He said 'I bring not peace but a sword.' Can I love the sword that strikes me?"

The old man did not understand much of what his companion was saying for he knew little about the other's faith. Still, he thought, he was a man of good family, well educated and pious, since, despite his rather singular ways, he was always talking of God and the Holy Scriptures. Very likely he had become a heretic only out of loyalty to his liege lord and his family. He did not believe him capable of having worshipped Satan in the shape of a black cat nor of having taken part in orgies. In his heart, Ansiau did not condemn Gaucelm.

"I, too," he said, "have been stricken by the sword. It will soon be twenty years since I lost my son and the wound bleeds still. It is a father's lot. But when we reach the Holy Sepulchre, there you will surely find consolation."

"What consolation?" Gaucelm cried out. "What shall I find there that I do not find here and in myself? Shall I be consoled by dead stones and sham relics? Am I a child to be diverted by such frauds?"

The old man made no answer. He was calling up from his memory an image of the road towards Jerusalem, the long file of crusaders and pilgrims, the hedge of crosses and banners extending over leagues and towards the great white city surrounded by cypresses and olives in the midst of blue hills. He saw again the great basilica of the Holy Sepulchre, the thousand candles, the brilliantly colored frescoes and mosaics decorating the walls; and once again, as at the time of his pilgrimages, an immense wave of joy lifted up his heart at the idea of being in the place itself, the unique and only place in the world, beside which all the kingdoms of the earth were but shadows. The place where the only true thing in the world had been accomplished, the place where the only true Friend of all men had transformed his dead flesh into flesh glorified. There is the place where death was vanquished, where there is no more death.

"Companion," he said, "when you are there, you will see. It is a hundred times more splendid than the joy of Christmas or of Easter Sunday, and there is no man so unhappy that he would not be consoled by it. God is not sparing of His gifts in the place where He suffered martyrdom."

"I shall die before we get there," Gaucelm said.

Sad autumn. Cold, rain and mud. Lulled by the horse's pacing the two blind men ride half-asleep, Gaucelm resting his forehead against the knight's wide back. United by the sadness of both their lives, formerly so rich—all lost, all done with, nothing but going forward in darkness and the cold, never again to meet those whom they loved, unless in another world. Neither living nor dead.

"Father, leave me—baron, I believe I am very far gone, send for the priest. Haumette, bring the candle, it is dark. Father, why do you allow yourself to be the Devil's tool? Father, I shall hang myself, I shall throw myself into the well, for I know very well that you hate me! Friend, friend, you will not see me again. Neither living nor dead."

And still after that there is whole life in the body, cold freezes hands and feet as it always did and hunger twists the bowels, and thoughts come and go in the mind.

"Lord God, Son of the Virgin without sin, Lord Son of the Immaculate Virgin, Lord God, mighty sanctuary, incomparable beauty, haven of peace, light in our darkness, warmth in frozen winter, nourishment of the starved, have pity upon two poor men out on the empty roads of autumn, for You are all that remains to us in the world."

And this thought was with Gaucelm always: "Alfonse, Alfonse my son."

He repeated it to himself like a litany, and it calmed him a little.

Part Three

BITTER BLOOD

Now the wind, which sings and weeps,
Down the dark road swoops and leaps.
Crow's wings ripping through the clouds
Tear the heavens into shrouds.
Naked tree with shaking boughs
Black and dreadful mops and mows.
Morgan the Fairy sings and sighs,
Morgan sings and Morgan cries,
Morgan moans and Morgan weeps,
Down the dark road swoops and leaps—
And within his dwelling creeps—
Morgan the Fairy's icy breath
Bringing him to dole and death.
Make him drink from your black cup,
Wine of mulberry make him sup.
So his pain may longer be,
Long his spirit's agony.
Fill his clothes with biting lice,
Curse his horse with stinging flies,
Crack his bones until he dies.
Strike his nerves with mortal cold
Rot his flesh with creeping mould—
So his pain may longer be,
Long his spirit's agony
And his body maggot's fee.

"O Morgan, the beautiful, daughter of kings, I shall deck your crown of mistletoe with cornflowers and buttercups, never again shall I weave crowns for Saint Odile—or Saint Catherine, for I am of the lost, drowned maids who haunt this wood.

"Teach me, Morgan, how to fashion his image, a likeness so like that it might be himself. Then will I pierce his eyes and his heart with my knife, first heating it red-hot in the fire. For see, I carry an image of his heart which all day long I pierce with needles, but I feel it is not enough, for do I know how his heart is fashioned? Does he even possess one? He is nothing but entrails. Not once did I feel the beating of his heart, so thick is his body.

"O vile soul, because I would have none of your bargain you flung me to the beasts. And if you made the same proposal again and threw in your love, I would reject it again. Better Macaire than a willing cuckold."

Her body had been abandoned to bestiality but not with her consent; she had not been an accomplice of that baseness.

He has a base soul, a villein's soul, finding his pleasure only in filth. Who could love so base-hearted a man? Surely he had bewitched her with charms brought from eastern lands, so that in that, too, he had cheated.

More than a lover, more than a husband, her own flesh and blood— yet he had betrayed her with charms, for not even for such a love had he enough heart in his coward, villein's soul. "His cruel love has cost me my life, but now he shall lose his life. I shall learn how to take it from him drop by drop, make his blood rot, send snakes to drink his eyes and leeches to suck his heart, and I shall so contrive that only I have power to save him, yet I shall not raise a finger to do it."

Since her great suffering Eglantine was no longer afraid of spirits or fairies. Five days and nights she had wandered in the forests, hiding among brambles when hunters were near. On the eve of Saint John fires were lit on village greens and in the meadows and lads and maids danced a farandole to the skirts of the woods, carrying branches of elm and willow. The woods and meadows were full of song. "Garin loves me, Garin lo . . ." By the last flicker of daylight and rising of the evening star, Eglantine had swallowed, at one draught, the brew which Jeanne the midwife had sold her for a silver brooch. Better to die than bear a villein's child.

On that Saint John's eve the moonlight was so strong that the colors of earth and stones were visible. Eglantine had lain down in the long grass of the fairies' clearing, for she needed the fairies' help in her purpose and Morgan herself sometimes came to dance in that clearing on Saint John's eve. By the light of the moon she had seen her dark blood and the tiny child, all red, which had come out of her in the midst of her great pains. Tiny, like a doll, with hands and feet smaller than small nuts, a head like a big nut, with huge eyes, closed.

She had wrapped it in bracken fern and had put it on the white stone so that Morgan would take its soul to make a small wanton sprite. It was so small its arms were like a child's fingers. Morgan had taken it to make a will o' the wisp. In the night of her great pain was born a spirit which would go neither to Heaven nor Hell, a sprite to dance on the marshes and frighten hunters.

For which reason Eglantine would never be afraid of spirits or of fairies.

> *Soul for soul, breath for breath*
> *Morgan keepeth me from death.*
> *Strong my will as any tower*
> *Over their bodies gives me power*
> *And over their souls.*

He was so small, with eyes like a dead squirrel's.

Three days after Saint John the lady saw Eglantine return to Bernon farmhouse; it was early morning, the servants were still sleeping, the sky only just lightening. The lady had just taken a light from her night-light to fire the faggots beneath the great saucepan in the hearth. Suddenly, Briffaut, the old, blind dog, had begun scratching at the door. He scratched and whined so persistently that at last the lady opened the door. Eglantine stood there, tall and lean, supported by one arm against the wall. The shadows under her eyes looked as if drawn with charcoal and her lips were blue; a ghost.

The girl had explained that she had fled from Bercenay because Macaire beat her and that she had seen fairies in the forest.

Since that day Eglantine had lived at Bernon; Macaire would certainly not try to fetch her away and Herbert was at Troyes. Joceran and little Marie were glad to have their sister back and competed in trying to amuse her as she lay in bed. Marie brought her flowers and berries, Joceran demonstrated his skill with the bow and presented her with the small birds which he caught in traps. The lady fed her on underdone meat and good wine and made her drink infusions of strengthening herbs. Little by little the invalid recovered her health and seemed to grow strong again.

The child was so like him—he who was gone—that the lady lacked the courage to speak harshly to her. Now that she was thinner, with her height and her wide shoulders she looked exactly like a boy. Her hair, formerly so thick, was falling out in handfuls, leaving her with poor, thin plaits, although short locks still fell forward over her face. She would toss them back with a brusque, fretful motion of the head and whenever she saw that gesture the lady suffered a pain in her heart, for there stood Ansiau as a young man. Eglantine had the same wide eyes, soft as a horse's, and the same big, flat-lipped mouth.

She might sit for hours on the threshold of the house, her long, thin arms clasped round her knees, her head bent to one side. Then she would get up and go into the forest, not to return until evening; the lady often sat up until midnight to let her in. Eglantine would return with brilliant, feverish eyes which seemed hardly to see the lady, obstinately speechless.

One day the lady said to her: "My girl, I am going to find a shift to break your marriage, since you say that Macaire has not touched you; and Macaire will readily swear the same. I am willing to give one-third of my dower to increase your dot and I will find you a husband suitable for your father's daughter."

Eglantine answered her: "It is too late."

"Come," the lady said, "there have been girls worse dishonored than you who've married and lived decent lives and borne fine children. You are only seventeen. I know that Pierre Guérin, the sire of Chesley's squire, would take you willingly and, with the dower you will have, his father will certainly consent."

"I don't want that," Eglantine said. "The lords of Chesley are my kinsfolk through my mother; I will not have them say that I have married a man who is their servant."

"Madness!" the lady said. "You know quite well you can never marry your equal."

"Then it would be better not to marry at all," Eglantine said, somberly. "Herbert thought me fit only to be flung to the dogs; and you are suggesting a servant. In any case, though a king asked my hand I should refuse, now."

And the lady could not get another word out of her. She believed that the child was out of her senses and consequently did not cross her . too often. But she was already beginning to have her suspicions: Eglantine did no work in the house, yet her hands were calloused and scratched and her nails broken. People who came across her in the woods heard her talking aloud and reciting what sounded like litanies.

Pierre Guérin had come to Bernon with his parents towards the end of October. Eglantine was seated, as usual, on the doorstep. Pierre had gone on his knees to her, saying:

"I adjure you, for the love of God, to raise the spell you put on me the day you touched me with your bouquet of nettles."

Eglantine had turned away her head and stared at the earth between her feet. Then, without saying a word, she had taken a lump of earth in her hands and begun to work it between her palms. The young man's mother and father watched her, terrified. The lady had said to them:

"Aren't you ashamed to believe in such stuff? So far as I know, it is not such a marvel to see a lad languish for a girl. At your age, you should have more sense."

But Pierre declared that the lump of earth was a model of his heart and that he had felt a pain, as if the girl were kneading his heart between her hands.

CRUSADE

For the first time in his life Haguenier was seeing the great misery of war. He would very much rather have been making war in a heathen land, especially since this was a crusade and they were under orders to give no quarter. He knew, of course, that a serving soldier is bound to bear arms against any enemy of his liege lord whatsoever, even his own kinsman or friend. And he was in the service of the Lord of lords. Since remission of sins was promised to every man who would do his forty days' crusading, he could not but believe that this was a holy war. Nothing but obedience is called for from a man under arms.

It was much easier for the Germans to fight without thinking, for they knew not a word of the language and chattered together in their harsh, northern jargon. Even many of the French and the Picards detested the people of the Midi as much as they did the heathen. Too much blood had been spilled in the past three years. The country was still resisting with dull obstinacy. In the places which had been taken the garrisons were not safe or at ease; the crusaders, foreigners in a strange land, constantly faced the threat of ambush and treachery. The first enthusiasm had begun to wane. The sack of Béziers had, all things considered, no doubt been profitable to God's cause; nevertheless it had scandalized many crusaders, good Christians though they were for, they said that never, even in a heathen country, had there been such carnage. It was beginning to be asked whether it was right to wage war in order to enrich the count of Montfort at the expense of the country's legitimate lord—whoever and whatever he might be, he was, after all, the count, holding his fief from the king and inheriting from his ancestors; these were rights of a free man which no one could take away from him.

Among the men of Champagne were many who felt goodwill towards the English, who took the part of the count of Toulouse. People were beginning to say:

"It's not surprising that Simon of Montfort should serve God so zealously, since by so doing he helps himself." And the older men, veterans of the Holy Land, were also saying:

"In our day we wore the cross on our shoulder, to give strength to our arm, and now they wear it on the breast, to ward off blows. The young men of today are degenerate."

In fact, the war was disappointing for the younger men; there were hardly any real battles that summer. There were brushes with badly armed troops and castles which yielded without striking a blow. The country was full of lawless men who pillaged and massacred the wretched people and there were bands of crusaders doing the same whenever they managed to convince themselves that they were in a village of heretics; heresy must be stamped out wherever it was found and many were too zealous for the good cause to be satisfied with garrison duty in abandoned castles.

The roads were crowded with refugee peasants, beggars, ex-soldiers; the glare of burning villages reddened the sky and it was pitiful to see so beautiful a country brought to such a pass.

Near Castres, however, the baron of Chantemerle's men had the good fortune to fall in with a troop of the count of Toulouse and to give battle. The men of Toulouse were more numerous but not so well equipped as the crusaders; moreover they had been taken by surprise and the battle was a bloody one for them. They lost more than twenty men. This was Haguenier's first battle; he had never yet killed men or had a combat lance aimed against him; the idea so confused him that he completely forgot why and for whom he was fighting. He could only think that if he did not achieve something altogether extraordinary that day he would be for ever discredited in the eyes of his own side and would bring his family into contempt. Unhappily for him Pierre felt just the same, and most of the other young men from Champagne were in an identical state of mind, so that each was almost ready to unhorse any comrade coming between him and the enemy in order to strike the first blow. They hurled themselves on the men of Toulouse with such violence that the latter had to withdraw hastily to avoid being smashed by the shock. At the critical moment Haguenier realized that his heart was going to play him false again; he felt such pain in his chest that he knew he could not bear it for long. He was seized by such despair that he nearly lost consciousness entirely. Then came the miracle: it was as if another man were born in him. When an axle breaks while the cart is moving at full speed, the wheels fly off, are hurled forward and crash through anything in their path. So too, Haguenier's body, strained past bearing, had, as it were, wrenched free from soul, thought and pain, and flung itself madly forward, spurring his horse, brandishing his lance, yelling death and destruction. He had reached the front rank of Toulousians, overthrown a mounted squire and driven his lance through the shoulder of a tall knight with a winged helmet—and all without knowing what he was doing, his martyred body no longer capable of feeling. He supposed that the effort might cost him his life, but the impulse was stronger than his will and he could not have stopped even if he would.

His madness was contagious; it spread, for each knight wanted to kill his man and the idea of serving God made everything possible, everything permissible. The count of Montfort's garrison had to make a sortie from the town to moderate the ardor of their impulsive allies.

Haguenier of Linnières was at first taken for dead and carried to the church at Castres with the four other crusaders killed in the battle. The bodies, washed and handsomely dressed, their wrists tied together on their chests, were laid out on a large catafalque in the middle of the nave, with a hundred candles burning about them, while their comrades took turns to watch beside them.

HAGUENIER:
IV. THE WIDENING RIFT

HAGUENIER was brought out of his syncope by a burning sensation in his right temple. A slightly leaning candle was dropping melted wax on him. Haguenier slowly opened his eyes, trying to make out where he was. The memory of the battle came back to him. "That pain . . ." he thought, and, "better to die than go through that again."

The ceiling of the church was quite low and by the light of the candles he could see above him a picture of the Last Judgment painted in bright colors picked out with gold. The wide, black-and-gold wings of the angels flashed all across the vault, about a Christ in Glory dressed in red and placed in a long medallion of gold and dark blue set with painted gems. The King of Glory's face was stern, the brows knit and the eyes starting. The closed mouth was threatening. Haguenier contemplated the Face, at once terrified and transported by love. The countenance spoke to him. It said:

"What suffering have I not undergone for you! And you are regretting the pain you suffered, fighting against my enemies. Did you take the cross to find pleasure? See—these men, worse than heathens, blaspheme my name and despise my Church. In the name of their master, the Devil, they kill my friends, in whose bodies I suffer. It is not for love of me but from vainglory that you find strength to fight. Your body's pain was needed to recall you to me, ungrateful servant."

"Lord, to you I owe all. Grant me the power to love my pain."

Somewhere, distant, a voice was reading from the Psalms. Haguenier, without much understanding of Latin, was trying to catch the words but his mind felt too weak. He tried to drive away the flies which were buzzing about his eyes and discovered that his wrists were tied. He told himself that he had, after all, been made prisoner, but then recalled that prisoners' hands were tied behind their backs, not in front. He made the effort of turning his head and saw, two inches from his face, the head of a corpse, purple, and with a gaping wound in place of the left eye. And he saw the candles and other bodies laid out on the catafalque.

"Am I dead, then?" he asked himself, more astonished than frightened.

At last he understood. Now the precentor was chanting litanies; the candles spluttered. Haguenier felt too weak to raise his head or turn over. He dared not speak, troubled at the idea of interrupting the precentor and perhaps giving him a terrible fright. Yet he was afraid of fainting again and being buried alive.

For a moment he was prey to a strange temptation, to let himself go, do nothing, since he was already counted amoung the dead; perhaps a sickness lay in wait for him, or great troubles; never, he felt, never would he possess Marie. Now the Christ in Glory was stooping over him with an expression of pity and sorrow. The gilding and deep reds of Christ's garments were more brilliant by candle-light than in full daylight, and dark-shadowed figures of angels with their small, stern mouths seemed to live and to come out of the ceiling. Haguenier suddenly experienced the sensation of rising—rising; he raised his head, straining his face towards the arms of the Saviour. He fell back, his breath harsh in his throat and, at that moment, the precentor uttered a shrill cry and ran for help to the knights who were watching by the dead.

Haguenier was resting, in the house of a nobleman of the town. His companions, their forty days of service done, had left the country. The knight whom Haguenier had been lucky enough to wound was considered to be his prisoner but the young man had declared that, for love of his lady, he would ask no ransom but only a promise not to bear arms again until this war was over. The knight, out of gratitude, arranged to install Haguenier in his sister's house in Castres.

Haguenier was seriously ill: despite the heat his hands and feet became very cold and turned blue and his legs were swollen. The palms of his hands and the soles of his feet were burned by his physician's cautery iron. He was also being treated with opium and belladonna. After ten days' rest his circulation became normal but the young man was so exhausted that he could no longer speak. He was deathly sad, telling himself that his father was quite right to despise him. And what lady would want to take so puny a being for her friend? He was very little consoled by the esteem in which he was held by his comrades and his hosts.

Slowly his strength returned, while he spent his days stretched on a cushioned seat in his hostess's room, chatting with the young girl of the household. The room was cool and gay, hung with striped tapestry, and the window was of glass, circular panes set in lead. The girl, seated on cushions placed on the ground, played her harp all day long. Haguenier spoke the *langue d'oc* well and knew songs by Marcabrun and Bernard of Ventadour and Jaufré Rudel. He tried his skill, singing them to accompany the girl. Her name was Agnès and her hair was dressed in fine black plaits falling to form a sort of trellis about her ears and neck. She liked to talk of love, and was always propounding difficult problems of gallantry for her guest to solve: a lover is urged to avow the secret of his love by his lady's husband; has he the right to name another lady, to ward off suspicion? When a man possesses a lady's heart and chaste affections, ought he to be jealous of her husband? Must a man keep faith with a woman who has taken the veil? Should you accept gifts from a lady who is pretending love for you in order to divert suspicion from the real lover? Haguenier found these discussions somewhat insipid but always answered with good grace. He would never have allowed a lady to see that he was bored by her company. Moreover Agnès was pretty to look at and of a gay disposition.

His hostess herself, the lady Marguerite of Figeac, had a very great notion of Haguenier's military ability. He had thought himself obliged to set her right:

"I do not," he had said, "want anyone from my own country, whom you may chance to meet, to think that I have been boasting unjustifiably. I have no reputation in my country, where I have only taken part in one tourney and that badly. I do not say this with any intention of being offensive to your brother, but if I did strike a good blow, it was by luck."

The lady Marguerite replied that modesty was a praiseworthy quality in a young man and persisted in her opinion.

SONGS AND REVERIES

WHEN the baron of Chantemerle left Castres to return to the north with his troop, Haguenier asked him to take a letter to the lady of Pouilli. In it he had rolled a paper of poetry which he had written, feeling sure that Aielot would guess for whom it was intended.

"Most dear and well-beloved sister, my very sweet friend before God and men, may Our Sweet Lord and King Jesus Christ and His Glorious Mother for ever hold over you their love, aid, and protection.

"A weariness of no great gravity, due to the blows I have received in God's cause, obliges me to remain in this country longer than I should have done and deprives me of the joy of seeing you this month. This separation is a great hardship and affliction to me. May it please God never to let you doubt, most beloved sister, the great tenderness which I feel for you, and the loyalty and faithfulness of my love. Know that your affection and your happiness are more precious to me than anything in the world but for one thing only. For my sake, be careful of your health, do nothing to cause yourself fatigue or anxiety, and above all do not worry about me, to do so would distress me. May God have your children and Jacques, my brother, in his keeping."

On the other sheet he had, after many spoiled papers, carefully copied out lines which he had composed to be sung to a well known tune belonging to a poem by the lord of Coucy.

Spring comes to flower on hills and vales,
And orchards blossom white as snow.

Winter within my soul prevails,
And naught but dole my heart can know,
Remote from her who makes my woe,
Banished, my heart is sick, and fails.

No hour nor day nor week goes by
Since love me in his bonds did bind,
But my heart's pain grows worse, and nigh
To burn my heart and slay my mind
No poison ever so unkind
As her serene and tranquil eye.

In a green field beside a stream
My eyes my fancy's freedom stole
I taste the sweetness of my pain
Will my heart ere again be whole?
She of my reason took her toll
I drank the potion of Brangaine.

For I love her who reason in me slew
More ere than Tristram loved Iseult the queen
Paris the lovely Helen and I ween
Aeneas loved the noble Dido true.

This song, ending with so unfortunate a line, had been composed by Haguenier in a state of exaltation of which he would not have believed himself capable, for his sickness had delivered him up to Marie more completely than he had wished or expected. To the extent that he was still too weak to control his thoughts, his imagination fed upon visions so marvellously beautiful as to be almost frightening in their intensity: it was as if he was only now discovering the quality of Marie's beauty. In her presence he had been awkward, over-anxious not to displease, distressed by her coolness. But now she was far away and out of reach, the barriers were down and he could give free rein to his madness.

Nothing now prevented him from dwelling at length upon her slender, creamy neck as he had seen it in the golden light of the awning

above her head, her large, blue-grey eyes flecked with emerald between
the delicate rosy lids, a little swollen, the small, dreaming mouth, the
pale light which the fine locks of her golden hair cast upon her face,
which changed color so easily and was radiant with a gentle warmth and
soft to the touch like some great flower; but what flower ever had eyes,
and eyes so bright and of a shape so pure that no jeweller could ever
have cut such perfect gems nor set them so perfectly as her eyes were
set between brown-lashed lids.

Never had Haguenier dared so much when he was in good health, for
now he imagined himself kissing each eyelash lingeringly, and the corners of her eyes and the delicate skin of her lips piece by piece, and the
hollow of the hand from which he had drunk, and the pulse of her
wrists. Nor could he grow tired, for he thought: "It is only a dream—
again and there again I press my lips to her eyes, gently, lest I hurt her,
then there between her eyebrows, then to her nostril, then there again,
to the corner of her mouth, and then no more." But then he wanted to
kiss her throat and the hollow of her throat, and then he dreamed of her
stretched by his side, gentle and loving, her eyes bright with tenderness, and he told himself:

"So that is what she is like. I did not know her. She is like that but
she wants to prove me." He tried to persuade himself that this was true
Would it dishonor her to love him, Haguenier? Perhaps he did not
amount to much, yet he, too, had a soul made by God and he knew
that if she loved him she would become, for him, even better and
nobler and purer. Had she not allowed him to kiss her? Had she not
come to him, that night, in the garden?

Sometimes he thought that he held her in his hands, minute and
fragile like a delicately wrought reliquary. What vessel could be more
beautiful than her body to contain the thing of wonder that her soul
must be? She seemed to him so young and so pure, so gently bred and
remote from the harshness and ugliness of life. If she wanted him, he
would ask her to be his only once, a single time—yet no, for after all
why? Not once, but always; and he would be faithful to her all his life.

Thus it was that Haguenier got better of his illness and rose, literally
sick with love and perceiving that all the songs of love and all that poets
had written of it were not vain words.

Nevertheless it seemed to him that he was failing in good sense and
he no longer dared give free rein to his reveries. All that he had formerly
read and learned now came back to him with a new force of meaning

and he experienced a brotherly tenderness for Tristram and for Gawain and for Lancelot of the Lake, imagining their beloved ones very like Marie; every love song he knew rang in his heart, each word taking on a magic sense, and he thought: "So this is what they meant!" and was astonished that these strangers had understood his own love so well. His heart was now so open that each word, each note of music penetrated and transfixed it. He wanted to talk to people, to animals, to the very walls of his room, and always of his love for Marie.

Yet when he was again strong enough to set out and realized that only two weeks of travelling separated him from Marie, he had a moment of sadness and hesitation. It was not without melancholy that he took his leave of the lady Marguerite of Figeac and the pretty Agnès. His heart informed him that there would be no more peace for him and that never again would he know those intoxicating dreams which had made a madman of him. After the courteous indifference of those two charming women, his hostesses, hard indeed would seem his father's welcome, money troubles, Ernaut's tortured expression, and Marie's incomprehensible whims.

> *My heart is sick with mortal wound*
> *Which no physician can defy,*
> *Love at her mercy leaves me bound,*
> *A thousand deaths she makes me die.*
> *Remote, recalling her, I sigh,*
> *Then how her presence shall I bear?*
> *Medusa she, Death in her eye,*
> *Yet Venus' lovely face doth wear,*
> *And chaste Diana's courage bear,*
> *And all that I may die.*

> *Never a work so fine and pure*
> *By Nature wrought, by Heaven blessed,*
> *Never a heart so hard, for sure,*
> *Beat in so soft and sweet a breast.*
> *Why by this love am I oppressed*
> *Although her glance my life deny!*
> *The poison in her eyes arrest*

My heart. Ah, that I yet may lie
Within her arms, and in her eye
Find mercy for my heart obsessed.

OBSTACLES

Dusty, travel-stained, exhausted by his journey and with his clothes drenched by rain, Haguenier presented himself at the door of Mongenost castle and asked to be received by the lady of Mongenost. Such was his impatience that he was beside himself and incapable of being sensible. "In any case," he told himself, "I should not be any handsomer for new clothes and she will not love me any the better for finery." Her husband was away hunting and the lady was reading, near to the fire, in her small, well-heated room. Her damsels were embroidering a stole. Haguenier, admitted to pay his respects, came in, lowering his head to avoid knocking it against the top of the low doorway. Marie sat up, put aside the lectern on which her book was placed and held out her hand to the visitor.

It was strange but he did not at first recognize her. She did not seem particularly beautiful in her dress of brown wool, her hair hidden by a coif, her face pale and her nose swollen by a cold. She appeared tired and sad, and, offering Haguenier a seat beside her, hugged herself into her cape.

"I have heard a great deal of your prowess," she said. "Your sister speaks of nothing else." She smiled kindly but Haguenier received the impression that Aielot's chatter had bored her.

"My sister, lady, is too kind, and you too good. I have done nothing worthy of praise." He did not quite know what to say and stared at her slender, beringed fingers grasping the cape about her shoulders. He thought: "She is cold," and the thought filled him with tenderness and desire.

He had been almost afraid that he would be stricken out of his senses

when he set eyes on his lady, but now Love, by a subtle ruse, was showing her to him stripped of her radiance, humbled and frail in her body;
so fragile, so delicate, simply a woman anxious to make herself pleasant
to a visitor. When he raised his eyes to the face which, in his day-
dreaming, he had tirelessly covered with kisses, he found it more touching than he had ever imagined it—so close to him, warm, a little moist
and reddened by the fire; now he no longer felt the fear and respect
with which she had formerly inspired him but only a mad desire to
take her in his arms, warm her, rock her like a child, stifle her with
caresses and speak over and over and over again all the tenderest words
—God knows why, at that particular moment the thing seemed to him
possible, and that in the very near future, and, indeed, inevitable.

Such was the gentle sweetness of this meeting that even Marie felt
herself invaded by the tenderness which radiated from her suitor's eyes.
Despite his travel-stained garments and his ill-shaven chin he was
radiantly handsome. He talked of indifferent matters, yet he had the
air of a man who has just taken Communion on an Easter Sunday.
Marie looked at him tenderly—how thin he had become, his eyes
grown larger, and his lids shadowed. To her he seemed to have about
him the aura of all the danger and toil of a crusade, he had passed
through the fire, he was a man, a warrior, and there could be no shame
in having a certain weakness for him.

Therefore she was charming to him. She did, however, reproach
him, with smiling and rather affected anger, for having likened her to
Dido and himself to Aeneas.

"I know, of course, that for poets the image or the rhyme are excuses
for every foolishness, but you should have realized that no lady would
wish to find herself in the situation of the unhappy Dido."

"Forgive me, lady," Haguenier said, smiling, "that was a mistake,
but do not forget that I wrote that I loved my lady *more* than Aeneas
loved Dido."

Marie burst out laughing.

"What a poor excuse! Anyone can see that you got your education
in Normandy. But peace! I forgive you, on condition, however, that
you write me a better song than the first one."

"I have one here, in my sleeve," he said. "I don't know that it is any
better but there is nothing about Dido."

"Give it to me and let us see."

Marie ran her eye down the parchment and frowned.

"No better, or hardly. Your lady, unless she be a woman without modesty, cannot be glad to find herself compared with Medusa, Venus and Diana, heathen goddesses and creatures of the Devil. Certain vulgar minstrels like writing that sort of thing to give an impression of learning but no well-born lady can allow herself to accept such songs."

When Haguenier rose to take leave, Marie suddenly became cold and curt and would not even give him her hand to kiss. He left her, sad and anxious, torn between his wish to return and ask the lady the reason for her coolness and his fear of angering her. He no longer saw where he was going, no longer dwelt upon his coming meeting with Aielot; his heart was like a heavy stone and his head like a clapperless bell. He knew that he would not have another moment's peace until he saw Marie again.

At his sister's he learned that his wife was four months gone in pregnancy and that Herbert was impatiently awaiting the birth of a grandson. Herbert himself was at Troyes; his brother-in-law, the sire of Buchie, had just died and Herbert, as uncle of the heir, wished to make sure of the guardianship, so that Haguenier was obliged to go and pay his respects to his father.

Herbert had lost weight and was dressed more elaborately than ever. His eyes were bright and he looked young. He seemed pleased to see his son and embraced him with simplicity.

"So!" he said. "So that's how you defend the honor of our name, son of a bitch! You deliver one stroke of your lance and fall ill for two months. You won't get far at that rate!"

His tone was bantering but nevertheless Haguenier was hurt.

"It can happen to anyone to be wounded," he said.

Herbert tapped him on the chest.

"There," he said. "Wounded—no, but it's the heart that's not up to the work. Pierre told me it was your heart. A bad business. If only your sister were a man, you could have taken your ease in a monastery. However, I hope that your wife will soon be giving me a grandson and I'm still young enough to live to see him grow up."

"To hear you speak," his son said, with rather a lop-sided smile, "one would think you had already buried me."

"God forbid! A fine lad like you! I shall keep you well in hand now and see that you don't get up to too much mischief. You're coming back to Linnières with me and I shall see that you don't spend all your time on horseback, backwards and forwards between Troyes and Mongenost."

Haguenier was so surprised to hear his father mention that name that he turned very red, which made his father laugh.

"Do you think I know nothing? The woman is beautiful, in fact very beautiful; I know what I'm talking about. But to succeed in sleeping with her you'd have to be different from what you are. That kind of woman does not want good looks and fine manners; a man like myself could get her easier than you. She'll just make you write her songs and look handsome, like a trained dog. Come, I'll find you a pretty little slut instead and you can bring her to Linnières."

Haguenier said:

"Thank you, I don't need that. And don't forget I'm of age and can go where I like."

"Very well, but you can't play the knight without money. You've spent your wife's whole income for two years and you've nothing left."

Haguenier asked his sister to lend him some money but she could promise him nothing before All Saints' Day.

"Jacques will receive what's due to him for the Païens bridge tolls then, and he'll be only too glad to lend you a part of it, for he's a great admirer of the lady of Mongenost. But until then we shall not even have enough to buy candles for Sunday mass. And then in any case you must go and see your wife; I am sure she knows a trick or two, and she is on excellent terms with the Chaource money-lenders."

Once again Haguenier crossed the Seine but this time only found the master of the castle at Mongenost. He had returned from hunting and was supervising the dressing of skins in the courtyard. Haguenier was forced to show an interest in the magnificent pelts of stag and fox which Mongenost complacently displayed. He left in very low spirits. Mongenost had told him that the lady was in bed and wished to be excused for not receiving him.

"So that's her master," the young man thought, boarding the ferry again. "It is no joking matter to be in love with a married woman. Whatever they may say, it's better to give your heart to a maid than a matron. I could never be resigned to the idea that that man can take her in his arms and caress her as much as he likes. And yet resign myself I must."

Mongenost might be about forty but he was not an ugly or disagreeable man; he was tall, lean, bore himself proudly, and wore a black beard well cared for and cut to frame his face. But surely it was against nature to marry so young a woman to a man older than Haguenier's father. He thought—"and she's already been married eight years." He tried to imagine what the relationship between Marie and that man could be, but he did not succeed.

He made the journey to Linnières in Herbert's company. Herbert was in a very good humor. He had just been awarded the guardianship of his young nephew, Garnier of Buchie.

"Which means," he said, "that I control Buchie, Bercenay, Hervi and Linnières, and Puiseaux is as good as dependent on me, since Joceran will be only too glad for me to have his roads repaired and protect his farms; so that I control all the roads skirting Othe forest. I am in negotiations with a captain of Swiss archers who is to put himself at my disposal from Christmas time, with one hundred unmounted men, twenty of them crossbowmen."

"What," Haguenier said, "then you're planning for war?"

"I don't know, son. It is certainly quite possible that there will be war soon, against your friends the English. It's possible we may be ordered to Île-de-France or even further afield. But God keep us from that for the time being, it would cost me more money than your knighting. Here is my idea: I am going to build a road by way of Puiseaux and Hervi and across Linnières forest and so down to Tonnerre, perfectly straight, and for people coming from Bar and from Chaource and Saint-Florentin it will be the best and shortest; it will be guarded by my archers. You'll soon see the big merchants from Burgundy and the south using it. In one year I shall get back the cost of construction in tolls."

"Oh, come, what about the count's toll-holders? They won't let you."

"It's clear you don't know me. I shall buy them all up and recover the cost from the merchants."

Herbert explained his projects for the next ten years to his son; he was going to build a church next to the castle, and fortify Hervi. Then, he was sure, all the surrounding nobility would send their sons into his service and would want to hold their land from him. Moreover, he was going to make a contract with the commune of Chaource, whereby he would furnish them with soldiers and in return would get the town's builders and masons cheaply. He was about carving himself a fief which would be among the most considerable in the country.

"If you have a son," he said, "I shall contrive to betroth him to the viscount of Bar-sur-Aube's daughter; she is three or four years old, I believe. We can celebrate the betrothal at Easter and I think I can see to it that her father will not dare break the engagement. In that case we shall hold half the Troyes lands in Bar-sur-Aube."

"Very well," Haguenier said, smiling. "And what if I have a daughter?"

Herbert flushed with irritation.

"Don't say it, don't speak of it, son of a bitch! It's a son I need, my plans are all made. In any case, all the midwives are agreed it will be a boy."

Haguenier asked his father for news of Ernaut and learned that his brother had set out for Rome to ask for a dispensation for his marriage with Ida of Puiseaux.

"At last!" Haguenier cried, joyfully. "So Joceran has consented?"

Herbert, looking embarrassed, frowned. "That's just it, it's not as simple as you think. What he said was: 'Let him get the dispensation, then we'll think about it.' I got him to sign a request in form for the marriage, but afterwards he denied it before witnesses, saying that he wished to leave his daughter free to make her own choice. All that he has promised is not to betroth his daughter to anyone else before Ernaut returns. Otherwise Ernaut would never have gone."

Haguenier went at once to Villemor, to visit his wife. She was in her bed, sewing swaddling clothes. She welcomed her husband with a tired smile; she was thinner, her nose was longer than ever and her brown face discolored by blotches.

"You have heard the good news from your father? He's growing thin with impatience."

There was a mocking gleam in her eyes. Haguenier wished her a happy delivery.

"Many thanks. You're very courteous. You will be good enough to excuse me for not receiving you in a proper manner myself, but I feel really tired. I think I am getting too old for this trade."

Isabeau bore her pregnancy very badly. She was unwell, and was becoming nervous and short-tempered and seemed no longer to have any affection for her husband. As for Herbert, she loathed him. She was afraid of dying in childbirth and regretted having allowed herself to be married. However, she made an effort and tried to be agreeable to Haguenier. He stayed with her for a week, at the end of which they were quite good friends again. Haguenier played draughts and chess with his wife and even at dice, Isabeau being a great gambler and winning throw after throw; Haguenier ended by losing far more than he could pay and Isabeau waived the debt.

"If I have a son," she said, "you shall pay me; if not, you'll have so many troubles that you will have every right to say that you owe me nothing." And she smiled her weary, mirthless smile.

THE INHERITANCE

Towards Christmas the lady Isabeau was prematurely brought to bed of a daughter who was christened Marguerite.

Herbert had assembled the whole family for the event and the dowager lady of Linnières, assisted by midwives, attended the mother. Haguenier had gone off to hunt wolves, for he could not bear the frightful cries coming from the women's quarters and filling the whole house. Isabeau's sufferings were so terrible that they several times gave her opium to put her to sleep. Her labor lasted twenty-four hours.

Herbert walked up and down the dining hall, emptying cup after cup of wine. When the cries ended there was suddenly such a silence that the lady was thought to be dead. Then the old lady of Linnières entered the hall, sweating, her handsome face still distorted by anguish.

"All is well, Herbert, thank God," she said to her son. "She is delivered of the child and no longer in danger."

"The devil take her," Herbert shouted. "I know what you mean: the child is dead."

"It is the most beautiful child I have seen, Herbert. But it is a girl."

"The bitch! The whore! She'd have done better to die."

He ordered his horse saddled at once and left for Linnières, to the great indignation of the lady's two brothers-in-law, who had come to Villemor with their wives.

Returning from his hunting Haguenier heard the news and ran up to his wife's room. Because of the pity which he had felt for her pain his heart was full of a poignant tenderness for her. He had not imagined that a human being could suffer so. And a woman! Perhaps Marie would have suffered as much had she borne a child. For him, every woman was Marie's sister.

Long and thin the lady lay, her face looking darker than ever against the white pillows. Her voice was weak and hoarse.

"It's over," she said, "there'll never be another child for me. Mother-in-law, give her to me."

The old lady put the swaddled white doll into her arms and Isabeau turned her head with an effort, squinting to see the child's face. Rather intimidated, Haguenier drew near. The child was the prettiest thing he had ever seen; her face was small as a flower, rose-pink and white, with enormous dark eyes, the tiny pink mouth a little swollen. Never had a newly-born child been so beautiful. Beside Isabeau's dark brown, almost masculine, head the baby seemed like a bud of apple blossom growing on a gnarled old tree.

"How happy you must be, lady," Haguenier said, "to have so beautiful a child. Such beauty is a real miracle."

Isabeau smiled gratefully, then closed her eyes again and turned away. Her lips drew together.

"Your father affronted me by leaving my house when he learned I had borne a daughter. I shall never forgive him."

"Lady, put it out of your mind, I shall manage to reconcile him, it was simply that he was so angry that it was not a son. But when he sees how lovely she is he will come and ask your pardon himself."

At that moment Haguenier felt well disposed to everyone but when, on the following day, he went to Linnières, he realized that things would not be so easy to arrange. Herbert was striding up and down the courtyard, swearing and kicking the dogs which got in his way. Seeing his son arrive, he shouted:

"Son of a whore! So that's the best you can do! A girl!"

"Father," Haguenier said, suppressing a smile with difficulty, "I swear it was not my fault."

"Nor is it your fault if you're nothing but some servant's bastard!"

Herbert was picking up lumps of earth and stones and hurling them
furiously on the ground. But seeing Haguenier about to remount his
horse, he calmed himself a little and said:

"Come with me. I have something to say to you."

He led him to the stables and said:

"I have been thinking during the night. I am going to give you the
chance to see your lady and as much money as you want. You will go to
Troyes, see the clerks at the bishopric and make your request for the
annulment of the marriage. You can say that your wife is barren and
that you need sons, being my only male heir. Between now and the
spring the thing can be done, and you can marry Ermessan of Rumilli;
her only brother died this summer, she has only one sister and they will
share the whole domain between them. She's already a grown girl and
can give you children at once."

Haguenier drew his father's attention to the fact that it would be
rather difficult to repudiate a wife for barrenness when she had just
been brought to bed of a child.

"That's not important. Given her age and the difficult confinement
she had, it's certain she can have no more children. We'll bring our
proofs afterwards; meanwhile, get the request in."

"I don't like the idea," Haguenier said, "furthermore I don't know
if my wife will agree."

"Her! Why the devil should she agree? But do you suppose I'll let
you trail round after any old hag with a lust for your white skin?"

"That will do," Haguenier said. "Do not speak of her in such terms.
She is my wife."

Herbert looked him up and down with surprise.

"Your wife, son of a bitch? And who made you marry that wife, eh?"

"Since it was you who chose her, that's another reason not to speak
ill of her."

"Rubbish! I've had time to change my mind twenty times since
then. How was I to know that young Garin of Rumilli would break his
neck before Saint-John? Ermessan will have half the land, the part
which marches with Chaource, which exactly suits my plans. Before
spring, I want you free."

"I shall not do it unless the lady Isabeau asks me herself."

"And if I order you to?"

"I shall not obey you."

Herbert raised his hand to strike his son, then thought better of it.

"You've time to reflect on it. I shall have the request sent in, in your name, by my clerk. I shall count on having your consent when it comes to signing the act."

"Do as you please," said Haguenier, shrugging his shoulders, "but you know quite well that nobody has ever been able to divorce a man who is of age against his will."

"Much more than that's been done, don't worry. When it's a question of family interest a man has no right to please himself. Now go up and greet your stepmother and your sisters. We'll speak of this again later."

After the siesta, Herbert sent for his son to come to the bath- and sweating-rooms, where he passed a good third of his time. The whole household made fun of le Gros's mania for constantly washing himself, saying that no doubt he felt the need to wash away his sins. Haguenier found him reclining on cushions with Ortrud busy perfuming his hair, which she then arranged in fat curls about his forehead. She had a tamed blackbird on her shoulder, and from time to time turned her head and gave it a little kiss. Haguenier admired the animal grace of her half-naked shoulders, and her fair hair, gathered at her back like a cascade of chains and rings of gold.

"And it's that man there," he thought, "who owns all that beauty. And why? Because he bought it as one buys a horse."

"My son," Herbert said, "I believe you to be a good son and I shall do nothing to cross you provided that you obey me. You saw for yourself that I equipped you like the son of a count. Nor did you disgrace me, I must admit that; you made it clear that you are as brave as the next man. Next spring, when you go to the countess's court, you shall have the means to live well and enjoy yourself."

"It would be no more than my due, since you hold my lands," Haguenier said, "but you will not get me to repudiate my wife that way."

"Your due! I paid a heavy enough price to enjoy it. We will speak of your divorce another time, and I may tell you that Ermessan of Rumilli is a very beautiful girl. If your health was good I should not be in such a hurry. But you must understand that I have not put myself to such trouble in order that the fief should descend by the distaff side. Hervi was half in ruins when your grandfather died. The fields of wheat which you have seen were going back to forest land, there had been nothing but brambles and nettles since the year of the smallpox, when I was still in the Holy Land. And you talk of your lands! Do you know how I won that land of yours? As true as I live I'm taken for a bad man and my father for a good one. But I am a better father to you than he was to me. *I* did not want to marry your mother, not me. I was fifteen and they forced me to. My father beat me until I nearly died of it—and why? I was a child, I had been seduced, more or less ravished in fact, by my lord's wife. I was not like Joseph, it's true. For that my father treated me as if I were a mangy cur; he nearly killed me; then he forced me to marry your mother, exactly as you give to the first comer a girl who's thrown away her virginity. It was only by chance that your mother's brothers died on crusade and I inherited everything. But I should just as soon not have been married in that style."

"Don't talk of my mother," Haguenier said, somberly.

"I'll talk of what I like. When I was your age I had to stay here, in this castle, biting my nails, with no amusement but hunting wolves. And all because my father was squandering the little that remained to us on trumpery for his mistress, while I had not even a mailed jerkin in decent condition. If I did not leave the country then it was because I knew that the Hervi land would come to me, and Linnières too, and I did not want to throw them away. I spent my youth in waiting. For these lands I spoiled my whole life, my lad."

"It seems to me you don't lead too bad a life," Haguenier said.

"Eh, son," Herbert, that day in sentimental mood, replied. "We say that and it's soon said. I love women more than a Christian should; well, that's my nature. I'm no happier for that. My father did not care for them and was faithful to my mother—excepting the Nangi affair and that was more the girl's fault than his—and he was no happier for that, either. I had a brother who died in the Holy Land and I have very often regretted that it was not I who died instead. He—my father loved him more than everything else besides. But nobody loved me. You can judge for yourself; you are my son, you ought to love me, and I know perfectly well that you loathe me."

Haguenier thought that his father must have drunk too much to say such things, but still he was touched.

"You are wrong to think so," he said. "I have never wished you any ill, only I don't want you to make me do anything dishonorable."

"You will do whatever I wish," Herbert said, with an air of weariness. "But I tell you this, in spite of everything I am very fond of you." Then, turning towards Ortrud, he slapped her thigh.

"Well, my two blackbirds, finished chattering together?" Ortrud gave her little throaty laugh, both capricious and excited, and resumed the combing of her master's hair. And once again Haguenier felt his heart contract, as he saw how young and how pretty she was.

He left his father after obtaining his promise to come to the child's christening. After an interview with his father Haguenier always found his mind dull and his thoughts vague, as if he were leaving a place of ill-fame. He did not loathe the man; he found him exhausting.

Back at his house he had to busy himself with preparations for the christening feast; the lady Isabeau was determined to make a great show before all their kinsfolk so that it was necessary to borrow money. All day long the wives of the petty nobility and farmers of the vicinity were arriving to admire the little girl, and they had to be received, offered refreshment and have room found for them. The little Marguerite, decked in embroidery and laid on her wet-nurse's knees, looked like a small reliquary, and her eyes were so lively that she seemed to understand everything. Haguenier could not have enough of looking at her.

On the day of the christening he promised Dame Isabeau to place the management of all the child's inheritance in her hand, should he die before her. Isabeau once again told him that she would never have another child but showed no wish for a divorce; in due course, therefore, Hervi must go, intact, to the little Marguerite.

MARIE: PORTRAITS

THE lady of Mongenost spent the long autumn evenings reading beside the fire and supervising the embroidery of a stole for the priest of the convent where her sister was a nun. She did little embroidery herself but her taste was good and she kept a close eye on the work,

choosing the colors and adding new elements to the design of crosses
and birds drawn on the silk. The work made slow progress but it was so
beautiful that all the ladies who came to see her, and Mongenost
himself, were not sparing of praise for the lady's art. Gold thread and
blue silk were worked together in such a fashion that not even a peacock's tail could be more radiant, and Marie caused edging of purple
and periwinkle blue to be worked into the design, and *appliqué* crosses
of white satin.

Marie put her whole heart into it, less for the love of God than
because of her taste for beautiful things. That autumn her mood was a
sad one and books no longer distracted her; it was necessary that the
stole should be perfect in beauty, so that she might look at it and not
think of anything else. "No beauty endures," she thought, "but the
beauty which one has in one's heart." And she tried to put into the
work all the beauty which might have sung in her heart, thinking:
"It will be consecrated to God, and will glow before the altar of the
Lord and will be used for the Most Holy Sacrament." But then her
thoughts would turn again towards something which was becoming a
torment and a shame to her: she believed herself in love with a man,
and a man who had not yet sufficiently deserved her love.

She did not wish to be blind to the facts; the lady of Pouilli's brother
had not yet done very much to win her. Henri of Bar was greatly his
superior in military prowess and in nobility and fine manners. Since
she did not love Henri of Bar, much less ought she to love Haguenier of
Linnières. He could write songs, but there was no lack of rhymers in
Troyes, even among the knights. The young man was heir to quite a
large domain, but was under the control of a father who was still young.
And he was married and had a child, which Marie considered a little
ridiculous and even humiliating for her. Moreover the father was
known for his irregular life and it might be like father, like son. In
short, she found so much fault with her official suitor that she was almost inclined to encourage Henri of Bar. "Can love tame a heart against
the will?" she wondered. "I should be ashamed, I who have always
been so proud, to give my heart to a man of little worth and no renown
simply because he is young and handsome. It would be behaving like
those ladies who, at the end of their maturity and on the threshold of
age, forget their pride and make do with what they can get. I am at
least four or five years older than he is; it's a great deal."

When she knelt in prayer before the image of the Virgin, she prom-

ised and swore never to love any man but with a pure and chaste love.
"If ever," she assured herself, "if ever I give my heart it will not be like
Iseult, Helen or Queen Guinevere, who brought shame upon their line;
I want to love without shame or remorse and to be proud of myself and
my love. Never shall any man be able to say that he treated me as his
strumpet."

Her relations with Foulque of Mongenost involved, for her, a painful
and shameful duty, and she was not inclined to mortify herself by
similar exercises with any other man; the more she loved a man, she
thought, the less inclination would she feel to yield to him.

From time to time she met Haguenier in Troyes or at Pouilli and
never failed to make clear that he had done nothing to deserve her. For
she thought:

"If he becomes discouraged at least I shall see that his love does not
amount to much."

He urged and begged her so earnestly to put him to the proof that at
last she said:

"Very well, fair friend, if you succeed in vanquishing and over-
throwing the count of Bar, I will yield you all my friendship."

It happened that Henri of Bar was then at Troyes, doing duty as
steward of the meats at the countess's table. Haguenier went the same
day to throw down his gauntlet, and the next day they met, on horseback, in the court before the castle. All the ladies had crowded to the
windows, admiring the young man's boldness. Naturally Haguenier
was beaten and, indeed, rather badly wounded in the leg. Henri of Bar,
knowing that he was dealing with a rival, treated him rudely, imposing
a ransom of ten marks and taking his horse and his hauberk. Herbert
refused to pay for his son, saying:

"He deserves a sharp lesson for his folly." And Haguenier had to
spend three months as a prisoner in one of the count of Bar's castles. It
was Jacques of Pouilli who undertook to raise the ransom money by
springtime.

Haguenier was mortally bored, for because of his wound he could not
even hunt. His only company was that of an old gentleman, the count's
squire and keeper of the manor. Henri of Bar came several times to
visit his prisoner and inquire after his wound. He was a strange creature; either love really had driven him mad or he had been mad already.

He never stopped talking, drank a great deal, and tried to get his guest drunk to make him talk. Sometimes he would drop his head in his hands and weep.

"The devil," he said, "created woman for our damnation. And I say this to you as to a brother, for we are brothers in misfortune. You see to what she has brought me. You must despise me for treating you as I did, since I am rich and honor required me to let you go without ransom. For you came against me in order to deserve your lady, who is mine also. I should have let you go and given you back your arms; but my feeling is too strong for me. I am so jealous that I would have imprisoned you for life if I could. And yet I am wrong to be jealous, I know it, for you'll have no more joy of her than I have had, she is a hard and perfidious woman who will never love anyone and will only make us a laughing-stock. And I should really be sorry for you and treat you as a friend. But my jealousy is stronger than my reason."

He proposed a bargain to Haguenier: he would waive the ransom if Haguenier would promise to give up all claim to the lady. Then he began talking of Marie again, and of all the sacrifices he had made for her.

After the count's visits Haguenier felt depressed; the man's exaltation infected him like a disease and his desire for Marie grew sharper and keener. He was tempted a hundred times to break his parole and make his way to Troyes to see Marie, if only from afar; only the fear of public obloquy kept him back. "Yet what matter, what can it matter? In any case I have lost her good opinion by my defeat and what does the opinion of the rest matter to me?" Yet he stayed, telling himself that it was really Marie who kept him there a prisoner, since it was her order which had made him fight. And as he now told himself that she would never have anything to do with him he allowed himself to think of her all the more, being no longer restrained by the respect due to realities. "The calm light of her eyes is deadly poison," he thought, seeing her again as she had been that last time, the day she had issued her cruel order—beautifully dressed and adorned, her face lucent with pale rose light. Thus she was—would be—when he would bear her off to some solitary tower, higher than Saint-Pierre's steeples, and see her at last unclothed, a radiant whiteness like a statue of alabaster lit from within; there he would say to her: "Lady, I want nothing from you who are at once my friend and my enemy, my life and death. I am not worthy to serve you, but only touch my heart with your naked foot and my heart will be burned as by a red-hot iron and I shall die. But if you will not do so, then let me look and look upon your beauty until my eyes are burned as by too strong a light, and then, blinded, I shall fall from this tower into the void. For I know that you are made to be no man's friend, you are a fairy and your body was formed of pink pearl and morning dew and set in the cradle beside your mother by Morgan the Fay. It is certain that Mongenost does not possess your body but only keeps you prisoner, else would he have been dead long since. But as for me, I desire to possess you and to die of it. Only tell me by what means to deserve you."

And he spent his time composing letters and songs, each more delirious than the others, but he committed none of them to paper.

FERRET HEART

Six weeks after Christmas Ernaut returned from his journey to Rome carrying his dispensation in a sealed box; learning that his brother was a prisoner, he hastened to visit him. Haguenier was so happy in his brother's joy that for a while he forgot his own troubles.

Despite a dark wind tan, Ernaut was now very handsome. He had even grown rather stout, his hair did not seem so straight, and his nose not so large. Yet he said that his life, for four months past, had been a hell, and he had lived on the free meals provided for beggars in the hostels for poor pilgrims. But nothing mattered since he had finally got what he wanted.

"You shall be my groomsman," he said, forgetting that his brother was married. "You will go with our father to ask for her hand formally. We shall soon see whether the swine will dare refuse when he sees the pope's letter."

Herbert himself went to Puiseaux, ostensibly to deal with a matter of some forage. But Joceran already knew what his visitor had really come for. The two cousins sat down on a seat beside the fire and Herbert twisted the rings on his fingers, a little thinner than they had been.

"You are well aware, fair cousin," he said, "of what I wish to say to you." It was strange that Joceran, his poor kinsman and a man of little renown, was the only man with whom Herbert ever experienced a certain diffidence.

"Yes, I believe I do know, cousin, but you are also aware of my opinion on the subject."

"Listen," Herbert said, "when my mother dies Ernaut will be master of Bernon, and I shall also leave him, as a fief, the tower of Seuroi. On his marriage I shall give him twenty marks of silver, in cash, which he will pay as a gift to his wife at the church door. Ernaut is brave and of good repute. Nor am I, myself, a man to be disdained."

"Not the pope himself can make a sin any the less a sin, and so I must tell you," Joceran said, chewing at the inside of his cheek. "Incest is incest. I've no wish to damn myself nor my daughter."

"Fair cousin, you know quite well that your father and my mother were not of the same bed. We have but one grandparent in common." He began counting on his fingers and added: "When it's a case of one common ancestor out of fourteen, there's no question of incest."

"If you like, cousin, as you please. But a dispensation is not an order. And I should not want to force my daughter into it, either."

"Does a girl know what she wants? And where would she find a better husband? He's loved her for ten years, that's to say he will not change. That is what counts in marriage, cousin."

Joceran looked into the fire with a hard stare and did not answer, and then turned to Herbert and said:

"Once and for all, fair cousin, you are richer and more powerful than I am and of my lands you are more or less master. But not in my house."

"You know well," Herbert said, "that I have always respected you as the eldest of our blood. What I ask, I ask as a friend; there is no question of forcing you."

Joceran's smile was sour, as if to say: "That's the last straw." Herbert went on:

"Fair cousin, tell me what it is you want. I shall not be ungrateful. Your son shall be my senior squire; I will make a knight of him when he is old enough, I will help him to make his way. That is not to be despised."

"I thank you, cousin. But I prefer to speak my mind frankly and I hope that thereafter the matter can be dropped between us and we need think of it no more: I am not yet either so poor or so inconsiderable that I need give my only daughter to the son of a Bernon peasant girl."

The eyes of the two men met; Herbert was the first to turn away his head, so much cold cruelty did he see in Joceran's look. And he realized that he would give way and in spite of everything they would remain friends; and he also realized that Joceran was pronouncing Ernaut's death sentence and that it was this which gave him pleasure. He, Herbert, who had neither pity nor consideration for anyone, was face to face with this man from whom he had no advantage to expect, whom he did not love and who did not love him and who enjoyed doing him harm—and he felt that the bond uniting them would be all the stronger, for he was attracted by cruelty as others by goodness and he was vaguely aware that this little, meager man whom nobody feared was, perhaps, worse than himself.

He rose, slowly stretched himself.

"Good," he said. "I could remind you that dame Brune's, your wife's, grandfather, was blacksmith at Jeugni, that your mother was not born in wedlock and that a Bernon peasant girl also comes from Adam's rib. But as your reasons are only pretexts, no purpose is served by talking about them."

Joceran had turned white with rage as he always did when his mother was mentioned, for she had, indeed, had the worst possible reputation.

"You are, nevertheless, very good not to call me bastard to my face, cousin. I know that Ernaut so calls me, my daughter told me so."

"Ernaut is an imbecile if he did, and your daughter a slut to repeat it. Let's drop the whole subject, since it makes you so angry."

But Joceran was not to be appeased. He sought about for a revenge and could think of nothing to the purpose. At last he said:

"Yes, let's talk of something else—a service you can do me and gain something yourself at the same time. Could you tell me to whom you sold your Arab thoroughbred, the roan horse with blue eyes? There's a banker at Bar-sur-Aube who saw it two years ago in Troyes and can't sleep for wanting it. He'd buy it regardless of cost and he's promised me a good commission on the deal. I'd give you half."

Herbert bit his lip to suppress a smile, for this tale of the thoroughbred evoked memories which were, after all, by no means disagreeable.

"I thought you more closely in touch with parish gossip," he said. "And I did not know my servants were so discreet. Your banker is wasting his time; I killed the horse at least a year ago."

"He had some disease, then?"

"He was faultless. I think you must know the story as well as I do. But I'll tell you the whole truth if you like: I learned, in a dream, that the horse was bewitched and brought bad luck and misfortune. I killed him and went and threw his eyes into the Armançon."

"You're very superstitious, cousin."

"It's one of the disadvantages of the soldiering trade."

Herbert was angry enough with Joceran to permit himself that insolent answer—Joceran, owing to poor health, had never served as a soldier and therefore his family had lost consequence in the country. The blow went home, for Joceran had too many weak points not to be excessively touchy. He smiled viciously and said:

"Nevertheless, cousin, I should advise you, for my part, to avoid such extravagant conduct; you'll be accused of sorcery or God knows what. I suppose you know that you're already accused of using dia-bolical charms to seduce the damsels of the whole region?"

"Silly, idle tittle-tattle! I've never needed that kind of thing. And if I knew of any such charms my son would not have to come begging for your good graces today."

"The old fox," Herbert was thinking. "He thinks he can frighten me with that old story. As if my mother would believe *him* if he went to her with his slanders. And he's certainly done worse himself. And, for all that, the thoroughbred was the finest animal I ever had in my stables—and I don't regret him." He seemed to see Eglantine as she was now, in a corner of the big room at Bernon, emaciated and dishev-elled, her eyes fixed for ever on some remote prospect. When she had seen him at Bernon, the first time after the business of her marriage, she had been ill and he had felt the old desire stir in him. He was a little regretful that he had broken with her so sharply. The adventure might have lasted a few months longer; he would have lost nothing by it. He had deprived himself of his last chance of passion for a whim—but still, after all, a little sooner or later, what did it matter? He would have got tired of it in any case.

Yet the sacrifice of his horse had not been for nothing; it would not have been necessary as a means to get him what he wanted, but he had done it willingly, with all his heart, as an offering to the girl's pride, to show her that the value he placed on her was not small; it had also been done for his own sake, to celebrate their union, the wedding of damned souls. Since his marriage to Aelis no woman had made him lose his head as Eglantine had done. And he was no longer young, it was not likely to happen again. Since even incest now seemed to him quite commonplace, in what could he find his future pleasure? He did not know. And he thought:

"Soon I must count myself among the elders. None too soon, perhaps; I've other things to do. But still, it's a pity. At least I can be satisfied that I put a proper end to that affair; the girl's done for; whether or not she still loves me, she's not ready to give me a successor."

To Joceran he said, finally:

"What is the use of our disputing, cousin? You know that I have not made you a bad kinsman. What could you have done had I carried off your daughter by force? If I don't do so it's not because I don't want to. But I've no wish to behave badly to you. I will ask you only one thing: to tell my son that you want to wait, that he must prove himself—in short, delay; I shall try to turn his attention elsewhere."

He managed to persuade Ernaut to leave and take service for a year with the baron of Chantemerle, over by Provins. Ernaut took the blow more calmly than Herbert had expected, but his face suddenly lost all its beauty and his eyes became dull and empty. He said to his father:

"I know that he desires my death, and he will get his wish. Understand that if you do not prevent him from marrying Ida to another man, you will share responsibility for my death."

Then he left for Provins and Herbert was not long in hearing that his son spent all his leisure time in brothels.

"Well, so much the better," the father thought, "it will make him get over this foolishness."

HAGUENIER: FIRST TRIAL.
THE OATH

HAGUENIER was set at liberty on the eve of Palm Sunday, Jacques of Pouilli having paid over the ransom to the count of Bar and himself, accompanied by Aielot, come to fetch his brother-in-law. It was a lovely spring day; the cherry trees were coming into flower, the fields were green or black and the woods still grey.

Aielot was wearing a dress of vivid green which made her almost white plaits look faintly pink. She amused herself by breaking off twigs from the cherry trees and weaving them into her horse's mane. Jacques of Pouilli told his brother-in-law about the Easter feasts which the countess was organizing. There were to be two great tournaments; first the chivalry of Reims would meet that of Troyes and thereafter the knights of Champagne those of Burgundy, for many renowned barons of Tonnerre and Dijon wished to measure themselves against Champagne's champions.

"There," Jacques said, "you will have a chance to take your revenge and gain the prize you hope for."

On Palm Sunday Haguenier was able to see Marie in Saint Peter's Church, among the ladies who attended on the countess. She was so different from all the others that he had no difficulty in following her through the crowd with his eyes, and he hung back by the court before the church so as to see her more closely as she passed. She came out with her branch of box leaves, which had been blessed, in her hand, talking gaily with a young woman dressed in mauve. She passed Haguenier without seeing him and he was almost glad of it. She had a scarf of blue muslin thrown over her hair, and Haguenier could see her profile and her chin, her long, slender neck and the amethyst jewel in her rosy ear.

He was able to talk to her in the countess's rooms, where the ladies of the court had organized a dance. She was dancing opposite Henri of Bar who, from a distance, looked very handsome. But when the dance was over the lady of Mongenost took Aielot by the hand and sat down with her on a seat near the window. Then Haguenier could approach her and bend his knee in greeting.

"Lord Knight," Marie said, "I am in your debt for I know that I caused you harm, although there is another at fault who did not treat you loyally. You may, therefore, ask something of me and I will undertake to grant it, if it be reasonable."

Haguenier answered:

"I have nothing to ask of you, lady, for you are nowise in my debt."

"You have done well to make me that answer," Marie said, "for I was putting you to the proof. It is true that I owe you nothing but, since you recognize that, and as we are on the eve of Our Lord's Passion, I want to give you a proof of my goodwill towards you. Tomorrow, after mass, I will receive you at my friend's, the lady of Chesley, in whose house I am staying."

During mass the following day, Haguenier was occupied with thoughts which had nothing to do with the Passion of the Saviour: he waited at the door of the church for the ladies of Mongenost and Chesley to come out and accompanied them to the house. They went up to a small, rather dark, richly carpeted room, with a window of small red and blue panes. The lady of Chesley seated herself on the bed, Marie in a large, high-backed chair.

"As you see, my friend," she said, when Haguenier was seated on a stool at her feet, "you were wrong in overestimating your abilities. It was for that reason I put you to such a proof, to teach you a lesson. For if it is not easy to overcome the count of Bar in jousting, how much more difficult it must be to vanquish the heart of a woman of honor. And yet you men think it can be done with words and songs and sighs. Were you to do battle with men with nothing but words and songs you would, very properly, be taken for a coward. Why, then, insult women by treating them as easier to vanquish than the first trooper you meet?"

"God forbid that I should ever have thought so!" Haguenier protested. "You judge me very wrongly. If I knew a way of winning your love—though it were to go and seek the Holy Grail—I would do it without hesitating."

"Meanwhile, nothing but words," Marie said, bitterly. "If you want to serve me, and if I accept your service, know that I shall submit you to harder and more painful trials than that stroke of the count of Bar's lance, to trials such as you do not expect and which may seem to you humiliating or annoying or ridiculous. I tell you, once and for all, I shall not accept your service unless you give me your word to submit to all my wishes whatever they may be, without an instant's discussion and without my promise of anything in exchange. In that case perhaps I may give you my love very soon, perhaps never. But if you will not give me your solemn promise to serve me unconditionally I shall not want ever to speak to you again."

"It is already done," Haguenier said, "for I have long been yours, unconditionally, but, if you wish it, I will swear to it now, upon the cross and my soul's salvation."

With her great, dreaming eyes Marie looked at him for a long time, and he was struck by the strange wisdom and motherly gravity of her look and the tender expression of her mouth. It seemed to him that this woman was infinitely his superior, that she must have a will of her own as incomprehensible as the will of God, and that she knew, better than himself, what was good for him and what bad. He thought she would order him to do nothing that was not for his good, since she was capable of wanting only what was good. He had now such confidence in her that it was almost a matter of indifference to him whether she gave him her love or not, for she embodied love, and each of her words and gestures was love.

Marie felt herself overwhelmed by the strange tenderness which this tall, grey-eyed lad inspired in her. It seemed to her a weakness, she was afraid of it and despised herself. "What of the trials I was to set him?" she thought. "May God refuse me salvation if I let myself be seduced by frivolous pleasures. As God is my witness, the more I love him, the harder will I be to him." And this resolution twisted her lips in a painful smile, for what joy there would be in harshness, knowing it was for love!

She said: "Friend, it is my wish to give you a week to reflect on it. Such oaths are not lightly taken. If I undertake to accept you as my vassal and to put you to the proof, it is not for a whim or out of vanity but to teach you to serve love, for that is a woman's duty. Think well on what you have said and make up your mind. If, after a week, you are still of the same mind, then God forbid that you should ever break your word; I should hold you coward and traitor."

That evening in the church, before the image of Saint Peter, Haguenier tried to concentrate his attention and prayed to the saint to enlighten him.

"Very well she knows that I shall not change my mind in a week," he thought, "and that I should look like a coward if I suddenly drew back in the face of her trials. No doubt she is thinking of things so profound and difficult that I should not be able to understand them. How, then, can I undertake to fulfill her conditions? Why, suppose she asks me, like Lancelot, to make myself ridiculous before the chivalry of the whole country, to play the coward in the lists, should I have the strength to do it? Especially since I have not a fine reputation to shield me? Well, so be it, I should do it, since I should not be dishonored in her eyes. Or suppose she asks me to go and live for three years in a cave and live on grass and not see her the whole time? I could not bear it, yet if I refused she would hate me, which would be even worse. And if I accept and after two months she came to see me and granted me her love? Or if, for example, she asks me to conspire against the count, betraying the faith I owe him? But she is surely too loyal to ask that of me. Even if she called on me to kill my father, I ought to obey, for at the last moment she would stop me and not let me do it. Whatever her demands, do I not know her to be too pure to wish me evil, for there is no evil in her?"

On Easter Monday, at the count's castle, in the presence of Aielot, the lady of Chesley, and two others of the countess's ladies-in-waiting, Haguenier solemnly swore fealty to the lady of Mongenost and received from her a ring set with amethysts to wear on the little finger of his left hand as a sign that now she was his lord and he her vassal.

Then Marie gave her new knight a mirror of polished steel the size of a plate set in a wide frame of engraved silver. She said: "It is my wish that henceforth you should bear no other shield but this in tournaments. If you succeed in vanquishing at least three knights without marring the steel, these ladies will award you the prize of your valor."

Aielot became very red but did not dare speak for the moment for fear of spoiling the solemnity of the occasion. Marie watched Haguenier's face avidly, thinking: "If he is distressed, then never will I love him." But Haguenier was no novice and knew that control over the expression is the first rule of good manners.

"I ask only one thing of you, lady," he said, turning his new shield towards her. "Look in this mirror, and for me your image will be for ever fixed in it; then I shall find strength to protect it and it will give me strength to conquer."

And Marie saw her own reflection before her—a little pale, the eyes enlarged by emotion, and it was so unexpected that it was as if she were seeing herself for the first time—the face seemed to be asking, "*What am I about? Where am I? What is this game in which you are involving me?*"

She thrust away the mirror and made an effort to smile.

THE BROKEN BODY

O N THE way back to the house where he was staying, Haguenier stopped at his armorer's to have a strong double strap fixed to the mirror for fastening it to his arm. The armorer was not particularly surprised; he had had a good deal to do with young men and their extravagant notions, but he said:

"It is a great pity. This is a very expensive article and at the first blow of a lance it will be shattered."

To which Haguenier said:

"I will wager my spurs that it will not receive the slightest scratch."

Nevertheless, he was not over-confident himself and spent the eve of the tournament having his body massaged and rubbed by Herbert's barber. Pierre and Ernaut, arrived in Troyes for the feasts, were also preparing for the tournament. They examined the mirror, turned it about, felt it, and shook their heads.

"Does she, at least, allow you to let the frame be damaged?" Pierre asked.

"I've no idea."

"Here's what you must do," Ernaut said. "You must try and manoeuvre to face the sun, use your mirror so that it reflects the sun on to your opponent and blinds him."

"I've already thought of that, but what about the rules?"

"Don't worry about them," Pierre said. "With a shield like this you're half disarmed; they won't be strict with you."

There was something which Haguenier had not dared admit to his brothers: he had sent his page to see Bernadine, a woman of Troyes who brewed all sorts of drugs and philters and was suspected of witchcraft. He had pawned his best cloak to pay the woman for a very strong cordial which was to set him up for the day's jousting. Bernardine did a brisker trade on the eve of tournaments than was generally realized, although the practice of taking such drugs was considered questionable and even impious and the cordial in question said to be a poison.

"It doesn't matter, provided I get through the day," Haguenier thought. "Afterwards—what will be, must be; but I must keep the mirror with my lady's image intact."

The tournament was the first of the year and the enclosure looked more like a fair-ground than a field of combat, so richly were posts and ropes and grandstands dressed with foliage and cherry branches in flower. The raised platforms were decorated with garlands of periwinkle and Easter daisies, and the damsels seated in the tribunes were weaving crowns of eglantine, cherry blossom, almond blossom and primroses in advance for the victors; they kept them fresh in jars of water. On boats moored along the banks of the Seine and decorated with flowers ladies of lesser rank, citizens' wives, and young people were preparing refreshments for both combatants and audience, singing as they worked to the music of rebecs.

In the enclosure, heralds cried the opening of the lists. As each knight rode by to enter the lists, the crowd, gathered on the river banks, commented on his equipment, the bright colors of his decorations, and the freshly painted lances which gleamed in the sunshine. Haguenier of Linnières's shield was certainly the brightest of all, but it was also the smallest and the subject of much comment in the grandstands. Veteran knights were saying that in their day a young man would not have behaved in such a manner, that it was nothing but drawing attention to oneself and was altogether too pretentious. The ladies about the countess knew all about the matter and many of them blamed Marie for what she had done; but the youngest said that she had behaved wisely, for how can love be recognized but by putting it to the proof?

Despite the fears of his father and his friends Haguenier succeeded in being among the victors in the tournament. He was lucky enough to

unhorse four knights from Reims, though not without having shivered
two lances and damaged his helmet and the left arm of his hauberk.
But no one could know what fortitude his victory had cost him. He
was even more grimly aware than he had been during his skirmish on
crusade that he must bear up, though he died afterwards. To begin
with, the cordial had given him uncommon speed and ardor, but at the
moment of hurling his second adversary out of the saddle he was near
fainting, as if something had suddenly broken in his chest. He could
still hear the heralds' cries, the shouts from the grandstands, and the
neighing of horses. But he could no longer see anything. He bit his lip
so hard that the skin broke and the blood welled out under his teeth;
his opponent's horse had been thrown back on its haunches, was slipping, unable to recover, while the man, stunned, still groped for his
lance. Haguenier pressed his lance against the other's chest and the
knight made a sign of surrender. The remainder of the tournament was
such torture for Haguenier that he no longer knew why he was fighting.
He was bleeding at the nose and mouth and the blood was not coming
only from his bitten lip. But once again he succeeded in surpassing the
limit of his strength, and he was not sustained by fear of dishonor nor
by the thought of the mirror he bore on his arm—for he could no
longer think of anything—but as if by the sense of an absolute and
categorical duty; it was as if his whole being, to the very marrow of his
bones, was aware that it was more important to overthrow two more
knights from Reims than to live.

He realized that his adversaries were trying to spare him and that he
must, therefore, press his attack with all the more determination to
force them to attack him properly. He received a blow on the head and
another on the left arm just above the shield but he remained firm in
the saddle and spurred his horse with such force that he made it
furious. The animal rode round the opposing horses and charged at
them, its mouth torn by the bit; it was an old stallion, well schooled and
afraid of nothing. The horse was so intelligent that he had quickly
realized that his rider was not very strong on his left side, and at each
charge he managed, by slight deviation towards the right, to enable
Haguenier to elude the lance aimed at the mirror of steel.

When the umpire had given the signal and the trumpets sounded
for the end of the jousting, Marie's mirror, although covered with dust,
was intact, and Haguenier wiped it clean with the end of the purple
scarf which decorated his helmet. And when he bowed before the

grandstand where the victorious knights received crowns of flowers from the ladies' hands he looked for Marie and turned the mirror towards her, wondering whether she could see herself in it. But she saw only the flash of sunlight which blinded her for a moment and made her put her hand up to cover her eyes. She passed the crown of eglantines to the countess's niece, who placed it on the knight's helmet. Haguenier could, by then, think of nothing but keeping in the saddle until he left the field, for his body's pain was already more than he could bear. Then the state of ecstatic ease and peace upon which he entered by way of pain penetrated to his thoughts and scattered them; he no longer thought of Marie nor of himself nor of his duty done; a wave as big as the universe swept his heart clear of love and pain and everything else.

When he opened his eyes again the first thing he saw was the large, badly shaven face of a middle-aged man; the thick, hard mouth and the eyes of too light a blue expressed so much anxiety that Haguenier was astonished, for the expression was out of place on that face—so out of place that he did not immediately recognize his father. But when he did recognize him he was moved, and tried to smile.

"Son of a bitch," Herbert said, but he could say no more and began to bite his lips.

Then Haguenier felt Aielot's too soft and perfumed cheeks against his own and felt his nose and mouth wet with her warm tears. This contact was disagreeable to him, tiring him so that he thought he was going to faint again. Strange, wordless songs were humming in his ears.

When he had recovered enough strength to speak he asked for his shield. Ernaut was sitting beside him and watching him with an air of sadness.

"A fine business!" he said. "I've kept it and put it in a safe place, but it cost me an effort to do it. You shall have it but I don't advise you to look at yourself in it. Father says there'll be no more jousting for you for two years."

"Bah! I'm of age. Not that I feel in any condition for great deeds at the moment. But it will get better."

"Please God. Father says you've been bewitched."

"Ernaut, friend, if you can do it will you go and see my lady for me? If, just once, she would walk past the window of the house—on her way to church, for vespers—or whenever she likes, without even stoping. Just go past the window."

"I'll do it," Ernaut said. And his fierce, determined expression made Haguenier suddenly realize that they must consider him very ill indeed, dying perhaps.

"Well, what does it matter, after all?" he asked himself. "One can only die once."

And when Ernaut had brought him Marie's shield, he was frightened by his own appearance; his face was blue and his nostrils swollen; there was a large black scab on his lower lip. His hands were also blue, but he had seen them like that before.

"And suppose I stay blue all my life," he thought, "that won't be very amusing. Still, I kept my word, and ought not to incur blame."

He was sick for a month; his heart finally recovered somewhat, but his complexion was still leaden with a tinge of violet, and there were pouches under his eyes. Moreover he had a large abscess in the armpit which caused him indescribable agony. Herbert came to see him quite often and was pleasanter than he had ever been, although he could not abstain from calling his son an idiot and a son of a bitch.

"You've got yourself involved for God knows how long with a woman who cares neither for your health nor your honor. If you managed to avoid making a fool of yourself at the tournament it was by the merest luck and you'd better be thanking God for it. Your sister has given a piece of her mind to that brainless chit, but you can never tell how far a woman's pride and vanity will take her."

"Don't talk of that, father. It is no one's business but mine."

"It's my business too, son of a bitch. Ernaut could talk like that, but not you. When you've got a son, then go and break your neck if you want to."

"You know my opinion about that," Haguenier said, "and you won't make me change it."

Marie had decided to remain in Troyes until Ascension and, by making a détour on her way to church, passed by the mansion where Herbert of Linnières was staying. Thus Haguenier saw her twice a day and lived for the sound of church bells ringing the services. Once Marie had even stopped, as if to adjust her shoes, and had raised her eyes apparently to look at the swallows' nests in the eaves. For a long time Haguenier retained the vision of her face, long, pure and pale, the eyes large and grave; it was thus that he now saw her in his dreams. He told himself: "I am not worthy of her, my body is too weak to make me a good servitor. But I will keep the promise I made her to the end, whatever she may require of me, for she did me the greatest honor she could when she did not treat me as a feeble creature to be spared and treated gently. Had she done that it would have been proof of contempt, not love."

Foulque of Mongenost had been greatly put out by his wife's latest fantasy. After Ascension he came to the lady of Chesley's house himself, to fetch Marie away to his castle.

"You do not seem able to distinguish between what is decent and honorable and what is not," he said. "While you accepted the homage of the others without involving yourself, I said nothing. But now you've accepted a man as your vassal, before witnesses, and set him a trial that the whole court is talking about; for I believe few people are ignorant of the fact that it was for you this lad fought without a shield. The least that can follow on all this is a lot of by no means pleasant gossip."

Marie said:

"There is no law which forbids a wife to receive a young knight's homage or put him to the proof. Many ladies have done so without losing consideration."

"If at least you had chosen a man of more renown and higher rank," Foulque said. "But this man does you no particular honor and people are likely to think you have fallen foolishly in love with him."

"Don't talk of love, foolish or wise," the lady said, with ill-humor, "for you know nothing about it. In the first place, if there had been any question of being madly in love I could have seen this man in secret and told nobody. There is no sin in a woman like me seeking the friendship of someone of my own age who shares my tastes. Is it my fault if I have little joy of you and that you like nothing I like? If I feel a pure and honorable love for this knight and want to help to instruct him in virtue and courtesy, what harm can that do you?"

"So ladies always say," Foulque replied, "but it is also said that that kind of friendship ends quite differently. It's all very fine for you to be thinking of nothing but virtue and courtesy; the man is always after something else."

"A man like you, perhaps," Marie said, disdainfully. "But there are men who know how to respect a woman."

"As to that, I don't believe a word of it. And in any case I do not care to hear your name associated with that of a man who has designs on my honor."

Marie looked him straight in the eyes.

"My friend," she said, "they say that it's a very bold man who relies on force to prevent a woman having her own way. Had I wanted to be unfaithful to you I should have had no difficulty in doing so. I swore on oath to you and before God never to yield my body to another man. Therefore, whatever happens, I shall not do so. But if you forbid me to see my friend openly, I shall do it secretly."

Foulque said:

"We shall see about that, we shall see about that," and closed the argument. But he determined to have his wife watched more closely than before.

Beautiful and delicate as she was, yet he did not love her. He was quite proud of having a wife who was so admired, courted by the count of Bar, the seneschal of Provins and by numerous young men of Troyes. But she was fifteen years younger than himself, cold, proud and capricious, and, on top of everything else, barren. Then her head was crammed with love romances as a result of which she thought that she had a profound knowledge of life. He did not pay her much attention, for she rather bored him, but now he began to feel a little jealous and to discover that, really, she was more beautiful and fresher than ever. After all, she was young and might well find herself seriously attracted to a young man.

As a measure of prudence he thought it as well to resume sharing his wife's room for a while. As a rule they had separate quarters, for Marie detested hunting, dogs, and her husband's table companions.

Dame Isabeau had come to Troyes when she learned of her husband's illness and had got him to make a formal will by the terms of which all property appertaining to the domain of Hervi would go to Marguerite and was to be managed by her mother. Herbert declared the will invalid and insisted that a family council must be called; Haguenier had no power to dispose of his property without his father's consent. Haguenier, very tired and suffering cruelly on account of his abscess, had not the heart to argue much, but steadily supported his wife. Since she had given him a child he had developed an almost admiring affection for her. At one time, when he was thought to be dying, the

child was brought in to receive his blessing, since when he asked for
her so often that the wet-nurse spent a good half of every day in the
sickroom. Marguerite, now more than three months old, had reached
the stage of smiling and warbling to herself, and her small fair head,
with pink cheeks and big round eyes, was so droll that Haguenier
laughed at each of the child's little grimaces. She smiled, stretched her
little neck, yawned, and rubbed her nose with a fist no bigger than a
nut. How so frail and nearly formless a being could be so graceful passed
Haguenier's understanding, and he wondered how the lady Isabeau had
contrived to make her.

"And after all," he thought, "it is better that I should have a
daughter, for I should not be a good model of chivalry for a son."

After Pentecost he was able to get up and Herbert, seeing no reason
to spare him any longer, told him:

"The request for repudiation has gone in long since but without you
I can do nothing. You must either write to the bishopric yourself or
go there with me."

And when Haguenier flatly refused, he said:

"Don't count on me to keep you or lend you money. And I shall
enter a complaint against you at the bishopric, since you're going
counter to the interests of your family."

Haguenier ordered his squire to get his effects together, mounted his
horse and went to stay with his sister at Pouilli. However hospitable
Jacques of Pouilli might be, Haguenier told himself that he could not
spend his life with him, but then—on the far bank of the Seine stood
the manor of Mongenost.

JOCERÁN AGAIN

For some months Herbert had been telling himself that he was
pursued by bad luck; Haguenier's two illnesses, the birth of a
girl where a boy was needed, Joceran's refusal, and other things less
important but which greatly displeased him. In the first place Archam-

baud of Ermele, Jacques of Pouilli's brother, had made several, very veiled, allusions to his daughter's conduct and Archambaud was not a man to jest. Herbert did not particularly blame his daughter; he thought it absurd that a woman's life should be forfeit for a fault in respect of which a man risked nothing whatsoever; but such was the custom, and he knew that Archambaud had the right to kill his sister-in-law without her father having any grounds for protest. Then he had had trouble with the count's provosts concerning the road which he was driving through his domains. Finally, the bishop of Troyes, in the course of his pastoral tour, had taxed him severely in Hervi church with his harshness towards his relations and his vassals.

"It can all be nothing but chance," Herbert thought.

For more than a year he had been master of his lands and he had thought that he would be able to arrange his life to suit his wishes; yet he felt that he was less happy than before his father had gone away. His sin with Eglantine was not yet expiated, since the man who was doing the pilgrimage for him had only left at Christmas and had not yet returned. Moreover, he was not sure that that would be sufficient expiation. He had therefore decided to beautify the chapel at Linnières, which, while it would please him, would at the same time be a pious work. He thought the chapel very ugly and less than worthy of him; since his grandfather's time nothing had been done to it except to give it a new coat of whitewash and to paint crosses and circles in red along the vaulting. Passing through Chaource, he asked the head of the town's guild of masons to visit Linnières to discuss the alterations.

Herbert somewhat exasperated the senior mason of Chaource with the largeness of his plans; he must have the three windows, which were nothing but slits, enlarged, turning them into true arched windows with small columns and he must have the two pillars which supported the vault made slenderer and provided with carved capitals. Then he wanted the walls and the vault covered with paintings—Herbert was already outlining the subjects for these, drawing in the sand at his feet: there must be a Christ in Glory, Hell and Paradise, as well as the whole life of the Virgin; and he explained how he had seen all this painted on the walls of the cathedral at Constantinople.

"In the first place," the senior mason said, "the cathedral at Constantinople must certainly have been bigger than this and what's suitable for a cathedral is not suitable for a castle chapel. I speak as a craftsman but any clerk or abbot will tell you the same."

"Master," Herbert said, sententiously, "understand that worldly grandeur is one thing and the service of God quite another. I am neither a duke nor a king, and I should not want to wear a crown even if I could. But when it comes to worshipping God I am as good as king or emperor and have as much need of holy images before my eyes when I am praying. My chapel is not large, but I wish it to be as beautiful as a count's oratory."

"It won't be suitable," the other said. "The vaulting does not lend itself to what you want done."

"The figures can be drawn longer and narrower—the essential is to have them all there. Send for your painter, he'll know how to manage it. I want every inch covered with painting."

"The whole project will involve you in endless expense and you'll be forced to leave it uncompleted. Piercing these walls, as thick as a fortress tower, just for the windows alone will entail weeks of work."

At that moment Joceran of Puiseaux came into the courtyard, which was cluttered with lime and beams, and, jumping lightly from his little, spindle-legged horse, went up to Herbert.

"God keep you, cousin! Still building the Tower of Babel? You must have sold your wine advantageously, from what I can see!"

"Fair cousin, greetings! You do my vineyards too much honor, I hardly got enough out of them to pay my men."

"I have come to consult you in a matter of great consequence for me, fair cousin. Milon of Jeugni has asked my daughter's hand for his son."

"So, so," Herbert said, without raising his head. "You're distantly related to them, if I remember rightly?"

"In the sixth degree. But is not the match an honorable one?"

"Very," Herbert said, drawing lines in the sand with the point of his knife to show the architect how he wanted the frescoes arranged.

"What would you have done in my place, fair cousin?" Joceran asked.

"I have no idea," Herbert said. And then he could restrain himself no longer but rose, dominating Joceran with all his vast bulk.

"If I wished, fair cousin, I should be able to stop this wedding, I should only have to say the word. Milon of Jeugni would not want me for an enemy. I should only have to say one word."

"That is exactly why I wanted to speak to you, cousin. Is it right that Ida should remain a maid all her life just because you are feared in these parts?"

"Consider one last time, cousin. It depends on you only to do me a service I shall remember all my life. Through me you can enjoy advantages that no one else can give you. You know this well."

Joceran let his quick, restless glance touch Herbert for a moment.

"And they'll say, throughout the country, that I've sold myself to you. Poor or not, I've the right to dispose of my daughter as I like."

"There are people who would hang themselves to prove that they've a right to do it." Herbert lowered his voice. "What you are doing is not Christian, cousin."

"Who will reproach me with it?" Joceran said, with a sour little smile. "Only tell me, frankly and candidly, whether I can have a free hand in this business?"

"It is your right," Herbert said, with an effort. "But understand that if any harm comes to my son I may not be as patient as I am now! You are the eldest of my line, the line of the womb which bore me. For the sake of the respect which I owe to my mother, I am bound to respect you. I must bear what you choose to put on me. But understand that I make this decision deliberately and might choose differently. If, for your sake, I bring my son to damnation, it will be a mortal sin, but the fault will be on your head rather than on mine.

"I am well aware, cousin, that it is Ernaut who is at fault in this business and that it is not right to want to wed a girl despite herself and her parents. But it is very difficult for me, his father, to recognize that. You may contract this marriage, cousin, but do not forget that it will be to me that you owe it, for it would have cost me nothing to prevent it. And now, go; and do not invite me to the feast, for I shall not come."

HAGUENIER: THE SECOND TRIAL.
A TASTE OF PARADISE

THREE days after Pentecost Haguenier was received by the lady of Mongenost in the little garden near the well. To do him honor she had had the red canopy decorated with flowers and had summoned two damsels, her kinswomen, to attend her. With her own hands she had woven a crown of rare beauty, for she was very skillful at such work: hyacinths, honeysuckle, yellow primroses and white daisies were woven together, following a regular pattern and so numerous that they hid the greenery. When Haguenier came and knelt before her, she placed the crown on his head, saying:

"Lord Knight, receive now the prize of your valor. You have served Love well, and it is he who, with my hands, crowns you."

Thereupon he seized her in his arms and kissed her mouth and her eyes and he said:

"O beauty and sweetness, treasure of purity, if you set me the same trial again, I will do your bidding tomorrow or even today. If it be your will, I will challenge the bravest knights of the land and fight without shield or hauberk."

"No," Marie said, withdrawing from his arms. "I do not ask it today. Come, that these damsels may also grant you the kiss of courtesy, and afterwards I will show you the new flowers I have had planted."

The damsels remained by the well and the lovers were alone together among lilacs and may trees. Haguenier went down upon his knees and took the lady's hands and pressed them to his brow. She withdrew them, so that he raised his head and for a long time she looked at him.

He had almost lost his beauty, his face was slightly puffy, his eyelids were swollen and his lips had a tinge of blue. But there was such adoration in his eyes that Marie did not see the rest. She stooped towards him, and he raised his arms and took her head in his hands, and they stayed thus, still, pressed against each other, without speaking. And she gave him a long kiss on the mouth.

For him, it was as if he were receiving Communion.

In that flowering garden, with the heavy crown of flowers on his head and Marie, alone, before him—he was like one of the blessed, entered at last into Paradise after earthly trials. But this Paradise was far from eternal and his joy in it was all the more poignant.

Marie drew him towards a rock garden where marigolds, pansies and pinks had been planted. Beyond the rockery was a quite low wall over which they could see the outer wall of the castle and the valley of the Seine. She said:

"Formerly, in this garden, I sent for you here, granting you a meeting of courtesy. But now that I have made you my vassal and the servant of Love, I can no longer grant you the same privileges; perhaps I may do so when I have proved you enough to give you my love. Now I am going to ask you to go and live for two weeks in your own part of the country with your kinsfolk and not to try to see me nor send me messages. For the time being I ask no more of you than this."

"I shall do as you wish, friend," Haguenier said, forcing himself to assume a calm and smiling air. Yet this was cruel: she might have allowed him to see her for two or three days more, have given him a little breathing-time after his months of hell. He had been in her company barely half an hour and his heart had already had time to establish itself in the midst of a happiness deriving from the idea that she was his wife, for always; life without her no longer seemed possible. He left after Vespers and returned to Pouilli to pack his things.

Marie, left alone in the garden with her damsels, gathered a bunch of marigolds and fixed them in her bodice; she felt her heart full of care.

"These flowers," she thought, "symbolize care. They are the color of the flame of jealousy, and in love care and jealousy are one. I sent him away that he might not see my attachment to him; now perhaps he will try to distract his mind from his discontent with light women, for men, they say, are like that. Since he cannot have me for his mistress, he will think he has the right to seek one elsewhere and I shall not even know. In any case, there's his wife, so that he'll think he can be unfaithful to me while committing no sin. Yet surely chastity is a lover's first duty? If he fails in that, I shall swear to love him no more.

"But, alas, I am already tormented by jealousy, while he does not even know whether I love him. But how can I put his love to the proof if I cannot know whether he is faithful to me? If I have accepted him as my servitor though he has neither the rank nor the renown to justify my choice, my honor requires, at least, that I be assured of the purity of the love he bears me."

And Marie did a thing which, formerly, would have made her blush: she asked her maidservant Isabelle to send her brother to the neighborhood of Linnières, there to remain a while and inform himself of the comings and goings of Herbert's son.

"All is fair in love and war," she told herself, "and is not a woman defenseless against any man who would wrong her?"

And she sent her lover a letter that same evening asking him not to go and live in his wife's castle.

So Haguenier settled himself temporarily at Bernon with his grandmother, for Herbert would not have him in his house.

THE BLACK MERE

SEATED in the long grass of a forest clearing Haguenier watched young Joceran and Eglantine match each other's skill with long batons of wood made into swords. He was saying:

"That stroke is not right, Uncle. Aunt, you're striking with the flat of your sword. Uncle, if you do not parry better than that, I shall fine you."

The two young people set their teeth and frowned, as if that helped them to fight better. Haguenier rose, laughing, and took Joceran's sword to show him how to handle it.

"It's simple enough," he said, "but don't poke with it as if it were a hay fork." Eglantine, more agile than her half-brother, parried quite well; red in the face, her hair loose, her skirt tucked up above her knees, she looked exactly like a boy.

"She's a witch, that's why she does it better than me," Joceran said, and Eglantine put out her tongue at him, as in the good old days when they were little.

"Rubbish! I'm no witch and I do it better than either of you,"

Haguenier said. "Come—time to rest, and Joceran shall fetch us water from the spring." He took a loaf of bread and a knife from his pocket and ran his hand over his sweat-damp hair.

"It's she who ought to fetch the water, she's younger than me," Joceran said, sulkily.

"Uncle, if you dispute my orders I shall not take you as my squire."

At this threat Joceran jumped up and vanished among the trees. Haguenier watched him go with a smile of amusement. These two were, in fact, his aunt and uncle, although they were his juniors by three years and he felt old enough to be their grandfather.

As he was, after Herbert, the head of his family, he considered it his duty to take an interest in his young relatives. Joceran was a sullen youth, pale in every sense of the word; everything about him was faint and ill-defined—coloring, features and mannerisms; he had been neglected always and by everyone, even by his mother, always and everywhere forgotten, and this made him curiously insignificant. Eglantine, on the other hand, contrived to be all too conspicuous, which was her misfortune. Haguenier was glad whenever he succeeded in making these two taciturn young creatures roar with laughter.

He had promised Joceran to make him his squire and was teaching him the management of weapons and military bearing; this had greatly changed the young man; it brought him to life again. And, what was stranger still, Eglantine was developing a strong taste for the military exercises in which they had included her for fun.

"Well, Aunt," Haguenier said, putting his hand on the girl's shoulder, "you would have made an excellent squire."

She looked him squarely in the eyes and he was surprised by the gravity of her expression.

"Would you take me, too, to Troyes, as your squire?" she said.

"What's this! What would my grandmother and all the family have to say? That's no trade for a damsel."

"A damsel—am *I* a damsel?" she said, bitterly. With her eyes fixed on remote emptiness she followed up her thought.

"They say there have been women who cut off their breasts and put on men's clothes to go and serve God in the Holy Land."

"Fair Aunt, such women certainly did not achieve salvation that way, for it is God's will that we should act according to our nature."

"It is easy to talk like that. As a woman, I don't count. I am—as you know—dishonored and moreover your father married me to a swineherd. No sort of life, as a woman, is now possible for me. Fair cousin, there are moments when I feel as if I were neither man nor woman but rather a creature of the accursed race, one of those who haunt woods and rivers."

"What an idea!" Haguenier said, yet he was somewhat uneasy. "What made you think of such a thing, friend?"

"Look, I'm willing to tell *you*." She put a hand on his shoulder with a moving look of candor and confidence. "I feel much better alone in the forest than among men. I know that the Little People watch over me and sometimes I go to the edge of the marshes and talk with them as if they were my sisters. I would tell you why, too, but it is not proper to speak of that to a man. Only the other evening I went to the fairies' clearing and I put my bread out on the white stones for the crows to eat. They will eat from my hand and are not afraid. And then I saw Morgan, who came and sat on the stone opposite to me. I was not frightened, and she spoke to me gently and told me she would teach me many things. If I had been like everyone else I should have been afraid, shouldn't I?"

"And what was Morgan like?" Haguenier said, still more curious than scared.

"Very pretty. Not as she's supposed to be; a lady, small, well-made, very fair and dressed in bright red. She has a crown of laurel on her head, and her eyes—so strange, and burning with a small red fire."

"You know," Haguenier said, "you should go and tell this to the priest at Saint Mary's, at Hervi, and stop going to the forest. It's very bad, what you tell me."

Eglantine bowed her head.

"No, I shall not tell. I know what they take me for here. They're going to shut me up for life in a convent, to weep for my sins. Oh, they despise me so here that I can't go on living. I'm like a dead woman among living men. And the worst of them all is your father, who has brought me to damnation out of jealousy, because my father loved me. Now, whenever he looks at me, it is as if he had killed and buried me."

Haguenier stared at her with an attention full of pity, as one looks at a sick child.

"Is it true, what they say, that he seduced you?" he said, without even thinking of the impropriety of the question. Nor did Eglantine notice it. She leaned her head against the young man's knees.

"Yes, it's true," she said. "You can see yourself that after that there can be no life for me among men. And I want to be revenged—how, I cannot tell you, but sometimes that frightens me too. If you could take me with you to Troyes and pass me off as a boy, afterwards I could leave the country and go and fight against the Turks. I think that would be better."

"Why change into a boy? I'll take you to my sister; you can serve her in her house."

"That—never! I'll serve in no one's house and especially not with my own kin. You, you're different. You are rather like a priest who would not be a priest. I feel calmer and quieter when you are here. But you'll leave and go to see your lady at Troyes and then it will be finished."

Joceran came back with a jug full of water. He gave the other two a strange look.

"And then what?" he said. "Supposing he is going to see his lady, what is that to you? You don't think yourself better than her, do you?"

"Idiot!" Eglantine said, shrugging her shoulders.

HAGUENIER: THE THIRD TRIAL. HARSHNESS

THE lady of Mongenost learned, through Isabelle's brother, that her knight was living at his grandmother's, at Bernon, and made frequent expeditions into the forest with a young person, his kinswoman, whose virtue was said to be easy. Marie felt so humiliated by this news that she at first determined to break completely with her suitor. Then she thought:

"After all, he has never promised to abstain from women and he may have done this thoughtlessly, without thinking that he was wronging me. First I shall punish him, but afterwards I shall forgive him."

When he presented himself after the specified time she announced that she did not wish to receive him and he had to keep a watch during three days before the castle; in the end she granted him a moment's interview. In the presence of three damsels and the lady of Chesley she cried shame on him for his treachery and declared him unworthy to serve her. He protested that she must have heard some calumny; she refused to believe him. To win forgiveness he had to undertake a public penitence, going barefoot and in his shirt from Mongenost to Troyes and there, before the cathedral, make honorable amends for having betrayed his lady.

Haguenier nearly protested, for, after all, could he thus brand himself guilty when he was not? But he told himself that she was putting him to yet another proof and that he had promised to obey without question. He therefore obeyed, but this time he bore Marie a slight grudge—did she so distrust him that she was setting spies on his movements and supposed him capable of lechery in his friendship with a close relative? At all events, he swore to himself that in future he would avoid all women like the plague, though they might be ten times the canonical age.

That summer Haguenier took service with the count of Brie, uncle of the count of Champagne; this did not oblige him to leave Troyes, since his new lord had a house there, but the service was exhausting, as he had to accompany the count's gentlemen at hunting all over Champagne, be present at all parades, mount guard at least once a week, and take part in every tournament—there were seven before Assumption. Haguenier did no fighting because of his health, but he had duties of organization and stewardship and, since he bore the count of Brie's arms, he had always to make a good showing, to be on his feet and on the move from morning to night at the count's table, in the count's ballroom, waiting by the grandstands, or to be in the courtyard with the other knights, his companions. He hardly got any rest except in church.

On the other hand his pay was good, enabling him to maintain three squires and a dozen servants. From time to time he took a day off to go to Mongenost; Marie hardly left her house now, for her husband wanted to prevent her from meeting her friend in Troyes.

After the great surge of jealousy which had made her treat her friend so badly, Marie had admitted to him that she loved him.

"I do not want to hide it from you," she had said, "for I see that my jealousy is stronger than my reason. Do not think that I shall change my conduct towards you nor that I shall not seek to put you to more proofs, for very often a man who knows himself loved, loves less, and that I will not have at any price. True love is only forged by time and proving trials."

"Oh, too wise and too prudent!" Haguenier thought. "If you knew what love is you would have no other thought than to spare me pain. What does it cost you to say that you love me, since for you love is no more than a word? As long as I have not the right to put you to the proof, as you do me, how shall I know that you love me?"

Sometimes he arrived so tired at Mongenost after a non-stop ride from Reims or Bar-sur-Seine that he hardly had the strength to speak; he dared not tell Marie that his strength was overtaxed and she, taking his silence for coldness, told herself:

"He loves me less since he knows I love him."

And then she did not dare be gentle with him but sent him away the same day and without granting him even one kiss. Later she would regret it and reproach herself with weakness, thinking:

"I am a cowardly woman, and weak, to cling to a man who has done so little to be worthy of me. As for the things he has done to please me, any man would have done them out of ordinary vanity or for the sake of his honor."

On one occasion, in the course of a journey to Tonnerre, it had occurred to him to stop at Dame Isabeau's; there he had seen the baby Marguerite, already sitting up in her cradle, and she had cut two teeth; she had learned how to laugh with all her heart, and to warble a little, and grab at her father's nose with her tiny hands. Haguenier was overwhelmed and he had given an account of it to Marie, for he was very proud of his child.

"I should like to live long enough to see her grow up," he said, "for she will certainly be a beauty. When she is seven or eight years old, I shall ask my wife to give her to you so that you can bring her up among your damsels; what better education could she have?"

"Men!" Marie said. "You swear to a woman that she's your whole life and that love of her is your only thought. Yet you have your house and your people, your brothers and children, and say that to love them is no treachery to your love of her. It seems to me that if you loved me as you should you could not love your child by this other woman."

"You know perfectly well," Haguenier said, "that for more than a year I have ceased to consider myself a married man."

"I know perfectly well," said the lady, "that you are so attached to that woman that you refuse to repudiate her in spite of your father's wishes."

"To repudiate her would be base, friend."

"Friend," Marie said, "if you wish me to trust in you, you should arrange that she cease to be your wife, even in name, since the thing is possible. And you should have done it without waiting for me to ask. Otherwise, I feel that you will become attached to this child and that in the end she will be more precious to you than I am. You will serve me from habit but your thoughts will be with your child and her smiles. If you love me, do not see her again."

"Very well, lady; since I promised to obey you, I will do it."

The next day Haguenier went to the bishopric of Troyes to enter his request for the annulment of his marriage. The business was delicate, since there was a child, proof that the marriage had been consummated; but Herbert had already completed the formalities and proved a kinship in the fourth degree, of which he claimed to have been left in ignorance. The annulment therefore seemed likely to be easily obtained, especially since the wife was now barren.

After that he had to go to Villemor to tell the lady Isabeau what he had done. Haguenier did not feel proud of himself. He still owed his wife a great deal of money and she herself did not want this separation. Moreover he knew that his father would now give him no peace and would begin negotiations for a second marriage; he would have to refuse, thereby offending the prospective in-laws, and, of course, Herbert. And he would have to give up seeing the little pearl of his heart, who suddenly became dearer to him than ever.

"After that," he thought, "I should no longer be a man if I don't succeed in making my rights recognized; although I promised to be hers unconditionally, I was relying upon her honor and fairness. Since she loves me she shall be mine or I'll damn my soul by taking another woman as my mistress—since she is so jealous, perhaps she would suffer if I did that. Yet ought I to be angry with her, having promised and sworn to serve her loyally in thought as in deed? In words I was ready enough for much harder trials than these. By the most pure Virgin, if she would give herself to me but once, never again would I be angry or impatient with her, though she had the sinews torn from my living body."

The lady Isabeau said to him:

"So at last your father has been too much for you. You have had enough of serving as a paid soldier; you prefer a new dot and a young bride."

"No, lady, I think I shall have to remain in service for the rest of my life. I shall not marry again. My father's property will go to the distaff side, unless my lady is widowed and I marry her, which I hardly dare hope for."

"Oh, so it's your lady?" Isabeau's look was hard and haughty. "Your relationship with her must be on a very advanced footing since she is able to make such demands on you. I have only to congratulate you. If I wished, I could bring a complaint against you for refusing to live with me. I shall not do so, for your life is already hard enough without that, my poor friend. Let us part in peace; it will be more decent."

"I should never have done it without being forced to, lady," Haguenier said, "for I believe you were the right wife for me. But what is the good of talking about it? Know, moreover, that I shall stand by my word in the matter of our daughter's inheritance and that you will enjoy the usufruct of it, so far as Hervi is concerned, until her majority. I understand sharp practice quite as well as my father and you may call me coward if I don't succeed in getting Hervi out of his hands as soon as I have repaid him the money he's spent on my lands. If necessary, I'll cheat at play."

"You're giving yourself a great deal of trouble to reassure me," Isabeau said, shaking her head. "Do not cheat, above all; and give no thought to all this for the time being. You have other things to think of and youth must indeed be served. Now go and see Marguerite; she must have finished her feed by now and will show you her most beautiful smiles."

"I don't think I will, lady. I must go, to be at Bernon before nightfall."

THE WORLD TURNED UPSIDE DOWN

Ever since the old master had gone away the peasants had begun to speak of Bernon as "the castle". People hardly came to Linnières at all except to pay their dues and have their bread baked and the bread was always badly baked since Dame Alis had left the great house. The lady Aelis, Herbert's wife, spent all her time hawking, and visiting the ladies of the neighborhood, while Herbert's bailiff was busy supervising the masons and painters. The lady Alis was still regarded as the real lady of the manor, and the peasants came to Bernon to ask for help when their wives lay in, for the accessories of bridal gowns and candles for their dead. Pilgrims seeking shelter at the castle were sent to Bernon and the relations and friends of the family preferred the lady of Bernon's hospitality to Herbert's. Haguenier came to his grandmother's house as if he were coming home and the lady treated him as her son: since he had taken Joceran to be his squire she had developed a great esteem for him.

"A pity," she said, "that your health is so poor. You would make a real head of the family, much better than the baron, my husband, or than Herbert. A pity, too," she added, "that you have involved yourself with another man's wife. Men who do that neglect the interests of their own flesh and blood."

Joceran showed off his horse, and his clothes as a squire, before Eglantine.

"Pooh," she said, "they suit you as peacock's feathers suit a jay. Cousin Haguenier only took you into his household out of charity."

"What! I'm his uncle. And no bastard, remember."

"Which doesn't prevent him liking me more than you."

"I should not be quite so stuck-up if I were you. Do you know that his lady made him do penance in a shirt and bare feet, because someone told her you were his mistress?"

"Then she's possessed by a demon!" the girl cried, indignantly. "To do such a thing to a lad who takes as much notice of women as if he were a monk! Do you know what—I ought to punish her. I shall cast a spell to give her the itch all over her body."

"No, it would give so much pain to Nephew Haguenier. It would be better to find some sort of philter to make her love him and agree to lie with him. If I had something of that sort I might pour it into her wine, if I ever happen to serve her at table."

"Why, but if it's you who pour it out, it would most likely be you she'd love. D'you see?"

Joceran blushed up to the eyes and laughed awkwardly.

"So!" Eglantine said. "You'd ask nothing better."

She pulled his hair. "I don't make those kinds of philters. Love is too ugly. I should like every beautiful lady to have a leprosy from head to foot."

"You're simply jealous because you're in love with Nephew Haguenier," Joceran said. Eglantine shrugged.

"Little idiot. I'm too old to be in love. But that's something you'll never understand."

Now the wheat is ripe, the oats and the barley. The golden month of rich harvest is here.

Oh, may the grain wither and fall from the ear, to be eaten by crows!

Seed accursed and youth lost, there will be no more rich harvests for me.

What is wheat for others is tares and nettle for me; may their bread also turn to tares.

They know not that black is white, white black; they see with different eyes.

They know not how hate can take the place of love and contempt do duty for honor.

And that it is easier than they think to turn all about, upside down and inside out. All that is necessary is to hold the head low and the feet high, to bring heaven down and raise earth up.

Every human creature seeks to be honored, but he who is despised to the uttermost must conclude that shame is honor or give up his life.

Morgan, my mother, I shall teach myself such words that when I utter them their wheat will rot as it stands, their cows be bloated, and the water grow foul in their wells.

For Heaven is below and Earth above, white is black and black is white. And what seems to them good is—naught.

Eglantine watched Haguenier who was standing before the door, talking to Joceran, as he drew on his gloves.

"How pale and grey he looks," she thought. "They say he will not make old bones. And since I wish so much harm to Herbert, I suppose I ought to be glad. God! how confused my mind is now. He was cut out to be my brother and my friend, yet we are forever apart, in this world and the next, for I see all about his body a kind of white aura of light, which shows that he is already set apart from the world, and because of that never will he have what his heart desires."

Haguenier started and turned, for Eglantine's stare had sent a kind of shock through his body. He remembered what she had told him about her meetings with the fairy Morgan, and was afraid.

"Are you trying to bewitch me, Aunt?" he said.

"Oh, no," she said, slowly shaking her head. "But listen: there are things I see; I see you beside a lady dressed in blue and violet and crowned with blue flowers. She kisses and caresses you, then weeps and is angry with you. And then I see you kneeling, as at prayer, and all about you streaks of flame."

"She's delirious," Joceran said. "You must not listen to her."

Eglantine sat down on the doorstep and put her hands in front of her eyes. Her head and all her body were aching. It was as if the streaks of flame she had seen surrounding Haguenier in her vision were penetrating her body and burning her. She no longer knew whether the pain was in him or in herself.

HAGUENIER: THE FOURTH TRIAL.
THE CUP WITHDRAWN

HAGUENIER did not find Marie at Mongenost. But Isabelle had a message for him. He was to dress himself as a pilgrim and go to the convent of Saint-Nicolas, beyond Traconne forest, where Marie was visiting her sister. There he could meet the lady without arousing suspicion.

Disguised, Haguenier entered the precincts of the convent, his face hidden in a hood and a staff in his hand. He had done half the journey on foot and was covered with dust. A dry, heavy heat lay upon fields and forest and crushed them. Throughout his journey he had really felt like a pilgrim, detached from all earthly ties, walking, alone and poor, in the dust of the road, on a pilgrimage towards his love.

Mixing with other pilgrims who had gathered there for the feast of the Assumption, he spent the night in the church. Tall candles burned all night long before the image of the Queen of Heaven. The church was small and the vaulting, painted blue, bore pictures of sun, moon and stars carried like lamps in the hands of long-winged angels. Pillars and arches were dressed with flowers and foliage, with human-headed birds, bird-headed beasts and other even stranger creatures, for all creation must be there to honor the Mother of God.

Two nuns, erect before the lectern, read litanies to the Virgin aloud, and worshippers uttered the responses in chorus. Then the thin, pure note of the convent bell rang for Matins, and the west door, which gave on to the cloisters, opened, and the sisters entered in file, erect beneath their white veiling; a number of ladies, there on a visit, came after them and placed themselves behind the sisters; their heads were veiled and they wore long, very full cloaks which completely concealed them. Haguenier knew that Marie was one of them but did not recognize her; but her blessed presence now filled all the church. And a kind of strange vision came to him: every one of the veiled ladies kneeling behind the nuns was Marie—a seven-fold Marie was praying to the Virgin; then he imagined that all the nuns likewise had Marie's face hidden beneath their white veiling; and the figure of the Virgin, decked with pearls and embroidery, wore Marie's radiant face beneath her crown but a hundred times more beautiful than the reality. For as every woman symbolizes, for every man, the mistress of his heart, so the lady of his heart is the symbol of The Lady.

"O Virgin Mother, Most Pure Lady, Star of the Sea, White Pearl of the bitter ocean, lovely with every splendor of creation, grant me, for the sake of Your Divine Beauty, that I may enjoy the beauty of my lady, that she may welcome me like a beloved spouse to her arms, for it was for that purpose that her beauty was made; if she act otherwise she would be false and cruel; and there should be naught but goodness in her."

The voices of the nuns were singing the canons for Matins in chorus.

After Matins the nuns resumed their litanies; the candles were still burning in the tall candlesticks but the rest of the church was in darkness. Pilgrims crawled on their knees to the steps of the altar and there remained, kissing the flagstones and weeping, hardly daring to raise their eyes to the decked image lit by small, wavering flames. Leaning against a pillar in a dark corner a woman was giving suck to her infant. It was hot and the smell of sweat and old clothes mixed with that of incense. Haguenier was not far from the door and he went out to breathe the night air. The courtyard, the convent precincts and the harvested fields softly glowed with the light of immense sheaves of stars, flung across the face of heaven. It was hot. Shooting stars furrowed the sky. Groups of peasants who had come from the neighboring villages for the feast were resting, seated or prone on the ground, behind the convent wall and even in the courtyard itself; they had brought sheep and poultry as offerings to the convent, and from time to time a bleating would break out, or the flapping of wings and a peasant's oath; then silence again, in which resounded the voice of the sister reciting the litanies within the church.

Then the bells began to ring for Prime.

After the office, the church and the courtyard of the convent became slowly more animated. In the sacristy nuns were arranging flowers and barley over the platform on which the statue of the Virgin would be borne in procession after mass. Novices were erecting tables outside the door for the offerings and were decorating the altar on which the first bunches of ripe grapes were to be consecrated to Our Lady.

Yet other sisters were setting up the long, low tables for the meals of the pilgrims and those of the visiting peasantry. The stars were paling and the sky behind the church lightening. The faces of all, from nuns to beggars, were marked by fatigue and excitement and the anxious anticipation of a great joy.

O day of the Lady of Mercy, Queen of the wheat and the vines and the humble meadow grasses! Herself, bright with ornaments, seated on her throne of gold and protected by the massive platform heavy with clusters of barley and flowers, went out across the dark gold of stubble and along by the vineyards dark with grapes; children bore crosses and banners and two priests wearing festal ornaments marched at the head of the choir. The white file of nuns followed, singing, and after them came the interminable procession of visitors, pilgrims, peasants, all singing with the choir, and the sound of their songs travelled far across the country and was answered by the convent bells. In the cloudless sky swallows were flying high, swooping together, gliding apart in a solemn, celestial ballet which God had taught them at the creation of the world. From sun-gorged fields arose the strident, staccato song of the crickets.

Throughout the feast Haguenier thought neither of his troubles nor of Marie, but only of the joy of feasting the Mother of God.

In the uproar of the courtyard, seated on the ground at the long, low tables, the peasants discovered that the long fast and waking night had made them hungry, and joyfully devoured bread and cheese, bacon and bowls of hot frumenty served to them by the lay sisters wearing coarse canvas aprons. Cups of beer passed from hand to hand, the clatter of knives on plates could be heard through the open windows of the refectory, mixed with the drawling, monotonous voice of the sister who was reading the account of the miracles performed by the Virgin.

Haguenier was caught by surprise when a young boy tugged at his sleeve and said: "I have a message for you." He at once recognized a little page in service at Mongenost.

"The lady sends to tell you that tomorrow she will walk in the forest and that she will rest when she comes to the spring of Saint-Elodie."

The child vanished, running, and Haguenier felt himself suddenly wide awake and almost disappointed. Now he would find himself counting the hours, languishing, filled with fears, whereas until that moment the world had been illuminated by the joy of being united with Marie, mankind and God, in prayer. And his desire to see Marie began to grow greater and greater, until it was almost pain.

Very early in the morning he came to the spring of Saint-Elodie and there installed himself. It was still cool. The grass about the spring was green and sweet and carpets of pale moss reached away beneath the pines. Haguenier fell into a deep sleep and was only awakened at last by the sound of women's laughter. A fair young girl, dressed in pink, was shaking a willow branch dipped in water over his face. He blushed and rose, letting his pilgrim's cloak fall from him.

Then he saw Marie standing before him, very upright, wearing a long purple cloak over a blue gown, with a crown of cornflowers on her hair.

"Where have I seen her like this before?" he wondered.

She was smiling and in a gentle mood. She dismissed her young attendant, and then they were alone together and so happy that they did not know what to say.

"You see," Marie said at last, laughing, "Mongenost would not let me bring Isabelle and he believes Guillemine faithful to him; but she is even more devoted to me than the other and I know that she will tell him nothing."

She dropped her cloak to the ground and beneath it she wore only a long, loose garment of a bright blue, and she pulled the cord which fastened the gathered neck so that the gown fell away revealing her shoulders and bosom. Haguenier stood astounded before a beauty such as he never yet imagined; she seemed to him so beautiful that it was frightening, all white and as if carved in alabaster, luminous, with golden lights, and the blue of her crown of flowers and her gown and the green of the forest made the blue of her eyes seem deep and radiant.

Marie, both troubled and fascinated by the look of almost demented admiration in her lover's eyes, moved a few steps towards the spring, gathered some blades of grass, then came and sat down on the cloak. So troubled was she that she had forgotten all the phrases she had prepared for this meeting and tried in vain to recall them.

"Well," she said, at last, "have you been bewitched by the fairy Vivian, friend? Have you lost your tongue?"

"Let me be," he said, "I cannot speak. I think this is the hardest trial yet. I am almost afraid of you."

"Of me, brother? But I am your friend. May God punish me if I am ever harsh with you. You can see for yourself how I trust you, since I come to you here, alone; it is I, rather, who would be afraid of you, if I thought you an ordinary, commonplace lover."

"And what *do* you think of me? I'll go away if you like."

She laughed.

"That would hardly be polite. Come here, beside me, friend; as God is my witness I am ready to grant you everything that is honorable."

Then he sat beside her and began kissing her shoulders and her throat, and she pressed herself against him and stroked his face. Then she realized that things might go too far, that he was making free with her in a manner offensive to her modesty. Red with shame, she pushed him away, rose and put her cloak about her shoulders again, and went and pressed her brow against the trunk of a tree to weep.

Haguenier had already so completely forgotten the respect with which Marie's body was surrounded, for him, as with a wall, that it seemed perfectly natural to follow her, to take her in his arms again, to press her body to his, to implore her and kiss her again, for, in his thoughts, she was already one flesh with him. But Marie felt herself wounded in her pride and modesty so that her cheeks had become bright red, which made her more beautiful than ever, and as she could not break out of his embrace she suddenly drew the hunting knife from Haguenier's belt and brandished it in his face.

Then he did let her go, and twisted her wrist until the knife fell to the ground. He picked it up and went away from her without saying a word.

For some time he walked in the forest, still holding the knife in his hand.

"Had I stayed," he thought, "I should have killed her. But she cannot be killed, she is a devil." Now he was certain that she hated him, yet his heart was torn with love for her, just as she was when he left her, her cheeks high-colored and her eyes darkened by anger. He could no longer see her otherwise, yet still desired her, burned with desire to go back to her, to implore her, threaten her—but no, never again; he would kill himself, rather.

He sat down on the moss and tried to think, to master himself.

"Did I not promise to undergo every trial without protest? And was not that one of them? Have I not broken my promise? I treated her brutally, left her like a blackguard, she will have the right to say that I broke my word. If I had behaved differently, perhaps she would have given way."

That he, her vassal, should have treated her thus! And how had he dared to believe that she did not love him, to doubt her word? He had left her, alone, offended, sad, perhaps, and weeping. What, Marie, his own lady, to be so treated by a man! He rose and began to run towards the spring. Perhaps she was still there, and would forgive him—if she loved him, surely she would be there still.

When he came to the spring he found nobody. Lying on his pilgrim's cloak, thrown on the grass, he found a little ring woven of grass and two corn-flowers. He made his way back to the convent and there learned from the portress that the lady of Mongenost had just left, on her way to visit an uncle who lived near Provins.

"Since she left me the ring and the two flowers," Haguenier told himself, "she had forgiven me. But she does not want me to see her, the two flowers must mean two months, unless they stand for two weeks. Yes, more probably two weeks. After that I'll go to Mongenost and make my peace with her."

Meanwhile, what was to become of him? After what had happened, he could not imagine life far from her for more than three days.

Slowly he followed the road under the oppressive sun-glare of afternoon. He felt himself greatly weakened and had, in fact, even forgotten to buy bread. He had four leagues to go to the inn where he had left his servant and his horse. The road was bordered by the forest on one side and on the other by the convent meadows where the hay had been cut a second time and grass was burned brown by the sun. The pilgrims would stay at the convent for another two days, and he travelled alone, lost between the silent forest and the deserted meadows. It was the day after the feast and no one was working in the fields or vineyards. He felt alone in the world, excluded from the feasts and days of rest ordained by God.

His legs began to hurt him, then his whole body became painful. He came to the feet of a crucifix, a wayside shrine at a crossroad, stopped, and fell on his knees before the cross.

"O Lord, Father, only true friend; I know that he who desires another's wife has no right to pray to You. But as You took pity on the woman taken in adultery, and on the thief, and on Saint Matthew and on Zacchaeus, have pity also on me, and call me to You, that I may be purified.

"For no man can come to You unless You summon him.

"I know that I am like a man who closes his eyes and ears that he may not be cured. Friend, tear away the veil that blinds my eyes and that is so close bound about them that it has become one with my flesh and the very pupils of my eyes. I have not the strength to tear it off for myself.

"My body and soul are perishing of hunger for a being who cannot nourish them; I eat stones instead of bread, and my mouth is broken by them.

"I know that my heart is made to love all who are near to me, yet I have neither mother, nor father, nor wife, nor child, the brother I loved is like one mortally wounded, and my bodily weakness sets me apart from my comrades. And she who should have been the friend of my heart has drawn a knife against me.

"Adultery is a sin, yet there is less sin in loving than in hating. If she has made me her thing only to cover me with wounds, she is a greater sinner than I am.

"Friend of all living souls, though she, the friend of my heart, give me stones in place of bread, make me to desire real bread with a true desire, the bread that You promised."

Haguenier raised his eyes to the image of the Crucified, crudely carved in wood. The appearance of the effigy was scarcely human, with arms strangely long and stiff, enormous hands with flat fingers, like batons, stiff folds in the tunic, and the face long and flat, with closed eyes, the mouth protruding, the nose long and as if flattened. The harsh light marked the shadows of the protuberant eyelids, the sharp cheek-bones and badly-carved beard. And Haguenier stared at that wooden face, fascinated, his mind absent, until suddenly, for an instant, he seemed to see Marie's face, living and vibrant, her cheeks flaming there before him. Thereupon an immense surge of pity filled him, pity near to pain, at the sight of that perishable beauty, that frail soul, imprisoned, ignorant, a pilgrim on earth: eternity was there, waiting, watching all about her. Before her and after her were thousands and thousands of years and in none of them so much as a trace of Marie or of her face, unique in the world.

"King of Mercy, I love her," Haguenier thought.

He was still contemplating the wooden face, without paying attention to the fierce sun which struck down at his head, and his heart was torn by love for the whole immensity of time, for every being, known or unknown, from Marie to the crows in the fields and the weeds growing there at the foot of the cross.

Later, he was unable to understand how, in so short an instant, he had been able to encompass so much with his mind—it is said that a drowning man thus sees his whole life in one second. But his vision had included much more; it was as if every human being he had ever seen, who had been anywhere on his way during the twenty-two years of his life, was there, present, and the object of his undivided love—even Herbert, even his cousin Joceran, even Mongenost. And he felt that his heart could never bear so much and every fiber of his being was stretched and taut like a cord on the point of breaking.

He seized the cross and clung to it, breaking his nails on the wood.

What happened thereafter he never knew exactly. He had not lost consciousness for he had been able to lie down in the grass at the foot of the cross and draw the hood of his cloak over his face. The sun still burned him, even through the worsted of the hood, and his nose was bleeding copiously. He remembered that Herbert was also subject to violent nose-bleeding and was accustomed to say: "It's healthy—better than being bled."

Then he saw himself a child again, in bed with a bad fever, and he could see the face of Jeanne, his nurse, stooped over him.

"How I loved her," he thought, "more than anything in the world. And now?" Would his love for Marie go the same way, passing away with his youth? Or at least with his life. No, no, no, that would never be. Then suddenly he was plunged into absurd day-dreams, their object a series of fantastic visions of a Marie made of snow, of fresh milk, of white flowers.

At sunset he rose and walked with more or less difficulty the league which separated him from the inn where Adam was waiting for him.

In the morning he awoke to a bad headache and the painful realization that he must again face the daily round, his difficulties and weariness, and the mortal boredom of being separated from Marie. After these four days lived, as it seemed, outside time, every ordinary encounter, every initiative to be taken, every obligation of his ordinary life seemed like so many thorns sticking into his flesh, and he knew a cowardly hope that another sickness would deliver him from all this—but to what end?

The company of Adam, whom, at the bottom of his heart, he preferred to Joceran, was a comfort. It was not unpleasant to find himself with his feet on the earth again, with a friendly face at his side. The memory of what he had experienced at the foot of the cross still lived in him; it was as if all his thoughts and feelings were phantoms, transparent veils beyond which burned a mysterious, inexplicable something, which was at once an object of terror and of temptation. He had prayed to be delivered from his love for Marie and now knew himself ten times more in love than before, for on one side of him there seemed to be a wall of flame and, on the other, Marie with her blue eyes, her childish shoulders and her blushing cheeks. He clung to the idea of her as to his very life, and knew that now he would meekly accept the worst insults from her without complaint, would ask of her nothing but to see her, for it seemed to him that he had the soul of a slave and no longer had any right to pride.

FAMILY TROUBLES

Passing by Pouilli manor he did not stop to visit his brother-in-law. To Aielot he was, indeed, more attached than to anyone in the world excepting Marie, but, such was his misfortune, he now felt himself separated from her also; for Jacques of Pouilli was most notoriously cuckold, and he adored his wife, for which reason the spectacle of his sister's home-life could not be pleasing to Haguenier. So he went to stay for a while with his comrade in arms, Gillebert of Beaufort, a young man somewhat frivolous, indeed, but well-bred. Haguenier was greatly esteemed by his comrades, for the purity of his life as much as for his affable yet thoughtful character. And since he had had the courage to enter the lists without a shield, he was much admired.

Haguenier learned from Gillebert of Beaufort that Ida of Puiseaux's betrothal was an accomplished fact and that the wedding would take place before the Christmas fasts. Gillebert had no idea how much pain this news was causing his friend, and was astonished to see him grow pale and bite his lip.

"Oh, come," Gillebert said. "You surely weren't in love with that little country miss?"

"It's as if I were," Haguenier said, "and even worse. For I can bear anything, but my brother Ernaut will never be able to bear it. I know that people who wish him ill have so managed things that he has not heard this, but I don't know whether to go and warn him or not. In either case he'll do something desperate. He's capable of going and killing Bernard of Jeugni to prevent the marriage."

"In your place," Gillebert said, "I'd certainly take on no such responsibility. No good ever comes of meddling in other people's love affairs."

"I think so, too," Haguenier said, "but I should not have an easy conscience. Since my father has done nothing to prevent this marriage, it becomes my business to do something."

Milon of Jeugni was at Troyes for the Feast of the Assumption, with his sons and sons-in-law. Haguenier sought them out and had private speech with the father, promising to find a better match for Bernard than Joceran of Puiseaux's daughter. Milon made it clear that he thought he was meddling in a matter which did not concern him. Haguenier said:

"The whole region knows that my brother has courted the damsel for years and that he has a dispensation to marry her from the holy father. You will be committing a great sin if you take her from him."

"Listen," Milon said, "everyone is in agreement in this business; the girl, her father, my son and myself. My son also loves the girl."

"He does not love her as Ernaut does," Haguenier said, obstinately.

"In the first place you cannot know that. And in any case that's no concern of mine."

"You will at least know that if you go on with this marriage you will have me for your enemy."

The old man said that he was sorry to hear it but that one could not please everybody. It then occurred to Haguenier to insinuate that Ida had already given herself to his brother but he dared not do it, knowing that it was not true. He said, therefore, that he wished to fight Bernard in single combat, the prize to be Ida's hand. Milon curtly refused, saying that such practices belonged to olden times. Much dissatisfied with himself, Haguenier withdrew, thinking of ways to meet Bernard alone and face to face. He would have been even more dissatisfied had he known that the result of his initiative was to be the hurrying on of Ida's marriage.

HAGUENIER: THE FIFTH TRIAL.
SACRIFICE

O N THE morrow he tried to find Bernard but learned that the Jeugni family had left Troyes. Fearing the worst, Haguenier returned to Gillebert of Beaufort's, intending to pick up his squires and go to Linnières by way of Puiseaux. On the threshold he met the young Guillemine, the girl in pink of Traconne forest. She was no longer in pink, but had a message for him from the lady: she was back at Mongenost and surprised at her knight's absence. Haguenier said that he had not expected her to return so soon, went up to change his clothes, had his horse saddled and left Troyes by the north gate.

Their meeting was bitter and sad. Marie reproached her servitor with having tried to treat her like a light woman, and with having taken her legitimate modesty for hatred.

"If I did not love you," she said, "I should not have forgiven such an outrage. I wanted to teach you what love really is, how different from the gross lust of the senses. I thought you capable of understanding. Ever since Adam and Eve were driven out of Paradise, carnal love has been impure and ugly and no purpose is served by lying to oneself about it. Would you have us become like the beasts?"

"I know nothing about that. But why refuse me what you grant to a man you don't love?"

"Ah, be silent!" Marie said, "don't speak of that. The law forces me and you've no right to reproach me with it. Tell me, rather, whether, without being forced to, you have ever lain with light and vulgar women for whom you had no respect? Can you say that you have not?"

"No."

"Well, then, and can you want to treat me in the same way?" she said.

"It would not be the same."

"Oh, you don't see anything! It ought to horrify you. Consider—I am your lady and your liege lord, can I be like any other woman to you? You are all the same, a woman is a chattel you can buy, the cheapest with money, the others with songs and promises and service and long waiting. But at bottom you can see no difference."

"If you can see no difference, may God forgive you, lady, for you do not love me."

"Oh, I know," she said, "you want proof. Well, I shall give you none. You are free to take my word for it. But after the oaths you swore to me I did not think you would be capable of speaking to me like any vulgar lover."

"You do well to recall my oath, lady, and I have no right to say anything. O falsely gentle and deceitful creature! Do you not see that you are doing something which, as between human beings, is not permitted? For you want to be served like God and you are only a sinful creature, like myself."

Troubled by this reproach, Marie turned pale and began weeping softly.

"God forgive me, yes, I am a sinner, like everybody, but why, then, would you have me sin even more? It is not for you to remind me of my sins. Go away, and do not come back unless I summon you, for you have wounded me, more even than the other time."

Haguenier left her, but he was entirely vanquished. Remorse, tenderness, desire and resentment made such a mixture in his heart that he no longer knew where he was, but knew one thing only—that he needed to see Marie again and that she would surely not recall him for several days.

On his knees before the chapel of Saint Peter, in the cathedral, Haguenier was praying, his clasped hands resting on top of the grille. He did not even know himself what he was asking for, only that he thirsted for comfort and appeasement and he believed that Saint Peter would help him. He recited his prayers in a murmur, wringing his hands meanwhile until the joints cracked. It was at that moment that a hand touched his shoulder. He turned, thinking that it was Marie, that she was come, having sensed his need. But it was only the priest who served that chapel, a man still young and of pleasant countenance, whom Haguenier already knew by sight.

"Excuse me," the priest said, "but I wanted to open this gate, to enter the chapel." He turned the key in the lock, then looked at Haguenier again.

"I see," he said, "that you pray with great fervor. May God grant

you what you ask, if it be a thing permitted. Should you need counsel
or confession, I am here. It sometimes helps to say what one has in
one's heart."

"Father," Haguenier said, "since you come to me at this moment, I
must believe that it is because God sends you. I shall hide nothing from
you. Especially since I have hardly any friend in whom I can wholly
confide."

Then he told the priest all his troubles, for he felt that the man
listened to him with interest.

"You are not very wise," the priest said, "if you think that God, who
so hates sin, will help you to drag a woman into adultery. You cannot
make requests of that kind to God."

"I know it well," said Haguenier, "but to whom shall I turn for
help?"

"You do not need me to tell you the will of God, for you know it.
Here is the command He lays upon you: since you have committed the
sin of repudiating your legal wife, that it may not have been done with
the end of deceiving the Church, take a young and beautiful spouse,
obeying your father, and cleave to her with the design of begetting sons.
Thus doing, you will at least be following worldly wisdom and exchanging for a guilty love one which is lawful."

Haguenier said:

"That would be as easy as ceasing to be myself in order to become
you."

"No," the priest said, "for we see this world's ties dissolve and change
even more quickly than they should. You are young, and if you make
an effort of will, and if the girl whom your father proposes is beautiful
and virtuous, you will find it will not be difficult for you to love her.
In any case you must understand that this other woman can be nothing
to you."

"Ah, Father, for you, who have the power to consecrate and hold in
your hands the body of God, everything must seem easy and simple, I
understand that. But I live in the world and according to the world's
laws."

"God refuses the power you speak of to no man who desires it in his
heart. It is, therefore, no excuse to call yourself a man of the world."

"Father, I, myself, know well that my way should be to do as you
did and renounce the world once and for all. But I know, too, that for
me this woman is meat and drink."

"If you do not give her up," the priest said, "God will send you a sign and then you will understand."

Thereupon he went away, leaving Haguenier perplexed and somewhat afraid. He would have liked to ask what the sign would be.

"Marie, Marie," he thought, "sweet and false, whatever you may be I shall love you; whatever you be, my chosen sister, who am I to judge you? Oh, my betrothed through all eternity, life had parted us before we met. I see clearly that that is my cross and that your honor prevents you from violating the law of God. Weak as I am, I should love you all the more for it instead of blaming you. But with God's help I shall never betray you for that reason nor turn to another woman. Rather will I live out my life like a monk."

Once again a thought which had already occurred to him seared his heart, a terrible thought which he had almost confessed to the priest without ever having admitted it even to himself. To die to oneself more thoroughly than by going down to the grave, to give up being and to hold in one's hands the divine body of the Master of worlds. But the prospect was so fearful that he entertained it only for a moment, then drove it from him again into the uttermost recess of his spirit; yet he knew that this was cowardice and he told himself: "Later. When I am old. Later. If Marie dies. God! What if the promised sign were Marie's death? No," he told himself, "I shall not wait for that. But I will only see her, see her once again, and then I shall know."

And, without waiting for the lady's summons, he returned to Mongenost.

She was willing to receive him, in the garden where yellowish weeds were now growing up between the paving flagstones. She was pale and sad and Haguenier anxiously sought for signs of disease in her delicate face and wondered whether his sacrilegious thought had not already weakened his sweetheart's life force.

"Sweet, cherished one, I ask your pardon for coming before you summoned me. Have pity. I know that you are as pure as the angels; I know that even if you wished it your nature would not allow you to sin. But I love you so much that I will gladly be content with whatever you wish to grant me."

Marie kissed him on the mouth without speaking and pressed herself so hard against him that he could hear the beating of her heart. They remained for a long time in each other's arms, unable to speak and hardly breathing, as if they were in the presence of the Holy Sacrament. But time was passing and Marie was afraid that a servant, sent to watch her, might appear. So profound was the silence within herself that she had even forgotten the use of her voice and when she tried to speak no sound issued from her lips. Then she burst into sobs.

Haguenier rose and removed the large baptismal cross from about his neck.

"You see this cross," he said. "It bears the sign of Our Lord's wounds. Lady, friend, if such is your will, I swear, this cross in hand, as true as God lives I swear never to wish for the possession of your body, whatever it may cost me." He was himself frightened by his own words, for he had spoken them almost involuntarily in a moment of exaltation but he knew that an oath is an oath.

"You see," he said, "it is too late and I can no longer take back my oath and be forsworn. It is too late and already I regret it. But at least God gave me the strength to speak the words. You will no longer be afraid lest I outrage you."

He spoke as if he were in a trance, with dilated nostrils and shaking lips. And his state communicated itself to Marie whose whole body was trembling. Something in herself was breaking down, she would have liked to snatch the cross from his hand, fling herself into his arms, deny the ban by giving herself to him—the wish was real enough at that moment. But her modesty and reserve were too strong and restrained her. She crossed her hands in front of her breasts and went swiftly away from him, stumbling against the shrubs and over the tufts of grass between the flagstones.

When she came to the well she sat down on the parapet and leaned over: deep down she saw the reflection of the iron arch, covered with climbing plants, and her own head, a dark shadow with hanging plaits. She was thinking: "I hate him. What right had he? He did it from pride, to force me to speak first; I shall not forgive him. Is this his obedience? I asked for no such oath. But I am mad—is it not exactly what I wanted? Then why reproach him for it?"

She heard Isabelle's voice and turned round, and was ashamed of her harrowed face which she seemed to see as it was, with her own eyes.

"Dear my lady, what has happened?" the girl asked.

"Nothing, Isabelle. Help me to arrange my hair. And tell the knight who is over there, in the garden, that I will not see him again for a fortnight. I shall go to the convent, to see my sister."

She told herself that Isabelle must have her doubts about her virtue and, strangely, the thought did not displease her. As for Haguenier, she no longer knew whether she loved him or hated him.

NIGHTMARE

HERBERT was in Linnières chapel, watching the masons at work on the new windows, when Gillebert of Puiseaux came to see him. The young man asked him for a week's leave of absence: his father had fixed Ida's wedding for the end of August, before the beginning of the vintage.

"So, your father's in a great hurry," Herbert said. "It's enough to make me believe that your sister cannot afford to wait. But, after all, perhaps it's better so. I am not one of the wedding guests, as you know —your father considers me a person of little importance. Well, there'll be gossip throughout the countryside. Go, and remind your father and your sister not to forget whom they have to thank for this wedding."

Gillebert departed, rather ill at ease; Herbert was even more so.

Ernaut was at Provins, thirty leagues from Puiseaux, but news travels fast and when a man wishes it he can cover thirty leagues in less than a day and a night.

"Even if the lad hears nothing until after the wedding, it will hardly be any better," Herbert thought, "for he will be mad with rage. God knows I would have given ten years of my life if things could have been arranged differently. I've given my word. But perhaps I could have the girl seized and carried off and pretend to know nothing about it. It would not be honest, but, after all, am I held to be an honest man in these parts?" Then he told himself that such things are not done among kinsfolk. For once in his life, it seemed to him, he had obeyed his conscience; yet his heart was full of anguish and remorse.

Haguenier was in Troyes, at Gillebert of Beaufort's house, in a state of almost complete prostration. As a result of his meeting with Marie he had suffered another heart-attack; it was not a bad attack but his illness had taken a new turn; he suffered palpitations and seizures which twisted and stiffened his limbs. After consuming a great quantity of soporifics, he had become so somnolent that he could hardly speak.

He remained in this condition nearly four days, telling himself that there was plenty of time to get up before the period prescribed by Marie was over, for now, despite his oath or perhaps because of it, his desire to see the lady was becoming a madness. The mere idea of touching her hand threw him into a kind of trance. He felt that there was, in this, something impure, yet he could not find the will to struggle against his desire.

On the day he was able to get up young Joceran came to announce that Ida of Puiseaux's wedding would take place in two days' time.

Haguenier struck himself on the forehead; how could he have forgotten? And perhaps it was his clumsy interference which had resulted in so hasty a marriage! He had not the strength to go and fight Bernard of Jeugni but at least Ernaut must be warned.

"If I don't do it," he told himself, "it will be treachery to him." Despite his weakness he determined to go to Provins.

Ernaut guessed everything at the first sight of his brother.

"I was keeping myself in ignorance on purpose," he said. "I've been careful not to ask for news. I felt it, I felt it in advance. I've tried to forget and God knows I have not seen her face for eight months—excepting every night, in dreams. Why does God allow a man to love like this?"

"Brother," Haguenier said, "I thought it my duty to warn you, but, if you can, let the thing go on. The girl is not worthy of you."

"Listen," Ernaut said, taking him by the arm and gripping it so hard that he hurt him, "come with me, we will start at once; we may arrive in time. I know what remains for me to do. I swore that she should not marry another man."

They set out at a gallop. Ernaut's horse went lame as they rode clear of Bercenay forest; he took his brother's horse and Haguenier got a fresh mount from his father's stables at Bercen. When Ernaut reached Puiseaux he waited at the cross-roads before the castle. He was haggard and his eyes were wild.

"They are at Jeugni," he said. "They're having the feast there. We'd have to get there before nightfall but it's already well past Lauds, the priest has blessed them." His voice was flat and dead and his eyes glittered with the feral terror of a beast hunted to death. But he was still struggling.

"Come on, and quickly. It may be we'll get there in time."

They tried to take a short cut through the forest, lost their way and were benighted. The horses were exhausted. The sky was overcast; no stars could be seen, no means of getting their direction. They came to a village and Haguenier knocked on a cottage door.

"In what part are we, good people?"

"Rumilli."

Haguenier said:

"For Jeugni, we'll have to make north, following the river. It's still a good league away."

Ernaut did not answer. But he refused to go any further.

The brothers dismounted and having tethered their horses lay down in the grass under a great oak. They watched a pale moon slipping behind clouds and giving little light. The square dark silhouette of Rumilli castle seemed as enormous as a mountain. An owl hooted mournfully nearby. In the distance was the vague, shifting sound of bells ringing for Matins. Ernaut's whole body was shaken by dry sobbing, he struggled like a bird taken in a snare and groaned aloud. At last he fell asleep, overcome by weariness, but Haguenier sat up and forced himself to keep watch, not knowing of what his brother might be capable.

It was already light when Ernaut opened his eyes. He seemed astonished, then his eyes grew large and dark with fear.

"God! It's starting again," he said. "I had almost forgotten. I've slept. Brother, don't leave me. I feel things are going badly with me, my bowels and brains seem to have turned to water. I can't believe they've done this to me. Suppose, nevertheless, we go to Jeugni?"

But when they drew near to Jeugni manor and could hear gay wedding-songs and the music of rebecs, Ernaut clung to his brother's arm and seemed about to fall from his horse. "No," he said, his voice muffled. "No. Let's go away from here, anywhere; I don't want to see anyone now. What's the use; it's over, finished."

They returned to Rumilli where Haguenier bought bread and beer. Ernaut tried to eat and could not. He was shaking with fever. Yet he was making great efforts to control himself.

"No," he said, "I shall not kill myself. They'd be only too happy. I know who has betrayed and sold me. I loved him, I was devoted to him, like a dog. He preferred Joceran, that crawling thing, to me. Everyone hates him, but I loved him. But he has betrayed me for Joceran, bastard Joceran. If I hang myself he'll say good riddance."

"Come," Haguenier said, "we'll go to the lady our grandmother, at Bernon. She is wise and will know the right words to say to you."

"As you please. My mother is also at Bernon and it is six months since I have seen her. I've not the heart to go and see her now. I wanted to give her half my pay so that she would have the means to live at ease in her old age. But I had to buy three horses and harness and then—brother, I don't know what I'm saying: see—I don't know what I've just been talking about. Repeat it to me."

"You were speaking of your mother."

"It's no good, I can't. . . . She'll be hurt, I know, but what's to be done? Oh yes, I know—if I had not been a bastard Joceran would not have refused."

He was talking quickly and copiously, yet seeking for words and constantly changing the subject. Above all, he talked of Ida.

"I was twelve, we were playing, she was my betrothed, we caressed each other like couples engaged to be married; she was very small, only eight. Yes, but for me it was not a game. They think I shall do God knows what. They'll be disappointed, especially le Gros. He gives you a horse and takes away ten. You know, I've never told you but he lends money at interest, like a Jew. He lent some to Foulque of Rumilli and the Chesley people—people of his own rank! Lending to merchants and townsmen, yes—but his own rank! Oh, I know all about him, and some things not very pleasant, I can tell you. I might have my revenge but I shall say nothing; what does it matter?

"I don't want to go to Bernon, let us stop at the Rainard tower, we shall be quieter there."

Haguenier would have preferred to take Ernaut to the old lady but he could not overcome his obstinacy. Ernaut insisted on stopping at the Rainard tower, now almost abandoned and somewhat dilapidated, where three old soldiers constituted a garrison. The place was always said to be haunted and, as he was passing near the stone which served as tomb for old Rainard of sinister memory, who had died excommunicate, Ernaut stopped for a moment and made a motion of greeting with his hand, as if a friend stood before him.

"What is it?" Haguenier asked. Ernaut's smile was hard and careless.

"Nothing. A prospective neighbor. You'll remember that."

"Ernaut, brother, for God's sake let us go to Bernon. You are not yourself."

"Indeed I still am. No, don't think anything bad," he added more gently, like a child who tries to hide some folly he is set on doing. "In any case, I shall stay with you. We'll drink. I want to rest."

The end of the day was as dreary as it could be. Secretly, Haguenier begged one of the soldiers to go to Bernon and tell the lady that Ernaut was at the tower and very ill. But Ernaut guessed his intention and was very angry.

"I've no need of grandmothers nor wet-nurses," he said. "If you bring the lady here, I shall go off into the forest." He paced the square room, then sat down on a seat and tried to drink but his throat seemed constricted. Towards evening he suddenly seemed to grow calm.

"Brother, I want to stay here, by your side. I am prey to a dreadful temptation. I don't want to give way to it. If you only knew how terrible I feel. Sometimes I tell myself that it's just pig-headedness that's driving me to it, to punish them. But to what end? Come, we'll sleep on the bed together and you shall hold me very tight; but I shall drink, that will make me sleep too."

He seemed in perfectly good faith, yet there was a little shifting light in his eyes, as if some other man were looking out of them.

Haguenier's strength was exhausted. He had determined to keep watch, but he had been two nights without sleep and now he was so tired that he had hardly lain down on the bed than he was asleep, with Ernaut's shoulders clasped in his arms.

In sleep a dreadful, formless nightmare oppressed him. Never, in sickness or at any other time, had he experienced a condition as frightful as this: it was as if his bowels had turned to lead and his bones were melting and such a sickness and disgust of life possessed him that Hell itself could not have been worse. Great toads, their bodies festering with pus, came from all sides to crush his body beneath them and watch him with dead eyes. He tried to wake up and drive them away but he could not. This state lasted so long that he thought he would die of horror, while all the time knowing that it was a dream. At last, with a tremendous wrench of will, he flung back his head and began to shout.

And he opened his eyes.

It was almost light. He was alone on the bed. He started up and peered about him. Ernaut's body was hanging from one of the low beams of the ceiling near to the loop-hole.

Ernaut had long been dead and his body was already cold. Haguenier cut the strap Ernaut had used to hang himself and the body slid on to him and was so heavy that it nearly knocked him down. He dragged it it to the bed and tried to close the dead man's mouth and eyes.

Strangely, his horror had left him and it seemed to him that his brother was there beside him, unchanged, no longer in this cold and leaden-hued body but somewhere apart, and that all Haguenier had to do was a friendly service in dealing with this strange object which still retained something of Ernaut's features. The jaws had to be tied with a scarf to keep them together. The eyelids were continually trying to open and reveal the whites of the eyes and Haguenier had to keep his fingers pressed on them for a long time. When at last the body was laid out on the bed, the hands crossed on the chest and face in repose, Haguenier sat down on the foot of the bed and wondered what he must do. There was no way of hiding that it was suicide. He was in no hurry to take the news to the soldiers nor to disturb the tranquillity of his dead. One does not pray for suicides, so that Haguenier's thoughts did not at once turn to God but only to Ernaut—damned or not, he was at least delivered from his anguish of the previous evening. How? God knows, but from the profundity of death Ernaut must be despising Ida's pretty body and her little empty head, for his suffering had been horrible and what human being was worth such suffering? "If a madman takes his own life, is it not as if he were dead by accident? What is sanity? Who is not mad? For I, too, am surely mad. And I am damning myself consciously and voluntarily. Who could refuse to forgive him? We have not the right to pray for such as he but surely the Mother of God has that right.

"Ernaut, brother," Haguenier thought, "forgive me, you who never, indeed, reproached me, forgive me for serving you so ill, guarding you so carelessly. I brought you here and exposed you to temptation and yet could not watch over you in your great anguish. Brother, friend, the Lord Jesus himself spoke with your tongue and asked me to keep watch with him and I fell asleep like a bad servant. I broke faith with you and with God and with everyone. What now remains to me, who am unworthy to look my father in the face, my father whom, in my madness, I despised?"

He sat down beside the body to arrange the hair on the brow and for a long time looked at that face, now tranquil and empty; the skin, stretched over the prominent cheek-bones and the strong jaws, was grey and smooth; a two-day beard covered the chin and the lower part of the cheeks. It seemed inconceivable that this severe mask was the face of so young a creature, a youth dead of despair. He seemed, rather, to be some rough warrior fallen in the service of his lord. Such would, no doubt, have been Ernaut's fate, had he not loved Ida. A simple, forthright soldier who would have asked no better than to serve without asking questions. And what was there in that plump little heavy-faced girl that she should have brought a strong, sound creature, whom she did not even love, to this? A great bitterness filled Haguenier's heart, not against Ida, but against Woman, Eve, drawn naked and innocent from Adam's flank to give life and death with the indifference of earth itself in which all life germinates and to which all life returns. Woman had killed his brother. Why did God so fashion us that we cannot but love this being, seemingly of our own flesh and wielding such power? Even Marie now seemed like an enemy, for she too was of that race—the race of Ernaut's executioners. Could he think well of any woman without betraying Ernaut? His treachery had been enough without that.

HERBERT

WHEN Herbert learned of his son's death he did not even spare time to go and see the body but mounted his big dappled horse, rode without stopping to Jeugni and there, breathless and without having himself announced, entered the hall where the bridal couple's kinsfolk were still at table, for it was the second day of the wedding-feast. He flung his cloak on to a seat and said:

"Cousin, Milon, fair sir, I am not one of your guests but am come nevertheless, for I, too, have my share of the feast: last night my son hanged himself."

Then he went towards Ida, who shrank, pale and frightened, and slapped her full in the face. Joceran and Milon's sons-in-law flung themselves on him; Herbert was one of those men about whom songs are written, capable of taking on twenty to one, but he was not as agile as he had been in his youth. There was a fierce brawl, he inflicted several dagger wounds, but in the end he was wounded in the arm and the thigh and thrown out.

He mounted his horse as best he could and left, losing blood but satisfied that he had at least caused a scandal which would reflect on Ida and her people. Moreover that was not to be the end of the matter. He would have Joceran's fields and forage barns burned. He would smoke him out like a wolf from his den.

"I warned him," he thought. "But he shall learn that it was not from weakness that I let him alone."

Oh, if only he could have seen Ernaut in time he would have tied him hand and foot for ten days, to give his madness time to pass. For once he had involved himself in an act of generosity and this was how God rewarded him.

He stopped in Bernon, at his mother's, to have his wounds dressed. There he saw Ernaut's body, laid out on a table and wrapped in a shroud. There were neither priests nor candles, the maidservants were huddled about the hearth, idle, not even daring to talk to each other. Haguenier was seated on a bench by the window between Eglantine and Joceran; the three were holding hands and their heads were bowed. The old lady was seated near the table, her brow resting against the dead lad's head.

When she saw Herbert alone, covered with blood and his clothes all dusty, she rose and ran to him.

"I am come from Jeugni. They'll not forget it," Herbert said. "I want to see him. Ah, the son of a whore, what has he done? I was going to make him lord of Linnières, instead of this milk-sop here."

He looked at the dead man's face and then drew the shroud over it again.

"Has Gauchère been told?" he asked.

"We don't know how to break it to her," the lady said.

"Well, she'll know soon enough. Don't fuss over me, they're only scratches. You"—he had suddenly seen Haguenier—"of course, you had to meddle. I hope you like your handiwork. Bastard. He was worth ten of you." Then his eyes met Eglantine's, frightened and reproachful and full of pity for her cousin. Herbert paled, then flushed.

"You," he said. "You're the witch, it's you who've done this. You've brought this on me, eh? You, the slut. You shall pay for it." Slowly, he advanced on the girl. Huge, bloody, hairy, he suddenly appeared so monstrous that Eglantine uttered a shrill cry and Joceran jumped up from the bench and ran for it. Haguenier rose, to protect the girl with his body, and Herbert rushed at him but, wounded and covered with bruises from his adventure at Jeugni, he had to give up the struggle.

"I'll have her burned alive," he gasped.

"Father, calm yourself," Haguenier implored him, "before his body!"

"Body? What body? A suicide, accursed, damned! He has damned himself! For me—on purpose to make me suffer, he damned himself!"

Herbert seized handfuls of his own hair above the temples, tugged at them, raging, shook his head violently and fell to the ground, sobbing.

MALEDICTION

Morgan comes ere he be up
Makes him drink from her black cup
From her black chalice makes him sup
So his pain may longer be
Long his spirit's agony
And his body maggot's fee.

"Morgan most beautiful, O Morgan my mother, make their wheat fall from the ear to dust and let there be nevermore a good harvest.

"I saw him, down, weeping, bleeding, humiliated, he who laughed at me and gave me to a dog. Oh, may my heart grow so hard that I shall have no pity for him and his. Strong, strong is he who can sing for joy because others are weeping. I will that my heart grow so strong that I can laugh, laugh though they bring me to judgment and the torture.

"His cup is of my making, his wine of my pouring. And he has drunk. He shall drink yet, to the dregs. You shall remember, Herbert le Gros, you shall remember, bull-face, your father's daughter and what she was to you. When your body and face are covered with leprosy, you will beg me to give you a remedy to cure you and I shall have the remedy in my pocket and I shall laugh at you and I shall go away and I shall not give it to you. I shall throw it into the Armançon. Damned and my brother, now he lies, Ernaut the Bastard, the beloved son, near the tomb of Rainard, with six inches of lime on his face. At night he will come and walk the marshes, with his deerskin strap about his neck, but I shall not be afraid of him. I shall tell him what words he needs that he may go seeking Ida of Puiseaux in her nuptial chamber and lie down between her and Bernard. Nights will not be merry for that pair!

" 'Come, Ida, open the door, I am your betrothed,' and the door will open of its own accord. 'Ida, sweet friend, make room for me beside you,' and the bed-clothes will turn back of their own accord. Every night she will sleep in the arms of the hanged."

On the Sunday before Septembrate the priest of Saint Mary of Hervi, Father Aubert, came in person to Bernon with his assistant and two deacons, saying that the house must be purified of the contamination due to the presence of a suicide. But the real reason for his visit was not this: the old lord's daughter had long been talked of in the countryside. The peasants were accusing her of having brought about the gales and hail which had damaged the apple trees in April.

The old lady received the priest with honor, had a white cloth spread on the table and sent to the cellar for a skin of old wine. But Father Aubert made no response to his hostess's welcoming smiles. He looked at her sternly. He was an old man and sour-tempered.

"Woman," he said, "I am aware that you are loved and honored in the countryside, but it is complained of you that your complaisance for your husband's family is excessive. It is well to love one's kindred but not so as to offend God."

"With what am I reproached, Father?" the lady Alis asked. "I am only an old woman with little influence, living on my dower. It is my son, the sire of Linnières, who is now head of the family."

"I do not reproach you with having done too much honor to the body of your grandson who has damned himself and caused such a scandal in the region. I knew him when he was only a child, a worthy lad who deserved a better end. After all, he was your own flesh and blood. But it is said that you are harboring a woman said to be possessed by the evil spirit. It was your duty to warn me if anything suspicious was happening in your household, and you have not done so."

"One cannot prevent people gossiping," the lady said. "If I thought any of my women possessed by the Evil One, you may be sure that I should have told you, Father."

"You well know, woman, that you are trifling with God, for I see in your face that you know whom I mean."

"Yes, Father, before God, I know. It is my daughter, the damsel Eglantine, of whom you speak."

"You are still seeking to cheat God and the world with vain words. The woman in question was conceived in sin and said to be the daughter of your husband and your daughter-in-law."

"Father, as true as I live, I shall let nobody, not the bishop, not the pope himself, touch a hair of the child's head. My husband and lord entrusted her to me and I shall have to answer to him for her, either in this world or the next."

"You have first to answer to God for her soul. Send for her. If, upon examination, I find that the rumors concerning her are false, I shall myself proclaim the fact in church and silence the slanderers."

Although anxious, the lady dared not disobey. She sent for Eglantine who had hidden herself in the loft when she saw the clergy arrive.

Father Aubert seated himself in the high-backed chair which the lady had brought for him and his assistants installed themselves on the bench behind him. The lady took Eglantine by the hand.

"Don't be afraid, daughter. Father Aubert won't eat you. Father, the child is not quite right in the head. She's been frightened with tales of devils and fairies. But as far as I know not everybody whose mind is deranged is declared to be possessed."

"We shall see. Let her speak and don't interrupt. My daughter, do you believe yourself to be a good Christian?"

Eglantine looked at the old man's face for a long time, then at the faces of the three men seated on the bench, who were staring at her avidly. Then, slowly, she went down on her knees.

"I have never cared to lie," she said. "I am not a good Christian. I was bewitched as a child."

"I've heard something of the sort," the priest said, turning to his assistant. "A serious matter. But, my daughter, that is not what I am talking about at present. We all have our own free will. Is it of your own free will and consent that you call yourself a bad Christian?"

To everyone's astonishment Eglantine nodded. "Yes."

"You see," the lady said, "she's not in her right mind. A witch would try to deceive you."

"Woman, do not interrupt. My daughter, tell me in what manner you believe yourself to have departed from God's law."

"I cannot tell you that."

"My daughter, you must tell me. If you wish it, I will hear it in confession."

"I shall not tell you in confession."

The old man bit his lip with anger.

"Then tell me, since you do not care to lie, if you do or do not believe yourself possessed by an evil spirit?"

"Yes," Eglantine said, "I believe that. I must have been bewitched as a child."

"Have you commerce with evil spirits or any other diabolical creature?"

Eglantine looked about her with an absent, lost air.

"I don't know," she said. "I have visions. They are perhaps diabolical creatures."

"Have you ever asked for their help with a view to doing certain persons harm?"

Eglantine suddenly rose, panting.

"I won't speak," she said. Father Aubert turned to his assistant, saying:

"It's an admission." The assistant demanded:

"Whom are you trying to harm with the aid of these creatures which you believe to be diabolical?"

"My enemies," the girl said. "Every man seeks to harm his enemies when he can."

"And who are your enemies, my daughter?" the priest asked.

"The whole country knows who is my enemy. He who, having all power over me, married me to a swineherd, me, the daughter of a noble father and a noble mother."

Her eyes glittered, her cheeks were burning, she was beautiful in her exaltation.

"It was Father Martin, the chaplain of Linnières, who married us. You knew that."

Father Aubert said:

"Then it was with the intention of harming your brother that you asked help of evil spirits?"

"Yes," she said. "Yes and yes! I did it and I shall do it. And I've a right to do it. Because he's a man who seduced me by black art, me, his father's daughter. Perhaps that, too, is a thing you have heard. Go and try Herbert for incest and witchcraft. But me you shall not have."

And before anyone had a chance to stop her, she was through the door and already running towards the forest.

The priest, the deacons and the lady stared at each other, petrified. At length Father Aubert asked:

"Have you heard anything of this?"

The lady was very pale, and trembling so that her teeth chattered.

"No," she said at length. "No. God knows I have not. Words of a madwoman, that's what it is. She knows no more about witchcraft than you or me. I shall have her shut up, that's all."

To his assistant Father Aubert said:

"The case seems to me suspicious and in any event scandalous. The girl is not quite sane, an idiot, but the Evil One sometimes makes use of such creatures. And the lady of Bernon may involve herself in serious trouble if she tries to cover both this girl and her son. I shall have to make a report to the bishopric."

As soon as the clergy had gone the lady Alis had her horse saddled to go to Linnières. The sun was already setting and the bells ringing for Vespers. For the first time in her life the lady was going to miss Vespers on a Sunday. She had not stopped to put on her cloak and her head-veil caught in the branches of trees. A dreadful fear gripped her heart at the thought of what she was going to do, yet she knew that she would do it. The cup had overflowed. She would no longer be accused of complaisance towards her family. It was not anger which possessed her, but a kind of holy horror, as if the world's order had been destroyed by that unnatural act and she must restore it in so far as it lay within her power to do so. She entered Linnières without speaking to anyone, crossed the hall, and asked where Herbert was to be found. He was in the chapel, which was half-covered with scaffolding, but one corner was kept clear for household prayers; four candles burned there in a branched candlestick below a bronze crucifix. Herbert, on his knees before his *prie-Dieu*, was finishing his devotions. The lady Aelis and her daughters were already rising to leave the chapel.

The old lady walked straight to the candlestick and took down the candles, extinguishing them one by one and putting them on the ground below the crucifix. Herbert had risen and was looking at his mother as if he had seen a ghost.

"There," the lady said. "You have no right to pray to God nor to light candles. Now hear me. You, Herbert of Linnières, whom I carried in my womb and gave suck from my breasts, you have tainted your father's flesh and violated the law of nature; therefore you no longer belong to the human race but to that of the beasts that perish. I, your mother, declare you outcast from the race of men. I deny you, you are no longer my son."

Horrified, Herbert moved towards her.

"Mother, mother, you have been hearing lies about me!"

"I am not yet in my dotage. Let me finish." With her eyes enlarged by fear, the lady laid her hand on the foot of the crucifix.

"Our Lady, Mother of the Saviour, help me. Flesh of my flesh, blood of my blood, life of my life—what nature made, I unmake.

"Before God I curse you!"

Livid with terror they stared at each other for a moment. Then Herbert fell on his knees and crawled to the old lady's feet.

"Mother, unsay what you have said, unsay it at once or you damn me. Why are you doing this to me at the very moment when I have lost my son? Unsay it; if I have done wrong as you believe I will make reparation."

"It is too late," the lady said, calm now, and with something like pity. "Farewell. You will not see my face again until your crime has been expiated."

She drew her veil about her face and went slowly out, crossing the hall under the terrified eyes of Herbert's household. The lady Aelis and her daughters had all heard the curse and were mourning aloud, as for one dead.

Herbert, left alone in the chapel, had prostrated himself at the foot of the crucifix and was staring fearfully at the candles which his mother had extinguished. He was thinking: "What have I done to deserve this? Eglantine? Was it such a sin? Women have no sense. Oh, that my mother had died before that!"

Accursed, he was a man accursed and degraded to the status of a beast. He thought that at any moment the thunderbolt would strike him down, that he was going to die without absolution, for he was now unprotected. Henceforth, as it seemed to him, he would stumble at each step, every mouthful of food would choke him; if he went out the very crows would swoop on him and peck out his eyes, his own dogs would devour him alive, since he was now outlawed from the natural order and denied by his mother. How many times had she not threatened him with this? But he had never believed that she would have the cruelty to do it. She had never loved him.

He remained there in the chapel without daring to move and night fell. He stared at the scaffolding and ladders not ten paces from him and an insane idea crossed his mind; no doubt the works had undermined the walls and the stones would collapse upon him and kill him instantly. How had he failed to think of it before? Taking a thousand precautions, he rose and went slowly towards the door.

Beyond, in the hall, all were silent or spoke in whispers, not daring to begin the meal without him nor to disturb him in his solitude, and it seemed to him that his own people would avoid him as if he were a leper, so that he dared not open the door.

"Well, but I am the master here," he thought. "A woman's words—nothing, she'll repent them by tomorrow. I'm not going to look like a whipped cur."

He went into the hall and the lady Aelis ran to him, then stopped, unsure of herself, only too familiar with her husband's rages.

"What's this," he cried, "do I look like a ghost? What's the matter with you all, you bunch of bastards? I'm hungry, and the meat's not on the table."

"I did not know . . . " Dame Aelis began.

"What? Is today a fast day? It's Sunday! And I'll have Cyprian wine, not Burgundy."

He strode forward into the hall, hustling Aelis, and brought his clenched fist crashing down on his butler's head; the man collapsed, unconscious.

"Take him away," Herbert said, and took his seat. "And talk, curse you, talk. I don't want to be served by a lot of mutes. Drink up or I'll banish the lot of you to the stables."

Herbert did not drink much at the meal nor did he invite any woman to share his bed that night. His youngest daughter, Hermine, his favorite and therefore the boldest, asked him:

"Father, is it true that the lady our grandmother has excommunicated you?"

"Hey!" he said. "Your grandmother's no bishop, that I know of. We shall see."

Leaving Linnières the lady felt so lost and without bearings that she did not know where to go. Night was coming on. She took the Hervi road and stopped before the old chapel in the skirt of the wood. There she dismounted and sat down on the stone bench in the chapel porch. She felt herself henceforth alone in the world, accursed herself, since she had cursed the fruit of her body. She had had so many sons and so many daughters and all were dead or estranged. Girard, her most beloved son, was a soldier in God knows what vagabond troop and sent no news of himself, and was he likely to be any better than Herbert, now, with the sort of life he led? Hélie, child of her sin, the gentlest and most beautiful, had lain in Saint-Florentin graveyard for nearly two years now. Mahaut, her eldest daughter, beautiful and proud, was now a widow at the turn of her life, soured, sharp-set for gain, and with no thought but for her ne'er-do-well son. Alette the gentle was a nun, spending her life shut in her cell, at prayer. Joceran—she did not love Joceran and was, for the moment, easy concerning his future. Marie, the baby, was growing up among peasants' children, wild and sullen. Out of her past life, only Herbert and Herbert's children were left to her; and also Eglantine, the accursed, the bitter fruit.

Had she not loved Herbert? Her second child, the first she had fed herself until he was weaned, the child she had borne when she was sixteen, the handsomest and strongest of all. She might have loved him —as she might have loved each of the twenty others she had brought into the world—if she had had the time to attend to them. No, God knows, she *had* loved him, loved him a long time, a very long time, and little by little he had worn out her love by his harshness and had become like a stranger to her. He was now thirty-eight, an age when a man has long passed the need for a mother. Yet of all her children this was the one who remained most attached to her. This was her child, the one who had bitten her breasts with his first little teeth, this and no other. This was the one who had fallen so low that she had had to curse him. What are years? He had grown tall and stout and had lost his beauty, and she no longer loved him. But a mother can do no otherwise than still to bear within her the bodies and souls of her children, even when they are grown, even when they are old. "God," she thought, "I understand only too well what has brought him to this. A madness for this girl must have possessed him, like the madness for the cakes I would not let him have when he was a child, when he would roll on the ground and scream for them like one demented. And now he's grown and it's no longer a question of mere cakes. And there it is—the way a man can cross the limit separating him from the beast. He took the fatal step," she thought, "and now he's like the beasts of the field, like the impious king. My son. But I am still in the order of humanity and could not do otherwise, for if I shut my eyes to this, too, I should be as bad as he, and that would be denying God. Accursed; and accursed the fruit of my body. It was I who moulded and nourished that accursed flesh. And now where am I to go, with my shame and my pain?"

To return to Bernon it was necessary to go through the forest. She had known the path for forty years and never travelled it alone at night. Thinking of the fairies and the ghosts, she dared not do it. She turned her horse towards Hervi but she did not want to ask for shelter at a castle belonging to Herbert; nor, after what had happened that day, did she want to go to the presbytery, where the little windows glowed with light while the church lights were extinguished. The lady made a half-turn and rode beside the cemetery. "What is there to be afraid of?" she thought. "Is this not consecrated ground?" Many a time had she been there, to weep upon her children's graves. She crossed the hedge where it was low and thin, near the graves of the poor and the beggars' graves; the tombstones were lost in weeds, the crosses awry. It was dark but the lady knew the way well. Near the small tomb of her children she stopped and sat down on the grass. Ala, the two twins, Marie, Garin, Henri . . . So many that she had buried in their swaddling clothes—and many and many the times she had pressed her aching breasts, swollen with milk, to their tombs, warm, sweet milk still flowing for small, cold mouths forever closed in the grave.

"Lord God," she thought, "ought I not to thank You for this? What would I not give to have Herbert, too, asleep in Your arms, a sweet, pure child? Here are fourteen who lived without sin.

"O Holy Mary, Most Pure Mother, what a Calvary is ours, mothers and sinners who spend our life watching the pure beauty of our angels of God grow daily towards vileness and degradation, year after year, until nothing remains but horror and shame. To have nourished and caressed them only to be brought to rejoice that they died so young! Oh, my angels, what shame, what crimes God spared you in taking you from me—for see how low are fallen those whom He left to me. Ah, Herbert, Herbert, Herbert, may God make you suffer so much that your expiation shall be in this world."

The night was calm and the sky heavy with stars. The graveyard grass was tough and faded and the ground still held the dry warmth of the day. It had not rained for six weeks. Even at night the air was stifling. An immense falling star crossed the sky to fall somewhere behind Linnières forest. In the distance stags could be heard belling with thirst, for the streams were dried up.

Herbert put on his most modest travelling clothes and went to Saint-Florentin priory. He had learned, through servants come from Bernon, what had happened there the previous evening and feared an inquiry. He could deny the incest; the word of a girl like Eglantine was not proof. As for witchcraft, he had never meddled with it; it was, on the contrary, the girl who was said—and rightly said—to be a witch, but after what his mother had done to him he was no longer sure of anything, and he might fail in whatever he undertook.

He was on good terms with the prior of Saint-Florentin and explained his case to him as briefly as he could: his mother, misled by calumnies, had cursed him. If he was innocent, would the malediction be effective?

"My son," the prior said, "you talk like a man full of the vain superstitions of the world. Think it out for yourself: the greatest saints were sometimes cursed by heathen and idolatrous parents, and it is clear that such a malediction has no validity against the power of God. Your mother is a good Christian but if she cursed you wrongfully and in a moment of anger she was behaving like a heathen. If what she has against you is true and merits such a punishment, the Church herself, mother of us all, would do the same and excommunicate you. But if—which might also happen—the Church exonerated you while, deep down in your conscience, you knew yourself guilty, you would be even more certainly damned than if you were put under ban by the Church."

"Ah, I understand nothing of your arguments, Father. Yet the case is simple: I am innocent and my mother believes me guilty. What can I do to nullify the malediction?"

"My son, such a curse is, in any case, a sin on her part but has no such maleficent power as the common people believe. I, a priest of the Church, can affirm that. But if you are a good son you ought to try and be reconciled with your mother."

Herbert promised the prior a gift out of the income from his vineyards and left, more perplexed than ever. He had thought the clergy knew more than that about exorcising curses. Most probably the prior did not want to say what he really thought and had used those trivialities to get rid of him. No doubt he was playing for a richer gift.

"Yet I cannot declare myself guilty of incest," he reasoned, "for in that case I should be forced to go to prison; at a pinch I could try to prove that Eglantine is not my sister, which, after all, is not impossible but difficult enough. In any case, she lives on my land and I can have her seized and deliver her to the ecclesiastical arm as a witch and demoniac. Meanwhile I am already in quite enough danger on my mother's account and the girl will call down God knows what on my head if I try to take my revenge on her. Ah, Ernaut, bad son that you are, why did you leave me? I knew that after your death I'd have nothing but ill-luck and unhappiness. Only you loved me and yet you abandoned me because of a wicked slut."

He went to Puiseaux to make his peace with his cousin Joceran, despite all the repugnance with which the man now inspired him, for he had great confidence in his cousin's resourcefulness.

In the grey and brown meadows beside the road lean sheep dragged themselves about, chewing at roots. From the neighboring villages the peasants were going up to Puiseaux castle with their wooden buckets—the great well of the castle was the only one in the neighborhood which still yielded drinking-water. Saint-Anne's spring, in the forest, now flowed only drop by drop, hardly enough to fill a bucket in a day.

"My vines will be ruined," Herbert thought. "It's not surprising that the prior was not delighted with my offer."

HAGUENIER: THE SIXTH TRIAL.
LIFE PARTS LOVERS

Haguenier had returned to Troyes immediately after Ernaut's burial. One thing tormented him until it was becoming an obsession—that he must not pray for his dead. He experienced such a need to do so that his heart was sore and aching; he was forever starting prayers, only to remember and stop at once so that they were forced back into him and weighed on his heart and stifled him. Calm and sad, the dead man rode beside him all his way, at once strangely absent and very close, so that Haguenier felt the sensation of having lost him less than ever. Ernaut was there but terribly preoccupied by a train of thought without issue or goal, yet still as full of affection for his brother as ever: this affection, together with his feeling of impotence, helplessness, was breaking Haguenier's heart. He could not stop thinking: "The misfortune is my fault and he'll soon be in a place where he will never enjoy peace again, and I can do nothing, just as I could do nothing before."

He stopped at Pouilli to see Aielot, who did not appear to be greatly afflicted by the loss of her half-brother.

"You know," she said, "Father wanted to make him heir to Linnières in your stead. It was a very dirty trick he was going to play on you."

"Bah! Father will outlive me, and may God give him long life. I've never been one to run after a legacy. I only remain in these parts for my lady's sake—always supposing she still wants me."

"You know," Aielot told him, "I think Mongenost has become more jealous than ever, you'll hardly see her alone." Laughing, she added: "You need the sort of husband that Jacques is."

"Sisterkin, I'm very fond of Jacques."

"And so am I very fond of him. There's not an ounce of jealousy in him."

"But his elder brother has enough for two. You should take care."

"Oh, I don't give a fig for the lot of them! I'm at least better than your lady—I'm not the one to torment a man as she's tormenting you."

Haguenier looked at her in silence for a long time. He would not have blamed her for just one lover but she was always changing and did not seem to be very particular in her choice.

She understood his silent reproach in her own way.

"Well, what?" she said. "If I happen to fall in love with a man beneath me in rank, where's the harm? We all come from Adam's rib. Because a man's poor is no reason to despise him."

"I don't say it is," Haguenier said, "but it might be as well to exercise one's charity elsewhere."

He did not reproach his sister any further, telling himself that only the pure had a right to judge. And pure he was not, for, despite all that had happened and the promise recently given to Marie, he could not prevent himself from having culpable thoughts. But what did it matter? You could not escape from your nature.

"The beast is the stronger. Since I was able to sleep like a brute while my brother was in agony, what can I expect from myself?"

He hesitated a long time before going to see the lady of Mongenost. From the manner in which she had received his promise to respect her he had understood that something had gone very wrong between them. But what, and how? He had thought to make her happy and become better himself; after that moment of heart's silence and pure tenderness, everything had seemed possible, he had thought they were both going to become like two saints together. He had sworn that oath not to desire her as he would have done to a saint come down from Heaven; then there had been that nervous, almost unhealthy, exaltation, in her as well as himself; then, after that, sickness again, followed by that nightmare ride with an Ernaut hunted by his own despair, and that horrible sleep in Rainard's tower.

Oh, yes, Ernaut had known how to resolve the problem; he had sworn to kill himself if Ida married another. Ida had married another and he had killed himself. It was simple and sharply clean. When it comes to living, not dying, it's another matter. Every step is a stumble and all the same you have your dignity as a man to keep and guard. He thought:

"Against heart and body, you can do nothing. Then what remains? The word of honor. There's not a man so weak and foolish but he can cleave to his oath, as to a pillar, to sustain him, for an oath is taken before God.

"Oh, Marie, how bitter is your friendship, yet I never loved you more than I do now. But now there is neither joy nor sweetness in my love, all turns to pain and disgust and you have become for me like bitter water which yet must be drunk to live. You are so pure, so good, the fault is not yours but in my sick soul which taints everything for me with the taste of gall, and you, who are all my soul, have become all bitterness."

To see her—not alone but in the presence of hostile women who would spy on her and denounce her to her husband. To see her—and be unable to quench his thirst for her lips. But not to see her—that was worst of all.

He was received in the lower hall; the garden was burned up by the sun and intolerable in the great heat. Marie was in company with her husband and an old lady whom Mongenost introduced as his aunt. Mongenost's presence was worse than anything Haguenier had anticipated. However, he sat down on a stool near the lady, after greeting his host and hostess courteously, and Guillemine brought him a cup of cold beer.

Mongenost was stripped to his shirt, his collar unfastened and his hair wet, and he kept wiping his neck with a towel soaked in cold water. The lady his aunt was fanning herself with maple leaves. Marie, also wearing only a shirt wide open at the throat, was lounging half-supine on a bench and dabbing at her forehead. Haguenier offered to fan her with his gloves and she accepted with a tired smile. Mongenost stared at them out of his black eyes, close-set like those of a miser.

"What weather," Marie said. "It does not seem possible this is September."

Mongenost spoke of the war between the king of England and the French king.

"We shall be in it too, this time," he said. "But the idea can hardly be pleasant to you, with your Norman connections and training."

"A man on service is not asked his opinion," Haguenier said. "He goes to war for his oath."

"But perhaps you'll send a substitute?" Foulque asked, with apparent casualness. Haguenier flushed.

"I'm not sixty yet," he said. Foulque said:

"Excuse me," but his look remained ironical.

Haguenier turned from his discourteous host and gave all his attention to Marie.

She was pale and sweating from the heat, her rather careless attire, justified by her husband's presence, suited her quite well; with her hair half uncovered, the plaits hanging down to her shoulders and her arms naked to the elbows, she looked like a mere girl. But her face was strained and sullen. Haguenier examined her face anxiously, the face which was so familiar but whose changes he never managed to understand. She was clearly embarrassed by Mongenost's inquisitorial air and hardly dared look at her friend. Haguenier gave her an account of his recent misfortune; she shook her head with an air of preoccupation.

"That's what a mad passion leads to. Should one not hate such a sentiment?"

Her manner was forced and affected and almost defiant.

"One should, rather, hate the girl who could be indifferent to such a love."

"If she did not love him, what could she do? Understand, Lord Knight, that the first rule of courtesy is not to reproach ladies nor the free choice of their hearts."

"Have I offended her?" Haguenier wondered, examining her pale, languid and indifferent face, against the dark red tapestry of the wall, with a tender anxiety—he was dying to press his cheek to the slender arm which lay along the leather cushion of the bench; he felt Mongenost's presence as an oppression of Marie and it was becoming a torment to him. He felt that, because of this man, she was suffering martyrdom. In his present condition every sensation was ten times more acute and painful than before and a feeling of horror and shame took possession of him in the presence of this swarthy, dry man with his round-clipped beard, his beaky nose, his hairy hands; never before had he experienced the other's being so acutely—but the man was his master, he possessed him body and soul, since he was master of Marie's body. To be there, exposed to the eyes of a man who had so humiliating an advantage over him, who was aware of everything and enjoyed his, Haguenier's, discomfort, was intolerable; it was obscene, as if some horrible bond of unnatural love bound him to this man. And such was the disgust which took possession of him that Haguenier felt the world was not large enough for both of them. That was the kind of disgust which had killed Ernaut.

"Well," Haguenier thought, "he was prouder than I am. I can't have much pride to have borne this so long." He despised himself, but Marie was there beside him, strained and taut; and he could not guess what she wanted and his uncertainty was such torment that he no longer had any will of his own.

Foulque rose and suggested to the ladies and to his guest that they accompany him to the orchard to pick some pears which would be exactly ripe. Then Haguenier discovered that the man's voice and gestures had something so false and vulgar about them that he could not bear his company any longer. He made his excuses, saying that he must go and see his sister at Pouilli. As Foulque made for the door, Marie offered her hand to her friend with a look at once tender and frightened, and said:

"Come again soon."

He kissed her hand and left.

Mongenost, alone with his wife in the lower hall, made a shocking scene, being now convinced that she had been unfaithful to him.

"One only had to look at your faces," he said. "Don't tell me there's nothing between you but virtue and courtesy. Well, I suspected something of the sort, you've become very odd in the last few weeks. He was my guest and I could not say anything, but the moment I see him elsewhere I shall kill him."

"By what sacred thing can I swear to you?" Marie cried. "I'll find twenty women of honor to swear with me, lay hands on red-hot iron if you like! Know that he has sworn on his cross never to touch my body. And if you do him any harm I shall put you to shame before the whole court, for everyone knows how pure his life is, and without reproach, and you'll be branded as a criminal."

"That's better than being branded a complaisant husband. Even if there is nothing between you, my honor's in question."

"You weren't quite so haughty when the man was Henri of Bar, although he was so crazy he talked of raping me. You would not have dared to do anything to him."

"At that time I trusted you. But now you're at the age when women become like mad bitches."

"If you dare attack this boy," Marie said, "I shall take the veil and make over my entire property to the convent."

"And a good thing too!" Foulque shouted. "I want nothing to do with you or your money! I've put up with you long enough. What good did I ever get of you? We've been living together nine years and you haven't been able to give me a child."

At these words Marie became very pale and seemed about to be taken ill. Foulque was softened.

"Come," he said, "that's not your fault. But, understand, there must be an end of this adventure, for it might take an evil turn."

Haguenier was very surprised to find his half-brother Pierre at Pouilli Manor, although Aielot detested him.

"I did not know where to find you," Pierre said. "Father is in trouble and would like to have you near him."

"I don't know how I can help him," Haguenier said sullenly. "He never asks my opinion in his business."

Pierre told him what had happened. The priest had been to Bernon about Eglantine; then the lady Alis had been angry with Herbert and had even cursed him, and he was anxious, seeing himself threatened by all kinds of troubles.

"He wants to make a pilgrimage to Our Lady of Puy and wants you to take his place in his absence. He thinks you'll handle matters better than he would if it comes to trouble with the Church authorities."

"Well, let him wait," Haguenier said. "I've some accounts to settle with a local chatelain here. Father has been making it clear for a long time that his business is none of mine. It happens that I also have other things to think of besides his troubles."

"You know, he'll hold it against you," Pierre said. "He seems to think he'll be struck by lightning if he doesn't leave before the end of the week."

"Not much danger of that," Haguenier said, "with this drought. I'll wager there'll be no storm for a fortnight."

Pierre found the witticism wanting in reverence. He had never before seen his brother so short and ill-tempered. The calm and measured tone of his voice failed to conceal his ill-humor.

"If you have a quarrel on your hands," he said, "count on me; I'll fight beside you if you need someone."

"A man asked me, today, whether, in case of war, I should send a substitute. That's an insult to our family, isn't it?" Pierre put his head on one side and reflected. He said:

"It's known that you've a weak heart. But even if the man meant no harm, he expressed himself very awkwardly. It would be better to put the matter on a proper footing."

"Thank you. We will discuss it together soon."

And the brothers returned to Troyes, to Gillebert of Beaufort's, where Haguenier had left his armor and his horses. That evening, after Vespers, they remained in the cathedral to go to confession. The priest who heard their confession was the young man with whom Haguenier had talked a fortnight earlier. Haguenier recalled his words "God will send you a sign" and wondered whether Ernaut's death was that sign or whether he must wait for another one. As he had not the strength of mind to renounce his evil thoughts and his hatred, he could not obtain absolution, and returned to the house in a condition of increasing sadness. The setting sun was red and the roofs and steeples of Troyes and the battlements and turrets of the walls were the color of copper and rust. The atmosphere was heavy and vilely tainted by the stench which rose from streets and courtyards.

In the morning Haguenier was present for Sext and left before the second mass. In the crowd at the door of the cathedral Guillemine accosted him.

"Come with me," she said, "to Audefroi the draper's."

"Oh, by the Holy Mother!" Haguenier told himself, "I am saved! I shall see her and speak to her." His anxieties vanished, he felt that the sight of Marie, alone and free to speak to him, would cure him—how, he did not know.

He found Marie seated in a corner of the shop examining a piece of red cloth. She was saying to the draper:

"I want to order a cloak for my husband, for his birthday, and this knight, who is my friend, will advise me about style, because I don't know very much about men's clothes."

In a low voice Haguenier said:

"I should have liked to make him a present of a red suit myself, but not of cloth."

Marie looked at him with surprise, there was so much hate in his eyes.

"I don't understand you," she said, gently. He looked at her, his eyes lightening.

"My only joy," he said, "because of you I am a lost man and I only love you the better for it. God keep me from ever causing you pain.

Yesterday I saw that you are being tormented because of me and I shall never forgive that man."

Her expression became severe and sad.

"Of what man do you speak? I see that you are indeed a lost man, for you do not keep your word."

"Sweet friend, if I have displeased you, tell me how. I will do whatever you wish."

"I sent for you," she said, "to take leave of you, for we shall not see each other again, at least for a long time; I absolve you from your promises; if you wish to remain my friend it must be secretly, in your heart, for it is no longer possible for us to meet."

Haguenier flushed and drew himself up.

"I know," he said. "That man is trying to forbid you. But I shall take such action that he is no longer able to do so."

She shook her head and looked at him as at a child who speaks foolishly.

"It is not only because of that," she said. "He cannot forbid me anything; it is I, myself, who want to send you away. You must leave Troyes and not be seen in this region. You will understand when you know why. I am pregnant."

That was the very last blow which Haguenier had expected. Disgust and anger so choked him that for a long time he could not speak at all; at last he rose and picked up his gloves.

"That," he said, "I cannot bear. I will rid you of this man whether you wish it or not. I have already spoken of it to my brother Pierre. We shall go and challenge him; he will only have to appear in the field in front of Pouilli with any friend of his choice; the thing will be settled in three days."

"Stop," Marie said, harshly. "Have you already forgotten your oath? Am I no longer your lady? Do you not know that your lady's husband should be sacrosanct? Have you forgotten that I am sworn to be faithful to him?"

"You are under no kind of obligation to him. He took you as a child without asking your opinion. I shall kill him and you will be mine without sin."

Marie's eyes flashed.

"How dare you use such words to me? I have been mistaken in you. You are vulgar. Is that love? Do you think me capable of marrying my husband's murderer? Are you trying to make me your accomplice in his murder? It would be worse than adultery."

Frightened by this outburst of anger Haguenier was silent and hung his head.

"I forbid you to touch so much as a hair of his head," she said, in a sharp voice. His answering smile was hard.

"You say that because you think he is stronger than I am. Thank you. I am now absolutely obliged to show you that I am capable of more than you think."

The face she turned up to him was softened and almost imploring.

"Friend," she said, "all I want is that you spare me shame and torment. An innocent child must not suffer because of us. Is it my fault that this has happened to me? I am a woman like any other. You should be sorry for me and realize the situation into which you are putting me."

Haguenier tried the piece of cloth between his hands to keep himself in countenance. He was tamed. And his heart was too full for speech. At last, with an effort, he asked:

"You will love this man's child?"

"I don't know," she said, sadly. "It's possible. At the moment I think I hate it. God forgive me!"

At the far end of the long, low shop the draper and his apprentice were unrolling bolts of silk for a richly dressed woman, some citizen's wife, who appeared to be bargaining outrageously; her attendant, a stout female of uncertain age, kept glancing curiously at this couple who took so little interest in cloth. Marie drew her veil across her face.

"Where shall I see you again?" Haguenier asked.

"Nowhere. You must leave Troyes today."

"To see you for the last time here, in front of all these people—lady, I will bear it all if I can see you once more, alone."

"Don't make conditions. You promised me. I love you more than anything in the world, now, and perhaps that's why God is punishing me. Friend, friend, what good has it done us to keep our love pure, since it has not spared us the humiliations which are the lot of guilty lovers? Now we can only love each other in secret, in our hearts, and each do our duty as we find it. Marry if you like. You will thus be obeying your father; I shall not hold it against you. It won't make me think that you love me any less."

"I shall remain faithful to you all my life, lady. I shall never touch another woman. I am going to enter the Church."

She looked at him fearfully.

"No. Make no such decision lightly. God keep you. My most dear friend, I must go, farewell. I shall never forget you."

He bent the knee, then stooped to the very ground and pressed his face against Marie's small violet shoes.

"Really," Pierre said, "it was hardly worth while putting me to trouble if you're not going to challenge the man. I went to confession for nothing. And your comrades already know you have this quarrel."

"I do not care what anyone thinks of me, now. We can go straight to Linnières, since Father is so anxious to see me. My term of service expires at Christmas but I should like to give it up earlier. You could take my place if you like; you would have a gayer life than at Linnières. I undertake to get father's permission. You can have my weapons."

"I certainly shall not refuse," Pierre said. "At Linnières I'm like a wolf in a cage. If the count of Brie will accept a bastard in his service, I'll pray for him all my life. And for you, too, brother."

The next day was wors than its predecessors: the air was heavy; it was like living in an oven. Reddish cl uds drifted on the horizon— forest fires somewher⌐ to the south. Towards the end of the afternoon— the brothers were n t f r from Hervi—the hazy sky suddenly flamed across its entire arch with an enormous flash of heat, which seemed to make the still and silent hills tremble. For an instant everything seemed to change color, then became grey again; there was no thunder, only a gust of hot wind. Staring at each other, terrified, the two young men crossed themselves. Both were thinking of Herbert.

THE FAIRIES

AT NIGHT beside their cold hearths, the village women of Bernon, Linnières and Hervi kneaded dough for unleavened cakes, as an offering to the fairies.

It had not rained by Septembrate. There had been a processional to Saint-Anne's spring, in the forest, then to Puiseaux; then, with the great cross of Hervi church and the parish priest at the head, a procession had gone to Saint Cydroine; men, women and children, all had marched along the dusty roads more than three leagues to Saint Cydroine. The priest had taken the relics of the saint into the fields; the peasants had brought their cows—their udders dry—and their mangy asses, with eyes inflamed, to soften the saint's heart. Small children, exhausted by the heat, dragged behind weeping or hung on to their mothers' skirts.

But no rain fell.

Mad dogs were at large in the countryside and had already bitten several children and a shepherd. They had shut the shepherd up in a hunter's lodge near the forest, rolling big stones against the door, and at night-time his howls reached the village and made the sheep tremble in their pen. Animals were being slaughtered by the dozen.

Herbert's provost had arrived, escorted by troops, on the eve of Septembrate to collect his dues; the harvest had been bad, part of the wheat and barley had burned because of the drought. On the advice of their priest the peasants of Linnières had hidden thirty hogsheads of barley in the cellar of the presbytery; the provost had guessed the trick and, by way of punishment, confiscated all the hidden barley. The soldiers had seized four men and three women, said to be responsible for the concealment, and flogged them with leather thongs; so that after the provost had gone, the village children sang nothing but songs composed to curse Herbert le Gros, bull-face, and the whole race of bloodsuckers. The masons, who had resumed work at the castle after the holy days, came down and beat and pestered the village girls and stole poultry, for Herbert paid them badly.

God keep the villein
from a lord who drinks
from a lord who builds
from a lord who makes war
from a lord who stays at home
from a lord who prays to God
from a lord who never prays
from rich lord, poor lord,
from grasping lord or prodigal.

Whether lord does well or ill
the villein never gets his fill
the Lord's well-doing goes to pay
his kin, the pilgrim on his way,
convent, clerk or holy day,
friars white and black and grey,
beggars, galley-slaves and they
all on the villein's back do lay.

Villein on earth ne'er makes good cheer
but on bitter watered beer,
ewe's-milk cheese, bread of pease
broth of dandelion—no spice,
but the hope of Paradise.

Country ladies crowned with mistletoe, dressed
in frocks of fleece from our lost sheep, ladies who
dance at night upon white stones, to the 'cursed
place within the forest go.

Ladies who frighten our goats and our sheep,
overlook children at night while they sleep,
tug at our distaffs to break off the thread,
throw snakes in our wells that the poison may spread.

Country ladies make it rain,
make water run from springs again,
in sun-baked earth make water flow,

to withered grapes the sap to flow,
and milk from our dry breasts to flow,
and water in dry wells to flow.
Country ladies, as a fee,
hot wheaten cakes we offer ye,
salted with our tears they be,
kneaded with our misery.
Country ladies give us rain,
bring water to our springs again.

Heads and feet bare, the village women advanced to the forest in single file. The moon was high in the sky. In the heat of the forest, the wild beasts howled the misery of thirst.

Near the white stones a human form lay stretched, long and lean, the arms crossed behind the head. The women had gone on their knees, each holding her cake before her with both hands, arms extended. They had not seen the long form lying in the grass or they had taken it for a fallen tree trunk. Then suddenly the form moved, sat up, slowly rose; and women cried out fearfully and some of them made to run away.

But the figure, the phantom, was also a woman, a tall, lean woman with wild hair—the damsel of Bernon. She was standing, motionless, staring at them fearfully. She was still hardly awake and thought she was dreaming. For three days she had been unable to distinguish between dream and waking reality.

"Damsel," cried Aubaine, the blacksmith's wife, "it is well known that you are friendly with the ladies of this place: make it rain."

The other women stretched out their arms towards Eglantine, somewhat reassured at seeing that the fairies had assumed the features of a familiar face. It was because this girl had allied herself with the fairies that it had not rained for two months.

"I can do nothing," Eglantine said. "Leave me alone. I can do no good." She tried to make off into the forest but the peasant women were already all about her, stopping her.

"Have pity, our beasts are dying of thirst, our men are going mad, our vines are ruined."

Eglantine struggled.

"Let me go, that is not what I ask of Morgan. I have no power over water. I am thirsty myself."

But Aubaine shouted:

"She drinks our tears at night and drinks the blood of our cattle. Woman, you shall give us rain or die."

"Damsel, your father was a good master. If you take after him, do it."

"We know you! It was you sent hail this spring-time!"

"Our men will rip out your guts with a pick if you still hold back the rain."

"They'll nail you to an oak with their pitchforks."

"Pity, have pity!" Eglantine cried, shielding her head behind crossed arms. "I am not like Flora, I am only a damned soul; I have no powers. I only damned my child to be friends with the fairies."

"If you are their friend, join us in praying to them for a storm within two days."

Eglantine stared at their faces, wild and haggard by moonlight, with a distracted air. Their hair was loose and hanging: she knew them all, formerly she had often seen them in church, but now they looked like witches and she was afraid of them. Heavy, bony women, squat or bent; beardless, long-haired men they seemed; only two among them were slender and still young. The night transformed their faces with great empty shadows where their eyes should have been. Eglantine felt her mind clouding, her head becoming void; she was no longer aware of her body. Then a violent shock made her body rigid, shook her from head to feet, and she fell, panting, across the white stone.

The village women moved back, frightened, and Eglantine lay there, stretched on the stone, writhing like a crushed earthworm. Then, after a violent spasm, she fell back, motionless, on to the stone. None of the women dared approach for fear lest the evil spirit which possessed the girl might strike at them. They stood there, round the great stone, their offerings in their hands, terrified in contemplation of this accursed being who disturbed and monopolized the ladies of the place. It was obvious that the springs and wells had dried up because this bewitched creature had diverted the power of the fairies to her advantage, as a stone placed at the source diverts the stream. They would have killed her had they dared to touch her. But she was in her own fortress, safer than within a strong tower. The moon threw a clear, cold light on her wide, haggard face, the enormous dark eyelids, the big, calm mouth, from one corner of which a thin trickle of black blood had run down her cheek.

The moon was already half-hidden by the tops of the trees when

Eglantine opened her eyes. She saw the erect shades all about her and uttered a cry.

"Morgan, Morgan, I see it all! There will be fire and water and blood! Your men will die in blood and your cattle in fire. And if I knew the words to bring rain I should not speak them, for my hour is not yet come."

In an instant she was on her feet; she leaped, thrust aside the terrified women and in three strides was among the trees and lost among the dark brushwood. Never had a woman been seen to leap and run like that; it was more like a wild beast. The women raised their hands to cross themselves but the power that was in that place prevented them; they could only place their useless offerings on the now empty stone and return slowly to the village, telling each other that evil was afoot, misfortune on the way and that this time the country ladies would do nothing good for them.

"O Morgan, I pray you, make me into a bird that I may fly away, an adder, that I may creep among the grasses; O Morgan, let me forever wander this wood with the soul of my damned child. Make me a nightingale that I may sing him songs, a thrush, that I may make him a nest of down, a weasel, that I may warm him with my body. For my place is no longer among men and there is not a human soul I can love. Here I shall die of hunger and thirst. Change my soul into a bird of the forest; I shall fly above the oaks, alight on bushes and brambles and on the marsh reeds, and sing to console the little damned soul as he dances over the bog."

That small living soul which she had lost gave Eglantine no peace since she had been living in the forest. Why, even the most wicked of women, whores who killed their living, new-born infants with their own hands, even they hid themselves at the end, so that they might be confined at the proper time, to baptize the child before it died. And she had killed her child before its birth-time and had given it to the fairies. Villein's child or not the little creature was a soul created by God. But perhaps he was an elf that the fairies had planted in her as a seed while she slept; or begotten by the rays of moonlight? Perhaps she had not really damned him; he had been damned already. It would explain why he looked like a little frog, with squirrel's eyes; and it seemed to her his eyes would have been like those of the hares or magpies in the forest, which was why the animals were not afraid of her.

The forest was hot and stank of decay, the streams turned to dried mud; from the evil-smelling bogs, partridge and woodcock rose on heavy wings, to fall after flying ten paces. Wild boars, the stench of their lair travelling far, dozed in fetid wallows of warm mud. Eglantine came across them while seeking a spring of water: with the mud over her ankles, she had put aside the brambles of a young willow coppice and had stood still, contemplating the great, motionless beasts which snorted noisily and stared at her out of tiny, blood-shot eyes. They looked as if the spirit of earth had modelled them there, out of mud and clay, for all eternity and had given them their red eyes to see to the end of time. To Eglantine it seemed that all this living community drew the same breath, saw with the same glance; that from the turgid soil sprang again mosses and grasses and trees and birds and beasts, all rotting and germinating at the same time, and that it was a single immense being which looked out through every eye, the knots on the trees, the pores of the leaves and her own eyes too. Perhaps, after all, it was not so difficult to be changed into a bird.

But thirst tormented her. At the edge of the marshes she had found nothing but rotten water mixed with slime when she plunged her hands among the blackened rushes. She had drunk a little from the hollow of her hand and had rubbed her forehead and her hair with it; but it smelled bad, it was warm and bitter and made her even thirstier. There, she found places where the sun had never penetrated; it was not so hot, but heavy and oppressive. At Bernon, the lady had a reserve of wine and beer. "She'll drive me away," Eglantine thought. "But first she will let me drink. She would have given drink even to a leper. I shall not even go in; I can drink a stoup of beer at the door and then go away. Ah, those women were mad, wanting me to make rain when Morgan will not even make the tiniest spring flow for me. But even if I could bring down rain for them, I should not do it; I would rather die of thirst myself. Change me, Morgan, into a bird, that I may not fall into the hands of these vile, low-born people, for I am well-born, of noble blood, daughter of a lovely, fair-haired damsel. Change me into a bird and I shall drink the eyes of their goats at night-time. I will fly round and round their children, leading them astray into the marshes. For they gave me to a villein, I, who am of noble blood."

A white haze was spreading over the sky but the sun still burned through it and pressed down more heavily than ever on the heat-stricken, panting forest. Eglantine dragged herself slowly along beside the dried and withering coppices.

The priest of Linnières was a countryman and very superstitious, believing in the fairies as firmly as he believed in the saints. That was why he had not prevented the women from going at night to make their offering to the fairies. He was a swarthy, rugged, horse-faced peasant. He was on his knees before the altar of his little whitewashed church, his massive hands clasped on his wooden rosary. He prayed to Saint Cydroine and Saint Madeleine and Saint Anne-of-the-Forest, reproaching them bitterly for their harshness to his poor people.

"Is it necessary, Saint Cydroine," he said, "that the poor people should suffer famine for the faults of one wicked and accursed man? He, le Gros, won't go hungry; on the contrary he'll take away our bread to the last mouthful and when we have no more he'll buy it elsewhere. Must the whole forest burn to smoke out one wolf?"

He began the office for None with revolt in his heart, and behind him the men of Linnières prayed in low voices, raising their eyes to the little square windows of the church; clouds which had seemed to be gathering were dispersing again; the day would end without rain. People were saying that it had rained between Troyes and Jeugni and that to the south, towards Auxerre, there had been a storm.

After None the priest took up the iron cross which was behind the altar and raised it above his head.

"My brothers, let us go to the fields once again, today. May God behold our misery. We will make the tour of the vineyards and meadows, reciting our prayers, bare-foot, like penitents."

And, leading the hymn with a sob in his voice, he moved off with the cross held high. The men's voices echoed their priest's, sounding like a dull, threatening murmur. They marched along the vineyards by dusty paths, the priest leading in his soiled cassock, his rudely cut hair falling from his tonsure in a fringe. The men followed him, their bonnets in their hands, their shoulders bent, raising a cloud of dust with their naked, blackened feet.

From the castle they could hear the quick, monotonous refrain of the masons' song and the shouted orders of the overseer. "Ho! ha! heave! Slip the rope!" A few women joined the procession. At each shout from the overseer they uttered oaths and curses. "Heathen! You won't find them in our procession. It's not their land."

Herbert's huntsmen came out of the forest carrying the bodies of two wild boars slung on poles. Overtaking the procession, two of them crossed themselves, but one shouted:

"Hey, scum! So your women have spent the night praying to the Devil!"

The priest went forward, with the cross raised, and the peasants followed in single file, making the tour of the vineyards and meadows.

THE STORM

NIGHT was falling. It had not rained, the air seemed more ponderous than lead; the well at Bernon was almost dry; there was no water for the horses and sheep to drink. Old Milon, the lady's intendant, had sent four servants to bring water from Linnières. The lady, her servants, and her little daughter stood at the door watching the clouds and thinking:

"Surely it will rain tomorrow."

A group of peasants—about twenty men and a few women—came out of the woods and advanced across the big clearing in front of the farm. "They're coming to ask for water," the lady thought. Then she saw that they were carrying bill-hooks and forks, not buckets. Most of them were from Linnières, but a few were from Bernon village and she recognized them as well-known trouble-makers. The lady took fright: the weather must have brought these people to the end of their tether and made them capable of God knows what mischief. She called Milon to stand beside her and ordered her maids indoors.

The peasants were now all round her. They had removed their bonnets:

"Lady, we don't want to offend you but we must have the damsel, the master's daughter. Because of her we get no rain in these parts."

"Come," the lady said, "that's an old wives' tale. You'd do better to go and pray to God."

"We've been doing nothing else. They say it's been raining over at Jeugni."

One of the men had stepped forward, a tall, loose-knit rascal, pock-marked, with a long, thin neck. This was André, the village spokesman.

"Lady, you can see for yourself, it's going to pass over us again today and go and rain on the convent. Our men—and the priest, too— say it will keep passing by us so long as the damsel is here. We don't want to offend you but we've got to do this for the country and the people. We can't stand any more."

"The damsel is not here," the lady said. "She has not been here for three days; she must have lost herself in the forest. I don't know where she is."

The men exchanged suspicious glances. The lady saw their hard faces, as if made of leather, their greasy hair, looming near to her; sun-blacked foreheads, low beneath ill-cut fringes, were covered with beads of sweat. Their weary bodies gave out a sour smell of wild animals. The lady looked at the forks in their hands and the sickles the women were carrying.

"If you fear sin, go away," she said. "The damsel is not here. Return to your homes. It will rain tomorrow, if not tonight."

"So she's not here," André said. "Well, we'll wait. We're not leaving here without her." The lady sent for a pin of beer and a stoup and offered them drink. But they refused. They stood there, looking at each other, as if asking each other what to do next. The lady guessed that they were thinking of searching the house. To the oldest woman present she said:

"Come, Mahaut, Madeleine shall take you over the house from cellar to loft; you can search everywhere, you will see for yourself that the damsel is not here and you will tell them so."

Mahaut came forward, suspiciously, then stopped on the threshold and refused to enter the house. The lady did not know what to do, for the servants had gone to Linnières; she had only two old men and a child of fourteen at Bernon. She tried to step swiftly into the house and shut herself in and at that moment a flash of lightning streaked the grey sky; the men raised their heads, their eyes full of hope. There was no thunder.

The forest was now a black mass, the clearing grey, and a reddish fog was trailing across the sky; there must be a fire over towards Tonnerre. It was like being in a furnace. The lady's face was running with sweat and she could feel her shift sticking to her body. She stayed there, her back against the door, beside Milon, with the peasants still standing before her, all waiting as if bewitched and unable to move. There was another flash of summer lightning, and another. And the lady, Milon, the peasants stood there like condemned men awaiting judgment, exhausted, breathing the air, which seemed too dense to enter their mouths, laboriously.

"You see!" one of the men said. "It's going round us again! It won't break here."

"Into the house!" André said, suddenly, shaking himself, "we'll soon see if she's there."

The lady barred their way.

"For God's sake, don't go in; you'll be tried for revolt."

André shouted:

"Who will try us? Who can judge us?"

"God will judge you," the lady shouted. "Look—more lightning. It will strike you."

Disconcerted, the men hesitated an instant. At that moment a more vivid flash, which threw a livid light over wood and meadow, picked out the tall silhouette of Eglantine coming slowly across the clearing. There was a yell of terror.

"The witch! There she is!" In the succeeding twilight she could still be seen; she had halted and seemed to be waiting. With raised forks the men rushed at her—she raised her hand to her mouth, cried out and began to run. She did not have time to reach the trees; the men had caught her and were dragging her away.

The lady and Milon ran towards the stables, shouting to the maids to get down the lances and the old sword from the wall. There were three sound horses; the lady, the intendant and Jean, the boy, mounted, the two old servants running after them brandishing massive, rusty lances. The lightning came more frequently, silent, terrible. Its yellow and white glare lit up the undergrowth of the wood and after it the gloaming light was like deep night; it was difficult to breathe. The air was full of yelling, shrill cries and the voice of a child calling thrice—"Father! Father! Father!"

The horses charged full into the group of peasants near the place where trees were being felled that year. Milon and Jean thrust and struck with their lances more or less at random and there arose such a wailing that the very forest seemed to moan. The frightened horses plunged and struggled, trampling bodies and heads. In the semi-darkness the villagers were under the impression that a troop of horse had fallen upon them. They defended themselves savagely, striking at the horses with their forks; the lady's horse, its entrails pierced, collapsed. She had just time to slip to the ground, flailing about her with her old sword without much idea of what was happening—never before had she used a sword and the blows she was striking frightened her. She could barely distinguish the people surrounding her and was afraid of striking her own. By the glare of a lightning flash she suddenly saw two men bleeding, a woman with her face smashed, raised forks, the trunks of dead trees and, in the grass, fallen against a felled trunk, the naked body of Eglantine, all lacerated with long wounds and covered with blood. Immediately thereafter came the first clap of thunder, a crash so tremendous that nobody grasped what it was; it was as if every tree in the forest had snapped off and great masses of rock been flung down, nearby, on to an iron roof. Followed a crackling, a sound of battering branches, the beating of wings and the outcry of terrified birds.

Terror-stricken, the small group of men in the forest became suddenly still, lances and forks raised, suspended. The horses snorted. Milon struck a man who was stooping over Eglantine full in the face with his lance. There was a scream of pain and the peasants began to ply their forks again. It was almost dark. The sky was lit by the red clouds of distant fires. And somewhere, quite near, where the lightning had struck, a crackling flame was rearing up at the heart of a cloud of smoke.

André had leaped on to a tree-trunk, wielding his fork furiously, striking at emptiness, and howling:

"Death! Death! Kill them, kill them all! They've sucked our blood! Death to the wolves!"

And all the men and women were about him, in that clearing encircled by fire, howling like animals with pain and anger.

Then another flash of lightning blinded them all. They were drowned in white glare and, in the uproar of thunder which followed, no one dared move or breathe. The lightning had struck towards Linnières and those men who could still move dropped their weapons and began running towards the village. One woman and three men were left on the field, writhing at the horses' feet.

Milon was wounded in the leg but able to sit his horse. He stooped and drew Eglantine's body up on to the saddle; she was still alive and began screaming horribly the moment he touched her. The lady took little Jean's horse, still unhurt, and they set off for the farm, too angry to think of the enemy wounded. In any case the lady herself was wounded in the shoulder, her head was bare, her dress torn. And Eglantine was still screaming and struggling in Milon's arms.

The wind was blowing from the west, towards Linnières. The dried grass, bushes and bramble thickets were burning like straw. The forest was on fire.

Then the rain came.

At Bernon they could smell the smoke and hear the nearby crackle of flame but the wind was blowing to the south-east and there seemed no immediate danger. Yet the village of Bernon, comprising about fifteen houses a little apart from the manor farm, was threatened, for the wind might change and, in spite of the rain, the fire was still gaining. The peasants were driving their sheep on to the new road, which led to Seuroi, to reach the meadows. Long streaks of driving rain were visible in the light of clouds of white smoke rising from the neighborhood of Linnières.

In the big room of the farmhouse two tallow candles were burning, set in tall candlesticks. A weird red light filtered in through the small, square windows. In the cattle-pens the sheep were bleating, the horses snorting and stamping and whinnying loudly, joyously—the beasts could smell the rain and seemed drunk with it. The maids were running with buckets, pots and troughs, putting them outside the door to catch the water and holding their burning faces and clammy hands out to the rain. Pale and haggard in the light from the curtain of white smoke hanging above the forest, they crossed themselves and recited their prayers. "O Holy Mary, Saint Anne, make the water fall and fall, that the fire may not reach the village." Maddened by the fire, hares, does and foxes came running into the clearing, ran round and round, seeking to hide themselves in the bushes or take refuge behind the barns; the air was alive with the heavy flight of marsh birds beating their wings, blundering into the roof, suddenly visible turning on their great, dark, vibrant wings against the curtain of smoke. Each flash of lightning bathed the whole scene in a white glare; the streaks of rain gleamed, then were unseen again as the deafening clatter of thunder covered the uproar from the forest; the women uttered piercing cries and covered their ears.

On the floor near the hearth Eglantine was lying on a bed of wolf

pelts and blankets. The lady was on her knees beside her, bathing her
wounds. Eglantine's breasts were badly hacked and her whole body
lacerated with sickle cuts. There were two deep wounds in her side
from which blood spurted rhythmically. She was still alive but the
lady told herself that the girl could not last the night. To fetch the
priest from Linnières it would have been necessary to cross the blazing
forest. Even the road to Hervi was not without danger. Milon was
coming and going restlessly, limping on his wounded leg. He went to
look at the horses, studied the sky, sat down and then got up again to
snuff the candles. There was no rest for anyone that night. Eglantine
groaned and her breath came harshly: "Father! O Father! Help me.
They're trying to kill me. Father, where are you, Father?"

The lady listened to the rolling thunder-claps and thought of
Herbert, on the other side of the forest. Who knows—perhaps the
castle had been struck by lightning. "Accursed," she thought, "accursed, I cursed him." The words went round and round in her mind
and she could think of nothing else.

Mounted men passed before the windows, there was the sound of
voices at the door. Pierre and Haguenier, followed by young Joceran
and Pierre's squire, entered the hall, all drenched with water, their
hair stuck to their pale faces.

"We've come to ask for shelter, lady," Haguenier said. "The road is
barred over by Linnières." Pierre shook himself, throwing his cloak
and gloves on the ground. His teeth were chattering.

"We rode slap into the sheep; we found your peasants on their way to
Seuroi. What a night! You'd think it was the Last Judgment."

The lady hastened to draw a blanket over Eglantine but Haguenier
had already seen the waxy flesh and the bloody wounds of her body.

"O, my sister, what have they done to you?"

"She is punished for her sins," the lady said. "She will commit no
more, by God's will."

Haguenier stooped over the dying girl. Her color was earthy and her
enormous eyes were ringed by dark circles of brown; her mouth was
bleeding and the lips dry. She recognized Haguenier and smiled at him
weakly.

THE WOLF

HERBERT lay on the chapel floor, a crucifix in his hands. Despite the storm he had sent his servants hastening through the night to Hervi, with horses, to bring back Father Aubert at once, for he had quarrelled with his chaplain, a timid and even servile man who had nevertheless no longer been able to bear his lord's jesting, careless manner. There was no priest at the castle. The priest of Linnières, a coarse and ignorant fellow, failed to inspire confidence in Herbert; that Seuroi peasant was of no use to him in the terror which had seized him.

The village was on fire. Lightning had struck the oak by the church. The peasants had not even had time to get their cattle out. They were now crammed into the castle courtyard, behind the new outer wall. There was not much danger of the fire spreading to the castle because of the wide moat which had recently been dug along the north wall. But Herbert was well aware—and others were thinking the same—that lightning might strike again, this time the keep itself. And the rain was not heavy enough to put out the fire. With the first lightning flashes of the storm Herbert had sent for his wife and ordered her to take her jewel-box and the small coffer in which he kept his gold pieces and his papers and go down to the cellars with her daughters. In the event of fire they could escape by the underground passage leading to Hervi. He had had it tunnelled, secretly, immediately following the death of the old Haguenier, his father-in-law, and he always carried the key of it on his person.

Then he had taken his leave of the lady Aelis, asking her forgiveness for all the wrongs he had done her. He had said:

"It is very likely I may die this night, and, if it is on my account that God is making this din, I shall not escape, wherever I go. I prefer to have you in safety. My testament apportioning Bercenay between our daughters has been drawn and each of them will have a small but sufficient dower. The rest, unfortunately, will go to Isabeau's daughter; there is nothing I can do about it."

Dame Aelis thereupon went down to the cellars, greatly astonished and hoping, in the bottom of her heart, that her husband was not mistaken.

Then Herbert had asked forgiveness for his faults of the whole household and had gone to lie flat in the chapel, in the attitude of a dying man, thinking that the most proper way to wait for death. His only fear was that the priest would not arrive in time.

He was not a fearful or timid man; he had been on two crusades and suffered more wounds than most people—nor had the fear of Hell tormented him overmuch, although he had committed a fair number of mortal sins. But he had always thought that he would be able to die in a manner sufficiently edifying to get him to Paradise, although perhaps after a rather long period of Purgatory. Now, owing to his mother's fault, this storm had burst on him, catching him unprepared without a priest in the house. Since the lady had cursed him he had felt himself to be a target for judgment and he had no illusions: he was going to be struck down; the main thing was to confess himself first.

In the last few days he had been busy with preparations for his pilgrimage and had hardly had time to make his peace with his conscience. After the malediction and having got over his first panic terror, he had faced the situation coolly.

"Provided the priest arrives in time, I shall just manage it," he thought. "I'll make a gift of all my Linnières lands to the Benedictine fathers, and with the money I have at Troyes I'll have a church built in honor of Saint Anselme, my father's patron saint. For all the good Haguenier's likely to make of my property, the Church might as well have it. I can be sure of masses and prayers for years, decades perhaps. They say the agonies of Purgatory are as bad as those of Hell, but if a man's sure of getting out of it, it should not be so terrible. But death? The body's agony? The parting of soul from body, so painful for everyone, even the best? It is a moment when the soul doubts and by doubting blasphemes; and the Devil is on the watch. Oh, nameless agony! Oh, lost soul! Can such a passage be travelled fearlessly because of a few words muttered by a priest and a scrap of unleavened bread? And I have not even a mother's prayers to help me on my death-bed."

Such a wave of self-pity rose in Herbert that it put the fear of Hell out of his mind. He saw himself as a child again, then as a young man, and all the injustices he had ever suffered seared his heart. Neglected by his parents, a younger son, misallied in wedlock. What else? That he, with strength and talents which would have done honor to the son of a king, should have so wretched a life, so empty and loveless, friendless; and now, at the very moment when it seemed he was to achieve something, he must die.

"Because of my mother," he thought. "Women understand nothing. I could have made reparation for my sins. And now it's over, done with. And the priest is taking a long time to come. O God, Lord, Master, I repent, I repent of everything"—yet at heart he felt no repentance, only a vague regret for a bad stroke of business, and, even then, it was his nature, he had never really intended to do evil.

The storm was passing over, Herbert began to think that the lightning had missed its aim, had struck some paces further to the south than was intended. Perhaps, this time, he would come off safely. Nevertheless he remained motionless, the cross pressed to his lips, and it was so that Father Arthème, curate to the priest of Hervi, found him.

"What's this, my son, I thought you sick unto death!" he said. "If we were fetched out in the middle of the night for every man who's afraid of lightning we should need as many priests as Christians!"

"This is no time for jesting, Father," Herbert said sullenly, raising himself on his elbow. "In the first place Father Aubert might very well have done me the honor to come himself, after all I've done to beautify his church. But one priest's as good as another, eh? You yourselves say so at all events. And, by the way," he added, "if you thought me dying, why have you not brought the Sacraments?"

The priest frowned and seemed embarrassed.

"Father Aubert had his reasons. In any case you can go to the church yourself in the morning. But if you insist I am ready to hear your confession."

Herbert knelt and said:

"Father, my soul is in great peril. But I am determined to repent and make reparation for my faults."

And the priest listened to an interminable confession, learning things concerning the burly nobleman which he would never have suspected. Herbert accused himself of having slily hastened the death of his father-in-law of Buchie by making him drink despite his diseased liver; of having had merchants from the south, using the county road, robbed and killed, behind Hervi; of having lent money on security, asking more interest than the Jews; of having lied in the confessional; of hav-

ing violated a boy, page to a knight of Troyes; of having watered the
wine he was selling; of having secretly broken fasts; of having committed incest with his half-sister; of having, one day when he was
drunk, himself performed a sacrilegious parody of the marriage service
between a dog and a sow—finally Father Arthème was wondering
whether Herbert was not inventing sins for himself, as happened occasionally to excessively scrupulous people who believe themselves to
have committed all the sins they have really only envisaged. But
Herbert was not the man to make himself out worse than he was.

"Never," said the priest, "will you receive absolution until you have
done penance and expiated. According to secular justice, you have deserved the death penalty."

"Ha! Then what use is confession? I've no need of a priest to go and
confess to the count's judges and get myself hanged."

"I tell you, my son, it would be better for your soul to make atonement before the world's justice. But we cannot force you to do it.
It is an error typical of a man of the world to find that way too hard.
Yet it is the easiest."

"Good. Then tell me the most difficult."

"Reparation, so far as that is possible, for the wrongs done to your
fellow men, renunciation of worldly things; and go and live in the
wilderness, fasting and weeping for your sins."

"I've been told that a hundred times already. But look you, Father,
I am a capable man, I've a head for building roads and bridges, castles
and churches. I can do good to the country."

"No good can come of ill-gotten money. And though you do good to
the country in that way, you do none to your soul and will not avoid
the tortures of Hell."

"Ah, Father, an old wolf doesn't fear fire, as long as it's not burning
him. I've heard too much about the tortures of Hell. And then, who
has ever seen them, that they should be thus spoken of as certain? It
may be very impious to say so, but it seems to me that it's a case of the
priests saying more than they really know."

"My son, it is said that certain holy hermits have received such terrible revelations of these tortures that their hair turned white in a
single night. Do you not know the parable of Lazarus and the wicked
rich man?"

"Certainly, certainly. I'm no holy hermit, and the Devil so darkens my spirit that I am no longer afraid of all that. It's of bodily death that I am afraid, Father, and if you could offer me Saint George's place in Paradise, I should refuse it."

"Words," said the priest. "Words most unworthy of a Christian, and especially of a soldier."

"It's obvious you've never used a sword, Father. Do you suppose a soldier is not afraid? He has more occasion to feel fear than other men. It's when you value your life that you insist on selling it dear. And don't tell me to bury myself in the wilderness, for I'd be a much worse hermit than I am a bad chatelain. Give me a punishment more suited to my nature. I'll do my best."

He bargained for a long time until finally Father Arthème made him understand that first he must make reparation. Thereafter, perhaps, he might receive absolution.

The dawn was cool and misty. The rain had extinguished the fire almost everywhere. Thin wisps of smoke rose from the black and russet forest; the village had been completely destroyed and the peasants were seeking here and there in the still smoking ruins for iron pots and other utensils which the fire happened to have spared and the charred or bloody corpses of sheep and goats. Foxes and wolves were already prowling in the nearby skirt of the woods, and crows turning above the carrion.

At the castle the normal routine was being resumed. Then the Linnières peasants learned from those of Bernon what had happened at the manor farm. The boy Jean arrived from Bernon on horseback to give Herbert the details.

Herbert was wearing the clothes he wore for fast-days and seemed weary and contrite.

"I forgive them everything," he said, in a dismal voice. "I am a worse sinner than any of them. If my mother is willing to receive me, I will go to Bernon and ask forgiveness for my faults. I am a changed man. I want her first to forgive me. Then will I make reparation for all the evil I have done."

And he sent the lady Aelis and his two eldest daughters and Garin his squire to plead for him with the lady.

Down in the village the Bernon incident was as much talked of as up at the castle; the storm and the fire were almost forgotten. The Linnières peasantry had already seen their houses burn more than once, and the lord was promising to compensate them for the loss of their cattle and to rebuild their houses. But the lady was well loved in that countryside—so, even, was Eglantine, despite her madness—and it seemed unjust that the local bad characters should have attacked two defenseless women; witch or not, once the rain had fallen the damsel appeared quite harmless; and she was dying.

Towards the hour of Sext a messenger returned from Bernon to inform Herbert of his mother's will; if the past night had really brought his wickedness home to him she might forgive him but she made no promises. In any case he must come to Bernon and publicly beg Eglantine's pardon.

"*Her* pardon," Herbert exclaimed, with disgust. "It's obvious that my mother knows me. That I should beg forgiveness of her! Yes—I'll go on my knees, I'll have myself flogged with rods if necessary. But let her not try to humiliate me before a whore!"

But Father Arthème, who was still there, advised him to obey.

"Really to become a new man, pride must be humbled, and perhaps this girl is no worse a sinner than yourself."

Herbert gave him an evil look but, throwing his cloak over his shoulders, he went down into the courtyard.

"After all," he thought, "if the girl's dying it might be better to beg her pardon—but yet, what for in Heaven's name? She's caused me nothing but trouble. I shall look fine indeed if she gets over it, and then what should I do with her? Well, so much the worse; we shall see."

He was so wishful to see his mother again that he was ready to swallow the bitter draught, but God knew his present feelings for the girl he had once loved madly were ferocious contempt and disgust. The time when he used to wait for her in the meadow behind the chapel, pacing up and down with his blood on fire, was too close—could he forget that he had allowed himself to be scratched, bitten and insulted and had almost taken pleasure in it? To him, a mistress who no longer pleased him was like an unclean object, like soiled linen—and this one, above all, this girl who, knowing that he was her brother, had given herself to him, really loved him. Now, it seemed, he was to ask her forgiveness for that!

"However, perhaps she'll be dead by the time I get there," he thought. And as he crossed the half-burned forest he tried to estimate the cost of the damage.

THE OTHER STRICKEN BIRD

EGLANTINE lay in the lady's own bed, surrounded with cushions and furs, her head tipped back, the breath snoring in her throat. Consciousness had returned and she had confessed to the priest of Linnières. She had been very surprised by the remission of her faults and now hardly knew what to think of herself. She was in great pain; one lung was perforated and breathing an agony. Her other wounds were already less painful, for her body was dying.

"So then," she thought, "I am going to die; they beat me at last. I've no longer the right to cast spells on them, since I've been confessed. They'll bury me in Hervi churchyard next to my baby sister Juliane. What shall I feel, under the sod there, with the white worms everywhere, everywhere, in my nose, in my eyes . . . Oh, how sad it is, it would have been better to be changed into a bird. They say the soul stays by the body forty days. After that, perhaps I shall go and see my father on the road to Jerusalem, if they'll let me. Or perhaps the devils will take me down under the earth to be eaten by snakes. It's funny, but I'm not frightened yet. And nothing seems to matter now!"

She opened her eyes. The lady was beside her and wiped her face with a cloth dipped in wine and water. Eglantine asked: "Lady, will it be long now?" She saw the old woman's lips tremble, then her mouth was distorted. "She is crying; why?" the girl thought, astonished. "Oh, yes, she must be thinking of my father; they say I'm like him." She tried to smile and asked, between two gasps: "Lady, did my father shave his chin when he was young?" The lady thought she was delirious and again pressed the wet cloth to her forehead.

It was very moving to watch that tall, still almost childish body sinking slowly into death. Eglantine seemed already disproportionately elongated and heavy, as corpses are. Her big hands were inert on the bed-cover and her wounds were no longer bleeding. But from time to time a bloody froth appeared about her lips. Her face, the color of dirty leather, was impassive and solemn; a childish gravity lent beauty to her

large, simple features, and the big brown eyes had the resigned, sa-
gacious expression of a wounded animal.

Eglantine had received the Host with indifference, almost without
understanding what was happening. Then she became slightly delirious.
She asked Haguenier to come nearer and to hold her hand. Towards
noon, as she seemed fairly quiet, the lady said to her:

"My daughter, Herbert is here, outside the house. If you wish it he
will come in and ask your forgiveness before all of us for the wrongs he
did you."

Eglantine let her head fall back with an air of weariness.

"What is that wild boar to me? Tell him I forgive him, if he wants
me to."

The lady had this answer conveyed to her son but did not allow him
to come in.

Herbert waited, sitting before the door on a bench still wet from the
rain. Servants came and went, watering the horses, cleaning out the
stables; hens were clucking in the farmyard, women passed with buckets
of water; life was being resumed as if nothing had happened, as if there
had been no great drought. The air was pure and cool, smelling of moist
manure and wet earth; animals and men breathed in these smells with a
tranquil joy—it was a moment of truce. The air seemed full of gentle
softness; the bad days were gone by or yet to come, but on this day no
man could do harm, if only because all had need of rest.

Herbert was whittling a piece of wood with his knife. They had left
him outside; so much the better. What was happening there, in that
room, did not interest him; he was sure that, in the end, his mother
would come to him. He was thinking of the time when he was little and
she could send him rolling with a swinging blow of her hand. Now she
would have had to be stronger than Roland to do it. But she could deal
him blows with a strength of a different order and he almost smiled with
admiring pride at the thought of the womb that had conceived him;
she still understood very well how to punish him—she had not forgotten that she was his mother. But she would forgive him and, seeing
him so changed, perhaps she would consent to come and live with him
at Linnières. He would know how to do her honor and see that she lived
as a great lady; the old man had never dreamed of that, he had made
her toil all her days like a plow-horse. But he—he would dress her in
vair and in sables, and she should eat off silver plate.

Within, tall candles burned beside the wooden bed where Eglantine lay, and by the hearth the women were preparing white sheets and the long shroud of linen to put on the body. The Linnières priest was on his knees at the bedside, saying the prayers for the dying in his rough, monotonous voice; when he was silent nothing was to be heard but the harsh breathing of the dying girl and the spluttering of the candles. The lady, on her knees at the foot of the bed, was praying in a low voice, her lips moving. Haguenier was still seated on the bed with Eglantine's hand in his, for she would not let it go.

All of them, Milon and Joceran and Pierre and the Bernon servants, were silent and not only out of respect for the conventions. It was as if all of them, suddenly, in that day of respite, had realized how much affection they had, without knowing it, for this creature so neglected and despised, seen how empty the countryside would be without her—half-boy, half-girl—haunting the woods and talking to the fairies. She was leaving them with the regal indifference of some great bird folding its wings in sleep. Her presence filled the room, and she seemed to be the only living being among so many phantoms, so solemn and austere was the fixed glance of her eyes. The death-rattle was soft in her throat.

At a certain moment she made an effort to raise her head and stretched out her hand towards the candles. She seemed to be trying to say something; it was as if she could not find the right words. It suddenly seemed to her that the room was very dark; she could hear a snoring sound, a broken whistling, and the sound was very disagreeable to her, as if it were preventing her from hearing something very important. She must make a painful effort to set the noise aside, to ignore it, but it was always there—she did not know it was the rattle of the breath in her throat. And it was so dark, so dark—how was it that night had fallen so soon? It saddened and surprised her. She heaved a great sigh and said: "What a short day!" They were her last words. For thereafter she could speak no more.

A voice, very remote, cried: "Eglantine!" She thought she had heard the voice before, but where?

"Who is it, Eglantine? My God, who is it? I knew it." Then she felt herself rising, still rising, and her body had become so large that she could have taken the farm in her hand, like a pebble. Only she no longer had hands.

The priest placed a cross on the dead girl's chest and the lady placed the dead hands, one upon the other, on the cross. The women were already beginning to mourn aloud. Then the lady Alis approached the bed, bearing a shift of white linen, and a maidservant set a jar of vinegar and water beside the bed. The priest bowed towards the body and departed. Haguenier, too, prepared to leave.

His hand was wet with sweat from holding the dying girl's hand so long. It was almost as if some essence of the girl had passed into him and that this body which the women were bathing now was a part of his own. He felt himself to be dead and shrouded. Marie—it was Marie they were going to bury with Eglantine's body; it was Marie who was keening in these women's voices, she who danced in the little flames on the hearth and who saw, through the open door, grey clouds and the branches of trees thrashing in the wind. Marie, sad, humiliated, scourged by life; it was Marie's sweet, pure body which had been lacerated with blows from forks and bill-hooks.

"Ah, sweet sister, though God knows I loved you well, yet now my heart is in too much pain. Oh, what have they done to her, my beautiful and tender, my only joy; they have parted us and I shall not see her again.

"Sister, farewell, I've your last sweat here, on my hand, and her hand, her warm and living hand, shall I never touch again. I shall see your dead face again, but her living one, all light, I cannot see. Oh, why is she not here, in your place, sister, that I might see her, pale and serene, and myself bear her to her grave; it would be better than to know her alive, in another man's arms, and bearing his child in her womb."

One of the young maidservants, who was with child, was leaning against the chimney-piece and wiping her forehead with the back of her hand. A vision of Marie pregnant flashed suddenly upon Haguenier, so that for an instant he saw the servant dressed in a long blue gown like Marie's, with Marie's face and, on that face, the servant's expression of exhaustion and indifference. He shook his head and blinked his eyes to banish the vision. "I'm going mad," he told himself. From the surface of the water in the bucket near the fire Marie's face stared at him with sad and feverish eyes. His head swam; he lay down on the floor.

"This has got to stop," he thought. "I've got to forget myself, drink, get bestially drunk. After the funeral I'll go to Troyes, disguised. I can see her in church. Nobody will know. My promise? To the Devil with that!"

Washed, combed and neat, her hair in two short plaits laid on her chest, Eglantine lay upon the table, calm and beautiful. She seemed to have returned to the time of her adolescence, the time when she still wore beautiful dresses and took care of her hair, and when her father was proud of her. But never before had such regal majesty been seen on her brow. The whole household, and the villagers who came to see the body, no longer remembered her past: this was the damsel Eglantine, the master's daughter they were burying, an innocent savagely slaughtered by brutes. It was said that those Linnières men who had taken part in the outrage were hiding away in the woods.

Herbert had also come to pay homage to the dead, and peasants and servants crowding into the room stretched their necks to see whether the corpse made any sign, for Herbert was held to be the one really guilty of all that had happened on the evening of the storm. Troubled, Herbert turned his eyes away from the dead girl's face: he suffered no remorse but he felt himself watched. The lady was present, but she had drawn her veil across her face. Herbert was thinking. "All this to-do over a girl who ended just as she deserved." He recognized no right but his own to judge her. She was his chattel, he had estimated her price and had done as he pleased with her. What need had these others, what right, to meddle?

The lady gave her adopted daughter a solemn funeral and required of Herbert that he punish those guilty of her death, naming them all. It had, in any case, been plain insurrection. She and Milon had been wounded, vengeance was called for. Herbert, the first moment of tenderness passed, did not need to be asked twice. On the day following Eglantine's death the strange state of peace and general pardon which had followed the storm was forgotten, as if no one had ever been aware of it. At Linnières the whole household was stirring: Herbert had sent for soldiers from Hervi; the burned houses were being demolished, losses calculated and search parties were beating the woods for the men who had fled. Herbert made a report to the viscount of Saint-Florentin and to the count's bailiff, and undertook to mete out justice himself. He was within his rights, his own serfs having murdered his half-sister and attacked his mother. With Pierre and Haguenier, Joceran of Puiseaux and Jacques of Breul, his nearest neighbors, at his back, he had the thirteen culprits caught by his men, tied and flogged with rods. Then he had them lacerated with bill-hooks and lances by his soldiers, each one receiving as many wounds as there were on Eglantine's body. Finally he had them all hanged from trees about the village. And for many a long year the bloody funeral rites of the damsel of Bernon were talked of in that country.

Then Herbert deputed the management of his domains to Haguenier and set out on pilgrimage to Our Lady of Puy without having persuaded his mother to show him her face again, by which he was much afflicted. But the days of blood and reprisals had restored him; he was his own man again, sure of himself and of his rights and sure of gaining from the Virgin the pardon due to his good intentions.

Moreover, as he thought, this pilgrimage fell out very conveniently. The priest of Hervi bore him a grudge for his cruelty to the Linnières peasants and might try to bring the matter of his incest into the open. It was better to arrange to be forgotten for a while. Furthermore, since he had got thinner, he was delighted to be able to ride again and enjoy a change of scene. He had never yet seen Le Puy.

Part Four

Part Four

MARSEILLES

I. THE UNCONSOLED

MARSEILLES, red and pink and grey in a brown countryside dotted with pines and cypresses.

On every side the sea—deep green, leaden grey, striped with thin white crests. In the port, behind the ramparts, hundreds of ships and barques, sails furled, awaiting fine weather. An icy wind.

Auberi had never seen the sea and felt a surge of fear at the sight of that horizon with the void beyond. It made him giddy. He had never seen a town as large as Marseilles—even Le Puy seemed small beside it; he was constantly afraid of getting lost in it, of losing his blind men. There were so many people, too, as if it were always a fair-day—so many people speaking languages you don't understand and wearing clothes no Christian ever wore. They said there were even unbelievers, and people come from China. They said, too, it's a town of thieves; but who has naught fears naught. Bernard of Castans's money had long been spent; they were living on alms.

He had supposed that you only had to get to Marseilles to set foot on a ship and sail straight to the Holy Land. But no; now the old master was saying:

"The most difficult, still, will be to find a ship's master who will have us. In any case, there'll hardly be any sailings before the spring."

There were hundreds of poor pilgrims there, hanging about the port, earning a few coins here and there as stevedores or porters—and even for that it was necessary to watch for the arrival of a ship, be first on the spot and fight for the job. That was not for Auberi.

Some of the pilgrims had been waiting their turn for two years and

more, always hoping to attract the attention of some charitable lord or
some ship's master in a pious mood who might take them aboard for
nothing—it was by no means uncommon. But, at the same time, there
were too many among the pilgrims who had nowhere to go, who trailed
from Saint-Jacques to Jerusalem, from Jerusalem to Puy, back to Saint-
Jacques or the Saintes-Maries or to Rome. For a vow or for the soul of
one dead or to expiate a sin—for these things a man may well wait one
or two or ten years, until at last he gets a taste for the life, perhaps
because he has lost his place in any other. A pilgrim, after all, is in good
repute with other Christians and has a right of asylum in hospices and
monasteries.

Ansiau had gone to pray in the great cathedral of Marseilles, the one
which contains relics of the Virgin and of Saint Lazarus, and he was
worried by the thought that he had already been there four times—
going to and coming from his two crusades—and that he had no
memory of these visits. More and more often the image of things past
was escaping him. Sometimes he was obsessed by this failure, and he
would beat his head with his fist as if to force out the image of a face,
a house, a painted shield or a flower—but all was becoming confused in
his mind, he felt himself going blind a second time.

Standing before the reliquary which contained threads from the
Virgin's mantle, he stayed there, gripping the grille, hearing the spluttering of the burning candles, feeling their heat, trying to imagine
them—that, at least, he could do—there were certainly fifty of them.
He had not the means to pay for a single one and he felt remorseful;
what sort of pilgrim was he, who could not even offer Our Lady a little
candle lasting a few hours, he who had been eating and drinking and
breathing God's air for half a century? And this was the condition in
which, having finally decided to consecrate his life to prayer, he presented himself before the good, Gentle Lady! Are there not beggars
who fast day after day and save up their alms so as to be able to offer
Our Lady a silver candlestick or a necklace of gold? Whereas he was
trailing that unbeliever around with him, always ill and always complaining, demanding—not to speak of Auberi who was always hungry
as only a thirteen-year-old *is* hungry. With them, two deniers were gone
quicker than they came; and they don't come every day.

"O most beloved Good Lady, only grant that I may reach the grave
of my child, and that I may succeed in having masses said for all the

companions to whom I owe them—for Thierri and for André who asked
me for a mass as he lay dying—and then I shall be free of all my debts
on earth. I can find a place for Auberi in the Holy Land and as for
Bertrand—let him go where he likes; he can beg his bread alone as well
as I—and I shall go and live in Acre that I may be buried in the same
tomb as my child."

For two weeks the three pilgrims stayed at the hospice of the monastery of Saint-Jacques; then the arrival of a crowd of pilgrims on their
way to Rome for Christmas forced them to move on. Monks are not
over-fond of vagabonds who overstay their welcome in their hostels on
the pretext of being pilgrims for Jerusalem. How many of them actually
reach the Holy Land, God knows; the majority spend their life hanging
about the port getting strangers to take pity on them with their tales
of Jerusalem. And then Bertrand was scarcely convincing as a pilgrim;
he hardly even troubled to cross himself when the Holy Sacrament was
carried by him and, excusing himself on grounds of ill-health, did not
attend mass every day.

Not that winter was hard at Marseilles; there was no frost nor snow.
But the wind was chill, the rain glacial, and cold gnawed the very bones
of those who had scant covering and meager rations and lacked the
strength to fight against it. Auberi fell ill a fortnight before Christmas.
An old woman who sold salt fish in the port undertook, out of charity,
to lodge the child in her house; but she was not exactly rich, for almost
every evening she brought home all her fish, calling down maledictions
in this world and the next on the French, Burgundian and German
pilgrims who found that her fish smelled bad.

"What do they want it to smell of? Cinnamon? Or vanilla? Naturally, it smells of fish!" And, in fact, Auberi was stifling in the midst
of that same fishy odor but at least he was warm. He coughed and
wheezed and was near dying of his fever. The old woman gave him a
tepid, greasy water to drink, which smelled of fish: to eat, fish again, but
he hardly ate any. The good old woman crossed herself placidly and
was already beginning the prayers for the dying. Then she took up her
fish—still the same fish—and went out to the port.

The two blind men had learned to find the church for themselves
and sat near the steps with the other beggars. Bertrand, because both
eyes had been put out, always received a few deniers. Even then it was
necessary to hold them tight lest they be snatched by his neighbors:

he passed them to Ansiau who hid them in his mouth; he was still burly enough to deliver a few telling blows with his staff on occasion. But the blind, begging without a guide, are never safe: twice the old man was attacked from behind and robbed of his money. In the evening the two men returned, exhausted and frozen, to the fish-wife, and handed over their takings. She gave them fish and bread.

Ansiau lay down beside Auberi's pallet and passed his hands over the child's face. It was like fire.

"Auberi, fair child, can you hear me?"

"Oh, yes, my lord."

"Are you any better today, Auberi?"

"Oh, yes, I think so, my lord."

But in that failing, resigned voice was naught but weariness and the wish to be left alone. Auberi was very ill. Yet in the end he recovered. On the day before Christmas Eve a warm breeze blew in from the sea; the sun was as warm as in April. Auberi, still very weak and leaning on the blind man's arm, was able to leave the old woman's hovel. A salt breeze was blowing up from the blue-green sea, caressing their faces and stirring their hair; the child and the old man walked slowly, along by the rows of moored fishing boats gleaming in the sunshine against dark water. Huge black nets were spread out everywhere on the bluffs around the harbor. There was a strong smell of seaweed and cuttle-fish and salt and stagnant water and good sea air. Out of habit, the child warned the old man:

"To the left, my lord, there are nets here; there's a stone in front of you." But the old man was aware of them before Auberi warned him. And he no longer asked him to describe the sea and the sky and the boats. He had given up thinking of them.

On the following day the old man had a strange adventure which was to leave its mark on him. As it was Christmas Eve the two blind men, escorted by Auberi, had decided to go and spend the night in the cathedral. True, they had little hope of getting in, but at least they could pray in the forecourt, not far from the door, and they wanted to take up their place early.

They went up by very narrow streets, encumbered by water-carriers, wine-vendors, poultry-wives, and dragging their feet through streams of mud. Then they stopped at the corner of a street, in front of a large inn, where Auberi wanted to slip into the kitchens and ask for a bowl of hot water. Although it was the eve of a holy day, sounds of men's and women's voices, songs, oaths and laughter, were coming from the hall of the inn. The old man was not listening, he was thinking of other things. Then, suddenly, he dropped his staff and fell, first on his knees, then backwards, dragging Bertrand, who had been leaning on his arm, with him; from within the hostelry a woman's voice had called, out of the tumult of other voices:

"Hey! Eglantine, come here!"

Before realizing what it was he had heard, the old man had lost consciousness. He was stretched out in the gutter, motionless as a block of stone.

Bertrand, beside himself, not understanding what was happening, shook him by the shoulder. A monk and a young, pregnant woman had stopped and were stooping over the old man.

"Poor man," the woman said. "He'll have fainted from hunger. He's nothing but skin and bones."

The monk raised the blind man's head, wiping away with the tail of his frock the mud which had splashed the big, livid face.

"He's not dead, is he?" Bertrand said. "Auberi! Where's the boy got to?"

A maid ran out of the inn and poured a jug of water over the old man's head. The monk said:

"Here you are, getting good things ready for your stomachs on this day of the great feast of God, and you let poor people die of hunger at your door! Quickly now, have this old man carried inside and get him a cordial wine. There's no fast so strict but it gives way when there's a life to be saved."

"They're quite capable of feigning sick in front of our door to arouse pity," the maid said. "A fine effect, indeed, to have the way blocked by stinking wretches just when we're all decorated and the good people all ready for church!"

Ansiau was still not moving but the cold water had revived him. He heard the sound of voices and was trying to understand what they were saying. He could not. He did not even know where he was nor why he had fallen. He opened his mouth and said: "Thierri," and memory was abruptly restored to him. He moaned and let his head fall back.

"God be praised, he's coming to," the monk said. "Quick, woman, call somebody to drag him inside. Who is with him? Nobody but this blind man?"

Auberi had pushed through the inquisitive crowd and was bending over his master, ready to weep from fear.

"Me, Father. I'll help him, but it will need someone else." And, shouting at the maidservant: "You—shut up! He's a nobleman and he wouldn't have had you to take care of his pigs. You heard what the good father told you—he must go inside and rest. We're three of God's poor, that's what we are!"

Somewhat disconcerted by the urchin's boldness, the woman stood back to allow the old man, whom they had now got on his feet, to pass.

But he had already recovered his faculties. An almost childish expression of fearfulness passed over his eyeless face. He shook his head.

"No," he said, "I shall not go in. Let us go away from here. Come, Auberi. Bertrand, companion, where are you?"

"But come in, come in!" the maid said; "don't be so proud! You shall have bread and soup, it will be no sin for a sick man."

"Yes, yes, my lord, come in," Auberi said.

"No. It's an accursed place. Come away."

And to the great indignation of the maid and the inn servants who had come to the door, the old man took up his staff and made off up the street with a dragging stride, followed by Bertrand and Auberi. Half an hour later they were installed beneath the porch of the cathedral.

Seated on the flagstones, elbows on his knees, chin in his hands, the old man listened, from afar, to the words of the office of Compline. The cathedral, ill-lit as yet, was swarming with a silent crowd, wrapped in meditation and yet excited; sighs, the creaking of shoes, sniffs, whispering, altogether made up a confused background of noise against which the priest's words did not always stand out clearly. But the grave melody of the psalms chanted by the choir rose to the vaulted roof and reached the porch, doubled by an echo.

Ansiau could not clearly distinguish the words, but he knew them without altogether understanding them.

Scapulis suis obumbravit tibi, et sub pennis ejus sperabis. For Thou, O Lord, art my refuge.

Non accedet ad te malum. There shall no evil befall thee.

In manibus portabunt te ne forte offendas ad lapidem pedem tuum.
Cadent a latere tuo mille et decem millia a dextris tuis.

A thousand shall fall at thy side, and ten thousand at thy right hand; but it shall not come nigh thee. . . . Lord, ten thousand and more are fallen and among them those whom I most loved, and what has it profited me to be spared? I must believe that it was Thy will.

They shall carry Thee on their hands—Lord, I have stumbled against every stone of the way and my feet are broken and my body likewise. My heart has stumbled and knocked against every stone of the way.

Super aspidem et basiliscum ambulabis.

Thou shalt tread upon the asp and the basilisk,

The young lion and the serpent shalt thou trample under foot.

Quoniam cognovit nomen meum—I have not known Thy name, for I am a poor man, and ignorant. Thy name spells bitterness for those who care for the things of the flesh.

When a man no longer has the right to love what he loves, then the heart must die.

For more than a year now my body has been worn with weariness by frost and burning sun, by wind and rain, by mud and stony roads, and my eyes are already dead and my head emptied by weariness and hunger; but it takes more than these things to kill the heart. A voice, heard by chance, in a tumult of strangers' voices—that was enough. Why, Lord! it's a name, like another, not common, to be sure, but there may well be a hundred women so called, and even a thousand. And even were it to be she, I should not turn my head nor stop for one second.

> *Thou shalt not be afraid for the terror by night,*
> *Nor for the arrow that flieth by day*
> *For the pestilence that walketh in the darkness,*
> *Nor for the destruction that wasteth at noonday.*

And it is true, Lord, that I no longer fear anything but it seems that my heart is weaker than I. I fear nothing now, Lord, and it is true; for I can no longer desire anything.

So that thy foot shall never chance to spurn at any stone. Lord, You Yourself refused to be carried by the angels and wounded Your beautiful feet against the stones of the way. It was for that that You came, born in a stable on a winter's night. Since it is true that You love my lost child more than I love her, You will welcome her as You welcomed the prodigal son; but, as for me, my heart is worn and my love like a wound when the flesh is already dead and rotting.

To the sound of the overwhelming song of triumph which presently rose from all about them, filling the square and the surrounding streets, the two blind men sat crushed into their corner and repeating with the rest the glorias and hallelujahs—lost and as if drunk. Then, groping, they felt for each other and kissed each other on both cheeks, tranquilly, as if they had been two brothers prepared, after the midnight mass, to join their family and friends in feasting and rejoicing. Nothing awaited them without but a cold night and the hope of alms. In convent and hostel courtyards the poor were already at blows for a seat at the tables. Auberi had not forgotten it; he was almost fainting from fatigue and hunger. But the two old men still had in their hearts a store of past Christmas Eves, all bright and full of beloved faces, of which nothing was left to them but the sound of songs and the odor of incense and candles. Yes, even Bertrand's memories of his youth were too splendid to allow him to pray with less fervor now than he had done as a child. They went into the church, now three-quarters empty, to hear the two masses which were to be sung. On their knees on the flagstones strewn with hay and olive branches they stayed so, their hands clasped upon their staves. The overpowering weariness in their aching bones prevented them from thinking, even from dreaming. And the chimes of bells and cries of "Hallelujah!" echoing from every quarter and in every key, now beat at them, penetrated their bodies, became mixed with the pain of numbed legs and bent backs—until there was no fiber of them which did not seem to repeat, like a cry of pain, each hallelujah.

They spent the remainder of the night in the house of a wealthy ship-owner who, as he was coming out of the cathedral, had the idea of inviting the three poor people to his table. There they were served by the daughters of the house: their feet were washed and they were seated on cushions. All three were falling asleep from weariness and hardly tasted the good wines and delicate meats which were served. But Auberi was as happy as a king and, between eyelids which kept closing, he could see an endless procession of white napery and embroidered garments and silver plate and candles and rosy, smiling faces. He was a little drunk and was laughing, his head falling forward over the linen cloth. Everything seemed to him so beautiful and the people so good and he thought:

"What a splendid Christmas the good God has sent me."

He thought also of the castle of Moustallet, of his lord, of his brother. He almost thought he was among them again.

The two blind men and the child were able to sleep for several hours on real mattresses, covered with woollen blankets.

Then they had to leave, going out into streets swept by the mistral. The windows of the burgesses' houses were decorated with colored hangings which fluttered in the wind like flags. Children in their Sunday best were running about the streets rivalling each other in singing Christmas songs and carols, and the air smelled of the sea and of spring. Long processions were leaving the churches to parade the streets and tour the ramparts; the wind blew out candles, swept and lifted the priests' robes, women's skirts and veils; the figure of the Virgin shook beneath her canopy of brocade ornamented with Christmas roses.

Seated on the ramparts above the port, the blind men listened to the sea and the tail-ends of songs which the wind carried to them. Auberi had gone to join in the procession.

"Three months," Ansiau was thinking, "and the pilgrim ships will be setting sail for Palestine. If we miss this spring, we shall have to wait here another year—unless we managed to board a merchantman calling in here—the crossing is not much more than a month and we could be in Acre by May. But still, little as they eat, three men cost something to feed for a month."

The idea of having to remain another year in Marseilles frightened him. While it had been a question of keeping walking he had kept up his courage, but to wait in one place—and without hope—trailing all day long from church to port, port to church, to change from a pilgrim into a real beggar—that would be rather a harsh trial for a free man. Then, somewhere in these parts, there was that unknown Eglantine, haunting him like a bad dream which is not clearly recalled yet will not be entirely forgotten.

Bertrand listened, unwearied, to the wash and backwash of waves in the harbor and the gurgling and slapping of water between the boats. Many years ago he had seen the sea, at Perpignan. He had no very exact memory of it but now he liked the sound of waves. Since they had been at Marseilles that was the only thing which succeeded in distracting his thoughts. His thoughts went forever around the same center—the same question, apparently so simple, so banal, which yet seemed to him more and more terrible: What was the good of living? Why was he still alive? "This fellow here," he thought, "this old child, would tell me: 'It's a sin,' and talk of hellfire. For him everything is simple. Go forward until you drop and ask no questions. Life has stunned him; yet there are days when I could wish to be like him. What is stopping me from going this very day down to the sea I hear calling me day and night and throwing myself in head first? It's not the sin I'm afraid of. It's no sin to free oneself from this accursed flesh branded and mutilated by the Devil.

"No, no, as true as God is good and did not will our sufferings, it was not He that created this mass of decay we call the body. And what is it, this body, under its deceptive look of beauty invented by the Evil One to seduce us, what is it but a heap of butcher's meat, greasy fluids, and excrement? Most pure God, if even Alfonse's lovely body has put off its form and turned to decay—O, my God, if I can think of that and not die of it, O my God, if even that is possible, how can I bear my own flesh one day longer? Yet here I am, eyeless, sick in my chest, my feet swollen, dragging myself about like a dog with a broken back, imploring pity from strangers and holding out my hand for a bit of bread.

"He had said to me: 'Let us die together.' And I did not die with him.

"There could be no salvation for me in this life, since I had, like a hog, profaned and fouled the Spirit which I had received into myself. But then, what prevented me from throwing myself into the Ariège, since, in any case, whatever I do, there is neither salvation for me in this life nor joy in this world?

"When I was young, happy and full of strength, I was a soldier and risked my life. Now that I have nothing to lose I sit and wait for the hour when I can eat."

The more he thought of it the further he was from answering his own question. What was there that he loved in this life that he should be afraid of quitting it? He did not believe in Hell. But the answer was there—he was still alive.

"Companion, have you ever thought of taking your own life?"

"Me? No, thank God. Never."

"Even when your son died?"

"God! I was thinking of very different things, then."

"Of what, companion?"

"How can I say? What do you think of in such cases? I was thinking of him."

"And you still wanted to go on living?"

"I don't know. I never thought of it."

"Well, I think of it. Does it seem to you, companion, that I have many reasons for living?"

"You always say the same thing. Am I a priest? Kill yourself, if your heart tells you to. It would need a more learned man than I am to console you."

"Come, friend," Bertrand said, putting his hand on the old man's shoulder, "there are neither men of learning nor doctors who can cure our wretchedness. One of these days, despite everything, I shall finish it all. I shall no longer be a burden to you."

The blind men listened for a while and in silence to the songs of the procession going down towards the harbor. Ansiau crossed himself and muttered a brief prayer.

"The unbeliever, he might have said a prayer, too," he thought. This Bertrand (or Gaucelm, he no longer knew what to call him), was still an enigma to him. Unbeliever he certainly was: no doubt he had been brought up so and one must not blame him too much. Yet he went into churches, knew the prayers, was, even, a man of education. Can a man have two faiths? In what manner did he, at the bottom of his soul, pray to God? Then, remembering what the poor man had undergone, the old man asked himself:

"Is it possible for me to understand? He seeks consolation where he can."

When the procession had passed on, he put his hand on his companion's arm.

"Brother, I want to ask you a question but don't take it in bad part."

"Ask, anyway."

"Why, really, do you want to go to Jerusalem? For I can see very well that it means nothing to you and that you have no wish to see the Holy Sepulchre."

"To see it!" Bertrand said, bitterly.

"Well, well, to go there, I mean."

"And you," Bertrand asked, "have you such a great wish to go there?"

"That, brother, is my business. I must go, in any case, because I no longer have anywhere else to go. I made a vow. It helps me to keep it. It's not the same for you."

"If I'm in your way," Bertrand said, "I can just as well stay in Marseilles. If I die quicker alone, so much the better."

"I knew it. You always come back to that. Did I go with you all the way to Castres and even Pamiers to be talked to like that?"

They both fell silent.

"Ah, brother!" Bertrand said, suddenly, in a broken voice. "Do you know the reason, brother? I'd go with you to Hell if you like, because in you only have I found a man to take pity on me. As long as one lives one wants to be treated as a man. And, for you, I am still a man."

"Yes, yes, it's true," the old man said. "For people who have their sight, we're nothing much, are we? Nothing much."

II. A PRODIGAL SON

Two days before the Feast of Epiphany which is also called the Feast of Kings the three pilgrims were sitting down by the harbor, eating their bread and garlic, when a girl, pretty enough, but decked out in loud finery and crude necklaces of painted wood, stopped in front of them, examining them through narrowed eyes, the lids darkened with charcoal. She moved on, then came back again, still looking at them with a puzzled air.

"Hi, you," Auberi said, furious. "If you've something to give us, give, or else be on your way. Or do you think yourself just pretty enough for blind men?"

"Why, you little ill-mannered brat," the girl said, "you've eyes in your head but it's not for the likes of you I'd be buying a new gown. Only—well, there's a lad here searching the whole town for a tall, one-eyed old man with an old wound scar on the right nostril, and an urchin who might be you. Well, the old man here may be the one he's looking for."

"A lad looking for us? What for? We haven't robbed anyone."

"That's none of my business, little chicken, but I'd like to do the lad a good turn because he's a very decent lad, and handsome, too, and a friend of yours, surely. Handsome, fair, chatters like a magpie. I fancy he's from Montélimar."

For a moment Auberi's excitement seemed to choke him. He ran to the old man and hugged him, then back to the girl and kissed her on both cheeks.

"Riquet, my lord, it's Riquet! I'm sure it's Riquet! Tell me at once where he is, take me to him, pretty lady, bring him to us—I'll go with you to fetch him. It's Riquet—he's here, Master Bertrand."

The two blind men had not followed the conversation and did not understand Auberi's excitement.

"Riquet? You can see Riquet?"

"He's here, he's here, I'm sure it's him! I'm going to fetch him. Wait for me, I'm going to fetch him at once."

"Hi, you don't suppose I know where he is now," the girl cried. "He'll be about the town somewhere with mountebanks of his own kidney. He's no bishop, to stay in one place in his own palace! I don't so much as know when I shall see him."

Auberi was already on the verge of tears.

"Oh, yes, come, we're sure to find him. Since you've seen him. You know who he's with, you can tell me."

"I've other things to do. If I see him I'll send him here."

"Oh, no, my beautiful, my pretty, my little dove! Come, you're sure to find him. It won't take long, you'll see, really it won't take long."

Confronted by the child's big, tear-filled eyes, the girl shrugged her shoulders and took Auberi by the hand.

"Come on, then, we'll try the market-place. If he's not there, I'm not looking any further."

Auberi ran so fast that the girl had difficulty in keeping up with him.

The blind men were left alone. The old man was thinking: "You'd think he'd found a treasure. A hare-brained fellow who abandoned us to run after a skirt. Well, well, youth will turn to youth."

"Brother?"

"Yes?"

"You were fond of this Riquet?"

"At that time I was fond of nothing and nobody. Nor now, come to that. I believe he had a fine voice."

Two hours later Auberi came back literally hanging from Riquet's neck. Riquet, tanned, lean, his head uncovered, with a fine, short, curly beard on his chin, carried himself proudly despite his strange outfit: he was wearing breeches cut from two pieces of cloth, so that one leg was blue and the other brown; over a woman's chemise of green silk he wore a coarse jerkin of sheep skin, and his shoes, of fine red leather, were too small and had holes in the toes. As he approached the two blind men he looked rather hang-dog. He even blushed.

Auberi said:

"Here's Riquet, my lord, he wants to stay with us now." His voice was soft with tenderness. The old man raised his head.

"So here you are, fair lad? What do you want with us?"

He would not have spoken so if he could have seen Auberi's horrified face.

"If you want my company," the young man said, "I'd like to go with you to Jerusalem."

"Words, my lad, words. There's no lack of pretty girls in Marseilles."

Riquet had turned away, his mouth looking sullen.

"If you don't want me, that's another matter," he said, at length.

"But of course he wants you! My lord, say you want him!"

"You think you're doing me a gracious favor, Riquet, in wanting to come with me who am old and infirm and with this worthy man, even poorer than I am. I've no need of your charity, Riquet. God will lead us where He wills and as He wills."

There was rather a long silence. Bertrand was inclined to be angry with his companion for thus turning away a sound man who might be of service. Auberi felt himself lost, his eyes shifting from Riquet to his master with an expression of desolation. Riquet, who had sat down beside the blind men, spoke at last.

"God knows I expected a different welcome, Master Pierre. For months I've been all over the country looking for you. I went as far as Pamiers. And it was not for my own pleasure. But you're too proud to understand that. I was very fond of you, you and my little Auvergnat piglet, who's not forgotten me, and the lord Bertrand, too, I was fond of him, because of all his misfortunes. I thought: 'I can still be useful to someone.' I wanted to serve you because I loved you like a father, God knows it's true, since I've lost my real father and the father abbot who was more than a father to me. I took no vow of obedience to you but I've come back all the same. Is that nothing, by your reckoning?"

The old man did not reply. Absently, Riquet was forming crosses with pebbles picked out of the sand. The old man raised his head and shook his mane of tangled hair.

"No, son," he said, slowly, "I'm not proud. But when you can't see any more, you find it hard to forgive those who can."

Riquet did not raise his head but still went on making his pattern of crosses in the sand. Then he wiped it all out with a stroke of his hand and took a piece of smoked ham from his pocket, and a knife.

"It's not a fast day," he said. "Would you like some? Auberi will, I'm sure. Ah, my Auvergnat piglet, it was you I played the dirtiest trick. But you don't bear me a grudge."

Auberi sighed and fell to devouring the slice of ham.

"And your leman—what was her name?"—Bertrand asked—
"Mahaut—the one who sold cheeses?"

Riquet raised his head, astounded to hear Bertrand raise so frivolous
a subject. Then he frowned and his face darkened. He said:

"These shopkeeping women don't understand love. What they want
is money, land, cattle. I wish her joy of them. I wouldn't take her for
twenty marks of silver."

"Good for you!" Ansiau said. Suddenly, God knows why, he felt
better disposed towards Riquet; yet he had other things to think of
than a young girl never seen and long forgotten. But there are shabby,
pitiful thoughts which may gnaw at the heart without a man being
aware of them. Abruptly, the old man was ashamed of his spitefulness
towards the young man.

Riquet got his living by singing in the streets but keeping a sharp
look-out, having no wish to be assaulted by singers belonging to the
organized brotherhoods—and played the fool for rich burgesses who
looked as if they enjoyed a good laugh; he would accost them in the
streets or slip into the courtyards of their mansions—he was not always
made welcome. But sometimes, by a stream of jokes at the expense of
the mayor, the bishop, the aldermen, the count of Montfort, the king
of Aragon, the king of France, and even the pope, he contrived really
to amuse his hosts, so that he was given a fowl or a goose or a few coins.
Once he was given a good woollen coat, another time a pair of shoes.
He also had a whole repertory of very scabrous stories, stories of monks,
priests and more or less loose women, stories which he had learned
from travelling minstrels on the road and which he recast in his own
style, in rhymed verses.

A big dealer in relics—but none the more pious for that—was so
fond of these stories that he would send for Riquet every Saturday and
keep him in his house until very late at night. Riquet had to share a
pallet with a half-idiot dwarf and a rebec player. The merchant was
much troubled with his nerves and suffered from insomnia. Little by
little, in the course of conversing of one thing and another, he came to
have an affection for Riquet and, knowing him to be a pilgrim bound
for Jerusalem, offered him a passage in a ship which he owned, which
was going to fetch relics from the Holy Land. He pulled a face when he
heard that Riquet had three companions. Riquet promised to get
money together to pay for at least part of the journey.

"The fact is, outward bound, I carry paying pilgrims," the merchant explained, "and then, after all, I should be very stupid to let you go; you amuse me."

"Oh, never fear, I shall come back with a much better lot of stories, about the sultan, and the king of Cyprus, and the merchants of Saint Jean d'Acre, and all the monasteries over there! You've got to travel a bit to learn anything new, eh? My head isn't a bottomless well."

"Get away with you! What's needed is wickedness, and you've enough for a score."

"Here! What do you take me for? I'm a pilgrim. I make nothing up. The stories I tell you are as true as holy writ. It's the world that's wicked, not me, I'm as pure as a new-born babe."

It was not always easy to make money by being funny. Sometimes Riquet's head would be splitting and his throat dry, his smile already becoming the fixed grin of the professional mountebank; his cheeks would become set in vertical lines, and there would be wrinkles of weariness under his eyes. He would return to his companions by no means as merry as he used to be, and he no longer cared to sing. But he was making money. Ansiau already had thirty silver halfpennies in his bag, for the journey, and both blind men had woollen cloaks and leather sandals.

After Shrove Tuesday Riquet was left idle; only his relic-merchant still sent for him, on Saturdays. Spring, always precocious in the south, was on the way; in March the gardens were full of flowers and the town smelled of jasmine and mimosa. The sun shone upon a sea already deep blue beyond the pink and red town. The first ships were fitting out from Egypt and the spice route. Ships full of new crusaders from Italy dropped anchor in the harbor, and the port was full of the clatter of hoofs, neighing, and the rattle of weapons; Easter drew near, as always, amidst a feverish anticipation, prayers, vague hopes of miracles, and ever-fresh anxiety—as if the Passion and the Resurrection were actually going to be repeated.

During Lent the churches were full and preaching friars were about the streets, stopping in squares and at crossways, crucifix in hand, haranguing the crowds which gathered about them. Marseilles had more need of such preaching than any other town, for God knows how many thieves, disguised heretics, escaped convicts, gypsies and mis-believers were numbered among its citizens, come from every country and established in the town for commercial or less reputable reasons.

Since the beginning of the crusade there were ten times as many preaching friars as there had formerly been, and all zealots, fanatics,

who never stopped describing the tortures of Hell with so much eloquence that sometimes women were seen to faint. There were, of
course, also the hard-headed who laughed and said:

"You'd think they'd been there themselves, they know the place so
well!"

But such as laughed were often no easier than the others: there had
been showers of falling stars seen in mid-winter; hardly a day passed
but a personal appearance of the Devil was reported—in a convent or
one of the town squares or in the port—he tangled the fishing-nets,
cut the moorings of ships and spread filth on refectory tables. And
never had want and misery been so great as in this third year of the
holy war.

Marseilles had never lacked beggars but now they came swarming
into the town—all the people from the country about Albi and
Toulouse, peasants, artisans, even burgesses, who could no longer get
food to eat in their own districts. It was not always safe to walk the
streets even in broad daylight and soldiers had to be sent to guard the
markets. Even during Lent people were murdered for a loaf of bread.
Many of the poor needed to hear the friars' preachings, to save them
from resorting to robbery, for God knows, many of them had been
through such suffering that it was necessary to keep the most terrible
tortures before their eyes if they were still to be kept in fear. Even so,
the stocks and gibbet drove a roaring trade.

But Easter was expected as a deliverance—as if the Saviour were
really coming, in person, to lead His poor into Paradise. For the
majority this paradise would be, at best, a bit of meat at some rich
man's table; but it would be given for the love of God—which was, at
least, something.

Riquet's return did not bring a spirit of peace and goodwill into the
little company. The two blind men often quarrelled, and also quarrelled
with Riquet. Ansiau was in charge of their exchequer. For fear of
thieves he kept the money sewn into his belt and once it was there it
was impossible to get a single denier out of him. Bertrand, and sometimes even Riquet, accused him of avarice.

"Then you should not have given it to me, my lad," the old man
said. "You know quite well that you could buy yourself a felt hat and
eat wheaten cakes in front of me; I should not know. Auberi would
never denounce you. The pair of you—you're free to live like fighting
cocks."

"That's right, call me a thief again," the young man said. "Left to yourself, you'd let this child die of hunger. He's not half the boy he was last winter and God knows he wasn't fat then!"

"Then, friend Riquet, you should never have left us. You, no doubt, would have taken better care of him than I."

When the two older men were alone, Bertrand said:

"You should not treat the lad like that, companion. He's brought us more money than we should have earned in three years. And remember, he's endangering his soul to do it. How do you suppose he could get so much by honest means?"

"I did not tell him to steal."

"But aren't you carrying his money he may have stolen about you?"

"Ah, I don't know. Who are we, now, to stand on our pride? I've had to do worse things in my time—or why should God be punishing me?"

Since his fainting fit on Christmas Eve Ansiau had felt that he was sinking without knowing quite why, for he was not brooding over Eglantine. Since that day the mad idea that she was in Marseilles had taken on substance within him and any young woman's voice could chill him with fear that he would not recognize her voice, that he would not be able to avoid her, that she would recognize him—and, what was strange, he was not conscious of thinking these things; his body was thinking for him, his body, so quiveringly alert ever since he had had no eyes to protect him. When he happened to pass the inn and hear the laughter within, his heart would flutter like a bird caught in a snare.

The horror of imagining the object of one's love soiled and degraded! He had found the strength to bear everything during a hard lifetime full of mourning, but this last thing his spirit could not accomplish and instinctively rejected. He did not want to be unfair towards Herbert nor to admit to himself that he had left his poor, sick ewe-lamb at the mercy of a wolf—what harm could Herbert do her? Marry her to a brute? Kill her? He should have done it himself, for his heart was aware of something worse, although he tried not to think of it, which is why the reminder had hit him so hard, and he was weary and his resistance lowered.

Sometimes memories still crowded upon him: the memory of Ansiet, still a young child, of his little hands, already rather heavy and wide, real boy's hands; of his little bare feet paddling in puddles. Then he remembered him as a youth, lean, perched up on a horse too big for him. But always his mind came back to the image of those big, bony hands, yellow as wax, crossed on the pommel of a sword; and of the waxen face, the chiselled, livid lips fixed in a proud, sweet smile. And that was the light of his life. It was for that he had lived twenty years. He who had never known how to count had yet counted the years, one by one, before and afterwards. Thirty-nine years. The child would have been thirty-nine this Easter, a man in his prime.

If he had thought, at the time, of dying—as Bertrand had suggested. Dying? But what had it mattered, then? He had no more given thought to dying than living.

What had happened to him that day when he began to love the child who should have been his son's daughter? Everything about her was contrary to nature, because she had been born of a union contrary to nature. Yet she was innocent. But accursed. There was nothing to be done. Neither forgiveness nor punishment. Only forgetting.

Had she wept very much when she heard that her old father had gone away?

At the confessional of the monastery of Mary Magdalene the poor formed long queues, waiting their turn, yet the confessions were hurried; there was hardly time to babble a *Confiteor*. But most of the priests of the monastery were busy elsewhere and were even advising those whose sins did not lay too heavy on them to await the general public confession at the churches before mass on Good Friday. Nevertheless, all preferred to wait for hours and slip their mite into the priest's hand, to receive a pardon personally.

"Father, I have sworn; Father, I have stolen. Father, I ate meat in Lent. Father, I drink, Father, I beat my wife and children." By thought, by word, by deed and by omission—there, one had put it into words, to be sure, but it was as if none of it had been said. Impossible to feel forgiven as long as one has not avowed it all—and there are no words—and no time.

When someone remains longer than is usual over his confession, the people look down their noses at him as he comes out, telling themselves: "He must have murdered someone, at least, or robbed a church."

Riquet had wept when he came to say his *Confiteor*. It was at least ten months since he had been to confession—ever since he had left his monastery.

"Hurry, my son, what is the good of crying? You can weep afterwards."

"Father, I have broken my vows."

"What vows, my son?"

"I was a monk in the Order of the Black Friars of Montélimar."

"You must return to your monastery, my son, and do penance."

Riquet promised to do so. There was not time to explain that, meanwhile, he planned a detour by way of Jerusalem.

Yet as he came out of the confessional he felt ashamed of himself: he was seized by such a nostalgic yearning for his monastery, his good father abbot, his old comrades in study and work, that he would have liked to abandon the old man and his unbeliever of a companion. After all, that was where his duty lay. He would never be reconciled with God until he went back. Had he, then, given up the monastery for an easy life? Another matter if it had been to live with Maguelonne in her hamlet near the walls of Castres—there he would have put up with hunger with a good heart and harnessed himself to the plow if they had no oxen. But honest young women are hard-hearted.

Now he had nothing but hunger, fatigue and, worst of all, humiliation and self-disgust. To begin with he had practiced his trade of buffoonery because he loved laughter and making others laugh and saw no harm in it, but within a few months had come this lassitude and, because he was obliged to be always laughing, now he would almost rather have been sorrowful and weeping for his sins. True, at the monastery he would be punished, and that severely, but, after all, he had deserved it. The shame of facing the father abbot seemed to him, at present, almost a kind of pleasure, so changeable is the heart of man. Yes, the very shame from which he had fled was now an attraction. Abandon his companions? He would regret Auberi, true. Not the other two.

He remained a long time in the church of Mary Magdalene, prostrate before the altar, near the massive iron candlesticks so loaded with candles as to rival daylight. By the brilliance of this great light, which shone upon the altar crucifix and lit up the stern countenances of the saints painted on the pillars, he seemed to see his own soul in a clear light, a soul degraded and made vile not so much by bodily debauchery as by that—so much worse—which he had had to impose upon his spirit. He thought of his evenings at the relic-dealer's house, of his clowning to amuse drunken noblemen.

"The greater the height, the lower the fall," he told himself. "The old man, who has never taken any vows, a soldier, no, even when young he would never have done what I've done. Nor Auberi either, he'll never do it. The old man, at my age, had rowed in a galley. But he hasn't the brains to do much more than that. It is well said: 'Blessed are the poor in spirit.' All my brains have been good for is to damn me a thousand times and more. O Lord God, let them send me to the pig-stys at the monastery or set me to clean the latrines for two years; I shouldn't find more filth there than I have in my head."

He had firmly resolved to take leave of his friends and set out for Montélimar.

It was not until late that night that he returned to the Saint-Lazarus hostel where the blind men and Auberi were then staying. He found his companions in a sorry state, seated on a pallet in the courtyard sur-rounded by others of the poor staying in the hostel and all arguing in raised voices. The old man's head was bandaged with rags; he was not talking and he was as motionless as a wooden statue. Bertrand, much moved, was giving an account of something or other through chattering teeth and Auberi was crying.

"Here now, what's happening?" Riquet said. "Have you had a quarrel?"

It was much worse: he learned that the blind men, having lingered in the streets waiting for Auberi who was coming back from confession, had been attacked by a thief who had knocked the old man down and torn off his belt with the money. Bertrand had received a violent blow on the chest and had not yet recovered, not so much from pain as from his feelings.

"Think of it," Auberi said, sobbing, "the eve of Palm Sunday! And blind men! And just while I was at confession! And God knows what I should be wishing the man, if I hadn't just confessed! Was there ever anything like it, Riquet? Such a town full of thieves? It's not a town, it's a cut-throat's lair!"

Riquet almost smiled at the spectacle of this childish anger and took Auberi's hand.

"There, don't start sinning, little puppy. I'll find some more money. Let's all go to bed and think no more about it."

He was thinking, at that moment, only of consoling the child but in reality he was greatly cast down; he had been not a little proud of the money he had got together and now it seemed he had been working for nothing—in that, too, the Devil had robbed and deceived him. "Finished," he thought. "Finished. They'll never take me back. This is another sign. I'm done for." At the same time the thought of the lost money made his heart ache.

He lay down on the pallet, beside Bertrand and Auberi. The old man remained sitting upright, without moving. He was so still that he might have been asleep or dead; spoken to, he made no answer.

"Yet it was not much of a blow," Auberi said, in a low voice. "He bled a bit, that's all. He said it did not hurt."

"Master Pierre, can you hear me?" Riquet said. "Hey, Master Pierre." He received no answer and lay down again. But he was unable to sleep.

It was late, the hour of Prime had just chimed, when Riquet felt a hand as heavy as a bushel fall on his arm.

"You're not asleep, Riquet?"

"No, how can I sleep?"

"Riquet, go back to your monastery."

"What?" The young man started up. How had the old man read his mind?

"Why are you telling me this now?"

"Riquet, my son, I ask your forgiveness. You must not bear me a grudge, Riquet."

"But for what? Was it your fault? Besides, the money was your own, since I'd given it to you."

"It's not so much that, Riquet. For that, too, of course, God has punished me, my son, for my pride and folly. Why should I try to get to Jerusalem on your back, poor lad?"

"What are you saying, and what's the good of saying that?" Riquet suddenly wanted to weep.

"I understand it very well now, you know. I'm a simple man, but I've had a lot of experience. Just now, I sat there like a log, unable to speak. Well, it was you I was thinking of, Riquet. It was pity for you, my mind was all at sixes and sevens. By what right do I claim your service? It is said: 'Let him who would be first among you be the servant of you all.' You did that, Riquet, and all you got from me was the rough side of my tongue."

"Oh, forget that; it will tire you out if you talk so much."

"No, my son, I'm not in my dotage. My head's clear enough. Only I was thinking about you a lot just now. I told myself that since you've a loyal heart, you must go and serve your father abbot, to whom you promised obedience. It'd be a pity for a lad like you to damn yourself so stupidly."

"Let's talk no more of it," Riquet said. "Tomorrow, we'll see." He did not know what to say; his heart was turning over in his breast at the sound of the old man's grave and broken voice. Because he felt that the blind man was right, he dug in his toes and wanted to do the opposite to what he was told, for he liked to have his own way.

"He'll think he's got round me with fine words," he thought. "He'll be saying to himself: 'This little monk's poor stuff, after all; you can twist him round your little finger.' Monk—what sort of a monk am I, now? Perhaps all I really want is to travel a bit more, see the world before I go back and face my penitence." He used these words to himself because he could find none to express the tenderness and pity which he experienced for the old warrior. Indeed what name exists for the tie which binds man to man and to account for which there is neither oath nor kinship nor gratitude nor even friendship—for could there be friendship between them as between men of the same age and rank? That which bound them together was deeper than all these, and simpler.

Came Palm Sunday and all Marseilles was covered with green, houses, streets, the port, and even the ships, all were covered with box and olive branches; the archbishop, mounted on a white mule and wearing a mantle embroidered with gold, made a tour of the main thoroughfares followed by priests and archdeacons, and monks from the town's monasteries; and women spread rugs and cloaks in their way for them to walk on.

Then came the longest week in the year, Holy Week, when every man forgets his cares, however heavy they may be, in the great agony of God, of the Virgin and the holy apostles. However long a man may live, every year he will live through that week, celebrated for more than a thousand years, as for the first time. God knows Ansiau was like a man who had never lost his son nor daughter nor house nor sight—for what do all these amount to when a man knows that God is about to be betrayed by one friend and denied by another, scoffed at and nailed to a cross? God knows that every year he wept more tears over Judas's treason, and for Saint Peter, and for Our Lady lamenting at the foot of the cross, than he wept in a whole year for his own sake. "For there," he thought, "were real unhappiness and suffering—not such mere shades of unhappiness as pass away with a man's life."

He could no longer see anything, could only hear the songs and the priests' voices, but he could have recited all the offices for Holy Week from beginning to end, for, although a man hears them but once a year, they became a part of his very substance when it is his heart that listens. He was now very little troubled by the priests' Marseillaise accent and by a manner of chanting different from that in use at Troyes. For more than a year he had not been able to get used to it, nor to the fact that the *cantilenas* were sung in the *langue d'oc*—for him it was rather like a profanation to hear the Virgin mourning in the *langue d'oc*.

"But then," he thought, "in any case, she did not speak French but Latin; this is done for simple folk." Only now, as it seemed, he was himself one of these same simple folk and was a little put out by it. The sound of the Latin psalms and prayers made him weep and pray all the more fervently in that he was not distracted by the sight of the candles and paintings—and his fellow-worshippers—and the words he understood least seemed to be most heavily charged with meaning and evoked an agony and a love which took away his breath.

Holy Week had been a time of respite. After the joy of Easter Sunday, the four pilgrims faced the fact that they had no money and were in a difficult situation—for the relic-dealer's ship was sailing in a fortnight, and her captain, as well as the owner, refused to encumber the vessel with so many useless mouths. There was, in any case, little room aboard, but even for a corner of the hold near the water-butts he was asking twenty sols a head. The merchant was willing to pay for Riquet but not for the others.

Riquet, in the hope of a miracle, prayed to Saint Mary Magdalene but he could hardly believe that the saint would produce one for so insignificant an individual as himself. What was to be done? Let the chance slip and continue to hang about Marseilles for God knows how long? Money? What, rob a shopkeeper or some travelling tradesman? Sleep with a rich woman so as to rob her afterwards? Slit some burgess's purse in the market place? Riquet did not feel bold enough for such trades as these. Yet he was so baffled that he did think of them quite seriously. He already had a certain amount of petty larceny on his conscience and told himself that there was no great sin in robbing a

rich man. But he needed at least fifty sols—and, also, he was afraid of
being caught. If he chose a woman as his victim the danger would be
less, especially if she were married—and was it not a woman who, in
the same manner, had been the cause of all his misfortunes? It seemed
to him that he had almost a right to do it, yet still the idea was re-
pugnant to him. Then—to go on a pilgrimage with stolen money was
hardly proper and could not have a fortunate issue.

Yet such was his need to see himself as one who inspired confidence
that he swore to his companions he would find the money and that all
was arranged with the captain.

One day—it was a Friday—towards the evening, he was on his
knees in the chapel of Saint Mary Magdalene Church, alone. He was
wringing his hands and tearing his hair at the temples, for he could not
win any rest or tranquillity in prayer.

"Saint Mary Magdalene, lady of sinners, take pity on me, a sinner;
help me, for I do not know which way to turn. Save me from sin.
Perhaps you think that my need for this money is not so very great.
But I swear to you that so strong is my desire for it that I would damn
myself to get it."

A sharp sound, like a stifled sob, made him raise his head. A woman
was there, on her knees, some paces away from him, raising clasped
hands towards the image of Saint Mary Magdalene painted on the wall
to the right of the altar. She was dressed in a long dark cloak and her
head was veiled. Riquet could see her pale profile, delicate and still
young; her slender fingers were covered with rings, not very valuable
but prettily worked. Automatically, the young man ran a hand over his
hair and adjusted his collar.

Now the woman was praying or rather talking in a low voice, her
shaking lips moving very quickly. Her eyes, the eyelids red, were
raised to the picture of the saint with an expression of such passion,
such ardent supplication, that Riquet was moved.

"Poor little thing," he thought, "she must be some squire's wife
who's cuckolded her husband, and that in the middle of Easter! And
it'll be the first time it's happened. Bah! She'll be at it again in another
week. That's how it goes. Still, there are plenty who would be a lot less
upset about it."

Abruptly, the young woman rose, stepped lightly over the wreaths of
flowers and foliage which covered the ground in front of the saint's
picture and stood face to face with the Magdalene, almost pressed to

the fresco. She raised eyes and hands swiftly towards the painted face, hesitated an instant, and dropped a light kiss first on the saint's mouth, next on the hand holding the jar of perfumed oil. Then she sank down to the ground and kissed the feet of the image. With a hasty motion she took something from about her neck and slipped some object among the flowers scattered before the picture, lowered the veil over her face and walked quickly out of the chapel, as if she feared to be caught there. Riquet had turned discreetly away.

Then he cast a swift glance all about, to make sure he was again alone, approached the picture, plunged his hand among the flowers, found the object, which seemed to be a necklace, slipped it into his pocket without looking at it. Then, greatly troubled, he again fell on his knees, not knowing which way to look. A miracle? Certainly it was a miracle. He must thank the saint. But he had not the courage. His cheeks and ears were red. He blinked, sketched a sign of the cross and left the church with his heart thumping, forcing himself not to walk too quickly.

"Sweet mother of sinners, sweet lady, thank you and forgive me for robbing you. You knew that the temptation was too strong; why did you let the woman do as she did just at that moment? She might have come half an hour earlier or later."

Hidden in an alley between two houses, he examined the necklace: it was of solid silver, encrusted with amethysts and turquoises.

"The Devil!" he thought. "She was no miser! There are richer than she who would not have given as much. It's worth at least ten marks but I shall be lucky to get two." He knew a Levantine shopkeeper in the port who dealt in stolen goods. He bargained for a long time and at last got two marks and six sols, telling himself that the necklace must be worth at least ten times as much.

Neither the two blind men nor Auberi ever asked Riquet where he had got his money. He did, indeed, try to spin them a yarn about a rich and charitable nobleman but then, seeing that they did not believe him, did not persist, feeling a good deal mortified.

"What do they think of me?" he wondered. But he did not dare admit that he had robbed Saint Mary Magdalene.

THE PROMISED LAND

I. THE VOYAGE

THE voyage in the ship's hold turned out to be an anguish which the blind men had by no means foreseen. Bertrand was sea-sick almost all the time and it was difficult to sleep at night because they had to fight off the rats. A score of other pilgrims shared the hold with them and the stench was such that women and the sick were always fainting: nor was it an easy matter to get them up on deck by means of the rope cradle which swung to each roll of the ship. Despite the season, the sea was rather rough and the pilgrims were constantly being flung against each other or against the water-butts and boxes of cargo. In calm weather, pressed against each other, they sang songs of Jerusalem together, to pass the time. This reminded them that the martyrdom they were suffering was not for nothing.

Riquet and Auberi, among others of the younger and stronger pilgrims, sometimes went up on deck; the captain did not like this much but Riquet was in his good graces and sometimes even ate at his table. It seemed to him that a sailor's life was a good one; he was interested in the masts and rigging and the great, patched sails with crosses and many-colored coats of arms sewed to them, the deck which was washed down daily, and the sea itself, blue in the daytime, white at evening or golden red and streaked with silver, sparkling like diamonds or glorious with swatches of liquid gold, according to time and weather. He would never have believed that the open sea was so different from the sea as seen from the shore. After dark, seated with Auberi on the poop, he watched the moon reflected in the ship's wake and foam breaking in thousands of tiny pearls against the dark water. And thousands of stars rocked slowly, slowly, above an horizon level in every direction and infinite.

Several times Bertrand thought he was going to die in the ship. On deck his spirits revived a little but he felt so ill that on one occasion he even thought of sending for a priest. For all he did not believe in Hell, there lingered in his spirit something which he himself called superstition.

"It seems my mind is weakening," he thought. And he told himself that Alfonse would have been ashamed of him, seeing him so cowardly. "Alfonse," he thought, "Alfonse had received the Consolation, whereas I cheapened the gift I had received. Although I die I shall never escape the curse of the flesh. I am condemned to wander for centuries among the Devil's phantoms and lies, but can that be worse than this present life? Perhaps, once freed of the burden of the flesh, I shall find my way better, find another body, stronger than this one. Their Paradise is naught but a lie, since you can buy it with masses and gifts, but at least they believe in it and are as happy as hogs in a wallow. Ah! Alfonse, where are you now, my son, delivered from what? And what was it, what splendor had you seen, that it enabled you to repulse me without pity, you who were all pity and gentleness? God knows, my beloved child, that even if I believed in their Paradise I should renounce it since you, in your purity, denied it. If it was your wish that I should die, I should have the courage to do it, even without Consolation. Ah, you say that I begot only your flesh, the body you wanted nothing to do with, but now your sweet body is broken and rotted, while I cling to mine as to God knows what treasure."

Up on deck the salt breeze played lightly with his hair and caressed his skin beneath his clothes; the sea sang to him and the wind hummed in the rigging. Must he return to the hold, the stench of bilges and vomit and filth, the feel of rats running over one's feet—and that for days, and more days? "Alfonse, would you not have been shamed to see your father in this state?" Who would not have been ashamed?

"Companion, lead me towards the side."

"Thank you very much! To help you to jump over? I'm not a murderer!"

"I want to vomit."

"No, no, I know you only too well. Go by yourself. After all, you can see as well as I can."

"I haven't the strength to walk."

"So much the better. Stay where you are."

Bertrand thought:

"If he'd lead me, I'd have the courage to do it. His charity won't stretch to that. And how far must he lead me before I make up my mind, then? My body is worn out, yet still I hang on to life."

In the morning, after a call at Cyprus, the Holy Land was in sight—the main-mast look-out had seen it first and had hailed the deck with the news. When land was visible from the deck, all, sailors and passengers, were there on their knees; the priests who were on board had set up an altar by the prow and fifty male voices thundered out the *Te Deum*. The priests said the prayers of thanksgiving and blessed the kneeling faithful.

Lost among the crowd, Ansiau prayed with the rest. He did not know that this land had more present reality for him than for these others who, having their eyesight, saw nothing but a thin streak of grey on the horizon. It seemed to him that he was already touching it with his fingers and for him it was like the bread which he was keeping in his wallet for the noon meal. His heart beat as if it would burst, but not for joy—from anguish, rather. He had waited so long for this day, yet without really believing he would live it. And afterwards? In a few days he would be in Jerusalem and there would cause to be said those masses which he owed. And then?

II. ACRE GRAVEYARD

That evening the ship dropped her anchor in Acre harbor.

Seated on the ramparts of the port, the four pilgrims felt the earth swing beneath their feet and thought themselves sea-sick. Auberi admiringly contemplated the handsome white town with its tall churches, their towers seeming to be carved like gems, its clumps of palm-trees and lemon-trees and the clear horizon broken by blue mountains. Since this was the Holy Land it had, of course, to be beautiful. How beautiful, the golden light over the sea, the many-colored sails in the port, the inhabitants' clothes—and what wealth! Even at Marseilles he had seen nothing of the sort. He had set foot in this port as one entering a church and he could hardly speak for enchantment. His spirit cast such a splendor about him that the very pebbles on the ground seemed to be precious stones.

Riquet, a little weary but dazzled too, thought that life was beautiful and that the old man was no fool. In this land there was, surely, sufficient holiness to burn up all the sins of the world like straw. A man who touches the Holy Sepulchre is made clean of his sins as the lepers were made clean of their leprosy by the hand of the Saviour.

Bertrand was the first to break the silence.

"Well, companion, where do we spend the night now we're here?" He was sad, feeling himself cut off from his friends at this moment. Ansiau did not answer; he was seized by the fear of not, after all, finding what he sought: he was thinking of the immense cemetery which lay behind the town.

It was almost twenty years since he had made his hostess, the widow Nicolai, promise to take care of the grave. Twice he had sent her money by the hand of friends on pilgrimage to the Holy Land, but for four years he had had no chance to send more, ever since the wedding of the baron of Brienne with the young queen of Jerusalem. Then, blind as he was, he would not easily find the widow's house again. She had remarried; her new husband was called Gherardi but it was a very common name. When Riquet suggested to him that they start looking for a pilgrim's hostel, he said:

"First I must find the house of the cloth-merchant Gherardi." Bertrand said:

"It's getting late."

"Very well," the old man said. "You go to the hostel with Auberi, while I take Riquet to look for the house."

"You must ask for the Pisan quarter, Riquet. We shall find it all right. It was not far from Saint Anne's Church. I remember the house well. But, as for describing it, no; they're all very much alike. There was an iron ring, in the form of two fishes, on the door."

"If I look at all the knockers on all the doors, it will take too long; it will be quite dark. Better to ask among the neighbors."

"Yes, that's safer. How do you like the town, Riquet?"

"A beautiful town. The people look prosperous here."

"I've seen it very badly damaged, God knows. And not only by the heathens. I've seen some ugly things in my time, Riquet. And the town cost us dear, too. It was here that our count, Henri, died after the war, when he had become king of Jerusalem. Are we far from Saint Anne's Church? I can hear bells very near, chiming Lauds . . . Now, you must ask for the house of Gherardi, the clothier. Knock at the windows, go on. They're sure to know him."

"They won't understand me."

"Yes, yes, everyone speaks a little French hereabouts. Try anyway: Gherardi."

A woman's face, very alarmed, appeared at a little square window.
"*Che volete? Gherardi? Gherardi Battista?*"

The old man summoned his memories of Italian.

"*Non sapere Gherardi, marito di vedova Nicolai.*"

The woman spoke a few more words, shook her head, and shut the window again.

"*Gherardi Andrea?*"

"*Gherardi marito di vedova—*"

"*Francesi?* No, this Gherardi not married."

". . . Husband of the widow Nicolai, Maria? Gian-Paolo? But he's been dead three years, Gian-Paolo! I have the business now." The man, a tall Genoese, lean and pock-marked, who happily knew French, stood at his door, looking at the pilgrims with a pitying expression.

"You've just landed, surely? You're welcome to sleep in the back of the shop tonight, if you like; but Gian-Paolo, God rest his soul, is no longer here."

"And his wife?" Ansiau asked.

"Also dead, God rest her soul." The man crossed himself. "They both died in the year of the smallpox. It was difficult even to give them decent burial. And then the—son, Ansellino, he joined a Venetian ship as a sailor and it's two years since he's been seen in these parts."

Ansiau had bowed his head and said nothing.

"Well, there it is, worthy man; it happens to all of us sooner or later. Say a prayer for their souls and think no more about it. It's the best way. No doubt you had some business with Gian-Paolo?"

"I was a crusader," the old man said. "It was about a grave."

"To be sure, to be sure, I understand. I am afraid it won't be easy to find it again. So many have been buried among the crusaders' graves and all round them. We had cholera ten years ago and then there was the smallpox three years ago. There it is, my friend, plenty of room is needed, and if there were no burying in old graves the local peasants would have no fields to plant their vineyards. These are hard times we live in, friend."

"Yes, hard times," the old man repeated. "Thank you for the information, friend. God keep you. Come, Riquet."

Slowly, the two men made their way down the steep, narrow streets of the town, and before them, between the roofs of houses and the rampart towers, was the blood-red sky already turning to violet and, at the horizon, dark blue shot with greenish light. Now the town seemed quite black. The church bells were ringing for Compline and the voices of the watch could be heard hailing each other all round the ramparts, announcing the hour of curfew.

"What's to be done now, Riquet? We shall not find a hostel now. We shall freeze."

"We might find some seafarers' inn, by the harbor."

"Take a good look at this town, Riquet. It's not so big, but it cost more men than Constantinople and Jerusalem. And the defenders were no cowards either, heathens though they were. . . . I don't know that we've much we can do here, Riquet. Might as well seek a needle in a haystack. Even if I could still see, how could I recognize a lost grave?"

"Was there, at least, a head-stone?"

"Yes, there was; I had one put up. With an inscription, but badly carved; I had not the means to employ a good workman. They'll have scratched it out and had something else carved on the stone. A big stone, it was, square, and damaged towards the left. It was taken from the ruins of the Accursed Tower. Aye, accursed, indeed, that cost us such a price! If the siege had not lasted so long, he might have had more strength to resist the sickness.

"Riquet, just now, when I knew we were right in front of the house, I had a kind of shock in my heart. He died in that house, Riquet. The very same house. His body was carried out through that door. . . . God knows, hearing she's dead, that touched me, too. She was a worthy woman. The lad who turned sailor—it's the sort of thing that happens in wartime—he was my son. It must seem funny to you. 'My son,' if one can call him so—it's probably the first time in twenty years I've thought of him. But her—I loved her, you know.

"I seem to myself like some sort of ghost, Riquet."

"We must both look like ghosts," the young man said. "I don't know how long it is since we've eaten. I'm wondering how you manage to keep on your feet."

"Sorrow, son; it's more nourishing than bread. That's something I learned some time ago. You forget the body's needs when you've something else to think of."

"We'll look for the grave together. You'll see, it'll be the devil indeed if we don't find it, since it was still there three years ago."

"It's not only the grave, son, it's everything. That grave is like a symbol for me. It's as if I had lost myself."

The next day the old man went down with Riquet to the Saint-

Nicholas cemetery. In that vast field, all covered with gravestones long and short, white and black, dotted, here and there, with big crosses and chapels, overgrown with weeds and thorn bushes and broken occasionally by fresh graves, black and green, the two men wandered, lost, not knowing which way to turn.

"It's to the east of the count of Flanders' tomb. That must be here still; you'll be able to find it. To the east, but a good hundred paces to the east, perhaps. And then, Auberi Clément's should not be far away. He was buried here—a fine man—with his face towards the town. He had a big slab stone, white marble. Thierri, my squire, was in the same group. And God has punished me for not having his grave cared for, since now I cannot find the other either."

"Auberi Clément—that's here, at all events," Riquet said. "Wait, here are some very dilapidated ones, but with names. And some clearer, too. Wait—Thibaut of Puiseaux—does the name mean anything to you? Was it far from yours?"

"My brother-in-law," the old man said, without showing the slightest feeling, however. "I know. He died in the final assault." He crossed himself. "Peace to his bones. We must look further. *Ansellus* is what we're looking for, *Ansellus miles. De Linneriis.*"

"Ansellus—I can see one but it's a long stone. Ansellus Ghisleberti. Wait, here again, a square stone but I can't make it out very well, *Andreas Salensis miles.*"

"André of Soulaines? I know who he was. We're going the wrong way; the man died before the assaults. Yet we're certainly among the Champagne men."

"*Arnoldus, miles.* No other name, but two crosses and an arrow under *miles.*"

"I know it. It was put up just before I left. We're not far."

"Now there are no more old stones. New graves. Here, a woman, Margherita. And then a whole lot of new graves, without stones."

"Look well, Riquet. It's not far. There may be more old ones."

"Yes, here's one. A long stone. *Richardus.*"

"*Richardus?* It was right beside it, Riquet! Look well again. Perhaps they've only stolen the stone."

"No, they're all new, here. Feel for yourself—the earth hasn't sunk yet."

For a long time they were silent. The old man had sat down on the ground near the graves, his arms clasping his knees.

"Then it's not worth searching any more, Riquet," he said, at last.

"It's here. He must be somewhere here, below. What does it matter that the stone has gone? Who cares about his name now? Even I no longer have eyes to read it.

"Riquet, it makes my heart ache to think that they have put other dead on top of him, crushing him. And yet that's stupid. What can it matter to him? In a hundred years who would have heard of it? And yet it hurts me."

"Come," Riquet said, "that won't stop him from hearing the angel's trumpet."

"That is what I think, too. Go, leave me, Riquet; I should like to stay here, alone. Come back and fetch me this evening."

The old man remained alone in the graveyard. He was worn-out by the long hours of inquiring and searching; the sun was already high and it burned his face and his naked arms. He was already thirsty and the idea of remaining there until evening without even a mouthful of water so troubled his mind that at first he could think of nothing else. Riquet had gone and he knew that, alone, he would never find his way out of the cemetery. It was the hour of the siesta—there would be no one about the cemetery between now and sunset. And Ansiau had good reason to know how vast the cemetery was.

"There was a spring, it's true," he thought, "near the northern boundary, where the Germans' tents were pitched. But I should never find it. And to think that I never even thought of filling my water-bottle."

He lay down on the ground, his arms behind his head, trying to recruit his strength and conserve the moisture in his mouth.

"Misery and wretchedness," he thought. "Here I am where I longed to be, a few feet from the body of my child, and now I can think of nothing but my own body's suffering. Had I any need to come all this way to suffer from thirst? God knows, I was just as thirsty, neither more nor less, in the country near Uzès. My child—who will never again feel hunger nor thirst, O nameless tomb—this earth, which I am touching with my body, is my body, nourished on my body; these thorns which have grown here were fed upon his flesh. It is all of him that is left to me, since the stone is gone, aye, and the very grave.

"My child, there you wait under the ground, wait for the trumpet of Judgment Day with your rusted sword in your hands; and I am thirsty and weary and my body is broken, but it was for you I travelled this

road and broke my strength. You are my weariness. Nothing remains
to me in all the world but my weariness and my thirst."

Suddenly he heard, quite near and above him, a whistling in the air
and the beating of heavy wings, then a cry both hoarse and shrill. The
sound of it pierced his heart like a knife—truly, being blind, he might
have been deceived about anything, anything save this; it was the cry
of the Holy Land's vultures. Those of Provence had not that cry, nor
did their wings, being shorter, make that sound.

How often, how much too often he had heard that cry during the
siege, not only in the graveyard but on the ramparts and earthworks, as
well as during his first crusade in the desert, when his comrades were
falling dead of sun-stroke and the Arab camel-drivers abandoned them
by the way and the caravan passed on.

"It's me they're watching," he told himself. "They think I'm dying."
And it suddenly came to him that he was, at that moment, alone there,
in the graveyard of crusaders, keeping watch over all these men who
had died for God during the siege. They were numbered by tens of
thousands, Frenchmen, men of Champagne, Englishmen, Germans,
Spaniards, Genoese and Pisans; men of the north, too, Danes—and
Provençals and Bretons. Yet, after twenty years, what remained even
of their graves? Very few had been so fortunate as to have their bodies
embalmed or their sealed coffins carried to their own country. The
counts and marquises, perhaps the Knights Templar and the Knights
Hospitaller still had their graves; one more siege, one more war, and
nothing would be left of all that company.

The earth, at least, must hold some memory of so much pain, of the
martyrdom of so many men; and it is earth, indeed, that remembers
them best, since it is earth that keeps their bones. And now, here he
was, alone among these bones, come there to watch over them; alone
with the vultures.

They, the vultures, had enjoyed fine feasting indeed, if you counted
only the ten thousand men-at-arms left unburied. On flesh, baptized
and circumcised alike, they had fed and grown fat, so that now they
must have little taste for other meat. Suddenly his spirit was lit by a
strange conviction; he, himself, was destined to no other sepulchre than
that. Well, if so, he would be sharing it with better men. But whence
came the idea, and why did it seem to him that he had already, somewhere, been like this, alone among the dead and surrounded by

vultures? Sometimes he had wondered what a wounded man, left for dead on a battlefield, must undergo. Thirst. Thirst must be the worst of it.

Oh, that the evening would come! The sun must still be high. If only Riquet might think of it—or Auberi. But they must be too busy seeing the town. They have their eyes. If only they knew how little there was to see and how the heavens are everywhere the same.

Riquet came at sundown with wine in his bottle and white bread.

"Master Pierre, we are going to have a high mass celebrated in Saint Anne's Church, for the repose of your dead. That's the best thing we can do, you know. It's only heathens and Jews who mourn at the grave, Master Pierre. That's not Christian. Come. A single mass is worth more than a hundred tombstones."

"Riquet, Riquet, you talk like a good monk; who would believe that you'd ever left your father abbot? Come, child, you are right. I am not making fun of you. God keep you from ever being a father."

"So now here you are, companion, in the Holy Land. Does it make you happier?"

"I did not come to be happier."

"What are we going to do now? Or do you expect to get your sight back in Jerusalem?"

"Companion, if God willed it, He could give back your eyes, even to you, such is His power. If He does not will it, it is because it must be so. It is not seemly to mock."

"I am weary of you, companion, and of your God who is always punishing for nothing. I did not deserve what has happened to me and nor did you. But you will not see where the evil lies."

"Am I a clerk, learnèd in argument? You complain all day long, like a woman, but women at least have their rosary to keep their tongues busy."

"Oh, cursed be the day I met you! If it had not been for you I should long since have been dead; you've been dragging me along for a year in misery and hunger and these two poor lads likewise, and to lead us where? To a still worse misery in a foreign country. If only you had stayed, stagnating and growing fat in your castle at your wife's side! Oh, God knows I was mad, even I, expecting God knows what miracle from this accursed Holy Land. It's nothing but dead stones and the dead burying their dead."

"It's just that you don't know the country, companion. And I tell you that, sinner though she may seem, this land, there's more praying and fighting here than everywhere else together, and perhaps there'll be yet more splendid feats of arms here than all that have gone before. This country has never lacked men of courage. As for the dead, after all, they must be decently buried; is it Christian to bundle them into the ground like dogs?"

"Oh, one cannot talk to you. You don't even know the Scriptures. You're just about able to babble a few words of Latin without understanding them. You call that prayer. When you find a decayed body from which the spirit has long since departed you worship it like an idol. If the Son of God had desired that, and if He had had a real body, He would have left it on earth to be worshipped. Since He did not leave it, and you nevertheless wanted to do your devil's work on Him, you have made an idol of His tomb and His Cross and of all the dead things which were used to humiliate Him on earth. Why do you not adore Pontius Pilate and Caiaphas and Judas?"

"Oh, you always come back to the same tale. Why talk of it? It's all a mystery. Who can talk of it? These things are not human."

Bertrand shrugged his shoulders and said no more. His arguments with the old man always ended in the same way. Each time he swore that never again would he talk seriously to so obtuse a creature. But he always tried again. He had become too attached to the man not to try and share his thoughts with him.

On the second day after their arrival Ansiau decided to go to the king's palace where he might find several knights of Champagne whom he knew slightly, having met them in Troyes, who were now members of the king's household. One of them was a brother-in-law of Haguenier of Hervi and Ansiau thought he might like to have news of his kinsfolk.

He therefore got Riquet to trim his beard and hair—for he was beginning to look like a desert hermit—and he made what improvements he could in his pilgrim's clothes.

"Am I very white now, Riquet?"

"Not white, no, but rather grizzled here and there. You cannot be very old, at that."

"Me? Indeed I am. Come, lad, we must get there before they go out to mass."

Herbert of Beaufort, brother-in-law of the deceased Haguenier, was not long in recognizing the old chatelain of Linnières.

"Ha!" he said, "I shall have good news to send to your son, my kinsman. I did not know you were in Palestine."

"What news from our part of the world?"

"Of your people, not much. I know that Herbert has made a knight of his son and married him to the widow of Thibaut of Villemor."

"Eh? Herbert might have found a better match; the widow in question is loaded with debts. And what about the Monguoz people, have you no news of them?"

"Gilles is now marshal of the chambers to the count of Brie and his son has become a Templar. Not here, there. Oh, yes, and I fancy your son-in-law of Buchie is dead."

Ansiau crossed himself and bit his lip.

"Aië! I should have thought of that. He was old and sick. I should have chosen a future husband for my daughter before my departure. Herbert has other worries on his mind and will not do it properly. Well, a man can't think of everything: God rest his soul, he was a worthy man."

After mass, Ansiau was given a place at table in the knights' room of the king's palace and talked about Holy Land matters with the other men of Champagne. They spoke of the sultan and of reinforcements from overseas. At Acre, this new crusade they had made in Provence was considered a great sin, keeping back crusaders who would have been better employed in Palestine. Apart from a few reinforcements from England and Spain and some isolated pilgrims, that spring had brought out no fresh men. The old ones were disappearing faster than new ones arrived. There were some who did not stand the climate well and succumbed to a fever in their first months. Then, even without a war, there were always some who got themselves killed in the hinterland; it was swarming with bandits and the sultan's guarantees were useless.

"Even the pilgrimage routes are not safe," Herbert of Beaufort said. "Several caravans have been attacked between Jaffa and Jerusalem. Last year a lady abbess was taken prisoner by these bandits and raped God knows how many times before being ransomed."

"Last month," said another of the Champagne knights, "a convoy of English pilgrims was caught and taken up into the mountains: one or two escaped and turned up here; no news of the rest."

"It couldn't have happened in Saladin's time," Ansiau said. "If the sultan cannot even guarantee the safety of the roads, then our own people should."

"How you newcomers do run on! We've barely enough men to maintain ourselves where we are. Why be surprised if our people are attacked in the middle of a heathen land, when in the heart of Champagne the roads are not always safe?"

Ansiau frowned and said no more: it occurred to him that that was a beam in his own eye, for Herbert had been several times accused of brigandage and he himself had twice gone bail for him without being any too sure of his innocence. He now felt himself obliged to leave his fellow-countrymen quite soon—a man may not tolerate an insult to his son, however veiled. Regretfully he took his leave of Herbert of Beaufort and the others; with how many of his friends had he not had to quarrel, because of Herbert?

Yet what a pleasant relaxation it had been for him to be seated there at his ease, talking with men for whom his poverty did not constitute a reason for treating him haughtily. The young man who served him with drink was the son of a count but saw nothing out of the way in remaining standing while he, Ansiau, ate. And, God knows, he was less at his ease even before Riquet than before this other lad, so much better born than himself. For Riquet he was only a poor wretch; for the other, the young squire, he was a knight.

He had himself taken back to the hostel by this same heir to a county, for he would not take advantage of Herbert of Beaufort's charity.

"I embraced poverty for the love of God," he said. "I made a vow."

With men of his own rank he liked to give his wretched condition an air of some nobility, but he thought:

"Pride and vanity, I shall never get over them. To think that Riquet probably stole the money to pay for the journey and that I accepted it!"

Riquet and Auberi were making a tour of the town, admiring everything uncritically, markets, shops, and palaces, turning round to stare after every richly dressed woman and every man in oriental costume.

The town hardly looked like a holy city, but to newly arrived pilgrims even the prostitutes appeared of different clay to those of Marseilles and, if not more virtuous, at least more attractive. The merchants' stalls seemed to them like the cave of Merlin the sorcerer; nowhere else had they seen such precious fabrics, such jewellers' work, carpets, vases and table-ware in engraved silver, glass and crystal, such a quantity of weapons ornamented with gold and precious stones. The houses of the city barons, worthies and merchants were most richly decorated with mosaics, with fences and gates of wrought iron as delicate as lace and silk curtains woven in patterns—it seemed to the two young people that the inhabitants of houses like these must be the sons of kings at least or marvellously beautiful ladies such as are celebrated in song. And Auberi felt himself ready to fall in love for life with every fair-haired damsel dressed in gold and pale-tinted muslin whom he saw, surrounded by maidservants, in the street leading to the church.

Long-bearded Armenians in embroidered robes, Turks in turbans, half-naked servants with faces black as coal, Levantine merchants in striped tunics—all reinforced the illusion that they had fallen into the very midst of the land of fables and dreams and Auberi would not have been in the least surprised to meet a man with a dog's head or catch a glimpse of a winged griffin through the iron grille of some garden gate. The noises of streets and the port, the ten different languages which they did not understand, the deafening uproar of the market where cheap-jacks and cattle-dealers' touts beat tabors to attract the crowd, the brawls round the inns and brothels, the songs and dances of seafaring men about the harbor—all this went to their heads and seemed to them a perpetual holiday, making them feel that in this country everything must be all ardor and joy of living. Riquet was deprived of all desire to return to his monastery and was already dreaming of seducing some princess of the land by his talent as a singer and establishing himself in one of those marble mansions with their gardens overflowing with roses.

It was decided that they were to leave for Jerusalem with a convoy under the command of the squire Jacques of Verneuil, which would leave on the next day but one. Most of their shipboard companions would be with the convoy and also a number of rich pilgrims who had disembarked that evening, an abbot, two Carthusians and three aged nuns. Jacques of Verneuil was taking an escort of ten soldiers for additional security; people from Jaffa had reported that a troop of armed men had been glimpsed among the hills the previous evening.

III. THE END OF A PILGRIMAGE

Having heard mass and taken Communion at sunrise, the pilgrims set out, singing psalms. The road followed the seashore and Mount Carmel rose before them, already drenched in sunshine, green and gold. The sun climbed swiftly in the east beyond the mountains, sweeping away the last traces of shadow, and the country, divided into vineyards and fields and dotted with olive groves, lay before them in its splendor—the air was so clear that as far away as the foothills it seemed possible to distinguish every tree and the very leaves of every tree. The hills were now colored a hard, vivid blue against a sky still golden at the horizon, turning to deep turquoise a little higher towards the zenith.

The two blind men with their guides were among those who lagged behind. During their stay in Marseilles they had lost the habit of long marches. Bertrand, already sick when aboard the ship, was near the end of his strength. His chest was painful, his breathing noisy, and he was spitting pus. For all its purity the air of that May morning seemed to him unbreathable and he was constantly stopping to get his breath. Moreover he had sores on his feet. But for his fear of being alone he would have stayed behind at the hostel in Acre. And now he was cursing the old madman who was in such a hurry to see this ill-starred Jerusalem of his.

"Riquet, friend, I can go no further. You know how to talk to people, run forward a little way and see if you can get a horseman to take me pillion."

"You're a bit late thinking of it; they've all got at least one man up behind them already."

"Not as sick as I am, surely. There's sure to be one who'll make way for me. Or if you could find me room in a litter, that would be even better."

"A litter! How you do run on!"

"Go and try, Riquet. Otherwise, you'll have to carry me."

Riquet began to run along the stony bank beside the road. One of the litters, hung with plain blue canvas curtains, looked to him more modest than the others; he caught hold of the long pole of painted timber from which it was slung. The man riding the rear horse raised his whip.

"Are you a Christian?" Riquet cried, "let me have a word with your master."

"Quickly, then, scamp, or you'll get a taste of this."

A woman's face, still pretty, and pink from the heat, appeared between the curtains; it immediately turned pinker than ever and promptly vanished. But Riquet was already hooked. He took off his bonnet, smoothed his hair and tapped gently on the wooden panel of the litter.

"What is it? What do you want, good pilgrim?"

"A great favor, lady, in the name of the Saviour of us all."

"What is it, friend? As between pilgrims, we must all try to help each other."

"A seat in your litter."

"Eh? That would hardly be decent, friend. I am alone with my two maids."

"Oh, it's not for me, beautiful and gracious lady. It's for a poor blind man with bad feet. That can't be an offense to your modesty, surely, and you'll be doing a good work."

The woman drew her lips together.

"I have no room."

"Come, you could make room. You said yourself we should help each other. I could see that you're good, being so beautiful."

"If I had to take every beggar with sore feet into my litter, it'd have to be as big as Noah's Ark."

"Not all, only one, sweet rose of Sharon. Being beautiful is not everything, lady."

"True—nor being handsome, either. You're very impudent. Yet I swear I'd even rather give you a seat than some wretch with rotting feet."

"That I do well believe, lady."

"Indeed? And what else do you believe, friend?"

"That your two maids will be going, this evening, to warm themselves by the fire and sing canticles."

"Whether they go or not is none of your business."

"Many thanks for your goodness, lady."

Riquet let the litter pass on and began seeking a charitable horseman. He did not find one and, until the evening, he had to take turns with the old man at carrying Bertrand on his back. That evening the convoy halted at a monastery near Jaffa; it was a poor house, not yet recovered from the damage inflicted by war. Only a few monks remained there, working hard to restore the chapel and maintain some part of the vineyards. They always had new bread, hot broth and wine for passing pilgrims, and profited from gifts made by the rich ones.

Fires were lit in the vast enclosure, fenced with stones gathered at random. The monks made the round of the fires with big saucepans of soup and rough wooden ladles. The richer pilgrims were given places at the refectory table.

A novice lit the candles in the chapel for Compline but very few of the pilgrims who were travelling on foot had the strength to attend that office. The night was cold and clear. Beyond the reddish smoke rising from the fires whose light made the surrounding night seem darker than ever, stars as large as pebbles shone with a hard brilliance and scarcely twinkled. Lying on the ground on their outspread cloaks, too exhausted to sleep, the men listened to the thorns crackling in the fires and the distant voices of the monks chanting their canticles.

"So here it is, the road to Jerusalem," Ansiau thought. "How it makes one's heart beat! Only two more days. I shall not see it, most beautiful of cities. Bah! What are eyes? Flesh. My heart will see it. Ah! the only place in the world which is true and sure. Neither living nor dead. Lady, farewell, for now I am near to every Christian's true spouse. Bitter are the nuptials, for I am come late.

"Forgive me, lady, for quitting you as a man quits house or garment. I never loved a woman. The bond which wore out your body and soul is broken. Forgive me, dear sister, that I could not find in you the nourishment of my soul.

"Jerusalem, image of the glorious city of God, since here below it is images we needs must love, which should we choose to love but Thee, the beautiful, the humiliated? It was upon Thee, and no other city, that God wept true tears as a man."

Until Matins Riquet lay in the litter with blue curtains. Then he went to chapel for the office. The monks, standing before the lectern, were singing the 104th psalm. The candles lit the blackened rafters and burned stones of the vaulting, the peeling and badly restored frescoes of the choir.

Thou deckest thyself with light as it were with a garment:
and spreadest out the Heavens like a curtain.

.   .   .   .

They go up as high as the hills and down to the valleys beneath:
even unto the place which Thou appointed for them.
Thou hast set them their bounds which they shall not pass:
neither turn again to cover the earth.

Intoxicated by the words, so familiar and so alien to all his miseries and shame, Riquet sang with the monks. "On the way back from Jerusalem," he thought, "I shall come here. Perhaps they will accept me. They need men. It was not for nothing that God brought me here, showed me these brothers who are in danger and need. This may be my true path."

He remembered the woman, and their meeting arranged for the morrow.

"Oh, what does it matter? I shall expiate everything at Jerusalem."

The march across the barren hill-country became harder and harder. By noon the sun burned with such a heat that they had to call a halt. Two men and one woman, victims of sun-stroke, had to be carried in a litter, the occupants of which mounted their servants' horses. The foundered horses could hardly get along. There were still two days' marching to accomplish.

The pilgrims had no impression of progress: the same mountains seemed to crowd in on them from all sides—vast, arid slopes grey and brown, rocks, hardly any trees. The road was stony, wide indeed but full of ruts and in places becoming one with a desiccated water-course. The blue of the sky was so vivid that it took the color out of everything else, rocks, road, faces. There was no sign of life but a number of eagles poised and gliding above the hilltops.

When a white-clad horseman appeared suddenly upon one of the great rocks near the road, Jacques of Verneuil hardly had time to utter a shout of alarm; apparently materializing out of thin air, half a hundred horsemen were galloping down the slope with long-bows drawn; the first arrows were among the convoy before most of the pilgrims had even seen the enemy. Less than a minute later there were more than a hundred, white on their small black horses and swifter than demons. The arrows whistled and the men uttered short cries, shrill and rhythmic, making an uproar which deprived even the boldest of their presence of mind. The horses of the men-at-arms were down in the first minute, their throats pierced, vomiting blood. The frightened litter horses got out of hand, tangled their harness, turned and reared, trampling litters and horsemen.

Jacques of Verneuil was the first killed; then it was the soldiers' turn. The pilgrims on foot, who had flung themselves to the ground to avoid the arrows and lay trembling for fear of being trampled by the horses, still barely understood what was happening to them when they found themselves seized, dragged along the ground, lifted by the shoulders, handled by dark, bony hands, tied together with their own belts or shirts. They hardly dared cry out their fear and pain, for these men, with their barking language, their dark faces half-hidden by white hoods, were really like creatures risen from another world, less human than the devils of the Last Judgment.

It was thus that, within a few minutes, the pilgrims, although still living men, were transported into another world and their souls wrenched by a change almost as total as death itself. For the richest among them it was a terrible adventure, full of anguish, suffering and fear for their lives; for the poor it was near certainty that their lives were forever lost. The unknown which awaited them now was more terrifying for some of them, and certainly stranger, than what they were accustomed to imagine as the hell or purgatory of the world after death.

Of them all, the two blind men were, if not the most wretched, certainly the most dumbfounded. They had seen nothing, and had suddenly found themselves plunged into a tumult of voices, shouts, running feet and hoofs. When all was over they had still not properly understood what was happening. An attack? But from where? By whom? Who had tied them? Where were the others? The old man at least had Auberi, who had clung to him and would not let go, gripping with such strength that they had not been able to separate him from his master and had tied them together. But he was too frightened to speak and did nothing but whimper and sob through chattering teeth.

"What can he see, poor little chap, to make him tremble so?" Ansiau wondered. "Perhaps they're torturing our people or cutting their heads off? But in that case I'd hear more cries. Bertrand? Where is Bertrand?"

Bertrand had been hit in the left arm by an arrow and the pain, as well as fear, had at first prevented him from thinking. Tied, dragged, he walked at random, his feet, covered with sores, knocking against stones. He could think of one thing only: let the pain stop. Fall? He fell on his knees, a kick brought him to his feet. A rope jerked at his waist, making the blood pour in gushes from his wounded arm which was twisted behind his back. Were the others also tied?

"Ah, let them kill me, I cannot go on walking like this." And he walked on still, his mind too clouded to give him the strength to stop.

This hellish march continued for two hours. One of the three nuns, wounded, fell, and was finished off with the stab of a lance. The body rolled down the rocky slope, dashing itself against large stones. The prisoners, tied together, marched in Indian file, following the troop of Saracen horsemen; a number of dismounted men, whips in hand, drove on those inclined to hang back with shouts and blows. Another troop of horse brought up the rear, with the pilgrims' horses and the booty taken from the litters.

The prisoners were led to a tented camp pitched about a well, where, at last, they could lie down on the ground and the horses were given water. The leader of the troop, wearing an engraved gilt helmet under his burnoose and a surcoat of chain-mail decorated on the shoulders with inscribed plaques, approached the prisoners, followed by a clean-shaven man in white with hard eyes: he was the interpreter. The emir signed to the prisoners to fall on their knees; all obeyed excepting the blind men, who had to be made to kneel by force. Thereafter he spoke briefly to the interpreter, who then raised a hand towards heaven and said:

"Blessed be God. This is what the son of Abdul instructs me to say to you; there is no God but God and Mahomet is his prophet. There are not three gods but one only. If there be men among you willing to recognize the true faith, to honor the Prophet and to be circumcised, they will be set at liberty and treated honorably. For we are all sons of the same Father."

The prisoners remained silent, too astonished by this opening to understand what was expected of them. Some wondered fearfully whether they would not have to undergo martyrdom. But it seemed that neither the emir nor the interpreter really expected any conversions, for they immediately went on to the question of ransoms. Only the abbot, a big wine-merchant and two burgesses of Dijon were able to promise the sum required; they were separated from the others and taken to a tent.

Next the warriors shared out the women who were still young— among them the fair-haired occupant of the blue litter, her two maids and a young novice. One of the soldiers also tried to take Auberi but the child still clung so frantically to his master that it was not easy to get him away. He kept shaking his head and saying: "He's my father." Ansiau tried to explain: "*Beni, ana bou,*" and the Saracen did not persist, not wishing to part father and son.

Thereafter it was decided that the young, strong men should be sent on to Damascus, to be sold in the slave-market. The others would be left to their own devices or to be picked up by anyone who had a use for them.

At sundown a servant brought the prisoners a large, narrow-necked jar of water. They had been untied: what was there to fear of men in their condition? The camp was guarded by armed sentries.

Now the prisoners were trying to regroup themselves, to join up with their friends. They huddled together to get warm. Two old women were wailing, lamenting aloud. Even some of the men, strong fellows in their prime, began suddenly to sob. More than one had a wife and children in France.

Riquet had sat down next to the old man and put a hand on his shoulder. The other had started, as if woken from a dream.

"It's me, Master Pierre—Riquet. You are not wounded, Master Pierre?"

"Where is Bertrand?"

"Lying on the ground beside the two weavers from Toulouse. I spoke to him but he doesn't move. I am afraid he's not long for this world."

"You must go to him, Riquet."

"Let be, Master Pierre. He'll know how to die without my help. This is the last night I shall spend with you, Master Pierre."

"Yes, Riquet."

For a long time Riquet looked down at Auberi, sleeping huddled against the old man's knees. He felt a lump in his throat. What would he not have given to hear the boy's frank laugh, or his voice, just beginning to break, again?

"They're taking us away at dawn, Master Pierre."

"Where?"

"Damascus. The weavers, the two monks and the Marseillais who was with us on board, and Landri, the blacksmith. We're to be sold, like horses at a fair."

"I too was sold, Riquet, at your age. As you see, I found a way out."

"Oh, I shall do the same, you'll see." Yet his voice was weary and sad. He was having to make an effort to keep up his courage.

"We shall never see each other again, Master Pierre."

The old man put his arm round the young man's shoulders. And in the face of this gesture of tenderness, the first his old companion had vouchsafed him, Riquet's self-control broke down and he began to sniffle and bite his lip. He was ashamed that the old man should hear him weep but he could think of no pleasantry to save his face. For a long time they remained thus, without speaking.

"*Or si defalt la loial compaignie*,"[1] the old man said, in a strangely gentle voice.

"Eh? I don't understand you very well when you use the northern tongue."

"It's from the *Song of Roland*. I thought of it because it suits our case. Our companionship did not last long, Riquet. If you manage to escape, have a mass said for me at Jerusalem. As for me, I shall not reach it. Yet we had not far to go."

"No. Less than from Montélimar to Avignon. What do you think they're going to do with you, Master Pierre?"

"How can I know? But they are men, after all, not brutes. There are men everywhere." He shook his head, to drive away the anguish which was clawing at him; why should these people burden themselves with a blind man? The dull, animal fear which griped his bowels was clouding his mind. He tried not to give way to it; but Riquet felt the fear in the uncertainty of his voice and it went to his heart.

"You know," he said, "you being so tall and strong, they're sure to use you to work in the fields. You can very well pass for being only blind in one eye and afterwards they'll always find a use for you."

"To be sure. Yes. Here you are, consoling me like a child, Riquet. And you're right, for I don't feel brave. It's something I've often experienced before but, then, I wasn't old. Yet I don't know—there's something in me which tells me this is still not the end, now. . . ."

[1] "Thus was dispersed this loyal company."

You're sure to escape, Riquet. But don't take their faith. Not even to escape later. It would be a great sin."

"God! What do you take me for? Am I a coward?"

"I've lived longer than you have. And so I can say this to you."

Auberi moaned softly and raised his head.

"My lord, it's still dark, my lord. It's too early to leave."

"Sleep, little one. Yes, it's too early."

The child dropped his head again and Riquet was thinking that he would have given his "Auvergnat piglet" a good hug and a kiss if he had not been afraid of waking him. "And when and where shall I sleep myself? Ah, Jerusalem, a fine pilgrimage I must make to you! Hands tied, and haltered like a beast. By what twists and turns, in how many years, in what state, shall I reach you? Grey-haired, perhaps, with torn nostrils and cropped ears, and my back half-broken by hard toil and blows. Youth gone, life lost! The friends I loved. Farewell. Now I'm a grain of sand in the desert. Ah, Father Abbot, do you still remember your Brother Frotaire?"

At sunrise, after the morning prayers, one of the soldiers mounted his horse, took two servants with him, and had the men destined for Damascus tied and roped in file. They hardly had time to take leave of their friends. Auberi only seemed to realize the position when Riquet was being led away: he rushed towards him, was thrust off by the guards and fell to the ground. The old man was straining his ears, still trying to hear his friend's voice. It was not easy to distinguish among those of the others, also shouting their farewells. At last he heard it, sonorous, vibrant with both tears and defiance.

"I'm off to Damascus, like Saint Paul, Master Pierre! Don't forget me, Master Pierre! Auberi! God be with you! Auberi!"

Then his voice was lost among the others and all of them were growing slowly fainter as the men moved off: those left behind followed the group with their eyes as it set off along the stony track beside the rock face. The men walked with drooping heads, stiff backs; they did not look back.

In the course of the day the emir's warriors struck their tents and went down into the valley, taking the rest of the prisoners. They hardly knew what to do with this mixed bag—either they must abandon them by the way or sell them in the settlements on the plain; there was no lack of Christian slaves in the region but their death rate was high and there had been no war in the country for twenty years. Most of this new batch were still capable of working. Two of their number—an old woman and Bertrand—seemed useless. But their captors, bandits though they were, hesitated to abandon an old woman and a wounded, blind man by the wayside, especially since Bertrand, with his nearly white hair and worn face, had the air of an old man and his distress inspired a certain respect even in these men without faith.

The road wound about the flank of an arid, sun-scorched mountain. The prisoners' hands were no longer tied; they had been given burdens to carry, jars of water and the booty taken from the convoy. Bertrand, although wounded, was consequently loaded with a parcel of clothes, which he carried on his shoulder, holding it in position with his sound arm. He was among the stragglers, far from the old man and Auberi. The child had, indeed, tried to lead him to the old man before their departure but Bertrand had refused, saying that he wanted no more to do with the madman who had caused his misfortunes. Now he was regretting it a little; he would have liked to march beside his old companion, if only to overwhelm him with insults and reproaches. He was almost fainting from hunger and pain and, now that the old man was no longer at his side, he felt lost and adrift, as if he had just lost his sight for the second time.

Never, before that bitterly cold night in the Saracen camp, had he really felt what revolt in a man's heart can be. He was frightened by it himself. True, when they had put out his eyes after killing his daughters, he had mourned and complained; and when Alfonse had repulsed him in favor of death he had become as if mad with pain, a pain which supported, even exalted him. But that which was now happening to him seemed to him so senselessly cruel that he did not even think of complaining. Almost, he could have laughed. To have undergone such miseries, such fatigues, to have made such efforts to get here for the sole purpose of being picked up by the Saracens, wounded, dragged along like an animal, his only prospect that of dying like a dog in a backyard of some Moslem village! His body's suffering was almost submerged in the dreadful, the intolerable astonishment which had taken possession of his whole soul. This, then, was truth; this was life, and not otherwise. This—that if there was still life before him it was that of a beast, without friends, language or name. Gaucelm of Castans—once again a bitter smile twisted his mouth—that this . . . this *thing* could still claim to be called Gaucelm of Castans—or Bertrand or Pierre or

Jacques—this whimpering, faceless, eyeless *thing*—hideous, yes, without seeing himself he knew it, hideous. Such was man. *Ecce homo.* Behold what a man could come to.

The old man. He must be there, a few steps away, among the others, walking with his heavy, regular stride, just as he had walked the roads about Albi. No doubt regretting his precious Jerusalem and the masses he could no longer have said. Throw him into boiling pitch and he'd still think of his masses. Hate this madman? He was not worth it. He was of those who know not what they do; he had dragged his companions into this hell and all he could say was: "God willed it."

"God, what does God will? Alfonse, Alfonse, it was you who condemned me to this martyrdom, because of your love of God. Cursed be you, Alfonse, and cursed be your God. It has needed all this to teach me to curse you indeed.

"My love is dead, Alfonse, my carnal love, the greed of eyes and heart. If you came down from Heaven like an angel to console me, should I suffer any less because of your beauty, your gentleness and the sweetness of your voice? Like the priest and the Levite, you have seen my misery and passed by on the other side, O cheat and liar, and now even the memory of you is naught but bitterness and vexation. You are nothing to me now. Wherever you may be, I curse you, Alfonse, and may my suffering poison your spirit forever; centuries may pass and worlds end but never can there be reparation for the injustice done to me. For the prince of this world has all power over souls and bodies and all has been delivered over to him. Never shall I go to God.

"If all this was needed to make me understand the nature of evil—well, I have understood. Shame upon him who has awaited this final humiliation before finding the courage to destroy the rottenness within him! I shall go no further. Let the old man march on, if he will."

Suddenly he halted and flung the parcel of clothes he was carrying on to the ground. With terrifying swiftness his mind became starkly clear—his inner eye saw so lucidly that he seemed to have recovered his sight. The man behind him knocked against him, then passed him. Bertrand made for the side of the road, groping, his feet stumbled against stones and he was astonished to feel no pain. It was as if he were drunk. He heard voices, the clatter of hoofs, shouts of anger. He went forward another three paces, both arms raised above his head.

A whip-lash curled about his shoulders, he felt a burning sensation, faltered, turned; there was a horseman near him, he could hear the animal breathing, the hoarse voice of the man three feet above him. Slowly, he stooped, picked up a stone which he had touched with his foot and, standing upright again, brandished it above his head. He did not have time to throw it; he hardly had time to feel something, which hissed and was cold, cut into his neck.

The convoy had stopped and the prisoners, mute with horror, were watching the scene. It had all happened so quickly; they had seen the horseman overtake the fugitive, whip in hand. And they saw the blind man's head rolling down the slope, bouncing like a ball, cracking against the rocks. For a few seconds the decapitated body remained upright, then collapsed, the black blood pouring out of it. The horse whinnied and reared; the convoy, which had halted for a moment, set off again.

A voice was raised, shrill, piercing, a wordless plaint, an interminable cry of horror, and this voice froze the prisoners' blood almost as much as the sight of the head loose from the body. The women began screaming; they had to be silenced with lashes of the whip. The road fell away among rocks glaring white under the sun and the sky was a crude, vivid, identical blue from zenith to horizon. The body, kneeling among the stones, the shoulders leaning forward, arms apart, was still moving, and the blood poured from the neck in gushes; it was that which Auberi was watching, his head turned to look back, as if he were hypnotized, and it was that which drew from him the long scream which he could not stop. The sound of the skull, ringing against the rocks, still rang in his own head.

The old man had not understood what was happening. He heard Auberi screaming and his heart contracted with anguish for the child.

"To what have I brought him? What is it he can see? They'll drive him out of his mind. Wretch that I am, what have I done to the child?"

Later, they told him how Bertrand had died.

"An old bird of ill-omen," he thought. "I've brought three to their deaths, three men who were nothing to me, who had taken no oath to me. O Jerusalem the deceitful, three lives lost for your sake and my own with them. A soul damned by my fault and for nothing—for I know that he killed himself in despair and he had trusted in me. Jerusalem, our only fatherland—I know that to reach you a man must first be worthy, yet many a man has completed that journey whose worth was no more than mine.

"So he's left me, my companion, my brother in misfortune. Without one last cry of farewell, he left me, cursing me in his heart. Aye, he was right, I should have done better to let him die on the day I met him beside the fountain near Uzès.

"Now there's Auberi and me, they'll surely take us to some village near here. Perhaps Auberi may be able to escape when he has got his strength back. What are they going to do with him, great God? The worst will be if, by my fault, he too comes to damnation. Yes, truly, rather than that I should prefer to kill him with my own hands."

Herbert? Yes, that night he had thought of Herbert, although God knows it was not to come begging help of his son that he had left his house. Yet, for his companions' sake, perhaps he ought to have done so. But, rich though Herbert might be, he would certainly not have been able to get together four ransoms in six months. To do it he would have had to ruin himself and charge himself with debt for life. No, no, the lady should never know that he was a prisoner in heathen hands.

When evening came, Ansiau and Auberi, with three companions in misfortune, were taken to a small fortified village in the mountains; a eunuch, intendant of the emir who held the village, examined them, felt their muscles, rapped them on the hams. They did not seem very strong, but there was a lack of men for rebuilding the ramparts and for the fruit harvest. The old man, the biggest of all and still sound, was set to carrying stones; several times he mistook the direction and finally stumbled into a heap of sand. It was only then that his blindness was realized.

After having abused him in Arabic and in French, the eunuch decided to use him for turning the mill.

A MASTERLESS HOUSE

THE mornings were becoming foggy and cold and the forest was all gold and bronze; the packs of white and russet hounds hunted across plowed land and meadows and the sound of the hunting-horns could be heard from afar in the forest. From the village the peasants watched the lady of the manor, tall and svelte in her close-fitting, red-lined blue gown, her roan horse all decked with colored fringe, crossing the fields with her neighbors, the lords of Breul, her damsels and her huntsmen. The whole country might be dying of hunger before they would allow a villager to kill a single stag in the forest; they would never lack meat to feed their dozen and a half couple of hounds; for all the master was away on a pilgrimage, his lady spent her time at chase of hare, boar or quail as in the autumn of any other year.

Grey and wet, the autumn advanced swiftly. The leaves of the trees, scorched by the drought, were already brown by the end of September. A hard winter was expected, the harvest had been poor and it was difficult to replace the beasts lost in the fire, cattle having been slaughtered over the whole region up to thirty leagues away because of the drought. And, in the village, the thirteen who had been hanged were not forgotten.

Haguenier had suddenly found himself desperately alone. Pierre had gone to Troyes to take his place in the count of Brie's service. And Haguenier had never had anything to do with his father's household. Nor had he any wish to see the old lady after she had cursed his father and, anyhow, since Eglantine's death Bernon no longer attracted him—it was as if the old master's daughter had carried off the soul of the house with her into the tomb.

Now he had to talk to the bailiffs, oversee the works, and pay the masons and soldiers who were much more exigent with the master's son than with Herbert himself. He had trees felled to rebuild the burned houses and had had thirty sheep and four cows bought in Tonnerre market at three times the ordinary price; despite this the peasantry continued to look down their noses at him, for he had stood at his father's side on the day of the executions; the children threw stones at him and called him hangman. And he was no better liked at the castle. The soldiers considered him miserly and the mason thought him haughty, for he spoke little. Herbert, despite his luxurious tastes and his brutality, always gave his men the impression of being one of themselves, wherefore they forgave him a great deal. Dame Aelis was forever taking offense at her stepson's want of deference towards herself, to which she sourly drew his attention; of all his father's household she was the one whom Haguenier could bear least easily, despite the fact that she was of noble blood, well-mannered and far from ill-tempered; she produced in him a mortal boredom. He got on better with the concubines; there were three of them, in addition to Ortrud, girls of little virtue but gay and by no means stupid; one of them was half Turkish and came from the Holy Land. It is well said that courtesans travel more than pilgrim friars; this girl had visited Germany and Hungary, spoke several languages and could sing the songs of every country. Haguenier had no taste for low company but he loved music.

In that house, which, for Haguenier, was full of Ernaut's memory, he was like a caged wolf; not two years had passed since they had been together there, throwing pails of water at each other by the well, cleaning their horses' harness in the stables; at that time Marie had been no more than one joy among many, a treasure to be won. Now Ernaut lay in the earth by Rainard's tomb and, as for himself, he had set out on a splendid adventure which was to last all his life, to raise him ever higher, cause him to accomplish miracles of valor. It had hardly begun, and now here it was, over and done with, in a manner most flat and humiliating for him—because of a jealous husband, for fear of gossip, she had dismissed him as one dismisses a worthless servant. This, then, was the proof to which she was to put him—O false, inconstant, weak woman who had required everything of him but had never reckoned with her own feebleness.

What, then, had she meant when she talked of serving Love?

"My trials are only beginning," he thought, "but I shall win her back despite herself, for my love will be with her everywhere and I shall love her so much that she will feel it, though she be a hundred leagues from me, and she will think of me unceasingly and will languish for me and weep all her tears for my sake. But I shall have erected a barrier between us which cannot be crossed."

He was thinking seriously of entering a monastery, and asking God to cure him.

He spent three weeks at Linnières, hardly ever leaving the castle, and despite his weak heart he got drunk almost every night.

"Fair son," the lady Aelis said to him one day, "you are setting people a bad example. It's shocking to see a lad of your age drink so much; it's that, surely, which makes you so ill. I have, indeed, been told that your mother also drank."

"And my father, too, I hear," Haguenier, already a little drunk, replied. "There are sons who follow their parents' example."

Vexed, the lady Aelis said:

"You could use a more civil tone to me. And let me tell you you're a deal worse than your father; you've neither friends nor mistresses but crouch in your corner like a wildcat."

"I should hardly look for friends and mistresses here. I had a friend and my father let him die to please his cousin. However, be easy; as soon as my father returns you will see no more of me here."

Yet he was a good deal disgusted with himself, for Dame Aelis's reproaches seemed to him justified. He went to pay a visit to the abbot of Saint-Florentin.

The abbot was a tall, stout man, with a brick-colored face devoid of beauty. He had a double chin, a powerful, hooked nose and thick black eyebrows. Despite his sixty years he had not a single white hair and he held himself upright. His reception room, which opened into the cloisters, was hung with striped cloth and furnished with taste; there was a great carved armchair, cushioned benches, a wrought-iron lectern and a great coffer covered with tooled leather. All these objects seemed to give out an odor of musk and lavender. A young lay brother brought Haguenier leather slippers, for the father abbot did not care for dirty boots on his polished floor and his carpets.

The abbot was noted as a lover of good cheer and Haguenier began by presenting him with some thrushes and hazel-hens taken in the forest the previous evening. Then, after the customary courtesies, he plunged at once into his business: as soon as his father returned he wished to enter the monastery for a period of trial. As a dower, he could bring with him one-third of the Hervi lands, the part which bordered on the monastery's property.

The abbot scratched his chin.

"Your father will not agree," he said.

"I am of age and the land is mine."

"You seem to me rather young to take such a decision," the abbot said, with a smile.

"No younger than the brother who was here a moment ago, Father."

"Quite another matter, my son. There are some who are called to God from childhood. You, you belong to the world, and have, as I have heard, led a very worldly life."

"Exactly, but I wish to renounce it."

"Very well," the abbot said, "let me hear your reasons."

He had the attentive yet somewhat detached look of a man who has heard hundreds of confessions and who is only the intermediary between the penitent and God: it was just such an expression that Haguenier needed; he was able to tell all that was in his heart without hiding anything and without fear of shocking or vexing the father abbot. When he had finished the abbot said:

"My son, I cannot accept you into this house, even for a trial. Think it out for yourself—a man who has just broken a leg is not accepted for a trial of prowess in leaping or running. When you have got over your attachment to this woman, then and then only I might consider whether you are worthy of God's service. Our house is not a hospital."

Haguenier bowed his head.

"Yet I should have thought, Father, that you could offer a refuge to those wishing to fly from the world's temptations. I feel that if I remain in the world I am lost."

"You are a child," the abbot said, and added, smiling: "Oh, I know that a young man of twenty does not like to hear himself so called. But I should have said the same thing to your father and even to your grandfather, whom I knew well and who was a man of excellent qualities, for a layman does not know what he is talking about when he speaks of withdrawing from the world to serve God. Few really have the call. And even those who have are exposed by the Devil to temptations and struggles beside which the world's miseries are naught but the vexation of a child who has broken his toy. If you had not the strength of character to fulfill your obligations in the world, obligations both human and natural, how will you fulfill those which are inhuman and against nature?"

"Your words are hard, Father," Haguenier said. "But I am not the light-minded man you take me for. I have not much strength, but

God can lend me strength if He will. He has already taken from me all that I had in the world. I come to Him like a beggar. You are right when you say that I am not cured of my love for this woman. How could I be cured? But I know that, in God's eyes, all this is very trivial. Even dogs have the right to snap up the crumbs which fall from their masters' tables. Only let me stand face to face with Him, making Him my only hope, since I, too, am His creature."

The father abbot looked at him for a long time out of his small, black, deep-set eyes.

"Remember, my son, what Our Lord said to the rich young man: commit not adultery, kill not, steal not, do not bear false witness, wrong no man, honor thy father and thy mother; and the young man, greatly your superior, had already accomplished these things. Only then did our sweet Lord tell him to sell all he had and to follow Him, and the young man, albeit so righteous, fell back in the face of such a decision. Now, you have committed all the sins which this man had not committed. For you have lusted after a married woman, you have become a soldier, consequently a murderer, you are rich with goods which belong to the poor, and you honor not your father. First, then, try to live honorably according to the world's wisdom."

"I know, however, that He called to Himself Saint Matthew and Saint Mary Magdalene," Haguenier said.

"Yes. But do you remember, my son, the manner of His calling Saint Matthew? He saw him seated among his evil companions, came to him and bade him follow Him. On the day when He calls you in the same manner, you will follow Him. Meanwhile, return home and do your duty in that station where God has placed you."

"How," Haguenier thought, "does he know that God has not ordered me to follow Him? Nevertheless, it must be as he says. In my pride I thought the place I sought easy to win, that I had but to offer my lands and they would be only too pleased to receive me. He treated me like a capricious child. I do not believe I am any such thing—yet there is surely some truth in his idea, for he is a wise man and one who knows the world. Only he's wrong; I could never continue to live the life I've led until now.

"It's all very well, but I cannot honor my father, and that's a sin, for did God say: 'Honor thy father only if he is good and just?' Fathers, in Moses' time, cannot all have been saints. And yet such is the incomprehensible wisdom of God that one must even honor a wicked man, and that without becoming a party to his wicked actions. They made a soldier of me because I come of a family of fighting men and God never said that a soldier should refuse to fight, and Saint George and Saint Theodore and Saint John Martyr were soldiers; yet it is said —thou shalt not kill. I never committed adultery and I took an oath to Marie not to touch her, so I should not be held guilty; yet I desired her so ardently that I committed adultery a thousand times in my heart. How could I ever understand all this?

"O only Friend, sole Father, unique Master, how hard is the love of You—yes, hard as prison walls. I turn and batter my head every way and cannot escape. For You have compassed me about on all sides and in this world I find no place nor refuge. And—it's no use lying—I shall never be able to fulfill my obligations in it without sinning; one might as well try to put harness on a goat. And for the time being I am forced to do it."

Riding slowly beside the Armançon, such were his reflections. Before him, in the pale blue sky, golden clouds piled themselves up into huge castles; high, square turrets rose, then slowly collapsed; gigantic keeps built themselves, crushing earth, woods and meadows beneath their mass.

Struck by their beauty, Haguenier dismounted and lay down in the damp grass in order to watch the spectacle at his ease. He felt as if he were present at the mystery of the Creation.

"For," he thought, "everything, even these masses of light vapor which lose their shape at the slightest breeze, all is an image of the created world. And the valleys shall be filled and the mountains levelled and all flesh shall hear the word of the Lord. If those clouds could suffer, what tears would they not shed to see themselves thus change and disappear? They are more beautiful than earthly valleys and mountains, they roll and fall, and out of all eternity only this instant will have been theirs and then they are no more. I am suffering to the point of death and shall never find consolation since I have lost that which was all my life. But it has no longer any importance, for, in an instant, I am gone with the clouds and exist no more."

The high towers had collapsed and in their place there was now nothing but an enormous block, grey below and coppery above, the whole drifting slowly like a huge ship on fire; then, from every side, it was penetrated by golden rays. Haguenier was still staring but without

thinking of anything. Suddenly he distinctly heard a voice saying:
"Haguenier, my brother." He was afraid, for it was Ernaut's voice.
"Brother," the voice said, again.

"Ernaut, friend, I am coming. Where are you?"

He rose and began walking haphazard towards the river.

The grass was already mixed with rushes under his feet. He drew
back, turned in his tracks and went towards his horse. Into what sin
was the Devil about to lead him? He crossed himself hastily several
times.

"O Holy Mary, Lady, most pure Virgin, protect me. I was about to
commit the unforgivable sin without even realizing it. Ah, to lie there
deep under the water, in the mud and the dark weeds; under the water
which has been flowing since the beginning and never returns to its
source. But this is but mirage and lies—O eternal beauty, welcoming
weeds and animals, ant and boar and crow into your deep restfulness,
yet you have nothing to offer man, who can find rest solely in God and
only torment everywhere else. It is quite true that as nature absorbs
and breaks down all flesh, so that it may be re-created to flower again,
the will of God takes souls to itself, giving them death that they may
burgeon again. But there is nothing in common between the world and
man; and he who seeks repose in death finds naught but torment.
Ernaut, Ernaut, my brother, you went to the very end and beyond it to
find rest in the body's death. May God give me the strength to realize
that I shall find peace nowhere and that it is futile to try to escape.
Better far to live wickedly in submission to the laws of the flesh which
God created, than to be like a man who spoils and sacks a land which
his lord has entrusted to him. His lord will say to him: 'You are worse
than a thief, for a thief enjoys what he has stolen, and may raise the
value of the stolen land and then repent and return the land to me on
the day when I shall require it of him; but the man who steals to
destroy is three times dishonest, for he robs me, and nature, and
himself.' "

HERBERT'S WIFE

THE lords of Breul and Vanlay had come to Linnières for the feast of Saint Denis, to organize a celebration in honor of Amaury, brother of the lord of Breul. He, single-handed, had just killed an old bear, long known in the region, whose den was in the northern part of Linnières forest. Haguenier had, indeed, pointed out to the lady Aelis that she would have done better, in her husband's absence, not to invite people to the castle, especially after what had happened in September. Aelis had replied:

"Fair son, the house is not, as far as I know, without a master. You are here to go bail for my honor. And what has happened that we should not hold up our heads before our neighbors?"

"As you say, the house has a master, although one whom you take no account of. But, since my father has always left you free to do as you please, there is nothing I can say to you."

"Yes," Aelis said, "he has always left me my freedom."

Haguenier had raised his head at that, surprised by the bitterness with which she had spoken. He looked at her for a long time—as always, she had an absent look, but there was something pitiable in the expression of her pale, almost colorless eyes, which were strangely reminiscent of Herbert's own.

"How young and pretty she is still," Haguenier thought. "Why had I never noticed it before?"

He was a good deal vexed at having to receive the guests she was imposing on him. But he thought: "After all, she's right enough; there's no reason for us to hang our heads before the Breul people. Whatever my father may have done, it's no business of theirs." He presided over the feast, next to Aelis and forced himself to play the host as courteously as possible.

The lord of Breul and his wife and brother were Dame Aelis's best friends and she was, indeed, almost always with them. Since her husband's departure she had sometimes stayed at Breul for several days running, despite her stepson's remonstrances. Now it was they who were staying at Linnières and the lady Aelis required wax candles to be lighted every evening, caused the best wines, the best spices and candied fruits to be served and was constantly making them presents of valuable objects—while Haguenier, who knew his father to have numerous debts, considered this prodigality very unseasonable. But he dared refuse nothing, and, out of politeness, even exceeded his stepmother's extravagance.

"After all," he told himself, "my father surely won't reproach me for it. He likes money to be spent." Nevertheless he began to look sourly on his stepmother's friendship with the Breul people.

He was not fond of this woman, primarily because she was his stepmother and his own mother would certainly have lived longer had his father not been in such a hurry to marry the Bercen heiress. And then Dame Aelis was a person so indifferent to everything that it was difficult to like her. Sometimes, indeed, it even seemed difficult to be aware of her at all, so listless were her movements, so dull her voice, so lifeless her expression. Several times since Herbert's absence, Haguenier had, greatly to his confusion, been called to order by her for omitting to greet her or to see that she was served before the others—he would hardly have believed himself capable of such a want of courtesy.

Yet she was the most elegant woman of the neighborhood—but although she was still pretty, it was her dress that was looked at, not her face. A rather pale face it was, with small, delicate features, the eyes too light under drooping lids. Sometimes Haguenier felt something like pity for her—unreasonably enough, since she led a gay, careless life, gayer, in fact, and more carefree than was proper in the mother of four daughters, the eldest twelve years old. But it really was a pity that a woman who spent her life amusing herself should always have such an air of boredom.

Perhaps one should have been sorry for her, with such a husband as hers. But everyone agreed that Herbert was, in fact, as good a husband as he could be to her. Some even thought him over-indulgent, for Aelis ran into debt without reckoning and quite neglected her duties as chatelaine, excepting that of entertaining guests, and Herbert never uttered a word of reproach. It was also well known that she was on a footing of excessively tender friendship with certain ladies and, according to the more scandalous tongues, these friendships were far from chaste. Herbert, who was not unaware of these rumors, preferred not to notice them, telling himself naïvely that, by this token, he ran no risk of being given a pair of horns. At all events, he showed a confidence in his wife sufficiently remarkable in a man of such jealous temper.

He took pride in believing that the fear which he inspired was worth all the locks and spies in the world.

Aelis had lived through the commonplace adventure of many heiresses of good family; she had been a girl like any other and had dreamed of a certain gay and handsome youth who came to whisper flowery words across her pet bird's cage or beside her embroidery frame. The young man was poor. Then a rich suitor presented himself, a knight, famous for his feats of courage under arms. When she was fifteen they had married her to this man of twenty-five, who seemed to her already old. She had wept. The young man she loved happened to be the younger brother of the bridegroom and had been present at the wedding as one of the groomsmen. She had realized, that day, that he had never loved her and had simply been after her dower.

As a last straw, her bridegroom had fallen in love with her immediately after their betrothal, and had become even more so after the wedding. What was a fifteen-year-old girl, already in love with another man, to make of this wild bull of a man? The wedding night had driven her nearly mad with fear. A few days later the brothers fell out, and Girard, the younger, having allowed himself some slighting remark about the bride, Herbert had disfigured him by knocking out his teeth with a blow of his fist.

A sensible young woman does not hate the man whom her father has chosen to be her husband. She was obliged to believe that the man loved her, since he overwhelmed her with presents and devoured her with kisses. She had children but was never allowed to attend to them herself, Herbert being too infatuated to leave her the time. The ladies of Troyes envied her her jewels and her wardrobe; she could not but suppose herself happy. After three years of marriage, Herbert set out on his second crusade. As, at that time, he was extremely jealous, he had incarcerated her in a convent, cautioning the mother superior not to let her out on any pretext whatsoever—and there, during two years, Aelis had had ample leisure to give herself up to that eternal, pointless day-dream from which nothing was ever to draw her again. After Herbert's return, life became spacious and handsome, but now she had to share her husband's favors with his concubines and take her part in veritable orgies; the old lady of Linnières had finally interfered and taken Aelis under her protection, and husband and wife thereafter went their own ways. Herbert could boast of having forever cured his wife of any wish to be unfaithful to him. For years she could not bear a smile or a glance from a man without shuddering.

She had involved herself in a world of dreams, composed solely of courtly ladies and noble damsels; she took part with the countess's ladies-in-waiting in all the courts of love and the hawking parties, and became infatuated with all the most beautiful and admired ladies of the court. She had her suitors, but always repulsed them, and, when they became importunate, complained to Herbert. She believed herself to feel if not friendship at least gratitude towards a husband who, no longer requiring anything of her, yet had the good taste and consideration to refuse her nothing, in memory of his past love.

On the night of the storm, when Herbert, supposing that he was going to be struck by lightning within the hour, had taken leave of her, she had realized for the first time that it would be a happiness for her never to see him again. Was that a sin? To her, at least, he had never done any harm. She had wept over her own hard-heartedness. He was her spouse in the sight of God. But then, for so long and so often had she listened to talk of a pure, tender and noble love, in which there was naught but sweetness and delight; and Herbert was no King Mark nor King Arthur; he would guess any secret from a look or a smile. A person who is afraid can hide nothing.

Since her husband's departure for Le Puy Aelis was aware that in order to go on living she found it necessary to hope that he would never return—at the mere idea of seeing him back in his place, beneath the armorial shields at the high table, she wanted to throw herself into the well—for since hope had found room in her heart, she felt that he would read its implication in her eyes.

She was very attached to the lord of Breul's wife, a woman very young, full of laughter and remarkably beautiful; and her friend talked to her a great deal about her brother-in-law, Amaury. Aelis did not feel particularly attracted to the young man, for all he was brave and gay and well-mannered; but Beatrix of Breul had so much affection for him and spoke so well of him that Aelis could not prevent herself from allowing her friend to think her in love; many are the women who thus take a lover in order to appear more interesting to their friends. It was true, too, that she was more and more inclined to dream of a secret love, composed of the language of flowers, of confidential talks with Beatrix, of embroidered purses, and kisses snatched between two rides, when they were out hawking. She had as yet granted Amaury nothing she need blush for, but she knew that Herbert would consider it far too much already and that he would immediately think the worst.

So tenaciously did she cling to the hope that he would return no more that it made her bold—she took to making up fantastic romances in her mind: if, indeed, Herbert came back one day, Amaury would carry her off with the help of his brother and Beatrix and all four of them would go to Germany and put themselves under the emperor's protection, for she imagined that anyhow, since she was giving countenance to a young man, all was already lost. Finally even the danger represented by Herbert was taking the vague and extravagant forms of a dream.

THE BAD STEWARD

HAGUENIER found himself in a sufficiently embarrassing situation: Dame Aelis had again invited her friends of Breul to Linnières and he could not avoid treating his stepmother with proper deference. But he perceived that Amaury was wearing a blue scarf about his wrist similar to that of the lady Aelis, that he always chose those pieces of the joint which the lady had just touched with her hands, and that his kiss lingered on her cheek longer than was called for by ordinary politeness. Haguenier was not greatly concerned over the honor of Jacques of Pouilli, although he was fond of him, but it was another matter when it was a question of his own father. His nature made him incapable of having his stepmother spied on, or anyone else for that matter, and he determined to come into the open.

He took Amaury of Breul on one side, on the pretext of teaching him the words of a song of which the young man was fond—he could not read well enough to learn from a written copy—and when they were seated together on a bench near the fire Haguenier said:

"Well now, Sir Squire, I did not bring you here only to talk of tunes and songs. I believe you are older than I am but, since I am a knight, I have the right to offer you a word of advice, without, I hope, causing you annoyance."

Amaury looked him straight in the eyes and replied:

"That depends on the nature of the advice."

Haguenier held the other's look for a long time without frowning. The lad had fine eyes, bold, very blue; he was red-haired, not notably handsome, but his face was high-colored, fresh and open, very pleasant to look upon.

"Hardly surprising," Haguenier thought, "if she prefers him to my father."

"Very good advice," he said, at last. "It is this—never behave in such a manner that a noblewoman may incur blame in consequence."

Amaury had drawn himself up.

"The advice," he said, "is good, but the manner of giving it is not. What woman have you in mind?"

"You know quite well. A woman closely connected with myself. That is why I have spoken."

"Is this a threat?"

"God forbid! I am giving you my opinion, that's all. A man who wrongs a woman without considering the risks she runs deserves to be treated no otherwise than a mangy dog. I prefer to believe that you are not that sort."

"I cannot see that you have any right to take this tone with me, when the whole countryside is saying that you yourself have got a married noblewoman with child."

Haguenier did not at once understand what the other meant, then suddenly his face became very red; too stifled by feeling to speak, he pressed his hands together behind his back for fear of striking out with them.

"I should like to meet the people who say so," he said at last, unable to keep his voice quite steady. "I should have to treat them as my worst enemies, and you also, for having believed them. If I have offended you, we are now quits. We will meet elsewhere."

That same evening he told the lady Aelis that her friends must be sent away; he was no longer willing to entertain them. Aelis, already informed of the quarrel by Amaury of Breul, told her stepson that she no longer wanted to speak to him. She said:

"Your father never distrusted me and you shall answer to him for this insult. You're trying to make me look ridiculous in front of my friends. What business is it of yours? Who made you my jailer? So long as your father remains away, I would rather seek hospitality of the lady Beatrix than stay here with you."

"That," Haguenier said, "I absolutely forbid. You will go to my aunt's, the lady of Buchie, or you can live at Bernon."

"Never, never! But, if you refuse to allow me to go to Breul, I shall leave tomorrow for Bercenay, which belongs to me. And if you come there, trying to spy on me, I'll have the door slammed in your face."

The following day she left the castle with her four daughters; and the lords of Breul and the lady Beatrix went with her to Bercenay and there stayed two weeks with her.

Haguenier now found himself with an affair of honor on his hands and even more troubled than before his quarrel with Amaury. At the time he had thought only of the insult to Marie and had told himself that he would have to gather together his friends and kinsmen and, weapons in hand, confound Amaury before the whole nobility of the country. On thinking it over he realized that such a course could only be harmful to Marie since the insult had not been public; nor must vengeance be public.

As for Dame Aelis, he had deprived himself of the means of keeping an eye on her and he had no right to attack a man simply because he suspected him.

"That's the misfortune of being too frank," he thought. "My father would not have thought twice about taking action and, since I am here in his stead, I should have taken the same line. But if this lad is innocent I should be doing a gross injustice in challenging him, for I am the better man when it comes to fighting."

He knew that it was useless to seek advice from the abbot of Saint Florentin. "He'll tell me it's all naught but sin and worldly vanity and that he who takes the sword will perish by the sword. But, since I have to live according to the world's laws, I'm surely obliged to defend the honor of our house and if that's a sin, well, I can't help it."

"O wretchedness of the flesh!" he thought. "Misery of us poor wretches, driven from one sin only to fall into another, avoiding the lesser temptations only to be confronted by the greater ones. I no longer know what I'm about. We are to forgive the wrongs which are done to ourselves but how can we not avenge the wrongs done to others? If my father and my lady are wronged, surely it's not my place to forgive? Why am I driven, now, into such a sin, driven to harm a man who is by no means wicked and who has done nothing to give me any right to blame him? If Foulque of Mongenost had a son, that son would have had the same suspicions of me as I have of Amaury of Breul."

A new temptation, worse than all the rest, now assailed him. Hitherto Marie's pregnancy had been, as it were, his own secret; painful though it was, he had ended by resigning himself to it, coming to terms with himself. Now, the fact was being flung brutally in his face and he felt more humiliated than if he had indeed been the father of her child. His resentment was turning against Marie. A frail vessel, truly, and a creature impure in her essence, since her body was so completely at the mercy of a will other than her own. Nature at work in her; her soul had nothing to do with it. Yet now, with her body seized upon by a life which was growing within her, could it possibly be that her soul remained untouched? Even she-wolves and sows are fond of their young; and women are, by nature's will, made after the same fashion. What a fool was the man who put himself at the mercy of this being made of flesh, formed to bring forth flesh.

"And it happened when she was saying that her love for me was at its height—but when, exactly, how—shall I ever know? At least I was faithful to her and still am. She tormented me, then sent me away remorselessly, and all this so that a little puppy of a squire can sneer at her to my face as a loose woman."

The more he thought of it, the more clearly he saw that there was no other issue, that his simple duty was to challenge Amaury of Breul; and yet he could feel neither hatred nor anger against the young man.

When he heard that the lords of Breul had returned home and were preparing to go to Troyes for Christmas, he had his horses saddled and set out with Adam and young Joceran to await his new enemies at Chaource crossroads. He had not put on armor and carried only a small lance and a light sword. But as it was cold he had put on a stout leather jerkin and thick gloves protected by iron scales.

It was snowing and the ground was covered with a thin layer of ice. The branches of the trees creaked in the wind, and the snow, swept by gusts of wind, was forming deep drifts against the banks and at the bends in the path. The two lords of Breul and the lady Beatrix, accompanied by three mounted servants and a damsel, had stopped at the crossroads, where the road was more slippery than in the forest, and the lady was busy shaking the snow from her cloak, laughing at the squall of wind which smothered her in her hood. The two Breul brothers had taken off their gloves and were blowing on their stiffened fingers.

Haguenier passed the turn and greeted the others with a raised hand.

"Here is the knight of Linnières," the lord of Breul said. "You are also going to Troyes for Christmas, sir?"

"I was waiting for you," Haguenier said. "I have two words to say to your brother."

"This is the county road we're on," the lord of Breul warned him.

"And I shall be responsible to the count if there should be anything irregular. If your brother refuses to fight with a knight, I am willing to accept you as my opponent, while he can fight Adam of Hervi, here, who is a squire."

Dame Beatrix seized her husband by the arm.

"André!" She turned to Haguenier.

"You are wanting in manners, Sir Knight, trying to settle your quarrels in a lady's presence."

"Let be, Beatrix," Amaury said. "He is right. I gave him cause for offense. There is not the slightest reason for André to fight. We'll settle the business between ourselves. I am perfectly satisfied to go bail for this man's honorableness, and I know that he'll fight as fairly there as before the countess. You can wait for us here."

The duel was short. Amaury was wounded in the thigh and forced to yield.

"If you wish," Haguenier said, "I will escort you home, if you'll give me your word that I need fear nothing from your people at Breul. This business ought not to prevent your brother and sister-in-law from going to Troyes—I am saying this in your own interest, and another person's."

Amaury was in great pain and had difficulty in speaking.

"That would be best," he said. "But it's two leagues. With this cold, we should have to stop before that."

"Don't worry, I'll take care of you. I'll have your wound dressed at Seuroi tower."

When they arrived at the manor of Breul Haguenier succeeded in getting the young man's promise to leave the lady Aelis alone and also his word never to doubt the lady of Mongenost's virtue. Poor Amaury was in very low spirits; his wound was serious and might cost him his leg. But it occurred to him that, if Haguenier had proof of his connection with the lady, he was, even so, getting off lightly.

"For my part," Haguenier said, "I promise you that the person you are thinking of will not be molested and that I shall not speak of this affair to a living soul. You can say that we fought in an affair of honor touching only myself."

And they parted very good friends.

Three days later the lady Aelis returned to Linnières. Haguenier expected reproaches. But she said nothing to him. She seemed, rather, anxious to restore herself in her stepson's good graces, spoke to him with somewhat excessive respect and watched him furtively, fearfully, as if she expected an affront from him. From time to time there burned in her colorless eyes the glow of an animal fear which exasperated the young man. He had to make an effort to be polite to her.

"The whore!" he thought. "The slut! So she did it after all! And because of her there's a decent lad damaged for life. My own lady, in her place, would have risked life and honor to come and nurse me, had I ever been wounded for her sake."

Nevertheless he had made up his mind to say nothing to his father when he returned. "If he hears of it from others, so much the worse for her; she'll certainly have asked for it."

THE STRICKEN MAN

Six days before Christmas, Giraut, Herbert's intendant, asked Haguenier's permission to go down to Tonnerre to buy a supply of candles for Christmas. Haguenier gave permission without paying any special attention. He did not like Giraut and was always glad to be rid of him: the man was Herbert's watchdog, one of those nameless, penniless soldiers Herbert was in the habit of picking up wherever he found them, devoted to his master as a man might be devoted to God. He would not have hesitated to prostitute his daughters to Herbert or perjure himself on Herbert's account, asking in return nothing but a bit of meat and some straw to lie upon.

Giraut had received a secret message from his master by the hand of a young apprentice of Tonnerre who was provided with Herbert's copper signet ring bearing the Linnières arms. Herbert was waiting for Giraut at Tonnerre, in the pilgrims' hostel near the great church.

Giraut provided himself with warm clothes and took two horses for the journey.

He found Herbert, thinner, bearded and hardly recognizable in his pilgrim's clothes. Giraut stooped to kiss his master's hand; then Herbert, quite simply, kissed him on both cheeks.

There was such an uproar in the long hall reserved by the monastery for pilgrims that they could hardly hear themselves speak; hundreds of men and women were gathered there, seated on the ground or on benches, lying down, eating, and all talking, questioning each other from one end of the room to the other and quarrelling over the places nearest to the fire. The ground was covered with rotten straw and melted snow, and a stench of sweat, sores and bad wine made the air almost unbreathable. Herbert went towards the door, putting aside with his staff the beggars who flocked about him.

"By the bowels of God, I'd like to know how they recognize me for a rich pilgrim," he growled. "These people can smell money as a dog smells game. Eh, Giraut? I've only just escaped being robbed a score of times."

Herbert sat down at the threshold and ran his fingers through his fair, tangled beard.

"We'll go to the barber presently. I'm overdue for a good bath and getting rid of this fleece; I'd never worn a beard before; it makes me feel like a peasant or some old dodderer. Apart from that, I feel younger—" he pounded his stomach "—nothing like a hundred leagues on foot to get a man's fat down. I shall resume military service when I get back to Troyes. And then, of course, I've fasted. Giraut, friend, if you only knew how pleased I am to see you; I can't stop talking. By and large, these pilgrimages are not at all a bad thing. I've learned a lot from this one. You wouldn't have thought that, would you? When I'm old I shall turn Templar and go off to the Holy Land to make a good end."

"Did you get your pardon?" Giraut asked.

"I should not be here otherwise. I don't know what line they're going to take here, at Troyes, but I am at peace with God, I've received absolution and been admitted to Communion, which is the thing that counts, isn't it? Since I've repented? I made my confession to a holy hermit who lives in a cave near Puy, and the penance he gave me was that I must beg, bare-footed and in rags, in the streets of the town until I had collected twenty marks to give to the cathedral treasury. Well—I had that twenty marks inside two months! As you see, begging's as good a trade as any other when one sets about it properly. I've a shrewd notion that the good people were giving readily out of fear that otherwise I might knock them on the head at the next street corner but, be that as it may, their charity enabled me to hand over twenty marks to the father treasurer, plus five marks of my own money. But do you know what, Giraut? The big church at Puy, the church of Our Lady, is built in such a fashion that the one our count is building to Saint Peter isn't worth a fig beside it. If I find I've any money I shall have Linnières chapel rebuilt rather in the same style; the Chaource masons are nothing but bunglers. I shall never employ them on a job again."

"Why," Giraut said, "your chapel's only just finished and it's already a lot too fine for the castle. It'd be better to improve the village church. It's all black from the fire."

"No. You'll see, I've more than one trick up my sleeve and with the new road I shall be one of the principal men in the country. I may even have a new church built to Our Lady, for she certainly deserves it. However, we are not there yet. Suppose I ruin myself, Giraut, well, what use is wealth to me? To eat and drink well? I'm not likely to want for bread, thank God. But if you build a church, it lasts, and you can be sure of the priests always saying masses in it, for your soul."

Herbert considered a visit to the public baths, to be bathed and shaved, then he thought better of it. His mother and Father Aubert had better see him as he was.

"I shall look more like a penitent. I'm not short of barbers and hair-washers at Linnières. It will look more pious, don't you think, if I preside over my first meal at home as a pilgrim? Piety—I'm an expert in it now! I've said so many *Ave Marias* that sometimes my tongue starts saying it when I mean something else. Well, now, let's see. I won't have myself shaved before Christmas and at Christmas, too, I'll put on new clothes; but they must be absolutely new, never been worn; how much time is there? Four . . . five days before Christmas, no, six days—I'll have a new shirt made by my seamstresses. That reminds me—Ortrud? Has she behaved herself? Let me hear what's been going on at the house. That's why I sent for you secretly. If there's anything wrong I don't want them to have the time to hide it before I get there."

Giraut, somewhat embarrassed, remained silent.

"I'll wager," Herbert said, "that my son's let the place take care of itself and gone off to Troyes after his fancy lady. In that case, I'll be asking you for a reckoning, so I'm warning you."

"I've nothing to say against the young master; he runs the place well. For such a young man, he even manages exceptionally well."

"Ah, if Ernaut were still alive, Giraut! It's as if the house were no longer mine since I lost him. Listen, if there's anything wrong, if you don't tell me, I shall find out later—and then watch out!"

"I don't know how to say it—" Giraut was biting his lip "—it's not that I did not keep my eyes open, but—well—it's hardly my place. It concerns the lady Aelis."

Herbert drew himself upright in a flash and seized Giraut by the throat.

"What! What about the lady Aelis, dog? What are you trying to say?"

"Let me go, I can't speak," Giraut croaked.

"There, speak—" Herbert was breathing stormily. "What about the lady Aelis?"

"There's talk about her and Amaury of Breul. And it looks as if there must be some truth in it, because your son fought the young man a week ago."

"Dog!" Herbert shouted. "Dog! Could you not have told me sooner instead of letting me sit here chattering like an imbecile? Where are the horses?"

The light was failing rapidly. At the meadow before the castle, near to the iron cross, Herbert's horse collapsed and fell dead beneath him, so that his rider barely had time to jump clear. Stunned by the fall, he rose and began shaking the snow off his clothes. He raised his eyes to the cross.

"A bad omen," he said, and his lips were shaking. "Come, Giraut,

we'll do the rest on foot. In any case I'm too heavy for your horse.
With this snow we shall not get on very fast."

He set off, panting, trying to find the way which had been hidden
by a fresh fall of snow. Giraut followed, leading his horse by the bridle.
Forced to go slowly, Herbert began to come to his senses. At a hundred
paces from the castle, he stopped.

"Suppose we go no further, Giraut?"

"What?" said the other. "Where to, then? The village?"

"Supposing we went to my mother's at Bernon? I know that there'll
never be any more happiness for me in this house."

"Listen," Giraut said, "with this snow we shall never get through the
forest; and there are wolves about."

"Oh well, so much the worse; it can't be helped then. You know,
Giraut, I should never have believed that she'd get herself talked about
because of a man. If anyone but you had told me I should not have
believed it. Do you think they've slept together?"

"How should I know? I don't sleep in the ladies' quarters. I think
they have. She went to Bercenay for a fortnight, with the Breul
people."

Herbert stopped dead and began to loosen his collar, for he felt as if
he were choking.

"Wait, wait, don't walk on my heels, idiot. Give me time to breathe.
You're driving me mad, Giraut. Do you think a man can be jealous of a
woman he doesn't sleep with himself?"

"It happens."

"It's not so much my honor, you understand. I live like a dog myself.
But I loved her so much, once. I thought it was a thing she'd never do.
It turns my inside over to think that she could do it. They're all the
same. Let's get on; we're not far.

"Giraut, I shall see it in her face, in a minute, I know her only too
well. And if it's true I shall kill her. It's all the same to me that she's of
noble blood and all the rest of it. If she's done that, she's a bitch and
nothing else. Afterwards I shall marry Ermessan of Rumilli myself; I
might get more sons of her. In that way, at least, I shan't have been a
complete idiot to the very end."

Surprised, Giraut whistled.

"You certainly don't waste any time."

"Of course not. Listen, shan't I be right? I rid myself of a bad wife
and, at the same time, make a sound deal—for in that way I shall be
even more sure of the Rumilli inheritance than I should be through my

son. Ah! the slut, what is she doing to me? She'll give me a stroke; it's certainly lucky I've been fasting so much in recent months."

Both men stopped at the castle door, Herbert to get his breath and shake the snow out of his shoes. It was almost completely dark and the door was closed for the night. This, also, seemed an ill omen to Herbert. He turned gloomy again.

"Go ahead, knock, Giraut, and give them the password. I don't want to be recognized at once. No one's to know I'm here. I want to see her face when she sees me; I shall know the truth from her eyes."

While Giraut was talking to the soldiers, Herbert studied the closed door and the raised drawbridge, which had been renovated and re-painted since he left, and he did not recognize them and had the feeling that he had become a stranger in his own house. He thought of the old story of the man returning from the war, disguised as a beggar, finding his place taken and his wife married again and all his people busy feasting and making merry in his absence, who then reveals himself and takes his revenge.

"There'll be blood for this Christmas," he thought, "and funeral mourning."

And he almost hoped that his wife had had twenty lovers, so that he might kill all of them.

As they were slow about opening the door, he felt an irrational uneasiness growing within him and wanted to turn in his tracks and cross the forest to Bernon. True, his mother had cursed him; but she seemed the only living soul, at that moment, who was not alien to him.

At the moment when the whole household was finishing the evening meal, they heard the bridge being lowered and the sound of the great door creaking on its hinges. Haguenier sent Adam to find out what visitors the porter was admitting without informing him. Adam had reached the door when he was knocked down by a bearded giant dressed in a rough woollen cloak and armed with a pilgrim's staff. The servants, astonished, stood looking at the man in the doorway, up-right, rigid, colossal, breathing hard after mounting the stairs too fast. He seemed to be looking for someone, his large, pale eyes taking in the room with a quick, penetrating glance.

In the instant of recognizing Herbert all of them felt a great weight fall upon them, for if he was already missed it was only in the hope that he would never be seen there again.

Dame Aelis, who was standing near the ladder which led to the bedrooms, uttered a loud cry and fell in a faint. Her little girls tried to support her or clung to her clothes.

There was a moment of silence, then Haguenier rose and went towards his father.

Herbert put him aside and strode across the hall towards the ladder where the lady had fallen. He said nothing, relishing the fear which he could read on every face. He was, in any case, too angry to speak. He stooped, seized the lady's head by her two plaits and battered it against the stone flags of the floor with all his strength. The sound it made was sinister—like breaking bone—and the little girls began to howl and the maidservants likewise.

Beside himself, Haguenier rushed at his father and twisted his wrist to make him let go his hold.

"Dog!" he shouted. "Leave her alone or I'll kill you!"

They stared into each other's eyes. Herbert was so astonished at this sudden rage in a lad usually so controlled that he did not immediately defend himself.

"Let go of me, son of a whore," he said. "Are you another of her lovers?"

"I am not the son of a whore!" Haguenier shouted. His face was of stone but his eyes flamed. "You are trying to kill her as you killed my mother! You have robbed me of my inheritance and dishonored our name! Now—get out of here."

"So," Herbert said, "you think you're already the master. Little reptile!" He raised his hand to strike.

Haguenier made no movement to avoid the blow and, receiving it full in the face, staggered and clung to the ladder, bleeding from the nose. Herbert stooped over the woman stretched out at his feet, her face to the ground; she was not moving and her face lay in a puddle of blood. Herbert, with a grimace of hate and disgust, again seized her by the hair, intending to fling her once more against the stone floor. Then Haguenier took him by the shoulders and the pair of them rolled over on the ground, Herbert swearing foully. Giraut shouted:

"Part them, in God's name!"

It all happened so quickly that nobody was able to say, afterwards, exactly what had occurred: father and son were on their feet again, a few steps apart, near to the hearth. In front of the hearth was a pair of massive andirons joined by a thick bar at a foot from the ground. Herbert rushed at his son, and he, with a violent blow of the elbow in his father's chest, flung him back so that Herbert fell with all his weight across the bar of the andirons.

He uttered a feeble cry, like a deep gasp, and slid forward until he was sitting on the floor, his shoulders against the bar. He seemed to be only stunned by the blow and his face was palely grey. Haguenier ran to him. "Father, have I hurt you?" Herbert put him aside with a motion of his hand: his wide-open eyes were full of limitless astonishment. He stared at his legs, felt his back.

"God's Blood!" he said. "Giraut, help me, devil take you. Pack of bastards."

Giraut, Haguenier and two servants took him by the arms to help him rise. He was so heavy that they could not get him to his feet; his legs, inert and flaccid, dragged on the ground. He panted and clung to the shoulders of the men holding him with all his strength.

"It's strange," he said. "I can't feel my legs. Lay me on the ground and fetch Jacques the barber."

Skins and cushions were spread on the floor near the fire. Herbert was stretched out on them, his head supported by a leather bolster, his arms apart to form a cross. His breathing was labored and he stared in front of him with a lost expression. He did not seem to be aware of what was happening about him.

The women were hoisting the unconscious Lady Aelis up the ladder, with her blood-soiled head wrapped in a wet cloth. The men crowded about the hearth, looking anxiously down at the enormous body with the wide-flung arms, not understanding what had just happened; hardly a few minutes ago it had been a winter's evening like any other, which no one would even have remembered afterwards. Yet now something irreparable had happened so swiftly that there had been no time to see it coming. The master had not even had the time to enter his own house, to resume his rights, before he was, as it were, turned again, transformed into a defenseless thing with which they did not know what to do.

All these men, for so many years accustomed to be without a will of their own in Herbert's presence, felt lost and uncertain as if they had received the great blow in the back. Jacques the barber stooped over his master, trembling, feeling that it was over his head that the injured man's anger would burst.

But Herbert barely glanced at him, hardly seemed to recognize him. Then, in a stifled voice, he said:

"You will bleed me from both feet, and quickly. God's Blood, what a crew! You have to tell them everything!"

Haguenier, on his knees beside his father, looked anxiously into his eyes.

"Father, are you in much pain? Perhaps you would like some wine to restore you?"

Herbert was not listening to him. He was frowning, as if he were trying to understand something.

"The bleeding," he said. "Get on with it, dog!"

"But I'm doing it, my lord."

Jacques had opened a vein below the ankle and a thin, dark trickle was running into the little copper bowl.

"Well, but—it's still bad, I can feel nothing. It's as if I no longer had my legs." And suddenly he yelled: "Ah-h! Dogs! Accursed be you, bastard! What have you done to me? You've killed me! Understand? Killed me!"

He raised his eyes to Haguenier, turned them towards Giraut, towards all these men who were staring at him with disconcerted expressions. And there was such terror, such distraction, in his look that, as a flash of lightning makes night as bright as day, so a whole truth was illuminated for an instant in the hearts of these men: in this sudden revelation of his misery, this broken creature was briefly closer to them than their friends and their own family. Saint or bandit, a man has but one life.

The embarrassment of their own feelings made these rough, burly, weather-beaten men lower their eyes, scratch their heads and fidget awkwardly. The silence became ponderous and Herbert suddenly felt himself sinking into such an abyss of loneliness and distress that he wanted to howl. With a broken back, a man might as well be dead. When a horse breaks its back, you finish it off. They would not put him out of his misery. He knew the manner of death awaiting him. Horrible pain. Young Robert of Monguoz had broken his back by falling off a wall at Troyes: he had screamed and howled like a stuck pig for eight days, yet, to begin with, they had thought there was nothing wrong with him. Herbert tried to understand and could not. The pain of some injuries is made tolerable by the hope of getting better. He would not even have that hope. It makes a terrible difference.

Such a short while ago he had been here, in this room, on his feet, walking about—desperately, he tried to recollect what had happened, as if he could go through the scene again and try, this time, to avoid the blow. Yes, he was holding Aelis by her hair, he was going to fling her down and trample her. To start with he ought to have dealt with Haguenier more thoroughly than he had done; he was the stronger, the other younger. Yes, it had been a mistake to wait for that blow on the chest; he had wasted three good seconds getting his breath and he ought to have minded the andirons.

"Ha!" he shouted, suddenly, looking towards the hearth. "Someone take that bar and give it to the blacksmith at Hervi. He can heat it up and break it in pieces. Ah! dog, cur, you deserve to have it driven, white-hot, through your body. What a welcome at your hands, what a Christmas!"

Terrified, Haguenier looked at him; he was only just beginning to understand what had happened and that his father's injury might be mortal. Into what nightmare was he to be plunged now? He seized his own hair, tearing at it with both hands.

"Oh, what have I done! What have I done! Ah! Saint Magdalene!"

He went on his knees and bowed his head to the injured man's very feet.

"Father, Father, forgive me. It was not intentional."

"Never," Herbert said. "I shall deliver you up to justice as a parricide. You'll be quartered. Ah, you cur, I always knew you'd bring me misfortune. What use are your regrets, now? You might just as well dance for joy; I shouldn't be any the worse. You've avenged your mother, eh? She'd have killed me herself if she could have done it. Go to the devil. I want to be taken upstairs, to my bed."

They tried to lift him but his back hurt him and he fell back, groaning.

"Not yet," he said.

Haguenier looked into that pitiable countenance, at the wide, color-less eyes slowly filling with tears, and felt such compassion take posses-sion of his soul that he could have covered the injured man's hands with kisses, wiped away his tears, been foremost in nursing him, watching by him; but he had not the right. His own father.

"O my God, if only he gets better, I'll spend my life as his servant. O God, what have you done to me? Did I ever wish for a different father?"

Under his son's burning look, Herbert felt himself moved, for an instant, to tenderness, and the expression of his eyes softened to one of sad reproach.

"Ah, bastard," he said. "To think I gave you the best I had. Horses. A Toledo hauberk. Your knighting was worthy of a count's son."

Haguenier burst into sobs.

Herbert, suddenly overcome by a mortal weariness, closed his eyes. He was falling into a heavy doze. They tried to make him drink but he could swallow nothing, rejected everything.

"I'm bad," he said, as if to himself. "It's beginning already." And: "I want my mother fetched from Bernon. She must raise the curse."

Servants had been sent to fetch the priest from Linnières. He came into the hall preceded by a child ringing a bell. It was snowing outside and the priest had snow on his hood and on the cloth covering the chalice which he carried in both hands.

Servants, squires and women, gathered in the hall, went down on their knees. Herbert, surprised by the ringing of the handbell and by the sudden silence which had fallen upon the room, painfully raised his head. Giraut and Adam had gone to meet the priest and, having bowed to the chalice, removed his cloak and led him to a coffer near the hearth on which Giraut's wife had spread a white cloth, which the priest blessed with one hand before setting down his precious burden.

When Herbert perceived the priest of Linnières, with his long, tanned face and his patched cassock, he experienced a surge of savage terror of which he would never have believed himself capable.

"Away with you, carrion-crow!" he cried. "I am not dying. I don't want to die! Away with you!"

The priest kneeled beside him and offered him his stole to kiss.

"I shall not confess myself to you," Herbert said. "No, no. Not yet. I want Father Aubert. Dogs! Dogs, I say! Send to Bernon for my mother. I'll make no confession until I've seen my mother."

The priest moved away and sat down near the fire to warm his feet. Giraut followed him.

"Here's a terrible state of affairs," he said. "It's my opinion, Father, that the count's provosts should be summoned."

"Then your own servants can fetch them, not me," the priest said, somberly. "The lord Herbert is perfectly capable of meting out justice within his own domains. Let him do as he likes."

"You'll be a witness," Giraut said; "there's been murder done."

"I was not a witness. I was sent for to a dying man. God knows, Master Giraut, that I shall do as much for him as I did for the men he hanged. That's my trade. But as for law and justice—manage it for yourself, I'll have nothing to do with it."

Haguenier, who was still on his knees beside his father, rose and drew near the fire.

"Father, I did it. I've no wish to cheat justice or anything of the kind. But you, who have attended so many dying men—do you think he's so far gone?"

"I don't know. I've had nothing to do with the dying of his sort, only poor folk. Your kind are of a different species. We must suppose he's not at death's door yet, since he refuses the rites."

Haguenier bowed his head and went to kneel before the coffer on which the chalice stood.

"O Lord, Who art here present, O treasure of purity and of life, O love eternal, out of Thy great pity, help us. Our unhappiness is great beyond our understanding. My God, if this thing happens, my life is over; my God, cure him. My God, all is over, I shall ask no more of Thee than his life spared."

Ortrud had come down from the women's quarters and had succeeded in making Herbert drink an infusion containing opium; he had fallen into a doze. The young woman sat beside him and stroked his hair, softly singing a German song.

Matins was chiming at Hervi when the lady arrived, out of breath and covered with snow, her nose reddened by cold. She let her cloak fall to the ground and, having thrown a quick glance at the dozing invalid, went hastily to the priest, still seated by the fire.

"Father, has he made his confession? Is he really bad?"

"You'd better ask that lost woman seated near him," the priest said. "He wouldn't speak to me."

Trembling, the lady approached the improvised bed where Herbert lay. He was asleep, his head tipped backwards, his hips supported by big down cushions. His hair and beard, a dirty yellow, were the same color as his wide and fleshy face on which pain had already had time to mark its lines; the nose seemed shrunken, dark creases were forming under his eyes and deep lines ran from the eyes to the bottom of the cheeks; his mouth was gaping. Never had the lady thought that she would see him looking so old; she hardly recognized him. This was not

Herbert, it was her father or her brother—he had always resembled both of them.

"O God, can he be dead already, to be so changed?"

But he was snoring gently in sleep.

Seeing the lady, Ortrud rose.

"If he is dying, my girl," Alis said, "it would be more decent for you not to remain beside him."

"It's what he would want, my lady," the young woman said. "He's used to me."

The lady sat down on the floor and looked at that face, become so strange to her. She knew there was no hope. A dreadful remorse gnawed at her: she had cursed her son and he was dying by his son's hand. This was what she had brought upon him. She did not want to think about Haguenier; there would be time enough for that afterwards.

Herbert opened his eyes and groaned. Then, seeing his mother, he looked into her eyes for a long time.

"Ah, lady," he said, "you cursed me, and now, as you see, I am dying."

"Be silent," she said, "don't speak. May God forgive us all. I am praying for you."

"Lady," he said, "I want to live," and his eyes were full of a humble supplication, as if he believed she could cure him. She turned her head slightly away, with trembling lips.

"Do you think I'm near death? Lady, lady, answer me!"

"No," she said. "No, my child, you will get better. My uncle Girard of Puiseaux lived ten years with a broken back; he could hardly move from his bed, but he did not have much pain."

"Ah!" he groaned, seized suddenly by a mad hope marred immediately by regret. "Me—to be ten years in bed, like a corpse, me, *me*, Mother! Is it over, then? Is it true? Yet miracles happen. Oh no, lady, no, it is not true. It cannot be true. Lady! Curse him, then, also, the dog who has done this. He is also of your blood, you have power to curse him."

The lady shook her head.

"I can curse no more, now. My heart and soul are worn out."

"Ah! Ortrud, give me something to drink. Mother, is it unlucky to confess when you think you're dying?"

"Of course not," the lady said. "It can cure the body in curing the soul. Extreme Unction has cured people sometimes."

He looked at her mistrustfully.

"You're saying so to make me confess. You think I'm dying."

She burst into tears.

"What can I say, son? You know it yourself. You're a man, and a soldier."

"Ah! I want opium, I shall be better after that. Don't cry, lady, I am not worth it. But I don't want to make my confession to this clodhopper. I shall wait for Father Aubert; I've time enough. First, I want to put my affairs in order. Call Giraut, and Laurent, my clerk, and let them bring ink and paper."

Towards morning the sick man began to suffer increasingly severe pains in the back; he breathed with difficulty and with a throaty rattling, and from time to time his chest was strained by a strange coughing, like a bark. He was losing control of his arms and he could swallow nothing. Infection had set in more quickly than could have been expected.

DEATH UNWELCOMED

THEN began a strange time when days were not separated one from another, when there was no morning, afternoon or evening, but time and all else was measured by pain. No rest was possible for anyone in the house while there, in the middle of the hall and visible to everyone, that man lay prostrate, bawling, his breath rattling in his throat, mourning his own death until nobody else had strength left to weep with him.

Yet many a man had already suffered and died in that house; but, just as Herbert had succeeded in emptying his household of life to fill it with his sole and ubiquitous presence, so, too, he filled the castle with his death and nobody seemed able to manifest an independent life while he remained there. Some days of struggling still faced him. On the morrow of the accident the abbot of Saint-Florentin had sent a

brother to Linnières, a man skilled in medicine, who treated the sick
man with cautery and massage; he succeeded in tranquillizing him by
means of calming potions and talk of miraculous cures. But he told the
lady that there was no hope; inflammation of the marrow had set in and
it could not be checked. The invalid might, at most, remain conscious
for two or three days; the important thing was to prepare him for
death.

Herbert of Linnières was not a man beloved in his country, yet, at
the news of his misfortune, the castle courtyard filled with visitors;
despite winter and the approach of the holy days the petty nobility,
kinsfolk or friends, had left their houses and business to find out what
was happening and pay their last respects to a man who would never
again do them good or harm. Was this curiosity or a sudden pity for
one whom all had thought so strong and whom God had stricken?
Visitors crowded into the stables, sweat-baths and barns, wrapped in
their mantles and furs, chattering of everything under the sun. Servants
and peasants warmed themselves about fires kindled in the courtyard,
ate their bread and passed judgment on each new visitor who crossed
the drawbridge under the great gateway.

"There's the lady of Buchie," they said. "She can't be sorry to be
rid of her guardian—how her youngster's grown! They grow like
asparagus at that age. . . . Here comes the lord of Jeugni, with his
son and Ida, the beauty, the one *he* slapped. . . . Hallo! The master-
mason of Chaource! I'll wager his reckoning hasn't been paid; he seems
in a hurry. . . . And did you see the lady of Pouilli making eyes at
George, Dame Mahaut's squire, and she with her father dying—ought
to be ashamed of herself! They say she didn't hit it off with her father."

"Bah! with these people, the rich, the father's the worst enemy.
That lad knew what he was about when he knocked his father down
over the andirons."

"He'll get away with it, you see if he doesn't. He'll be our next
master."

"Well, now, I'll tell you . . . the lad's not very strong and the
other, the master, well, you know what he was like; if our little Niot
was able to deal him such a blow, it's my opinion he didn't do it alone."

"Not alone? But everyone saw it! He was the only one who struck a
blow."

"Aye—but the help he had was the kind you can't see—unless
you've light to see by better than the eyes in your head."

Several men crossed themselves. The old man who had spoken of "our little Niot" went on:

"The one who helped him has wings on his back, all white and shining. It's a judgment of God, that's what it is."

"Judgment of the Devil more likely," another said. "You're daft, old 'un. God doesn't make a son kill his own father."

"Le Gros," said another servant, "thought he could cheat God, like the wolf disguised as a pilgrim. And when God realized that he was as wicked as ever, under his Lenten beard and his pilgrim's cloak—well, he just struck him down once and for all; that's how I see it."

"All right, Roger, and what would you have done if you'd got back from a pilgrimage to find your wife in bed with another man?"

"Far as I know, she wasn't in bed with anyone."

"It comes to the same thing. Everyone was talking about it. Their lordships don't take that sort of thing as a joke."

"And what about their ladyships, then? Le Gros used to have upwards of three women in his bed at once, not counting his German fancy girl. Do you suppose his lady liked that?"

"It's not the same thing, Roger. With these sort of people, it's a matter of honor."

"You can't help being sorry for the youngster. They say he's on his knees in the chapel night and day and that he won't eat or drink."

"Well, of course, such a sin! It's the worst sin there is."

"Oh, no. The worst is killing your mother. That's been known, too, and in our time. Four years ago it was, over at Bar-sur-Aube, a wheelwright was broken on the wheel for killing his mother."

"Well, this one's no wheelwright, and he'll be neither broken on the wheel nor hanged. Justice isn't the same for them as for you. You'll see, they'll all say it was an accident, them as were there; that le Gros fell of his own accord—for the honor of their name!"

The lady and Giraut had had beds made up in the upper chambers for the closest kin and noblest ladies who could not be left in the barns. Entertaining so many people entailed much work. And Herbert would have nobody in the hall.

"Coming here as if it was to a feast!" he said. "I hate the lot of them. I don't want them to hear me yelling."

The lady said that it was not decent to turn out their close relations.

"Nor is it decent to suffer as I'm suffering. I want peace and quiet.

Oh, very well, do as you please; let them all come, my pain will be no worse. Ah! lady, lady, God punish you, it's you who have brought this on me."

Whenever Herbert had a moment of respite from pain he experienced a sensation of awakening—but from what? From a dream which had lasted all his life. He awoke from his life to be confronted by the only truth: the certainty of death. Only a few days ago he had been on the road, shivering with cold and thinking of the wine which he would drink when he came to the inn. He had walked, as it were, tranquilly, like a man who has yet thirty years of life in his body. And he had had only four or five days.

From those thirty years he had still to live, thirty years which were his by right, he was waking now—what was his life without those lost years? Half a life, the stump of a life. Yes, there it was—he had lived thirty-eight years for nothing. He had not known that his life would be only half a life, that his maturity and his old age were going to burn out in his body in three days, as, in a fire, the candles prepared for a whole year are consumed in a single hour.

So little did he grasp the truth of this that he was already settling down in his three days of life as if they had been three months or three years. He issued orders for the funeral, for the management of the property after his death, about the gifts to be made to his men, the amounts to be paid in reparation of damage, but in the midst of them he would awake and find himself in a void—nothing, nothing more. For him there would be no funeral, no funeral mass, for he would not be there, would not see it; all would be over, there would no longer be a man called Herbert of Linnières on earth. And he was seized by such terror that he began wailing aloud, unashamed, since he thought it would be put down to his body's pain which, God knows, was keen enough!

He had often risked his life. Even here, in the castle chapel, he had prepared himself to die, believing that he would be struck by lightning during the night; but he had not been really afraid. His body, intact, had guarded him against fear—a body which, being built for a long life, assured him that death was a lie. But it had been his body which lied—the body into which death had smuggled itself and now watched and waited, the stupid body which God had lured into a trap and which had broken itself—all because of an awkward blow and a badly placed andiron. That was how God had caught him. The first attempt, with the storm, had missed, but what are three months to God? Less than three seconds. He had won three months' respite and, like a fool, had spent them in tiring himself out, fasting, praying and playing the beggar for love of God; the whole pilgrimage had been nothing but a fraud contrived to draw him into the trap. Ah! That mad, obstinate woman! She had denied him the sight of her face; because of that Our Lady, too, had withheld the light of Her countenance and had sent him straight to his death.

This monk here, beside his bed, for ever talking to him of the next life, of Paradise and Hell—Herbert had always distrusted priests; for him their talk was no more than the patter of a huckster vaunting his wares. He believed, of course, in masses and prayer and all that the Church taught. How could he not have done so? He was not an un-believer. But he had good reason to know that, in his own life, holy things had never been of much help to him.

The next life—could this man promise him a Paradise full of splendid feasts, beautiful girls, hunting, battles, a Paradise where he would be lord and master, with knights to serve him?

"Even when dead," he thought, "I should still want it all, for what else could I wish for?" Was it his fault if everything he loved was held sinful? A greasy, bearded hermit, without desires or blood in his veins, such a man may be happy in Paradise and have what he wants there. A man, a real man with a zest for life, cannot expect anything but the tortures of Hell. Was that fair? If, to avoid those tortures, he must cease to be himself, was that fair either? To transform oneself to the extent of liking their Paradise, without women, goods or ambitions, their Paradise of—lazybones—why, it was as dismal as dying!

Ah! his body, his own body, lost for ever! There it was—he had his two legs, long as beams, before his eyes, but they were no longer a part of him, he could not feel them, he was cut in two. Of the rest—his head, for instance—he still had that and his eyes, but soon not even these. The soul? A shade, less than a shade—how can the soul see, having no eyes, hear without ears? The priests could say what they liked, a soul isn't much.

"Our Lady, if I had to give the life of my son and my daughters to ransom my own, I should do it. And if I had to give up my mother's life to save my own, I'd do it. Yes, even if I had to cause the death of our countess Blanche and the young count, I'd do it. For of what use is it to me that they be alive if I am dead? If I am dead, it is for me as if they were dead, they and all men and all the earth. Even mutilated as I am I would rather live another ten years, one year even, than go straight to Paradise, though it was to the highest place beside Saint John the Baptist. My God, though you made me cup-bearer to Our Lady I should not want it but would prefer to be Herbert of Linnières, lord of Hervi.

"Lord, Lord, soon, now, there will be no more Herbert of Linnières, nowhere, never, never, nevermore. Lord, do not let this thing happen, not, at least, until I am old and tired of life, and then I shall be fit to go to Paradise."

He made up his mind to receive the sacraments. He did it, with death in his soul, out of respect for the conventions, for he knew himself to be so ill-prepared for death that he was living for a miracle and at the bottom of his heart rejected the sacraments. This death which was to be his portion he did not accept. He would have made a good end had God let him live his three-score years and ten. This good end God had filched from him and the death he was dying was not really his proper death at all; theft and sleight of hand, that's what it was, a throw with loaded dice, and it was God who was cheating, not he.

When he heard that Dame Aelis was on the mend and no longer in danger, he dictated to his clerk, in Father Aubert's presence, a letter in which he denounced his wife as an adulteress and debauchee, lodging a complaint against her and Amaury of Breul with the bishop of Troyes.

"Whether I die or not," he said, "she must be tried and condemned. I should turn in my grave if her name ever appeared on any document whatsoever as my widow."

He was also able to talk to the county judge, who had come from Troyes. He had, at his mother's instance, agreed not to lodge a complaint against his son, and he declared that there had been an accident and that he had himself been the aggressor in the business; the young man was guilty of nothing more than insubordination and want of respect for his father and his misdemeanor was a matter for the ecclesiastical courts, not the count's justice.

Haguenier spent his time before the altar in the chapel where, night and day, the chalice containing the Host was displayed. From time to time he slipped into the hall, keeping close to the wall so that Herbert would not see him, and watched the dying man from as near as he dared approach. He was still hoping for a miracle. His mind was so clouded by fasting, fatigue and anguish of spirit, that he recognized nobody and talked to himself aloud. A few days had strangely altered him. It was as if a slow fire were consuming him internally, remodelling his features, burning away that thickness which time and weariness were already giving them: but for the brownish bristle on his chin, he would have looked like an adolescent who has outgrown his strength. And his face was taking on a beauty so radiant, despite the wildness of eye and gesture, that even Giraut, meeting him at the door of the chapel, had put a hand on his shoulder and said:

"Come, don't eat your heart out: anyone can see that God forgives you."

"But *he* does not forgive me," Haguenier thought, "nor do I forgive myself. If he dies, how can I face living?"

Once, on the evening of the third day, when Herbert seemed calmer and when the monk who was nursing him had fallen into a doze, Haguenier plucked up his courage and drew near to the bed. Herbert saw him but did not at first recognize him. Then his wide-open, pale eyes filled with tears and, at the same time, with an expression of such hatred that Haguenier's heart was harrowed. In a low, whistling voice, Herbert said:

"Cur!"

"Forgive me."

"There can be no forgiveness between me and you. The dead do not forgive."

Haguenier bowed his head and said no more.

"Wait," Herbert said. "I wanted to tell you. I do not wish you to take my place here. I prefer to leave all my property in Dame Isabeau's hands."

"Yes," Haguenier said. "I shall go away."

"You will enter a monastery to weep for your sin."

"I shall go."

And suddenly Herbert felt no more rancor. While the youth was out of his sight he had been able to bear him malice; now his paternal feeling came uppermost.

"To the very end he'll have disappointed me," he thought. "If he had only done it on purpose, the idiot, or if, at least, he enjoyed coming

into his inheritance. In his shoes, Ernaut would have called me a bad
father and accused me of trying to kill him. Woe to the man who,
wanting sons, is forced to get them by way of a woman! He's Bertrade's
son; it's to her flesh and blood my inheritance must go and there's
nothing I can do to alter it. Well, let him go to his monastery! It's all
he's good for."

Yet, in spite of everything, he was fascinated by the splendor of that
young countenance which suffering was sharpening and transfiguring,
for there was in it a forgetfulness of the self so complete that it seemed
to reveal another and different world. Beneath all his contempt and dis-
appointment, Herbert was aware that there might be more in this lad
than he had supposed. He wanted the boy to remain there, beside him.
He said:

"And yet I loved you well, son of a bitch."

"Forgive me," Haguenier said, again.

"Foolishness. Of what use is my forgiveness? I cannot. Stay where
you are. Tell me—if, now, I were to bid you marry again, to get sons,
would you obey me?"

"Yes," Haguenier said, "but I should prefer to become a monk."

"Well then, turn monk. I've always said it's all you're good for. But
before doing so, speak to the viscount and find a good husband for your
daughter. With the dowry she'll have, she could have the count of
Bar's second son or, better still, the seneschal of Bar-sur-Aube, who'll
be exactly forty when she's old enough to marry. He'll maintain the
land properly. But have the wedding performed before you enter the
monastery. How old is she exactly?"

"One, since she was born just before Christmas."

"Yes, the seneschal's the more reliable man. Have a full marriage,
not just a betrothal—it's much less easy to break off, after all. Wait, tell
me now, before I forget, that lady—who was your mistress or whatever
she was—the daughter of the late Erard of Baudemant who turned
Templar—I can't remember names, now—you've left her?"

"Yes."

"And that's why you want to turn monk?"

"Yes."

"Stay where you are. Listen—the seneschal of Bar-sur-Aube is to be
responsible for our armed levy, since he'll hold the fief, but don't let
him forget Pierre; he's to set aside a part of the Linnières revenues for
him. Pierre can do him homage, since I have not the right to make him

my heir. And then don't forget Ortrud. You must find her a husband.
I bought her as a virgin from her mother, a proper old procuress. I
don't want her cast adrift. Besides, she's your unofficial stepmother,
eh?"

"Don't talk; you'll tire yourself," Haguenier said.

"I shall have time enough to be silent. I feel better. I should like to
see your sister, too, but later. It's strange, but while you're here I almost forget the whole thing's your fault. My brain must be softening.
Wait—see this monk, here, snoring away—I can't recall what his face
looks like. Nor Father Aubert's. And then, I'm beginning to forget
names. You, now—at first I took you for my brother Ansiau. Yet you're
not like him; his hair was not curly."

He went on talking for some minutes but he began wandering. He
thought he was in the Holy Land and talked of an assault on the Accursed Tower and of the marquis of Montferrat, saying: "The dog!
He's trying to starve us. He's sold himself to Saladin. Jacques of Hervi
owes me a bowl of beans; since he's dead his brother should return
them. Ah! they say there are some who are still alive, the vultures are
eating them alive. Me, I want to be buried." He uttered a loud cry of
terror which woke the friar-physician.

"He's delirious," Haguenier said.

"It won't be long now," the monk said. The young man looked at
him with so much distress that the monk regretted the words.

During the night Herbert again became sensible of his surroundings
for some time. He saw priests kneeling by his bed, and the lady, and
Pierre and Aielot and Mahaut of Buchie and Joceran of Puiseaux and
all his family kneeling about him, praying. Such hatred of all these—
still among the living, watching him, on the look-out for his death—
such hatred possessed him that he began to howl like an animal, unable
to articulate a single word. The lady sat beside him and took his head
on her lap.

"Ah! let me be," he cried, "and send these vultures away! Ah!
Christmas! Christmas! Christmas without me!"

"Calm yourself, little one, you will get better," the lady said.

"I curse you, lady. I curse all of you. Curse God. I spit on Him. And
on the Virgin. Give me the Host that I may spit on It! Without me!
Without me! Christmas without me!"

"There, there, it'll be better presently. I'm here," the lady said.

"It'll never be better! Keep your lying consolations! Death blast you all, you've killed me between you!"

Thereafter he saw nothing but disconnected images. Vultures hovered about him, as they had over the field of the dead at Acre. Then their wings seemed to draw circles, to close like pincers. Endless circles of vultures with white and empty eyes swooped down to crush him from all sides. He still had an instant to think: "Such are men—I am a vulture. God is a vulture. Mother! Mother!"

His unconscious body struggled throughout another day and until Christmas morning. That night it was not possible to celebrate the feast of Christmas at Linnières.

STILL LIFE

FINE gilt candles lit the new chapel whose creator had never seen it finished. It was the first day of Christmas. On a catafalque raised before the dressed altar lay Herbert of Linnières, surrounded by a pomp worth of a baron of high lineage. This, his last bed, was covered with silks embroidered with golden birds, stolen from Constantinople. His body, stiff, massive, seeming long almost past belief, was dressed in a red habit decorated at collar and cuffs with braid as wide as a hand and all of gold thread. His feet were shod in white leather encrusted with silver, his fingers covered with heavy gold rings, so that his big, waxy hands, laid flat one upon the other and tied to his chest, gleamed like fire in the light of the candles.

The great mane of ash-blond hair was washed, combed and arranged in curls about his brow and cheeks, supported by an embroidered cushion and leaving the ears exposed to reveal Arab earrings set with turquoises.

A long Spanish sword, the ivory hilt inlaid with jet and enclosing a relic of Saint Jacques, was placed flat, naked and shining, upon the body. The hilt was secured under his wrists and the point touched his feet. Golden spurs gleamed on his heels and a white belt was about his waist.

All the carpets and dyed cloths from the house had been laid upon the chapel floor, and the ladies had hung their colored scarves and embroidered sleeves from the high chandeliers, the walls and the windows to make this lying-in-state the more sumptuous. The candles gave out such a light, reflected from the newly painted roof vaulting, that those entering were dazzled and closed their eyes.

The lady and the dead man's sons had ransacked their coffers for treasures to honor his lying-in-state. The things he had loved in his life would not be wanting on this day when his body was saying farewell to the earth. On that dreadful Christmas Day his soul, having left the body in so evil a fashion, at least could not complain of a poor funeral.

Six men nobly born, knights and squires, took turns to watch by the body: Pierre of Linnières, Joceran of Linnières, Joceran of Puiseaux, Jacques of Pouilli, Manesier of Puiseaux, André of Chapes. Three priests—Father Aubert, the prior of Saint-Florentin and the vicar of Linnières took turns to pray for the repose of the dead man's soul.

The body, which had been emptied, cleaned, filled with unguents and rubbed with balm that night, looked more like a marble idol than a human body. The face was yellowish, smooth, shaven, the handsome lips pouted, the nose was wide and straight; it was unrecognizable. The complete absence of expression was striking—there was not even that fugitive look with which chance often enlivens features deformed by death. Herbert's face, in death, showed neither peace nor sorrow nor anguish. Nothing. An idiot born might have looked like this. In consequence, despite the beauty of feature, the face was frightening to look upon.

On the third day of Christmas the body of Herbert of Linnières, placed in a large coffin of oak sealed with lead at the corners and covered with rich cloths, made its last earthly pilgrimage. It was placed upon a big cart and drawn by six horses along the new road from Linnières to Hervi: the sweating horses skidded on the wet snow. A priest went first, followed by choirboys carrying candles. Immediately behind the cart the lady walked, erect beneath a full white veil and a black woollen cloak. The family and friends of the deceased followed in pairs. Last in the procession, behind the men and women servants, came Haguenier, wearing grey woollen cloth like a peasant and with shorn hair.

He walked a dozen paces behind the rest, not daring to make himself part of the cortège. At each bend in the road he stopped and climbed the bank to get a distant view of the coffin.

During two more days the coffin remained on view at the church of Saint Mary of the Angels, where in that time more candles were consumed than were used in a whole year at Linnières. Father Aubert told himself that the master of Linnières had well chosen his time for dying, for had he waited another month he might very probably have died excommunicate; the inquiry into the manner of his life was still going on but now there was nothing to do but drop it. Nevertheless he was shocked by the pomp with which the family were celebrating this funeral: neither the thirteen who were hanged nor the damsel Eglantine had been forgotten in the neighborhood.

While the body was in the church, an enormous dray drawn by four oxen appeared at the crossing of the road leading to Puiseaux and came slowly down towards Hervi. It was preceded by a man on horseback and there were servants pushing behind and pulling the oxen by their harness. The crowd gathered about the church and in the cemetery watched it in astonishment: and Pierre of Linnières mounted his horse and rode to meet the newcomers, telling himself that friends from Troyes must be sending funeral gifts.

The horseman removed his hat when he saw the young man and Pierre recognized the senior journeyman of one of the great masons of Troyes, Master Jacques Hervieu.

"I have come," he said, "to deliver the order. Excuse the delay, lord knight, but the roads are bad. It's his lordship your father's fault, God rest his soul: he asked us not to deliver it until the day of his death." And he indicated the enormous object covered by tent cloth which he had on the dray. Pierre then heard for the first time that as long as ten years ago, before his second crusade, Herbert had put in hand a large stone sarcophagus, to be closed by a sculptured slab, in which he wished to be buried.

"Didn't you know?" the journeyman asked. "Why, only six months ago your father called on my master and went down to the cellar to see the slab-stone. He often came to look at it and he seemed to be very pleased with it."

Pierre wiped his eyes with the palm of his hand and got off his horse to help the servants to push.

The crowd gathered round the huge stone trough which was being unloaded by means of planks and logs to be placed in the narrow Lin-nières vault. There was, indeed, hardly any room left in the vault and it had not been used for a long time, but Herbert had worked every-thing out in advance. There was still just room between the tomb of his grandfather and that of Herbert, called the Red; it was the space re-served for Rainard the accursed, who had not been permitted Christian burial.

While the stone coffin was being removed from the dray, one of the logs rolled too quickly and the enormous mass of stone slipped and fell with all its weight on one of the workmen, crushing the lower part of his back. The unfortunate man died later that day. And the country folk said:

"He's still doing evil, even from the grave."

Then the sculptured slab, the closure of the coffin, was uncovered. It depicted—carved in relief—a knight, fully armed, sword on breast and shield at side. It was a beautiful work. The details of the armor, even to the stitches of the hauberk, were carefully carved, and the knight's face, beneath a helmet with the beaver raised, was handsome and serene, a likeness of Herbert with his dimple in the chin, his sensual lips and straight nose. Deeply engraved Latin letters made a border all round the slab. The beaver joints of the helmet, the joints of the hauberk and the spurs, were painted gold, the rest of the armor grey. On both sides of the chest, beginning at the crossed wrists, were carved two ribbons, also painted gold, on which letters were engraved: on the right, *Regina coeli*, and on the left, *Ave spes mea*.

Herbert's coffin was placed in the sarcophagus, the slab placed in position and there sealed with lead. Everyone felt a kind of confusion to which the uneasiness caused by the accident contributed: it was as if, at the last moment, Herbert himself had returned to upset all the arrangements and, once again and finally, make an impression by the insolent luxury with which he had liked to surround himself. No one in that countryside had ever had such a coffin: it must have cost a fortune; where had the money come from? Jacques Hervieu's journeyman said that Herbert had paid cash down when he returned from Constan-tinople. He had visited the workshops to supervise the work, corrected details, had insisted that the face must, at all costs, be a likeness, and had composed the inscriptions himself.

At Hervi castle was held a great wake, gloomy and luxurious. The old lady, once more mistress of the great house, hung with heavy, dark jewellery beneath her crimped white mourning veil, seemed more anxious to see her guests satisfied than to weep for her son. The family affected a decent sorrow but the fact was that each of them had the same single idea—to return home as soon as possible. They were all mortally bored by the long and tedious funeral rites after that long-drawn-out dying.

Moreover the thought of the life now so brusquely and cruelly cut off left an impression of uneasiness. For twenty years they had been thinking: " 'Ware the day that sees Herbert master." The day had come, the old man had been gone two years, Herbert had hardly begun to spin his spider's web over the countryside: the neighbors were beginning to say: "Now for it, we shall all be his vassals one day." The rancor they felt for him had been accumulated for a score of years in advance. And at the height of his powers, in his very prime, he had vanished, leaving behind him only a void and disorder—not even a son to keep his house, for Haguenier, a prisoner on parole, must go to Troyes and give himself up to the ecclesiastical justices. He had already renounced the succession, saying that such was his father's will. The whole of Herbert's fortune must now pass to the little Marguerite's future husband, with the exception of Bercenay, which returned to the lady Aelis. The husband in question was not yet chosen, so that for the time being the property was masterless.

Haguenier had no wish to make his journey in the company of kith and kin. Despite Aielot's prayers—she was determined to accompany him—he declared that he wished to be alone. To avoid any meeting on the way with his sister or his aunt or other relations returning to Troyes he asked the journeyman stone-mason to take him on his dray, among his workmen. There, dressed as a poor man, his head covered with a coarse, hempen hood, shaken about on the boards among the tent cloths, he was sure of not being recognized.

Was it all a bad dream from which he would soon wake? He could not understand how he, who thought he had already lost everything, had now lost a hundred times more. Oh, why had he not thrown himself into the water that October evening when he had heard Ernaut's voice? Was it likely that Ernaut, the good and pure, would have given him evil counsel? At least he should have left his horse and cloak and gone away, alone, leaving his father's house forever, since he was destined for such a sin. How is it that, without wishing to do evil, a man may do naught but evil? The whole thing had been his fault from the beginning; probably it had been by challenging Amaury of Breul that he had forced his stepmother to go further than she intended. And since, after all, he believed her guilty, why rush to her defense as if his own mother were in question?

"Ah, Marie, sweet friend, had I loved you less I should not have done it."

For he was well aware that, before he had loved Marie, he would never have been roused to such anger at the sight of a man striking a woman. And why interfere?

Was it to fly into a rage like a beast that he had spent three months praying and playing the saint? There it was—let a man but try to kill the evil within him by his will and it was sure to grow all the greater.

His father. The only man against whom he should never have raised his hand. His father had the right to strike his wife; yes, and his son.

"He cannot have been a bad man, since he was able to speak gently to me after what I had done. There have been great saints who led a wicked life before being called to God and perhaps he was on the point of being converted and becoming good, and I prevented him forever and so killed his soul at the same time as his body. What! Was I to expect him, so violent and jealous, to be gentle with a wife who had dishonored him? Perhaps I might have done the same in his shoes. At the very moment of his return, without giving myself time to see how thin and tired he was, I, who was keeping his house, had to give him a welcome like that! And now it's all over forever, he's there in his coffin and I shall never see his eyes nor hear his voice again.

"And, God knows, I loved him, not as a man ought to love his father but still I loved him. And, although I never did him honor as I should, he loved me. He forgave all my weaknesses and follies and I took his forgiveness for granted and still found him too hard."

To what man in all the world should his loyalty have been engaged, if not to the one who had engendered him? Do we not call God "Father"? And can he who does not love the father he has before his eyes love the invisible Father?

"I was incapable of understanding the father I saw before me, yet flattered myself that I loved God. And now it is too late to honor him. And too easy. The dead are always respected. It was while he lived that I should have honored him."

His sin seemed to him so irreparable that he almost regretted that he was not to be found guilty of parricide and condemned to death. As it was he would suffer only a fine and a public penitence. And thereafter? Go and pray for his soul? But what is a sinner's prayer worth?

He had such a need to hear his father spoken of that at the first halt he moved up to sit beside the stone-mason—his name was André Guillaume—and asked him to tell the story of the monument and in what manner Herbert had been led to bespeak it. He had hardly spoken a word to a soul for a week and he felt like a leper. But the stone-mason was a new face for him and the man's polite indifference calmed him and slowly restored him to command of himself. And then he had this especial hunger to learn a little more concerning his father's life.

"Had you known him long?" he asked.

"Ever since I've been at the workshop. That'll be nine years. I'm a Reims man. And the Reims shops do better work than the Troyes ones, I can tell you—no offense, of course. Master Jacques Hervieu had need of a journeyman with a thorough understanding of the finer work—being that he'd got a contract to decorate the great church of Saint Peter. So for nine years now I've been a Troyes man."

André Guillaume was a man of about forty, fair, stooping, gnarled, and with a look which, while it seemed absent-minded, contrived to be penetrating.

"Yes, indeed, I had a very high opinion of your late father. That's why I came myself to deliver the work; Master Jacques could quite well have sent an apprentice. It was also I who carved the head. I wanted to supervise the proper placing of the job and all. I may say, between ourselves, your vault's nothing to boast about—it's damp, and the floor's sinking. It ought to have been repaved."

"I'll see to it. Did my father often come to see you?"

"Oh yes, indeed, we got to know him really well. A very nice gentleman, and not a bit proud. And the first time I ever saw him he was still a very handsome man, getting a little fat already, but a kingly head and fair as a woman. When he came back from Constantinople, what a change, even then! I mentioned it to him. And, as I recall it, he replied: 'I'm ripening. When I'm master of my lands, then watch me grow twenty years younger.'"

Haguenier sensed a reproach in these words and turned away his head. Then he resumed his questioning:

"Did he ever tell you why he did not want to mention the monument to anybody?"

"No, not that I can remember. I think he was afraid that the existence of a portrait of himself after death might be unlucky and he did not want anyone to see it. He used to come and look at it after it was finished—that's a long time ago, now. He'd sit down in front of it, so, on a block of stone, and stare and stare and ask to be left alone with it, in the cellar. And then he'd say:

" 'A man ought to be a count or a duke to have such a statue made. Well, I am neither count nor duke, but it's my pleasure to have it, all the same. We're all equal in the face of death.'

"And he'd also say:

" 'This, at least, is something the worms won't eat.' Aye, and he had a very high opinion of our guild, too. He was a man who really appreciated fine workmanship.

"There was a figure of Our Lady he was also very fond of. It was being carved for the church porch at Bar-sur-Aube. And while it remained in the workshop, he always went out of his way to call on us—admittedly there was another attraction, the master's daughter—and he'd sit down before the statue with his chin on his hand, and then he'd say:

" 'Yes, that's her, that's what she's like, Our Good Lady. Not a hair more or less. How good it must be to pray to her when you've got her like this, carved and painted in front of you.'

"And then, after the master's daughter was married, he never came again."

PITY

HAGUENIER awaited judgment on his case, which would not be forthcoming until after Easter, in the episcopal prison. He was shut up in a rather dark cell and the food was bad, but at least he was able to hear mass three times a week. Aielot came to see him almost every day. It was not customary but the lady of Pouilli did not care for that; she treated the prison staff as her servants, made the warders presents, threatened to complain to the countess, even to the bishop, until at last everyone, weary of struggling, had given way to her and let her do as she pleased. Ignoring Lent, she brought her brother delicacies, of which he ate a little, to please her; in any case she invariably finished them up herself in the course of the visit.

"It's shameful," she said, "that you've allowed yourself to be shut up here like a beggar. You're a knight, you've the right to a light room, among well-born people, and a bed. In my opinion nobody had any right to interfere in this business at all; it was up to the family to deal with it. If the count and the bishop are going to take a hand in every family quarrel, they're going to have their work cut out."

"Sisterkin, it was father himself wished it."

"And you, of course, had to listen to him! He was out of his mind. You're the head of the family, after him, and he had no right to put this shame on you."

Haguenier said:

"Little sister, you're talking like a child. You don't stop to think how it hurts me to hear you say such things. When you've done what I have done, you can think of nothing but expiation."

"Are you a man?" Aielot said. "Done what you've done, indeed! You did not even do it on purpose! And, if you had, you've done nothing since but pray and fast and repent, so much so that your sin's ten times forgiven by now. Father was right to call you a milksop. *Expiation!* Did father expiate when he killed our mother? He married again three months later."

In the end Haguenier gave up answering her and concentrated on concealing the extent to which she wearied him.

When he was alone he spent hours stretched on his pallet, not thinking of anything. He was very depressed; from a distance prison had looked like asylum, but now he would have given a great deal to be out on the highroad again with André Guillaume and his workmen. Ever since being shut up his legs had ached with the desire to be out, walking free in the open air, and his eyes had ached with desire for something other than grey walls to look upon. All his wandering, active life seemed to throb in his body as the blood throbs and flows towards an amputated limb, so that it made him forget his crime to the point of wondering, sometimes, why he had been thus shut up. He, who had never wished to harm a soul. He had not wished it; and he had done it. Against his own will he had done evil and against his own will must now suffer it in his turn. In this world he had become like a cork tossed about on the waters, at the mercy of the winds, and nothing remained of his will but suffering.

Sometimes he would begin to lament the stupid bungling of his life, a life which was only beginning and yet was already without a future. The monastery to which he had aspired as to a place of salvation appeared to him like a new prison now that it was imposed upon him by his dying father's will. He no longer had any choice. None whatever. And he wanted to live. He had lost his place among men forever, for he was not of those who can fly from their country and their vows to go and make a new life in a strange country. His place was here, all ready for him: the first monastery willing to accept him without goods or dower. Some poor monastery, with a hard superior and coarse peasants as comrades. And that for his whole life.

"Perhaps it will not be long," he thought. "My health is bad. But now I don't want to die. Less than ever."

At night, since he could not sleep and seemed to be stifling when he lay down, he spent his time in prayer, with his hands clasped on the bars of his window. He heard Matins chime, then Prime, then Terce, and thereafter the sky would begin to lighten. He would try to recall the words of the psalms for each office and to sing them softly, under his breath, finding a real joy in this, for he was passionately fond of music and, as a child, had used his hours of leisure to join the church choir. He had lost his voice since that day of tournament when he had fought without a shield and suffered the second attack of his sickness.

"A pity," he thought. "It would have been of service to me now. But there, what vanity! Even if they set me to work in the dung-yard, should I not accept the task joyfully for the love of God? Someone has to do it; why should it not be me?"

He was taken to hear mass every Tuesday, Thursday and Sunday in the prison chapel. There he saw the other prisoners, clerics for the most part, monks, false or real, and a certain number of laymen condemned for offenses against morals or for heresy. Haguenier had been a good deal surprised to find one of the count of Brie's falconers among them, a worthy fellow some forty years old whom he had met several times during great hunting-parties.

"So, we meet again, Sir Knight," the man said. "Me, I've been rotting in here for six months. But I'll wager you have friends who'll have you out of here before Easter."

And he told Haguenier that he had been imprisoned for adultery with the head falconer's wife. The sight of his ruddy, placid face made it difficult for Haguenier to imagine him as a seducer; he was more inclined to laugh than to pity the man.

"Well, that's life," he said. "Your own wife, then, was very ugly?"

"Not at all, but she lives in Provins. Now she's on her own with our three boys and I've still got a year to do. On top of which I was flogged in the main square of Troyes in the middle of the market and on market day. That wouldn't happen to people of your rank, eh?"

"You've certainly been unlucky," Haguenier said. "If everyone in your case got the same treatment, we'd have half the town here!"

"But you, Sir Knight, I'm wondering how the Devil managed to get you in here."

Haguenier turned away, saying:

"You're too curious. You should know that the reasons which land a man in here are nothing he wants to boast about."

He did not have occasion to speak with the falconer again but from that day he noticed that, during mass, his fellow prisoners were inclined to look down their noses at him; it was now known that he was a knight, and the too-garrulous falconer had no doubt imagined and propagated the most horrifying account of his case. He felt that he was despised and loathed by these people who did not even know him and who did not look spiteful. And that hurt him, for his nature was benevolent; he was so lonely that he felt a need for affection. So long as he had been free, rich and gay he had been well liked, better, indeed, than he realized. Now, every hostile glance was like a knife thrust—not that he attached importance to it, for, after all, he believed himself to have deserved it; but hostility seemed to cause him physical pain since now his soul lay naked. So a horse, flayed alive, must suffer if the tiniest gnat alights on it.

On Ash Wednesday he was at last admitted to Communion. The prison chaplain consented to give him absolution, telling him that his sin, although terrible in its consequences, was venial and need not exclude him from the sacraments. Haguenier had asked him:

"Do you think, Father, that I shall be condemned to remain here for long?"

"Such matters are not within my province," the chaplain had said, "but, in any case, you may be sure that holy Church, our Mother, will not impose any chastisement which is not for your own good. You should consider yourself fortunate to have escaped the secular courts of justice."

Nevertheless Haguenier found it hard to imagine that this prison, in which he was languishing so, really stood for the Church's maternal love. He could think of nothing but the day of his release and the brief interval between prison and monastery. He took Communion in a spirit of resignation but, for the first time in his life, not joyfully: in that, too, God was abandoning him.

Back in his cell, he fell into a strange condition: he felt incapable of thinking, as if his brain had been removed; he had just enough awareness to be conscious of the void within his mind. He lay down on his pallet; his eyes opened wide and at three paces from him, in the corner near the door, he saw Ernaut, on his knees and with his head raised, as if for prayer. He was trying to raise his hand, as if to make the sign of the cross, and he could not do it. He went on trying and his awkward, clumsy motions and the disturbed expression of his lean, tanned face were so painful to see that Haguenier rose, wishing to help him to cross himself. Ernaut asked him:

"Brother, shall I be able to do it? Shall I ever be able to do it?"

"I will help you," Haguenier said.

"No, I have to do it alone. I don't know how to do it. It's hellish."

Then Haguenier could no longer see him. "That's the trouble," he thought, "he has to do it by himself. There's no way to help him. And yet something must be done. I don't see my way. It's at once black and white. It's not possible, yet so it is."

And he closed his eyes, fixing all his thoughts on Ernaut's face and his inert hand. Then he lost consciousness.

He had other visions and even complained of them to the chaplain, for the experience was terribly exhausting and his heart was becoming more and more painful. On most occasions he saw Ernaut. Once, too, he saw Eglantine, naked and covered with wounds, as he had seen her on the eve of her death. But it was Ernaut who recurred time and again, sad, distracted, a mortal distress in his wide-open eyes. The chaplain took pity on Haguenier and allowed him to sleep, with other invalids, in the side aisles of the chapel. From there he could go and pray before the altar whenever there was no service being held.

He prayed, now, almost incessantly. His prayer was one which he hardly dared admit to himself and of which he could speak to nobody but which imposed itself upon his will. He prayed for the souls of the damned, those for whom even God Himself could do nothing. He knew perfectly well that this was futile, yet nevertheless he went on praying, as if convinced that it was necessary and he could not do otherwise. He sensed his father and Ernaut near to him, no longer such as his memory represented them, yet still living and sunk in an eternal nightmare; and he said to them:

"I am here. I shall always be here, watching. See, I fix my eyes on this cross and I watch. Everywhere and always I shall be there, watching the cross for you. Lord, on earth I was the bad steward; now there is naught I can do but look at You, You who are always faithful to the end, to all of us. Lord, there is no soul under heaven but is in Your hands, even the damned."

So passed three weeks. Haguenier spent all his time in the chapel, which was pleasanter than staying in his cell. It was cold but the air was pure. There were three other invalids, one half-idiot, the other two almost paralyzed. They stayed at the far end of the chapel, the brother who swept out the church brought them their food and, as it was in Lent, visitors who came to the services gave them alms. Aielot was very shocked to find her brother in such pitiful company; but Jacques of Pouilli was more understanding, saying: "Let him be, each one of us saves his soul as best he can." And Haguenier asked no more than to be left in peace, provided that, between services, he could walk about for a while to stretch his legs, thereafter to kneel facing the altar where the Holy Sacrament was exposed.

Towards mid-Lent the new rector found him one morning at prayer on the altar steps and shook him roughly.

"Listen, my lad," he said. "You don't look much like a sick man to me and I can see no reason for your being here. You're just another of the kind who report sick so as to loaf away their time in a holy place, like pigs in a kitchen garden! I'm wondering why the father chaplain allowed you in here."

"I believe, Father," Haguenier said, "that he thought me a bit off my head."

"Mad, you? Look at me. It's no use telling me the tale, I've seen too many real madmen; and, let me tell you, it's not quite so easy to pass yourself off as mad. I warrant you you'll be back in your cell within the hour."

The rector was a good deal put out when he learned that the prisoner he had treated so harshly was a man of distinction and good family and, moreover, more unlucky than guilty; but he did not reverse his decision.

"The fact that he is rich in the world's goods does not entitle him to more consideration than a poor man," he said. "Since his case is *sub judice*, let him remain in his cell and eat the bread of penitence."

So Haguenier was sent back to his cell; but this did not arouse in him as much bitterness as he expected. His three weeks spent in prayer, while he had thought himself sunk in distraction and despair, had nevertheless brought him appeasement. He realized that his prayer, bitter though it tasted, had become for him a nourishment as real as bread and that it had entered into him without his perceiving it. He maintained his prayer in his cell, still standing with his hands grasping the bar of the window; it gave him strength and his spirit became firm and his mind no longer wandered. But he was aware of a great change in himself and a detachment from everything which was happening to him. He no longer even felt remorse for his sin. It was such a small matter in comparison with the suffering it had caused; his sin was like a wisp of straw which, catching fire by accident, burns down the house. His own house had been burned down, his father, and his own life. Now let God help him.

THE SEVENTH TRIAL or
MARIE CROWNED

ON THE fifth Sunday in Lent Haguenier, having returned from mass, was waiting for Aielot; he was hoping that Jacques of Pouilli would come too: for Jacques, at least, never reproached him and prevented his wife from speaking too much. The door opened and the warder showed in a woman smaller than Aielot, wrapped in a large, green mantle, her head covered with a veil.

Haguenier jumped to his feet and ran to the door to prevent the warder from closing it but he was too late, he heard the latch fall. He stayed where he was, his back against the door, his head bowed, for he did not dare to look at the woman standing before him. It was only now that he realized how surely, in the remotest part of his being, he had expected her. And there was nothing in the world which could frighten him more.

But the first instant of terror over, his good sense returned.

"Am I a lout," he thought, "that I should receive her so ill, when she is doing me so great a favor?"

And, with an effort, he raised his eyes.

She had lifted her veil to reveal a thin, pale face, the eyelids discolored, the features drawn. Only the noble lines of the mouth, the nose and the deeply sunken eyes bore witness to her erstwhile beauty, for, apart from these, this tired and mortally sorrowful face retained nothing of its former splendor. And pity and tenderness swept Haguenier's mind clean of all power to think of himself.

"O my most lovely and most sweet," he said. "How could you. . . . For the love of God, don't stay here, call the warder. Why come here and torture yourself even more?"

She threw back her cloak and put her hands on his shoulders.

"A sister has the right to come and see her brother when he is in misfortune. I would do very much more for you."

He said:

"You should not be here. I will not have you incurring blame for my sake."

"Who could blame me? Everyone knows that you loved me. What! —one may visit prisoners one doesn't know out of ordinary charity, but I, your friend, must refuse to see you? Should I be something less to you than your sister? The only reason I have not been before is that I was ill."

"O God! And I did not know it! O my own lady, my most beautiful, to have made the journey to Troyes in your condition and in such bad weather! And you're not better yet, this is going to tire you out again— and all this for me, and you knowing what I've done. It was madness; you should not have done it."

"Oh," she said, sadly, "I see how it is—you were not overanxious to see me again."

Haguenier was at his wits' end, in an agony at the idea of her having to remain standing, worn out as she was, and with that weight in her body. There was not even a bed. In the end he drew the red blanket, which Aielot had given him, over his pallet and took both his lady's hands to lead her to it and help her to sit down.

"You'll be more comfortable like that," he said. "How could they let you into this hole, the dogs, cold as it is and evil-smelling! Don't take off your cloak, whatever you do. Perhaps I had better put my jerkin over your shoulders. You're shivering, I can see."

Impatiently, she said.

"Am I a child? Cannot you talk of anything else?"

He sat down in front of her, at her feet, and began picking off the wisps of straw which had stuck to the hem of her mantle.

"The first time you ever came to see me and this is how I must receive you! Well, I won't reproach you any more if it vexes you. But tell me about yourself. It—it will not be very long now, will it?"

Involuntarily his eyes strayed to her swollen belly, which she did her best to conceal in the ample folds of her cloak. She turned away her head.

"No," she said, "and I could wish to die of it. Life is a burden to me, now. And I can see that you do not love me any more."

He looked at her, dumbfounded.

"I?" he said. "But how could I not? Do you suppose I can change so quickly? Then you do not know what love is. Yet it was you who drove me away from you and forbade me to see you."

She looked at him again, her eyes full of rancor and a kind of sad mockery.

"There are lovers," she said, "who would not have been quite so obedient as you. But I am wondering if it was love made you so obedient, or because—it was not very hard to stay away."

"That is for you to judge. I have only one tongue and one thought, not two. I did what you told me and thought I was doing rightly."

"Forgive me, friend," Marie said. "I am easily irritated because I am sick. But is it true, as I've heard from your sister, that you have renounced your heritage and are planning to enter a monastery?"

"It is true."

"If you really loved me you would not have done it."

"Don't say that, lady. I have no choice. Had you been free, I might have hesitated. I am not even sure of that."

Her smile was somewhat hard.

"A great change from the time when you talked of going and killing Mongenost so as to marry me."

"It was a vile thought and it was you who told me so. False friend, have you two hearts? Think of it—if it is true, as you say, that you feel some love for me, would you rather see me living in the world, parted from you and married to another woman? You're talking like a child."

"Because I love you," she said, "and it's hardly your place to reproach me with it. Do you suppose that I gave you my love for fun? I swear to you that when I accepted you into my service, it was not out of worldly vanity but because I esteemed you and wanted to teach you love. But it was I who was burned and it is I who am undergoing, now, the trials I was to set you. And now life is parting us, leaving me with nothing but my bitter love, without even the consolation of knowing you happy.

"You are my vassal and took a vow of obedience to me. How could you know that the separation I imposed on you was not just one more trial, an artifice of love? Could you be certain that I did not intend to grant you, one day, that which you wanted?"

"Sweet friend, artifice is not my strong point and I am easily deceived. You bade me renounce you and I renounced you. What it cost me to do so concerns nobody but myself. Am I a glove, to be turned about at will, to be taken or left? I am no longer your vassal; you freed me from my oath."

Marie hid her face in her hands and began to cry. And Haguenier had not the strength to bear that; he took her in his arms and drew her to him.

"Sweet loveliness, I know that my words are hard but they are not spoken in anger or bad feeling. You do not even know how high I place you: and what goodness must be yours to have been able to love a man who has brought you neither honor nor glory nor any joy, and has not known how to deserve you? At the height of my madness and weakness you were able to point out to me what I ought to do; now it is my turn to help you, for your pity for me makes you weak. Since we cannot, without sinning, love one another in the flesh and the world, it is better that we no longer try to live as we did before, like two fools who would and yet would not and know not whither they are bound. You may be sure of one thing: I shall not cease to love you and I shall always be faithful to you. But my life belongs to God even more than to you."

"And I," she said, "what sort of a life is mine to be?"

He took her in his arms and helped her to rise.

"True," he said, "I am mad, I think only of myself. Beloved friend, forgive me. I do not know how I am to live without you. Above all, may God keep you. You must go, you have already stayed too long. It's strange, but while you are here with me it seems as if it must be for always."

"So it seems to me, also," Marie said. "But I shall not come again."

He began rapping on the door to summon the turnkey. Timidly, Marie held out her arms to him and he threw himself into them, pressing her to him, kissing her hair and her brow.

"Mother, sister, refuge! Oh, what can we do, what can we do? I shall die without you."

He heard the latch being raised and a sudden rage seized him at the brutality of a life which was parting them like this. He opened the door himself. Marie had drawn her veil over her face. He bowed and kissed her hand.

"So," he thought, walking up and down his cell, "she has been ill. While I would not ask my sister for news of her because I did not want to think of her! How thin she has got! Fragile creatures, women. And still fretted with care because of me. And I hurt her. And she'll be brought to bed soon. If Dame Isabeau, strong as she is and having had so many children, suffered so. . . . At the very thought of that, a man ought never to dare touch the woman he loves. There are some who die of it. And she's so good, thinking and talking only of me. Ah, what a lesson!" he told himself. "How shall I ever measure her charity! Such a love—and for a worthless man—that is true love, indeed. It is thus that God must love. I should be no better than a beast if I took advantage of her goodness to try and drag her into sin."

All night long he meditated on his lady's profound wisdom, finding lessons and symbols designed to guide him towards God in all that she had asked of him and in all the trials she had imposed on him. She had shaped him to meet life, sometimes without even knowing it, as a mother unwittingly shapes the child in her womb. Yes, she had required of him everything, thereafter to leave him without hope and with empty hands—but had this been cruelty? Her soul must have had an awareness of what he really needed. She had done it all to make him understand what God requires of man.

"For I am not yet ripe for understanding what the love of God means and He sent my lady to me as an earthly symbol of His love. Not that I should worship her as an idol, nor desire her beauty for my pleasure, but that I might lose all, lose her, and still and always keep my faith in her most pure love.

"O subtle friend, your charity is more painful than your harshness! Why did you ever beguile me with an empty hope? For it meant a useless suffering, made worse by knowing you tormented, you, to whom, of all things, I wanted to bring peace. Your fine spirit is humiliated, your soul tempted by my fault, and I could not find the way to console you but only to hurt you yet again. I shall have done harm even to you. But only as a child hurts the mother who is bringing it into the world. Is it my fault if I can no longer make your will the law of my life?"

Haguenier came out of prison on the Saturday preceding Whitsunday. His sentence had been quite a light one, since his trial had taken place so soon after Easter—a fine, a public penitence and a flogging of thirty strokes of the rods; in addition he was to be branded with a hot iron on the lips which had abused and in the hand which had struck his father; the branding on the lips, however, had been more or less symbolic, leaving only a slight wound which was already healing over. He walked the muddy streets of Troyes, looking up in astonishment at the blue sky where the swallows were tracing their arabesques above the grey roofs of the houses. He had asked his sister and his friends not to try to see him during his first days of freedom but now he almost regretted it, for such a fear of solitude had suddenly possessed him that he was tempted to speak to the first person he passed in the street. At the same time, he experienced difficulty in talking, not only because of his burned lip.

The humiliation of his punishment still burned in his cheeks. Because of it he seemed to be aware of no part of his body but his back, lacerated by the flogging, and his palm, branded with a red-hot iron; and it seemed to him that he was naked and that everyone could see his back. He had not expected a slighter punishment and believed himself to have deserved much worse; but his body revolted in spite of his mind and he felt as taut and feverish as he had been at the moment when the iron was burning his lips. It was for this reason that he was denying himself to his friends, so that after two days in the prison infirmary he found himself launched, solitary, into the streets of Troyes, without past or future, on leave from life. He still had family business to attend to; after that he wanted to see the abbot of Saint Florentin again before setting out, on foot, for Vézelay. Even the mere idea of all that he had to do inspired in him such a disgust that he preferred not to think of it.

Finally he went into Saint-Nizier Church where the bells were ringing for Lauds. In church he did not feel his humiliation so keenly.

"My God," he thought, "it was You, after all, Who chastised me by those men's hands. How can I learn submission? You, Yourself, were beaten. It seems that what I suffered was necessary to teach me the power of the body over us. For my body cannot bear shame, but now this hand, with which I make the sign of the cross, is branded—it was so even before, since I used it to strike my father, but I did not feel it; now it seems to me as if accursed. By way of the body, the soul is branded.

"O my God, grant that my whole body be so branded by You, for it is not of my own treacherous will that I give myself to You, but because Your will has compassed me about and closed all other ways to me.

"And grant, O God, that I may not bring You this broken, branded body as a man may give away waste goods which no one wanted. For my will had nothing to do with it and I have seen Your hand at work where I little thought to see it, even in my sin. My God, if I be so wholly Your creature that You brought me to commit the worst of sins that I might learn of how little account was my own will, then You will take me such as I am and I shall ask nothing of You but the right to obey."

At Hervi, Haguenier gave a feast in honor of his departure for the monastery. It was a modest feast, for he did not wish it to be thought that he was forgetting his father's death. But he had to do honor to his name and family and avoid any imputation or appearance that he was slinking away like a guilty creature since he had received remission for his sin. He must take leave of his family and of his worldly life worthily.

He had invited all his family and the seneschal of Bar-sur-Aube with whom he had caused his daughter's wedding to be celebrated. The viscount of Paiens had given his consent and had been present as a witness, the lady Isabeau standing proxy for her daughter, giving and receiving the promises in the child's name.

The seneschal of Bar-sur-Aube was a knight of the region, Pons of Traînel by name, a man of about five-and-twenty and already renowned for his strength—he could bend an iron horse-bit with one hand and could stun a bull with a blow of his fist. Herbert had not made a bad choice of successor; none of his vassals would blush to serve this man, dark, handsome, proud of his bearing, who, despite his youth, had only to be seen to be obeyed.

Haguenier had seated him in the master's place, in a high-backed chair with a stool for his feet, and, at his side, the lady Isabeau with the child Marguerite on her knees; and all the men of Hervi, as of Linnières, of Bernon and Seuroi, knelt before Pons of Traînel. Each in turn put his hands in those of Pons, all taking their oath to him and thereafter kissing the little white, plump hand of his infant bride, their lawful lady. The child, gorgeous in golden embroidery, her cap of silk sewed with pearls, jumped up and down on her mother's knees, uttered small, excited cries and tried to pull the hair of all these strange men who came to stoop over her hand. She was a beautiful and lively child; her gold or auburn curls showed beneath the cap which she tried to snatch from her head. She sucked her embroidered clothes and laughed aloud when she succeeded in getting a firm grip on the hair or collar of one of her "vassals." They were all enchanted with her, looking upon her as a man contemplates the Infant Jesus in His Mother's arms, and grew tender, saying:

"See, she already has seven teeth. And what long hair! And how merry she is, afraid of nothing—you can see she comes of noble stock."

Haguenier, standing beside the lady Isabeau, also watched her and then turned his eyes to the man seated in the high chair, stiff and grave, repeating, for each man, the formula for the acceptance of homage, taking hands in his, exchanging formal kisses. "A sound man," Haguenier thought, "who'll take good care of land and men; he'll be a father for my little beauty—but in fifteen years, well, he'll be a man worn out, accustomed to his concubines. If I had married again, to get sons, my daughter might have lived free and chosen a man after her own heart. Even on this innocent I am imposing the burden of my sin and my renunciation. Will she say, in years to come, that I spoiled her life?

Ah, may God protect her, this Pons is a true man and it may be I am leaving her in better hands than my own."

The ceremony over he took the child in his arms and carried her towards the hearth to show her the flames. She squirmed and kicked so much that he had difficulty in holding her and was constantly afraid of hurting her. She managed, at last, to get her cap off and dropped it in the ashes. Her auburn curls caught in the clasp which fastened her father's collar and she began to cry, pulling at it.

"How I should have loved you if I could, my pink pearl. If only I could leave you with my lady, to be brought up with her own child, but Dame Isabeau would never hear of it; it's a thing women can be hard about. Keep still, little demon, or I shall drop you."

Then he began to kiss the baby's cheeks and eyes and forehead, thinking that these were the last carnal kisses, the last kisses of human love, which he would give in his life; and the touch of those flawless cheeks, of the mouth which could not yet speak, of eyes which had nothing to hide, was very sweet to him.

"There's a heavy heritage, little one, already loaded on you. Shall I ever see you again, my treasure?"

Her laughter was loud under his kisses and she beat with all the strength of her small hands against her father's cheeks and forehead.

Haguenier bent the knee before his grandmother and asked for her blessing. Then he bade farewell to all his companions. When it came to kissing Pierre and Adam he wanted to cry but he restrained himself. Then he went to visit the cemetery, entering the vault to look once again at Herbert's memorial stone—it was already covered with a layer of dust fixed by the damp and he rubbed it clean with the skirt of his coat. He contemplated the calm, handsome face of the figure and thought of that which lay within the coffin until it made him afraid and he rose and went out. The grass between the graves was acid green and there were buttercups and daisies growing in it. Behind the church two plum trees spread their branches, which seemed to droop beneath the weight of creamy blossom.

A few paces from the vault was Eglantine's grave, covered with green grass and wild flowers. Haguenier fell on his knees. "Farewell to you, also, Sister. Do not forget me." And he remounted his horse and, after a detour by way of Rainard's tomb, he took the road to Troyes.

There yet remained one more earthly pilgrimage he must make, before his final departure.

A west wind was blowing, driving grey and pink clouds across a pale sky. The grey waters of the Seine were ruffled into small waves and the road was covered with the white petals of cherry blossom. Beside the banner of Champagne on the round tower of Mongenost a red flag fluttered in the breeze—it had just been hoisted, signifying that a son had been born to the master of the house.

Haguenier walked slowly along the river bank, leading his horse by the bridle.

"A son; may God grant him a long and splendid life, may he be everything I have failed to be, and may he grow daily more beautiful under his mother's eyes; may he be, for her, the jewel she wears about her neck, the treasure she bears in her heart—she who has undergone so much that he might become a living soul. Pure friend, bright star, I shall not see you again, for bitter is the taste of our earthly encounters, forcing us always to want and not to want, drawing each to the other by one hand, only to repulse with the other.

"You are forever my betrothed and my spouse, yet belong to another. These two things are both true, yet cannot be contained in a single thought. Therefore I must never see you again, O crown of stars, for there is not, in this life, room for two truths contrary to each other."

At the bend in the Seine, opposite the islands, Haguenier stopped to look, once again, at the red banner fluttering in the wind. It was the last of Marie that he would ever see. And he took the thin purple scarf, from which he had not been parted for two years, from about his neck, and broke off some branches of wild apple and wild rose which grew beside the path and swiftly wove them into a huge crown, tying it, as best he could, with the scarf; because of the wild rose thorns his hands were covered with blood. Then he threaded into the crown all the wild flowers he could find upon the bank—periwinkles, anemones, daisies and buttercups, as if he were decorating a reliquary for a holy day. The sun was setting and the Seine below Mongenost was turned to gold; the clumps of willow growing along the banks had taken on tints of copper and silver, the colors everywhere had been transformed and the whole scene seemed unreal. The wind had fallen and behind the castle long, thin clouds were melting into the burning gold.

Haguenier made the sign of the cross, took his amethyst ring—the ring which bound him to Marie—from his little finger and hung it upon one of the branches of the floral crown. Then he went down to the Seine, leaned over the rushes and placed his crown on the water. Pink, green and white, as if made of lace and stars, the vessel of flowers tilted a little and then began to float away with the current. For an instant it was caught in the reeds, then freed itself and, spinning gently, swung out towards the middle of the river.

Haguenier watched it float away, his hand shielding his eyes, for the sun was shining directly upon the water and blinding him. Tears hung upon his lashes, yet a strange tranquillity was possessing him, confronted by the glory of the sunset. The crown was still floating, now a tiny dark islet in the river of gold.

"Perhaps it will get as far as Mongenost," he thought, without attaching much importance to the idea. "Or else it will sink. It comes to the same thing. In any case, she will understand."

Part Five

Part Five

THE END OF AUBERI'S SERVICE

THEY had fastened a heavy beam to the old man's shoulders, like a yoke. This bar was fixed to the wheel, at the height of a man's shoulders, but the old man was so tall that he had to work stooping, his back crouched; this became so painful that he would certainly have fallen, exhausted by pain, had he not been tied to the beam. He even told himself that had the beam been high enough to suit him he would not have found his work too hard—and what else, indeed, could they set him to do? They could not be expected to feed him for nothing.

On the first day the sense of being tied and harnessed like an ox, doing the work of a draft animal, had seemed to him somewhat hard, indeed. It had even made him weep—tears were all that his dead eye was good for. Not that he had never known worse; rowing in a galley was worse. But then he had been young. Once in a galley a man has little enough hope of ever leaving it, God knows, except on the day when they throw him to the fishes to be eaten. Still, at last, and by a miracle, he had come out of that alive. But now he could be more or less certain of ending his days at the beam of this mill.

It had been all very well to be prepared, in his thoughts, for anything, but when a man is spat on, kicked, tied to a beam, his legs lacerated with lashes to drive him forward—was that easy to accept, old and tired as he was? Why, even an ox, in his own animal language, would have complained.

The first day had seemed very long to him. But for the sun, eternally pressing down upon his head, he could have believed that he had been laboring round and round for a week. The pain in his back became worse and worse, spreading to his shoulders and legs and finally his whole body; one step forward, two, three, four—he tried to count his steps and lost count; the buzzing in his ears was so loud that he did not even know whether there was a man there to watch him. His bleeding legs, on which the flies clustered thick, still experienced a lively fear of the lash, so that he would not have dared to stop however much he wanted to; it was because he could see nothing and could not know where the blows would come from that his body stiffened, more fearful than his soul, for there was no longer room in his mind for either fear or sorrow but only pain; he thought he no longer knew how to speak and could not have found a single word to complain of his lot.

It must have been past noon when the man he called the guard brought him a drink. He drank, bent over as he was, avidly, in two great gulps; the water was tepid. Between his lips he felt the clay lip of the jug to which so many other mouths must have glued themselves recently; vaguely it disgusted him—the mouths of infidels—well, but to them, *he* was the heathen. Mechanically he thanked the man, in Arabic, without thinking that it might be as well not to be recognized here as an old crusader. The guard spoke a few words to him which he did not understand—his Arabic was strongest in the matter of insults and abuse.

Then he had to resume his plodding. After a while the time no longer seemed to pass so slowly. It seemed to him that he had always been walking in a circle with this weight on his shoulders; he had forgotten everything else. He no longer had hopes or wishes. They came to untie him; he tried to straighten his back, could not manage it and stood there, still bent, not daring to move, wondering what was expected of him.

He was led to a kind of hole dug in the ground, covered with planks, in which men lay in heaps, pell-mell; these must be the other prisoners. He lay down on the earth and remained there. He tried to find a position in which his body was free from pain. The flies—the country was infested with troublesome flies. It began to be cold and, instinctively, the old man huddled up to his nearest neighbor to warm himself a little.

He was already asleep when he felt a hand touch his arm. "It's morning," he thought, and sat up, trying to rise. Two thin arms went round his neck and a wet cheek was pressed against his own. Auberi! He had forgotten Auberi. "I am going mad," he thought. The child did not speak. Weeping, he pressed himself against his master. The old man stroked the boy's hair absently, too absorbed in his own wretchedness and weariness to think of his little companion. Presently Auberi fell asleep, still sniffling like a very young child.

Auberi had not yet brought himself to believe what had happened: he could not believe that it could have happened to him, Auberi, this terrible thing—being taken prisoner by the infidels. Formerly he had imagined that it must be as frightful as dying and going to purgatory; even worse. After all, in Christian lands, death is the lot of every man in the end, and all the comment it receives is "God rest his soul." But prisoners—everyone is sorry for them. There are even special prayers for them in church, as for martyrs.

Almost he had imagined infidels to be horned and furry monsters with fire coming out of their mouths, but those who had fallen upon the pilgrim caravan were, after all, ordinary men, although, indeed, very dark of countenance, as was to be expected of unbelievers. These village people were not even so very dark, and he had seen young boys among them with whom he would have liked to play and fight; and they had women, tall and beautiful, wearing trousers but with veiled faces, who put on striped garments and wore bright bracelets on their wrists and ankles on holidays. There were little children who ran about mother-naked and old women who carried tall jars of water on their heads.

The men were artisans, and manufactured leather bottles and pottery, just like Christians.

He had been there, out in the blazing sunshine, for a week, with no garment but a clout of rough canvas about his loins. He had to carry stones to the top of the hill where the lord of these territories was having his village fortified, rebuilding an old wall which had been demolished. There were about thirty of them working at it. The stones were heavy and the men enfeebled; most of them were native Christians. Auberi could not readily distinguish them from infidels and thought they could not be real Christians. There were also two old Genoese sailors with whom, in the end, he managed to establish more or less comprehensible communication in Provençal.

In the evening the exhausted men took advantage of the time of prayer to lie down on the ground against the wall. From there they could see the mosque, the white, flat-roofed houses, a few cypresses in front of the wall of the lord's castle and, beyond it, the olive groves against a background of violet hills. At the hour of evening prayer everything became tranquil; the translucent gold of the sky, the silvery olives, the black candles of the cypresses and the flat whiteness of the houses—so much beauty took the breath away. Auberi stared in front of him, dazed, his mind empty of thought, a hand playing with the wild locks of his sweat-soaked hair. He began to like the shrill, drawling voice of the muezzin. Amused, he would watch the man's strange motions up there on his tower, the shaking of his ruddy beard and his heavy turban of white muslin.

"It would be fine," he thought, "to see the priest of our village shouting like that or even the sacristan; you can see that these people worship the Devil; they'd rather let their priest shout himself hoarse than buy a bell."

Then his astonishment at being among the infidels would overwhelm him again—among them for good and with no means of escaping—how could he escape, with a blind man? It would be necessary to climb the wall, jump down into the ravine. . . . And Auberi would measure up the wall with his eyes, trying to recall the little he had seen of the road from the slope where he was working. The enterprise seemed to him perfectly possible and his imaginary escapes gave him so much satisfaction that it never entered his mind to try and carry them out in practice.

"O my brother, my companion, God is punishing me for having abandoned you in the depths of your great misery, brother in misfortune whom God placed in my way because our misfortunes were the same. By burning roads I led you, and icy ways, in wind and frost; together we extended our hands for alms outside churches, together lay down in straw or upon the bare earth. Brothers in the body's night, brothers in mourning. Rather than be parted from me you submitted to weariness and misery although towards other men your spirit was haughty and your heart was hard.

"And, brother, you can never have known how much I loved you, for I myself knew it not. And your noble head rolled down among the stones, that head beneath whose eyelids not even the crows could find sustenance, your tortured head full of hard thoughts.

"I brought you here, brother, only to betray you and abandon you, although you trusted me as you trusted no other man in the world.

At the end I was not beside you; you died alone because I failed you; my heart did not lead me to you.

"Brother, you chose to die rather than be what I am now, a slave and almost a brute beast. May your sin be upon my head only and I will endure while I can.

"Brother, you would have had good cause to mock me now, but you are beside me no longer and never again will I hear your reproaches.

"That life, which to the end you despised, I suffer still and cling to still, although, God knows, it seems empty enough without you— you whom I failed, brother, you who abandoned me. Has the man who has failed to guard his friend from evil still the right to pray to God?

"As the ox for his yoke-mate, so do I yearn for you, brother in misery, but, as God is our judge, you would not have left me so had you been a true friend. Lord God, Only Friend, we, he and I, might have turned this mill, been harnessed to this beam together—I would have taken all its weight upon myself. Bertrand, my companion, false friend, may God forgive you as I forgive you; may He judge you as I judge you, friend.

"Aye, may He think of you as I think of you; may He love you even though you do not love Him."

Long days. Little by little the habit of holding himself stooped had been formed, the old man had grown used to his yoke and thought that his task was one which left him more tranquillity than any other would have done. Sometimes it seemed to him that he was simply walking, advancing along an interminable road not much different from the roads of Provence, Guyenne and Palestine where for nearly two years now he had been on the move; and here there were neither stones nor puddles of mud and he need not fear to fall.

Each evening Auberi was there and whenever he heard the child's voice Ansiau remembered that he himself was still living, and this was a bitterness. In Auberi's absence he seemed to himself to be dead and buried, so that he was freed from hope and fear. Only Bertrand's absence weighed upon him; it was as if he had been deprived of his arm, the arm which would never again support the weight of the other, his companion, he who also knew how stones sound, how walls sound and how one may recognize a man by the touch of his hand; his companion with the bitter tongue.

Never would he have thought that the world in which he lived still had so much color, so much movement, and was still so full of living men.

"They are harvesting the olives," Auberi said. "The women are bringing in basket after basket on their heads. Wicker baskets as tall as that. The olives growing here smell good, they must be good eating. . . . This country round here is called Saint Joseph, Naplouse is the nearest town. . . . On the other side of the hill they're having their vintage. They're some kind of Jews but not real Jews. They worship the stones on the hill beyond this hill with the olive groves; they call it the Hill of Healing—" (for Auberi thought *Garizim* was *guérison*, as he had made Saint Joseph of *Yasuf*). "It was the Genoese told me so. I'm going to bring the Genoese to you, you're sure to be able to talk to him. He had three sons in Genoa—the eldest was like me. . . . It seems that one of the emir's wives is a Frenchwoman of these parts, only she doesn't worship the true God; I expect she was forced not to. Is that a great sin, would you say?"

"A great sin, Auberi."

"They must have tortured her. But even so—what must her thoughts be when she prays at evening?

"Today," Auberi would say, "we saw the emir go by, off hawking with his falcons . . ."

Listening to him, the old man would let himself fall into daydreams . . .

"What was his horse like?" he would ask.

"If you climb up on the ramparts you can see the Jordan. At evening it's like a golden saber."

The old man crossed himself.

"Please, my lord, is it true what the Genoese says, that it's the Jordan where God was baptized by Saint John?"

"Certainly. What other Jordan do you suppose it could be?"

"It's really, really true that it's the same?"

"Yes, yes. There aren't two of them."

Auberi's deep sigh was melancholy and incredulous.

"You know, I'd never have believed it." Then, after a long silence, puzzled, he added: "How was it, then, that that Frenchwoman turned infidel, if the country is so holy? . . . And then—well, that isn't all; it seems there are men who have done it, too—had themselves circumcised and everything, so that now they're no better than dogs and worship Mahomet—not only local people but proper Frenchmen as well. What do you think of that?"

"Why, lad, I wasn't born yesterday. These things happen. Some of them escape and do penance afterwards. People will do almost anything to save their skins."

Auberi thought it over, his chin in his hand.

"So they do penance afterwards," he repeated, surprised and thoughtful. There followed a long silence which the old man broke at last:

"Auberi, you must escape."

"How can I? I can't go without you."

"Needs must. I free you from your oath. I may live another five years; you cannot stay here five years."

The child put his arms round the old man's neck and clung to him wildly.

"I'll stay twenty years and more, if you live. I've nowhere to go, except with you."

The old man burst into sobs, sharp and clear like the barking of a dog. Never would he have thought that the child held such a place in his heart. Now he began to think more and more of the danger to which Auberi was exposed until the thought gave him no peace even during the daytime. He told himself: "At the Last Judgment I shall have to answer to his mother. What have I done to him? Was he entrusted to me only that I should damn his soul?"

The more he thought of it, the more he realized how fearful he was of the day when he would no longer hear the child's voice each evening after the muezzin's call to prayer. "Yet go he must," he thought. "He is young and the Devil is strong." At last he said:

"Auberi, I am your master. You must do what I tell you. One comes to this country to serve God, not these dogs of Moslems."

Sullen, his eyes lowered, Auberi listened.

"I do not know how to serve God. If I left you I should be a traitor. I shall not go anywhere away from here without you. And in any case I shouldn't know how."

"Ah! son of a bitch! If only I had my eyes! Those Genoese of yours are villeins and the sons of villeins. Were you, yes or no, born a free man? Why, even Riquet, who's the son of a peasant,—do you think he has not already escaped from wherever they took him, though it were the Arabian desert? There must certainly be a way."

Auberi shook his head without answering. A part of his mind was thinking: "Having eyes is not everything."

His ankles were tied by a stout cord which prevented him from taking long strides. He could have got it off without overmuch trouble, but he was never alone and he distrusted most of his companions who, although they were Christians, loathed him as a Frenchman. Then he would have to climb over the wall, not very high but guarded, jump down about twelve feet, crawl out of the moat, and then—the worst was still to come: an unknown country. In any of the scattered villages he might come to he would be quickly spotted and seized as a runaway slave; he only knew a few words of the native language; and, finally, his hair was now bleached fairer than it had ever been.

JERUSALEM

THE night was cold and moonless but there were so many stars that there seemed to be no room for the smallest corner of dark sky. You only had to stare at the sky to see more and ever more of them appear; among the big ones, with their starshine of yellow, blue or green winking and twinkling, there were thousands of small ones like the silver thread in a brocade; the great Saint Jacques' Way was spread out all dotted with starry gems, like a long white altar-cloth. Lying on the ground in the withered grass, his face turned to the sky, Auberi stared upwards, trying to understand how all these lights held together; he seemed to hear the cascades of the stars, as they fell slowly to pour down beyond the earth into a great gulf on the far side of the world.

He was drunk with the feeling that the rope no longer hobbled him and that walls no longer hemmed him in, although never, in the mortal terror of the moment of escape, could he have supposed that he would be happy that night. Had he even realized how much the inability to go and come as he pleased had irked him? There had been food to eat, up there in the village; they were not unkind to him; and his lord was there.

Now, all that was done with—lost forever the kind countenance of his master with its big, sightless eyes and his smile, still youthful by reason of its goodness.

"Lost forever," he thought, "for even if they recapture me they will kill me and I shall not see him again. Ah—provided only they don't torture me, don't force me to turn heathen!"

Where to go? And how? He had no call to fear the highroad or hunger, old familiars. But how many days' journey might he be from a Christian country? He had no idea. He was exhausted, the scratches on his knees and elbows were bleeding; he had been crawling for hours through the bush.

He was thirsty. He had succeeded in stealing a skin of water from the sleeping sentry but he did not want to touch it yet. Rolled in a fold of his sash, about his waist, he had ten barley cakes which his master had been saving for him during the past week instead of eating them—his morning meal. Now, at all events, the master could eat again. Auberi had sworn not to eat the cakes until the next day; they seemed more precious than gold to him. If it had been possible he would have kept and cherished them, like relics. Hunger, thirst, sleepiness? He no longer felt them; God was protecting him.

His nerves were as taut as the strings of a lute and beneath that icy and glittering sky it seemed to him that his whole body was vibrant with the music of the stars. Jackals were barking about the foot of the hill and crickets chirping in the grass. He was free as the wild beasts of the fields, alone in the world, in this land without the cross, hunted, like a wolf, by men. For what? Yet they were men, who ate, sang, bounced their babies on their knees like other men. And they would kill him without pity, like a dog, because he did not speak their language and claimed the right to walk the highroad without a rope about his ankles.

Ah, and he would take that right, it would need more than these dogs of heathens to deprive him of it again!

"Oh, my lord, my father, may it be in Paradise that I see you again, for on this earth it was too bitter; in Paradise your eyes will be open again, father, and you will see me.

"Like the beasts that perish, but like the sparrows, too, of which not one falls in vain. *In te Domine speravi.* By the great joy there is in

Heaven this night and every night, have pity, O Lord! Lord God, Our Lady Holy Mary and all the saints be my witness I never did harm to a single soul."

Painfully, he opened his eyes. His face was burning, his eyelids swollen, his mouth gummy. Where was he? He could see stalks of bramble and long, dry, yellow grass sharp against a vivid blue sky. At first he thought he was in Provence, on the road to Les-Saintes-Maries. Then he remembered, and was overwhelmed by such a feeling of distress that he wanted to die. True it is that had wishing been enough to kill, he would have died at that moment. Then a great pity for himself overcame him and he began weeping noisily, like a very young child, sniffing and swallowing his tears. He felt so weak, his whole body ached and he was quite without hope of coming alive out of this adventure. His head felt like a clapperless bell, dreadfully heavy, enormous; as soon as he moved it he was overcome by a feeling of nausea and the world was lost in darkness before his eyes. There was a buzzing and ringing in his ears so insistent that he could no longer hear the song of the cicadas.

The sun was high towards the zenith; it must be noon.

He remembered the skin of water hanging from his belt, and his supply of barley cakes. The water was tepid and smelled of camel, but he drank and drank and felt as if fresh blood were flowing through his body. He ate three cakes, one after the other, until his stomach was swollen like a bladder; then he fell back upon the ground again, unable to stir. At that moment it seemed to him that the only thing to do was to stay there until his provisions were exhausted and thereafter to die of hunger. He knew very well that if he risked only a few steps any shepherd or a stray horseman wandering over the hills would very soon overtake him; they had a way of suddenly materializing out of thin air, like phantoms; God knows how many there might be on watch behind the rocks. When he shut his eyes he would see Bertrand's head again, rolling and dashing itself against the stones. He did not know where he was, but he believed himself to be lying on the hill which rose from the bed of the *nullah* they called the *oued-el-Attara*.

He slept until nightfall and once again his awakening was painful and again he was thirsty. And so cold. He was shaking with fever. He drank a few mouthfuls of water, then rose and set off.

While still in the village he had given much thought to the route he must follow, steering by the stars. He had told himself that to go towards the sea he must take as his guide a star between the Great Bear and a southern constellation. But there was a great outcrop of rocks across his way and in working round them he perceived that he was turning his back on his star. The rocks were now so close together that he could no longer make any progress. Slowly, bleeding from a score of cuts, torn by thorns, he went down again towards the valley where, among boulders, tufts of cactus and clumps of small willows, lay the dry bed of the torrent. Soft, gurgling, the water skin beat against his thighs. Each gurgle rang like a reproach in Auberi's heart; he could not forgive himself for having drunk so much the previous evening. He was tormented by thirst but he had sworn to drink no more until the morning.

A thin crescent moon rose behind the rocks. In no other sky, no other country, had Auberi ever seen moon and stars so brilliant. This crescent moon hurt the eyes like a new sickle reflecting the sun at noon, and after looking at it Auberi could see nothing but little white crescents everywhere. He clambered over the boulders and slipped like a shadow between the clumps of trees. How good it was to go straight forward without being caught at by brambles! The boulders and pebbles of the watercourse and the foliage of willows and oaks composed black arabesques against the backcloth of hills lit up by the moon. The long mountain crowned with rocks loomed, a vast shadow, over the valley and, seeing it always the same, Auberi had no sense of making progress but seemed rather to be walking forever on the same spot like a man bewitched.

The sound of branches shifting, light footsteps just beside him, sent a shock through his whole body and made him throw himself flat on the ground; he caught a fleeting sight of a small head, horned and delicate, and of two enormous eyes in which the moon was briefly reflected; then the shadows of two antelopes leaped and vanished soundlessly among the mountain undergrowth. Auberi smiled with delight; he would have liked the power to recall the two animals, to talk to them; their proximity alone was reassuring. Getting to his feet again, he drew a deep breath and looked once more upon the moon-drenched mountains and the radiant sky; it all seemed to have been unchanged, dead for centuries and yet more alive than a town on market day. Every stone and blade of grass seemed vibrant, bewitched; he would not have been surprised to see the pebbles change into diamonds, the foliage glow with the colors of the rainbow, and all the stars pour out of the sky and rain down upon the hills. Oh, to be able to remain forever in this enchanted world! Regal solitude. How much more clearly the eyes see when the body is exhausted, the soul hunted by fear and sadness. Nothing then remains of body and soul but the eyes still see.

He must get back on to his way towards the sea. Leaving the watercourse he took to a mule path, although fearful that it might lead to an Arab village. The longer he walked the larger seemed the mountain range he had to cross, and it seemed to him that he was losing instead of gaining ground. Behind him mountain crests began to stand out more and more sharply against a white sky. The starlight waned and presently the rocks above him began to glow with rosy light and, turning about, he saw a long purple streak on the horizon.

All about him trees, shrubs and boulders, still deep in darkness, took on monstrous forms and seemed to move. Collecting the little strength which remained to him, Auberi began to run. In the deep shadows already gathering beneath each clump of bushes he seemed to see evil spirits lurking, goblins awaiting the sunrise to vanish into the air; it was the hour when they would be only too glad to find a living creature in whom to take refuge. Muttering prayers, he ran on and, as the first ray of sunshine touched his head, he stopped and made a great sign of the cross.

He was already on the other face of the mountain which he had worked round during the night. In the distance, still in deep shadow, · he could see a valley full of cypresses and fig trees, a little town of flat roofs perched on the side of the mountain among olive groves. Wisps of smoke, shot with pink light, rose into the lightening sky and the muezzin's call to prayer came clear through the pure and icy air.

Auberi clambered up among the rocks and found a hiding-place at the foot of a bush of brambles. He ate another of his cakes and drank a few mouthfuls of water. He now had hardly a day's supply left. A single night's travel would never enable him to reach the far side of the valley and he did not know which way to take if he was to avoid the village. His head was burning, his lips crusted and so dry that the skin was peeling away. Licking them was useless; he seemed to have no saliva left in his mouth. His tongue was swelling and it hurt him.

During the day he heard peasants moving along the pathway, leading mules loaded with baskets of olives; he saw a mounted lookout materialize like a phantom and vanish among the rocks on the crest of the hills. With shrill cries a number of men dressed in white and armed with spears passed along the slope towards the valley.

The fourth night. The fifth night. Now the surrounding country was arid desert. Countless boulders, stones without end. Withered bush. Auberi was certain now that he was not going towards the sea; his star lay well to his right hand and he had not the strength to make towards it, for he would have had to start climbing again and clamber over bare rock. He was dying of thirst. He still had one cake left, hard as a stone, at which, from time to time, he nibbled. Ah, if only God could make water gush from one of these stones for him, as he had done for Hagar! Sometimes he lay down upon the ground and pressed his mouth to the stony soil, in search of moisture.

"My lord, it was to my death you sent me. My lord, I am dying.

"Ah, I should have done better to stay where I was, where I had food and drink. Better to have turned infidel than endure this torture. In their villages they've wells full of water. They have stone jars full of water. Skins all swollen with cold water. Yes, yes, I'll go to the nearest village, let them kill me or make a heathen of me, provided they first give me water to drink."

And now he was in Hell. He managed to take refuge once again in a dried-up water-course which was used as a road by caravans; there were bushes and cactus and tufts of tall, stinging grass. He tried to dig beneath the roots in search of water; he tore off cactus leaves, trying to bite and suck them. They were bitter and the spines lacerated his lips. Nevertheless he persisted in sucking until he felt aching pains in the region of his palate and his throat contracted.

Then he began to see visions.

He saw heathen horsemen, the lower half of their faces covered with a black veil, scimitars at their side, their naked arms bending black long-bows. He saw white camels racing towards him. He did not know where to hide and began waving his hands in front of his eyes to drive these visions away. Then he saw springs of water, streams gurgling over cool pebbles, so clearly that he could have counted the pebbles and could make out the sandy banks from which the water trickled.

He thought he would be unable to bear another day of it. Yet, in the hope of finding a stream or even a village, he summoned the strength to set out again and found himself, the next morning, among rocks, with a wide flat valley stretching below him. Through it wound a road, yellow with dung, between grey bushes. Auberi lay down among the rocks, wondering how many leagues there were between him and the road. Two hours' walking should bring him to it—"By the Grace of God," he thought. And—"Someone is sure to pass along the road. I shall ask for water. For the rest, we shall see."

The day passed more quickly than he had expected. The fear of being killed had again been stronger than his thirst. He had seen a few Arab horsemen, dressed in white and mounted on their small, black horses, with their long-bows slung from their shoulders. Thereafter, crawling between boulders, he had lost sight of the road.

The stings of mosquitoes and gad-flies brought him back to full awareness of his surroundings. He stumbled over the skeleton of a camel, frightening two large vultures with bare necks which rose and flew about in the air above his head; then a swarm of blow-flies, heavy and green, was all about him, alighting upon his eyes and his lips. He beat at the flies with his arms and began to run, to fall over something which must have been the corpse of a mule; it was black, sticky, crawling with flies, and in the heat of the afternoon the unstirring air was laden with a stench so foul that the boy lost consciousness.

A sharp pain in the arm brought him to himself again. A vulture was perched on his body and staring into his face out of eyes as round and yellow as jewels. This look, the first living glance he had encountered for five days, so fascinated Auberi that he did not immediately realize what it was he was seeing and even forgot the pain in his arm. Then suddenly he understood and uttered a cry so piercing that the bird, frightened, beat its wings and rose slowly into the air. Auberi jumped to his feet and began running straight before him, his arms raised, yelling and screaming like a madman in a voice as shrill as a bird's. He saw carrion all about him, felt the wings of vultures beating about his ears and saw their dead, unwinking eyes wherever he looked. He dared not stop, sure that he had only to lie down to rest to be devoured alive by vultures.

At nightfall he was still walking, although certain that each step was his last and still finding strength for just one more, but without knowing whither he was bound. At last he lay down on the ground for he could no longer see, although the night was not dark. But everything had turned to blackness before his eyes; he could not even see the moon.

The sound of singing came to him from somewhere in the distance, a song sung by several voices, male voices, rough and harsh, and with them the thin thread of a higher voice. They were singing in unison, with a deep breath at the end of each phrase, and the voices seemed to wax, hesitate, then wane and wax again, like the flame of an altar lamp. Where did these voices come from? Auberi thought he must be delirious, yet still listened more and more eagerly, for the words were familiar.

Ave regina coelorum
Ave domina angelorum

Mentally, he sang with them, keeping time with the voices but sometimes surprised by their way of singing, for, although the tune was the one he knew, the accent and intonation in which the words were pronounced seemed strange to him.

"Oh, let it go on and on, let me hear it so all my life, hear this song of peace and light!" It seemed to him almost that he was back in his own house and in his mother's arms.

Now he was no longer afraid; never again would he be alone. For the song informed the rocks and filled the valley and the whole sky. Never in all his life had he prayed with such ardor. He prayed with all his thirst, not to ask for water but because the feeling of thirst was all that remained alive in him, and at the same time he wanted to say something to Our Lady and to greet her, since her presence was all about him: "Our Lady, I am thirsty."

The song came to an end on a long *Amen*. As in a dream Auberi rose and began to walk. Twenty steps from him three hobbled horses were snorting, and stamping to keep warm. Beyond them was a long, dark shadow the outlines of which enabled Auberi to guess that it was a campaign tent and beside it a four-wheeled cart, more or less effectively extending the tent with staffs and cloaks; between the chinks shone an unsteady light. From the cart he could hear the dull sound of voices and the weeping of a child.

"Pilgrims," Auberi told himself. "It was they who were singing. God wanted to save me, after all. The master was right, he knew what he was doing."

Auberi drew slowly nearer to the horses, who shied away from him, whinnying nervously.

"There," he said, "quiet, good beasts, quiet." He wanted to stroke them, to kiss their big eyes, as if they had been Christians.

Then two sturdy fellows came out of the tent, carrying lances which must surely date from the crusade; the two men did not look very accommodating, yet Auberi began laughing with joy at the sight of them and went towards them with raised arms. He could not understand what they were saying. Heads were poked out from the cart and the tent. The men were saying:

"*Wer da? Wer da?* Halt!"

English? German? Auberi ran towards them, was dazzled for a moment by a lamp shining behind the half-open tent flap; one of the men pointed his lance at him.

"Brother," Auberi said, shaking his head, "brother. French, *Francesi, pellegrino.*"

The men, two burly soldiers, fair and bearded, looked at each other, lowering their lances.

"*Ja so, ein Welscher. Komm.* Come."

Auberi entered the tent; he was laughing, out of his mind with weariness and excitement, shaken by a nervous hiccoughing. He could not take in his surroundings. He sank to the ground, on to skins, saying:

"A drink, thirsty."

He was aware of someone pressing a bowl of wine to his cracked lips.

Shaken by the motion of the cart, Auberi lay shivering in a high fever: the sunshine through chinks in the canvas cover hurt his inflamed eyes.

"I, too, am going blind," he thought. The pains in his head and his belly were so bad that he could hardly eat. He was constantly asking for something to drink and his companions were grumbling at being obliged to reduce their already meager ration of wine and beer because of him. Their supplies were almost exhausted; they were one day's journey from Jerusalem.

They were German pilgrims who had been forced to delay their journey at Jaffa because of the heat; among them were old men, some sick, and a woman who had been brought to bed of a child on shipboard. The convoy was led by four soldiers and three monks.

At evening the monks took Auberi out of the cart and laid him on sacks, which also served as their own beds, in the tent which they pitched for the night. The air was fresher than in the cart and there was more room. The people in the cart slept crowded on top of each other; there was an old man all covered with sores who stank like a corpse; a fat man, paralyzed in both legs, who never stopped groaning and abusing his neighbors. An old woman, driven half-mad by the journey, sang obscene songs in a low voice; the men laughed at her.

The woman with the infant was also installed in the tent and was undoing the child's swaddling-clothes. Two monks had hung an oaken cross, decorated with wrought iron, to the tent pole and surrounded it with palm branches whose long, withered leaves were like lances. They had fixed candles of yellow wax in two narrow-necked earthenware jugs and lit them from the flame of their little oil-lamp. The third monk stood outside, leaning against the cart, watching for the Shepherd's star to rise so that they could begin to sing Compline.

His mind dulled by fever, Auberi watched, indifferent. But the singing, rough and rhythmic, revived his interest a little. All the evenings of his past lived again in this one evening, in the words, which were unchanging, in the melody, which had been in his very blood since he could walk. It is something one never escapes from: the song was as necessary to him as bread and salt.

He raised his body slowly on his elbow; then got on his knees; to remain lying there during a religious service was as impossible as to attend a service stark naked or with his head covered.

Erect, stiff-backed and with their arms crossed, the monks sang as tranquilly as if they had been in the oratory of their monastery. They were Black Friars, wearing coarse woollen frocks very worn and dirty; they were badly shaved and had the sour, harsh faces of peasants. Their heads wagged and their shoulders swayed slowly in time with their singing.

Nunc dimittis servum tuum,
Domine, secundum verbum tuum in pace.

And at these words their voices faltered a little, and all who were present, the soldiers, Auberi, the woman and the few pilgrims who had climbed down from the cart to pray, trembled and drew closer together, suddenly possessed by the anguish of an imminent joy; it was as if they realized only at that instant that they were celebrating their last twilight watch before arriving at Jerusalem.

The ragged canvas of the tent, the dried-up palm leaves, the candles in their jugs, the physical miseries of their own bodies, all of these, on that great night spent at the portal of the treasury of holiness they were about to enter, became more sacred than the finest ornaments of a saintly festival. For they alone knew what tears, what sweat and bitter suffering Jerusalem had cost them. Now they felt themselves to be richer than bishops and noblemen who make the pilgrimage on horseback, with servants and provisions. More than one of them had lost a comrade by the way; more than one was far from sure of ever being able to return home. To give his all, a man must be poor.

In manibus portabunt te—ne forte offendas ad lapidem pedem tuum.

Super aspidem et basiliscum ambulabis—et conculcabis leonem et draconem.

Quoniam in me speravit—

The youngest of the monks extinguished the candles, the soldiers rose, stretching stiff legs.

"*O du Herzliebster Herr Jesu. Du Seelenheil.*"

The infant was crying in his reedy voice and persisted in working his small, supple arms out of the swaddling-clothes. He had a long oval head and the grave eyes of a bird. His mother rocked him in her arms, drawing her cloak about him and casting furtive looks at the monks, not daring to give the child suck until after the benediction.

Then, seated on the ground, the mother offered the nipple of her long, flabby breast, greyish-white, holding it before the child's mouth with her fingers. She was a woman who had passed her thirtieth year, lean, and with a handsome, sensitive face; long, straight, black hair fell from under her kerchief. The child clung to the breast with his little pink hands.

"*Du Minne,*" the woman said. "*Du Minne.*"

For her, at that moment, Jerusalem did not even exist. Strangely, a brief silence had fallen over the tent, as if the baby's crying had also been a song which must not be interrupted.

Auberi had lain down in his place again, flat on his stomach, his chin in his cupped hands; he was suddenly astonished to feel soft hair against his palms; he had never thought of such a thing. How had he suddenly grown so much older? A mustache—rather thin, however—covered his upper lip; he stroked it thoughtfully with the tip of his finger.

As if he were reciting a litany, he said over all the names which his master had made him learn before his departure, the names he would have to include in his prayer when he stood, at last, before the Holy Sepulchre: Ansiau, Thierri, Garin, Garnier, Thibaut, another Ansiau, another Garin, André, Pierre, Aioul, Jacques, Jacques again, Herbert, Aubert, Jean, Thibaut, Bernard; there were still at least twenty more and not a single one must be forgotten. Bertrand, too, although the master had not said so.

And it seemed to him that life was beautiful and that no more harm would come to him ever, since, on the morrow, he would behold Jerusalem.

BROTHER ERNAUT

O SOLE, true coronation with the crown of thorns, Father, see me now, free at long last and the world all mine, as it is Yours. What is there, now, which I do not possess? I am freed from all the bonds which limited my wealth—from name, goods, friends, desires. The crows of the fields are not poor, nor the flowers which scatter their petals on the road; the wind is no pauper who carries off the petals and sows the seed as he wills. Father, I am Your heir and all Your domains are mine.

"Father, each of these candles burning before Your altar is mine and burns in my heart. Each flagstone I tread is mine, and the stone which is wearing out my knees is part of my body, my staff and the rock to which I cling. Like the bread I eat and the water I drink, all Your world is my sustenance, earned with the sweat of my brow. Father, my sin is no more—for it is true that the boulder which crashes down a mountain side, crushing all in its way, does not fall unless You have willed it; and if such be Your will, others may take the same stone and dress it and make it the plinth of a pillar.

"Father, grant that I may be as docile as that stone and like the tree which I fell, the axe with which I fell it and the hand that holds the axe. And may my heart be to You like my hand is to me, obeying me though I do not give it a thought."

It was a small community of White Friars in the mountains near Avallon, built at the top of an uncleared valley; for ten years the monks had been clearing land by cutting the trees and already had a field for grain, a vineyard and a small herd of cows which they took into the forest clearings to graze. Work on the land will not wait; the monastery buildings were not yet completed. Only the chapel and the cloister, the part of the house reserved for the abbot, and the hostel for casual guests were finished. The brothers and novices slept in dormitories more like barns and not so well protected against cold and damp as the byres; however, the monks did not spend much time there. It was a monastery with a very strict rule. The offices were recited and sung right through, with additional readings almost as long as the offices, and, between Vespers and Vigils, Vigils and Matins, not much time was left for sleep. The single small copper bell, hung from the oratory rafters, did not always awaken the sleepers and the prior himself would come and do it, using his cane and not sparing the lazier brothers. He was an ex-peasant from Auvergne, of the freeholding yeomanry, a rough, tight-fisted man but a tremendous worker.

The brothers were for the most part young and neither the cold nor the hardness of their plank beds prevented their falling dead asleep the moment the offices were finished; they were not allowed to sleep more than three hours at a stretch. After Vigils came Matins and Prime, and the morning mass and the chapter; then toil in the farmyard and the byres, in the fields and the forest and at the building work. The newest enclosure must be cleared and the dormitory finished before winter. In the wide yard, deep in shavings and cluttered with tree-trunks, the saw was at work from dawn until dusk, only still during the offices; the men, with sleeves and frock-skirts tucked up, their faces red and their hair sticky with sweat, worked all the harder to make up for their want of skill; they brought the solemnity of apprentices to their work but spoiled planks and bad cuts were not rare.

They barely gave themselves time to straighten stiff backs, suck a finger skinned by the saw or remove a bit of sawdust or a gnat from an inflamed eye. They all sang in chorus as they worked—that was the rule. The Devil is everywhere on the lookout for monks; even while you're lifting a plank or handling the saw or the axe, *he* is there to jog your elbow, or display some profane figment before your eyes—so you must follow the song or, when short of breath, repeat the words in your head—even the words of the songs had been changed, so that nothing could be found in them but God's praises.

Despite want of sleep and a frugal diet, youth asserted its rights; in the two quarters of an hour allowed for recreation, after None and after Vespers, the novices organized ball games and skittle games which assumed the aspect of serious brawls, such passion did the players bring to them; often enough the balls were confiscated and the games replaced by meditation or reading, although it was not thought wise to forbid them entirely to the novices and lay brothers.

The abbot was supported by four veteran monks who had been there since the foundation of the monastery and fifteen others who had taken their final vows since that date. Others had died of fever or of the privations of the first four years; among the lay brothers none was more than thirty years old and the majority was barely more than twenty. The novices were increasingly numerous; that year there were seventeen. All of them were stout lads and hard workers, and when, during the offices, they raised their voices in chorus, the thunder of their singing shook the roof of the oratory. Not all of them had fine voices but they sang just as they worked, heartily, without undue care for their throats or their lungs.

It was after Pentecost that the abbot had, for the first time, received the tall lad with the Norman accent in his parlor, sent to him by the abbot of the monastery at Pontigny. Without his brother abbot's recommendation he would not have accepted the lad, who seemed too exalted and whose health was poor; but he was full of goodwill and there was a sweetness in his manner which it was difficult to resist. The abbot had not a heart of stone; he had conceived a strong and personal affection for the newcomer—so much so that he had, from the start, made him a concession which was contrary to his principles. The young man was extremely anxious to bear, even in his novitiate, the name of Ernaut, although that was not his real name; it was, he said, "in memory of a brother he had lost and whom he had gravely wronged."

When his request was denied he had fallen into such a melancholy that in the end the abbot had given way.

The young man wished to dedicate himself to God in expiation of a crime, an involuntary one it is true, but grave—no less than parricide. But he had by no means the air of a penitent. He was a lad of very equable temper, inclined, indeed, to laughter and making the best of things. The master of the novices, who kept a sharp eye on him, was inclined to find fault with his somewhat worldly manners; the youth came of a rich and noble family. But he was forced to admit that he could find neither vanity nor light-mindedness in the lad and that, despite his poor health, he was an excellent worker; during his childhood he had undergone a training so harsh that he was apt at any kind of work, thanks to the quickness and adaptability of his mind and his natural agility.

He could both write and calculate; to begin with he had been set to keep the accounts; but one day the prior found him asleep, his head on the desk and the ink upset on his hair. As a punishment he was sent to the forest to fell trees; there was no risk of his falling asleep at that work. There he proved himself so apt that he was soon able to direct the work and got more done than Brother André, a lay brother and a woodman by trade.

"The trade of arms is a thing which is bad in itself," the master of novices, Brother Izembard, thought, "but there is this to be said for it —it prepares a man for monastic discipline. Here's a lad I would not have given two sous for had he been born a burgess but, being what he is, he has obedience in the blood and can in his turn command obedience when necessary."

And he could not forget the smile of gratitude and childlike delight which had lit up that lean, wide, handsome face on the day when the young man first heard himself called Brother Ernaut.

"How attached he still is to the vanities of this world," Brother Izembard had thought. "But we must not expect too much of a beginner. Since he loved his brother, perhaps he can learn to love God."

He did not know that Haguenier was still even more attached to the vanities of this world than he supposed, for he had not dared to admit that his brother had hanged himself and this lie of omission had been due to the hope that he might thus trick them at the monastery into praying for the dead man's soul. Yet this was trying to cheat God. He knew it, but in the excessive ardor of his piety he supposed himself to know a great deal about the goodness of God. God, he thought, could not want to damn Ernaut.

He liked his new life. That, to be sure, did not prevent him from cursing the prior, the abbot, the monastery and the rule every time he had to get up in the night for Vigils. That was his worst temptation. But on the way from the dormitory to the chapel, to the regular chime of the little bell, he recovered control of his mind and he was never seen to yawn or rub his eyes during the offices. The brothers' voices, rather slow and dull with sleep at first, grew clearer, stronger, and, as if borrowing strength from each other, finally swept all away together, sleep, fatigue and thought alike; for in the ring of those voices was all the intoxication of sleep sacrificed, of the silent night and in almost every case a deep love of singing—well or ill—was reinforced by that sudden and violent dragging of the mind from sleep. These men put into their singing all the ardor they would have put into sleeping, and that was no small matter. Matins was the office at which the singing was most fervent. Brother Ernaut felt secretly humiliated at being among those who did not sing, but then that was one of the means used by God to put him to trial. What use had he made of his fine voice in the world? If he had lost it, it was because he had richly deserved to do so.

Haguenier was finding the conditions of his childhood repeated—as when, after a day of hard practice with the master-at-arms and other tutors, he had had to wait at table until nightfall and when he had had to awaken before dawn to light the fire and prepare his master's clothes. With every fiber of his body he was living again through the experience of intense waiting for the hour of rest, of waking in darkness when the idea of only one more minute in bed seemed to him a happiness worthy of Paradise. Now he was rediscovering the simple and precious paradise of every living man—a dreamless sleep, sleep tight and entire, the flawless refuge.

"In that, too, I am discovering You again, O my God—in the sleep You grant me and the sleep You deny me; for I am Yours forever, the breath of my nostrils is Yours, the darkness behind my eyelids and the light I see when I open them—and my laziness and the failure of my will are Yours also; and Your thing am I."

It had been drilled into him that, tired or not, a man must keep his shoulders squared and his face smiling; here, nobody required him to have a smiling face but he retained the good humor which was the primary duty of the nobly born towards his comrades, the other novices, very far from nobly born for the most part but yet, now, quite as much so as himself since they were all brothers and equals. Did he like them? He could not have said. Their freedom to talk together was strictly limited; they had, indeed, barely time, between work and prayer, to tidy their clothes and wash themselves in the big bucket at the spring near the cattle pond. Most of the novices liked Brother Ernaut because he was good-humored and contrived to smile even when anyone else would have been angry, when a tree trunk fell awkwardly or the oxen became obstinate and refused to move. He was an excellent work-mate, although it was not obvious why the work progressed better when Brother Ernaut was present; he had the quick, sure eye and common sense of a good foreman, and directed the work without seeming conscious that he was doing so.

The novices and lay brothers were allowed to converse during working hours, at least in so far as it was necessary. But on one occasion Brother André, whose business it was to parcel out the work in the woods, had chided Brother Ernaut in front of all the others, saying:

"Brother Ernaut fancies himself still on his own land and among his own men."

The other had answered him:

"No, we are on your land, Brother André, and among your men."

At the chapter meeting the next day they both had to answer for these vain and uncharitable words. Brother Ernaut pleaded that mockery had not been his intention: the land belonged to all the brothers and they were all of them each other's men—apart from any question of obedience to their superiors. The abbot found them both at fault, Brother André for having started a dispute, Brother Ernaut for having answered back and thereafter for having tried to justify himself. He therefore decided, with the agreement of the master of novices, that Brother Ernaut should be in sole charge of the forest work one day out of two; on the other days he would take his orders from Brother André, without having the right to open his mouth even for a yes or a no.

Brother Ernaut was more afflicted by this latter part of his punishment than he could have expected, not out of a taste for chatter but because of his zeal for the work. He frequently had to bite his lip to prevent himself from shouting: "Slacken that rope a little, Brother Garnier!" or "Haul to the left, Brother Pierre!" And as, on alternate days, he was in full command, it was all the harder to see the work being done otherwise than the way he thought best.

For the monastery was now his own land, his native country, and nothing seemed more important to him than good progress in the tree-felling and construction of the buildings. Sometimes he even found himself bearing a real grudge against Brother André who, to his way of thinking, was slowing down the work. When he had confessed his evil thoughts to Brother Izembard he was condemned to work every day under Brother André's orders and to maintain complete silence every day instead of every other day.

"You must learn," the master of novices had told him, "that God has no need of your mind to build His monastery and that it is better that the buildings should remain incomplete yet another year than be finished with the help of unclean hands and a will full of pride, even if it were true, as you think, that the work makes better progress under your orders. God requires of you not work well done which fills you with pride, but obedience and charity."

"So," Haguenier thought, "they give me work to do such as I've never done before in my life, and I do my best, and yet I'm to be reproached for doing it too well. This house is God's house and our business is to build it. If everyone does not do his best—and God knows it's not much I'm doing in any case—where will the monastery be? The work is so hard and the hands so few, what with three more novices down with fever and bedridden."

He was dangerously near to blaming Brother Izembard for being insufficiently concerned about the interests of the monastery. "My God," he thought, "my heart binds itself wherever it can. I love this house and this church and even the very planks of wood which are sawed in the courtyard and the nails we use to secure them." And of his brother novices: "God knows, I have no right to love them otherwise than as Your servants; but if we do not have the time to finish the new buildings before winter, some of them will fall ill from the cold through sleeping on the bare earth. I should not have been able to make much difference but, through no virtue of mine, the fact remains that the work makes better progress when I am in charge.

"O my God, why was I reared to take care of other men? I cannot escape a sense of responsibility for them, although I know that You alone are responsible for all of us." And he asked Brother Izembard to set him the lowest and vilest task, which was normally done by lay brothers as a punishment for disobedience—he was ready to clean out the stables and latrines or cart dung to the fields.

"Stay as you are," the old man had said. "It's there that you will best fight against your temptation."

Brother André set his rival to the hardest work. From morning until night Haguenier labored with his axe to fell the great beech which was to be sawed into planks for the roofing. The axe was small and worn and the work did not make much progress. Haguenier attacked the task with an ardor which verged upon rage. He had come to identify the beech with all his sins, all the temptations he had to overcome, and no good came of it, for the tree was the victor; before he had cut even halfway through the trunk, he had a fainting fit at Vespers, as he was entering the oratory.

He was thought to be dying. There were neither physician nor medicines at the monastery nor was the death of a brother thought of as a misfortune excepting in so far as it reduced the labor force. There were already fourteen graves behind the cloisters and five in the chapel itself. A monastery is founded on its dead as well as on its living brethren, and those whose names were called over every day in the chapel were, for their comrades, not absentees. Brother Ernaut's grave was dug behind the cloisters and his shroud prepared, and the brothers who watched beside him recited the prayers for the dying. He, himself, seemed remote, yet kept enough consciousness of his surroundings to utter *amen* in the right places. He gave proof, under his sufferings, of a great gentleness and self-disregard which impressed even the prior, who did not like him. Then, contrary to all expectation, he began to mend, and the novices, especially the younger ones, began talking of a miracle, for they thirsted for miracles, not from vanity, but out of love for their community, so new and still so poor, and of which they were so proud.

Brother Ernaut thus found himself, on his bed of pain, the object of an esteem which he had neither sought nor deserved; his comrades affirmed that they had seen his countenance grow luminous at the moment when the father prior placed the crucifix to his lips. It was true. But he himself knew nothing about it. And he was tempted to accuse his brothers of want of common sense and of frivolousness, for he was ashamed of his illness.

As soon as he was strong enough to lift his arms he begged the master of novices to give him some work, writing, or accounts to keep. He was present at the offices on a stretcher but between these services he was obliged to be idle and was afraid of falling into temptation. Sickness was too bound up with memories of Marie, and he was particularly anxious not to become involved, by the weakness of his body, in day-dreams which he might not be able to control.

Brother Izembard ordered him to say his rosary and he did so very conscientiously, but in the prayers which he whispered over and over again the name of Marie recurred hundreds and thousands of times: *Ave Maria gratia plena—Sancta Maria, mater Dei;* he would have preferred to meditate on the Rule.

"*Ave Maria gratia plena*—Marie full of grace, O cornflower-crowned friend, friend and mother of pain, mother of my heart. I had no mother but you. What use is it that I no longer desire your body if my heart returns to you and it is your hand I want on my brow to still my pain?"

Saying over his rosary he was afraid lest, envisaging Our Lady with the features of Marie, he commit the most dreadful sacrilege.

He had borne these same pains in chest and legs while thinking of Marie, because of her, and for her, and now here was his body, more persistent than his heart, plunging him back into that love of which he had thought himself cured.

"O my God, I thank You for the grace conferred upon me in having given me a broken body which resists my will, like an image of my sinful soul, so that I feel all the ugliness of sin even in my very veins and nerves. If I can win no command over my body, what chance have I over my soul? You alone can say to me: 'Take up thy bed and walk.' You alone can deliver me from my heart.

"Oh, I am indeed my father's son since even when doing the simplest of tasks I manage to think not of God, but of the tree; that, I shall never be cured of. I made both an idol and an enemy even out of that splendid tree which God planted as an ornament of the earth and for the service of mankind. When a man has passion in his body, what matter the object it chooses?

"Father, accept me as I am, for I know that everything about me is unclean and even my love for You is impure and mixed with evil thoughts. Order me not to think of You, since my thinking is impure.

"O God, You gave me a father whom I judged wicked—and who was so—may I say it without sinning! And that father You gave me, O Father, in order that I should not dare imagine You with an impure mind: the man on earth to whom, above all, I owed loyalty, Your image for me in this world, was that man and none other. And You caused him to suffer martyrdom by my means and under my eyes, O God, that I might judge You to be even more cruel than he was; that I do not understand, O God, and I swear to You that this was cruelty to Yourself; but still I obey You even so, for I know, I know for certain, that You are such that a man can love no other thing in this world but You.

"None but You can a man love, You whom he can neither see nor imagine with his mind.

"Kill, then, my mind.

"May it be like the mirror which, in her wisdom, my lady gave me to make me understand that nothing could protect me unless it might be that shield on which there was no device but that which could contain all the heavens and the sun. May my shield in Your sight, O God, be that plain, polished steel, reflecting Your light back to You even though I cannot see it.

"O my God, our will is no more than that of the stone which rolls and falls where it has been pushed; our heart, like the beast of the woods, seeking warmth and sustenance wherever it can find them, without being able to see reason. I have naught but my body to bring to You, Lord, and it is broken. But You can take it even from the grave, if it be Your will to make use of it."

One day, during mass, while the brothers were singing the *Sanctus*, Brother Ernaut rose from his stretcher and took his place beside the other novices and began to sing at the top of his voice as he had not sung for two years; he had a strong and beautiful voice, like his father's, and at the castle of Coucy, in Normandy, it had always been he who led the singing in the choirs. All the brothers turned their heads, surprised at the sound of that splendid voice which they had never heard before. But he himself was too intoxicated with the song to notice their surprise or even to realize that this was the first time for so very long that he had sung in this fashion.

The novices were singing the plain chant in the vernacular, an indulgence which was permitted them at mass on weekdays.

> *Cist aigneaus est li sires qui onques ne menti,*
> *Agnus Dei qui tollis peccata mundi, miserere nobis.*

C'est cil que le péchié effaça et tolli
Agnus Dei qui tollis peccata mundi, miserere nobis.
C'est cil qui se beaux bras en la croix estendi.
Agnus Dei qui tollis peccata mundi, miserere nobis.
C'est cil qui par sa mort la nostre mort perdi
Et en resuscitant la vie nous rendi. . . .
Et remonta au ciel là d'où il descendi.[1]

Domine non sum dignus.

And although he had not been to confession since the day when he had received Extreme Unction, Brother Ernaut was among the first of the novices to step forward to take Communion, receiving the Host from the abbot's hands.

He remained on his feet until the end of the mass, singing the prayers of thanksgiving, and his full, grave voice dominated the others. After the mass and the kiss of peace, he took his place in the file of his comrades as they left the chapel and walked round the cloisters on their way to the chapter house with folded arms and bowed heads. His expression was so tranquil that no one would have recognized in him the invalid who had lain prostrate on his stretcher an hour before. Such was the power of this inward tranquillity, reflected in his face, that his comrades no longer stared at him as they had at the moment when they had first heard his voice; all of them looked, as he did, as if nothing at all unusual had happened.

Nobody, not even the abbot, ever dared speak to him of his sudden cure. After None, Brother Izembard sent for him and told him that the abbot had need of him to keep accounts and write letters.

"But," he said, "if I ever find you fallen asleep again I shall have you set to cleaning out the byres."

Brother Ernaut said nothing but he could not prevent himself from smiling his wide smile, so full of goodwill and good-humor that it was infectious. And the old man, although by no means a happy-natured man, was tempted to put his hand on the novice's shoulder and to say a

---

[1] This lamb is the Lord who never lied—
He who washed out and abolished sin—
He who stretched out his beautiful arms on the cross—
He who purchased life for us with his death.
Who gave us life by his resurrection
And ascended to Heaven whence he had descended.

few words of smiling friendliness; but he controlled the too profane impulse and frowned to keep himself in countenance. It was, however, a wasted effort: he was well aware that the other had read his feelings in his eyes and was doubly grateful for them, albeit he was barely able to detect the slightest glimmer of conspiratorial banter in Brother Ernaut's grey eyes.

Thenceforth Brother Ernaut became the abbot's accountant and secretary and addressed himself all the more keenly to the work in that he was competent; not for nothing had he managed the estates of the lady Isabeau and his father. As a novice he was not barred from dealing personally with the peasants in the matter of harvesting, and he supervised the handing over of gifts promised to the monastery by its lay or religious friends. As a monk he still retained the scrupulous and somewhat miserly qualities he had shown as an intendant and bailiff, nor did he regret this, contenting himself with confessing it to the master of novices for whom he had developed a sincere affection. He was inclined to stick a little too closely to the letter of the words, *super pauca fidelis*. The monastery's material assets were, altogether, not very impressive. He knew it, but they had been entrusted to him and it was a question of increasing them in so far as that lay within his power.

Since he knew himself to be forgiven he was no longer afraid of falling into sin—which he did, however, a hundred times a day and paid no attention to it. It was not for becoming more virtuous that God had forgiven him—he had no opportunity of becoming more virtuous than he was. He had his eight hours a day of divine services which nourished him more than the bread he ate and he was as grateful for the one as for the other; nor was it a trifling thing to be able to sing as he sang now and thus to glorify God by means of his body. What is a wicked thought? A splinter in the hand, a sty on the eye, and the brother who is prevented from working and praying by such small matters is not worth his salt.

"Marie, loyal friend, may God grant that I be such a man that you will not need to blush for him whom, in your great goodness, you chose. You will never know, my sole treasure in this world, the good you have done me. Had it been permitted, I should have written to tell you, but still you will manage to understand; for God guided you in spite of yourself, as He guided me in spite of myself.

"O candid friend, if only you could know that you are here, present in all my prayers, in my blood and my flesh, and that I take not a mouthful of bread without wishing to share it with you. You are my sister in God and I shall remain your knight until Judgment Day. As the flower on the bank and the sun in the heavens, so is your pure beauty. God did not order us to put out our eyes; but that man would be raving mad who wanted to eat the sun.

"That is why I know, now, that there is no more sin in loving you than there is in living; may God deliver you from all suffering, friend; to you I owe my rebirth into life.

"May you suffer no remorse or pain because of me. O weak woman, I should prefer to be forgotten by you forever rather than that the memory of me should cause you pain. I know that I can never right the wrong I did you in trying to sully your purity. But I should be happy if God gave me the means to make you think of me without bitterness, as of a friend who trusted you.

"Sweetheart, it is a great deal to be like the sun in a man's heaven, O proud one who tried to be my God because you knew that I could love none but God."

Now his particular sin was that of excessive yearning after the white frock of a brother and thinking with too much passion of the day when he would put off his own clothes and place his petition on the altar. So much was this the case that the master of novices, happening to catch a look of too eloquent concupiscence for a white frock, was obliged to point out:

"Brother Ernaut, it is well said that it is not the frock that makes the monk. If that holy garment should be, for you, an object of greed, there is a great risk that you may never wear it."

The novice bowed without speaking, to thank him for his observation, but the other detected something like an involuntary reproach in his large, lively eyes: "How can I not be greedy for it? Should I be here, otherwise?" "Novice fervor," the old man thought. "But he's quite capable of keeping it up for two years."

On the eve of Saint-Martin's Day Brother Ernaut was in the court-yard with the prior, busy measuring pieces of coarse worsted with an ell-stick; the woollen cloth had been brought as a donation and was destined for the poor of the neighboring village on the occasion of the holy day. Brother Ernaut was stretching the cloth a little, counting up the number of cloaks which could be cut from it. At that moment a stranger entered the courtyard, accompanied by a brother leading a horse by the bridle. The unknown was a young man, dark and lean, with the stiff bearing of a military man. Brother Ernaut raised his eyes at the sound of the horse's hoofs and immediately, forgetting the rule, and the prior's presence, threw himself into the newcomer's arms.

"Adam!"

The two young men kissed and looked long at each other, surprised, and unable to recover from the effect of their feelings. Then Brother Ernaut introduced his one-time squire to the prior and apologized for his incorrect behavior.

"You are but a novice, Brother Ernaut, and still belong to the world," the prior said. "If this young man has news for you, I give you permission to interrupt your work."

Brother Ernaut led his friend to the guest room, where there was a fire.

He could do nothing but repeat: "Adam, Adam, lad." And he was so happy that he did not even think of asking the reason for this unexpected visit. Adam, also, was too glad at this reunion with his old friend and master to be able to speak.

"Here, warm yourself, take off your gloves. Lauds will be ringing shortly, but we have a little time. Let me look at you. You've been to war, that's obvious. We hardly hear any news here, but we had a high mass of thanksgiving and everything. Adam! tell me: you didn't come simply to see me? No, don't tell me. Wait: if Pierre or my son-in-law had been killed in the battle, I'd have heard of it before, shouldn't I? Don't tell me anything. My daughter—she's well, isn't she?"

Adam lowered his eyes.

"She is in good health."

"And—and my sister?"

"She also is well. I might as well tell you at once. The lady Isabeau died last Sunday at Matins. God keep her soul. They say she had something wrong internally since her confinement."

"Adam!"

Haguenier laid his head on the table and burst into tears.

Never would he have believed that the death of this woman, to whom, very much in spite of himself, he had been faithful as a husband, would hit him so hard. He bit his lip and stiffened his muscles, trying to recover his calm, swallowing the tears which were running into his mouth.

"Tell me Adam, did she suffer much pain?"

"I think she did. I was not there. I am in Master Pierre's service at Troyes. She was buried on Wednesday. Your son-in-law, the knight of Traînel, our lord, sent me to you about your daughter. You have not yet taken your final vows, so it is for you to decide. Do you want to make her a ward of the lady of Bernon or of your sister? Both of them want to be her guardian. His lordship said: 'So long as she is not of age, it's for her father to decide.' "

"He'd have done better to make the decision himself. I am not on the spot. And I don't want to annoy either my grandmother or my sister."

"Sir Pons of Traînel is of the same opinion."

"Of course. There's Lauds chiming. We will talk after the service."

Brother Ernaut wiped his eyes and went to join the other novices, who were entering the chapel. He applied himself to singing the psalms, trying to master his voice broken by tears. Dead. He had dreamed of her several times—unclean dreams. Fortunate, at least, that the Devil only sent the figment of his legal wife to tempt him. But now she was dead. He had had a certain affection for her. He had wronged her; she had not forgiven him the divorce. And she had always behaved very well to him.

"O God, tell me what I ought to do. Now, once again, I have decisions to make touching a life; once again you are confronting me with my sin. Why did you have to leave my child an orphan, without either mother or father? I know that it is not Your will that I return to the world. And my little daughter is left without a mother, at the mercy of strangers."

After Lauds he asked Brother Izembard's permission to write a letter to his son-in-law, to settle a family matter.

"To Pons of Traînel, knight, seneschal at Bar-sur-Aube. Most beloved son-in-law and brother in Christ.

"Noble and beloved son-in-law, you have done me the service of informing me, through Adam, of the death of the lady of Villemor, who was formerly my spouse and friend. God rest her soul in Paradise. In the matter of my daughter, you are united to her by promise of marriage and you are her lord and her protector, therefore it is my duty to refer to you any matter concerning her education. I have the fullest confidence in you, and if you consider, upon your honor, that she will be better in the care of the lady your mother or any other person among your kinswomen I shall defer to your decision joyfully.

"But since you have been so courteous as to inquire my wishes in the matter, I will inform you of them frankly and thereafter leave you to act as you think best. I should not wish to hurt the lady my grandmother nor the lady of Pouilli, my sister. But I am bound to think first of my daughter and to ensure that she be brought up suitably to her rank and acquire all the perfections of her sex: piety and courtesy and all the accomplishments of mind and body, such as writing, music and the art of speaking well, and all fine needlework, hawking and venery. But above all I am bound to think of her soul, to ensure that she learn to think nobly and beautifully and have an honest heart. In all these matters I can think of only one person who could be to her at once a guide and an example, and that is the lady Marie of Baudemant, wife of Sir Foulque of Mongenost near Troyes. You are aware that, when in the world, I myself took an oath of chaste and courteous devotion to this lady; and, since she accepted me as her vassal, she could not refuse my request.

"She is a lady of such exalted qualities that not even a duke need blush to entrust his daughter to her; nor do I believe that either my grandmother or my sister would be angry, knowing my child to be in such good hands. It would be my wish that henceforth, from the age when she is beginning to talk and to recognize people, she might live under the influence of this lady and learn to love her. I shall therefore beg you to allot, on my behalf, a good pension to Oda, my daughter's wet-nurse, and to appoint a maidservant for the care of her clothes; and to make a gift to the lady of the necklace of beryls which I inherited from my mother; and to Sir Foulque, her spouse, my ceremonial harness of Toulouse work, with the silver plates and turquoises, that they may accept these gifts as a token of my gratitude. For I shall owe them a thousand times more if the lady agrees to accept my daughter into her care and to make an accomplished woman of her. Let neither the lady nor the knight, her spouse, take this for presumption on my part, but as evidence of my great esteem for them.

"If, for any reason, you consider this arrangement unsuitable, most beloved son-in-law, I leave you at liberty to follow your own judgment.

But I repeat that as far as I am concerned my wishes are positively as I have written them and not otherwise.

"With this, I pray that God our Lord, His glorious Mother and Saint Mary Magdalene may keep you always under their holy care and protection, you and all your kin.

"Haguenier deceased, lord of Linnières and of Hervi, now Brother Ernaut, novice."

Before giving the letter to Adam, Haguenier asked Brother Izembard to read it. He frowned and said that he understood nothing of family matters, especially among the nobility. "It does not seem right to me," he said, "that you should try to take your daughter out of the hands of her natural relations, but I suppose that you know them better than I do. You are still free and I leave you to judge for yourself whether or not what you are doing is a sin. But I should wish you to give me your word that there has been no sin between this woman and you."

"Should I have dreamed of entrusting my daughter to her otherwise? I give you my word since you insist."

Adam left on the morrow, with the letter. When saying goodbye to him Haguenier's heart was full; never had he thought to be so fond of his squire. Indeed Pierre and their grandmother and Aielot and all his friends were now dearer to him than they had ever been, and nearer. But now there was more peace in his heart: it was as if the sight of Adam and news from his own part of the world had made him realize more clearly how firmly he was planted in his new life; he had not experienced an instant's regret nor any wish to resume his old life.

It was Brother Ernaut who had talked to Adam and wept over Dame Isabeau. It had not even occurred to him that this resurgence of his past could be a temptation. A great delight and a great grief—and he had accepted both as the gift of God. But his life was so filled with work and prayer that he no longer had either the right or the leisure to think of it.

He did not know that his hardest trials were yet to come.

THE LAST PILGRIMAGE

THE months passed. The rainy season had come and the old man had long ceased from turning the mill. He had fallen ill and a villager, a potter named Ali, had taken him into his house out of charity, his house being a kind of dark and stinking hole, half dug out of the cliff face, where he lived with his wife, his children, his goats and his dog. The prisoners who had been working on the fortifications were no longer there. They had been taken to Naplouse for resale.

The old man stayed huddled in his corner beside the goats which, from time to time, licked him and rubbed against him. He no longer noticed the strong smell of urine which pervaded the house and liked the breath and warmth of the two animals. The fever was exhausting him and he shivered under the cover which his host had thrown over him. Sometimes one of the potter's little girls brought him water or came and crouched beside him to pick off his fleas, for he had not the strength to do it himself and was so infested with vermin that they even got into his mouth and nostrils. The little girl—she was five or six years old—greatly enjoyed catching them and making them pop between her teeth. For her the *nazir* was an unusual but nowise frightening object, whose company entailed no risk of a wound from horns or claws or even of a slap, and who sometimes uttered strange words which made her laugh. Sometimes, if she pulled his beard or beat him with a willow twig, he muttered mechanically, "*Il an' dînak,*"[1] without anger. It was like an agreed sign; this conventional and familiar swearword made the Christian a man like other men, only not ill-natured, and the child would show all her pretty, white teeth in a smile and bring her thin, malicious face close to his, trying to catch a look from his eye, not understanding that he could not see her.

But he was aware of her look, like a touch, and her sweet breath and the child's warm laughter, and began to be fond of her. A score of times every day he would call, "*Ya, Munira,*" and the child would

[1] God curse your faith!

come running to crouch beside him, tucking her little bare feet into the hollow under his shoulder and resuming her hunt for his fleas.

Little by little the potter's whole family had become accustomed to the Christian. Like the wife and children, he ate the remains of the master's meals. Munira brought him his share on an earthenware plate and laughed to see him make the sign of the cross before lifting the food to his mouth, and was rewarded by a round oath which made her laugh all the more, delighted to discover that the Christian was not as stupid as he looked.

The potter's wife did her cooking on a charcoal fire near the door. Neighbors sometimes came to crouch round her for a gossip while giving suck to their infants or delousing their little girls. The old man listened to their sharp, scolding voices and to their speech, sounding, to him, like a yapping, and he thought: "Women are certainly the same everywhere—no need to understand what they say—baptized or not, there's as much sense in magpie's chatter as in theirs."

On the whole it diverted him.

Children, too, were the same everywhere; as a child Eglantine had cried in the same way as these little unbelievers and laughed like Munira. Sometimes he would bounce Munira on his knees and sing her songs and kiss her cheeks; and the little girl, never caressed by her parents, had at first been frightened, then, going to the other extreme, had become passionately attached to the Frank and came to take refuge in his arms when she was sleepy or after a beating. Then he would cradle and warm her in his arms.

The mother said nothing; the man was not dangerous for the excellent reason that, being blind, he could not have the evil eye. And she would give him her last-born to nurse and rock when the infant would not stop crying.

Ansiau, chatelain of Linnières, was even more humiliated by this task of being a nurse to children than by that of turning the mill—unbaptized children are, after all, little better than animals; even baptized children are women's business and he would never have thought that the end of his days would see him doing a woman's work. But the flesh is weak, and that little, dirty body inspired in him more pity than disgust. He had always felt a tenderness even for the young of animals; how many little bear cubs had he not brought in and tamed, and antelope fawns, after the mother had been killed? He shifted the baby from one arm to the other and gave him his finger to suck, and mocked at himself a little, thinking: "Lucky, at least, that they don't ask me to suckle him!"

When the baby Omar was asleep at last he was glad, and not only because the child's crying wearied him.

But Munira was quite another matter: he imagined her swarthy, with large, dark eyes and white teeth, for thus are the children of the heathen. There had been a touch of the heathen about Eglantine, for all she was baptized; yes, to be sure, it was absurd to become attached to this creature, given up to the demon, a hand-maiden of Mahomet.

Well, but am I, myself, any better than an animal, now?

He was an object of ridicule to those Arab peasants who sometimes came to the potter's house and threw lumps of mutton, already gnawed to the bone, to the Frankish slave. He did not deign to pick them up or he gave them to the dog. The men laughed and called him a "wood worshipper." Ali was a not entirely ill-natured man; he was still young and one who enjoyed a joke; he was not fond of the Franks, to be sure, but this one was a poor, blind wretch whom he had taken into his house like a stray dog; one does not require a famished animal to believe in the Prophet, nor a Christian. But sometimes, after a good meal, he amused himself a little at the Frank's expense, not maliciously, but as a man may laugh at a child.

He would give him bits of wood, saying that they were wood from the True Cross and that he ought to worship them. The old man could understand quite well that their jesting was not ill-natured, even though they despised him a little as being addicted to a crude superstition—for them, *he* was the infidel, and he could hardly be angry with them. Nevertheless it was hard to hear his religion made game of. As a kind of defiance, he had collected all their bits of wood and had carved them with the blade of a broken knife so that they fitted into each other and together composed a cross. This cross he had hung on the wall in the corner which he shared with the goats. Let them learn, poor ignoramuses, that since the day when God had allowed himself to be nailed to a wooden cross wood had become holier and nobler than the purest gold. How could their laughter profane his cross? Was not God Himself spat upon? When he prayed, he touched his cross so fervently that the potter and his friends no longer dared laugh at him; and when, out of curiosity, they gave him more bits of wood—remains of a broken beam or a rotten rafter—he accepted them calmly and used them to enlarge or decorate his cross.

The rains were over. Winter was come with frost, winds and snow which lashed the faces of the sentries on the wall and those of the travellers going to Naplouse, their mules loaded with jars and pots for sale in the town. The old man had learned to regulate his life by the muezzin's calls to prayer, to which he had become so accustomed that as soon as he heard them he made the sign of the cross and began to say his own prayers—without ever forgetting to begin by cursing the faith of Mahomet. On his knees, with his hands upon his big wooden cross, he prayed, ignoring the potter's family who, engaged in their own devotions, left him in peace. Munira sometimes came and cuddled up to him but at these times he would push her away quite roughly, whereupon she would kneel beside him and copy all his movements, crossing herself and bowing down to the ground and casting covert glances at the Frank to see whether he approved of her. Her parents, who had spotted this little trick, merely laughed at it—a girl, well, it's not like a boy. Let her amuse herself aping the Christian as long as it kept her out of mischief.

Since none of the children fell sick that winter, Salma, the potter's wife, had taken it into her head to regard the Frank as a kind of holy man and, without her husband's knowledge, gave him olives and dried figs, and sometimes combed his hair and beard and washed his feet; she firmly believed in the miracles performed at the graves of Christian hermits and venerated Our Lady of Tortosa; like all women of the people she believed that there could not be too many saints and holy places to protect children from sickness and the harvest from bad weather and pillage.

Her husband laughed at her superstition but he had become very attached to the Frankish slave. The man had a wide and simple smile, a grave voice, and knew enough Arabic to answer back to abuse or say thank you, never forgetting to touch head and heart in token of gratitude, as believers do, so that one could not quite look on him as a mere savage. And Ali, while he could not but consider the worship of a piece of wood as ridiculous, was not far from regarding the old man's cross as a kind of talisman which might bring his house good luck. Allah could inform even idolaters with his wisdom. This particular idolater certainly had a pure heart and might well have become a convert if only there had been a learned man available to teach him the true faith.

One day Fatima, Ali's neighbor, came to Salma carrying her newly born son in her arms. It was only five days since his eyes had been uncovered; he would not take the breast and was fading away. She said that she wanted to have him blessed by the Frank. Let him sprinkle the child with water and say the sacred words of the Christians over him; it was known that the Christians saved their own children after this fashion. All the muezzin's prayers had been unavailing.

The old man flatly refused. He was not a healer and knew no incantations of that sort; he had a certain skill in the right words to say for horses but not for children. He became even angrier when he realized that they were asking him to baptize the child. That was a sacrament of God, "a holy thing pertaining to Allah," he explained, "and he could not do it if the child was to live like a dog thereafter and pray to Mahomet. Did they have empty jars in place of heads? Did they not know that the thing was forbidden by their faith?"

It must be supposed that the old man did not know enough of the language to make the women understand the difficulty. The mother was weeping. Her other children were only daughters. This was her first son. She had been full of joy at his birth. Ibn' Ismail, her husband, had given a sheep to be sacrificed. Was she condemned to be forever without a son, an object of contempt in her family? Here was little Yousouf, the light of her life, dying before her eyes, and there was nothing left for her to do but to put out those same eyes that she might not see him die and to tear open her breasts to rid herself of her now useless milk. Salma, too, was lamenting, and her daughters crying at the tops of their voices; the old man, stupefied by their noise, waited patiently for them to finish. He felt pity for them. But what can a man do against women's foolishness? Fatima put the infant on to his knees.

"There, he's dying, he's hardly breathing. If you bless him, perhaps he will live."

And the old man ran his hands over the cold and emaciated little body and told himself that there could not, indeed, be much hope for the child.

Thereupon he made up his mind and called for a jug of water.

"Since he's dying, I shall at least save his soul," he thought. "Why should an innocent child go to Hell?" And he trickled water on to the child's forehead and baptized him Jean, in the name of the Father and the Son and the Holy Ghost. The women, crouching in front of him, watched him do it, open-mouthed and full of terror. Then Fatima, shaking all over, took back her son and offered him her breast, and he took the breast and began to suck.

That same evening Ibn' Ismail, Fatima's husband, came to see the Christian to present him with a woollen cloak as a token of gratitude. He was sure, he said, that his son was saved and would live. And the old man was more put out than pleased, for he had no wish whatever to be taken for a village sorcerer and moreover now found himself responsible for a Christian soul who was going to be forced to deny God and serve Mahomet. He refused the gift and sent Ibn' Ismail away with harsh words; it was Allah whom he should thank; he himself had done nothing and did not know how to do anything—all that was naught but women's superstitions. The other swore that he was his servant forever and that he wished to treat him as his father and give him a place in his house. Ansiau wasted his breath calling him the son of a Jew and even the son of a Christian and invoking on his head the curses of Allah for this foolishness; Ibn' Ismail persisted in believing that the Frank was a holy man who denied himself the gratitude of others only out of humility.

"O my God, I know very well that Your sacrament is a mighty matter, for the body as for the soul, and that You take pity even upon a fledgling fallen from the nest. I know that I should praise You for having taken pity on this woman and allowed her baby to live. But then my own child is dead, for all my prayers. My own beautiful child. O God, if this child is to be to his heathen father what mine was to me, grant that he may grow up and not die when he is twenty years old. But it is a great pity that Your holy sacrament was profaned like that. I swear to You that it was through no fault of mine.

"O my God, why do You make me live among these heathen folk who know not Your name? To be sure, I do not despise them, they are Your creatures. But it is hard when I think that I shall never again hear Your name uttered by a Christian tongue. Where is Auberi? Perhaps I sent him to his death; and I still live. Christmas is past and

I did not hear the song sung, the song in which the angels glorified You on that night; Easter is coming, but for me there will be no Holy Week."

With the approach of spring the old man asked to be led out upon the ramparts which gave on to the south, over the valley, that he might pray there with his face towards Jerusalem. The winter had weakened him; he had lost the habit of walking and was now suffering from more and more frequent bouts of coughing and fever. It seemed that staying still and resting for four whole months had exhausted him more than two years of walking and fatigues. By now all the potter's family were attending to him as if he were one of them and Ibn' Ismail sent him the best pieces from his table every day. He was no longer infested with vermin and slept upon a mat which was more or less clean, but he clung to his corner, with the goats and his wooden cross. And he languished like a caged eagle. Not even Munira could make him smile often. He thought: "My strength is gone, my life done; it will not be long now." And a sadness overcame him, a mortal sadness, animal in quality, the sadness of a beast which knows that it is going to die, and die far from its lair.

Never before had he felt anything like it. It was as if he had forgotten his past life and its misfortunes. He hardly even thought of Bertrand any more. He would, he thought, like to be lying in a wood, beside a stream, smelling the scent of damp earth and moss and hearing the cuckoo call. He would have liked to eat wood strawberries again and to rest upon fresh-cut hay smelling of mint and clover. He even found it difficult to pray; he would have liked to hear the sound of bells instead of the muezzin's call to prayer.

When Munira led him, his hand in hers, along the narrow village street, he walked slowly like a very old man, dragging his numbed feet. The children in the street, the women carrying jars of water on their heads and the craftsmen working at the doors of their houses drew back a little at the passage of this tall, swarthy man, wide-shouldered, lean, who walked stiffly with his head held high and who, with his long, curling beard, had the look of some prophet of antiquity. It was known that he had cured Ibn' Ismail's son by a miracle and he was considered to be a magician, if not a holy man. The women stopped their chatter when he came in sight and prevented the children from teasing him, while the men greeted him with a deferential *essalamlik*, to which he felt obliged to reply. But nothing, not even the camel-driver's blows nor his work at the mill, had humiliated him so much as this respect by which he felt himself surrounded. He was, to be sure, no more modest than the next man; he would have enjoyed being respected as a good soldier by other soldiers, even heathen. But a respect inappropriate to a man's qualities is an insult, and what could the esteem of peasants who took him for something other than he was be worth to him? That, too, he was forced to suffer without too ill a grace, for after all these people were good to him. It was not their fault that they were stupid.

Arrived on the ramparts he turned his head in the direction of Jerusalem, opening wide the lids of his dead eye as if he might still hope to see the holy city. It was a few leagues away. Local men made pilgrimages there, to the mosque of Omar; men from Naplouse were passing along the road below the ramparts and the old man could hear the bells on their camels and the cries of the mule drivers. He breathed the mountain air, which must come from there, possessed again by his absurd and obstinate desire, even stronger than homesickness, to lay his head upon the stones of the Holy Sepulchre and to hear mass there, where the body of Jesus Christ had rested. He had seen Jerusalem for the first time when Baldwin the leper was king, when it was a Christian city full of churches and monasteries; the second time, under Saladin, it had been decorated with green flags bearing the crescent, and the churches had been transformed into mosques. But though they had razed the city, the Holy Sepulchre would still have been there, and Calvary, and the Mount of Olives. Lord, our bodies are born wherever You may will; but our souls are born in Jerusalem.

Munira, seated at the old man's feet, was playing with her wooden doll and singing it an old lullaby of Champagne which the Frank had taught her. From time to time she would tug at the old man's hand to ask him whether her doll was not beautiful. He said:

"*Ma'ma, ya sghyrat*—Yes, little one." For her, at least, he was not blind. She would call out to him to look at an eagle gliding overhead or a horseman passing along the road, laughing and clapping her hands when he "looked" the wrong way: she was astonished that he could be so silly, and he would join in her laughter.

"Little heathen one, you'll have been more charitable to me than anyone else ever has and you don't even know it. And I *do* see you, Munira. You are the prettiest little girl in the world and your doll the prettiest doll; you can believe your old Frank when he tells you so. Perhaps I shall die before you come to understand that the Frank has nothing behind his eyes but a hole full of darkness."

The hills were bright with anemones and fragrant with lavender, thyme and rosemary and in the bush every shrub bore pink or white or yellow roses; their scent was so strong that the whole village was drenched with it. The slightest breath of wind carried the scent of flowers to mix with the stench of urine and rancid fat and fresh manure and cooking; all these smells, in the sharp, pure air of spring, were pleasant to the nostrils and filled the heart with joy. The sky was full of migrant birds of passage, herons, storks and swallows, and the air vibrant with their calls. "Will some of them be on their way to my country?" the old man wondered, thinking of the swallows which nested beneath the roof of the keep. "My life's finished. Neither living nor dead, lady. O my country! Spring in Champagne—lavender has a sweeter smell there, and thyme and rosemary—water a sweeter taste, the very manure a sharper odor."

The season of Easter drew near and the old man was in despair, not knowing exactly which day it would be. He attempted to calculate it from the Moslem months and asked Ali where the moon was; there were Syrian Christians at Naplouse, there must be some means of knowing when they were to celebrate their Easter. At the beginning of Holy Week—or the week he took to be such—he asked Ali to lead him, out of courtesy, to some place apart where he could devote himself to prayer in solitude, and also to give him the means to wash his body and to trim his hair and beard. Ali did not dare take one of the uncircumcised to the baths or the village fountain but he took him beyond the fortifications to a little cedar wood, bringing him a jar of water, a little oil and some wool-shears. For several days Munira led him there each morning, returning to fetch him at evening. There, alone, far from the noises of the village, for hours at a time he stayed prostrate, his face pressed to the earth, or on his knees, calculating the time by the muezzin's calls, saying over to himself as well as he could whatever he could recall of the psalms and chants of the day. He had cleared a small area at the foot of one of the cedars and had hung a cross made of branches against the trunk and above it his own body-cross containing relics of Saint Peter, so that he might at least say his prayers before a consecrated object.

Washing himself had been far from easy; he was so encrusted with dirt that he had ended by almost flaying himself through rubbing his body with sand and ashes, for he could not afford to waste water. His clothes were rotten, so that after being washed they were nothing but rags and so stiff that they chafed his skin. Fine raiment, indeed, in which to appear before God on an Easter Day! And on Good Friday he could not prevent himself from cursing the infidels, whom he could hear chanting their prayers for a longer time than on other days; he knew that these were impious prayers, in which the Holy Ghost was denied and the true faith cursed.

"O my God, may You confound them, who jeer at Your Passion on so sacred a day!

"O God, here all the earth is in mourning; the trees weep their sap, the flowers close up, the birds call sadly. And there were men who denied You, O God, even most faithful Saint Peter. My God, I abandoned You, and I am far from You and surrounded by heathen. Yet even so forget not, I pray You, Your bad servant, unable to honor You as he should, profaned as he is by contact with unclean infidels."

Munira led him back to the house and he remained silent, speaking neither to Ali nor to his wife, that he might not soil his mouth with a heathen tongue during such a solemn time.

On the morning of Easter Sunday Salma placed upon his knees, without saying a word, a woollen shirt, new and clean. And he bowed his head, not daring to thank her, because he was ashamed—had he not been living on the charity of these people for six months? Slowly, he traced with his hand a big sign of the cross over the shirt.

Seated at the threshold of the door, the old man heard wedding processions passing, the bridegroom going to the baths to the sound of tambourines and cymbals and returning at evening amidst singing and dancing, escorted by boys carrying torches. Then came the long choruses and chants of the wedding feast, filling the whole village with their monotonous refrain which, to the old Frank, seemed sad rather than gay—*ya habbabah, ya habbabah*—and the piercing, stunning noise of the tambourines which beat and beat interminably, late into the night. From the mountains could be heard the mournful cry of owls and the howling of jackals.

Then came the season of hard work; mules came up to the village loaded with baskets of olives and figs and the earth reverberated with

the blows of flails thrashing the barley and millet. Little Omar, Ali's
son, could already crawl and could clamber up on to the old man's
knees, and Salma had a new son at her breast. Halimah, Ali's eldest
daughter, had already left her father's house to the sound of cymbals
and by the light of torches.

During spring the old man had decorated his wooden cross with
flowers, and at harvest time he had woven a wreath of ripe barley for
it which delighted Munira and also the goats who, during the night,
nibbled both flowers and grain. To the *mullah*, who had reproached
Ali with encouraging heathen practices, the potter had answered that
the Frank was his guest.

After *Ramadan*, exhausted by obligatory fasting, the old man suffered
another bout of fever; he sent for Ibn' Ismail and said to him:

"You are my *habib*, my friend, as you told me. Order your nephew
to guide me to Jerusalem, that I may die there. I am a burden here,
not a servant; they will let me go."

Ibn' Ismail was very glad to be able to do a service to the man who
had saved his son; but the Frank was the emir's property, and only
the emir could liberate him. The emir, well informed by the eunuch,
his major-domo, refused to give liberty to a man who was said to be a
healer. On the contrary, he would bring the man into his palace,
especially since his favorite wife had been born a Frank and would be
glad to have a holy man of her own country in the house. When Ibn'
Ismail reported this answer to the Frank the old man could not hold
back his tears, turning away in silence and pressing his forehead to the
cross fixed to the wall.

Old, blind and sick, were still more demands to be made on him?
He would not have complained if he had had to remain in Ali's house,
sharing his corner with the goats. But now, because of silly women's
chatter, he was again to become an object of ridicule, like an ape at a
fair, to be a pastime for a female renegade, and she the concubine of a
heathen. To think that he had believed himself to have plumbed the
depths of humiliation on the day that he was harnessed to a beam, like
an ass! He had been born free and dubbed knight and no man had any
right to ask more of him than his mere body.

Once shut up in the palace, he would no longer be allowed to go up
to the ramparts, would no longer have Munira to guide him. A "holy
man," indeed! Aye, he was just the kind of holy man they deserved,

the imbeciles, and in fact even a man like him was too good for them. Since they would not even leave him there in peace, a crazy idea recurred to him, an idea which he had often had before but which he had rejected as too absurd. He would set off for Jerusalem alone. He had a staff. He would go out by the main gate with the shepherds, early in the morning, just to take the air on the hill with Munira. Who would suspect him of trying to escape? He would go down to the road and wait to be picked up by the first travellers who saw him. He could very well pass for a native beggar. Even if he were recaptured, what had he to lose?

That evening, Ali and his wife ate their meal in silence, sad at having to part with their guest. The emir's servants were to come for him in the morning to take him to the palace. "You'll be better off there than here," Ali said. The old man made him no answer, he had not opened his mouth all day long. Munira had fallen asleep on his lap and he stroked her hair.

That night he concealed, in his sash, a few dried figs which he had put aside, with a few handfuls of barley, took down one of Ali's gourds from where it hung on the wall and filled it with water from the big jar which stood by the door. He always felt at his best at night; he had learned to move noiselessly and to tell from the sound of their breathing whether his hosts were asleep or not. He knew that they could not see him and were, as it were, disarmed, whereas he could feel and hear as well as in broad daylight. He hung the gourd on his belt; nobody would see it under his ample woollen cloak.

Then he set himself to take his wooden cross to pieces, bit by bit, for he did not want to leave it to the mercy of infidels. He tore his shirt in two, put the pieces of wood into one half and made the whole up into a package easy enough to carry on his shoulder. It occurred to him that it would be rather heavy to carry, but he would not have far to go. The road was only three hundred paces below the village.

Then he lay down and, too excited to sleep, began stroking the horns and muzzles of the two goats and to speak to them softly in their animal language, as he was accustomed to do. The goats were very fond of him; they rubbed against him and licked his face.

"Who will talk to them at night now? Surely animals, too, need friendship. Tomorrow I shall be far away, my pretties. I hope, in fact, that you will never see me again."

And he felt young again, and wanted to laugh like a child contemplating mischief. "No doubt about it," he thought, "I'm in my second childhood. What sensible man would do what I'm doing? If old people did not turn foolish life would be too sad for them. What have I to lose, now?"

He was sorry that he would not be able to take leave of Ali and his wife and Ibn' Ismail; he could not allow himself to do so. He knew that Ibn' Ismail would have made it a point of honor to escort him personally to Jerusalem; he had no right to involve the man in disloyalty to his lord. Munira? She would forget him in a week.

Morning: the sun was beginning to warm up and the mountains beyond the olive groves were blue. The village of Yasuf lay white and stone-grey within its walls, its little houses seemingly piled one upon the other, and the white and azure palace of the emir gleamed, surrounded by lemon groves and myrtles. The herd of goats had wandered off on to the hill. Munira was running about the hillside, gathering teasel heads and sticking them together to make a necklace and sucking her little fingers, pricked by the spines. She was also sticking teasels on to the Frank's back and throwing them to stick in his hair, then running to clamber all over him and laughingly put her arms round his neck. She had been given permission to guide the Christian out on to the hill as far as the old cedar tree; she did not very often have the chance to leave the village and it was such fun to hide behind the bushes and jump up on to the big boulders; she thought the Frank very good to have brought her there.

Meanwhile he was thinking only of some means of finding a hiding-place among the rocks and cliffs and getting rid of the child. Then, at nightfall, he would move down to the road; he thought he knew which way to go in order to reach it.

"Once on the road," he thought, "I'll have nothing to do but walk. At night nobody will see me and in the morning I'll join the first party going to Jerusalem."

"Munira, there is the *mullah* calling *az-zuhr*, go back to your mother for your meal. You can come back for me afterwards."

"Munira wants to stay with the Frank."

"No, *ya sghyrat*, the Frank wants to be left quite alone, to pray."

"Munira can pray like the Frank."

"No, she cannot. Go, little dove, go and eat."

Biddable, the child set off running towards the village. He called her back.

"*Ya, Munira!*"

She returned and ran into his arms. He said:

"Munira is pretty. Your dress is pretty, too. Your doll is pretty, Munira. *Kahla, Munira, kahla bezzaf.*"

As if aware of something untoward, the child began to cry; then she ran off, jumping on to big stones and humming a song which the Frank had taught her: *Vante l'ore et li raim crollent. Vante l'or-ore-e.* . . .

It was hot, the air was dry. He had to walk slowly, feeling for obstacles with his staff. He thought he must be among thickets of bramble; he had passed the trees and no longer knew how long he had been walking, in the grip of an old man's obstinate determination. First, to hide, to hide so that he could not be found: at night he would go down to the road; it should not be too difficult, he was sure that there were no very steep slopes nor cliffs. To be sure, he would not get on very fast. But he would get there. He lay down among some bushes, placed the package containing the pieces of his cross on the ground and ate a few figs. Now he had only to wait for the evening. Nobody would look for him here. He fell asleep, to be awakened by cold.

It was only then that he realized the risk he was running: it would, perhaps, have been better to risk being found by the villagers than to get lost in the mountains. Below and in the distance he could hear the dismal howl of jackals. Taking his chance, he began the descent, holding on to the thorn bushes; the heavy package containing the cross swung at each step he took and bruised his back. His feet were torn by brambles and seemed on fire and he was so cold that his teeth were chattering. No night had ever seemed so long to him. He was almost crawling, working his way round outcrops of rocks, becoming involved in thickets of bramble until he could not extricate himself by going down, and he was forced to climb upwards again, trying to find another way out.

"Come now," he thought, "it's night. I've only to suppose it's a very dark night, the sky overcast, and that I can still see better than a man with eyes. I can feel the smallest stone. I know that this way goes up and over there must be a slope down. I've only to let myself slide a bit; I've been coming down for a long time, I am bound to end up by reaching the road."

The package got in his way but he did not dare to jettison it. It was, after all, the cross before which he had prayed for so long. He would put it together again and have it blessed at Jerusalem.

"If I go downwards I can't help coming to the road. I am certainly not on the other face of the hill. The road follows the valley and there is sure to be someone passing along it early in the morning. I shall hear them coming from a distance and can sign to them to stop. Who would stop a beggar from getting to Jerusalem? I'm so dark, I'll be taken for a native Christian."

Exhausted, he stopped at the foot of a bluff, offered up a brief prayer and drank a mouthful of water. "Never drink much while on the road. Allowing six mouthfuls, three times a day, I should have enough for two days." In spite of himself he began to reckon with the possibility that he might not find the road that morning.

He rose, drenched with dew. The ground, bushes, grass and weeds were all wet, as after rain; he licked his hands and sucked leaves, preserving his reserve of water. After that bitter cold night he was shaken by fever, and the day warmed up quickly until everything was dry and fiery hot, even the leaves of acanthus and rosemary which he picked to chew. He made another attempt to go downhill and was stopped by thickets, had to go up again and get round them, until at last he no longer knew whether he was going up or down.

He knew that the valley was somewhere below, to his right, but no sound came to him, not the faintest tinkle of a mule bell, not a single cry. The village must be far away, for he had not heard the call to morning prayer.

He came out on to a clear slope, stumbled on loose stones, nearly dropping his burden and his staff; now there were few bushes and no trees. He found something which seemed to be a path and walked on for quite a long time, his strength restored by the thought that he was at last going towards the road. Time passed; heat and thirst tortured him more and more. The silence of the mountains, broken only by the hoarse cries of crows and vultures, filled him with an uneasiness growing towards anguish at every step. Now he was quite sure that he had mistaken the way; the road was on the other side, beyond the mountain, and he was in a deserted valley.

A night had passed and another day. The old man had no more figs nor barley, no more water in his gourd, and was waiting for the morning dew to ease his thirst a little. The sudden change from heat to cold was so exhausting that he could no longer walk. In the morning he drank all the dew he could find and sucked it out of his clothes, which, however, dried with heart-breaking rapidity. He then lay down.

It was finished. He would go no further than this stone. He had not
the strength to move. In a painful half-sleep, struggling against un-
consciousness, he seemed to hear bells chiming endlessly, tolling the
knell, each tolling echoed by a score of others. Mosquitoes stung his
face and got into his eye, but he had not the strength to drive them
away; they did not leave him alone when he tried shaking his head.
Towards evening he rose and tried to walk on again, ridden by a fear
which was almost an obsession: he could see nothing, for all he knew
the road was not two paces away, the buzzing in his ears might have
prevented him from hearing passing travellers and he might yet encounter someone willing to take him to Jerusalem. It was cowardice to
give up when he was, perhaps, so near. God had not brought him so far
only to abandon him.

The package on his shoulder became as heavy as if the wood had
changed to lead. It was breaking his back and still he dared not jettison it; it was, after all, a cross, although neither blessed nor consecrated.

Then he tripped on a stone and fell and dropped his staff: he could
hear it rolling down the slope away from him, twenty paces from him.
And he began to swear as he had not sworn for years, in French and
Arabic; tears of rage flowed from his eye; he drank them, as he drank
the blood flowing from his cut knee.

"O my God, my strength is all gone. God, what have You done to
me? I'm going to die. O God, I should like to drink, for I am thirsty.
Only True Friend, do not let me die here and now. I am afraid. I well
know that my time has come, Lord, and more than come—I am old;
but I want to hear mass once more, and I want to hear my native
speech.

"Only Friend, don't let me die now. I don't want to die all alone.
Not one night since my cradle have I slept without a companion, but
now it is three days since I heard a human voice and it is driving me
mad. My mind and heart pant with desire for the voice of a man. A
man on his own is no better than a beast.

"Lord God, for three days I have gone forward, seeing nothing and
my body broken, seeking brothers in the Faith, and You have not led
me to them. Why not have left me among the heathen, who were
like brothers to me?

"I do not want to die, O God. I cannot die seemly in the state I am
in. I have none to pray beside me and my mind is confused. I am so

thirsty I can think of nothing. If, at least, God, You would send me rain, since the month of rains is near. Send it two or three days early, it's a small matter to You. O God, I am so thirsty. If I get no relief I shall be howling like a beast. Don't turn me into a brute beast."

The night was cold but the old man was so tormented by fever and thirst that he no longer knew whether it was night or day. The immense silence of the mountains crushed him; he was almost glad when he heard jackals barking or the hoot of an owl. It seemed to him that his body was absorbed into the mountain range, that it was enormous, like a mountain, that it filled the whole valley and that a river was not enough to quench his thirst. The whole earth was thirsty, drying and cracking everywhere, gasping for water. His agony became such that he no longer knew what to do with his body; the marrow seemed to dry up in his bones, his tongue was swollen and his throat tortured by spasms of pain. Drink his own blood while waiting for the dew? He bit into his wounded knee where a scab had formed, and sucked the blood for a long time when it began to trickle, but it was warm and salty and sticky. He was becoming giddy and he was possessed by the fear of not having time to say his last prayers. When morning came, and with it the dew, he licked it up wherever he could find it until his tongue and mouth were sore.

Drinking the dew had given him back a little strength—not enough to enable him to get up on his knees, but at least he managed to turn his body to face south—towards Jerusalem—guiding himself by the heat of the sun. With his hands clasped on the pieces of his wooden cross, he tried to bring some order into his mind. A man's last duty. All the others he had accomplished so badly.

"O Bertrand, my brother, worst of all was my betrayal of you. Farewell, now, brother and unbeliever, may my plight in this hour, if you can see it, serve you in reparation. My dying is worse than yours.

> *Confiteor Deo omnipotenti,*
> *Beatae Mariae semper Virgini,*
> *Beato Michaeli Archangelo,*
> *Beato Joanni Baptistae,*
> *Sanctis Apostolis Petro et Paulo.*
> *Omnibus Sanctis. . . .*

"I forget the words. *Peccavi.* What sins? Very great sins and they must be recalled once more. *Quia peccavi. Cogitatione. Verbo et opere. Verbo.* . . . No, first the deeds, they were more serious."

He tried to remember his sins, or at least the worst of them, so that there would be time to get himself forgiven for those at least. The worst of it was that he could now never make reparation.

"Baudouin of Puiseaux—to revenge myself I caused him to be castrated. Guillaume of Nangi—I dishonored his daughter, although he was the sponsor of my knighthood, and again, after he was dead. Bertrand—I allowed him to damn his own soul."

So many others—but those were surely the worst of his sins.

He tried saying over to himself, in a low voice—*I did thus and thus:* and shame seared him, a shame greater than if there had been a priest there to hear him. It was the first time he had made his confession directly to God, without a priest. And it was very terrible, as if the heavens had suddenly fallen upon the earth, burning and massive, and compassed him about on all sides, cutting off his breath, beating at his ears. Strong and awful as thunder, tremendous as the sea, was the Presence he became aware of, receiving the admissions from his lips.

"O God, You know all in any case. Why, then, must I suffer this shame?" But he knew that it was important to make the effort to the bitter end, for otherwise he would not be forgiven.

"I have killed men. I cannot remember how many. I have forgotten You, a hundred, a thousand times. I have missed going to mass. I have been too indulgent to my own flesh and blood. I have loved wickedly, like an animal."

He could have told it all to a man without blushing over-much. But confronted by Him whose presence he could sense and Who was listening to him, he felt stripped naked, flayed, raw. That which, in a man's eyes, is barely a sin, becomes a nameless vileness when face to face with that dreadful Power which sears the heart.

"You know everything, Lord God, and how can I talk to You? I am afraid. I don't know how. *Mea culpa, mea culpa, mea maxima culpa. Ideo precor beatam Mariam semper virginem, Beatum Michaelem Archangelum.* . . .

"*Orare pro me ad Dominum Deum nostrum.*

"There is no priest to absolve me. Absolve me, O God, Thyself, I pray Thee. It is said that You do this, for those who die alone."

Never had he supposed it could be so terrible to be alone with God.

Alone, and he could feel Him with his hands; alone, and he could touch Him with his lips.

"My God, I cannot die without having received Your most pure Body. You will have to forgive me, in order that what I shall do may not be a sacrilege."

Then he stretched out his hand, seeking for a blade of grass which he might pick and consecrate—his fingers did not obey his will properly, he could feel nothing, but at last grasped a thin, dry grass which cut his fingers; he tore it off, however, and placed it on the ground before him. He was panting with exhaustion.

The sun was burning his face, which was swollen with mosquito bites, and a dry wind blew dust over his face and hands. He hardly felt it, absorbed in his effort to obey the commandments of the One who stood before him.

"O my God, You are here, it is You who will do what must be done. For You are also a priest, the only true Priest. Here is this grass, grown where You, perhaps, once walked, for You lived in these parts. Now I make the sign of the cross upon this thing which You created. The bread which is Your body is also made of a grass.

"By the power I possess in virtue of baptism I consecrate this grass which I hold in my hands that it may be the image and likeness of Your body. The words of power I do not say, I have not the right, but You will say them for me.

"A man dying alone has no choice. You will not let me die of hunger.

"And my hunger for Your body is as great as my thirst, God. I have no power, but bless, I pray You, this thing of Your creation, that I may receive it as Your image."

Slowly, he broke the blade of grass in two and raised it to his bruised and swollen lips.

"My God, the worst is now to come for me. Take me in Your arms. You are here, the Source of the water of life, and I am thirsty. Grant that I may drink of You and eat of You; here, my body breaks and opens to admit You, and it is agony without name. My Water, living Water, You deny me water for my body. I no longer know what I should be saying; do not let my mind grow clouded.

Libera me Domine
De morte aeterna.

"*In die illa tremenda*. O God, You also suffered thirst, and know what it means.

"O Saint Peter, Saint Michael, Saint George; Saint John the Baptist, Saint Andrew, Saint James, Saint Stephen, Saint Laurence and Saint Nicholas; Saint Catherine, Saint Lucie, Saint Valerie; Saint Martin, Saint Saturnin and Saint Potentien—I have forgotten, I no longer know, I—"

At all costs he must continue praying, for great is the temptation of pain. And despite himself he groaned and writhed on the stones like a crushed earthworm, trying to ease his suffering by this rhythmic rubbing of his body against the rock. Without realizing it he had torn open his wrist with his teeth and was sucking the dry, chapped skin and the slow drops of blood. The pain of feeling within himself something which resisted so grimly, which refused to yield, to break, was unbearable. Exacting struggle of the body laboring to give birth to death! Struggle—with what? What is it that will not yield?

"Lord, You are here, do not take from me what little I have, this body mortally stricken."

"*Miserere mei Deus*, I forget the words. Is it, then, so hard, so very hard, for the heart to cease from beating? Jesus, Lord Jesus, Lord Jesus."

The remnant of his memory clung to those two words. They entered into his body, contracted his throat, twisted his entrails; they were the name of his agony.

Those bells, ringing in his ears.

"Let it be over, finished. I cannot breathe, everything is sinking, the soul is being dragged from my body with pincers of lead. Oh! let it be quickly done! Auberi, tell me, is the sun up? I cannot recall your face. Goodbye, lamb without blemish. Lord Jesus, God, I'm done, my body is void, I'm going—"

For a little while he could feel—feel trickles of cold water drenching his face and his neck. It was good. He breathed and drank the water which soaked his mustache and ran down off his nose. He snorted and hawked, unconscious of everything but the water which flowed and still flowed, drenching his hair and his clothes, freezing his already numbed body. In the end he realized what it was. "Rain," he thought, and smiled, as if he had heard good news. He was setting out for somewhere and there was something he had to take with him, someone, he could not remember. Munira—she was also Eglantine—pressed a cold and tear-wet cheek to his cheek.

"Don't cry, little sweetheart, I'm here. *Munira ḳahla bezzaf.* I am here, little one, don't cry any more. This time I will take you with me."

He thought he felt himself rising.

O only Friend, all is transcended.

For a long time the rain lashed the mountains until torrents of water poured off the bluffs, washing the long dark body, which lay out on the stones, clean of blood and sweat. It was stiff and cold, the left hand gripping the iron cross, the single eye and the mouth gaping open, the beard, running water, plastered flat to the chin.

Lying out on those vast stony slopes covered with grey withered bramble, the body was the only dark object and it looked as small as an ant. Two shepherds, caught by the rain, were driving their flock quickly homeward along the valley; they stopped for a moment to look up at it, protecting their eyes against the rain with their hands. They agreed that it was an ass which had strayed and broken its back, falling among the rocks, and went on their way, huddling into their white woollen cloaks.